Alasdair Gray was born in Glasgow in 1934. He still lives there and works mainly on painting portraits and mural decorations. He was until recently Glasgow's Official Recorder, painting portraits of local dignitaries and celebrities, and he was Glasgow University's Writer in Residence from 1979 to 1981. Prior to the publication of *Lanark*, his first novel, which met great critical acclaim, his best known writings had been television, radio and stage plays. He has also written a collection called *Unlikely Stories Mostly* and two novels, *1982, Janine*, and *The Fall of Kelvin Walker*.

LANARK

'Has all the makings of a "cult" book . . . obsessional energy, a relish for archetypes, a nightmarish imagination . . . I salute it'
Hermione Lee *The Observer*

'Fluent, imaginative, part vision, part realism . . . the writing is easy and elegant . . . a book of undeniable quality'
Hilary Bailey *The Guardian*

'Fantastic quality . . . all finely written, with passion and wit'
Publishers Weekly

'A major Scottish novel by a major author . . . chillingly prophetic'
Scottish Field

'The most remarkable first novel I've read for years . . . the nearest I've come to a Scottish version of James Joyce's *ULYSSES*'
Evening Times

'The reader is carried along in grand style by his infectious wit. In every way this is a big book. It is also an extremely honest book and perhaps one of the best pieces of prose fiction to have appeared in Scotland in the last twenty years'
Trevor Royle *Times Educational Supplement*

'Extraordinary . . . an exciting, unusual book'
Daily Express

'Haunting and powerful . . . the writing is sharp and the dialogue true and the observation acute . . . handled remarkably'
Northern Echo

'Gray is a fantastic writer (and his own fantastic illustrator) who owes something to Kafka but not much . . . Scotland produced, in Hugh MacDiarmid, the greatest poet of the century (or so some believe); it was time Scotland produced a shattering work of fiction in the modern idiom. This is it'
Anthony Burgess *Ninety-Nine Novels: The Best in English since 1939*

'Undoubtedly the best work of fiction written by a Scottish author for decades . . . a popularity which is growing steadily . . . By turn funny, nightmarish and provocative, it has already acquired the trappings of cult status'
Time Out

ALASDAIR GRAY

Lanark

A Life in Four Books

PALADIN
GRAFTON BOOKS
A Division of the Collins Publishing Group

LONDON GLASGOW
TORONTO SYDNEY AUCKLAND

Paladin
Grafton Books
A Division of the Collins Publishing Group
8 Grafton Street, London W1X 3LA

Published in Paladin Books 1987
Reprinted 1989
Previously published in Panther Books 1982
Reprinted 1982, 1984 (twice), 1985

First published in Great Britain by
Canongate Publishing Limited 1981

Chapters 6 and 7 of this work appeared in *Scottish
International Review* in 1970, Chapter 12 was a runner-up
in the 1958 *Observer* short story competition under
the pseudonym Robert Walker, the prologue was in
Glasgow University Magazine 1974 and Chapters 35 and
41 were in *Words* magazine, Fife, 1979 and 1978.

ISBN 0-586-08613-7

Printed and bound in Great Britain by
Collins, Glasgow

Set in Garamond

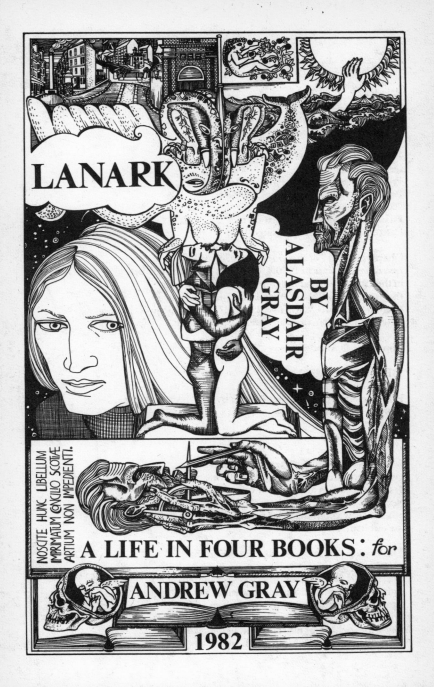

Creatures shall be seen on the earth who will always be fighting one another, with the greatest losses and frequent deaths on either side. There will be no bounds to their malice; by their strong limbs the vast forests of the world shall be laid low; and when they are filled with food they shall gratify their desires by dealing out death, affliction, labour, terror, and banishment to every living thing; and from their boundless pride they will desire to rise towards heaven, but the excessive weight of their limbs will hold them down. Nothing shall remain on the earth or under the earth or in the waters that shall not be pursued, disturbed, or spoiled, and that which is in one country removed into another. And their bodies shall be made the tomb and the means of transit of all the living bodies they have slain.

O earth, why do you not open and hurl them into the deep fissures of thy vast abysses and caverns, and no longer display in the sight of heaven so cruel and horrible a monster?

—From Leonardo da Vinci's Notebooks

VLADIMIR: Suppose we repented.
ESTRAGON: Repented what?
VLADIMIR: Oh . . . *(he reflects)* We wouldn't have to go into the details.

—From Beckett's *Waiting for Godot*

TABLE OF

BOOK   CHAPTER 1: The Elite   Page   3
THREE   CHAPTER 2: Dawn and Lodgings   Page   10
              CHAPTER 3: Manuscript   Page   16
              CHAPTER 4: A Party   Page   24
              CHAPTER 5: Rima   Page   34
              CHAPTER 6: Mouths   Page   40
              CHAPTER 7: The Institute   Page   50
              CHAPTER 8: Doctors   Page   59
              CHAPTER 9: A Dragon   Page   72
              CHAPTER 10: Explosions   Page   84
              CHAPTER 11: Diet and Oracle   Page   97

PROLOGUE telling how a nonentity was made
and made oracular. . . . . Page 107

BOOK   CHAPTER 12: The War Begins   Page 121
ONE   CHAPTER 13: A Hostel   page 130
              CHAPTER 14: Ben Rua   Page 136
              CHAPTER 15: Normal   Page 146
              CHAPTER 16: Underworlds   Page 156
              CHAPTER 17: The Key   Page 167
              CHAPTER 18: Nature   Page 177
              CHAPTER 19: Mrs. Thaw Disappears   Page 190
              CHAPTER 20: Employers   Page 204

INTERLUDE to remind us that Thaw's story
exists within the hull of Lanark's . . . . Page 219

CONTENTS

BOOK TWO
CHAPTER 21: The Tree   Page 223
CHAPTER 22: Kenneth McAlpin   Page 240
CHAPTER 23: Meetings   Page 253
CHAPTER 24: Marjory Laidlaw   Page 268
CHAPTER 25: Breaking   Page 278
CHAPTER 26: Chaos   Page 293
CHAPTER 27: Genesis   Page 305
CHAPTER 28: Work   Page 317
CHAPTER 29: The Way Out   Page 335
CHAPTER 30: Surrender   Page 350

BOOK FOUR
CHAPTER 31: Nan   Page 357
CHAPTER 32: Council Corridors   Page 364
CHAPTER 33: A Zone   Page 375
CHAPTER 34: Intersections   Page 387
CHAPTER 35: Cathedral   Page 398
CHAPTER 36: Chapterhouse   Page 408
CHAPTER 37: Alexander Comes   Page 419
CHAPTER 38: Greater Unthank   Page 431
CHAPTER 39: Divorce   Page 455
CHAPTER 40: Provan   Page 468

EPILOGUE annotated by Sidney Workman, with
an index of diffuse and imbedded Plagiarisms .... Page 479
CHAPTER 41: Climax   Page 500
CHAPTER 42: Catastrophe   Page 517
CHAPTER 43: Explanation   Page 534
CHAPTER 44: End   Page 549

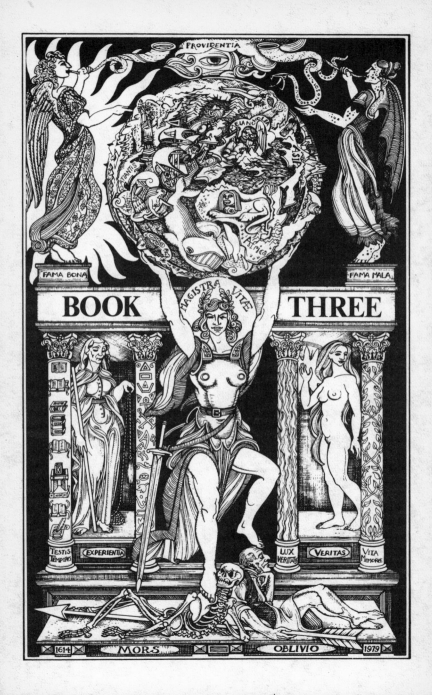

CHAPTER 1. The Elite

The Elite Café was entered by a staircase from the foyer of a cinema. A landing two thirds of the way up had a door into the cinema itself, but people going to the Elite climbed farther and came to a large dingy-looking room full of chairs and low coffee tables. The room seemed dingy, not because it was unclean but because of the lighting. A crimson carpet covered the floor, the chairs were upholstered in scarlet, the low ceiling was patterned with whorled pink plaster, but dim green wall lights turned these colours into varieties of brown and made the skins of the customers look greyish and dead. The entrance was in a corner of the room, and the opposite corner held a curved chromium and plastic counter where a bald fat smiling man stood behind the glittering handles of a coffee machine. He wore black trousers, white shirt and black bow tie and was either dumb or unusually reticent. He never spoke; the customers only addressed him to order coffee or cigarettes, and when not serving these he stood so still that the counter seemed an extension of him, like the ring round Saturn. A door by the bar opened onto a narrow outdoor balcony above the cinema entrance. This had room for three crowded-together metal-topped tables with parasols through the middle. Coffee was not drunk here because the sky was often dark with strong wind and frequent rain. The tabletops had little puddles on them, the collapsed cloth of the parasols flapped soddenly against the poles, the seats were dank, yet a man of about twenty-four usually sat here, huddled in a black raincoat with the collar turned up. Sometimes he gazed in a puzzled way at the black sky, sometimes he bit thoughtfully on the knuckle of his thumb. Nobody else used the balcony.

When the Elite was full most languages and dialects could be heard there. The customers were under thirty and sat in cliques of five or six. There were political cliques, religious cliques, artistic cliques, homosexual cliques and criminal cliques. Some cliques talked about athletics, others about motor cars, others about jazz. Some cliques were centred on particular people, the biggest being dominated by Sludden. His clique usually occupied a sofa by the balcony door. An adjacent clique contained people who had belonged to Sludden's clique but grown tired of it (as they claimed) or been expelled from it (as Sludden claimed). The cliques disliked each other and none liked the café much. It was common for a customer to put down his coffee cup and say, "The Elite is a hellish place. I don't know why we come here. The coffee's bad, the lighting's bad, the whole dump teems with poofs and wogs and Jews. Let's start a fashion for going somewhere else." And someone would answer, "There is nowhere else. Galloway's Tearoom is too bourgeois, all businessmen and umbrella stands and stuffed stags' heads. The Shangri-la has a jukebox that half deafens you, and anyway it's full of hardmen. Armstrong had his face slashed there. There are pubs, of course, but we can't always be drinking. No, this may be a hellish place but it's all we have. It's central, it's handy for the cinema and at least it's a change from home."

The café was often crowded and never completely empty, but on one occasion it nearly emptied. The man in the black raincoat came in from the balcony and saw nobody but the waiter and Sludden, who sat on his usual sofa. The man hung his coat on a hook and ordered a coffee. When he left the counter he saw Sludden watching him with amusement.
Sludden said, "Did you find it, Lanark?"
"Find what? What do you mean?"
"Find what you were looking for on the balcony? Or do you go there to avoid us? I'd like to know. You interest me."
"How do you know my name?"
"Oh, we all know your name. One of us is usually in the queue when they shout it at the security place. Sit down."
Sludden patted the sofa beside him. Lanark hesitated, then put his cup on the table and sat. Sludden said, "Tell me why you use the balcony."
"I'm looking for daylight."
Sludden pursed his mouth as if tasting sourness. "This is hardly a season for *daylight*."

"You're wrong. I saw some not long ago and it lasted while I counted over four hundred, and it used to last longer. Do you mind my talking about this?"

"Go on! You couldn't discuss it with many people, but I've thought things out. Now you are trying to think things out and that interests me. Say what you like."

Lanark was pleased and annoyed. He was lonely enough to feel flattered when people spoke to him but he disliked condescension. He said coldly, "There's not much to say."

"But why do you like daylight? We're well lit by the usual means."

"I can measure time with it. I've counted thirty days since coming here, maybe I've missed a few by sleeping or drinking coffee, but when I remember something I can say, 'It happened two days ago,' or ten, or twenty. This gives my life a feeling of order."

"And how do you spend your . . . *days*?"

"I walk and visit libraries and cinemas. When short of money I go to the security place. But most of the time I watch the sky from the balcony."

"And are you happy?"

"No, but I'm content. There are nastier ways of living."

Sludden laughed. "No wonder you've a morbid obsession with daylight. Instead of visiting ten parties since you came here, laying ten women and getting drunk ten times, you've watched thirty days go by. Instead of making life a continual feast you chop it into days and swallow them regularly, like pills."

Lanark looked sideways at Sludden. "Is your life a continual feast?"

"I enjoy myself. Do you?"

"No. But I'm content."

"Why are you content with so little?"

"What else can I have?"

Customers had been arriving and the café was nearly full. Sludden was more casual than when the conversation started. He said carelessly, "Moments of vivid excitement are what make life worth living, moments when a man feels exalted and masterful. We can get them from drugs, crime and gambling, but the price is rather high. We can get them from a special interest, like sports, music or religion. Have you a special interest?"

"No."

"And we get them from work and love. By work I don't mean

shovelling coal or teaching children, I mean work which gives you a conspicuous place in the world. And by love I don't mean marriage or friendship, I mean independent love which stops when the excitement stops. Perhaps I've surprised you by putting work and love in the same category, but both are ways of mastering other people."

Lanark brooded on this. It seemed logical. He said abruptly, "What work could I do?"

"Have you visited Galloway's Tearoom?"

"Yes."

"Did you speak to anyone there?"

"No."

"Then you can't be a businessman. I'm afraid you'll have to take up art. Art is the only work open to people who can't get along with others and still want to be special."

"I could never be an artist. I've nothing to tell people."

Sludden started laughing. "You haven't understood a word I've spoken."

Lanark had an inner restraint which stopped him displaying much resentment or anger. He pressed his lips together and frowned at the coffee cup. Sludden said, "An artist doesn't tell people things, he expresses himself. If the self is unusual his work shocks or excites people. Anyway, it forces his personality on them. Here comes Gay at last. Would you mind making room for her?"

A thin, tired-looking, pretty girl approached them between the crowded tables. She smiled shyly at Lanark and sat beside Sludden, saying anxiously, "Am I late? I came as soon as—" He said coldly, "You kept me waiting."

"Oh, I'm sorry, I really am sorry. I came as fast as I could. I didn't mean to—"

"Get me cigarettes."

Lanark looked embarrassedly at the tabletop. When Gay had gone to the counter he said, "What do you do?"

"Eh?"

"Are you a businessman? Or an artist?"

"Oh, I do nothing, with fantastic ability."

Lanark looked hard at Sludden's face for some trace of a smile. Sludden said, "Occupations are ways of imposing yourself on others. I can impose myself without doing a thing. I'm not boasting. It just happens to be the truth."

"It's modest of you to say so," said Lanark, "but you're wrong to say you do nothing. You talk very well."

Sludden smiled and received a cigarette from Gay, who had returned meekly to his side. He said, "I don't often talk as frankly as this; my ideas would be wasted on most people. But I think I can help you. Do you know any women here?"
"None."
"I'll introduce you to some."
Sludden turned to Gay and lightly pinched the lobe of her ear, asking amiably, "Who will we give to him? Frankie?"
Gay laughed and at once looked happy. She said, "Oh no Sludden, Frankie's noisy and vulgar and Lanark's the thoughtful type. Not Frankie."
"What about Nan, then? She's quiet, in a will-'oo-be-my-daddy sort of way."
"But Nan's crazy about you!"
"I know, and it's a nuisance. I'm tired of seeing her weep in the corner whenever you touch my knee. Let's give her to Lanark. No. I've a better idea. I'll take Nan and Lanark can have you. How would you like that?"
Gay leaned toward Sludden and kissed him daintily on the cheek. He said, "No. We'll give him Rima."
Gay frowned and said, "I don't like Rima. She's sly."
"Not sly. Self-contained."
"But Toal is keen on her. They go around together."
"That means nothing. He has a sister fixation on her and she has a brother fixation on him. Their relationship is purely incestuous. Anyway, she despises him. We'll give her to Lanark."
Lanark smiled and said, "You're very kind."
He had heard somewhere that Gay and Sludden were engaged. A fur gauntlet on Gay's left hand stopped him seeing if she wore a ring, but she and Sludden exhibited the sort of public intimacy proper to an engaged couple. Lanark had been impressed unwillingly by Sludden but now Gay had come he felt comfortable with him. In spite of the talk about "independent love" he seemed to practise a firmer sort than was usual in the Elite.

Sludden's clique arrived from the cinema. Frankie was plump and vivacious and wore a tight pale-blue skirt and had pale-blue hair bunched round her head. Nan was a small shy uncombed blonde of about sixteen. Rima had an interesting, not pretty face with black hair drawn smoothly from her brow and fixed in a ponytail at the back. Toal was small, haggard, and pleasant, with a young pointed red beard, and there was a large stout pale boy called McPake in the uniform of a first lieutenant. Sludden, an arm round Gay's waist, neither paused nor glanced at his friends but continued talking to Lanark as they sat down on each side of him. Frankie was the only one who paid Lanark special attention. She stood staring at him with feet apart and hands on hips and when Sludden stopped talking she said loudly, "It's the mystery man! We've been joined by the mystery man!" She stuck her stomach forward and said, "What do you think of my belly, mystery man?"

"It probably does its work," said Lanark.

Sludden smiled slightly and the others looked amused.

"Oh! He makes little jokes!" said Frankie. "Good. I'll sit beside him and make McPake jealous."

She sat beside Lanark and rested her hand on his thigh. He tried not to look embarrassed and managed to look confused. Frankie said, "God! He's gone as tense as . . . hm. I'd better not say. Relax, son, can't you? No, he can't relax. Rima, I'll change seats with you. I want to sit with McPake after all. He's fat, but he responds."

She changed seats with Rima. Lanark felt relieved and insulted.

Two or three conversations began around him but he lacked the confidence to join one. Rima offered a cigarette. He said, "Thank you. Is your friend drunk?"

"Frankie? No, she's usually like that. She's not really my friend. Did she upset you?"

"Yes."

"You'll get used to her. She's amusing if you don't take her seriously."

Rima spoke in an odd, mewing, monotonous voice, as if no words were worth emphasis. Lanark looked sideways at her profile. He saw black glossy hair drawn back from a white brow, a large perfect eye slightly emphasized by mascara, a big straightish nose, a small straight mouth without lipstick, a small firm chin, a neat little bust under a black sweater. If she felt his glance she pretended not to but tilted her head back to breathe smoke from her nostrils. This so reminded him of a little girl trying to smoke like a woman that he felt an ache of unexpected tenderness. He said, "What was the film about?"

"It was about people who undressed soon after the beginning and then did everything they could think of in the circumstances."

"Do you enjoy those films?"

"No, but they don't bore me. Do they bore you?"

"I've never seen one."

"Why not?"

"I'm afraid of enjoying them."

"I enjoy them," said Sludden. "I get genuine pleasure from imagining how the actors would look wearing flannel underwear and thick tweed skirts."

Nan said, "I enjoy them too. Except the best bits. I can't help closing my eyes during those, aren't I silly?"

Frankie said, "I find them all very disappointing. I keep hoping to see a really surprising perversion but there don't seem to be any."

A discussion began about the forms a surprising perversion might take. Frankie, Toal and McPake made suggestions. Gay and Nan punctuated these with little screaming protests of horror and amusement. Sludden sometimes contributed a remark, and Lanark and Rima remained silent. Lanark was embarrassed by the conversation and thought Rima disliked it too. This made him feel nearer her.

Later Sludden whispered to Gay and stood up. He said, "Gay and I are leaving. We'll see you all later."

Nan, who had been watching him anxiously, suddenly folded her arms upon her knees and hid her face in them. Toal, who was seated beside her, put a comforting arm around her shoulders and smiled at the company in a humorous mournful way. Sludden looked at Lanark and said casually, "You'll consider what I said?"

"Oh, yes. You gave me a lot to think about."

"We'll discuss it later. Come on, Gay."

They went out between the crowded tables. Frankie said mockingly, "The mystery man seems to be replacing you as court favourite, Toal. I hope not, for your sake. You'd have to take up your old job of court jester. Rima never sleeps with the court jester."

Without taking his arm from Nan's trembling shoulders Toal grinned and said, "Shut up, Frankie. You're the court jester and always will be." He said apologetically to Lanark, "Pay no attention to what *she* says."

Rima took her handbag from the seat beside her and said, "I'm going."

Lanark said, "Wait a bit, so am I."

He edged round the table to where his coat hung and put it on. The others said they would see him later and as he and Rima went out Frankie shouted after them, "Have fun!"

CHAPTER 2.
Dawn and Lodgings

The foyer downstairs was empty apart from the girl at the cash desk. Through the glass doors Lanark saw lamplight reflected in a rain-wet street. Sometimes the wind dunted the doors extra hard and made them swing inward and admit a hissing draught. Rima took a plastic raincoat from her handbag. He helped her put it on and said, "Where do you get your tram?"

"At the cross."

"Good. So do I."

Outside they had to struggle against the wind. He took her hand and forced himself to go fast enough to feel he was dragging her. The cross was not far away and the tram stop was near the mouth of a close. Laughing breathlessly they stepped into this and sheltered from the wind. Rima's hair had unloosed from its clasps and her composed, large-eyed face glanced at him between two falls of moist hair. She combed it back with her fingers, grimacing and saying, "A bother."

"I like your hair that way."

They were silent for a while, standing against opposite walls and looking out into the street. At last Lanark cleared his throat. "That Frankie is a *bitch*."

Rima smiled.

He said, "She was very nasty to Toal."

Rima said, "She was under a strain, you know."

"Why?"

"She feels the same about Sludden as Nan does. Whenever Sludden and Gay go off together, Nan weeps and Frankie is rude to people. Sludden says it's because Nan has a negative ego and Frankie a positive one."

"My God!" said Lanark. "Do all of Sludden's girlfriends love him?"

"I don't."

"I'm glad to hear it. Oh, look! Look!"

"Look at what?"

"*Look*!"

The cross was a place where several broad streets met and they could see down two of them, though the dark had made it difficult to see far. And now, about a mile away, where the streets reached the crest of a wide shallow hill, each was silhouetted against a pearly paleness. Most of the sky was still black for the paleness did not reach above the tenement roofs, so it seemed that two little days were starting, one at the end of each street. Rima said again, "Look at what?"

"Can't you see it? Can't you see that . . . what's the word? There was once a special word for it. . . ."

Rima looked in the direction of his forefinger and said coldly, "Are you talking about the light in the sky?"

"Dawn. That's what it was called. Dawn."

"Isn't that a rather sentimental word? It's fading already."

The wind had fallen. Lanark stepped onto the pavement and stood leaning forward and staring along each street in turn, as if wanting to jump to the end of one but unable to decide which. Rima's indifference to his excitement had made him forget her for the moment. She said with slight distaste, "I didn't know you were keen on that kind of thing," then, after a pause, "Good, here's my tram."

She went past him into the road. An antique-looking almost-empty tramcar came groaning along the track and stopped between Lanark and the view. It would have taken him to his lodgings. Rima boarded it. He took a step to follow her, then hesitated and said, "Look, I'll see you again, won't I?"

As the tram started moving Rima waved offhandedly from the platform. He watched her settle in an upstairs seat, hoping she would turn and wave again. She didn't. He looked along the two streets. The wan watery light was perceptibly fading from the ends of them. He abruptly crossed over to the broadest and started running up the middle of it.

He ran with his gaze on the skyline, having an obscure idea that the day would last longer if he reached it before the light completely faded. The wind rose. Great gusts shoved at his back making it easier to run than walk. This race with the wind toward a fading dawn was the finest thing he had

done since coming to that city. When the sky had grown altogether black he stopped, rested up a close mouth to recover
his breath, then trudged back to the tramstop at the cross.

The next tram took him along a succession of similar tene-
ment-lined streets. The stop where he got off had tenements
on one side and a blank factory wall on the other. He entered
a close, climbed ill-lit steps to a top landing and let himself
quietly into the lobby of his lodgings. This was a bare room
with six doors leading from it. One led to Lanark's bedroom,
one to the lavatory and one to the kitchen where the landlady
lived. The other doors led to empty rooms where bits of the
ceiling had fallen in opening them to the huge draughty loft
under the roof. As Lanark opened his bedroom door the landlady shouted from the kitchen, "Is that you, Lanark?"
"Yes, Mrs. Fleck."
"Come here and see this."
The kitchen was a clean, very cluttered room. It contained
armchairs, a sideboard, a scrubbed white table, a clumsy gas
cooker with shelves of pots above it. An iron range filled most
of one wall and there was a sink and draining board under
the window. All horizontal surfaces were covered with brass
and china ornaments and bottles and jam-jars of artificial flowers, some made of plastic, some of coloured wax, some of paper.
One wall had a bed recess and Mrs. Fleck, a small middle-
aged lady, stood beside it. She beckoned Lanark over and said
grimly, "Look at this!"

Three children with serious wide-open mouths and eyes
lay in a row under the quilt. There was a thin boy and girl
of about eight years and a plump wee girl of four or five.
Lanark recognized them as children from the house across the
landing. He said, "Hullo you lot."
The older ones grinned, the young one giggled and spread
her hands on her face as if hiding behind them. Mrs. Fleck
said morosely, "Their bloody mother's disappeared."
"Disappeared? Where to?"
"How do I know where folk disappear to? One minute she
was there, the next she had gone. Well, what could I do? I
couldn't leave them to look after themselves. Look at the size
of them! But I'm too old, Lanark, to be pestered by bloody
weans."

"But surely she'll come back?"

"Her? She won't come back. Nobody comes back who disappears when the lights go out."

"What do you mean?"

"I was standing at the sink washing dishes when the lights went out. I knew it wasn't a power cut because I could see the streetlights through the window, and right away I thought, 'Somebody's disappearing,' and then I thought, 'Oh, what if it's me?' My heart was thumping like a drum, though I don't know why I should be scared. I get so tired and my back is so sore that I often feel I'd be glad to disappear. Anyway, the lights went on again, so I went and had a look in your bedroom. I *thought* you were out but you might have come back without letting me know and it might have happened to you."

Lanark said uneasily, "Why should I disappear?"

"I've told you already I don't know why folk disappear."

"If I had been in the bedroom and . . . and disappeared, how would you have known?"

"Oh, there's usually a sign. My last lodger left a hell of a mess, bedclothes all over the room, the wardrobe on its side, half the plaster out of the ceiling—I haven't been able to let that room since. And his screams! They were awful. But I knew you wouldn't go like that, Lanark. You're the quiet type. Anyway, you hadn't been in so I crossed the landing. The door was open so I stuck my head in and shouted 'Susy!' I was always friendly with her even if she was a tart and didn't look after the kids. Sweets, sweets, sweets, that was all she fed them on, and look at the result. Open your mouth!" she commanded the smallest girl, who obediently opened her mouth to show, on the top and bottom gums, a row of little brown points with gaps between them.

"Look at that! Hardly older than a baby and without a sound tooth in her head."

"What happened then?" said Lanark.

"I shouted 'Susy!' and the kids yelled to me that their mammy had disappeared. Isn't that so?"

She glared at the children, who nodded vigorously.

"Well, Lanark, that house is a bloody midden. It's like a pigsty. I couldn't leave them in it, could I? I brought them here and washed them and put them to bed and now I'm washing their clothes. But you'd better look out if I'm going to see to you!" she told the children fiercely. "I'm not soft like your mammy!"

They grinned at her and the youngest giggled.

Mrs. Fleck leaned over the bed and groaned as she tucked the blankets round them. She said, "Oh Lanark I hate bloody kids."

Lanark shook his fist at the children and pulled such grotesquely threatening faces that they shouted with laughter, then he went back to his bedroom.

It was a high-ceilinged corridor of a room with the door at one end and a curtainless window at the other. A chair, camp bed and wardrobe stood against one wall, the wallpaper and linoleum were brown, there was no carpet, and only a small rucksack on top of the wardrobe suggested the place was used. Lanark took off his jacket and coat together, hung them on a hook behind the door, then lay on the bed with his hands behind his head. Weariness would eventually make him undress and get between the sheets, but he had a disease which made sleep unpleasant and he usually tried to postpone it by thinking of recent events.

There were the disappearances. The lights had gone out and the mother of three children had vanished. Lanark knew the woman well. She had been a friendly dirty attractive woman who often brought strange men to her house. He could think of no reason why she should vanish. He dismissed that matter and thought of the Elite. He would never again go there to sit on the balcony for now he had acquaintances who expected his company. This was not a wholly pleasant thought. The Sludden clique lacked dignity. Surely it was nobler to sit outside it, watching the sky and waiting for the light? Then he recalled how often he had sat on the balcony pretending to watch the sky but really wishing to sit in the warmth talking to the sexual-looking well-dressed women. "Admit!" he told himself, "You watched the sky because you were too cowardly to know people."

He remembered Rima, who sat with the group but seemed aloof from it. He thought, 'I must get to know her. Ach, why did the damned dawn come when I might have arranged to take her home?'

He thought of Sludden. Like Rima, Sludden seemed aloof from the emotions around him. Though loved by three women he was faithful to one, and Lanark thought this rather fine. Furthermore, Sludden had ideas about life and had suggested something to do. Lanark did not wish to be an artist but he felt increasingly the need to do some kind of work, and a writer needed only pen and paper to begin. Also he knew something about writing, for when wandering the city he had visited public libraries and read enough stories to know there were two kinds. One kind was a sort of written cinema, with plenty of action and hardly any thought. The other kind was about clever unhappy people, often authors themselves, who thought a lot but didn't do very much. Lanark supposed a good author was more likely to write the second kind of book. He thought, 'Sludden said I should write to express myself. I suppose I could do it in a story about who I am and why I have decided to write a story. But there's a difficulty.'

He became restless and started walking up and down the room.

This restlessness happened whenever his thoughts blundered on the question of who he was. "What does it matter who I am?" he asked aloud. "Why should I care why I came here?" He went to the window and pressed his brow to the glass, hoping the cold pressure would banish that problem. It did the opposite. The window overlooked a district of empty tenements, and he saw nothing through it but the black silhouette of his face and the bedroom reflected dimly behind. He remembered another window with only a reflection in it. Distaste and annoyance flooded him and some sexual fantasies about Rima.

Suddenly he went to the wardrobe and opened the single deep drawer at the foot. It was empty but for brown paper lining the bottom. He took the paper, folded it into neat rectangles and by careful tearing along the creases produced a sheaf of about twenty sheets. Removing the drawer he stood it on end beside the chair and laid the paper on top, then took a pen from the jacket pocket, sat down and wrote in small precise letters on the first page:

The first thing I remember is

After a few more words he scored out what he had written and started again. He did this four times, each time remembering an earlier event than the one he described. At last he found a beginning and wrote steadily until he had filled thirteen pages, but rereading them he noticed half the words had no definite meanings, having been added to make the sentences sound better than they were. He scored these words out and copied the rest onto the remaining pages with whatever improvements occurred to him. And then, completely tired for the first time since he came to that place, he undressed to his underwear, slid between the sheets and fell into a profound sleep.

CHAPTER 3. Manuscript

The first thing I remember is a thumping sound, then either I opened my eyes or the light went on for I saw I was in the corner of an old railway compartment. The sound and the blackness outside the window suggested the train was going through a tunnel. My legs were cramped but I felt very careless and happy. I stood up and walked about and was shocked to see my reflection in the carriage window. My head was big and clumsy with thick hair and eyebrows and an ordinary face, but I could not remember seeing it before. I decided to find what other people were on this train.

A cold wind blew along the corridor from the direction of the engine. I walked into it, looking through the windows of the compartments. They were empty. The wind at the end of the corridor was so strong that I had to grip the loose rubbery stuff on the walls of the doorway which usually leads to the next carriage. I could not go farther, for the entrance opened on a dark surface of wooden planks rocking from side to side. It was the back of a goods truck. I returned along the corridor with the wind at my back and recognized my own compartment by the open door. The compartments beyond were empty and the far entrance opened onto a metal tank of the kind used for transporting oil. So I returned to my compartment and noticed, as I shut the door behind me, a small rucksack on the rack above the corner seat. This made me wary. Since waking up I had felt wonderfully free and comfortable. I had been pleased to see I was alone and amused to find the carriage coupled in a goods train, but the knapsack frightened me. I knew it was mine and held something nasty but I was reluctant to throw it through the window. So I took it cautiously down, telling myself there was nobody looking and I need not be bound by what I discovered.

I first looked in the two outside pockets and found safe things, a shaving kit in a plastic envelope, some socks and a magnetic compass which didn't work. I opened the top of the knapsack and found a rolled-up black raincoat, dirty underwear and a suit of pyjamas. Underneath was a folded map and a wallet stuffed with papers so I opened the window, dropped them out and pulled the window shut. Feeling safe again, I repacked the knapsack and returned it to the rack and then (for the rucksack business suggested this) searched my pockets. They all held some grit and tiny seashells. I also found a handkerchief, pen, key and pocket diary. I threw the key and diary after the wallet and map. After that the train tooted its whistle and came out of the tunnel.

It ran along a viaduct among the roofs of a city. Rainclouds covered the sky and the day was so dull that lamps were lit in the streets. They were broad streets, and crossed at right angles, and were lined with big stone buildings. I saw very few people and no traffic. Beyond the rooftops were rows of cranes with metal hulls among them. The train travelled toward these and crossed a bridge over the river. It was a broad river with stone embankments, cracked khaki-coloured mud on the bottom and a narrow black stream trickling zigzag down the middle. This worried me. I felt, and still feel, that a river should be more than this. I looked down into a yard where two hulls stood. They were metal cylinders with rusty domes on top, and a rattle of machinery inside suggested they were being worked on. The train entered another tunnel, slowed down, came out into a marshalling yard and stopped. Through the windows on either side I saw lines of goods trucks with railway signals sticking out of them. The sky was darker now.

I sat for a while in my warm corner, not wanting to leave it for the bad weather outside. Then the light went out, so I shouldered the knapsack, went into the corridor, opened a door and jumped to the ground. I stood between two lines of trucks. Thin rain was falling, so I put down the knapsack and unpacked my coat. As I put it on I saw a man in black overalls and peaked cap come toward me looking closely at the trucks of the train and pencilling in a notebook as he passed each one. He stopped beside me, marked his book and asked if I had just arrived. I said I had. He said, "They needn't have provided a whole carriage for one passenger. They could have brought you in the guard's van."

I asked what time it was. He said, "We don't bother much with time now. The sky is lighter than normal but that sort of light is too chancy to be useful."

I asked if he knew where I could go. He said someone was coming who usually helped with that sort of thing then went on along the train.

A small figure ran toward us and passed the railwayman without a look. He stopped beside me and stared up with a feeble ingratiating smile. He had a weak-chinned handsome face and greasy hair sloping wavily back to a paltry wisp of curl on the nape of his neck. He wore a maroon bow tie, a jacket with maroon lapels which came down to his knees, tight black trousers and maroon suède shoes. His accent was soft and whined on the vowels. He said, "You're new here, aren't you?"

I said yes.

"I've come to help you. You can call me Gloopy. You don't have a name yet, I suppose. Is anybody with you?"

I said no.

"I'll take a look, just to be on the safe side. Give me a hitch up, will you?"

He insisted on entering every compartment and looking under the seats. And he giggled when I helped him down and said I was very strong. Then he offered to carry my knapsack but I shouldered it and asked if he would tell me where I could spend the night. He said, "Of course! That's why I'm here! I'll take you to my boardinghouse, we've got a spare room."

I said a boardinghouse was no use, I had no money.

"Of course you've no money! We'll leave your knapsack in my boardinghouse and then we'll go to the security place and they'll *give* you money."

We emerged from among the trucks and crossed some railway lines. The city lights glittered between a pair of black hills ahead of us. It was dark now and raining heavily and my guide turned up the sodden collar of his fancy jacket. He was far worse dressed for this weather than I was. I asked who paid him to meet people and he said in a hurt voice, "Nobody pays me. I do this job because I like people. I believe in friendship. People ought to be nice to one another."

I pitied him. I knew it was wrong to dislike people for their appearance and way of speaking but I disliked him very much. I explained that I wanted to collect the money before I did anything else. He said slyly, "If I take you to the security place first, will you promise to come to my boardinghouse after?" I told him I promised nothing and walked fast to get away. He trotted behind shouting, "All right! All right! I never said I wouldn't take you to the security place, did I?"

We continued side by side till the way grew narrow then he walked in front. The path went down a steep embankment between the two hills which seemed to be rubbish dumps. Where it twisted sharply I sometimes walked forward and found myself wading in what felt like ashes and rotten cloth. We crossed the dry bed of an old canal and reached the end of a street. The city did not seem a thriving place. Groups of adolescents or old men stood in occasional close mouths, but many closes were empty and unlit. The only shops not boarded up were small stores selling newspapers, sweets, cigarettes and contraceptives. After a while we came to a large square with tramcars clanging around it. The street lamps only lit the lowest storeys of the surrounding buildings but these looked very big and ornamental, and people sheltered between pillars on their façades. Some soot-black statues were arranged round a central pillar whose top I couldn't see in the black sky. In spite of the wet a man stood on a high part of the pillar's pedestal and spoke to an angry crowd. We passed through the edge of the crowd and I saw the speaker was an anxiously smiling man with a clergyman's collar and bruised brow. His words were drowned by jeering.

A street leaving the square was blocked with long wooden huts joined by covered passageways. The lit windows of these huts had a cheery look when compared with the black windows in the solider buildings. Gloopy brought me onto a porch with a sign over it saying SOCIAL SECURITY—WELFARE DIVISION. He said, "Here it is, then."
I thanked him. He kicked his heels and said, "What I want to know is, are you even going to *try* and be friendly? I don't mind coming in and waiting for you, but it's a hell of a long wait and if you're going to be nasty I don't think I'll bother." I said he shouldn't wait. He said sorrowfully, "All right, all right. I was only trying to help. You don't know what it feels like to have no friends in a big city. And I could have introduced you to some very interesting people—businessmen, and artists,

and girls. I've some lovely high-class girls in my boarding-house."

He eyed me coyly. I said goodnight and turned but he grabbed my arm and gabbled into my ear. "You're right, girls are no use, girls are cows, and even if you don't like me I've got men friends, military gentlemen—"

I pulled myself free and stepped into the hut. He didn't follow.

It was not a big hut but it was very long and most of the floor was covered by people crowded together on benches. There was a counter partitioned into cubicles along one wall, and the cubicle near the door had a seat in it and a sign saying **ENQUIRIES.** I stepped in and sat down. After a very long time an old man with bristling eyebrows arrived behind the counter and said, "Yes?"

I explained that I had just arrived and had no money.

"Have you means of identifying yourself?"

I said I had none.

"Are you sure? Have you searched your pockets thoroughly?"

I said I had.

"What are your professional qualifications and experience?"

I could not remember. He sighed and brought from below the counter a yellow card and a worn, coverless telephone directory saying, "We can't give you a number before you've been medically examined, but we can give you a name."

He flicked through the directory pages in a random way, and I saw each page had many names scored out in red ink. He said, "Agerimzoo? Ardeer? How about Blenheim. Or Brown." I was shocked at this and told him that I knew my name. He stared at me, not believing. My tongue felt for a word or syllable from a time earlier than the train compartment, and for a moment I thought I remembered a short word starting with *Th* or *Gr* but it escaped me. The earliest name I could remember had been printed under a brown photograph of spires and trees on a hilltop on the compartment wall. I had seen it as I took down the knapsack. I told him my name was Lanark. He wrote on the card and handed it over saying, "Take that to the medical room and give it to the examining doctor."

I asked the purpose of the examination. He was not used to being questioned and said, "We need records to identify you. If you don't want to cooperate there's nothing we can do."

The medical room was in a hut reached by a passageway. I undressed behind a screen and was examined by a casual young doctor who whistled between his teeth as he wrote the results on my card. I was 5 feet 7¾ inches high and weighed 9 stone 12 pounds 3½ ounces. My eyes were brown, hair black, blood group B (111). My only bodily markings were corns on the small toes and a patch of hard black skin on the right elbow. The doctor measured this with a pocket ruler and made a note saying, "Nothing exceptional there."

I asked what the hard patch was. He said, "We call it dragon-hide, a name more picturesque than scientific, perhaps, but the science of these things is in its infancy. You can dress now."

I asked how I could get it treated. He said, "There are several so-called medical practitioners in this city who claim to have cures for dragonhide. They advertise by small notices in tobacconists' windows. Don't waste money on them. It's a common illness, as common as mouths or softs or twittering rigor. What you have there is very slight. If I were you I'd ignore it."

I asked why he had not ignored it. He said cheerfully, "Descriptive purposes. Diseases identify people more accurately than variable factors like height, weight, and hair colour."

He gave me the card and told me to take it back to the enquiry counter. And at the enquiry counter I was told to wait with the others.

The people waiting were of most ages, none well dressed and all (except some children playing between the benches) stupid with boredom. Sometimes a voice cried out, "Will Jones"—or another name—"go to box forty-nine," and one of us would go to a cubicle, but this happened so rarely that I stopped expecting it. My eye kept seeking a circular patch of paler paintwork on the wall behind the counter. A clock had been fixed there once and been removed, I felt sure, because people would not have borne such waiting had they been able to measure it. My impatient thoughts kept returning to their own uselessness until they stopped altogether and I grew as unconscious as possible without actually sleeping. I could have endured eternity in this state, but I was roused by a woman who sat down beside me, a new arrival still in the restless stage. Her legs were encased in tight discoloured jeans and she kept crossing and recrossing them. She wore an army tunic over a plain shirt, and glittery earrings, necklaces, brooches, bangles and rings. Thick black hair lay tangled down her back, she smelled of powder, scent and sweat and she brought several of my senses to life again, including the sense of time, for she kept smoking cigarettes from a handbag which seemed to

hold several packets. When she lit the twenty-third I asked how long they would keep us waiting. She said, "As long as they feel like it. It's a damned scandal."
She stared at me a moment then asked kindly if I was new here. I said I was.
"You'll get used to it. It's a deliberate system. They think that by putting us through a purgatory of boredom every time we ask for money we'll come as seldom as we can. And by God they're right! I've three weans to feed, one of them almost a baby, and I work to keep them. When I can get work, that is. But not everyone pays up the way they should, so here I am again. A mug, that's what I am, a real mug."
I asked what work she did. She said she did things for different people on a part-time basis and gave me a cigarette. Then she said, "Are you looking for a place to stay?"
I said I was.
"I could put you up. Just for a wee while, I mean. If you're stuck, I mean."
She looked at me in a friendly sideways assessing way which I found stirring. I liked her, she was pleasant to be with, yet she was the first woman I had met and I knew most of my lust came from loneliness. I thanked her and said I wanted something permanent. After a moment she said, "Anyway, a neighbour of mine, Mrs. Fleck, has just lost a lodger. You could get a room with her. She's old but she's not too fussy. I mean she's very respectable, but she's nice."
I thought this a good idea, so she wrote the address and how to reach it on a used cigarette packet.

Someone shouted that I should go to box fifteen. I went there and was received by the bristling old clerk who returned the card saying, "Your claim is being allowed. Report to the cash desk for the money."
I asked how long the money was meant to last. He said, "It should last until you find work, but if you spend it before then this card entitles you to present another claim, which we shall be obliged, in due course, to honour. Eventually. Have you any other questions?"
After considering I asked if he could tell me the name of the city. He said, "Mr. Lanark, I am a clerk, not a geographer."
The cash desk was a small shuttered hatch in the wall of a room full of benches, but few people were sitting on them. The shutter was soon raised. We queued and were swiftly paid by a woman who asked our names in turn, then shoved out

between the bars a heap of notes and coin. I was surprised by the size of these heaps and the careless way the clerk handled them. The notes were creased and dirty and drawn from several currencies. The coins were thick copper pennies, worn silver with milled edges, frail nickel counters and plain brass discs with holes through the centre. I distributed this money into several pockets but I've never learned to use it for everyone has a different notion of its value. When buying anything I hold out a handful and let the waiter or shopman or conductor take what he thinks right.

The directions on the cigarette packet led me to the house where I write this, thirty-one days later. I have not looked for work in that time or made friends, and I count the days only to enjoy their emptiness. Sludden thinks I am content with too little. I believe there are cities where work is a prison and time a goad and love a burden, and this makes my freedom feel worthwhile. My one worry is the scab on my arm. There is no feeling in it, but when I grow tired the healthy skin round the edge starts itching and when I scratch this the scab spreads. I must scratch in my sleep, for when I waken the hard patch is always bigger. So I take the doctor's advice and try to forget it.

CHAPTER 4. A Party

Lanark was wakened by someone bumping up and down on his chest. It was the small girl from next door. Her brother and sister stood astride his legs, holding his coat aloft on the head of a floor brush and swaying from side to side so that the struts of the frail bed creaked. "The sea! The sea!" they chanted. "We're sailing into the sea!"

Lanark sat up rubbing his eyes. He said, "Get away! What do you know about the sea?"

They jumped to the floor where the boy shouted, "We know all about the sea! Your pockets are full of seashells, hahaha! We searched them!"

They ran out giggling and slammed the door. Lanark arose feeling unusually fresh and relaxed. The hard skin on his elbow had spread no farther. He dressed, rolled up the manuscript and went outside.

There was a surprising change in the weather. The dreary rain, the buffeting winds had given way to an air so piercingly still and cold that he had to walk quickly, flapping his arms to keep warm, the breath snorting from his nostrils in jets of mist. His toes and ears were painfully chilled aboard the tram and after climbing the cinema stairs the crowded Elite seemed wonderfully warm and homelike. In the usual corner sat Sludden with Gay, McPake with Frankie, Toal with Nan, and Rima reading a fashion magazine. Rima nodded to him and continued reading but the rest looked surprised and said, "Where have you been?" "What have you been doing?" "We thought you'd disappeared."

Lanark dropped the manuscript on the table beside Sludden who raised an eyebrow and asked what it was.

"Something I've written. I took your advice."

There was no room near Rima so Lanark squeezed onto the sofa between Sludden and Frankie. Sludden read a couple of pages, flicked through the rest, then handed it back saying, "It's dead. Perhaps you're more naturally a painter. I mean, it's good that you've tried to do something, I'm pleased about that, but what you've written there is dead."

Lanark blushed with anger. He could think of nothing to say which wouldn't show injured vanity so he pressed his lips into a smile. Sludden said, "I'm afraid I've hurt you."

"No no. But I wish you had read it carefully before judging."

"No need. Two pages showed me that your prose is totally flat, never departing an inch from your dull experiences. If a writer doesn't enjoy words for their own sake how can the reader enjoy them?"

"But I do enjoy words—some words—for their own sake! Words like river, and dawn, and daylight, and time. These words seem much richer than our experiences of the things they represent—"

Frankie cried out, "Sludden, you're a sadist, leave the mystery man alone! Don't bother about Sludden, mystery man. He thinks he's God but he can only prove it by torturing people. Isn't that true, Sludden?"

Sludden raised an imaginary hat from his head and bowed, but her wrath was too impressive to seem a joke. She stood up saying, "Anyway, McPake's taking us to this party, so come on, everybody. Rima, you don't care about fashion, give up pretending to read that magazine and look after Lanark. Try to stop rotten things happening to him. I can't do it."

She walked off toward the stairs. Toal, McPake and Sludden grinned at each other and pretended to wipe sweat from their brows. Everybody stood up. Sludden said to Lanark, "Come along, it might be fun."

"Who's giving this party?"

"Gay and I. It's our engagement party. But the house belongs to a friend and the army is providing the booze."

"Why?"

"Prestige reasons. The army likes to be liked."

Outside the cinema a steel-grey truck was parked beside the pavement and they scrambled through the sliding door into the narrow seats. Only McPake, in gauntlets and fleece-lined jacket, was dressed for the intense cold. He gripped the wheel and the truck charged smoothly forward. Sludden hugged

Gay to his side with one arm and Frankie with the other. Frankie resisted fretfully until he said, "I need you both, girls. This frost is killing me."

Toal and Nan embraced in the seat behind but Rima sat so forbiddingly erect that Lanark (who was beside her) folded arms on chest and clenched his teeth to stop their chattering. Gradually the heater raised a comfortable temperature. The truck nearly had the streets to itself but when passing a tramcar or pedestrian McPake sounded a clanging blast on the horn. Lanark said, "Rima, will there be dancing at this party?"

"I suppose so."

"Will you dance with me?"

"I suppose so. I'm not selective."

Lanark clenched his fist and bit hard on the thumb knuckle. After a moment he felt his arm touched. She said quietly, "I'm sorry I said that—I didn't mean to be nasty. I'm more nervous than I seem."

He almost laughed with relief and drew her gently against him saying, "I'm glad you told me. I was deciding to leave the truck and walk home."

"You're too serious."

The truck travelled down broad streets between over-grown gardens, then entered a drive which curved through a shubbery. The headlights made points of frost glisten among the dark leaves. McPake sounded his horn and stopped before a large mansion and everyone got out. The mansion was a square three-storey building with outhouses and a conservatory at the sides. The enclosing larches, hollies and rhododendrons gave it a secret look, although the windows were lit, music resounded and many cars were parked on the gravel near the porch. The front door was open, but Sludden pressed the bell before leading his party into the hall. This was heavily magnificent, terrazzo tiled and oak panelled, with a pair of black marble columns separating a space where the staircase began. A small figure looked out of a door on the right. It was Gloopy. He was shorter and fatter than Lanark remembered, his hair was streaked with grey and he wore a silver lamé jacket. He said, "There you are, Sludden. Leave the coats in here, will you?" The room was hung with paintings of fruit and lobsters in gilded frames. There was an oval table in the centre nearly covered by coats and scarves. As Lanark helped Rima remove her coat Gloopy gazed at him with a grin and said, "Hello, hello! So you've arrived after all. You'd have been here sooner if you'd come with me."

"Is *this* your boardinghouse?"

"It's not mine in the sense of owning it. I suppose you could call me the concierge."

"What's a concierge?"

"Why must you be nasty to me? I haven't hurt you."

"You don't understand our mystery man, Gloopy," said Sludden, who was straightening his tie at a mirror. "He's never nasty. He's just very very serious all the time. Where's the revelry tonight?"

"We're in the downstairs drawing room."

The interior walls and doors of the house seemed soundproof, for nothing could be heard in the hall but the click of their feet on the tiles, yet the opposite door opened into a crowded room where couples were dancing to loud jazz. The people were the kind who visited the Elite, though the girls were more exotically dressed and Lanark noticed a few elderly men in dark business suits. He took Rima's hand and led her onto the floor.

He couldn't remember enjoying music before but the rhythm excited him and his body moved to it easily. He kept his eyes on Rima. Her movements were abrupt yet graceful. Her dark hair lay loosely about her shoulders, she was smiling absentmindedly. The record came to an end and each stood with an arm round the other's waist. Lanark said, "Will we do that again?"

"Yes, why not?"

Suddenly he stared across the room, his mouth open. A table laden with food and drink stood in the curve of a bay window and a girl sat on the edge chatting to a stout spectacled man. Lanark muttered, "Who is the girl—the big blonde there in the white dress?"

"I don't know. One of the camp followers, I suppose. Why has your face gone that colour?"

"I've met her before."

"Oh?"

"Before I came here—before I came to this city. I know her face but I can't remember anything else."

"Does it matter?"

"How can I speak to her?"

"Ask her to dance."

"Do you mind, Rima?"

"Why should I?"

He hurried through the crowd to the table and reached it as

the music started. The girl was sipping from a glass while the stout man laughed heartily at something she had said. Lanark touched her shoulder. She set the glass down and let him lead her onto the floor. She was a vivacious girl with gaudy makeup and a rich brown tan. Lanark held her urgently and said, "Where have I seen you before?"
She smiled and shook her head. "I couldn't say."
"I think I know you well."
"I doubt it."
"I killed you, didn't I?"
She stepped violently back from him and said, "Oh my God!" People stopped and looked. She pointed at Lanark and said loudly, "How's this for party conversation? We've just met and he asks if he killed me once. How's that for small talk?" She turned to an onlooker (it was McPake) and said, "Take me away from that bastard."
They joined the dance, McPake winking at Lanark as they passed him. Lanark looked desperately round for Rima, then pushed to the door, stepped outside and closed it behind him.

The hall was completely empty and silent. It was also rather cold. Lanark strolled up and down wondering what to do. He could not think why he had blurted such words to the blond girl, but he would go far to avoid anyone who had been in the room at that time, excepting Rima. Yet he had no wish to leave. His elbow itched and he wondered if a wash would cool it. There was sure to be a bathroom in the house, a tiled bathroom with clean towels warming on heated towel rails, and soap crystals, and sponges, and all the hot water he could use. There was no bathroom in his own lodgings, he had not bathed since arriving there, and now (feeling dirty inside and out) he thought a bath would be beautifully soothing. He walked to the end of the hall and climbed the softly carpeted stairs. The upper floors were in darkness and he found his way by light from the hall below. At the second landing a corridor began. Halfway along it a triangle of light was cast on the floor from an ajar door. He moved toward this, his steps silent in the thick carpet, then stopped and peeked through the narrow door-slit. A vertical ribbon of wallpaper was visible, the light on it flickering slightly. Lanark pushed the door wide and stepped through.

The room was a library illuminated by a vivid fire burning beneath a carved mantelpiece. Above surrounding bookcases hung massive portraits with antique weapons crossed on the walls between them. There were many high-backed leather arm-chairs, and a standard lamp with a red silk shade shone beside one with a man getting up from it. He smiled at Lanark and said, "Why, it's the writer! Come on in."

He was nearly seven feet high and wore a polo-necked sweater and well-cut khaki trousers and, though perhaps fifty, gave an impression of youthful fitness. He had a bronzed bald head with tufts of white hair behind the ears, a clipped white mous-tache and good-humoured, boyishly alert features. Lanark said awkwardly, "I'm afraid I don't know you."

"Quite so. Not many of your crowd know me. Yet the whole place belongs to me. Funny, isn't it? I often have a laugh about that."

"Does Sludden know you?"

"Oh yes, Sludden and I are great buddies. What would you like to drink?"

He turned to a sideboard with bottles and glasses on it.

"Nothing."

"Nothing? Well, sit down anyway, I want you to tell me some-thing. Meanwhile I will pour myself . . . a drop . . . of Smith's Glenlivet Malt. Here's health."

The warm fire, the mild light, the host's calm manner made Lanark feel this a pleasant place to relax. He sat in one of the chairs.

The tall man returned with a glass in his hand, sat down and crossed his legs. He said, "What makes you chaps tick? What satisfaction do you, personally, get from being a writer?" Lanark tried to remember. He said, "It's the only disciplined work I remember trying. I sleep better after it."

"Really? But wouldn't you sleep better after other kinds of discipline?"

"I don't know. I suppose it's possible."

"And you've never thought of joining the army?"

"Why should I?"

"Because in a couple of terse, commonplace sentences you connected the ideas of work, discipline and health. So I suspect that, in spite of your association with sponges and leeches, you are still a vertebrate. Am I wrong?"

Lanark thought about this for a while, then asked, "What use is the army?"

"What use to society, you mean? Defence and employment. We defend and we employ. I believe you lodge with a woman called Fleck in a tenement beside Turk's Head Forge."

"How do you know?"

"Aha! There's not much we don't know. The point is that
the Turk's Head Forge produces components for our Q39.
Industry is slack just now, as you may have noticed. If it wasn't
for the Q39 programme the Forge would have to close, thousands would be unemployed and they'd have to cut the social
security allowance. Think of that next time you feel like knocking the army."

"What is the Q39?"

"You've seen them. They're being assembled in the yards near
the river."

"Do you mean these big metal constructions like bombs or
bullets?"

"You think they look like bombs, do you? Good! Good! That
cheers me greatly. Actually they're shelters to protect the civil-
ian population. Each one is capable of housing five hundred
souls when the balloon goes up."

"What do you mean?"

"About the balloon? It's a figure of speech derived from an
outmoded combat system. It means, when the sign goes out
that the big show is starting."

"What show?"

"I can't tell you precisely, because it could take several different
forms. We could be on the receiving end of any one of sixty-
eight different types of attack, and I don't mind telling you
that we're only capable of defending ourselves against three
of them. 'Hopeless! Why bother?' you say, and miss the point
entirely. The other side is as badly placed as we are. These
preparations for the big show may be pretty inadequate, but
if we stop them the balloon will go up. Am I depressing you?"

"No, but I'm confused."

The tall man nodded sympathetically. "I know, it's difficult.
Metaphor is one of thought's most essential tools. It illuminates
what would otherwise be totally obscure. But the illumination
is sometimes so bright that it dazzles instead of revealing."

It struck Lanark that in spite of his smooth flow of words
the tall man was drunk. Somebody grunted nearby. Lanark
turned and saw a stout elderly man sitting immobile in one
of the chairs. He wore a dark blue suit and waistcoat. His
eyes were shut but he was not asleep, for his hands were grasp-
ing his knees. Lanark gasped and said, "Who is that?"

"That is one of our city fathers. That is Baillie Dodd."

The man in the chair said, "No."

"Well, actually he's more than just Baillie Dodd. He's Provost Dodd." The tall man began to laugh. "Yes!" he said between gasps, "that's the Lord Provost of this whole, fucking big metropopolis."

He silenced his chuckles by drinking what was left in the glass, then went to the sideboard to refill. The Provost said, "What does he want?"

The tall man looked over his shoulder. "Yes, Lanark, what do you want?"

"Nothing."

"He said he wants nothing, Dodd."

After a moment the Provost said flatly, "Then he's no use to us."

The tall man returned to his seat saying, "I begin to fear you're right." He smiled at Lanark and sat down. "I suppose in the end you'll join the protest people."

"Who are they?"

"Oh, they're very nice people. No bother, really. My daughter is one. We have great arguments about it all. I had hoped you were a vertebrate, but I see you're a crustacean. You'll be at home with the protest people because most of them are crustaceans. Now you're going to ask what crustaceans are, so I'll tell you. The crustacean isn't a mere mass of sentient acquisitiveness, like your leech or your sponge. It has a distinct shape. But the shape is not based on a backbone, it derives from the insensitive shell which *contains* the beast. In the crustacean class you will find the scorpion, the lobster and the louse."

He smiled into his whisky. Lanark knew he had been insulted and stood up, saying sharply, "Could you tell me where the bathroom is?"

"Third on the left as you go out."

Lanark went to the door but turned before reaching it. He said, "Perhaps the Provost could tell me what his city is called?"

"Certainly he could. So could I. But for security reasons we're not going to."

Lanark opened the door to step through but was arrested by a cry of "Lanark!"

He turned and saw the man standing up gazing at him intently. "Lanark, if you ever come to feel you would like (how can I put it?) like to strike a blow for the good old vertebrate Divine Image, get in touch with me will you?"

There were tears in his eyes. Lanark went quickly out, feeling embarrassed.

The corridor was still in darkness. He turned left and moved toward the staircase, counting doors. The third one did not open into a bathroom but into a luxurious, brilliantly lit bedroom. On the quilt of the double bed moved a huge knot of limbs with the heads of Frankie, Toal and Sludden sticking out. Lanark slammed the door and clapped his hands over his eyes but the image of what he had seen stayed inside the lids: a knot of limbs with three crazily vacant faces, and Sludden's mouth opening and shutting as if eating something. He hurried to the stairs and ran down them to the cloakroom. He was looking for his coat among the heap on the table when a slurred voice said, "I feel we've never really understood each other."

Gloopy stood grinning emptily in the doorway. His legs were together and his arms pressed to his sides, his oiled grey hair and silver jacket glistened wetly. He took a few steps nearer, walking as if his thighs were glued together, then fell forward onto the floor with a sodden slap. He lay in the posture in which he had stood, except that his face was tilted so far back that it grinned blindly at the ceiling. Without moving his limbs he suddenly slid an inch or two toward Lanark along the polished floorboards, and then the light went out.

The darkness and silence were so complete that for a moment Lanark was deafened by the noise of his own breathing. Then he heard Gloopy say, "People ought to be nice to one another. Why can't you and I—"

The words were cut short by a chilling draught which blew up suddenly from the floor bringing with it a salt stench like rotting weeds. Lanark felt he was on the lip of a horrible pit. He grew dizzy and crouched to the floor, afraid to move his feet and terrified of falling down. He squatted in the darkness like this for a very long time.

At last he saw light from the hall shining through the doorway. A bulky figure appeared in it, grunted and switched the light on. It was Provost Dodd. Lanark stood up, feeling sick and foolish, and said, "Gloopy. He's disappeared. Gloopy's disappeared!"

The Provost stared about the room as if Lanark were not in it and muttered, "No great loss, I would have thought."

Lanark was filled with the conviction that every footstep in that room might land in an invisible trap. He managed to move

to the door without running. The Provost said, "Wait."
Lanark stepped into the hall before turning to him. The Provost pushed out his lower lip, frowned down at his shoes, then said, "You came with a girl. She had black hair and wore a black sweater and her skirt was . . . I forget the colour."
"Black."
"Quite so. Do you know where she is?"
"No."
The Provost stared at him for a while then turned away, saying heavily, "Anyway, it's all the same. It's all the same."
Lanark hurried out, slamming the door hard behind him.

CHAPTER 5. Rima

There was fog outside. The light from the windows saturated it so that the mansion seemed wrapped in a cocoon of milky light, but outside the cocoon Lanark walked in total obscurity and only found his way down the drive by the crunch of gravel underfoot and the touch of rimy leaves on his hands and face.

On the pavement it was possible to steer through the murk by the glow of the street lamp ahead. The clammy air made his footsteps resound loudly but after five minutes he decided that what seemed like echoes were the footsteps of someone behind. His back prickled apprehensively. He stood against a hedge and waited. The other footsteps hesitated, then came boldly on. In the fog's cloudy dimness a shadow appeared and developed an unusual density of black, then the slim black figure of Rima passed by giving him only the flicker of a glance. He hurried after her crying gladly, "Rima! It's me!"

"So I see."

"Provost Dodd was looking for you."

"Who's Provost Dodd?"

The question seemed meant to stop conversation rather than aid it. He walked beside her, thinking of what he had seen of her friends in the bedroom. This memory no longer horrified. It combined with his words to the blond girl, with Gloopy's disappearance and with the fog; it cast around her an odour of exciting malign sexual possibility. He asked abruptly, "Did you enjoy the party?"

"No."

"What did you do?"

"If you must know I spent most of the time in the bathroom with Gay. She was very sick."

"Why?"

"I don't want to talk about it."

"Do you want to talk to me at all?"

"No."

His heart and penis hardened in angry amazement. He gripped her arms and pulled her round to face him saying softly, "Why?" She glared into his eyes and yelled, "Because I'm afraid of you!"

He was hit by a feeling of shame and weariness. He let her go, shrugging his shoulders and muttering, "Well, maybe that's wise of you."

Half a minute later he was surprised to find her walking beside him. She said, "I'm sorry."

"Don't be. Maybe I am a dangerous man."

She began laughing but quickly smothered this and slipped a hand through his arm. The light pressure made him calmer and stronger.

They came to a street corner. The fog was very thick. A tramcar clanged past a few feet in front of them, but nothing could be seen of it. Rima said, "Where's your coat? You're shivering."

"So are you. I'd take you for a coffee but I don't know where we are."

"You'd better come with me. I live nearby and I stole a bottle of brandy from the party."

"You shouldn't have done that."

Rima withdrew her hand sharply and said, "You, are a very, big, wet, drip!"

Lanark was stung by this. He said, "Rima, I am not clever or imaginative. I have only a few rules to live by. These rules may annoy folk who are clever enough to live without them, but I can't help that and you ought not to blame me."

"All right, I'm sorry, I'm sorry, I'm sorry. You can make me apologize by breathing on me, it seems."

They turned the corner. Lanark said, "But I can frighten you too."

She was silent.

"And I can make you laugh."

She laughed slightly and took his arm again.

They seemed to enter a lane between low buildings like private garages. Rima unlocked a door, led him up a steep narrow wooden stair and switched a light on. Her austere man-

ner and clothing had made Lanark expect a stark room. This
room was small, with a sloping ceiling and not much furniture,
but there were many sad little personal touches. Childish crayon
sketches of unconvincing green fields and blue seas were fixed
to the walls. There was the only clock Lanark remembered
seeing, carved and painted like a log cabin, with a pendulum
below and a gilt weight shaped like a fir cone. The hands were
missing. A stringless guitar lay on a chest of drawers and a
teddy bear sat on the bed, which was a mattress on the floor
against the wall. Rima clicked the switch of the electric radiator,
removed her coat and became busy with a kettle and gas ring
in a cupboard-sized scullery. There were no chairs, so Lanark
sat on the floor and leaned on the bed. The radiator heated
the small place so quickly that he was soon able to remove
his fog-sodden jacket and jersey, yet though his skin was warm
he was still shaken from inside by spasms of shivering. Rima
carried in two large mugs of black coffee. She sat on the bed
with her legs folded under her and handed a mug to Lanark
saying, "You probably won't refuse to drink it."
The coffee flavour was drowned by the taste of sugar and
brandy.

Later Lanark lay back on the bed, feeling comfortable and
slightly drunk. Rima, her eyes closed, rested her shoulders
against the wall and cradled the teddy bear in her lap. Lanark
said, "You've been kind to me."
She stroked the old toy's head. Lanark tried to think of other
words. He said, "Did you come to this town long ago?"
"What does 'long' mean?"
"Were you very small when you came?"
She shrugged.
"Do you remember a time when days were long and bright?"
Tears slid from under her closed lids. He touched her shoulders.
"Let me undress you?"
She allowed this. As he unfastened her brassière his hands met
a familiar roughness.
"You've got dragonhide! Your shoulderblades are covered!"
"Does that excite you?"
"I have it too!"
She cried out harshly, "Do you think that makes a bond between
us?"
He shook his head urgently and placed a finger on her lips,
feeling that words would move them farther apart. His anxiety
to be tender to someone who needed and rejected tenderness

made his caresses clumsy, until genital eagerness sucked thought out of him.

He felt relieved afterward and would have liked to sleep. He heard her rise briskly from his side and start dressing. She said curtly, "Well? Was it fun?"

He tried to think then said defiantly, "Yes. Great fun."

"How nice for you."

A nightmare feeling began to rise around him. He heard her say, "You're not good at sex, are you? I suppose Sludden is the best I'll ever get."

"You told me that you didn't . . . . love . . . . Sludden."

"I don't, but I use him sometimes. Just as he uses me. He and I are very cold people."

"Why did you let me come here?"

"You wanted so much to be warm that I thought perhaps you were. You're as cold as the rest of us, really, and even more worried about it. I suppose that makes you clumsy."

He was drowned in nightmare now, lying on the bottom of it as on an ocean bed, yet he could breathe. He said, "You're trying to kill me."

"Yes, but I won't manage. You're *terribly* solid."

She finished dressing and slapped his cheek briskly saying, "Come on. I can't apologize to you again. Get up and get dressed."

She stood with her back against the chest of drawers, watching while he slowly dressed, and when he finished she said inexorably, "Goodbye, Lanark."

All his feelings were numbed but he stood a moment, staring stupidly at her feet. She said, "Goodbye, Lanark!" and gripped his arm and led him to the door, and pushed him out and slammed it.

He groped his way downstairs. Near the bottom he heard her open the door and shout "Lanark!" He looked back. Something dark and whirling came down on his head, heavily enfolding it, and again the door slammed. He dragged the thing off and found it was a sheepskin jacket with the fleece turned inward. He hung this on the inside knob of the bottom door and stepped into the lane and walked away.

After a time the dense freezing fog and his arctic brain and body blended. He moved along streets in them, a numb kernel of soul kept going by feet somewhere underneath. The only thing he felt very conscious of was his itching right arm, and several times he stopped and rubbed it backward and forward against corners of walls to scratch it through the sleeve. The sounds and lights of tramcars passed him frequently now, and after crossing a street he was puzzled by a complicated shape between himself and the flow of a high lamp. Going nearer he discerned a queen with a long train riding side-saddle on a rearing horse. It was a statue in the great square. He considered going for warmth to the security office but decided he needed something to drink. He crossed other streets till he saw red neon shining above the pavement. He opened the tinkling door of a small aromatic tobacconist shop, crossed to a staircase and went down into Galloway's Tearoom. This was a low-ceilinged place much bigger than the shop upstairs. Most of it was alcoves, some opening from others, each with a sofa, table and chairs in it and a stag's head on a plaque. Lanark ordered lemon tea, sat in the corner of a sofa and fell asleep.

He awoke long afterward. The glass of tea was cold on the table before him and he was listening to a conversation between two businessmen. His ear was an inch from a thick brown curtain separating his sofa from where they sat and clearly they had no sense of being overheard.
". . . Dodd is on our side. After all, the Corporation has nothing to do but light the streets and keep the trams running, and these services don't pay for themselves. They have to be subsidized by the sale of municipal property, so Dodd is selling and I'm buying."
"But what will you do with it?"
"Sublet. The smallest of these rooms could contain sixteen single apartments if we divided them up with matchboard partitions. I've measured."
"Don't be mad! Why should anyone want a tiny apartment just because it's on the square? There's no profit in being a landlord with a third of the city standing empty."
"No profit at the moment. I mean to sublet these eventually."
"Don't be mysterious, Aitcheson. You can trust me."
"All right. You know the population is smaller than it used to be. Have you faced the fact that it gets smaller all the time?"
"Why?"
"You know why."
There was a silence. "What about the new arrivals?"
"Not enough of them. You live in a hotel, don't you?"
"Of course."

"Of course. So do I. Nobody notices disappearances in a hotel. In the normal way you expect the man in the next room to disappear after a while. Life is different in a tenement. Suddenly the house across the landing is empty. A little later the one upstairs goes empty too. Then you notice there are no lights in half the windows across the street. It's disturbing! Mind you, people are still pretending not to notice. Wait till they have no neighbours left. Wait till they're lonely and the panic starts! They'll crowd to the city centre like drowning men onto a raft. If the city chambers are still empty they'll break in and squat. But they won't be empty because I'll be subletting them."

After a pause, the other voice said grudgingly, "Very clever. But aren't you being a bit optimistic? You're gambling on a trend that may not continue."

"What is there to stop it?"

Lanark stood up, feeling terribly afraid. A short while ago he had told Sludden he was content. Now everything he heard or saw or remembered was pushing him toward panic. He desperately wanted Rima beside him, a Rima who would smile and be sad with him, a Rima whose fears he could soothe and who would not fling words at him like stones. He paid for the tea and went back to his own room and undressed. When jacket and jersey were removed he saw the right shirt-sleeve was stiff with dried blood, and on taking off the shirt he found the arm was dragonhide from shoulder to wrist, with spots of it on the back of his hand. He put on his pyjamas, got into bed and fell asleep. There seemed nothing else to do.

CHAPTER 6. Mouths

With no will to see anyone or do anything he immersed himself in sleep as much as possible, only waking to stare at the wall until sleep returned. It was a sullen pleasure to remember that the disease spread fastest in sleep. Let it spread! he thought. What else can I cultivate? But when the dragonhide had covered the arm and hand it spread no further, though the length of the limb as a whole increased by six inches. The fingers grew stouter, with a slight web between them, and the nails got longer and more curving. A red point like a rose-thorn formed on each knuckle. A similar point, an inch and a half long, grew on the elbow and kept catching the sheets, so he slept with his right arm hanging outside the cover onto the floor. This was no hardship as there was no feeling in it, though it did all he wanted with perfect promptness and sometimes obeyed wishes before he consciously formed them. He would find it holding a glass of water to his lips and only then notice he was thirsty, and on three occasions it hammered the floor until he waked up and Mrs. Fleck came running with a cup of tea. He felt embarrassed and told her to ignore it. She said, "No, no, Lanark, my husband had that before he disappeared. You must never ignore it."

He thanked her. She rubbed her hands on her apron as if drying them and said abruptly, "Do you mind if I ask you something?"

"No."

"Why don't you get up, Lanark, and look for work? I've lost a husband by that"—she nodded to the arm—"and a couple of lodgers, and all of them, before the end, just lay in bed, and all of them were decent quiet fellows like yourself."

"Why should I get up?"

"I don't like talking about it, but I've an illness of my own—
not what you have, a different one—and it's never spread very
far because I've had work to do. First it was a husband, then
lodgers, now it's these bloody weans. I'm sure if you get up
and work your arm will improve."

"What work can I get?"

"The Forge over the road is wanting men."

Lanark laughed harshly and said, "You want me to make components for the Q39."

"I know nothing about factory work, but if a man gets pay
and exercise by it I don't see why he should complain."

"How can I go for work with an arm like this?"

"I'll tell you how. My husband had the same trouble on exactly
the same arm. So I knitted him a thick woollen glove and
lined it with wash leather. He never used it. But if you wear
it along with your jacket nobody will notice, and if they do,
why bother? There are plenty of men with crabby hands."

Lanark said, "I'll think about it."

He was prevented from saying more by the hand's raising the
teacup to his lips and holding it there.

Sometimes the children played on the floor of the room.
He liked this. They were quarrelsome but they never explained
what life was or persuaded him to do something, their selfishness did not make him feel wicked. At these times he felt
ashamed of his great arm and kept it below the covers, but
once he awoke to find it lying outside with the children squatting round it staring. The boy said admiringly, "You could
murder someone with that."

Lanark was ashamed because the thought had occurred to himself. He drew the arm out of sight and muttered without much
conviction that two human hands would be better. The boy
said, "Yes, but not in a fight."

Lanark found the limb beginning to fascinate him. The colour
was not really black but an intensely dark green. It looked
diseased because it grew on a man, but considered by itself
the glossy cold hide, the thorny red knuckles and elbow, the
curving steel-blade claws looked very healthy indeed. He began
to have fantasies about the damage it could do. He imagined
entering the Elite and walking across to the Sludden clique
with the hand inside the bosom of his jacket. He would smile
at them with one side of his mouth, then expose the hand
suddenly. As Sludden, Toal and McPake leapt to their feet
he would knock them down with a sweeping sideways blow,

then drive the squealing girls into a corner and rake the clothes
off them. Then the image grew confused, for each of his fantasies tended to dissolve into another one before reaching a climax. After these dreams he would become dismally cold and
depressed. Once he discovered himself stroking the cold right
hand with the fingertips of the left and murmuring, "When I
am all like this. . . ." But if he was all like that he would
have no feeling at all, so he thought of Rima and her moments
of kindness: the time in the truck when she touched him and
said she was sorry, the dance and how they held each other,
the moment in the fog when she laughed at him and slid her
hand round his arm, the coffee she had made and even the
jacket she had flung. But these memories were too feeble
to restore human feeling, and he would return to admiring
the feelingless strength of the dragonish limb until he fell
asleep.

At last he wakened in pain which made him scream aloud.
Mrs. Fleck ran in. A ragged wound had been torn in his side
through the pyjama jacket, blood from it flooded the blankets.
Lanark bit the thumb knuckle of his left hand to prevent further
screaming and glared at the bloodstained claws of the right.
Mrs. Fleck ran to get bandages and water but when she returned
dragonhide had crystalized over the wound and Lanark sat on
the bed pulling his clothes on. He said, "You spoke about a
glove. Can I have it?"
She went to a lobby cupboard and took out her husband's
glove and an old waterproof coat. She helped Lanark put them
on and he left the house.

Snow had fallen but thin rain was reducing it to slush.
He had gone to bed because the alternatives were detestable
and now he walked the streets because sleep was dangerous,
choosing streets where the slush lay thinnest. Once again he
came to the square. The ground-floor windows were alight
in a building along one side of it, and hammering and sawing
resounded within. Arched doors stood open, showing a marble-
floored entrance hall with a red wooden hut in the middle.
It was covered with posters saying **YOU HAVEN'T MUCH
TIME—PROTEST NOW.** The words seemed meant for him,
so he crossed the marble to the hut and stepped inside.

A thin, bearded man wearing a clerical collar and an old
woman with wild white hair sat behind a counter putting pamphlets into envelopes. A young man with bushy hair typed

rapidly at a table behind them, and an attractive girl sat on the table plucking idly at a guitar. As Lanark approached the counter the woman clasped her hands below her chin and looked at him with an encouraging smile. After hesitating awhile he said in a low voice, "I'm frightened of what's happening to me."

She nodded vigorously. "Yes! No wonder. If you've been looking around you'll see we haven't much time."

"What can I do?"

"The primary need is to persuade others of the danger. When we have a majority we can act. Would you care to distribute some pamphlets for us?"

"That wouldn't help. You see my arm is all—"

"Oh, we understand that! And we're glad you came, even so. Please, please don't believe we don't care. We have launched this campaign because we care deeply. But for troubles of that personal kind hard work is the only answer, hard work for a decent cause. I'm sure if you sit down calmly and address those envelopes it will help more than you believe."

Lanark pulled the glove off and showed her the right hand. Her round, pleasant face grew red but she smiled determinedly into his eyes and said, "You see, the only cure for these—personal—diseases is sunlight. Which our party is trying to restore. The artificially inflated land values at the centre have produced such overbuilding on the horizon that the sun is barely able to rise above it. As soon as we have a majority we can persuade the authorities to act."

The bushy-haired young man had stopped typing to roll a cigarette. He said, "Ballocks. If we had a majority tomorrow the situation would be the same. A city is ruled by its owners. Nine tenths of our factories and houses are owned by a few financiers and landlords, with a bureaucracy and a legal system to defend them and collect the money. They are a minority and they are in power. Why should we wait until there are more of us before we seize it? Numerically there are more of us already."

The girl looked up from the guitar and said, "I think you're being too hard on the boss class. They feel in their bones that the system is unfair and unwieldy, so the intelligent ones get terribly bored and join us. That's what I did. My daddy's a brigadier."

"We contain all shades of opinion," said the white-haired woman, becoming flustered, "but we are agreed upon one thing: the need for sunlight. You need that too, so why not join us?"

Lanark stared at her and she smiled bravely back but eventually shrugged her shoulders and resumed work with the envelopes. The clergyman beside her leaned forward toward Lanark and said in a low voice, "You're on the edge of a pit, aren't you?" In spite of the beard his face looked childish and eager, with a blue mark like a bruise above the right eyebrow. He said quietly, "People in this organization see the pit a long way ahead, so put your glove on, we can't help you." Lanark bit his underlip and pulled on the glove. The man said, "If you get out of the pit I hope you'll join us all the same. You won't need us then but we will certainly need you." Lanark said heavily, "I don't know what you're talking about," and walked away.

He crossed the square and walked to the Elite because it was the only other place he could think of and Rima might be there. Her kindly moments had become radiant in the coldness he moved through, and she had dragonhide too, and what had it made of her? He leaped flooded gutters and plunged through ridges of slush; he pushed open the glass doors of the foyer and rushed upstairs, and the café was empty. He stood in the entrance and stared unbelievingly around but nobody was there, not even the man who had stood so fixedly behind the counter. Lanark turned and went downstairs.

Crossing the halfway landing he saw a girl below in the foyer buying cigarettes at the cash desk. It was Gay. He called her name and hurried down. She looked whiter and thinner but greeted him with surprising vivacity, bobbing lightly up to kiss his lips. She said, "Where have you been, Lanark? Why those mysterious disappearances?"
"I've been in bed. Come upstairs with me."
"Upstairs? Nobody goes upstairs nowadays. It's so horrible. We use the downstairs café now, the light is more soothing." She pointed to a thick red curtain which Lanark had thought covered a door to the cinema. She pulled it slightly aside, saying, "Come and join us. All the old gang are here."
Beyond the curtain was perfect blackness. Lanark said, "There's no light here at all."
"Yes there is, but your eyes take a while to get used to it."
"And is Rima in there?"
Gay let the curtain go and said uneasily, "I don't think I've seen Rima since my . . . . my engagement party."
"Then she's at home?"

"I suppose so."

"Could you tell me how to get to it? I went there in the fog and I couldn't find it now."

Gay's face seemed suddenly ancient. She folded her arms, bowed her head and shoulders, looked at him sideways and said faintly, "I could take you there. But Sludden wouldn't like it."

"Take me there, Gay! She helped you when you were sick at the party. I'm afraid something is happening to her too."

She gave him a sly, frightened look and said. "Sludden sent me to buy cigarettes and he hates waiting for anything."

Lanark saw that his dragon hand was clenching to strike her. He thrust it into his pocket where it squirmed like a crab. Gay did not notice. She said wistfully, "You're very solid, Lanark. I can go with you if you hold me, I think. But Sludden never lets go."

She held out a hand to him. He seized it gladly and they went into the street.

Gay's footsteps were so feeble that he put his good arm round her waist to help her onward. At first they went quickly, then the pressure on his arm began to increase. Her feet were not engaging the slippery pavement, and though her body was light it felt as if an elastic cord fixed to her back were making forward movement more difficult with each step. He paused for a moment under a lamppost, breathing hard from exertion. Gay put an arm round the pole to steady herself but seemed wholly placid. With a coy sideways look she said, "You're wearing a glove on your right hand. I've got one on my left!"

"What about it?"

"I'll show you my disease if you show me yours!"

He began to say he was not interested in her disease but she pulled off her fur gauntlet. Surprise gagged him. He had expected dragon claws like his own, but all he could see was a perfectly shaped white little hand, the fingers lightly clenched, until she unclenched them to show the palm. He took a moment to recognize what lay on it. A mouth lay on it, grinning sarcastically. It opened and said in a tiny voice, "You're trying to understand things, and that interests me."

It was Sludden's voice. Lanark whispered, "Oh, this is hell!"

Gay's hand sank to her side. He saw that the soles of her feet were an inch above the pavement. Her body dangled before him as if from a hook in her brain, her smile was vacant and silly, her jaw fell and the voice which came from the mouth was not formed by movement of tongue or lip. Though it had a slightly cavernous echo it was Sludden's voice, which said glibly, "It's time we got together again, Lanark," while a tiny identical voice from her left hand cried shrilly, "You worry too much about the wrong things."

"Oh! Oh!" Lanark gabbled. "This is hell!"

He pressed gloved and ungloved hands to his mouth and without ceasing to stare at Gay's dangling image stepped backward away from her. Like something sliding on a wire she quivered and moved backward too, slowly at first, then accelerating till he saw her emptily grinning face recede and dwindle to a point in the direction of the café.

He turned and ran.

He ran blindly till his foot slipped and he fell on the slushy pavement, bruising hip and shoulder and soaking his trousers. When he stood up the panic had been replaced by desperation. His wish to leave this city was powerful and complete and equalled by a certainty that streets and buildings and diseased people stretched infinitely in every direction. He was standing near railings with a bank of snow beyond them which the rain had not dissolved. Some naked trees grew out of it. The trees and snow had such a fresh look that he climbed the railings and waded upward between the trunks. The lamps in the street behind showed a dim hillside laid out as a cemetery. Black gravestones stood on the snowy paleness and he climbed between them, amazed that the ground of this place had once swallowed men in a natural way. He reached a path with a bench on it, brushed snow from the seat with his sleeve, then knelt and banged his brow hard there three times, crying from the centre of his soul, "Let me out! Let me out! Let me out!" After a moment he stood up, dazed by the blows but indifferent to sodden clothes and aching body. He felt strangely buoyant. There was a yellow radiance among some obelisks on the hilltop, lighting the base of a few and silhouetting others, so he ran uphill.

The slope below the summit was unusually steep, and Lanark kept rushing up and slithering back until he gained the momentum to reach the top and stumble between two monuments onto flat ground. The summit was a circular plot with a ring of obelisks round the edge and a cluster of them in the middle. They were old and tall with memorials carved on the pedestals. He was puzzled by the light. It was a glow like the light from a steady fire, it lit nothing over five feet from the ground and cast no shadows, and Lanark walked round the central monuments without discovering a source. The glow was brightest on a pedestal near the place where he had entered the ring, so he examined it for a clue. It was a marble block erected by the workers and management of the Turks Road Forge in gratitude to a doctor who had rendered them skilled and faithful service between 1833 and 1879. Lanark was reading the inscription for a second time when he noticed a dim shadow across the centre of the stone. He glanced over his shoulder to see what cast it and saw nothing, though when he glanced back it looked like the shadow of a bird with outspread wings. But the colour deepened and he saw that the shape forming there was a mouth three feet wide, the lips meeting in a serene, level line. His heart beat now with an excitement which was certainly not fear. When the lips had fully formed they parted and spoke, and just as a single intense ray can dazzle an eye without lighting a room, so this voice pierced the ear without sounding loud. It pierced so painfully that he could not understand the syllables as they were spoken, but had to remember them when they stopped. The mouth had said, "I am the way out."

Lanark said, "What do you mean?"

The lips pressed together in a line which seemed ruled on the stone and moved swiftly to the ground, crossing the projections of the base as simply as the shadow of a gull passes over a waterfall. It sped over the snow, then stopped and opened into an oval pit in front of his feet. The edges of the lips were shaded lightly on the snow but curved steeply down to the projecting tips of the perfect teeth. From the blackness between these rose a cold wind with the salty odour of rotting seaweed, then a hot one with an odour like roasting meat. Lanark shuddered with dread and giddiness. He remembered the mouth in Gay's hand which had nothing behind it but a cold man being nasty to people in a dark room. He said, "Where will you take me?"

The mouth closed and became dim at the corners. He saw it was fading and would leave him on a hilltop in a city more sterile and lonely than anything a pit could hold. He shouted, "Stop! I'll come!"

The mouth grew distinct again. He asked humbly, "How should I come?"

It replied. When the sound stopped hurting his ears he found it had said "Naked, and head first."

It was hard to remove the coat and jacket because his side had grown thorns which pierced the cloth. He ripped them free and threw them down, then looked at the mouth which lay patiently open. He rubbed his face with the good hand and said, "I'm afraid to go head first. I'm going to lower myself backwards and hang by the hands, and if I'm too scared to let go I will consider it a kindness if you let me hang till I drop."

He stared at the mouth but no part of it moved. He sat on the rags of the coat and removed his shoes. Fear was making him slow, he grew terrified of its stopping him altogether so he went to the mouth without undressing further. The hot breath alternating with the cold one had melted the surrounding snow into a margin of firm moist gravel. Moving fast to avoid thinking, he sat with his legs in the mouth, gripped the teeth opposite and slid down until he hung from them. Since the right arm was longer than the left he hung by that alone, buffeted by hot roast and cold rot blasts and waiting for the hand to weary and loosen. It didn't. His claws gripped a big incisor as if screwed to it, and when he tried to loosen them the muscles of the whole limb began to contract and lift him toward the oval of dark sky between the teeth. In a moment his head and shoulders would have come through them, but he yelled, "Shut! Bite shut!"

Blackness closed over him with a clash and he fell.

But not far. The cavity below the mouth narrowed to a gullet down which he slithered and bumped at decreasing speed as his clothing and thorny arm began catching on the sides. The sides began to tighten and loosen, heating as they tightened, cooling as they loosened, and the descent became a series of freezing drops from one scalding grip to another. The pressure and heat grew greater and gripped him longer until he punched and kicked against it. He was dropped at once but only fell a few feet, and the next hold was so sickeningly tight that he could not move his arms and legs at all. He opened his mouth to scream and a mixture of wool and cloth squeezed into it, for the pressure had dragged vest, shirt and jersey over his face. He was suffocating. He urinated. The great grip stopped, he slid downward, the garments slid upward, freeing mouth and nose, and then the sides contracted and crushed him harder than ever. Most senses abandoned him now. Thought and memory, stench, heat and direction dissolved and he knew nothing but pressure and duration. Cities seemed piled on him with a weight which doubled every second; nothing but movement could lessen this pressure; all time, space and mind would end unless he moved but it had been aeons since he could have stirred toe or eyelid. And then he felt like an infinite worm in infinite darkness, straining and straining and failing to disgorge a lump which was choking him to death.

After a while nothing seemed very important. Hands were touching his sides, softly sponging and softly drying. The light was too strong to let him open his eyes. Some words were whispered and someone softly laughed. At last he opened his eyelids the narrowest possible slit. He lay naked on a bed with a clean towel across his genitals. Two girls in white dresses stood at his feet, clipping the toenails with tiny silvery scissors. Between their bowed heads he saw the dial of a clock on the wall beyond, a large white dial with a slender scarlet second hand travelling round it. He glanced toward his right side. Growing down from the shoulder was a decent, commonplace, human limb.

CHAPTER 7. The Institute

The food was always a lax white meat like fish, or a stronger one like breast of chicken, or pale yellow like steamed egg. It was completely tasteless, but though Lanark never ate more than half the small portion on his plate the meals left him unusually comfortable and alert. The room had milk-coloured walls and a floor of polished wood. Five beds with blue coverlets stood against one wall, and Lanark, in the middle bed, faced a wall pierced by five arches. He could see a corridor behind them with a big window covered by a white Venetian blind. The clock was over the middle arch, its circumference divided into twenty-five hours. At half past five the light went on and two nurses carried in hot water and shaving things and made the bed. At six, twelve and eighteen o'clock they brought meals in a wheeled cabinet. At nine, fifteen and twenty-two o'clock a cup of tea was given him by a nurse who measured his temperature and felt his pulse in a slightly offhand manner. At half past twenty-two the neon tubes in the ceiling faded and the only light filtered in through the corridor blind. This was a pearly mobile light from several sources, all moving and growing or dimming as they moved, yet the movement was too stately and suggestive of distances to be cast by traffic. Lanark was soothed by it. Each pillar between the arches threw several shadows into the room, every one a different degree of greyness and all sweeping at different slow rates in one direction or another. The dim, rhythmical, yet irregular movement of these shadows was reassuringly different from the horrifying black pressure which the pressure of the pillow on his cheek still brought to mind. One morning he said to the nurses making the bed, "What's outside the window?"

"Just scenery. Miles and miles of scenery."
"Why are the blinds never raised?"
"You couldn't stand the view, Bushybrows. We can't stand it and we're perfectly fit."
They had begun calling him Bushybrows. He examined his face in two square inches of shaving mirror and noticed that his eyebrows had white hairs in them. He lay back thoughtfully and asked, "How old do I look?"
One said, "A bit over thirty."
The other said, "No chicken, anyway."
He nodded glumly and said, "A short while ago I seemed ten years younger."
"Well, Bushybrows, that's life, isn't it?"

He was visited that morning by a bald professional man wearing a white coat and half-moon-shaped rimless glasses. He stood by the bed surveying Lanark with a grave look which did not completely hide amusement. He said, "Do you remember me?"
"No."
The doctor fingered a piece of sticking plaster on his chin and said, "Three days ago you punched me, just here. Oh yes, you came out fighting. I'm sorry I haven't had time to see you since. We have hardly enough staff to deal with the serious cases, so the totally hopeless and the nearly fit are left much to themselves. Can you go to the lavatory yet?"
"Yes, if I hold onto the beds and walls."
"I suppose your sleep is still pretty troubled?"
"Not very."
"You're recovering fast. You would be running around already if you'd undressed properly and come head first. At present you are convalescing from severe shock, so take things easily. Is there anything special you would like?"
"Could you get me something to read?"
The doctor slid each hand up the opposite sleeve and stood for a moment with his lips pursed, looking like a mandarin. He said, "I'll try, but I can't promise much. Our institute has been isolated since the outbreak of the second world war. There is only one way of coming here and you've seen yourself how impossible it is to bring luggage."
"But the nurses are young girls!"
"Well?"
"You said the place was isolated."

"It is. We recruit our staff from among the patients. I expect
you'll be joining us soon."

"When I get better I intend to leave."

"Easier said than done. We'll discuss it in a day or two, when
you're able to walk. Meanwhile I'll hunt out some reading
material."

The nurses who brought the midday meal also brought
a children's cartoon book called *Oor Wullie's Annual for 1938*,
a crime novel with the covers missing called *No Orchids for
Miss Blandish*, and a fat squat little book in good condition,
The Holy War, in which the *s* was usually printed *f* and half
the pages were uncut. Lanark began reading *Oor Wullie*. It made
him smile in places but many pages had been spoiled by someone's colouring them with a blunt brown crayon. He began
No Orchids and was halfway through it that evening when the
nurses hurried in and set screens around the bed beside him.
They brought metal cylinders and trolleys of medical equipment
and went out saying, "Here comes a friend for you, Bushybrows."

A male nurse wheeled in a stretcher and the room was
filled with the sound of hoarse guttural breathing. The figure
on the stretcher was hidden by two doctors walking alongside,
one of them Lanark's doctor. They went behind the screens
and the stretcher was taken away. Lanark could read no longer.
He lay listening to the tinkle of instruments, the murmur of
professional voices, the huge harsh breathing. His evening cup
of tea was brought and the lights went out. Except for a lamp
behind the screens the room was bathed in moving shadows
cast by the corridor windows. The breathing became a couple
of quietly repeated vocal sighs and then grew inaudible.
Screens, trolley and instruments were wheeled out and everyone left except the doctor with the rimless glasses, who came
to Lanark's bed and sat heavily on the edge wiping his brow
with a piece of tissue. He said, "He's cured of his disease,
poor sod. God knows how he'll recover from the journey here."
Under the bed lamp, propped against a bank of pillows, was
a face so shockingly like a yellow skull that the only indication
of age and sex was a white moustache with drooping corners.
The sockets were so deep that it was impossible to see the
eyes. A skeletal arm lay on the coverlet, and a rubber tube
carried fluid from a suspended bottle to a bandage round the
biceps.

The doctor sighed and said, "We did what we could, and he

should be comfortable for eight hours at least. I wish you would do us a favour. You still sleep pretty lightly, I suppose?"

"Yes."

"He may gain consciousness and feel like talking. I could leave a nurse here but their damned professional cheerfulness depresses introspective men. Talk to him, if he feels like it, and if he wants a doctor call me on this."

He took from his pocket a white plastic radio the size of a cigarette packet. There was a circular mesh on one surface and a red switch at the side. The doctor pressed the switch, and a small clear frantic voice asked Dr. Bannerjee to come to delivery room Q. The doctor switched it off and slid it under Lanark's pillow. He said, "It works two ways. If you speak into it and ask for me they'll pass the message on; I'm called Munro. But don't try to stay awake, he'll waken you if he needs you."

Lanark could not sleep. He lay at the edge of the glow surrounding the sick man, turned his back to the bony head and played the radio under the pillow. Munro had said his institute was understaffed but the staff was still very large. In ten minutes he heard forty different doctors summoned in tones indicating an emergency to places and tasks he was wholly unable to picture. One call said, "Will Dr. Gibson go to the sink? There is resistance on the north rim." Another said, "Ward R-sixty requires an osteopath. There is twittering. Will any free osteopath go at once to deterioration ward R-sixty." He was greatly puzzled by a call which said, "Here is a warning for the engineers from Professor Ozenfant. A salamander will discharge in chamber eleven at approximately fifteen-fifteen." At last he switched the clamour off and dozed uneasily.

He was wakened by a low cry and sat up. The sick man was craning forward from his pillows, moving his head from side to side as if seeking something, yet Lanark was still unable to see eyes in the black sockets. The man said loudly, "Is anybody there? Who are you?"

"I'm here. I'm a patient, like yourself. Should I call a doctor?"

"How tall am I?"

Lanark stared at the thin figure beneath the blue coverlet. He said "Quite tall."

The man was sweating. He gave a dreadful shriek. *"How tall?"*

"Nearly six feet."

The man lay back on the pillow and his thin mouth curled in

a surprisingly sweet smile. After a moment he said languidly, "And I don't glitter."

"What do you mean?"

"I'm not covered with . . . you know, red, white, blue, green sparkles."

"Certainly not. Should I call a doctor?"

"No no. I expect these fellows have done what they can."

The man's skull was no longer a reminder of death. Feeling had softened it and now it seemed a daringly austere work of art commemorating human consciousness. The thin lips still curved in a faint smile. They opened and said, "What brought you here?"

Lanark considered several answers and decided to use the shortest. "Dragonhide."

The man seemed not to hear. At last Lanark asked, "What brought you?"

The man cleared his throat. "Crystalline hypertrophy of the connective tissue. That's the medical name. Laymen like you or I call it rigor."

"Twittering rigor?"

"I did not twitter. All the same, it came as a shock."

He seemed to become thoughtful and Lanark fell asleep. He was wakened by the man crying out, "Are you there? Am I boring you?"

"I'm here. Please go on."

"You see, I loved the human image and I hated the way people degraded it, overdeveloping some bits to gain temporary advantage and breaking others off to get relief from very ordinary pain. I seemed surrounded by leeches, using their vitality to steal vitality from others, and by sponges, hiding behind too many mouths, and by crustaceans, swapping their feelings for armour. I saw that a decent human life should contain discipline, and exertion, and adventure, and be unselfish. So I joined the army. Can you tell me what other organization I could have joined? Yet in spite of five dangerous missions behind enemy lines, and in spite of launching the Q39 programme, I grew to be nine feet tall and as brittle as glass. I could exert fantastic pressure vertically, upward or downward, but the slightest sideways blow would have cracked me open. We do crack, you know, in the army."

Indignation had entered his voice and exhausted it. He lay breathing deeply for a while; then his lips curved in the surprising smile. He said, "Can you guess what I did?"

"No."

"I did something rather unusual. Instead of waiting till I cracked
and leaving the pit to eat up the pieces I *invoked* the pit. I
asked for a way out, and the pit came to me, and I entered it
in a perfectly decorous and manly fashion."

"So did I."

For a moment the man looked indignant again, then he asked
in a low voice, "How many of us are there in this room?"

"Just you and I."

"Good. Good. That means we are exceptional cases. Depend
on it, not many pray for that way out. The majority spend
their lives dreading it. Did you lose consciousness coming
down?"

"Yes, after a while."

"I lost consciousness almost at once. The trouble was, I kept
coming back to it, again and again and again. I wish I had
taken their advice and removed my uniform."

"You came down in a uniform!" cried Lanark, horrified.

"Yes. Belt, boots, braid, brass buttons, the lot. I even had
my pistol, in a holster."

"Why?"

"I meant to surrender it to the commander here: a symbolic
gesture, you know. But there isn't a commander. That pistol
made a trench as deep as itself across my right hip, which is
why I am dying, I suppose. I could have survived the uniform
but not the revolver."

"You're not dying!"

"I feel I am."

"But why, why, why should we suffer that pit and blackness
and pressure, why should we even try to be human if we are
going to die? If you die your pain and struggle have been
useless!"

"I take a less gloomy view. A good life means fighting to be
human under growing difficulties. A lot of young folk know
this and fight very hard, but after a few years life gets easier
for them and they think they've become completely human
when they've only stopped trying. I stopped trying, but my
life was so full of strenuous routines that I wouldn't have noticed
had it not been for my disease. My whole professional life
was a diseased and grandiose attack on my humanity. It is an
achievement to know now that I am simply a wounded and
dying man. Who can be more regal than a dying man?"

His languid voice had become a very faint murmur.

"Sir!" said Lanark fervently. "I hope you will not die!"

The man smiled and murmured, "Thank you, my boy."
A moment later sweat suddenly glittered on the visible parts
of him. He clawed the coverlet with both hands and sat upright
saying in a harsh commanding voice, "And now I feel very
cold and more than a little afraid!"
The lamp went out. Lanark leaped onto the polished floor,
slipped, fell and scrambled to the man's side. Some pearly light
from the window passed over the body half sprawling from
the covers, the head and neck hanging off the mattress and
an arm trailing on the floor. A dark stain was spreading on
the bandage where the rubber tube had been wrenched out.
Lanark ran to his bed, grabbed the radio and flicked the switch;
he said, "Get Dr. Munro! Get me Dr. Munro!"
A small clear voice said, "Who is speaking, please?"
"I'm called Lanark."
"Dr. Lanark?"
"No! No! I'm a patient, but a man is dying!"
"Dying naturally?"
"Yes, dying, dying!"
He heard the voice say, "Will Dr. Munro report quickly to
Dr. Lanark, a man is dying naturally; I repeat, a man is dying
naturally."
A minute later the ward lights went on.

Lanark sat on the bed staring at his neighbour, who looked
crudely and insultingly dead. His mouth hung open and it was
now obvious that his sockets were eyeless. By the hand on
the floor a tiny puddle was spreading from the nozzle of the
rubber tube. Dr. Munro came in and walked briskly to the
bedside. He lifted the arm, felt the pulse, hoisted the body
farther onto the mattress, then turned off a tap on the suspended
bottle. He looked at Lanark sitting on the edge of his bed in
a white nightshirt and said, "Shouldn't you cover yourself up?"
"No. I shouldn't."
"Did he speak to you?"
"Yes."
"Did he recognize himself?"
"Yes. What are you going to do with him?"
"Bury him. Strange, isn't it. We can find a practical use for
any number of dead monsters, but a mere man can only be
burned or shovelled into the ground."
"I don't know what you're talking about."
"Get into bed, Lanark."
"I want to see out the window."

"Why?"

"I feel enclosed."

"Can you walk there?"

"Of course I can walk there."

The doctor opened a locker beside the bed, took out dressing gown and slippers and handed them to Lanark, who put them on and walked to the window, ignoring a feeling of floating above the floor. He was surprised to find the corridor hardly longer than the room he had left: to right and left it ended in a blank wall with a circular door closed by a red curtain. Lanark hesitated before the slats of the blind until Dr. Munro appeared at his side and placed a hand on a green cord hanging from the top. He said, "I'll raise the blind, Lanark, but first I want you to repeat certain words."

"What words?"

"If I lose my way I will shut my eyes and turn my head."

"If I lose my way I will shut my eyes and turn my head."

Munro raised the blind.

It was a view of mistily moving distances with the sun shining through them. Snowy ranges of cloud divided snowy ranges of mountain and silvery skies lay so near to sparkling oceans that they were hard to tell apart. The institute seemed drifting toward the sun between the precipices of a canyon and he peered forward and down, trying to catch sight of the bottom, but when the mist below the window thinned and parted he saw a dark violet space containing stars and a sickle moon. Feeling dizzy he looked back at the sun for reassurance, for though dimmed by haze it shone solidly in the centre of the scene, illuminating and uniting it; but now he wondered if the sun was maybe far overhead and this a reflection in the sea, or perhaps it was behind him and he was seeing it mirrored in a glacier among the mountains in front. Nothing was visible now but sunlight and milky cloud with a single peak rising from it. Streams like silver threads poured through gullies in the lower slopes and white lines of waterfalls fell from cliff tops into the clouds. He saw this peak was not a simple cone but a cluster of summits with valleys between them. One valley was full of lakes and pasture, another was shaggy with forests, through a third lay a golden-green ocean with a sun setting behind it. The act of seeing became an act of flight. He raised his eyes to the horizon but above the level lines of every sea and plain lay islands, mountains, storm clouds, cities, and setting or ascending suns. He tried to escape this recession by staring at a village on a little hill in a shaft of morning light. A cloud passed overhead and he only saw the village by the light sparkling on windows and roofs, then the sparkles shifted and drifted sideways like snowflakes into silvery blueness where they circled like gulls above a steamship, then changed colour and became black specks circling like aeroplanes in a flashing red glow above a bombed city. So Lanark clapped a hand over his eyes, turned round and returned soberly to the room.

The body of his neighbour, swathed in blankets, was wheeled past on a stretcher by a male nurse. Lanark put the slippers and gown in the locker, climbed into bed and pulled the covers to his chin. Dr. Munro had lowered the blind and gone to the locker beside the dead man's bed. He took out a pistol and stood examining it thoughtfully. He said, "This is why he died, you know. He wore it on the way down."
"Yes, he told me."
"Still, he came head first, which not many do."
"Where is this institute?"
"We occupy a system of galleries under a mountain with several peaks and several cities on top. I believe you come from one of these cities."
"Under a mountain?"
"Yes. That screen isn't a window. It shows images caught by a reflector on one of the peaks. This ward has one because patients of your kind sometimes do feel enclosed. If I showed that view to other patients they would curl up like watchsprings."
"How deep down are we?"
"I don't know. I'm a doctor, not a geologist."

Lanark had received more than he could consciously absorb. He fell asleep.

CHAPTER 8. Doctors

He wakened next morning feeling tired and sick, but the nurses brought a bland omelette which restored vitality. On a chair by the bed they laid clothes with the same soft glazed texture as the food: underwear, socks, shirt, dark trousers, a pullover and a white coat. They said, "You're joining us today, Bushybrows."

"What do you mean?"

"You're a doctor now. I hope you aren't going to bully us poor nurses."

"I am not a doctor!"

"Oh, don't refuse! The ones who refuse at first always bully us worst."

When they left Lanark arose and dressed in all but the coat. He found shoes of suède-like stuff below the bed. He put them on, entered the corridor, lifted the blind and saw a white flagpole in the middle of a warm, sunlit terrace of level grass. Children ran about playing anarchic ballgames and on the far edge two older boys sat on a bench gazing across a great valley, the valley-floor covered by roofs made prickly by smokestacks. On the right a river meandered among fields and slag bings, then the city hid it though the course was marked by skeletal cranes marching to the left. Beyond the city was a bleak ridge of land, heather-green and creased by watercourses, and the summits of mountains appeared behind that like a line of broken teeth. This view filled Lanark with such unexpected delight that his eyes moistened. He returned and lay down on the bed, wondering why.

"Anyway," he told himself, "I'll go there."

Munro came through an arch and Lanark sat up to face
him saying, "Before you speak, I want to assure you I will
not be a doctor."
"I see. How do you intend to pass the time while you stay
here?"
"I don't want to stay. I want to leave."
Munro flushed suddenly red and pointed to the window. Outside it grey waves were rising and falling against a great cliff
with mist on the summit.
"Yes, leave! Leave!" he said in a controlled voice, "I'll take
you to an emergency exit. It will let you out at the mountain
foot, and after that you can find your own way through the
world. Men used to find homes like that, leaving the safe oasis
or familiar cave and crossing wildernesses to make houses in
unknown lands. Of course these men knew things you don't.
They could plant crops, kill animals, endure pains that would
deprive you of your wits. But you can read and write and
argue, and if you go far enough you may find people who
appreciate that, if they talk the same language."
"But a minute ago I saw a habitable city out there!"
"And have you never heard how fast and far light travels?
And how masses warp it and surfaces reflect it and atmospheres
refract it? You have seen a city and think it in the future, a
place to reach by travelling an hour or day or year, but existence
is helical and that city could be centuries ahead. And what if
it lies in the past? History is full of men who saw cities, and
went to them, and found them shrunk to villages or destroyed
centuries before or not built yet. And the last sort were the
luckiest."
"But I recognized this city! I've been there!"
"Ah, then it lies in the past. You'll never find it now."
Lanark looked miserably at the floor. The view had given him
dreams of a gracious, sunlit life. He said, "Are there no civilized
places I can reach from here?"
Munro had regained his mandarin calm and sat down beside
the bed. "Yes, several. But they won't take you without a
companion."
"Why?"
"Health regulations. When people leave without a companion
their diseases return after a while."
"Am I the only healthy individual who wants to leave this
place?"
"One woman doctor hates her work so much that she'll leave

with anyone, but take care. Entering another world with someone is a form of wedding, and this woman will hate any world
she lands in."
Lanark groaned and said, "What can I do, Dr. Munro?"
Munro said cheerfully, "That is your first sensible question
Lanark, so stop worrying and listen. You can look for a companion among three classes of people: the doctors, the nurses and
the patients. Not many doctors want to leave, but when they
do, it is with a colleague. Nurses leave more often, with men
they thoroughly trust, and doctors have proverbial advantages
where they are concerned. But the biggest class are the patients,
and you can only know them by working on them."
"I'm not qualified to work on anybody."
"And were you not nearly a dragon? And are you not cured?
The only qualification for treating a disease is to survive it,
and right now seventeen patients are crushing themselves under
belligerent armour without one reasonable soul to care for
them. Don't be afraid! You need see nobody whose problem
is not a form of your own."

They sat in silence until Lanark stood up and put the white
coat on. Munro smiled and produced a hospital radio saying,
"This is yours. You know how to make contact through it,
so I'll show how it contacts you."
He flicked the switch and said to the mesh, "Send a signal to
Dr. Lanark in ten seconds, please. There's no message, so don't
repeat it."
He dropped the radio into Lanark's pocket. A moment later
two resonant chords from there said *plin-plong.*
"When you hear that, your patient is near a crisis or a colleague
needs help. If you need help yourself, or lose your way in
the corridors, or want a lullaby to soothe you to sleep, speak
to the operator and you'll be connected to someone suitable.
Now get your books and we'll go to your new apartment."
Lanark hesitated. He said, "Has it a window?"
"As far as I know this is the only room with a viewing screen
of that kind."
"I prefer to sleep here, Dr. Munro."
Munro sighed slightly. "Doctors don't usually sleep in a patients' ward, but certainly this is the smallest and least required.
All right, leave the books. I'll show you something of the insti-
tute's scope then we'll visit Ozenfant, your head of depart-
ment."

They went through an arch to one of the circular doorways.
The curtain of red pleated plastic slid apart for them and closed
behind.

The corridors of the institute were very different from
the rooms they connected. Lanark followed Munro down a
low curving tunnel with hot gusts of wind shoving at his back,
his ears numbed by a clamour of voices, footsteps, bells going
plin-plong and a dull rhythmic roaring. The tunnel was six feet
high and circular in section with a flat track at the bottom
just wide enough for the wheels of a stretcher. The light kept
brightening and dulling in a way that hurt the eyes; dazzling
golden brightness slid along the walls with each warm blast
and was followed by fading orange dimness in the ensuing cold.
The tunnel slanted into another tunnel and grew twice as large,
then into another and grew twice as large again. The noise,
brightness and windpower increased. Lanark and Munro travelled swiftly but doctors and nurses with trolleys and stretchers
kept overtaking and whizzing past them on either side. Nobody
was moving against the wind. With an effort Lanark came beside
Munro and asked about this, but though he yelled aloud his
voice reached his ears as a remote squeaking and the reply
was inaudible; yet amid the roaring and gongings he could
hear distinct fragments of speech spoken by nobody in the
vicinity:
". . . is the pie that bakes and eats itself . . ."
". . . . . is that which has no dimensions . . . . ."
". . . is the study of the best . . ."
". . . . . an exacting game and requires patience . . . . ."
They entered a great hall where the voices were drowned in
a roaring which swelled and ebbed like waves of cheering in
a football stadium. Crowds poured over the circular floor from
tunnels on every side and disappeared through square doors
between the tunnel entrances. Among white-coated nurses and
doctors Lanark saw people in green dustcoats, brown overalls,
blue uniforms and charcoal-grey business suits. He looked upward and staggered giddily. He was staring up a vast perpendicular shaft with gold and orange light flowing continually up
the walls in diminishing rings like the rings of a target. Munro
gripped his arm and led him to a door which opened, then
slid shut behind them.

They were in a lift with the still air of a small ward. Munro
looked up at a circular mesh in the middle of the ceiling and

said, "The sink, please. Any entrance."
There was a faint hum but no sense of movement. Munro said, "Our corridors have confusing acoustics. Did you ask something?"
"Why do people only walk in one direction?"
"Each ward has two corridors, one leading in and the other out. This allows the air to circulate, and nobody goes against the current."
"Who were the people in the big hall?"
"Doctors, like you and me."
"But doctors were a tiny minority."
"Do you think so? I suppose it's possible. We need engineers and clerks and chemists to supervise lighting and synthesize food and so on, but we only see those in the halls; they have their own corridors. They're a strange lot. Every one of them, even the plumbers and wireless operators, think their own profession *is* the institute, and everyone else exists to serve them. I suppose it makes their work seem more worthwhile, but if they reflected seriously they would see that the institute lives by purging the intake."
"Purging the intake?"
"Doctoring the patients."

The lift door opened and Lanark's nostrils were hit by a powerful stink, the foul odour he had first noticed when Gloopy vanished in the dark. Munro crossed a platform to a railing and stood with his hands on it, looking down. To right and left the platform curved into distance as though enclosing an enormous basin, but though searchlights in the black ceiling cast slanting beams into the basin itself Lanark was unable to see the other side. From high overhead came huge dismal sounds like a dance record played loudly at an unusually low speed, and from the depths beyond the railing came a multitudinous slithering hiss. Lanark stood at the door of the lift and said shakily, "Why did we come here?"
Munro looked round.
"This is our largest deterioration ward. We keep the hopeless softs here. They're quite happy. Come and look."
"You said I need see nobody whose problem is not a form of my own!"
"Problems take different forms but they're all caused by the same error. Come and see."
"If I look over that railing I think I will be sick."
Munro stared at him, then shrugged and re-entered the lift.

He said to the mesh, "Professor Ozenfant," and the door closed and the air softly hummed. Munro leaned against the wall with his hands tucked into the opposite sleeves. He frowned at his shoes for a moment then looked up with sudden brightness saying, "Tell me, Dr. Lanark, is there a connection between your love of vast panorama and your distaste for human problems?"
Lanark said nothing.

The door opened and they entered another huge roaring ceilingless hall. Pulses of sound and bright air beat down from above and flowed out into the surrounding tunnels with crowds of people from the surrounding lifts. Munro led the way to a tunnel with a block of names on the wall by the entrance:

McADAM	McIVOR	McQUAT	McWHAM
McCAIG	McKEAN	McSHEA	MURRAY
McEVOY	McMATH	McUSKY	NOAKES
McGILL	McOWEN	McVARE	OZENFANT

They sped along it hearing bodiless voices conversing among the clamour:
". . . glad to see the light in the sky . . ."
". . . . . frames were shining on the walls . . . . ."
". . . you need certificates . . ."
". . . . . camels in Arabia . . . . ."
". . . annihilating sweetness . . ."
They reached a place where half the names were printed on one wall and half on the other, and here the tunnel forked and diminished. It forked and diminished three more times until they entered a single low tunnel labelled OZENFANT. The red glossy curtain at the end opened on a surface of heavy brown cloth. Munro pulled that aside and they stepped into a large and lofty apartment. Tapestries worked in red, green and gold thread hung from an elaborate cornice to a chequered floor of black and white marble. Antique stools, chairs and sofas stood about in no kind of order with stringed instruments of the lute and fiddle sort scattered between them. A grand piano stood in a corner beside a cumbersome, old-fashioned X-ray machine, and in the middle Lanark saw, from behind, a figure in black trousers and waistcoat leaning over a carpenter's bench and sandpapering the edge of a half-constructed guitar. This figure stood up and turned toward them, smiling and wiping hands on a richly patterned silk handkerchief. It was a stout young man with a small blond triangular beard.

His sleeves were rolled well above his elbows exposing robust hairy forearms, but collar and tie were perfectly neat, the waistcoat unwrinkled, the trousers exactly creased, the shoes splendidly polished. He came forward saying, "Ah, Munro, you bring my new assistant. Sit down both of you and talk to me." Munro said, "I'm afraid I must leave. Dr. Lanark has tired of my company and I have work to do."

"No, my friend, you must stay some minutes longer! A patient is about to turn salamander, an always impressive spectacle. Sit down and I'll show you."

He gestured to a divan and stood facing them and dabbing his brows with the handkerchief. He said, "Tell me, Lanark, what instrument do you play?"

"None."

"But you are musical?"

"No."

"But perhaps you know about ragtime, jazz, boogie-woogie, rock-and-roll?"

"No."

Ozenfant sighed. "I feared as much. No matter, there are other ways of speaking to patients. I will show you a patient."

He went to the nearest tapestry and dragged it sideways, uncovering a circular glass screen in the wall behind. A slender microphone hung under it. He brought this to the divan pulling a fine cable after it, and sat down and said, "Ozenfant speaking. Show me chamber twelve."

The neon lights in the ceiling went out and a blurred image shone inside the screen, seemingly a knight in gothic armour lying on the slab of a tomb. The image grew distinct and more like a prehistoric lizard on a steel table. The hide was black, the knobbly joints had pink and purple quills on them, a bush of purple spines hid the genitals and a double row of spikes down the back supported the body about nine inches above the table. The head was neckless, chinless, and grew up from the collarbone into a gaping beak like the beak of a vast cuckoo. The face had no other real features, though a couple of blank domes stuck out like parodies of eyeballs. Munro said, "The mouth is open."

Ozenfant said, "Yes, but the air trembles above it. Soon it shuts, and then *boom!*"

"When was he delivered?"

"Nine months, nine days, twenty-two hours ago. He arrived nearly as you see him, nothing human but the hands, throat and sternum mastoid. He seemed to like jazz, for he clutched the remnant of a saxophone, so I said, 'He is musical, I will treat him myself.' Unluckily I know nothing of jazz. I tried him with Debussy (who sometimes works in these cases) then I tried the nineteenth-century romantics. I pounded him with Wagner, overwhelmed him with Brahms, beguiled him with Mendelssohn. Results: negative. In despair I recede further and further, and who works in the end? Scarlatti. Each time I played *The Cortege* his human parts blushed as pink and soft as a baby's bottom.''

Ozenfant closed his eyes and kissed his fingertips to the ceiling. "Well, matters remain thus till six hours ago when he goes wholly dragon in five minutes. Perhaps I do not play the clavichord well? Who else in this wretched institute would have tried?"

Munro said, "You assume he blushed pink with pleasure. It may have been rage. Maybe he disliked Scarlatti. You should have asked."

"I distrust speech therapy. Words are the language of lies and evasions. Music cannot lie. Music talks to the heart."

Lanark moved impatiently. Light from the screen showed Ozenfant's mouth so fixed in a smile that it seemed expressionless, while the eyebrows kept moving in exaggerated expressions of thoughtfulness, astonishment or woe. Ozenfant said, "Lanark is bored by these technicalities. I will show him more patients."

He spoke to the microphone and a sequence of dragons on steel tables appeared on the screen. Some had glossy hides, some were plated like tortoises, some were scaled like fish and crocodiles. Most had quills, spines or spikes and some were hugely horned and antlered, but all were made monstrous by a detail, a human foot or ear or breast sticking through the dinosaur armour. A doctor sat on the edge of one table and studied a chessboard balanced on a dragonish stomach.

Ozenfant said, "That is McWham, who is also unmusical. He treats the dryly rational cases; he teaches them chess and plays interminable games. He thinks that if anyone defeats him their armour will fall off, but so far he has been too clever for them. Do you play any games, Lanark?"

"No."

In another chamber a thin priest with intensely miserable eyes sat with his ear close to a dragonish beak.

"That is Monsignor Noakes, our only faith healer. We used

to have lots of them: Lutherans, Jews, Atheists, Muslims, and others with names I forget. Nowdays all the hardened religious cases have to be treated by poor Noakes. Luckily we don't get many."

"He looks unhappy."

"Yes, he takes his work too seriously. He is Roman Catholic and the only people he cures are Quakers and Anglicans. Have you a religion, Lanark?"

"No."

"You see a cure is more likely when doctor and patient have something in common. How would you describe yourself?"

"I can't."

Ozenfant laughed. "Of course you can't! I asked foolishly. The lemon cannot taste bitterness, it only drinks the rain. Munro, describe Lanark to me."

"Obstinate and suspicious," said Munro. "He has intelligence, but keeps it narrow."

"Good. I have a patient for him. Also obstinate, also suspicious, with a cleverness which only reinforces a deep, deep, immeasurably deep despair."

Ozenfant said to the microphone, "Show chamber one, and let us see the patient from above."

A gleaming silver dragon appeared between a folded pair of brazen wings. A stout arm ending in seven brazen claws lay along one wing, a slender soft human arm along the other.

"You see the wings? Only unusually desperate cases have wings, though they cannot use them. Yet this one brings such reckless energy to her despair that I have sometimes hoped. She is unmusical, but I, a musician, have stooped to speech therapy and spoken to her like a vulgar critic, and she exasperated me so much that I decided to give her to the catalyst. We will give her to Lanark instead."

A radio said *plin-plong.* Ozenfant took one from a waistcoat pocket and turned the switch. A voice announced that patient twelve was turning salamander.

Ozenfant said to the microphone, "Quick! Chamber twelve."

Chamber twelve was obscured by white vapours streaming and whirling from the dragon's beak, which suddenly snapped shut. Radiant beams shot from the domes in the head, the figure seemed to be writhing. Ozenfrant cried, "No light, please! We will observe by heat alone."

There was immediate blackness on which Lanark's dazzled eyes projected stars and circles before adjusting to it. He could hear

Munro's quick dry breathing on one side and Ozenfant breathing through his mouth on the other. He said, "What's happening?"

Ozenfant said, "Brilliant light pours from all his organs—it would blind us. Soon you will see him by his heat."

A moment later Lanark was startled to feel Ozenfant murmuring into his ear.

"The heat made by a body should move easily through it, overflowing the pores, penis, anus, eyes, lips, limbs and fingertips in acts of generosity and self-preservation. But many people are afraid of the cold and try to keep more heat than they give, they stop the heat from leaving though an organ or limb, and the stopped heat forges the surface into hard insulating armour. What part of you went dragon?"

"A hand and arm."

"Did you ever touch them with your proper hand?"

"Yes. They felt cold."

"Quite. No heat was getting out. But no heat was getting in! And since men feel the heat they receive more than the heat they create the armour makes the remaining human parts feel colder. So do they strip it off? Seldom. Like nations losing unjust wars they convert more and more of themselves into armour when they should surrender or retreat. So someone may start by limiting only his affections or lust or intelligence, and eventually heart, genitals, brain, hands and skin are crusted over. He does nothing but talk and feed, giving and taking through a single hole; then the mouth shuts, the heat has no outlet, it increases inside him until. . . watch, you will see."

The blackness they sat in had been dense and total but a crooked thread of scarlet light appeared on it. This twitched and grew at both ends until it outlined the erect shape of a dragon with legs astride, arms outstretched, the hands thrusting against darkness, the great head moving from side to side. Lanark had a weird feeling that the beast stood before him in the room. There was nothing but blackness to compare it with, and it seemed vast. Its gestures may have been caused by pain but they looked threatening and triumphant. Inside the black head two stars appeared where eyes should be, then the whole body was covered with white and golden stars. Lanark felt the great gothic shape towering miles above him, a galaxy shaped like a man. Then the figure became one blot of gold which expanded into a blinding globe. There was a crash of thunder and for a moment the room became very hot. The floor heaved and the lights went on.

It took a while to see things clearly. The thunder had ended, but throughout the apartment instruments were jangling and thrumming in sympathy. Lanark noticed Munro still sitting beside him. There was sweat on his brow and he was industriously polishing his spectacles with a handkerchief. The blank screen was cracked from side to side but the microphone hung neatly under it. Ozenfant stood at a distance examining a fiddle. "See!" he cried. "The A-string has snapped. Yet some assert that a Stradivarius is without a soul."

Munro said, "I am no judge of salamanders, but that vibration seemed abnormally strong."

"Indeed yes. There were over a million megatherms in that small blast."

"Surely not!"

"Certainly. I will prove it."

Ozenfant produced his radio and said, "Ozenfant will speak with engineer Johnson. . . . Johnson, hello, you have received our salamander; what is he worth? . . . Oh, I see. Anyway, he cracked my viewing lens, so replace it soon, please."

Ozenfant pocketed the radio and said briskly, "Not quite a million megatherms, but it will suffice for a month or two." He bent and hoisted up a harp which had fallen on its side.

Lanark said sharply, "That heat is used?"

"Of course. Somehow we must warm ourselves."

"That is atrocious!"

"Why?"

Lanark started stammering then forced himself to speak slowly. "I knew people deteriorate. That is dismal but not surprising. But for cheerful healthy folk to profit by it is atrocious!"

"What would you prefer? A world with a cesspool under it where the helplessly corrupt would fall and fester eternally? That is a very old-fashioned model of the universe."

"And very poor housekeeping," said Munro, standing up. "We could cure nobody if we did not utilize our failures. I must go now. Lanark, your department and mine have different staff clubs but if you ever leave the institute we will meet again. Professor Ozenfant is your adviser now, so good luck, and try not to be violent."

Lanark was so keen to learn if the last remark was a joke that he stared hard into Munro's calm benign face and let his hand be gravely shaken without saying a word. Ozenfant murmured, "Excellent advice."

He uncovered a door and Munro went through it.

Ozenfant returned to the centre of the room chuckling and rubbing his hands. He said, "You noticed the sweat on his brow? He did not like what he saw; he is a rigorist, Lanark. He cannot sympathize with our disease."

"What is a rigorist?"

"One who bargains with his heat. Rigorists do not hold their heat in, they give it away, but only in exchange for fresh supplies. They are very dependable people, and when they go bad they crumble into crystals essential for making communication circuits, but when you and I went bad we took a different path. That is why an exploding salamander exalts us. We feel in our bowels the rightness of such nemesis. You were exalted, were you not?"

"I was excited, and I regret it."

"Your regret serves no purpose. And now perhaps you wish to meet your patient."

Ozenfant lifted the corner of another tapestry, uncovered a low circular door and said, "Her chamber is through here."

"But what have I to do?"

"Since you are only able to talk, you must talk."

"What about?"

"I cannot say. A good doctor does not carry a remedy to his patient, he lets the patient teach him what the remedy is. I drove someone salamander today because I understood my cure better than my invalid. I often make these mistakes because I know I am very wise. You know you are ignorant, which should be an advantage."

Lanark stood with his hands in his pockets, biting his lower lip and tapping the floor with one foot. Ozenfant said, "If you do not go to her I will certainly send the catalyst."

"What is the catalyst?"

"A very important specialist who comes to lingering cases when other treatments have failed. The catalyst provokes very rapid deterioration. Why are you reluctant?"

"Because I am afraid!" cried Lanark passionately, "You want to mix me with someone else's despair, and I hate despair! I want to be free, and freedom is freedom from other people!"

Ozenfant smiled and nodded. He said "A very dragonish sentiment! But you are no longer a dragon. It is time you learned a different sentiment."

After a while the smile left Ozenfant's face, leaving it startlingly impassive. He let go the tapestry, went to the carpenter's bench and picked up a fretsaw.

He said sharply, "You feel I am pressing you and you dislike it. Do what you please. But since I myself have work to do I will be glad if you waste no more of my time."

He bent over the guitar. Lanark stared frustratedly at the corner of the tapestry. It depicted a stately woman labelled *Correctio Conversio* standing on a crowned and sprawling young man labelled *Tarquinius*. At last he pulled this aside, stepped through the door and went down the corridor beyond.

CHAPTER 9. A Dragon

Lanark was not a tall man but he had to bend knees and neck to pass comfortably down the corridor. The differences between bright and dull, warm and cool were slight here and the voices were like whispers in a seashell: "Lilac and laburnum . . . . marble and honey . . . . the recipe is separation . . . ."
The corridor ended in a steel surface with a mesh in the centre. He said glumly, "Please open. I'm called Lanark."
The door said, "Dr. Lanark?"
"Yes yes, Dr. Lanark."
A circular section swung inward on a hinge. He climbed through, raised his head, banged it on the ceiling and sat down suddenly on a stool beside the table. The door closed silently leaving no mark in the wall.

For more than a minute he sat biting his thumb knuckle and trying not to yell to be let out, for the observation lens had not prepared him for the cramped smallness of the chamber and the solid vastness of the monster. The tabletop was a few inches above the floor and from the crest on the silver head to the bronze hooves on the silver feet the patient was nearly eight feet long. The chamber was a perfect hemisphere nine feet across and half as high, and though he pressed his shoulders against the curve of the ceiling it forced him to lean forward over the gleaming stomach, from which icy air beat upward into his face. Soft light came from the milk-coloured floor and walls and there were no shadows. Lanark felt he was crouching in a tiny arctic igloo, but here the warmth came from the walls and the cold from the body of his companion. The hand at the end of the human arm was clenching and unclenching, and this was a comfort, and he liked the wings folded along

the dragon's sides, each long bronze feather tipped with the
spectrum of rich colour that is got by heating copper. He leaned
over and looked into the gaping beak and was hit in the face
by a welcome gush of warmth, but he saw only darkness. A
voice said, "What have you brought this time? Bagpipes?"
The question had a hollow, impersonal tone as if transmitted
through a machine too clumsy for the music of ordinary speech,
yet he seemed to recognize the fierce energy beating through
it.
"I'm not a musician. I'm called Lanark."
"What filthy tricks do you play on the sick?"
"I've been told to talk to you. I don't know what to say."
He was no longer afraid and sat with elbows on knees, holding
his head between his hands. After a while he cleared his throat
and said, "Talk, I suppose, is a way of defending and attack-
ing, but I don't need to defend myself. I don't want to attack
you."
"How kind!"
"Are you Rima?"
"I'm done with names. Names are nothing but collars men
tie round your neck to drag you where they like."
Again he could think of nothing to say. A remote faint thudding
noise occupied the silence until the voice said, "Who was
Rima?"
"A girl I used to like. She tried to like me too, a little."
"Then she wasn't me."
"You have beautiful wings."
"I wish they were spikes, then I wouldn't need to talk jaggedly
to bastards like you."
"Why do you say that?"
"Don't pretend you're not like the others. Your technique
will be different but you'll hurt me too. I'm helpless in this
freezing coffin so why not begin?"
"Ozenfant didn't hurt you."
"Do you think these noises made me happy? Ballet music!
Sounds of women flying and floating in moonlight like swans
and clouds, women leaping from men's hands like flames from
candles, women disdaining whole glittering audiences of czars
and emperors. Yes, the liar talked, he left nothing to my imagination. He said *I* could have done these things once. 'Open
your heart to my music,' he said. 'Weep passionately.' He could
not reach my skin so he raped my ears, like you."
"I haven't raped your ears."
"Then why shout?"

"I haven't shouted!"

"Don't get hysterical."

"I'm *not* hysterical."

"You certainly aren't calm."

Lanark bellowed, "How can I be calm when . . ." and was deafened by the reverberation around the narrow dome. He folded his arms and waited grimly. The uproar faded out as a faint ringing with perhaps (he wasn't sure) an echo of laughter in it. Eventually he said in a low voice, "Should I leave?"

She murmured something.

"I didn't hear that."

"You could tell me who you are."

"I'm over five and half feet tall and weigh about ten stone. My eyes are brown, hair black, and I forget the blood group. I used to be older than twenty but now I'm older than thirty. I've been called a crustacean, and too serious, but recently I was described by a dependable man as shrewd, obstinate and adequately intelligent. I was a writer once and now I'm a doctor, but I was advised to become these, I never wanted it. I've never wanted anything long. Except freedom."

There was a metallic rattle of laughter. Lanark said, "Yes, it's a comic word. We're all forced to define it in ways that make no sense to other people. But for me freedom is . . ."

He thought for a while.

". . . life in a city near the sea or near the mountains where the sun shines for an average of half the day. My house would have a living room, big kitchen, bathroom and one bedroom for each of the family, and my work would be so engrossing that while I did it I would neither notice nor care if I was happy or sad. Perhaps I would be an official who kept useful services working properly. Or a designer of houses and roads for the city where I lived. When I grew old I would buy a cottage on an island or among the mountains—"

"Dirty! Dirty! Dirty! Dirty!" said the voice on a low throb of rage. "Dirty bastards giving me a killer for a doctor!"

The blood boomed in Lanark's eardrums and his scalp prickled. A wave of terror passed over him in which he struggled to get up, then a wave of rage in which he sat, leaned forward and whispered, "You have no right to despise my bad actions without liking my better ones."

"Tell me about these, were they many? Were they pretty?"

He cried, "Dr. Lanark is ready to leave!"

A circular panel opened on the other side of the chamber. He stepped carefully across the body and paused with one foot on each side of it, his shoulders against the height of the dome.

"Goodbye!" he said with a conscious cruelty which startled him. He stared down at the clenching and unclenching hand for a while, then asked humbly, "Are you very sore?"

"I'm freezing. I knew you would leave."

"Talking doesn't help. What can I say that won't annoy you?" After a moment she spoke in a voice he just managed to hear. "You could read to me."

"Then I will. Next time I'll bring books."

"You won't come back."

Lanark climbed out through the opening into a tunnel where he could stand erect. He leaned into the chamber and said cheerfully, "I'll surprise you. I'll be quicker than you think." The panel closed as he turned away.

At the end of the corridor a red curtain admitted him to a passage between a large window and a row of arches. Through the arches he recognized, with a sense of homecoming, the five beds of his own ward. It seemed strange that the silver dragon had been so near him since his arrival. He went to his locker, lifted the books and hurried back to the curtain. From the other side it had slid open at the touch of a finger, he knew it was a paper-thin membrane with no locking device, and yet he couldn't open it; and though he stood back and ran his shoulder into it several times it only quivered and rumbled like a struck drum. He was about to kick it in a fit of bad temper when he noticed the view from the window. He was looking down on a quiet street with a skin of frost over it and a three-storey red sandstone tenement on the far side. The windows glinted cleanly in early morning sunlight; smoke from a few chimney-pots flowed upward into a pale winter sky. A boy of six or seven with a dark blue raincoat, woollen helmet and schoolbag came down some steps from a close and turned left along the pavement. Directly opposite Lanark a thin woman with a tired face appeared between the curtains of a bay window. She stood watching the boy, who turned and waved to her as he reached the street corner and banged the side of his head into a lamppost. Lanark felt inside himself the shock, then amusement, which showed on the mother's face. The boy went round the corner, rubbing his ear mournfully. The woman turned and looked straight across at Lanark, then lifted a hand to her mouth in a startled puzzled way. He wanted to wave to her as the boy had waved, to open the window and shout something comforting, but a milk cart pulled by a brown horse came along the street, and when he looked back from it the bay window was empty.

This vision hit Lanark poignantly. He lowered the blind to prevent a new scene from replacing it and wandered into the ward feeling very tired. It seemed many days since he had been there, though the clock showed it was not three hours. He put the books and white coat on the chair, slid his shoes off and lay on the bed, intending to rest for ten or fifteen minutes.

He was wakened by the radio saying *plin-plong, plin-plong, pin-plong*. He reached across, took it from the coat pocket and switched it on. Ozenfant said, "My dear fellow, sleep is not enough, sometimes you must eat. Come to the staff club. Leave the white coat behind. Evening is a time for mirth and gaiety."

"How do I reach the staff club?"

"Go to the nearest hall and enter any lift. If you ask it nicely it will bring you direct. Mention my name."

Lanark put on the shoes, took the books under his arm and passed through the curtain into the noise of the exit corridors. This time he ignored the voices and studied how to move as swiftly as those around him. The usual laws governing the motion of bodies seemed not to apply here. If you leaned backward against the force of the current you were certain to fall, but the farther you bowed before it the faster it carried you with no danger of falling whatsoever. Most people were content to move rapidly at an angle of forty-five degrees, but one or two flashed past Lanark's knees like rockets, and these were bent so far forward that they appeared to be crawling. The great hall was less crowded than last time. Lanark entered a lift which seemed waiting to be filled before ascending. Two men carrying a surveyor's pole and tripod were chatting in a corner.

"It's a big job, the biggest we've handled."

"The Noble Lord wants it ready in twelve days."

"He's off his rocker."

"The creature is sending tungtanium suction delvers through the Algolagnics group."

"Where will we get power to drive those?"

"From Ozenfant. Ozenfant and his tiny catalyst."

"Has he said he'll give it?"

"No, but he can't oppose the president of the council."

"I doubt if the president of the council could oppose Ozenfant."
The lift filled and the door closed. Voices said: "The drawing
rooms." "Leech-dormitory Q." "The sponge-sump club."
Lanark said, "The staff club."
The lift said, "Whose staff club?"
"Professor Ozenfant's."
The lift hummed. The people near Lanark were silent but the
farthest away whispered and glanced at him. The door opened
and sounds of Viennese dance music floated in. The lift said,
"Here you are, Dr. Lanark."

He entered a softly lit restaurant with a low blue ceiling
and thick blue carpet. The tables were empty with their cloths
removed, except for one on the far side where Ozenfant sat.
He wore a light grey suit with yellow waistcoat and tie; the
corner of a white napkin was tucked between two buttons of
the waistcoat. He was cutting a small morsel on his plate with
obvious pleasure, but he looked up and beckoned Lanark over.
The light came from two candles on his table and from low
arches in the walls, arches of a moorish pattern which seemed
to open into bright rooms at a lower level. Through the nearest,
Lanark saw a section of dance floor with black trouser legs
and long skirts waltzing over it. Ozenfant said, "Come, join
me. The others have long finished, but I am somewhat addicted
to the joys of the feeding trough."
A waitress came from among the shadowy tables, pulled out
a chair and handed Lanark a menu. The dishes were named
in a language he didn't understand. He returned the menu
and said to Ozenfant, "Could you order for me?"
"Certainly. Try Enigma de Filets Congelés. After the slops of
the invalid ward you will appreciate stronger meat."
Ozenfant gulped from a tulip-shaped glass and pulled his mouth
down at the corners.
"Unluckily I cannot recommend the wine. Synthetic chemistry
has much to learn in that direction."

The waitress placed before Lanark a plate with a cube of
grey jelly on it. He cut a thin slice from a surface and found
it tasted like elastic ice. He swallowed quickly and the back
of his nose was filled by a smell of burning rubber, but he
was surprised by a sense of friendly warmth. He felt relaxed,
yet capable of powerful action. He ate another slice and the
smell was worse. He laid down the knife and fork and said,
"I can't eat more than that."
Ozenfant dabbed his lips with the napkin. "No matter. A mouth-

ful gives all the nourishment one needs. As you learn to like
the flavour you will come to take more, and in a few years
you will be overeating like the rest of us."
"I won't be here in a few years."
"Oh?"
"I'm leaving when I find a suitable companion."
"Why?"
"I want the sun."
Ozenfant began laughing heartily then said, "I beg your pardon,
but to hear such a sober fellow declare such a strange passion
was a little unexpected. Why the *sun?*"
Lanark was irritated beyond normal reticence. He said, "I want
to love, and meet friends, and work in it."
"But you are no Athenian, no Florentine, you are a modern
man! In modern civilizations those who work in the sunlight
are a despised and dwindling minority. Even farmers are moving indoors. As for lovemaking and friendship, humanity has
always preferred to enjoy these at night. If you wanted the
moon I could sympathize, but Apollo is quite discredited."
"You talk like Sludden."
"Who is he?"
"A man who lives in the city I came from. The sun shines
there for two or three minutes a day and he thinks it doesn't
matter."
Ozenfant covered his eyes with a hand and said dreamily, "A
city on the banks of a shrunk river. A city with a nineteenth-
century square full of ugly statues. Am I right?"
"Yes."
"Excuse me but the temptation is too great."
Ozenfant reached for Lanark's plate, placed it on his own empty
plate and ate slowly, talking as he did so.
"That city is called Unthank. The calendar in Unthank is based
on sunlight, but only administrators use it. The majority have
forgotten the sun; moreover, they have rejected the clock. They
do not measure or plan, their lives are regulated by simple
appetite varied by the occasional impulse. Not surprisingly nobody is well there. Politically, too, they are corrupt and would
collapse without subsidies from healthier continents. But do
not blame its condition upon lack of sunlight. The institute
has none, yet it supports itself and supplies the staff with plenty
of healthy food and exercise. The clock keeps us regular."
"Have you a library?"
"We have two: one for film and one for music. I am in charge
of the latter."

"What about books?"

"Books?"

"I want to read to my patient and I have only these three."

"Read! How Victorian. Let me see them. Hm. That seems a well-balanced selection. I don't know how you could add to it unless you borrowed from poor Monsignor Noakes. He always has a fat little book with him. It might be a Bible. Bibles are full of funny stories."

Lanark said, "Where could I find him?"

"Don't be in such a hurry—I want to dissuade you from leaving us. Think of the time you could lose by it."

"What do you mean?"

"In this universe every continent measures time by different calendars, so there is no means of measuring the time between them. A traveller going from the institute to a neighbouring continent—Unthank, perhaps, or Provan—must cross a zone where time is a purely subjective experience. Some make the transition and hardly notice it, but how many years did you lose when you came here?"

Lanark was troubled by a feeling of dread which he hid by standing up and saying abruptly, "Thank you for the warning, but a patient is expecting me. Where is Monsignor Noakes?"

"At this hour he is usually in the smoking room watching the bathers. Go through the arches behind me and walk straight ahead. Turn left when you enter the third room, he will be behind the arch facing you."

Lanark walked from the restaurant into a brilliant room where older people were playing bridge. The room beyond was dim and full of billiard tables with low lights over them. The next room contained a swimming bath. Amid raucous echoes some men and women with the even brown tan that comes from exposure to ultraviolet light were diving or racing or chatting on the edge. Lanark turned left along the tiled slippery platform until he reached a wall pierced by the usual arches. He climbed a few steps into a softly lit, thick-carpeted room full of leather armchairs. Noakes sat near the steps smoking a slim cigar and glancing furtively at the brown bodies refracted by the blue-green water. Lanark sat opposite him and said, "I am Dr. Lanark."

"Oh yes."

"A patient of mine needs reading material and I'm collecting books. Professor Ozenfant suggested you could lend me one."

Noakes gave no sign of noticing Lanark was there. He glanced

from the bathers to his cigar and spoke quietly and listlessly.
"Professor Ozenfant is a noted humorist. He knows I have
only my breviary. If your patient had been interested in prayer
she would have been my patient."
"He thought you had a bible."
"Another joke. I have a Greek testament, and I suppose your
patient understands Greek as little as you do. What have you
gathered so far?"
He looked at the books Lanark held out and waved wearily
toward *The Holy War*.
"The other two are trash, but that one is good in parts. The
main message, I mean, is true. I knew the author slightly. He
wrote me as a character into one of his books—not that book,
another. His description was malicious but insignificant. He
described Ozenfant too, but more truthfully and at greater
length. Ignore what I say. Ozenfant has warned you against
me."
"Ozenfant has said nothing against you."
Noakes stared at the floor and whispered, "Then he has come
to despise me as much as that."
He raised his chin and spoke almost loudly.
"He owes his position to me, you know. It was I who cured
him. Ozenfant was a very difficult case, half leech, half dragon.
(Nowadays he pretends he was pure dragon. I know otherwise.)
I believed that the Mass had cured him, and my prayers and
sermons, but it was the music. Ah, what music we had in those
days! When I discovered that he had no sense of holiness apart
from music I made him our organist. He has risen since then,
and I—I have declined. You notice, I suppose, a fretful queru-
lous note in my voice?"
"Yes."
"Then try to understand why. All these professors and artists
and heads of department have become powerful by tearing
tiny bits off the religion which cured them and developing
these bits into religions of their own. No God unites them
now, only mutual assistance pacts based upon greed. Where
we had Christ's vicar upon earth we have now"—he spat the
words at Lanark accusingly—"Lord Monboddo, president of
the council!"
Lanark said defensively, "I'm new here. I don't understand
you."
Noakes bowed his head and murmured, "You like your work?"
"No."
"Then you will come to like it."

"No. When I've cured this patient I'm going to leave with her, if she wants me."

Noakes jerked upright and shouted, "What nonsense!" then leaned forward and grabbed Lanark's hands, speaking in a low quick gabble of words. "No, no, no, no, my child, forgive me, forgive me, it is *not* nonsense! You *must* cure your patient, you *must* leave with her, and if—forgive me, I mean *when*—you leave, you will do something for me, will you not? You promise to do this one thing?"

Lanark pulled his hands free and asked irritably, "What thing?"

"Tell people not to come here. Tell them they must not enter this institute. A little more faith, and hope, and charity, and they can cure their own diseases. Charity alone will save them, if it is possible without the others."

"Why should I warn folk against coming here when coming here cured me?"

"Then tell them to come willingly, in thousands! Let them enter like an army of men, not wait to be swallowed like a herd of victims. Think of the institute with twenty staff to every patient! We will have no excuse for not curing people then! We will be like"—his voice grew wistful—"a cathedral with a congregation of priests. It would burst the institute open to the heavens."

Lanark said, "I don't think telling people things helps them much. And if you are still working here after so many years, you can't think it much worse than it was."

"You are wrong. In all the corridors there are sounds of increased urgency and potency, and behind it all a sound like the breathing of a hungry beast. I assure you, the institute is preparing to swallow a world. I am not trying to frighten you."

Lanark was more embarrassed than frightened. He stood up and said, "Is there a lift near here?"

"I see you will not try to save others. Pray God you can save yourself. There is one in the far corner."

Lanark passed between the chairs and found an open lift in a wall between two arches. He entered and said, "Ignition chamber one."

"Whose department?"

"Professor Ozenfant's."

The door opened on a familiar surface of brown cloth. He thrust it aside and stepped into the high-ceilinged tapestry-hung studio, almost expecting to find it in darkness. It was lit as before, and in the middle Lanark saw from behind a familiar figure in black trousers and waistcoat leaning over the carpenter's bench. Lanark tiptoed uneasily round the walls looking for the figure of *Correctio Conversio* and sometimes glancing sideways at Ozenfant. The Professor was fixing the bridge on his guitar with a delicacy and concentration it would have been wrong to disturb. Lanark was relieved to lift the tapestry and, stooping, enter the low tunnel.

He sat in the tiny chamber pressing his back against the warm curve of the wall. The only movement was the silver creature's clenching and unclenching hand, the only sound the remote and regular thumping. Lanark cleared his throat and said, "I'm sorry I'm late, but I have a book here which someone who knew the author tells me is very good."
There was no answer so he began reading.

"A RELATION OF THE HOLY WAR. In my travels, as I walked through many regions and countries, it was my chance to happen into that famous continent of Universe. A very large and spacious continent it is; it lieth between the heavens. It is a place well watered, and richly adorned with hills and valleys, bravely situate, and for the most part, at least where I was, very fruitful, also well peopled, and a very sweet air."

"I refuse to listen to lies!" cried the voice, making a ringing echo. "Do you think *I* don't live in the universe? Do you think I don't know what a stinking trap it is?"
"My own experience supports your view rather than the author's," said Lanark cautiously, "but remember he says 'for the most part, at least where I was.' Frankly, if I felt there were no such places and we could never reach them, I wouldn't be reading to you."
"Then read something else."
"Here is a story about a small boy called Oor Wullie, and it is told in pictures. The first picture shows him coming with his father out of the front door, which is separated from the pavement by a single step. His hair is brushed and his boots are shining. His mother looks after them and says, 'Since it's Sunday, ye can tak Wullie a walk before dinner, but see he doesnae dirty his good claes, Paw.' His father, who is tall and thin with a flat cap, says, 'Leave it tae me, Maw!' Wullie is thinking, 'Crivens! Some fun this walk is going to be!' In the next picture they're walking beside a fence made of upright

pieces of timber joined edge to edge. I can't read what Wullie is saying because the words have been scored out with crayon, but his father—"

"Is this meant to be entertaining?"

"I wish you could see the pictures. They have a humorous, homely look which is very comforting."

"Have you no *other* book?"

"Only one."

He opened *No Orchids for Miss Blandish* and read:

"It began on a summer morning in July. The sun up early in the morning mist, and the pavements already steaming a little from the heavy dew. The air in the streets was stale and lifeless. It had been an exhausting month of intense heat, rainless skies, and warm, dust-laden winds.

Bailey walked into Minny's hash-house, leaving Old Sam asleep in the Packard. Bailey was feeling lousy. Hard liquor and heat don't mix. His mouth felt like a birdcage and his eyes were gritty. . . ."

He read for a long time. Once or twice he asked, "Are you enjoying this?" and she said, "Go on."

At last she interrupted with a harsh rattle of laughter. "Oh, yes, I like this book! Crazy hopes of a glamorous, rich, colourful life and then abduction, rape, slavery. That book, at least, is true."

"It is not true. It is a male sex fantasy."

"And life for most women is just that, a performance in a male sex fantasy. The stupid ones don't notice, they've been trained for it since they were babies, so they're happy. And of course the writer of that book made things obvious by speeding them up. What happens to the Blandish girl in a few weeks takes a lifetime for the rest of us."

"I deny that," said Lanark fiercely. "I deny that life is more of a trap for women than men. I know that most women have to work at home because people grow in them, but working at home is more like freedom than working in offices and factories; furthermore—"

His voice raised an echo which competed with the words. To end the sentence audibly he began shouting and caused a deafening explosion which took minutes to fade. Afterward he sat scowling at the air before him until the voice said, "Just go on reading."

CHAPTER 10. Explosions

He visited her chamber twice a day and read aloud there, only stopping when he was hoarse. He soon lost count of the times he had read *No Orchids for Miss Blandish.* Once, to have a different story to tell his patient, he watched a cowboy film in the staff club cinema, but mention of it threw her into a cold violent rage. She only believed in repetitious accounts of brutal men and humiliated women and thought anything else was deliberate mockery. Lanark left her chamber each time with a sore throat and a determination not to return, and had there been anywhere to go but the staff club he might have stayed away. The soft, brightly lit rooms with their warm air and comfortable furniture made him feel oppressively enclosed. The members were polite and friendly but talked as if there was nothing important outside the club, and Lanark was afraid of coming to believe them. At other times he suspected that his own ungraciousness made him dislike gracious people. He spent most of his free time on his bed in the ward. The window was no longer enjoyable for it had begun giving views of small rooms with worried people in them. Once he thought he glimpsed Mrs. Fleck, his old landlady, tucking the children into the kitchen bed. After that he preferred watching the lights move mysteriously between the slats of the half-shut blind and listening idly to the radio. He noticed that the requests for doctors were increasingly varied by a different kind of message.

"Attention, please note! Attention, please note! The expansion committee announces that after the hundred and eightieth all twittering is to be treated as a sign of hopelessness."

"Attention, please note! Attention, please note! The expansion committee announces that after the hundred and eightieth the sink will take no more softs. All helpless softs will be funnelled

into the compression sluices under the main wards."
But none of this urgency showed in the staff club unless it
was displayed through increased jollity at mealtimes. People
sat at tables smiling and talking loudly in groups of four. Ozenfant's booming laughter sounded among them; he was always
to be seen there wearing a light suit, talking hard and eating
hugely. Only three people sat quiet and alone: himself, Monsignor Noakes, and a big, strikingly sullen girl wearing khaki
overalls who ate almost as much as Ozenfant.

One evening Lanark had entered the restaurant and seated
himself when Ozenfant sat down beside him saying cheerfully,
"Twice today, at breakfast and at lunch, I beckon you to my
table and you do not notice. And so"—he passed a hand down
the yellow curve of his waistcoat—"the mountain comes to
Mahomet. I want to tell you I am pleased, very pleased indeed."
"Why?"
"I am a busy man, even at mealtimes I am working, so I have
only had time to observe closely two of your sessions, but
believe me, you do well."
"You're wrong, I do badly. She's freezing, I don't warm her
and everything I talk about increases her pain."
"Well, of course you are treating an impossible case, a case I
would have judged hopeless had you not needed someone to
practise on. But you have employed a tact, a tolerance, a patience which I never expected from a novice. So now I want
you to withdraw from this case and start on someone more
important."
Lanark leaned forward over the table and said, "You mean
those hours of reading that bloody book were *for nothing?*"
"No, no, no, my dear fellow, they have been very valuable;
they have shown me the sort of doctor you are and the kind
of patient you should treat. There are layers of stolid endurance
in you which make you a perfect buffer for these tragic intelligent females whose imagination exceeds their strength. We
have just such a patient in chamber thirty-nine who would, if
cured, be a delightful addition to our staff, and her head and
limbs are unarmoured. If you still wish to visit chamber one
you can do so, but I want you to spend most of your time in
chamber thirty-nine."
"What if my first patient gets well and wants to leave with
me? Do I simply abandon the second?"
Ozenfant made an impatient gesture. "Those are the scruples
of a novice. Patient one will not get well, and you have no

reason to leave. Suppose you did leave, and reached (which
is unlikely) a more sunlit continent, how would you earn your
bread? By picking up litter in the public parks?"
Lanark said in a low voice, "I shall visit my first patient, and
nobody else, until she doesn't want me."
Ozenfant drummed his fingers on the tablecloth. His expression
was blank. He said, "Dr. Lanark, what will you do when you
have failed to reclaim your Eurydice?"
"I am too ignorant to understand your jokes, Professor Ozenfant," said Lanark, rising and walking away.

He was angry and upset and felt that his patient's rage
against life would be a consolation. Instead of going to bed
he entered the lift and said, "Ozenfant's studio."
"Professor Ozenfant is recording just now. If I were you I
wouldn't disturb him."
Lanark seemed to recognize the voice. He said, "Is it you,
Gloopy?"
The lift said, "No. Only part of me."
"Which part?"
"The voice and feelings and sense of responsibility. I don't
know what they've done with the rest."
This was said with a stoical dignity which filled Lanark with
pity. He laid his hand against the lukewarm wall and said hum-
bly, "I'm sorry!"
"Why? People need me now. I'm never alone and I hear all
kinds of interesting things. You'd be amazed at what happens
in a lift between floors. Why, yesterday—"
Lanark said quickly, "I'm very glad. Will you take me to Ozenfant's studio?"
"But he's recording."
"He can't be, I've just left him in the restaurant."
"Don't you know that heads of departments can feed and work
at the same time? And he gets really poisonous when his music's
interrupted."
"Take me to the studio, Gloopy."
"All right, but I warned you."
The door slid open and Lanark heard the complicated squealing
of a string quartet playing very badly. He pulled the tapestry
aside, went in and struck a hanging microphone with his shoulder. He was confronted by four music stands with people behind
them. A gaunt woman in a red velvet gown was grappling a
cello. Three men in tailcoats, white waistcoats and bow ties
scraped on a viola and fiddles. One of them was Ozenfant.

He silenced the others with a hoarse cry and marched toward
Lanark, fiddle under elbow and bow clutched in the right hand
like a riding crop. When his face was an inch from Lanark's
he stopped and whispered, "Of course you knew I was recording?"

"Yes."

Ozenfant began speaking in a quiet voice which grew steadily
to a deafening yell: "Dr. Lanark, you have been allowed very
special privileges. You use a public ward as a private apartment.
You employ my name in lifts and they take you everywhere
direct. You ignore my advice, disdain my friendship, sneer at
my food and now! Now you deliberately ruin the recording
of an immortal harmony which might save the souls of thousands! What other insults do you plan to heap on me?"

Lanark said, "Your anger is misplaced. You have bullied me
into trying to cure a difficult patient and now you try to stop
me reaching her. If you don't want to see me you should contact
the engineers. Get them to fix that door in my ward so I can
go back through it, and we need never meet again."

Ozenfant's rage-swollen features relaxed into astonishment. He
said faintly, "You want the current of the whole institute thrown
into reverse for *that?*"

He wiped his face with his handkerchief and turned away, saying wearily, "Get out of here."

Lanark quickly lifted the tapestry and stooped into the corridor.

     He crouched in the ignition chamber feeling too discour-
aged to pick up the book where he had left it. He stared at
the slim human arm, noticing silver freckles above the elbow
and wondering if they had been there before. He tried to
hold the moving hand but it clenched into a fist.

The voice said, "Yes I'm unprotected there. Why not use
force?"

"Rima!"

"I'm not your Rima. Go on reading."

"I'm sick of that book. Couldn't you talk to me? You must
be lonely. I know I am."

There was no answer. He said, "Tell me about the world before
you came here."

"It was like this."

"It was not."

"Take care! You're afraid of the past. If I told what I know
you would go mad."

"Sinister hints don't frighten me now. I don't care about the past and future, I want nothing but some ordinary friendly words."

"Oh, I know you, Thaw, I know all about you, the hysterical child, the eager adolescent, the mad rapist, the wise old daddy, oh, I've suffered all your tricks and know how hollow they are so don't weep! Don't dare to weep. Grief is the rottenest trick of all."

Lanark was too disturbed to feel the tears on his face. He said, "You don't know me. I'm not called Thaw. I've been none of these things. I'm something commonplace that keeps getting hurt."

"So am I but I have courage, the courage not to care and clutch. Go away! *Can't you see what's happening?*"

From shoulder to wrist her arm was spotted with silver blots and stars. Lanark had a horrible feeling that each of his words had caused one. He whispered, "Dr. Lanark wants out." The panel swung open and he climbed through.

Someone had raised the blind in the ward and he looked out on a dingy plaster wall with brickwork showing through big cracks in it. For a moment he turned giddy and almost fell, then remembered he had left the staff club without eating. It seemed the one comfort he could get was the institute's nasty, invigorating food, so he returned to the restaurant. It was nearly empty but Ozenfant sat at his usual table talking intensely with two other professors. Lanark went to a table in the farthest corner and was approached by a waitress. He said, "Have you anything brown, dry and crumbly?"

"No sir, but we've something pink, moist and crumbly."

"I'll have a quarter of a plateful, please."

He had begun to eat when a hard, slightly hesitant voice said, "Can I sit here?"

He looked up and saw the big girl in the khaki overalls. She stood with hands in pockets staring at him fiercely. With a sense of relief he said, "Oh, yes."

She sat opposite. Her face had straight clear handsome lines like a Greek statue, though the chin was heavy and forward-jutting. She did not hold her fine shoulders erect but slumped and hunched them forward. Her brown hair was twisted loosely into a thick plait which hung over her left breast. Her fingers stroked it with short quick movements. She said abruptly, "Do you hate this place too?"

"Yes."

"What do you hate most?"

Lanark considered. "The manners of the staff. I know they have to be professional to keep things clean and orderly, but even their jokes and smiles seem to have professional reasons. What do you dislike?"

"The hypocrisy. The way they pretend to care while using the patients up."

"But they could help nobody if they didn't use their failures." The girl bent her head so that he only saw the top of it and muttered, "You don't hate this place if you can say that."

"I do hate it. I'm leaving, when I find a companion." She looked up.

"I'll go with you. I want to leave too."

Lanark was confused. He said, "Well, thank you, but—but— I have a patient, not a very hopeful case, but I can't leave until I've definitely cured her or failed."

She said disgustedly, "You *know* nobody is ever cured, that the treatment only keeps the bodies fresh until we need fuel or clothes or food."

Lanark looked at her, said "Foooo?" and dropped his spoon in the plate.

"Of course! What do you think you've been eating? Have you never looked into the sink? Has nobody shown you the drains under the sponge-wards?"

Lanark rubbed his clenched fists into his eye sockets. He wanted to be sick but the pink stuff had nourished him well: he had never felt stronger or more stable. He told himself wildly, "I'll never eat here again!"

"Then you'll leave with me?"

He looked at her blindly, not thinking of her at all. She said, "I frighten you, I frighten most men. But I can be very sweet for short times. Look."

He looked vaguely round the room for a way out until there was nowhere to look but in front, and the expression on her face made him lean forward to see it clearly. She had a slight, disdainful smile but within her defiant eyes he saw discontent, and beyond that a vast humility and willingness to become, for a while, anything he wanted. Looking into her eyes became like a rapid flight across shifting worlds, all of them sexual, and when he returned from the flight he saw that her fierceness was pleading and the smile timid. He began trembling with feelings of dizzy power. She said anxiously, "I can be very sweet?"

He nodded and whispered, "Where can we go?"

"Come to my room."

They stood together and she led the way out, Lanark walking
awkwardly because of the pressure of his penis against his trousers. As they passed Ozenfant's table the Professor cried in
mock alarm, "Oh, Dr. Lanark, you must not deprive us of
our little catalyst!"

   In the lift she said, "The specialist apartments."
The lift vibrated. They embraced and the feel of her strongly
female body made him mutter, "Let's stop the lift between
floors."
"That would be silly."
"Give me that contemptuous smile you're good at."
She gave it and he kissed her fiercely. She pulled her mouth
away and said, "Open your eyes, you must look at me while
we kiss."
"Why?"
"I'll do anything but you must keep looking."
The door slid open and she led him by the hand into one of
the halls. It was circular and gigantic like the others but seemed
deserted and silent until Lanark recognized the silence listening
makes. A number of men and women in overalls stood against
the walls gazing upward. Lanark looked up and saw the perspective of gold and orange rings sliding toward him, and in the
centre a black triangular shape swaying and growing bigger.
It seemed to be the base of a piece of machinery lowered
from above. It was only slightly narrower than the shaft, for
a grinding hum came briefly from the walls as if a metallic
corner had scraped them, but it must have been more than a
mile overhead for it looked very small. He squeezed the girl's
hand.
"What is that?"
"A suction delver. The creature's lending some to the expansion
project."
They were speaking in whispers. Lanark said, "Where do you
get power to drive things like that?"
"From the current, of course."
"What drives the current?"
"Please don't be technical. Come to my room. You'll like it,
I decorated it myself."
As she led him over the floor he tried not to picture what
would happen if the immense machine fell. No corridors led
out of this hall. The lift doors had smaller doors between them,
and she whispered to one of these, "I'm home," and it opened
inward.

The room was a cube and walls, ceiling and floor were
sheets of pure mirror. A low double bed in the centre was
covered with velvet cushions, a spot lamp on one wall cast a
beam of light on it, and that was all the furniture. Lanark stood
stupefied; he seemed to be standing among a hundred gleaming
glass boxes, each holding a bed, girl and himself. Looking down
he saw his feet resting on the soles of a dangling self looking
up. He stepped to the bed making figures advance on each
side of him toward a row approaching in front. He knelt on
the quilt and tried to see only the girl, who lay against a bank
of pillows, watching. She said shyly, "Do you like it?"
He shook his head.
"Then you think I'm hard and brazen?"
He thought of the silver dragon and felt a gush of affection
for this girl who had nothing to protect her but abrupt manners
and a few defiant expressions. He said, "I know you aren't.
Tell me your name."
"Let's not be personal until afterward."
He undressed quickly. Sympathy for the girl, and the many
movements his actions caused all round, made his lust less
greedy. He gently opened her overalls and drew them down
to her hips. She whispered, "How should I look?"
"Smile as if you were seeing me after waiting a long time."
She smiled so sweetly that he leaned forward to kiss her shoul-
ders. With her thumbs she pulled his eyes open, saying, "You
must look at me, I go blank when I'm not watched."
A radio sounded: *plin-plong, plin-plong, plin-plong, plin-plong!*
She murmured, "Ignore it."
"Let me turn it off."
"You can't, you can only turn it on."
The musical braying continued until he stretched and grabbed
the radio from his coat pocket. He turned the switch and Ozen-
fant said cheerfully, "Forgive if I interrupt but I thought you
would like to hear that your patient is about to go salamander."
"What?"
"There is nothing to be done, of course, but hurry along if
you wish to enjoy the spectacle. Bring your friend."
Lanark dropped the radio and sat biting his thumb, then stood
up and started automatically dressing. The girl stared from the
bed. She moaned, "You're leaving me to watch *that?*"
"Watch what?" He glanced at her hauntedly and added "I'm
sorry" and pulled the shirt over his head. He hurriedly finished
dressing, muttering at intervals, "I'm really sorry." He grabbed
the radio from the bed and looked about for the door, but

the gleaming glass was perfectly smooth. He said, "Dr. Lanark
wants to leave."
Nothing happened so he shouted it. She said, "This is *my*
home."
"Please let me out."
She stared at him stonily. He knelt on the bed, gripped her
shoulders and said pleadingly, "You see a friend is—is—is going to burn up; you must let me go."
She hit him hard on the side of the face. He shook his head
impatiently and said, "Yes, yes, that's all right, but you must
let me go."
She cried out, "Oh, open for him! And slam behind him as
hard as you can!"
A door opened and he ran out shouting, "I'm sorry! I'm sorry!"

If the exit slammed behind he did not hear for the noise
outside was too great. This hall had a pit in the centre and
two vast cables running into it from above and vibrating thun-
derously. Lanark rushed round the walls looking for a lift, but
all the doors had **OUT OF ORDER** signs on them. At last
he found a little tunnel with pulses of warmth and brightness
flowing out and forced his way in against the current. This
was almost impossible until he lay on the floor and drove forward by shoving with hands and feet against the narrow walls.
After several minutes of struggling he advanced about three
yards. "Oh, Rima!" he cried and had begun banging his head
on the floor and weeping with frustration when the pressure
against him stopped. He sat up. Before and behind the tunnel
had gone a dim orange which suddenly went completely black.
It was cold, and the noise had stopped, though there was a
distant twittering and occasional voices called forlornly:
"Dloc ma I ho."
"Sthgil! Teah dna sthgil!"
"Redloc ylnellus worg I won."
He got up and ran gladly forward through the dark until prevented by a surface which rumbled at the impact of his body.
It was one of the curtains. He drew back to fling himself on
it again when it opened and out poured a deafening noise
like many flocks of starlings' crashing through plate-glass win-
dows. In the door's bright circle he saw three white-faced men
staring at him, two in overalls and one a doctor. They shouted,
"You were going against the current!"
Lanark said, "There was no other way through."

"But you've blacked out the staff clubs! You've jammed the suction delvers!"

The doctor said, "I don't give a damn about those but you've caused an epidemic of twittering and God knows how many fractures. If it had happened after the hundred and eightieth you'd have been a murderer! A mass murderer!"

"I'm sorry, but I have to reach Ozenfant's studio."

The men in overalls glanced at each other. The doctor said, "Ozenfant may be a big man but if he starts letting his staff block the current he's in trouble."

The doctor turned and walked away and Lanark was about to follow when one of the men put a hand on his sleeve and said, "No, no, Mac, you've done enough damage. We'll go the way you came."

The normal movements of light and air resumed in the tunnel as they went down it, one of the men in front of Lanark, the other behind. When they reached the hall even the noise was normal. The leader opened one of the lifts with a key, led them inside and said, "Professor Ozenfant's place, then the sink." He looked accusingly at Lanark and said, "The sink is iced over."

"I'm sorry."

The door opened. Lanark was pushed into the studio but the men did not follow.

The quartet sat on chairs before the observation lens chatting and sipping from glasses. Ozenfant looked round smiling and cried, "Aha, so you are in time! There was a temporary power cut which we feared might delay you. But my dear fellow, your brow is bleeding!"

A silver figure glowed in the lens, air faintly trembling above the gaping beak. Looking back from it to the cosy social group, Lanark was gripped by rage. He quickly crossed the studio, passed between Ozenfant and the lady cellist, raised his right leg and struck his heel into the centre of the lens. It cracked and went black. The room was completely silent as he crossed to the wall, lifted the tapestry and entered the tunnel behind.

He leaned into the chamber through the open panel. All her limbs were metal now and she was bigger, head pressing the wall on one side and hooves on the other, the wings spread so that the tips of the plumes touched the walls all round and not an inch of floor was visible. The air was chokingly hot and a white line like cigarette smoke rose from the beak. He said, "Rima."

The voice answered with a throb of delight. "Is that you, little Thaw? Have you come to say goodbye? I'm not cold now, Thaw, I'm warm and soon I'll be shining."

"I am not little and I have not come to say goodbye."

He climbed in, crawled across the rigidly quivering copper wings, sat astride the silver thorax and gasped breathlessly. The chamber was getting dim with whirling steam. She laughed exultingly and said, "Are you still there? I'm glad you came. I like you now I'm leaving but you mustn't stay any longer."

"Listen! listen to me!" he shouted and could think of nothing to add. He lay flat and shoved his head desperately into her jaws. The heat scorched his face and made his hair stream upward. There was a crackling sound and Ozenfant's voice said sharply, "You have ten seconds to leave, the dome must soon be sealed, it should have been sealed already, you have seven seconds to leave."

She laughed again and her voice rang directly in his ears. "Are you angry that you'll have nobody to read to, Thaw? But I've spread my wings, I'll fly everywhere and you can't come, I will rise with my flaming hair and eat men like air."

"Soon her jaws will shut," said Ozenfant. "Listen, you dislike me but I give you five more seconds, five unofficial seconds to leave starting *now.*"

A moment later there was a faint hiss and such a blast of steam from the mouth that Lanark jerked his head back with a yell. She said, "You're not here?"

"Yes, I'm here."

"But I'll kill you."

"I don't care."

"I don't want to kill you."

He felt a wave of heat go through the cool metal under him then the beak shut with a crack like a gunshot. There was a second crack then a clang. The clouds of steam began clearing, yet he was unable for a moment to see the great beak, for the head had fallen off. There was a black hole between the shoulders from which poured a pale shining stream. It was hair. There was another clang as the thorax split. He fell sideways onto a wing and lay listening to sounds like buckets and kettles falling downstairs. The silver body and limbs cracked and fell apart until they covered the floor like ornate scrap metal.

A naked girl crouched weeping in the middle, rubbing her cheeks with her hands. She was blond and tall but she was Rima for she shook her head at him and said, "You should have taken that coat. I didn't want you to be cold."
There was a crackling and Ozenfant said, "What is happening? What is happening? I can see nothing without the screen."
Lanark was too stunned to think or feel but he could not stop gazing at her with open mouth and eyes. Her skin looked drenched and she curled her knees up and hugged them, trembling. Lanark took his coat and jersey off, pushed away some cracked armour and crawled to her side saying, "You'd better put these on."
"Lay them round me please."
Ozenfant said, "Stop whispering! I demand to know what has happened!"
Lanark said, "I think we're all right."
After a moment Ozenfant said, without expression, "I wash my hands of the pair of you."
Lanark put the clothes round her shoulders and sat by her side with his arm about her waist. She leaned her head on him and said drowsily, "You look as if you've been in a fight, Lanark."
"I'll be better soon."
"I wonder if I can forgive you for breaking my wings. It's nice to be human again but they were beautiful wings."
She seemed to fall asleep and he passed into a kind of stupor.

Later she kissed his ear and murmured, "Should we try to leave?"
He roused himself and said, "Dr. Lanark is ready to leave."
The ignition chamber said sternly, "You are allowed to leave but you are no longer a doctor."
A line appeared dividing the milky dome in two and each half sunk into the floor and left them squatting in a small room with an entrance on each side. Down the low tunnel from the studio ran, stooping, a nurse with a broom, followed by a stretcher pushed by another nurse. The first swept the metal shards to one side while the second brought a plain white nightshirt to Rima and helped her on with it, and all the time they laughed and chattered excitedly.
"Poor Bushybrows looks stunned."
"He's found a girlfriend but he needs a wash."
"Can you stand up, dear? Lie on the stretcher and we'll take you gently to a lovely, lonely ward together."

"The Professor is cross with you, Bushybrows. He says you've
been sabotaging the expansion project."
They wheeled Rima down the corridor to the ward and Lanark
followed. The blind was raised. There was a deep green sky
outside with a couple of stars in it and some feathery bloody
clouds. The nurses fetched towels and basins and washed Rima
in bed. Lanark took his dressing gown and undressed and bathed
in the ward lavatory. When he returned the nurses were putting
screens round the bed. He said, "Leave an opening so that
we can see the window, please."
They did that, then one patted his cheek, the other said, "Have
fun, Bushybrows," and both pressed fingers to their lips and
tiptoed out with exaggerated stealth. Lanark went to the bed.
Rima seemed to be sleeping. He slid gently in beside her and
fell asleep himself.

Someone seemed to be shining a torch on his eyes so he
opened them. The ward was dark but the window through
the arches was filled with stars. A nearly full moon had risen,
and its clear wan light shone upon the bed and Rima, who
leaned on an elbow watching him with a grave small smile,
nibbling the tip of a lock of silvery-gold hair. She said, "Were
you the only one who could help me, Lanark? Nobody special?
Nobody splendid?"
"Have you known many special men?"
"None who weren't pretenders. But I used to have fantastic
dreams."
"I can imagine nobody more splendid than you."
"Take care, that makes me stronger. I may not find a better
man but I'll always be able to imagine one."
"But that makes me stronger."
"Don't talk."
They did not sleep again until he had explored with his body
all the sweet crevices of her body.

CHAPTER 11. Diet and Oracle

They lay in bed for three days for she was weak and he liked
to be near her. The window showed azure skies with distant
birds in them or sunlit or sullen cloudscapes changing before
a wind. Lanark read *The Holy War* and looked at Rima, who
slept a lot. He had been near beauty before but had never
expected to touch and hold it, and being held and caressed
by it was so luxurious that it made his insides feel golden.
That she, delighting him, delighted in him was a reflection
multiplying delight until it shone round them like a halo. Her
clear lovely body glowed, even in sweat, as if the silver once
containing her was softly breathing under the skin. When he
told her this she smiled sadly and said, "Yes, I suppose good
looks and money are alike. They make us confident but we
distrust folk who want us for them."
"Don't you trust me? I said that as a compliment."
She stroked his cheek with a fingertip and said absently, "I
like making you happy, but how can I trust someone I don't
understand?"
He stared, astonished, and cried, "We love each other! What
could understanding add to that? We can't understand ourselves, how can we understand others? Only maps and mathematics exist to be understood and we're solider than those, I
hope."
"Take care! You're getting clever."
"Rima, which of us came out when that shell cracked? My
thoughts are bigger than they used to be, I'm afraid of them.
Hold me."
"I like big men. Hold me instead."

He refused all food on the first day, saying he had over-
eaten the day before. When the nurse brought breakfast next

morning he cut his pale sausage into thin slices while Rima
ate, then tried to hide them by laying her empty plate on his.
She said, "Why are you doing that? Are you sick?"
"I'll be all right in a day or two."
"We'd better get a doctor."
"I don't need one. I'll be fine when we leave the institute."
"You're being mysterious about something. What are you hid-
ing?"
She interrogated him for an hour and a half, pleading, threaten-
ing, and at last tugging his hair in exasperation. He fought
back and the tussle grew amorous. Later, as he lay quiet and
unthinking, she murmured, "Still, you'd better tell me."
He saw the argument like a ponderous boulder about to roll
over him again. He said, "I'll tell you if you promise to keep
eating."
"Of course I'll keep eating."
"You know that the institute gets light and heat from people
with our kind of sickness. Well, the food is made from people
with a different sickness."
He watched her anxiously, dreading an outcry. She looked
thoughtful and said, "These people aren't deliberately killed,
are they?"
He remembered the catalyst but decided not to mention her.
"No, but the staff don't cure people as often as they pretend."
"But without the staff they would go bad anyway."
"Perhaps. I suppose so."
"Anyway, if I stop eating I'll die, and nobody extra is going
to be cured. Why shouldn't I eat?"
"I want you to eat! I made you promise to eat."
"Why won't you eat?"
"No logical reason. I have instincts, prejudices, that stop me.
But don't worry, I'm fit enough to go without food for two
or three days."
She glared at him and cried, "I'm not!"
"But I want you to eat."
"And then you'll despise me."
Lanark grew confused and uneasy. He said, "No, I won't exactly
despise you. . . ."
She turned her back to him and said coldly, "Right. I won't
eat either."
She neither moved nor spoke for many hours, and when the
nurse brought lunch she ordered it away.

That afternoon the window showed pearly fog and a tiny
hard white sun. He could sense that Rima wasn't sleeping.

He tried to embrace her but she shook him off. He said abruptly, "You know that if I eat this food you'll have defeated me in a way I'll always remember?"

She said nothing. He took the radio and said to it "Dr. Lanark needs to speak to Dr. Munro."

"I'm sorry. There is no doctor called Lanark on the staff register."

"But Dr. Munro delivered me. I desperately need his advice."

"I'm sorry Mr. Lanark, the doctor is off duty just now, but we'll give him your message first thing after breakfast tomorrow."

Lanark put down the radio and bit his thumb knuckle. When the nurse brought the evening meal he tried to persuade Rima to eat without him, but again she told the nurse to remove it. He rose and walked up and down the ward for a long time, then returned to bed, lay down wearily with his back to her and said, "Don't worry. I'll eat."

A little later her arm slid round his waist. She kissed him comfortingly between the shoulderblades, pressed her breasts to his back, stomach to his bum, and knees to the backs of his knees. They lay like that till morning, fitted together like a couple of spoons in a drawer.

They were wakened by the nurse, who tidied the bed and helped Rima wash. Lanark shaved and washed in the lavatory, feeling relieved and happy. He had been foodless for two days and ached with hunger and was glad to have a reason for breaking his promise to himself, especially as Rima was not triumphant about it but gentle and grateful. When he returned to the freshly made bed the nurse brought in breakfast and placed on his knees a plate holding a small transparent pink dome. He stared at it, gripped the knife and fork, then looked at Rima, who waited, watching steadily. Feeling cold and lonely he handed the plate back, saying, "I can't. I meant to eat, I want to, but I can't."

Rima handed back her own plate, then turned away from him and started weeping. The nurse said, "You're nothing but a couple of babies. How can you get well if you won't eat?"

She pushed the trolley out and the radio *plin-plonged*. Lanark switched it on. Munro said briskly, "Are you there, Lanark?"

"Yes. When can we leave, Dr. Munro?"

"As soon as your partner is strong enough to walk. Four days of rest and proper feeding will put her on her feet. Do I hear someone sobbing?"

"Yes, you see we can't eat the food. Or I can't and she won't."

"That's unfortunate. What are you going to do?"
"Is there no way of getting decent food?"
Munro sounded angry.
"Why should you demand a superior diet to the rest of us?
The Lord Director eats nothing better. As I told you, the institute is isolated."
"Yet a certain creature is sending in tons of expensive machinery."
"That's different, that is for the expansion project. Stop talking
about what you don't understand. If you and your partner want
to leave you must eat what you're given and not fight the
current."
The radio went dead. The craving in Lanark's stomach had
vanished while he surveyed the food but now it came back
harder and stronger. It mixed with the woe of Rima's weeping
and filled him with dense, concrete misery. He folded his arms
on his chest and said loudly, "We must stay like this until
things improve or deteriorate further."
Rima turned on him, shouting, "Oh, what a fool you are!"
and scratched at his face with her hands. He slipped out of
bed and said fiercely, "I'd better leave, you'll be able to eat
then! Just say the word and I'll clear out for good!"
She pulled the coverlet over her head. He put on his dressing
gown, went out through the screens and walked aimlessly up
and down the ward. At last he returned and said soberly, "Rima,
I'm sorry I yelled. I was being selfish and brutal. All the same,
you would probably eat if I wasn't here. Should I go away
for a couple of days? I promise I'll come back."
She lay below the cover, giving no sign of hearing. He slipped
in beside her and dozed.

He was wakened by having a shin kicked. Her head was
still covered but a tall figure in a black cassock sat stiffly by
the bed. Lanark sat up. It was Monsignor Noakes, who sucked
his lower lip and said, "I apologize if I intrude, but I believe
the matter is urgent."
His voice was listless and quiet and he seemed to be talking
to a brown suitcase on his knees. Lanark was wondering what
to say when Noakes went on.
"A certain person (I name no names) has certainly told you
of the very considerable powers I once wielded here. I was
director of this institute once, though not called that, for in
those days the titles were different. Never mind. The only
relic of my ancient status is the privilege of attending ecclesiasti-

cal conferences in continents where the connection between feeding and killing folk is less obvious. This has enabled me to stock a small larder of delicacies which you may find useful. I hear you are refusing our meals."

Rima sat up and leaned on Lanark's shoulder and they stared while Noakes unpacked his case and laid upon the coverlet:

a carton of cheese with red cows and green fields on the label
a big block of chocolate wrapped in gilt foil   a date-pack
a salami sausage over two feet long   a tin of ravioli
four squat black bottles of stout   a tin of sliced apricots
a small bottle of cherry brandy   a tin of condensed milk
a tin of smoked oysters   a big paper poke of dried figs
cutlery,   plates,   a tin-opener

Rima cried, "Oh how kind you are!" and began eating figs. Lanark said passionately, "You are a decent man," and opened the carton of cheese. Noakes sat watching them with a faint wistful smile. He said, "Cannibalism has always been the main human problem. When the Church was a power we tried to discourage the voracious classes by feeding everyone regularly on the blood and body of God. I won't pretend the clergy were never gluttons, but many of us did, for a while, eat only what was willingly given. Since the institute joined with the council it seems that half the continents are feeding on the other half. Man is the pie that bakes and eats himself and the recipe is separation."

Lanark said, "You're very good to us. I wish I could do something in return."

"You can. I asked you, once, and you weren't interested."

"You wanted me to warn people against the institute."

"I want you to warn everyone against the institute."

"But Monsignor Noakes, I can't, I'm too weak. When I leave the institute I'll certainly denounce it in conversation and I'll certainly vote for parties opposing it, but I won't have time to work against it. I'll be working to earn a living. I'm sorry."

Noakes said drearily, "Don't apologize. A priest must always urge people to be better than himself."

Rima stopped munching and asked, "What's wrong with the institute? I got better here, don't others?"

Lanark said abruptly, "You were cured against the instructions of my department. The institute is a murder machine."

Noakes shook his head and sighed.

"Ah, it could be easily destroyed if it was a simple murder

machine. But it is like all machines, it profits those who own it, and nowadays many sections are owned by gentle, powerless people who don't know they are cannibals and wouldn't believe if you told them. It is also amazingly tolerant of anyone it considers human, and cures more people than you realize. Even the societies who denounce it would (most of them) collapse if it vanished, for it is an important source of knowledge and energy. That is why the director of the institute is also president of the council, though two thirds of the council detest him."

"A specialist told me nobody is ever cured."

Noakes glanced furtively at Rima and said in a low voice, "That specialist is employed to do what others try to prevent. Her view of our curative functions is necessarily pessimistic."

"If all that is true, why warn folk against it at all?"

Noakes sat upright and said strongly, "Because it is mad with greed and spreading like cancer, because it is fouling the continents and destroying the handiwork of God! It is horrible for a priest to confess this, but sometimes I care less for those the institute eats than for the plants, beasts, pure air and water it destroys. I have nightmares of a world where nothing exists outside our corridors and everyone is a member of the staff. We eat worms grown in bottles. Between meals we perform Beethoven's Choral Symphony for hours on end with Ozenfant conducting, while the viewing screens show ancient colour films of naked adolescents dancing through flowers and sunlight that no longer exist."

Rima stopped eating and Lanark stared fearfully at the window. A dazzling sun rested on the horizon of a sea of clouds with an eagle speeding across it. Lanark pointed and said, "That is not? That is not a . . . ?"

Noakes wiped his brow and said, "That is not a film. What I dread has not yet happened."

He shut his suitcase and stood up, saying, "My health is poor. I embarrass you and embarrass myself. God bless you, my children."

With thumb and forefinger he sketched a cross in the air above their heads and hurried out in a posture so like someone escaping that it would have been brutal to shout thank you or goodbye. Rima said, "Do you think he's mad?"

"No. He's been too decent."

"Yes, he's sweet, but I bet *he* never cures anyone."

The nurses brought lunch and were told to take it away and not bring food again. Lanark and Rima ate a quarter of the salami, a little cheese and a few figs; then he helped her walk to the lavatory, where she bathed and he washed her back. They returned to bed and drank cherry brandy and kissed drowsily. The silver was starting to glow under her skin when he thought of something and said, "Rima, in the ignition chamber you sometimes called me Thaw."

She pondered and said finally, "Yes, I dreamed a lot of strange things in that armour. You were called Thaw, or Coulter, and we stood on a bridge at night with the moon above us and an old man watching from among some trees. You wanted to kill me. I don't remember the rest."

"I wonder how I could discover more."

"Why bother? Aren't we happy, when we don't quarrel?"

"Yes, but I'll have to work soon and I've forgotten what I'm able to do. I should have asked Noakes if there was a way of learning about life before Unthank."

"Call him on the radio."

"No, I'll call Munro. I've more confidence in Munro."

He was linked to Munro with surprising speed and said, "I called to tell you we're all right: we've our own supply of food."

"Quite so. Is that your only reason for calling?"

"No. I'm wondering about the past, you see I can't remember it. . . ."

There was crackling and a smooth voice said, "These are the archives. May I help?"

"I'm trying to find out about my past. My name is Lanark. . . ."

There was a loud whirring then the voice spoke in a quick monotone: "You reached Unthank on the 3rd day of the 10th month of the 1956th solar year of the Nazarene calendar. Calling yourself Lanark you attended the central social security office, were registered as a dragon and awarded 8 pounds, 19 shillings, and 6 pence. You lodged with Bella Fleck, 738 Ashfield Street, Unthank N. 2 for 30 days and then applied for admission to the institute. You were delivered in human form on the 75th day of the 4999th decimal year from the foundation and on the 80th became a junior assistant to Professor Ozenfant in the energy division. Your talent was vitiated by acts of aimless violence. On the 85th you interrupted a recording session, insulted the catalyst, blocked the current and shattered a viewing lens. Your relocation is scheduled for the 88th subject to confirmation by Lord Monboddo, director of the institute, moderator of the expansion project and president of the council."

There was a brief, unexpectedly noisy fanfare of trumpets.

Lanark said irritably, "I know that. I want to learn what I did *before* I came to Unthank."

"You reached Unthank through water, which is outwith the jurisdiction of the council. Do you wish to consult an oracle?"

"Of course, if that will help."

The cool white plastic of the little radio went red hot. Lanark dropped it on the coverlet, Rima screamed, he brushed it with his sleeve to the floor, it exploded with a loud bang.

The space round the bed was dim with blue smoke which hurt the eyes. Rima lay staring at him. He pulled his scorched fingers from his mouth and asked if she was all right, but the detonation had numbed his eardrums. Her reply was remote and interrupted by a distant voice saying Help help, can nobody hear me?

Rima asked who was there and a moment after the voice spoke directly into his ear. It was sexless and eager but on an odd unemphatic note, as if its words could never be printed between quotation marks.

It said I am glad you called.

Lanark shook his head very hard then said firmly, "Could you tell me about my past, please? Starting with childhood?"

The voice said I'm very keen on this kind of work but you'll have to give me a clue. Have you anything belonging to that past?

"Nothing."

No clothes, for instance?

"My clothes were dissolved on the way here."

Had you nothing insoluble in the pockets?

"There was only . . . wait a minute."

Lanark remembered Munro's taking the pistol from the drawer in his dead neighbour's locker. He opened his own drawer and looked in. Most of the space was filled with food but in a corner he found a tiny fluted cockle and a quartz pebble with grey and cream veins through it. He said, "I've found a seashell and a stone."

Hold one in each hand. Yes, I can see the way backward now. You were called Thaw. Will I start the story when you're five or fifteen or ten?

"Five, please."

Lanark lay down comfortably and the oracle, in the voice of a precocious child, said Duncan Thaw made a blue line along the top of a paper and a brown line at the bottom. He drew a giant running along the brown line with a captured princess,

but as he couldn't draw the princess beautiful enough he made
the giant carry a sack. The princess was inside it. His father—
"Excuse me," said Lanark. "That's a very abrupt beginning.
Could you not start by telling me something of the geographical
and social surroundings?"

After a moment of silence the voice said in a dry academic
voice The river Clyde enters the Irish Sea low down among
Britain's back hair of islands and peninsula. Before widening
to a firth it flows through Glasgow, the sort of industrial city
where most people live nowadays but nobody imagines living.
Apart from the cathedral, the university gatehouse and a gawky
medieval clocktower it was almost all put up in this and the
last century—

"I'm sorry to interrupt again," said Lanark, "but how do you
know this? Who are you anyway?"

A voice to help you see yourself.

"But I've heard too many of these voices. None of them belonged to liars, even Sludden and Ozenfant told a lot of truth,
but only the truth which suited their plans. What plans have
you? What bits will you leave out?"

The voice said mournfully I've no plans at all. The only things
I'll try to leave out are the repetitions, and I'll probably fail.
I've grown obsessed with detail since I faded into nothing.

"I don't understand."

Then I'll tell you my history before I go on to yours. It's less
amusing but the lack of detail makes it shorter, and since I
once lived in your country it will tell you something about
the economics of the place.

The oracle began speaking in a male, pompous elderly
voice and Lanark settled comfortably to listen. Rima yawned
and snuggled against his back. Five minutes later he noticed
she was asleep.

PROLOGUE

From an early age I only wanted to deal with what I was sure of, and like all thinkers I soon came to distrust what could only be seen and touched. The majority believe that floors, ceilings, each other's bodies, the sun, etc. are the surest things in the world, but soon after going to school I saw that everything was untrustworthy when compared with numbers. Take the simplest kind of number, a telephone number, 339-6286 for example. It exists outside us for we find it in a directory, but we can carry it in our heads precisely as it is, for the number and our idea of it are identical. Compared with his phone number our closest friend is shifty and treacherous. He certainly exists outside us, and since we remember him he also, in a feeble way, exists in our heads, but experience shows that our idea of the man is only slightly like him. No matter how well we know him, how often we meet him, how conservative his habits, he will constantly insult our notion of him by wearing new clothes, changing his mind, growing old or sick or even dying. Moreover, my idea of a man is never the same as someone else's. Most quarrels come from conflicting ideas of a man's character but nobody fights over his phone number, and if we were content to describe each other numerically, giving height, weight, date of birth, size of family, home address, business address and (most informative of all) annual income, we would see that below the jangling opinions was no disagreement on the main realities.

On leaving school my teachers suggested a career in physics, but I rejected the idea. Science certainly controls the physical world by describing it mathematically, but I have already mentioned my distrust of physical things. They are too remote from the mind. I chose to live by those numbers which are most purely a product of the mind and therefore influence it most strongly: in a word, money. I became an accountant, and later a stockbroker. It puzzles me that people who live by owning or managing big sums of money are commonly called materialistic, for finance is the most purely intellectual, the most sheerly spiritual of activities, being concerned less with material objects than with values. Of course finance needs objects, since money is the value of objects and could no more exist without them than mind can exist without body, but the objects come second. If you doubt this, think which you would rather own: fifty thousand pounds or a piece of land valued at fifty thousand pounds. The only people likely to prefer the land are financiers who know how to increase its value by renting or reselling, so either answer proves that money is preferable to things. Perhaps you will say that in some circumstances a millionaire would give his wealth for a cup of water, but these circumstances happen more in arguments than in life, and a better indication of how folk regard money is the instinctive reverence which all but ignorant savages feel toward the rich. Many deny this, but introduce them to a really wealthy man and see how unable they are to treat him casually.

I was thirty-five when I became really wealthy, but long before then I was living in a service flat, driving a Humber, playing golf at weekends and bridge in the evenings. People who did not understand financial reports thought my life a dull one: they could not see the steep determined climb from one level of prosperity to the next, the excitement of the barely avoided loss, the triumph of the suddenly realized profit. This adventure was purely emotional, for I was physically secure. I feared the greed of the working classes and the incompetence of governments, but only because they threatened some of the numbers in my accounts; I did not feel in danger of hunger or cold. My acquaintances lived like myself in the world of numbers rather than the muddle of seeable, touchable things which used to be called reality, but they had wives, which meant that as they grew richer they had to move into bigger houses and buy new cars and reproduction antique cocktail cabinets. These things naturally occurred in their conversation, but I also heard them gloat on other objects with an enthusiasm which seemed greater the more useless the object was. "I see the daffodils are with us again," they would say, or "My God! Harrison has shaved his moustache off." Where I saw a leaf they saw a "lovely green" leaf. Where I saw a new power station they saw "technological progress" or "industry ravaging the countryside." Once at a party a couple started fighting. I was explaining something to a client and the noise made me raise my voice, but the other guests were greatly excited and began whispering and spitting adjectives: "disgraceful," "pathetic," "ludicrous," "distressing," "inconsiderate." I saw that most people had excessive funds of emotion which they got rid of by investing in objects they could not use. I had no excess emotion, my work absorbed it all, but now I know that these casual investments showed a profit. Like vain women, the objects postured before their admirers in light and colours

I was never allowed to see. They showed me just enough of themselves to let me know they existed. And one day they began to stop doing even that.

I was studying a document when my attention was nagged by some difference outside the printed paper. I examined the top of my desk. It had been polished wood with a slightly rippled grain, but now the grain had vanished and the surface was as blank as a sheet of plastic. I looked round the office, which was furnished in the modern manner for I detested fussy details. The white walls and plain carpet were as usual but the view through the window had altered. What had been a typical street in the business centre of an old-fashioned industrial city, a street of elaborately carved and pillared façades, was now bordered by blank surfaces punctured by rectangular holes. I saw at once what was happening. Not content with showing itself in poorer materials than it kept for others, reality was economizing further. Where I had once seen irrelevant details and colours I saw none at all. Stone, wood and patterned surfaces became plain surfaces. The weaves of cloths were indistinguishable, and all doors looked flush-panelled.

Yet I did not feel ill-treated, for there was still enough outer reality for me to work with and in some ways I could work better. On entering a room of employees before this I usually had to look at several before recognizing the one I wanted, which wasted time, especially if I felt obliged to smile or nod at the men I noticed first. Now, when I entered a room, everyone but the man I wanted was as faceless as an egg, so I knew him at once. And later I only saw the man I wanted—nobody else was visible, unless they were slacking or wanted to speak to me, in which case they displayed enough substance to let me deal with them. You may wonder why I never collided with those surrounding me. Well, in my office it was other people's business to keep out of my way, and when driving there I noticed traffic signs and adjacent vehicles, though pedestrians and scenery were invisible. But one day I parked the car in the usual side street, opened the door to walk to the office and could see neither street nor pavement, just a clear general greyness, and leading through it to the dim silhouette of my office (there were no other buildings) a line of solid, pavement-coloured stepping stones, each the size and shape of the sole of my shoe. I could only leave the car by walking along these; each vanished as I took my weight from it; I had spasms of vertigo and was in terror of what would happen if I stepped *between* the stones. On reaching the office doorstep (which was completely visible) I squatted and moved the palm of my hand experimentally down into the emptiness. A piece of pavement the shape of the hand appeared underneath it. Simultaneously three clerks solidified round me, asking if I felt unwell. I pretended, not convincingly, to tie a shoelace.

Later I sat on a swivel chair above fathoms of emptiness, grey emptiness all around except where, six feet to the right, a pencil moving on its point across an angled notepad showed where my secretary was taking down the words I dictated to her. My right hand felt as if it rested on my knee, but I could see nothing but the dial of the wristwatch. At half-past five a line of carpet-coloured stepping stones appeared which released me from the chair, but walking on them was hard for I could no longer see my feet, and when I reached the end, instead of the linoleum-coloured stepping stones of the lift floor I saw nothing: the emptiness before and behind was total and complete. I saw nothing, heard nothing and felt nothing but the soles of my feet pressing the floor under them. Suddenly I was too tired and angry to continue. I stepped forward and nothing happened, except that the pressure on my feet vanished. I neither fell nor floated. I had become bodiless in a bodiless world. I existed as a series of thoughts amidst infinite greyness.

At first I was greatly relieved. I have never been afraid of loneliness, and the previous days had been more of a strain than I had let myself believe. I slept almost at once, which means that I stopped thinking and the surrounding greyness went black. After a while it grew light again and for the first time in my life I was idle. Every life has blank moments when we stand waiting for a bus or a friend and there's nothing to do but think. In the past I had filled these moments by calculating how an unexpected war or election would affect the wealth entrusted to me, but I had no zest for calculation now. Money, even imaginary money, needs the future to give it force. Without future it is not even ink in a ledger, paper in a purse. The future had gone with my body. There was nothing to do but remember, and I was depressed to find that the work which had given my life a goal and a decent order now looked like an arithmetical brain disease, a profit-and-loss calculation lasting years and proving nothing. My memory was a catalogue of things I had ignored and devalued. I had enjoyed no definite friendship or love, no intense hatred or desire; my life had been stony soil in which only numbers grew, and now I could do nothing but sift the stones and hope one or two would turn out to be jewels. I was the loneliest and most impotent man in the world. I was about to turn desperate when a lovely thing appeared in the air before me.

It was a cream-coloured wall patterned with brownish-pink roses. A beam of early morning summer sunlight shone on it and on me. I was sitting in bed with the wall on one side and two chairs on the other. It seemed a very big bed, though it was an ordinary single one, and two chairs had been placed to stop my falling out. My legs were covered by a quilt on which lay a tobacco pipe with a broken stem, a small slipper and a book with bright cloth pages. I was perfectly happy and singing a song on one note: *ooloolooloolooloo*. When tired of that I sang *dadadadada* for I had discovered the difference between *loo* and *da* and was interested in it. Later still, having tired of singing, I took the slipper and thumped the wall until my mother came. Each morning she lay in bed with a thin solemn young man on the other side of the roses. Her warmth reached me through the wall so I was never cold or lonely. I don't suppose my mother was unnaturally tall but she seemed twice the size of anyone else, and brown-haired, and regally slender above the hips. Below the hips she changed a lot, being often pregnant. I remember seeing her upper body rising behind the curve of her stomach like a giantess half-hidden by the horizon of a calm sea. I remember sitting on that curve with the back of my head between her breasts, knowing her face was somewhere above and feeling very sure of myself. I can't remember her features at all. Light or darkness came from them according to her mood, and I am certain this was more than the fantasy of a small child. I remember her sitting very still in a room of chattering strangers and steadily reducing them to whispers by the sullen silent fury she radiated. Her good moods were equally radiant and made the dullest company feel gallant and glamorous. She was never happy or depressed, she was glorious or sombre, and very attractive to modest dependable men. The men I called father were all of that kind. Apart from loving her they had no peculiarities. She must have attracted them like an extravagant vice for she was a poor housekeeper; on coming to live with a man she tried to prepare meals and keep things tidy, but the effort soon waned. I think the first house

I remember was the happiest because it had only two small
rooms and my first father was not fastidious. I believe he was
a garage mechanic, for there was a car engine beside my bed
and some huge tyres under the recess bed in the kitchen. As
I grew older my mother was less ready to come when I thumped
the wall, so I learned to crawl or stagger to the bed next door
and be pulled in. She would lie reading newspapers and
smoking cigarettes while my father made a hill under the
blankets with his knees and suddenly flattened it when I had
climbed on top. Later he would rise and bring us a breakfast
of tea and fried bread and eggs.

The house was in a tenement with a narrow, busy street
in front and a cracked asphalt yard at the back. Behind the
yard was the embankment of a canal, and on sunny days my
mother dragged me up this by straps fastened to a harness
round my chest and we made a nest in the long grass beside
the mossy towpath. The canal was choked with rushes and leafy
weeds; nobody passed by but an old man with a greyhound
or boys who should have been at school. I played with the
tobacco pipe and my slipper, pretending I was my mother and
the pipe me and the slipper my bed, or pretending the slipper
was a car with the pipe driving. She read or daydreamed as
she did at home, and I know now that her power came from
these dreams, for where else could an almost silent woman
without abilities learn the glamour of an enslaved princess,
the authority of an exiled queen? The place where we lay was
level with our kitchen window, and when my father returned
from work he would prepare a meal and call us in to eat it.
He seemed a contented man, and I am sure the quarrels were
not his fault. One night I was wakened by noise from the dark
wall at my ear, my mother's voice beating like high waves
over protesting mutters. The noise stopped and she entered
the room and lay with me and hugged me hungrily. This
happened several times, filling the nights with anticipation and
delight and leaving me stupefied all day, for her thundering
kisses exploded like fireworks in my ears and for long spells
annihilated thought entirely. So I hardly noticed when she
dressed me, and packed a suitcase, and took me away from
that house. I don't remember if we travelled by train or bus,
I only remember that as night fell we walked along a track
between trees whose high branches crashed together in the
wind, and the track brought us to a farmhouse where we lived
for over a year. My sister was born soon after we arrived.

My mother's ominous attraction is shown by the fact that even in a visible state of pregnancy, with a two-year-old son, she was employed as a housekeeper by a thrifty farmer whose wife had died. For the first few weeks I was happy. We slept together in a small low-ceilinged room at the back of the house and ate by ourselves. I remember us sitting furtively in a corner of the cosy parlour while the farmer and his children dined before the fire. My mother was singing softly in my ear:

> "Wee chooky birdy, tol-lol-lol
> laid an egg on the window sol.
> The window sol
> began to crack,
> Wee chooky bird roared and grat."

Soon afterward we all began eating together and I slept in the little low room by myself. My mother spent most of the time in an upstairs room I could never visit and an old woman came each day to do the housework. I believe the old woman was first employed as temporary help while the baby was born, but she was still cleaning the house and making meals many months later, and carrying eggs and toast upstairs on a tray while the farmer, his children, and I breakfasted on porridge at the kitchen table. All my memories of the farm have eggs in them. When exploring the barnyard one day I found a great cluster of brown eggs in a clump of nettles behind an old cart. It was a surprising sight, for our eggs usually came from wooden henhouses in a nearby field. I trotted into the kitchen to tell someone. The farmer was there, and he explained that hens sometimes laid astray in an effort to get their eggs hatched instead of eaten. I led him to the eggs; he gathered them in his cap, praised me and gave me a peppermint. Whenever I felt lonely after that I would crawl into a henhouse through one of the tiny doors the hens used, steal an egg from under a sitting fowl and go to the stackyard or byre and pretend to find it under hay or among the cowcake. Then I took it to the farmer, who always patted my head and gave me a peppermint. I think he must have known where I got the other eggs, but it was friendly of him to pretend otherwise. He probably liked me.

His children did not. There was a garden of tangled grass and stunted fruit trees behind the house, and on warm summer evenings I played there, building nests in the ivy round my

bedroom window. One evening the farmer's daughter came
and said, "What do you think you're doing?"
She may have been less than twelve but she seemed a grown
woman to me. I said I was making a nest for a bird to lay an
egg in. She said, "A wee chooky birdy? That's daft. And where
did you get the straw?"
I said, "On the ground in the yard."
"Then it belongs to my daddy and you stole it so put it back
there."
Since I continued building she gripped and twisted my wrists
until I kicked her ankle, then she went off screaming she would
tell my mother and I would be sent away. I ran crying to the
henhouse field, squeezed through a hen door on hands and
knees and squatted in a corner of the grain-sprinkled floor till
it grew dark. I meant to starve to death there but I heard my
mother distantly calling, sometimes nearer and sometimes farther, and at last I felt that the misery in her breast and the
misery in mine were the same thing. I squeezed through the
door and moved among the black henhouses under a high
ceiling of stars. An owl was hooting. Suddenly I found her
and wrapped my arms round her big stomach and she was
kind to me. A few nights later I was wakened by a great uproar
and she entered the room and climbed into bed. This was less
pleasant than it had been in town, for she brought my sister
and the bed was overcrowded. The loving heat she baked me
in was still deliriously exciting, but my mind was now too strong
to be unmade by it. I was worried, because I liked the farm
in some ways. A week later the farmer took us in his ponycart
to a railway station, gave me a bag of peppermints and left
us on the platform without saying a word.

I understand my mother now. She expected splendour.
Most of us expect it sometime or other, and growing old is
mainly a way of learning to do without. My mother could never
learn to do without so she kept altering her life in the only
way she knew, by shifting to other men. She shifted when
pregnant because pregnancy made her more hopeful than usual,
or because she feared that bearing a child when living with
the father would fix her to one man forever. If this is so then
I never saw my real father. The third substitute was a bank
manager who lived with his widowed sister in a mansion in a
small fishing port. He was a gentle, dismal, kindly man; she
was an abrupt, unhappy, slightly acid woman, and my mother

(with a four-year-old son, one-year-old daughter, five-month-old embryo) charmed and dominated both of them. But three is the smallest number that can make a series, and she no longer dominated me. Perhaps she no longer wanted to. At any rate, when she moved on I was left with the bank manager. My life became calm and dependable. I went to school, was good at lessons, and every evening the manager and his sister developed my powers of concentration by playing three-handed bridge with me, for small stakes, from half-past six till bedtime. That was how I learned to dread the body and love numbers.

Having relived these memories I saw that the path from the sunlit roses to the grey void had been inevitable, yet I was not content. I was appalled at having nothing to do but remember a life like that. I wanted madness to blot out the memories with the strong tones and colours of a delusion, however monstrous. I had a romantic notion that madness was an exit from unbearable existence. But madness is like cancer or bronchitis, not everyone is capable of it, and when most of us say, "I can't bear this," we are proving we can. Death is the only dependable exit, but death depends on the body and I had rejected the body. I was condemned to a future of replaying and replaying the tedious past and past and past and past. I was in hell. Without eyes I tried to weep, without lips to scream, and with all the force of my neglected heart I cried for help.

I was answered. A sullen, determined voice—your voice—asked me to describe *his* past. My experience of void had made me able to visualize things from very slight cues, and that voice let me see you as you were. From the pebble and shell in your hands I deduced the shore where you grasped them, and from the shore I saw a path stretching back through mountains and cities to the house where you were born. You know now why I am an oracle. By describing your life I will escape from the trap of my own. From my station in nonentity everything existent, everything *not me,* looks worthwhile and splendid: even things which most folk consider commonplace or dreadful. Your past is safe with me. I can promise to be accurate.

Lanark thought for a while, then said, "Your story contains a contradiction."
Oh?

"You said money can no more exist without objects than mind without body. Yet you exist without body."

That puzzles me too. Sometimes I think my body is in the world where I abandoned it, lying in bed in some hospital, kept going by infusions into my veins. If so, I have hope of coming alive one day or dying utterly. And now I'll tell you about Duncan Thaw.

Rima stirred slightly and murmured, "Yes, go on."

The oracle began speaking. His voice sounded so far inside the head that the story seemed less narrated than remembered. It was not delayed by eating, or going to the lavatory, or sleeping: at night Lanark dreamed what he could not hear and woke with no sense of interruption. All the time they saw through the window people moving in the rooms and streets of a city, though sometimes there were glimpses of mountains and sea, and at last huge waves moving slowly at the foot of a cliff.

CHAPTER 12. The War Begins

Duncan Thaw drew a blue line along the top of a sheet of paper and a brown line along the bottom. He drew a giant with a captured princess running along the brown line, and since he couldn't draw the princess lovely enough he showed the giant holding a sack. The princess was in the sack. His father looked over his shoulder and said, "What's that you're drawing?"

Thaw said uneasily, "A miller running to the mill with a bag of corn."

"What's the blue line supposed to be?"

"The sky."

"Do you mean the horizon?"

Thaw stared dumbly at his picture.

"The horizon is the line where the sky and land seem to touch. Is it the horizon?"

"It's the sky."

"But the sky isnae a straight line, Duncan!"

"It would be if you saw it sideways."

Mr. Thaw got a golf ball and a table lamp and explained that the earth was like the ball and the sun like the lamp. Thaw was bored and puzzled. He said, "Do people fall off the sides?"

"No. They're kept on by gravity."

"What's ga . . . gavty?"

"*Grrrrr*avity is what keeps us on the earth. Without it we would fly up into the air."

"And then we would reach the sky?"

"No. No. The sky is just the space above our heads. Without gravity we would fly up into it forever."

"But wouldn't we come to a . . . a thing on the other side?"

"There *is* no other side, Duncan. None at all."

Thaw leaned over his drawing and drew a blue crayon along the line of the sky, pressing hard. He dreamed that night of flying up through empty air till he reached a flat blue cardboard sky. He rested against it like a balloon against a ceiling until worried by the thought of what was on the other side; then he broke a hole and rose through more empty air till he grew afraid of floating forever. Then he came to another cardboard sky and rested there till worried by the thought of the other side. And so on.

Thaw lived in the middle storey of a corporation tenement that was red sandstone in front and brick behind. The tenement backs enclosed a grassy area divided into greens by spiked railings, and each green had a midden. Gangs of midden-rakers from Blackhill crossed the canal to steal from the middens. He was told that Blackhill people were Catholics with beasts in their hair. One day two men came to the back greens with a machine that squirted blue flame and clouds of sparks. They cut the spikes from the railings with the flame, put them in a bag and took them away to use in the war. Mrs. Gilchrist downstairs said angrily, "Now even the youngest of these Blackhill kids will be able to rake our middens." Other workmen build air-raid shelters in the back greens and a very big one in the school playground, and if Thaw heard the air-raid warning on the way to school he must run to the nearest shelter. Going up to school by the steep back lane one morning he heard the siren wailing in the blue sky. He was almost at school but turned and ran home to where his mother waited in the back-green shelter with the neighbours. At night dark green blinds were pulled down over the windows. Then Mr. Thaw put on an armband and steel hat and went into the street to search for houses showing illegal chinks of light.

Someone told Mrs. Thaw that the former tenants of her flat had killed themselves by putting their heads in the oven and turning the gas on. She wrote at once to the corporation asking that her gas cooker be changed for an electric one, but as Mr. Thaw would still need food when he returned from work she baked him a shepherd's pie, but with her lips more tightly pursed than usual.

Her son always refused shepherd's pie or any other food whose appearance disgusted him: spongy white tripe; soft penis-like sausages, stuffed sheep's hearts with their valves and little arteries. When one of these came before him he poked it uncertainly with his fork and said, "I don't want it."

"Why not?"

"It looks queer."

"But you havnae tasted it! Taste just a wee bit. For my sake."

"No."

"Children in China are starving for food like that."

"Send it to them."

After more discussion his mother would say in a high-pitched voice, "You'll sit at this table till you eat every bit" or "Just you wait till I tell your father about this, my dear." Then he would put a piece of food in his mouth, gulp without tasting and vomit it back onto the plate. After that he would be shut in the back bedroom. Sometimes his mother came to the door and said, "Will you not eat just a wee bit of it? For my sake?" then Thaw, feeling cruel, shouted "No!" and went to the window and looked down into the back green. He would see friends playing there, or the midden-rakers, or neighbours hanging out washing, and feel so lonely and magnificent that he considered opening the window and jumping out. It was a bitter glee to imagine his corpse thudding to the ground among them. At last, with terror, he would hear his father coming *clomp-clomp* upstairs, carrying his bicycle. Usually Thaw ran to meet him. Now he heard his mother open the door, the mutter of voices in conspiracy, then footsteps coming to the bedroom and his mother whispering, "Don't hurt him too much."

Mr. Thaw would enter with a grim look and say, "Duncan! You've behaved badly to your mother again. She goes to the bother and expense of making a good dinner and ye won't eat it. Aren't ye ashamed of yourself?"

Thaw would hang his head.

"I want you to apologize to her."

"Don't know what 'polgize means."

"Tell her you're sorry and you'll eat what you're given."

Then Thaw would snarl "No, I won't!" and be thrashed. During the thrashing he screamed a lot and afterward stamped, yelled, tore his hair and banged his head against the wall until his parents grew frightened and Mr. Thaw shouted, "Stop that or I'll draw my hand off yer jaw!"

Then Thaw beat his own face with his fists, screaming, "Like this like this like *this?*"

It was hard to silence him without undoing the justice of the punishment. On the advice of a neighbour they one day undressed the furiously kicking boy, filled a bath with cold water and plunged him in. The sudden chilling scald destroyed all his protest, and this treatment was used on later occasions with equal success. Shivering slightly he would be dried with soft towels before the living-room fire, then put to bed with his doll. Before sleep came he lay stunned and emotionless while his mother tucked him in. Sometimes he considered withholding the goodnight kiss but could never quite manage it.

When he had been punished for not eating a particular food he was not given that food again but a boiled egg instead. Yet after hearing how the former tenants had misused their oven he looked very thoughtfully at the shepherd's pie when it was brought to table that evening. At length he pointed and said, "Can I have some?"
Mrs. Thaw looked at her husband then took her spoon and plonked a dollop onto Thaw's plate. He stared at the mushy potato with particles of carrot, cabbage and mince in it and wondered if brains really looked like that. Fearfully he put some in his mouth and churned it with his tongue. It tasted good so he ate what was on the plate and asked for more. When the meal was over his mother said, "There. You like it. Aren't ye ashamed of kicking up all that din about nothing?"
"Can I go down to the back green?"
"All right, but come when I call you, it's getting late."
He hurried through the lobby, banged the front door behind him and ran downstairs, the weight of food in his stomach making him feel excited and powerful. In the warm evening sunlight he put his brow to the grass and somersaulted down a green slope till he fell flat from dizziness and lay with the tenements and blue sky spinning and tilting round and round his head. He keeked between the stems of sorrel and daisies at the midden, a three-sided brick shed where bins were kept. The sound of voices came indistinctly through the grass blades to his ears, and the scratchings of a steel-tipped boot on an iron railing, and the rumble of a bin being shifted. He sat up.

Two boys slightly older than himself were bent over the bins and throwing out worn clothes, empty bottles, some pram wheels and a doormat, while a big boy of ten or eleven put them in a sack. One of the smaller boys found a hat with a bird's wing on it. Mimicking the strut of a proud woman he put it on and said, "Look at me, Boab, am I no' the big cheese?

The older boy said, "Stop that. You'll get the auld wife after us."

He dumped the sack over the railings into the next green and the three of them climbed over to it. Thaw followed by squeezing between the railings then lay down again on the grass. He heard them whisper together and the big boy said, "Never mind about him."

He realized he was frightening them and followed more boldly into the next green, though keeping a distance. He was slightly appalled when the big boy turned and said, "What d'ye want, ye wee bugger?"

Thaw said, "I'm coming with you."

His scalp tightened, his heart knocked on his ribs but this boy had never eaten what he had eaten. The boy with the hat said, "Thump him, Boab!"

Boab said, "Why d'ye want tae come with us?"

"Because."

"Because of what?"

"Nothing. Just because."

"Ye'll have tae carry things if ye come with us. Will ye collect the books?"

"Aye."

"All right then."

After this all magazines and comic papers were left to Thaw, who soon learned which were worth picking from the garbage. They visited every back green in the block, leaving some refuse scattered across each, and were chased from the last by a woman who followed them through her close shouting breathless promises to call the police.

A girl of twelve waited in the street outside holding the handle of a pram with three wheels. She pointed at Thaw and said, "Where did ye pick that up?"

Boab said, "Never mind him," and loaded his sack onto the pram which bulged with rubbish already. The two wee boys harnessed themselves to it with strings tied to the front axle, then with Boab and the girl pushing and Thaw running alongside they went quickly down the street. They passed semi-detached villas with privet hedges, a small power station humming behind aspen trees, allotments with beds of lettuce like green roses and glasshouses glittering in the late sunshine. They went through a gate in a rusty fence and climbed a blue cinder path through a jungle of nettles. The air was thick with vegetable

stink, the wee boys groaned with the effort of pulling, a low thundering vibrated the ground under them and at the top they reached the brink of a deep ravine. One end was shut by double doors of huge rotting timber. A glossy arch of water slipped over this, crashed to the bottom, then poured along the ravine and flowed through open doors at the end into a small loch fringed with reeds and paved with lily leaves. Thaw knew this must be the canal, a dangerous forbidden place where children were drowned. He followed his companions uphill among structures where water spilled over ledges, trickled through cracks, or lay in rushy half-stagnant ponds with swans paddling on clear spaces in the middle. They crossed a plank bridge under the shadow of so high a waterfall that the din of it was deafening. They crossed stony ground and then another bridge and heard dimly a distant bugle blown in a caricature of a battle call.
"Peely Wally," said Boab.
They went quickly down a cinder path, through a gate and into a street.

Thaw found it a foreign kind of street. The tenements were faced with grey stone instead of red, landing windows had broken glass in them, or no glass, or even no window frames, being oblong holes half bricked up to stop children falling out. The men who had taken the spikes away to the war from Riddrie (where Thaw lived) had removed all the railings here, and the spaces between pavement and tenement (neat gardens in Riddrie) were spaces of flattened earth where children too young to walk scratched the ground with bent spoons or floated bits of wood in puddles left from last week's rain. In the middle of the street a pale lipless smiling young man sat on a donkey cart with a bugle on his knees. His cart held boxes of coloured toys which could be bought with rags, bottles and jam jars, and already a crowd of children surrounded him wearing cardboard sombreros, whooping on whistles or waving bright flags and windmills. When he noticed Boab and the pram he shouted, "Make way! Make way! Let the man through!"

While these two haggled Thaw and the smaller boys stood round the donkey and admired the mildness of its face, the hardness of its forehead and the white hair inside the trumpet-shaped ears. Thaw argued about the donkey's age with the boy wearing the hat.

"I bet ye a pound he's older than you onyway," said the boy.
"And I bet ye a pound he isnae."
"Why d'ye think he isnae?"
"Why d'ye think he is?"
"Peely!" shouted the boy. "How old is your donkey?"
"A hundred!" shouted Peely.
"There ye are—I wiz right!" said the boy. "Now you've tae
give me a pound." He held his hand out, saying, "Come on
now. Pay up!"
The children who had heard the argument whispered and gig-
gled, and some beckoned friends who were standing at a dis-
tance. Thaw, frightened, said, "I havenae a pound."
"But ye promised! Didn't he promise?"
"Aye, he promised," said several voices. "He bet a pound."
"He's got to pay."
"I don't believe the donkey is a hundred," said Thaw.
"Ye think ye're awful clever, don't ye?" a thin girl shouted
venomously and sarcastic voices cried, "Oh, Mammy, Mammy,
I'm an awful smart wee boy."
"Why does the smart wee boy no' believe the donkey's a hundred?"
"Because I read it in an ENCYCLOPAEDIA," said Thaw, for
though he was still unable to read he had once pleased his
parents by saying encyclopaedia without being specially taught
and the word had peculiar qualities for him. Pronounced in
the service of his lie it had an immediate effect. Someone at
the edge of the crowd jumped into the air, clapped hands above
head and cried, "Oh, the big word! The big word!" and the
mob exploded into laughter and mockery. Waving flags and
blowing whistles, they raved and stamped around the frightened
stone-still Thaw until his lips trembled and a drop of water
spilled from his left eye.
"Look!" they yelled. "He's greeting!" "Crybaby! Crybaby!"
"Cowardy custard, stick yer nose in the mustard!" "Riddrie
pup with yer tail tied up!" "Awa' hame and tell yer mammy!"
Thaw was blinded by red rage and screamed, "Buggers! Ye
damned buggers!" and started running down the darkening
street. He heard the clattering feet of pursuers and Peely Wally
laugh like a cock-crow and Boab roar, "Let him go! Leave
him alone!"
He turned a corner and ran down a street past staring children
and men who paid no attention, through a small park with a
pond and the sound of splashing water, then down a rutted
lane, going slower because they weren't following now, with

longer intervals between his sobs. He sat down on a chunk of masonry and swallowed air until his heart beat more calmly.

There was empty ground in front of him with the shadows of tenements stretching a long way across it. Colours had become distinctions of grey and close-mouths' black rectangles in tenement walls. The sky was covered with blue-grey cloud, but currents of wind had opened channels through this and he could see through the channels into a green sunset air above. Down the broadest of these flew five swans on their way to a lower stretch of the canal or to a pond in the city parks.

Thaw started back the way he had come, sniffing and wiping tears from his nose. In the small dim park only the splashing of water was distinct. It was night in the streets. He was glad to see no children or grown people or any of the adolescent groups who usually gather by street corners at nightfall. Black lampposts stood at wide intervals on either kerb. The tenement windows were black like holes in a face. Twice he saw wardens cross the end of some street ahead, silent helmeted men examining blinded windows for illegal chinks of light. The dark, similar streets seemed endlessly to open out of each other until he despaired of getting home and sat on the kerb with his face in his hands and girned aloud. He fell into a dwam in which he felt only the hard kerb under his backside and awoke suddenly with a hushing sound in his ears. For a second this seemed like his mother singing to him then he recognized the noise of waterfalls. The sky had cleared and a startling moon had risen. Though not full there was enough of it to light the canal embankment across the road, and the gate, and the cinder path. He went gladly and fearfully to the gate and climbed the path with the hushing growing in his ears to the full thunder of the falling stream. Several trembling stars were reflected in the dark water below.

As he stepped off the bridge Thaw seemed to hear the moon yell at him. It was the siren. Its ululations came eerily across the rooftops to menace him, the only life. He ran down the path between the nettles and through the gate and past the dark allotments. The siren swooned into silence and a little later (Thaw had never heard this before) there was a dull iron noise, *gron-gron-gron-gron,* and dark shapes passed above him. Later there were abrupt thuddings as if giant fists were battering a metal ceiling over the city. Beams of light widened, narrowed

and groped above the rooftops, and between two tenements
he saw the horizon lit orange and red with irregular flashing
lights. Black flies seemed to be circling in the glow. Beyond
the power station he ran his head into the stomach of a warden
running the other way. "Duncan!" shouted the man.
Thaw was picked into the air and shaken.
"Where have ye been? Where have ye been? Where have ye
been?" shouted the man senselessly, and Thaw, full of love
and gratitude, shouted, "Daddy!"
Mr. Thaw tucked his son under one arm and ran back
home. Between the jolts of his father's strides Thaw heard
the iron noise again. They went up steps into the close-mouth
and Thaw was put down. They stood together in the dark,
breathing hard; then Mr. Thaw said in a weak voice Thaw
hardly recognized, "I suppose you know the worry you've given
your mother and me?"
There was a shriek and bang and pieces of dirt hit Thaw on
the cheek.

From the living-room window next morning he saw a hole
in the pavement across the street. The blast had shaken soot
down the chimney onto the living-room floor, and Mrs. Thaw
cleaned it up, stopping sometimes to talk with neighbours who
called to discuss the raid. They agreed that it might have been
worse, but Thaw was very uneasy. His adventure with the midden-rakers was a horrider crime than not eating dinner so he
expected punishment on an unusually large scale. After closely
watching his mother that day—noticing the way she hummed
to herself when dusting, her small thoughtful pauses in the
middle of work, her way of scolding when he was stupid during
a lesson on clock reading—he became sure that punishment
was not in her mind, and this worried him. He feared pain,
but deserved to be hurt, and was not going to be hurt. He
had not returned to exactly the same house.

CHAPTER 13. A Hostel

The house was changing. Obscure urgency filled it and in bed at night he heard rumours of preparation and debate. Coming home from a friend's back green he stuck with his head on one side of the railings and his body on the other. Mr. and Mrs. Thaw released him by greasing his ears with butter and pulling a leg each, laughing all the time. When free he flung himself howling on the grass but they tickled his armpits and sang "Stop Yer Ticklin', Jock" until he couldn't help laughing. Then one day they all came out onto the landing and the house was locked behind them. His father and mother carried his sister Ruth and some luggage; Thaw had a gas mask in a cardboard box hanging from his shoulder by a string loop; they all went up to his school by the sunlit bird-twittering back lanes. Murmuring groups of mothers stood in the playground with small children at their side. The fathers spoke in noisier groups and older children played halfheartedly between.

Thaw felt bored and walked to the railings. He was sure he was going on holiday and that holidays meant the sea. From the edge of the playground's high platform he looked across the canal and the Blackhill tenements to remote hills with a dip in the middle. Looking the opposite way he saw a wide valley of roofs and smokestacks with more hills beyond. These hills were nearer and greener and so distinct that along a gently curved summit a line of treetops joined like a hedge and he saw the sky between the trunks underneath. It struck him that the sea was behind these hills; if he stood among the trees he would look down on a grey sea sparkling with waves. His mother shouted his name and he strolled toward her slowly,

pretending he had not heard but was returning anyway. She
adjusted the string of the gas mask which had got across his
coat collar and was cutting the side of his neck, then made
the coat sit better on his shoulders with tugs and pats which
shook his head from side to side. He said, "Is the sea behind
there?"

"Behind where?"

"Behind where those trees are."

"Who told you that? Those are the Cathkin Braes. There's
nothing behind there but farms and fields. And England, eventually."

The sparkling grey sea was too vivid for him to disbelieve. It
fought in his head with a picture of farms and fields until it
seemed to be flooding them. He pointed to the hills behind
Blackhill and asked, "Is the sea over there?"

"No, but there's Loch Lomond and the highlands."

Mrs. Thaw stopped tidying him, lifted Ruth on her left arm
and stared straight-backed at the Cathkin Braes. She said
thoughtfully, "When I was a girl those trees reminded me of
a caravan on the skyline."

"What's a caravan?"

"A procession of camels. In Arabia."

"What's a procession?"

Red single-decker buses suddenly came into the playground
and everyone but the fathers climbed on board. Mr. and Mrs.
Thaw said goodbye through the window and after a long wait
the buses drove out of the playground and down to the Cumbernauld Road.

A dim broken time followed when Thaw and his mother,
with Ruth on her lap, sat in buses at night hurling through
unseen country. The buses were always badly lit with windows
blinded by blue-black oilcloth so that nobody saw out. There
must have been many such journeys, but later he remembered
a single night journey lasting many months in a cabin full of
hungry tired people, though the movement of the bus was
interrupted by confused adventures in dim places: a wooden
church hall, a room over a tailor's shop, a stone-floored kitchen
with beetles crawling over it. He slept in strange beds where
breathing became difficult and he woke up screaming he was
dead. Sores appeared on his scrotum and the bus brought them
to the Royal Infirmary where old professors looked between
his legs and applied brown ointment which stung the sores

and smelled of tar. The bus was always crowded, Ruth crying, his mother weary and Thaw bored, though once a drunk man stood up and embarrassed everyone by trying to get them to sing. Then one evening the bus stopped and they got out and met his father, who led them onto the deck of a ship. They stood in the dusk near the funnel which gave out comfortable heat. The air was cold between slate-dark clouds and a heaving slate-blue sea. A reef lay among the lapping water like a long black log, and at one end an iron tripod upheld a lit yellow globe. The ship moved out to sea.

They came to live in a bungalow among low concrete buildings called the hostel. This stood between sea and moorland. Munition workers slept there and it held a canteen, cinema and hospital and had a high wire fence all round with gates that were locked at night. Each morning Thaw and Ruth were taken in a car along the coast road to the village school. This had two classrooms and a kitchen where a wife from the village made flavourless meals. A headmaster called Macrae taught the older pupils and a woman called Ingram the small ones. The pupils were all children of crofters excepting some evacuees from Glasgow who lodged in farms on the moors.

On his first day in the new school the other boys rushed to be Thaw's neighbour in the queue to go out to play, and in the playfield they gathered round to ask where he came from and what his father did. Thaw answered truthfully at first but later told lies to keep their interest. He said he spoke several languages and when asked to prove this could only say that "wee" was French for "yes." Most of the group went away after that, and next day in the playfield he had an audience of two. To stop it getting smaller he offered to show them round the hostel, then other boys approached him in threes and fours and asked if they could come too. Instead of going home that night in the car with Ruth, Thaw trudged along the coast road at the head of a mob of thirty or forty who talked and joked with each other and, apart from an occasional question, totally ignored him. He was not sorry about this. He wanted to seem mysterious to these boys, someone ageless with strange powers, but his feet were sore, he was late for tea and afraid he would be blamed for arriving with so many friends. He was right. The hostel gateman refused to allow the other boys in. They had walked two miles and missed their

tea to accompany him and though he walked back with them
a little way apologizing they were still very angry and the evacuees began to throw stones. He ran back to the hostel where
he was given a cold meal and a row for "showing off."

Next morning he pretended to be ill but unluckily the
asthma and the disease between his legs weren't troublesome
and he had to go to school. Nobody spoke to him there and
at playtime he kept nervously to the field's quietest corner.
On queuing to re-enter the classroom he stood beside an evacuee called Coulter who pushed him in the side. Thaw pushed
back. Coulter punched him in the side, Thaw punched back
and Coulter muttered, "A'll see you after school."
Thaw said, "A've to go straight home after school tonight;
my dad said so."
"Right. I'll see ye the morra."
At home that night he refused to eat anything. He said, "I've
a pain."
"You don't *look* sick," said Mrs. Thaw. "Where *is* the pain?"
"All over."
"What kind of pain is it?"
"I don't know, but I'm not going to school tomorrow."
Mrs. Thaw said to her husband, "You deal with this, Duncan,
it's beyond me."
Mr. Thaw took his son into the bedroom and said, "Duncan,
there's something you haven't told us."
Thaw started crying and said what the matter was. His father
held him to his chest and asked, "Is he bigger than you?"
"Yes." (This was untrue.)
"Much bigger?"
"No," said Thaw after a fight with his conscience.
"Do you want me to ask Mr. Macrae to tell the other pupils
not to hit you?"
"No," said Thaw, who only wanted not to go to school.
"I knew you would say that, Duncan. Duncan, you'll have to
fight this boy. If ye start running away now you'll never learn
to face up to life. I'll teach ye how to fight—it's easy—all ye
have to do is use your left hand to protect your face. . . ."
Mr. Thaw talked like this until Thaw's head was full of images
of defeating Coulter. He spent that evening practising for the
fight. First he sparred with his father, but the opposition of a
real human being left no scope for fantasy, so he practised
on a cushion and went confidently to bed after a good supper.

He was less confident next morning and ate breakfast very
quietly. Mrs. Thaw kissed him goodbye and said, "Don't worry.
You'll knock his block off."
She waved encouragingly as the car drove away.

That morning Thaw stood in a lonely corner of the playfield
and waited fearfully for the approach of Coulter, who was playing football with friends. Rain started falling and gradually
the pupils collected in a shelter at the end of the building.
Thaw was last to enter. In an agony of dread he walked up
to Coulter, stuck his tongue out at him and struck him on
the shoulder. At once they started fighting as unskilfully as
small boys always fight, with flailing arms and a tendency to
kick each other's ankles; then they grappled and fell. Thaw
was beneath but Coulter's nose flattened on his brow, the resulting blood smeared both equally, each thought it his own and,
appalled by the suspected wound, rolled apart and stood up.
After that, in spite of encouragement from their allies (Thaw
was surprised to find a cheering mob of allies at his back)
they were content to stand swearing at each other until Miss
Ingram came up and took them to the headmaster. Mr. Macrae
was a stout pig-coloured man. He said, "Right. What's the
cause of all this?"
Thaw started talking rapidly, his explanation punctuated by
gulps and stutters, and only stopped when he found himself
starting to sob. Coulter said nothing. Mr. Macrae took a leather
tawse from his desk and said, "Hold your hands out."
Each held his hand out and got a hellish stinging wallop on
it. Mr. Macrae said, "Again!" "Again!" and "Again!" Then
he said, "If I hear of you two fighting another time you'll
get the same treatment but more of it, a lot more of it. Go
to your class."
Each bent his head to hide his distorted face and went to the
next room sucking a crippled hand. Miss Ingram didn't ask
them to do anything for the rest of the morning.

After the fight Thaw found playtimes more boring than
frightening. He would stand in the lonely corner of the field
with a boy called McLusky who didn't play with the other
boys because he was feebleminded. Thaw told long stories with
himself as hero and McLusky helped him mime the actable
bits. The vivid part of his life became imaginary. Thaw and
his sister slept in adjacent rooms, and at night he told her
stories through the doorway between, stories with the adven-

tures and landscapes of books he had read by day. Sometimes he stopped and asked, "Are you asleep yet? Will I go on?" and Ruth answered, "No, Duncan, please go on," but at last she would fall asleep. Next night she would say, "Go on with the story, Duncan."

"All right. Where did I stop last night?"

"They . . . they had landed on Venus."

"No, no. They had left Venus and gone to Mercury."

"I . . . don't remember that, Duncan."

"Of course you don't. Ye fell asleep. Well, I'm not going to tell *you* stories if you don't want to listen."

"But I couldnae help falling asleep, Duncan."

"Then why didn't ye tell me you were falling asleep instead of letting me go on talking to myself?"

After bullying her some more he would continue the story, for he spent a lot of time each day preparing it.

He bullied Ruth in other ways. She was forbidden to stott her ball indoors. He saw her do it once, and terrified her for weeks by threatening to tell their mother. One day Mrs. Thaw accused her children of stealing sugar from the livingroom sideboard. Both denied it. Later Ruth told him, "you stole that sugar."

He said "yes. But if you tell Mum I said so I'll call you a liar and she won't know who to believe." Ruth at once told their mother, Thaw called Ruth a liar, and Mrs. Thaw didn't know who to believe.

During the first few weeks at school he had looked carefully among the girls for one to adventure with in his imagination, but they were all too obviously the same vulgar clay as himself. For almost a year he resigned himself to loving Miss Ingram, who was moderately attractive and whose authority gave her a sort of grandeur. Then one day when visiting the village store he saw a placard in the window advertising Amazon Adhesive Shoe Soles. It showed a blond girl in brief Greek armour with spear and shield and a helmet on her head. Above her were the words **BEAUTY PLUS STAMINA,** and her face had a plaintive loveliness which made Miss Ingram seem commonplace. During the dinner intervals Thaw walked to the store and looked at the girl for the length of time it took to count ten. He knew that by looking too hard and often even she might come to seem commonplace.

CHAPTER 14. Ben Rua

Mr. Thaw wanted a keener intimacy with his son and liked open-air activities. There were fine mountains near the hostel, the nearest of them, Ben Rua, less than sixteen hundred feet high; he decided to take Thaw on some easy excursions and bought him stout climbing boots. Unluckily Thaw wanted to wear sandals.

"I like to move my toes," he said.

"What are ye blethering about?"

"I don't like shutting my feet in these hard solid leather cases. It makes them feel dead. I can't bend my ankles."

"But you arenae supposed to bend your ankles! It's the easiest thing in the world to break an ankle if you slip in an awkward place. These boots are made especially to give the ankle support—once a single nail gets a grip it can uphold your ankle, your leg, your whole body even."

"What I lose in firmness I'll make up in quickness."

"I see. I see. For a century mountaineers have gone up the Alps and Himalayas and Grampians in nailed climbing boots. You might think they knew about climbing. Oh, no, Duncan Thaw knows better. They should have worn *sandals.*"

"What's wrong for them might be right for me."

"My God!" cried Mr. Thaw. "What's this I've brought into the world? What did I do to deserve this? If we could only live by our own experience we would have no science, no civilization, no progress! Man has advanced by his capacity to learn from others, and these boots cost me four pounds eight."

"There would be no science and civilization and all that if everybody did things the way everybody else does," said Thaw. The discussion continued until Mr. Thaw lost his temper and Thaw had hysterics and was given a cold bath. The climbing boots lay in a cupboard until Ruth was old enough to use them. Meanwhile Thaw was not taken climbing by his father.

One summer day Thaw walked briskly along the coast road until the hostel was hidden by a green headland. It was a sunny afternoon. A few clouds lay about the sky like shirts scattered on a blue floor. He left the road and ran down a slope toward the sea, his feet crashing almost to the ankles among pebbles and shells. He felt confident and resolute, for he had been reading a book called *The Young Naturalist* and meant to make notes of anything interesting. The shingle gave onto shelving rocks with boulders and pools among them. He squatted by a pool the size of a soup plate and peered in, frowning. Below the crystalline water lay three pebbles, a small anemone the colour of raw liver, a wisp of green weed and several winkles. The winkles were olive and dull purple, and he thought he saw a tendency for the pale ones to be at the edges of the pool and the dark ones in the middle. Taking out a notebook and pencil he drew a map on the blank first page, showing the position of the winkles; then he wrote the date on the opposite page and added after some thought the letters:

SELKNIW ELPRUP NI ECIDRAWOC

for he wished to hide his discoveries under a code until he was ready to publish. Then he pocketed the notebook and strolled onto a beach of smooth white sand lapped by the sparkling sea. Tired of being a naturalist he found a stick of driftwood and began engraving the plans of a castle on the firm surface. It was a very elaborate castle full of secret entrances, dungeons and torture chambers.

Someone behind him said, "What's that supposed to be?" Thaw turned and saw Coulter. He gripped the stick tightly and muttered, "It's some plans."
Coulter walked round the plans saying, "What are they plans of?"
"Oh, they're just plans."
"Well, mibby you're wise no' to tell me what they're plans of. For all you know I'm mibby a German spy."
"You couldnae be a German spy."
"Yes I could."
"You're just a boy!"
"But mibby the Germans have a secret chemical that stops

folk growing so they look like boys though they're mibby twenty or thirty, and mibby they've landed me here off a submarine and I'm just pretending to be an evacuee but all the time I'm spying on the hostel your dad is managing.''

Thaw stared at Coulter who stood with feet apart and hands in trouser pockets and stared back. Thaw said, *"Are* you a German spy?''

"Yes," said Coulter.

His face was so expressionless that Thaw became convinced that he was a German spy. At the same time, without noticing it, he had stopped being afraid of Coulter. He said, "Well I'm a British spy.''

"You are not.''

"I am so.''

"Prove it.''

"Prove you're a German spy.''

"I don't want to. If I did you could get me arrested and hung.''

Thaw could think of no answer to this. He was wondering how to make Coulter think he was a British spy when Coulter said, "Do you come from Glasgow?''

"Yes!''

"So do I.''

"What bit of Glasgow?''

"Garngad. What bit do you come from?''

"Riddrie.''

"Hm! Riddrie is quite near Garngad. They're both on the canal.''

Coulter looked at the plans again and said, "Is it a plan of a den?''

"Well . . . a sort of den.''

"I know some smashing dens.''

"So do I!'' said Thaw eagerly. "I've got a den inside a—''

"I've got a den that's a real secret cave!'' said Coulter triumphantly.

Thaw was impressed. After a suitable silence he said, *"My* den is inside a bush. It looks like an ordinary bush outside but it's all hollow inside and it stands beside this road in the hostel so you can sit in it and watch these daft munition girls passing and they don't know you're there. The bother is''—truth made him reluctantly add—"it doesnae keep out the rain.''

"That's the bother with dens,'' said Coulter. "Either they're secret and let in rain or they don't let in rain and arenae secret. My cave keeps the rain out fine, but last time I went there the floor was all covered with dirty straw. I think the tinkers

had been using it. But I could make a great den if I had some-
body to help me."
"How?"
"Will ye promise no' to tell anyone?"
"Aye, sure."
"It's up a place near the hotel."
They crossed the beach to the road and walked along it chatting
amiably.

Before reaching the village they turned up a track which
ascended to the tall iron gates and yew trees of the Kinlochrua Hotel. Past this the track became a path half covered
by bracken. It led them precariously higher and higher between
boulders and bushes until Coulter halted and said triumphantly,
"There!"
They were on the lip of a gully sloping down to the waters
of the burn. It had been used as a rubbish dump and was
half filled by an avalanche of tins, broken crockery, cinders
and decaying cloth. Thaw looked at it with pleasure and said,
"Aye, there's plenty of stuff here for a den."
"Let's get out the big cans first," said Coulter.
They waded among the rubbish, collecting materials, then carried them to a flat place beneath two big rocks. They used
petrol drums for the walls of the den and roofed it with linoleum
laid across wooden spars. They were finishing by stuffing odd
holes with sacking when Thaw heard a footstep and looked
around. A shepherd was passing downhill waist deep in the
bracken to their left. "Good afternoon, lads," he said.
Thaw began working more and more slowly. Until then he
had been chatting enthusiastically, now he became silent and
answered questions as shortly as possible. At last Coulter threw
down a piece of pipe he had been trying to make into a chimney
and said, "What's wrong with ye?"
"This den's no use. It's too near the path. Everybody can see
it. It's not secret at all."
Coulter glared at Thaw then gripped the linoleum roof,
wrenched it off and threw it down the gully.
"What are ye doing?" shouted Thaw.
"It's no use! Ye said so yourself! I'm taking it down!"
Coulter pushed down the walls and kicked the drums into the
gulley. Thaw watched sullenly until nothing was left but a few
spars of wood and a distant clanking sound. He said, "Ye neednae have done that. We might have camouflaged it with
branches and stuff and hidden it that way."

Coulter shoved through the bracken to the path and started walking down it. After a few yards he turned and shouted, "Ye bugger! Ye damned bugger!"

"Ye bloody damned bugger!" shouted Thaw.

"Ye *fuckin'* bloody damned bugger!" yelled Coulter, and disappeared from sight among the trees. Brooding blackly on the den, which had been a good one, Thaw walked up the track in the opposite direction.

The glen had taken all the streams of the moor into its gorge where they tumbled and clattered among boulders, leaves and the songs of blackbirds, but Thaw paid little attention to the surroundings. His thoughts took on a pleasant flavour. Expressions of grimness, mockery and excitement crossed his face and sometimes he waved an arm imperiously. Once he said with a bleak smile, "I'm sorry, madam, but you fail to understand your position. You are my prisoner."

It was a while before he noticed he had left the glen behind but there was an uneasiness in the quiet of the open moor which daydreams couldn't shut out. The main sound was the water flowing clear and brown, golden brown where the sun caught it, along runnels which could have been bridged by a hand. In places the heather had knotted its twigs and roots across these and it was possible to follow their course by a melodious gurgling under the purple-green carpet which sloped and dipped upward to the humps and boulders of Ben Rua. Thaw suddenly saw himself as if from the sky, a small figure starting across the moor like a louse up a quilt. He stood still and gazed at the ben. On the grey-green tip of the summit he seemed just able to see a figure, a vertical white speck that moved and gestured, though the movement might have been caused by a flickering of warm air between the mountaintop and his eye. To Thaw the movement suggested a woman in a white dress waving and beckoning. He could even imagine her face: it was the face of the girl in the adhesive shoe-sole advertisement. This remote beckoning woman struck him with the force of a belief, though it was not quite a belief. He did not decide to climb the mountain, he thought, 'I'll follow this bit of stream,' or, 'I'll go to the rock over there.' And he would reach the top of a slope to find a higher one beyond and the ben looking nearer each time. Sometimes he climbed on a boulder and stood for minutes listening to small noises which might have been the distant scrape of a sheep's hoof on a stone, or the scutter of a rabbit's paw, or

the fluttering of blood in his eardrum. From these pedestals
the summit of Rua sometimes looked vacant, but later, with a
pang, he would see on it the flickering white point. He advanced onto the mountain slope and the summit passed out of
sight.

The lower slopes were mostly widths of granite tilted at
the angle of the mountainside, level with the heather and
cracked like the pavements of a ruined city. Higher up the
heather gave way to fine turf, where grasshoppers chirped and
flowerets grew with stalks less than an inch high and blossoms
hardly bigger than pinheads. Becoming thirsty he found a shallow pool collected from last week's rain in the hollow of a
rock. Stopping to drink he felt rough granite under his lips
and warm sour water on the tongue. The mountain steepened
into nearly vertical blocks with ledges of turf between. For
half an hour he used his hands as much as his feet, squirming
and wriggling up crooked funnels, pulling himself over small
precipices, then lying flat on his back on a ledge under the
shadow of the summit to let the sweat dry out of his damp
shirt. At this height he heard noises that had been shut off
from him on the moor: a barking dog on one of the farms, a
door slamming in the hostel, a lark above a field behind the
village, children shouting on the shore and the murmuring
sea. He contained two equal sorts of knowledge: the warm
lazy knowledge that above on the mountain a blond girl in a
white dress waited for him, shy and eager; and the cooler knowledge that this was unlikely and the good of climbing was the
exercise and view from the top. There was no conflict between
those knowledges, his mind passed easily from one to the other,
but when he stood up to begin the last of the climb the thought
of the girl was stronger.

He was at the foot of a granite cliff about four times his
height with a ledge sloping up it made by a lower stratum
projecting beyond the one above. As he climbed his fear of
height made the excitement keener. The ledge was decayed
and gravelly, each step sent a shower of little lumps rattling
and bouncing down into the sky beyond the edge. Gradually
it narrowed to a few inches. Thaw pressed his chest against
the granite, stood on tiptoe and, reaching up, brought his fingertips within an inch of the top. "Hell, hell, hell, hell, hell,"
he muttered sadly, gazing at the dark rock where it cut against
a white smudge of cloud. A face suddenly stuck over this edge

and looked down at him. It was a small, round, wrinkled almost
sexless face, and the shock of it nearly made Thaw lose balance.
It took him a moment to recognize Mr. McPhedron, the minister from the village. The minister said, "Are you stuck?"
"No, I can go back."
"Aye. The right way up is round the other side. But bide
there a minute."
The face was withdrawn and Thaw saw something black and
straight with a curled end poke over the edge and slide toward
him. It was the handle of an umbrella. Swallowing the fear
that slid up his gullet Thaw gripped the handle with his left
hand and tugged. It stayed firm. He put the toe of his sandal
against a bump in the rock face, gripped the handle tighter,
heaved himself at the edge and got an arm across. The arm
was grabbed and he was pulled onto the summit. He sat up
and said, "Thank you."

     The summit was a rock platform as big as the floor of a
room and tilted so that one side was higher than the others.
On the highest corner stood a squat concrete pillar like a steep
pyramid with the top cut off. With a sad pang he saw that
this had seemed the beckoning white woman. The minister,
a bald dry little man in crumpled black clothes, sat nearby
with his legs over the edge, fists resting on thighs and back
as upright as if sitting in a chair. The rolled umbrella lay behind
him. He turned and said, "Now you have your breath back,
give me your opinion of the view."
Thaw stood up. The moor lay below with dots of sheep grazing
on it, some shrub-filled glens and the green coastal strip beyond.
The village was hidden by the trees of the largest glen but
its position was shown by the hotel roof among its conifers
and by the end of a pier sticking into the Atlantic. To the
left of this, between the beach and the white road, the hostel
stood in neat rectangular blocks like a chess game, human specks
moving on the straight paths between. Farther off still, the
road—a bus moving down it like an insect—turned from the
coast into a district of moorland with small lochs and blue-
grey bens paling into the distance like waves of a stone sea.
The ocean in front, however, was as shining-smooth as slightly
wrinkled silk. It stretched to the dark mountains of the Isle
of Skye on the horizon, and the sun hung above these at the
height of Thaw himself. It was dimmed and oranged by haze
but firing golden wires of light from the centre. Thaw stared

at it miserably. The minister was someone he tried to avoid. On coming to the hostel his mother, who went to church, sent him to a Sunday school held by Dr. McPhedron after the morning service. He had expected to sing little hymns and draw little pictures of Bible stories; instead he was given a book of questions and answers to learn by heart so that when Dr. McPhedron asked a question like "Why did God make man?" Thaw could give an answer like "God made man to glorify his name and enjoy his works for ever." After the first day of Sunday school he didn't want to go back and his father, who was an atheist, said he needn't if he didn't enjoy it. Since then Thaw had heard his parents discuss the minister several times. His mother said there was too much Hell in his sermons. She thought churches were good because they gave people something to look up to and hope for, but she didn't believe in Hell and it was wrong to frighten children with it. Mr. Thaw said he saw no reason why people shouldn't believe what pleased them but McPhedron was a type found too often in the highlands and islands, a bigot who damned to Hell whoever rejected his narrow opinions.

To hide embarrassment Thaw turned and examined the pillar.
"Do you wonder what that is, now?" asked the minister. His voice was soft and precise.
"Yes."
"It is a triangulation point. Your name is still on my Sunday school enrolment book. Would you have me remove it?"
Thaw frowned and rubbed his fingers round an odd depression in the pillar's top.
The minister said, *"That* is to hold the base of an instrument used by government mapmakers. I notice you don't come to kirk with your mother any more. Why?"
"Dad says I needn't go to something I don't like if it isn't educational," muttered Thaw. The minister gave a slight friendly laugh.
"I admire your father. His notion of education embraces everything but the purpose of life and the fate of man. Do you believe in the Almighty?"
Thaw said boldly, "I don't know, but I don't believe in Hell."
The minister laughed again. "When you have more knowledge of life you will mibby find Hell more believable. You are from Glasgow?"

"Yes."

"I was six years a student of divinity in that city. It made Hell very real to me."

A muffled blast came to their ears from a distance. A white cloud drifted up from a dip in the moorlands to the south, shredding and vanishing as it rose. The sound was batted back and forth between the mountains, then trickled into echoes among far off glens.

"Yes," said the minister. "They are testing at the munition factory down there. The country must be preserved with all the Hell we can muster."

Thaw was filled with baffled anger. He had bitten into the splendid fruit of the afternoon and found a core of harsh dull words. He muttered that he'd better be getting home.

"Aye," said the minister. "It is late for a wee lad to be far from bed."

He got up and led Thaw from the summit by a fall of granite blocks which presented so many horizontal surfaces that he went down it like a flight of giant steps, hopping nimbly from one to another, using the umbrella to balance him in awkward places. Thaw jumped and scrambled sullenly after him. When they reached the more grassy slopes Thaw let the distance between them increase until the minister vanished behind a boulder; then he turned left and scrambled round the mountain-side until a sufficient girth of it was between them and then set off toward the hostel.

The sun had set by the time he reached the road but it was still the gloaming, a protracted summer gloaming with the land dim but the sky lively with colours. He limped in at the hostel gate, the hard tarmac hurting his feet, and went by two straight paths to the manager's bungalow. His mother sat knitting on a deck chair on the lawn. Nearby his father stabbed casually with a hoe at weeds in a small rockery. As Thaw approached Mrs. Thaw called reprovingly, "We were beginning to worry about you!"

He had meant to keep quiet about the climb as he had made it wearing sandals, but standing between his parents he said, "I bet you don't know where I've been!"

"Well, where have you been?"

"There!"

Behind the hostel's low straight roofs Rua showed like a black wedge cut out of the green rotund-looking sky. Soft stars were beginning to shine between a few feathery bloody clouds.

"You were up Ben Rua?"

"Aye."

"Alone?"

"Aye."

His mother said gently, "That could have been dangerous, Duncan."

His father looked at his sandalled feet and said, "If you do it again you must tell someone you're going first, so we know where to look if there's an accident. But I don't think we'll complain this time; no, we won't complain, we won't complain."

CHAPTER 15. Normal

The Thaw family came home to Glasgow the year the war ended. They arrived late at night as thin rain fell, took a taxi at the station and sat numbly inside. Thaw looked out at a succession of desolate streets lit by lights that seemed both dim and harsh. Once Glasgow had been a tenement block, a school and a stretch of canal; now it was a gloomy huge labyrinth he would take years to find a way through. The flat was cold and disordered. During the war it had been let to strangers and the bedding and ornaments locked in the back bedroom. While his father and mother unpacked and shifted things he looked at his old books and found them dull and childish. He asked his mother, who was dusting, "How long will it be before we get back to normal?"

"What do you mean, normal?"

"You know, settled down."

"I suppose in a week or two."

He went to the living room where his father was looking through letters and said, "How long will it be before we get back to normal?"

"Maybe in two or three months, if we're lucky."

Mr. Thaw spent the next months typing letters at his bureau in the living room. With each post he got back letters with printed headings which he gave to Thaw, who drew on the blank backs. Thaw sat drawing and writing for hours at a tiny desk in the back bedroom, wearing a dressing gown and an embroidered smoking cap which had been his grandfather's. He seldom looked at the letters whose backs he used, but once his eye was caught by the heading of the factory where his father had worked before the war. He read:

Dear Mr Thaw,

It would seem that a prophet is not without honour save in the city of his birth! I congratulate you on having done so well with the now defunct Ministry of Munitions.

Unfortunately we have no vacancy for a personnel officer at present. However, I am sure your manifest abilities will have no difficulty in finding employment elsewhere. Our hearty good wishes to you.

Yours faithfully,
John Blair
Managing Director

One day at dinner Mr. Thaw said to his wife, "I took a walk out Hogganfield way this morning. They're building a reservoir to serve the new housing scheme." He swallowed a mouthful and said, "I went in and got a job. I start tomorrow."
"What doing?"
"The walls of the reservoir are made by pouring concrete between metal shuttering. I'll be bolting the shutters into place and taking them down when the stuff has hardened."
Mrs. Thaw said grimly, "It's better than nothing."
"That's what I thought."
After this Mr. Thaw cycled to work each morning wearing an old jacket and corduroy trousers tucked into his stocking tops, and now when Thaw was not at school he scribbled at Mr. Thaw's bureau or lay reading on the hearth rug, enjoying his mother's proximity as she went about the housework.

One day Mr. Thaw said, "Duncan, you sit your qualifying exam in six weeks, don't you?"
"Yes."
"You realize how important this exam is? If you pass you'll go to a senior secondary school where, if you work well at your lessons and homework and pass the proper exams, you'll be able to take your Higher Leaving Certificates and work at anything you like. You can even do another four years at university. If you fail the qualifying exam you'll have to go to a junior secondary school and leave at fourteen and take any job you can get. Look at me. I went to a senior secondary school but I had to leave at fourteen to support my mother and sister. I think I had the ability to do well in life, but to do well you need certificates, certificates, and I had no certificates. The best I could become was a machine minder in Laird's box-making factory. During the war of course there was a short-

age of men with certificates, and I got a job purely on my abilities. But look what I'm doing now. Have you any notion of what you would like to be?"

Thaw considered. In the past he had wanted to be a king, magician, explorer, archaeologist, astronomer, inventor and pilot of spaceships. More recently, while scribbling in the back bedroom, he had thought of writing stories or painting pictures. He hesitated and said, "A doctor."

"A doctor! Yes, that's a good thing to be. A doctor gives his life to helping others. A doctor is always, and will always be, respected and needed by the community, no matter what social changes take place. Well, your first step is the qualifying exam. Don't worry about anything but that first step. You're good at English and General Knowledge but bad at Arithmetic, so what you must do is stick in at Arithmetic." Mr. Thaw patted his son's back. "Go to it!" he said. Thaw went to his bedroom, shut the door, lay on the bed and started crying. The future his father indicated seemed absolutely repulsive.

Whitehill Senior Secondary School was a tall gloomy red sandstone building with a playing field at the back and on each side a square playground, one for each sex, enclosed and minimized by walls with spiked railings on top. It had been built like this in the eighteen-eighties but the growth of Glasgow had imposed additions. A structure, outwardly uniform with the old building but a warren of crooked stairs and small classrooms within, was stuck to the side at the turn of the century. After the first world war a long wooden annexe was added as temporary accommodation until a new school could be built, and after the second world war, as a further temporary measure, seven prefabricated huts holding two classrooms each were put up on the playing field. On a grey morning some new boys stood in a lost-looking crowd near the entrance gate. In primary school they had been the playground giants. Now they were dwarfs among a mob of people up to eighteen inches taller than themselves. A furtive knot from Riddrie huddled together trying to seem blasé. One said to Thaw, "What are ye taking, Latin or French?"

"French."

"I'm taking Latin. Ye need it tae get to university."

"But Latin's a dead language!" said Thaw. "My mother wants me to take Latin but I tell her there are more good books in French. And ye can use French tae travel."

"Aye, mibby, but ye need Latin tae get to university."

An electric bell screeched and a fat bald man in a black gown appeared on the steps of the main entrance. He stood with hands deep in his trouser pockets and feet apart, contemplating the buttons of his waistcoat while the older pupils hurried into lines before several entrances. One or two lines kept up a vague chatter and shuffle; he looked sternly at these and they fell silent. He motioned each class to the entrances one after another with a finger of his right hand. Then he beckoned the little group by the gate to the foot of the steps, lined them up, read their names from a list and led them into the building. The gloom of the entrance steeped them, then the dim light of echoing hall, then the cold light of a classroom.

Thaw entered last and found the only seat left was the undesirable one in the front row in front of the teacher, who sat behind a tall desk with his hands clasped on the lid. When everyone was seated he looked from left to right along the rows of faces before him, as if memorizing each one, then leaned back and said casually, "Now we'll divide you into classes. In the first year, of course, the only real division is between those who take Latin and those who take . . . a modern language. At the end of the third year you will have to choose between other subjects: Geography or History, for instance; Science or Art; for by then you will be specializing for your future career. Hands up those who don't know what specializing means. No hands? Good. Your choice today is a simpler one, but its effects reach further. You all know Latin is needed for entrance to university. A number of benevolent people think this unfair and are trying to change it. As far as Glasgow University is concerned they haven't succeeded *yet.*" He smiled an inward-looking smile and leaned back until he seemed to be staring at the ceiling. He said, "My name's Walkenshaw. I'm senior Classics master. Classics. That's what we call the study of Latin and Greek. Perhaps you've heard the word before? Who hasn't heard of classical music? Put your hand up if you haven't heard of classical music. No hands? Good. Classical music, you see, is the *best* sort of music, music by the best composers. In the same way the study of Classics is the study of the *best.* Are you chewing something?"
Thaw, who had been swallowing nervously, was appalled to find this question fired at himself. Not daring to take his gaze from the teacher's face he stood slowly up and shook his head.
"Answer me."
"No sir."

"Open your mouth. Open it wide. Stick your tongue out."
Thaw did as he was told. Mr. Walkenshaw leaned forward,
stared, then said mildly, "Your name?"
"Thaw, sir."
"That's all right, Thaw. You can sit down. And always tell
the truth, Thaw."
Mr. Walkenshaw leaned back and said, "Classics. Or, as we
call it at university, the Humanities. I say nothing against the
study of modern languages. Naturally half of you will choose
French. But Whitehall Senior Secondary School has a tradition,
a fine tradition of Classical scholarship, and I hope many of
you will continue that tradition. To those without enough ambition to go to university and who can't see the use of Latin, I
can only repeat the words of Robert Burns: 'Man cannot live
by bread alone.' No, and you would be wise to remember it.
Now I'm going to read your names again and I want you to
shout Modern and Classics according to choice."
He read the list of names again. Thaw was depressed to hear
all the people he knew choose Latin. He chose Latin.

The Latin students queued at the door of another classroom
opening out of the hall. The girls who had chosen Latin were
already there, giggling and whispering. It took Thaw a second
to notice and fall in love with the loveliest of them. She was
blond and wore a light dress, so he looked loftily round the
hall with an absent-minded frown hoping she would notice
his superior indifference. The hall was like an aquarium tank,
the light slanted into it from windows in the roof. On a wall
at one end a marble tablet showed a knight in Roman armour
and the names of pupils killed in the first world war. Photographs of headmasters hung between surrounding doors:
shaggy bearded early ones and neatly moustached recent ones,
but all with stern brows and clenched mouths. From a balcony
above came the horrible detonation of a leather belt striking
a hand. Somewhere a door opened and a voice said querulously,
"Marcellus animadvertit, Marcellus noticed this thing, and at once
into battle line formed the forces, and did not reluctantly, er
reluctantly take the opportunity of recalling to them how often
in the past they had borne themselves, er, nobly. . . ."

A lank young teacher led them into the classroom. The
girls sat in desks to his right, the boys to the left, and he faced
them with hands on hips leaning forward from the waist. He
said, "My name is Maxwell. I'm your form teacher. You come

to me first period each day to have the class register called
and to bring reasons for having been absent or late. They'd
better be good reasons. I'm also your Latin teacher."
He stared at them a while, then said, "I'm new to teaching.
Just as I'm your first senior secondary school teacher, you are
my first senior secondary school class. We're starting together,
you see, and I think we'd better decide here and now to start
well. You do right by me and I'll do right by you. But if we
quarrel about anything *you're* going to suffer. Not me."
He stared at them brightly and the frightened class stared back.
He had a craggy face with a rugged nose, trimmed red moustache and broad lips. Thaw noticed the undersurface of the
moustache was clipped to exactly continue the flat surface of
the upper lip. This detail frightened him even more than the
grim, nervous little speech.

Through the morning depression gathered in his brain
and chest like a physical weight. Each forty minutes the bell
screeched and the class moved to a different room and were
welcomed by a few unfriendly words. The Mathematics teacher
was a small brisk woman who said if they tried hard she would
help them all she could, but one thing she could not and would
not stand was dreaming. There was no room for dreamers in
her class. She gave out algebra and geometry books in which
Thaw saw a land without colour, furniture or action where
thought negotiated symbolically with itself. The science room
had a pungent chemical smell and shelves of strange objects
which excited his appetite for magic, but the teacher was a
big bullying man with hair like a beast's fur and Thaw knew
nothing *he* taught would bring an increase of power or freedom.
The art teacher was mild and middle-aged. He talked about
the laws of perspective, and how these laws had to be learned
before true art became possible. He gave out pencils and got
them to copy a wooden block onto a small sheet of paper. In
each class Thaw sat in the front row and stared at the teacher's
face. He was in a world where he could not do well, and he
wanted to give an impression of obedience that would make
the authorities treat him leniently. All the time he felt the pale
blaze of the blond girl somewhere behind him on the left.
Twice he dropped a book as an excuse for looking at her while
he picked it up. She seemed an unstill flickering girl, always
moving her shoulders, shaking her head and hair, smiling and
glancing from side to side. He noticed with surprise that her
oval face had a thrust-forward, slightly clumsy jaw. Her beauty

lay more in the movement of her parts than the parts themselves, which was maybe why she was never still.

The boys from Riddrie stood chattering in a queue for the tram which would take them home at noontime. One said, "That big Maxwell—I hate him. He looks mad enough to murder ye."

"Ach, naw, he'll be all right if ye do as he says. It's the science man I'm feart from. He's the sort that'll hammer ye jist because he's in a bad mood."

"Ach, they're all out to terrorize us today. The theory is that if they scare us enough at the start we'll give them nae trouble later. They've got a hope."

There was a reflective silence; then somebody said, "What dae ye think of the talent?"

"I care for that wee blond bird."

"Aye, did ye see her? She couldnae keep still. I wouldnae mind feeling *her* belly in a dark room."

Everyone but Thaw sniggered. Someone nudged him and said, "What do you think of her, moon-man?"

"Her jaw's too ape-like for me."

"Is it? All right. But I wouldnae give her back if I got her in a present. Does anyone know her name?

"I do. It's Kate Caldwell."

Things improved in the afternoon for they had English and the teacher was a young man with a comforting likeness to the film comedian Bob Hope. Without any introductory speech he said, "Today is the last day for handing in contributions for the school magazine. I'll give you paper and you can try to write something for it. It can be prose or poetry, serious or comic, an invented story or something that really happened. It doesn't matter if the result isn't up to much, but maybe one or two of you will get something accepted."

Thaw leaned over the paper, elated thoughts flowing through his head. His heart began to beat faster and he started writing. He quickly filled two sheets of foolscap then copied the result out carefully, checking the hard words with a dictionary. The teacher collected the papers and the bell rang for the next lesson.

Next day the class had geometry. The Maths teacher talked lucidly and drew clear diagrams on the blackboard, and Thaw gazed at her, trying by intensity of expression to make up for inability to understand. A girl came in and said, "Please, miss, Mister Meikle wants tae see Duncan Thaw in room fifty-four." As she led him across the playground to the wooden annexe, Thaw said, "Who's Mr. Meikle?"

"Head English teacher."

"What does he want me for?"

"How should I know?"

In room fifty-four a saturnine man in an academic gown leaned on a desk overlooking empty rows of desks. He turned toward Thaw a face that was long, lined and triangular under the oval of a balding skull. He had a small black moustache and ironical eyebrows. Lifting two sheets of foolscap from his desk he said, "You wrote this?"

"Yes sir."

"What gave you the idea?"

"Nothing, sir."

"Hm. I suppose you read a lot?"

"Quite a lot."

"What are you reading just now?"

"A play called *The Dynasts.*"

"Hardy's *Dynasts?*"

"I forget who wrote it. I got it out of the library."

"What do you think of it?"

"I think the choruses are a bit boring but I like the scenic directions. I like the retreat from Moscow, with the bodies of the soldiers baked by fire in front and frozen stiff behind. And I like the view of Europe down through the clouds, looking like a sick man with the Alps for his backbone."

"Do you do any writing at home?"

"Oh yes, sir."

"Are you at work on anything just now?"

"Yes. I'm trying to write about this boy who can hear colours."

"Hear colours?"

"Yes sir. When he sees a fire burning each flame makes a noise like a fiddle playing a jig, and some nights he's kept awake by the full moon screaming, and he hears the sun rise through an orange dawn like trumpets blowing. The bother is that most colours round about him make horrible noises— orange and green buses, for instance, traffic lights and advertisements and things."

"You don't hear colours yourself, do you?" said the teacher, looking at Thaw peculiarly.

"Oh no," said Thaw, smiling. "I got the idea from a note Edgar Allan Poe wrote to one of his poems. He said he some-

times thought he could hear the dusk creeping over the land
like the tolling of a bell."
"I see. Well, Duncan, the school magazine is rather short of
worthwhile contributions this year. Do you think you could
write something more for us? Along slightly different lines?"
"Oh yes."
"Don't write about the boy who hears colours. It's a good idea—
perhaps too good for a school magazine. Write about something
more commonplace. How soon could you manage it?"
"Tomorrow, sir."
"The day after will do."
"I'll bring it in tomorrow."
Mr. Meikle tapped his teeth with a pencil end, then said, "We
have a debating society in the school every second Wednesday
evening. You should come to it. You may have something to
say."

      Thaw ran leaping back across the empty playground. Out-
side the maths room he paused, took the grin from his face,
frowned with his brows, smiled faintly with his mouth, opened
the door and went to his seat with the eyes of the class on
him. Kate Caldwell, who sat across the passage from his desk,
smiled and flickered questioningly. He bent over a page of
axioms, pretending to concentrate but working inwardly on a
new story. The elation in his chest recalled the summit of Rua.
He remembered the sunlit moor and the beckoning white speck
and wondered if these things could be used in a story and if
Kate Caldwell would read it and be impressed. Taking a pencil
he began to sketch furtively a steep mountain on the cover
of a book.
"What is a point?"
He looked up and blinked.
"Stand up, Thaw! Now tell me what a point is."
The question seemed meaningless.
"A point is that which has no dimensions. You didn't know that,
did you, yet it's the first axiom in the book. And—what's this?
You've been drawing on the cover!"
He stared at the teacher's mouth opening and shutting and
wondered why the words coming out could hurt like stones.
His ear tried to get free by attending to the purr of a car
moving slowly up the street outside and the faint shuffle of
Kate Caldwell's feet. The teacher's mouth stopped moving.
He muttered "Yes miss" and sat down, blushing hotly.

He took four nights to finish the new story properly. He gave it to Mr. Meikle with many apologies for the delay and Mr. Meikle read it and rejected it, explaining that Thaw had tried a blend of realism and fantasy which even an adult would have found difficult. Thaw was stunned and resentful. Though not satisfied with the story he knew it was the best he had written; the words "even an adult" hurt his pride by suggesting his work was only interesting because he was a child; moreover he had quietly told a few classmates of Mr. Meikle's request, hoping word of it would reach Kate Caldwell.

CHAPTER 16. Underworlds

Partly for pleasure, partly to save money, he walked to school each morning through Alexandra Park, mistakenly thinking a twisting path through flowerbeds was shorter than the straight traffic-laden road. The path crossed a hillside with a golf course above and football pitches below. The sky was usually pallid neutral and beyond the pitches a grey pragmatic light illuminated ridges of tenements and factories without obscuring or enriching them. Past the hill a boating pond lay among hawthorn and chestnuts. Often a film of soot had settled overnight on the level water and a duck, newly launched from an island, left a track like the track a finger makes on dusty glass. Crossing the flood of trucks and trams clanging and rumbling on the main road, he picked his way through a grid of small streets by a route which passed two cinemas with still photographs outside and three shops with vividly coloured magazines in the window. The women in these gave his daydreams a more erotic twist.

He had crossed the main road one morning and was descending a short street when Kate Caldwell came out of a close mouth in front of him and walked toward school, her schoolbag (a wartime gas-mask container) bumping at her hip. He followed excitedly, meaning to overtake but lacking the courage. What could he say to her? He imagined his stammering voice saying dull, awkward things about lessons and the weather and could only imagine her saying conventional things in response. Why didn't she turn and smile and beckon? Surely she knew he was behind? If she beckoned he would smile faintly and approach with eyebrows questioningly raised. She would say, "Don't you like my company?" or "I'm glad you come this way, these morning walks are a bit dull," or "I liked your story in the school magazine; tell me about yourself." He glared furiously at her dancing shoulders, willing her to turn and beckon, but she didn't, and they reached school without getting nearer together or farther apart. After this he hoped each day she would come from the close at the exact moment he passed it so he could speak to her without lowering himself, but either he didn't see her at all or she emerged ahead and he had to follow as if towed by an invisible rope. One morning he had just passed the close when he heard light quick footsteps overtaking from behind. A confusion of hope and distress hit him, and a nervous prickling in the skin of his face. Before the steps reached him he abruptly crossed the road to the opposite pavement, defiance and self-pity mingling in a sense of tragic isolation. Then he saw pass him, across the road, not the contemptuous dance of Kate Caldwell's shoulderblades but a small, vigorous old lady with a shopping bag. He reached the playground feeling baffled and disappointed, and afterward went to school by a route which bothered him with fewer emotional complications.

Doing well in some subjects, learning to do badly in others without offending the teachers, he came to accept school as a sort of bad weather, making only the conventional complaints. He was friendly with other boys but had no friends and rarely tried to make them. Apparent life was a succession of dull habits in which he did what was asked automatically, only resenting demands to show interest. His energy had withdrawn into imaginary worlds and he had none to waste on reality.

A small fertile land lay hidden in a crater made by an atomic explosion. Thaw was Prime Minister of it. He lived in an old mansion among lawns and clumps of forest on the shore of a loch ornamented with islands. The mansion was spacious, dim and peaceful. The halls were hung with his paintings, the library full of his novels and poems, there were studios and laboratories where the best minds of the day worked whenever they cared to visit him. Outside the sun was warm, bees hummed among flowers and fountains, the season was midway between summer and autumn when the trees showed their matured green and only the maples were crimson. Political work took little of his time, for the people of that country had such confidence in him that he had only to suggest a reform for it to be practised. Indeed, his main problem was to keep the

land democratic, for he would have been crowned king long
before if his socialist principles had not forbidden it. He looked
young for a Prime Minister, being a boy in early adolescence;
at the same time he had ruled that land for centuries. He was
a survivor of the third world war. The poisonous radiations
which had killed most of his contemporaries had, by a fluke,
given him eternal youth. In two or three centuries of wandering
about the shattered earth he had become leader of a small
group of people who had come to trust his gentleness and
wisdom. He had brought them to the crater, protected by its
walls from the envy of a bygone age, to build a republic where
nobody was sick, poor or forced to live by work they hated.
Unluckily his country was surrounded by barbaric lands ruled
by queens and tyrants who kept plotting to conquer it and
were only kept out by his courage and ingenuity. As a result
he was often involved in battles, rescues, escapes, fights with
monsters in the middle of arenas, and triumphal processions
of shocking vulgarity which he only took part in to avoid hurting
the feelings of the queens and princesses whose lives and countries he had saved. When these adventures were over he invited
the main characters home to stay with him, and since he annexed
the plot of every book and film which impressed him the house
by the loch was always crowded with the celebrities of many
different races, nations and historical phases. In the simplicity
of his spacious rooms they were amazed by the quiet friendliness
of a way of life more civilized than their own, and they learned
the true duties of a ruler by seeing him spend an afternoon
drawing the plans of a new reservoir or university. The women
guests usually fell in love with him, though some of the more
barbaric came to hate him for his friendly indifference, an indifference which clothed a deep shyness. He could only feel near
to women when rescuing them, and often envied the villains
who could humiliate or torture them. His position made it
impossible to imagine doing such things himself. Yet when
walking home from school or public library, these adventures
filled his head and chest with such intoxicating emotions that
he had to run hard to be relieved of them and often found
he had come through several streets without remembering anything of the people, houses or traffic.

His other imaginary world was enjoyed in the genitals.
It was a secret gold mine in Arizona which a gang of bandits
worked by slave labour. Thaw was bandit chief and spent his
time inventing and practising tortures for the slaves. The mine

got outside stimulus, not from the shelves of the library but, cryptically, from American comics. He never bought these, and had courage to look at their enticing covers only when the shop contained something else he could pretend to examine, but he sometimes borrowed one at school and in the privacy of the back bedroom copied out pictures of men being whipped and branded. He kept these pictures between pages of Carlyle's *French Revolution,* a book no one else was likely to open.

One evening he knelt by his bed with the pictures on the quilt before him. There was a familiar tension in his genitals but tonight, by a coincidence of positions, his stiffened penis touched a girder upholding the mattress. The contact fired a bolt of white-cold nervous electricity into him in a shock so poignant that he had to press harder and harder against the source of it until something gushed and squirted, the kicking mechanism broke down, shrunk and went limp and he was left feeling horribly flat and emptied out. All the while his mind had sat feebly aghast, wondering what was happening with the slight energy left to it. Now he looked disgustedly at the drawings, took them to the lavatory, flushed them down the pan and opened his trousers.
A grey slug-shaped blob of jelly lay on his stomach just under the navel. It was transparent, tiny milky wisps and galaxies hung in it and it smelled like fish. He wiped himself clean and went back to the bedroom, not knowing what had happened but sure it had to do with the sniggers, hints and sudden silences which instinctive distaste made him ignore among his classmates. He felt numb and disgusted and swore not to think again the thoughts that led to this condition. Two days later they came back and he gave way to them without much resistance.

And now the flow of his imaginative life was broken by three or four orgasms a week. His pleasure in the mine had once lasted indefinitely, for it never reached a climax. After drawing or brooding awhile he would be called to a meal, or to homework, or would go for a walk and return from it the humane triumphant Prime Minister of his republic. Now after brooding on the mine a few minutes his penis would yearn to touch something, and if denied this help often exploded by itself, leaving a sodden stain in his trousers and a self-contempt so great that it included all his imaginary worlds. He was as much estranged from imagination as from reality.

The asthma returned with increasing weight, by day lying on his chest like a stone, at night pouncing like a beast. One night he woke with the beast's paw so hard on his throat that he moved in a moment from fear to utter panic and leaped from bed with a cawing scream, stumbled to the window and clutched back the curtain. A gold flake of moon, a dim wisp of cloud hung above the opposite chimneys. He glared at them like words he could not read and tried to scream again. His father and mother came beside him and gently pressed him back to bed. Mr. Thaw held him tightly while his mother gave an ephedrine pill and brought first hot milk, then hot whisky, and held the cups to his mouth as he drank. His frightened grunting got less. They left him wrapped in a dressing gown, sitting cross-legged against a pile of pillows.

At the height of the panic, while glaring at the irrelevant moon, his one thought had been a certainty that Hell was worse than this. He had not been religiously educated and though he had a tentative faith in God (saying at the end of prayers "If you exist" instead of "Amen") he had none in Hell. Now he saw that Hell was the one truth and pain the one fact which nullified all others. Sufficient health was like thin ice on an infinite sea of pain. Love, work, art, science and law were dangerous games played on the ice; all homes and cities were built on it. The ice was frail. A tiny shrinkage of the bronchial tubes could put him under it and a single split atom could sink a city. All religions existed to justify Hell and all clergymen were ministers of it. How could they walk about with such bland social faces pretending to belong to the surface of life? Their skulls should be furnaces with the fire of Hell burning in them and the skin of their faces dried and thin like scorched leaves. The face of Dr. McPhedron came to him as abruptly as when it was thrust over the edge of the rock. He turned for help to a bookcase beside the bed. It held books got secondhand for sixpence or a shilling, mostly legends and fantasies with some adult fiction and nonfiction. But now the fantasies were imbecile frivolity, and poetry was whistling in the dark, and novels showed life fighting its own agony, and biographies were accounts of struggles toward violent or senile ends, and history was an infinitely diseased worm without head or tail, beginning or end. A shelf held his father's books, works by Lenin and the Webbs, *The History of the Working Classes in Scotland, Humanities Gain from Unbelief, The Harmsworth Encyclo-*

paedia and books about mountaineering. Putting out a desperate
hand he took from among these a general history of philosophy,
opened at random and read:

All the perceptions of the human mind resolve themselves into
two distinct kinds, which I shall call IMPRESSIONS and IDEAS.
The difference between these consists of the degrees of force
and liveliness with which they strike upon the mind, and make
their way into our thought or consciousness. These perceptions,
which enter with the most force or violence, we may name *impressions;* and under the name I may comprehend all our sensations, passions and emotions, as they make their first appearance
in the soul. By *ideas* I mean the faint image of these in thinking
and reasoning. . . .

He read on with increasing relief, brought more and more
into a world which, though made of words instead of numbers,
was almost mathematical in its cleanness and lack of emotion.
Looking up from the book much later he saw between the
disordered curtains that the sky was pale and heard a faint
distant music, a melodious thrumming which grew louder and
louder until it seemed above his head, then faded into the
distance. It was too rhythmical for birdsong, too harmonious
for aircraft. He was puzzled but oddly comforted and fell into
a smooth sleep.

　　At seven an alarm rang in the living room where his parents
slept in the bed settee. Mr. Thaw had breakfast and carried
his bicycle downstairs to the street. Mrs. Thaw brought to the
bedroom a tray set with porridge, fried egg, sausage, brown
bread with marmalade and a cup of tea. She watched as he
ate and said, "Is it any better, son?"
"A bit better."
"Ach, you'll be all right when ye get to school."
"Mibby."
"Take another pill."
"I have taken another. It's not doing much good."
"You've made up your mind it's not doing good! If you wanted
it to work it *would* work!"
"Mibby."
After a while he said, "Anyway, I don't want to go to school
today."
"But, Duncan, the exams are two weeks away."
"I'm tired. I didn't sleep well."
Mrs. Thaw said coldly, "Are you trying to tell me you *can't*

go to school? You weren't very well yesterday but you were well enough to go to the library. You've always enough breath for what you want to do; none for what's important."

Thaw laboriously dressed and washed. Mrs. Thaw helped him on with his coat and said, "Now take your time going down the road. It's church first period so it won't matter if you're a bit late. The teachers understand. And straighten your back. Stop walking about like a half-shut penknife. Look the world in the face as if you owned it."

"I own none of it."

"You own as much of it as anyone! You can own *more* of it if you use your brain and learn to do well in the exams. You have a good brain. Your teachers say so. They want to help you. Why don't you want to be helped?"

There was no special position for praying in. People sat with legs apart or crossed, arms folded, hands clasped or clenched as they pleased, but all shut their eyes to suggest concentration and bowed their heads as a mark of respect. For a long time Thaw had stopped shutting his eyes but lacked the courage to lift his head. Today, arriving late and breathing uneasily, a great carelessness filled him and he impatiently raised his head during a lengthy prayer. He was seated on one side of the gallery with a clear view down on the bent heads of the congregation, the choir, the minister in the octagonal tower of his pulpit and the headmaster at the foot of it. The minister was a fat-faced man whose head wagged and nodded with every phrase while his raptly shut eyes gave it a blind empty look, like a balloon blown about in a draught. Thaw felt suddenly that he was being watched. Among the rows of bowed heads in the gallery opposite was an erect, slightly clumsy, almost expressionless face which, if it noticed him (and he was not sure it did) did so with a faint sarcastic smile. Something in the face made him feel he knew it. Later that day the stranger was introduced into the class as Robert Coulter, who had been promoted to Whitehill Secondary School from Garngad Junior Secondary School. He fitted into the class easily, making friends without effort and doing fairly well at the things Thaw did badly. He and Thaw exchanged embarrassed nods when accident brought them face to face and otherwise ignored each other. Once, in the science room, the pupils stood talking by their benches before the teacher arrived. Coulter approached Thaw and said, "Hullo."

"Hullo."

"How are you getting on?"

"Not too bad. How are you?"

"Ach, not too bad."

After a pause Coulter said, "Would you mind swopping seats?"

"Why?"

"Well, I'd like a closer view. . . ." Coulter pointed at Kate Caldwell. "After all, you're not interested in that sort of thing." Thaw took his books to Coulter's bench filled with black rage and depression. Nothing could have made him admit his interest in Kate Caldwell.

One day after the exams the teachers sat at their desks correcting papers while the pupils read comics, played chess or cards or talked quietly in groups. Coulter, at a desk in front of Thaw, turned round and said, "What are ye reading?"

Thaw showed a book of critical essays on art and literature. Coulter said accusingly, "You don't read that for fun."

"Yes, I read it for fun."

"People our age don't read that sort of book for fun. They read it to show they're superior."

"But I read this sort of book even when there's nobody to see me."

"That shows you arenae trying to make *us* think you're superior, you're trying to make *yourself* think you're superior."

Thaw scratched his head and said, "That's clever, but not very true. What are you reading?"

Coulter showed him a magazine called *Astounding Science Fiction,* with a picture on the cover of tentacled creatures manipulating a piece of machinery in a jungle clearing. Green lightning leaped from the machine into the sky where it split open a planet which seemed to be the earth. Thaw shook his head and said, "I don't like science fiction much. It's pessimistic." Coulter grinned and said, "That's what I like about it. I was reading a great story the other day called *Colonel Johnson Does His Duty.* This American colonel is in a hideout miles underground. He's one of those in charge of fighting the third world war, which is all done by pressing switches. Everybody aboveground has been killed, of course, and even a lot of the army folk have had their hideouts blasted by special rockets that bore into the ground. Well, this Colonel Johnson, see, has been out of touch for months with the folks on his own side, because if you use the radio these special rockets can work out where your hideout is and come down and blast you. Anyway, this Colonel Johnson invents a machine that can find out where people are by detecting their thought waves. He starts using the machine on America. No good. Everyone in America's dead. He tries Europe, Africa, Australia. Everybody's dead there too. Then he tries Asia and here there's only one other man left alive in the world, and he's in a city in Russia. So he gets into this plane and flies to Russia. Everything he passes over is dead—no plants or animals or anything. He lands in this Russian city and gets out. Everything's wreckage, of course, but he creeps through it till he hears this other man moving inside this building. It's eight years since he's seen another human being, he's going mad with loneliness, see, and he's been hoping to talk tae another man before he dies. The Russian comes out of the building and Colonel Johnson shoots him."

"But *why?*" said Thaw.

"Because he's been trained tae kill Russians. Don't you like that story?"

"I think it's a rotten story."

"Mibby. But it's true tae life. What do you do after school?"

"I go to the library, or mibby a walk."

"I go intae town with Murdoch Muir and big Sam Lang. We stage riots."

"How?"

"D'ye know the West End Park?"

"The park near the Art Galleries?"

"Aye. Well, they don't lock it up at night like other parks and folk can walk through it. There's a few lights in it but no' many. Well, big Sam'll stand near some bushes and light a fag, and when someone comes we charge out from the bushes and pretend to kick big Sam in the guts and he lashes out with his fists and we all fall down and roll about swearing. We don't touch each other, but in the dark it's hellish convincing. You get lassies running away screaming for the police."

"Don't the police come?"

"We run away before they come. Murdoch Muir's dad is a policeman. When we tell him about it he roars and laughs and tells us whit he would dae tae us if he caught us."

Thaw said, "That's anti-social."

"Mibby, but it's natural. More natural than going walks by yourself. Come on, admit you'd like tae come with us one night."

"But I wouldnae."

"Admit you'd sooner look at that comic than read your art criticism."

Coulter pointed at the cover of a neighbour's comic. It showed

a blonde in a bathing costume being entwined by a huge serpent. Thaw opened his mouth to deny this, then frowned and shut it. Coulter said, "Come on, that picture makes your cock prick, doesn't it? Admit you're like the rest of us."
Thaw went to the next classroom alarmed and confused. "That picture makes your cock prick. Admit you're like the rest of us." He remembered other words heard long before but carefully ignored: "I wouldnae mind feeling *her* belly in a dark room."

He had known from the age of four that babies hatched from their mothers' stomachs. Mr. Thaw had described the growth of the embryo in detail, and Thaw had assumed this process occurred spontaneously in most women above a certain age. He accepted this as he accepted his father's account of the origin of species and the solar system: it was an interesting, mechanical, not very mysterious business which men could know about but not influence. Nothing he heard or read later had mentioned inevitable links between love, sex and birth, so he never thought there were any. Sex was something he had discovered squatting on the bedroom floor. It was so disgusting that it had to be indulged secretly and not mentioned to others. It fed on dreams of cruelty, had its climax in a jet of jelly and left him feeling weak and lonely. It had nothing to do with love. Love was what he felt for Kate Caldwell, a wish to be near her and do things that would make her admire him. He hid this love because public knowledge of it would put him in an inferior position with other people and with Kate herself. He was ashamed of it, but not disgusted. And now, jerkily, under the influence of Coulter's remark, his separate pictures of love, sex and birth started to become one.

He was crossing the hill in the park when he heard musical throbbing come from the sky. Five swans flew over his head in V formation, their thrumming wings and honking throats blending in one music. Lowering their feet they dropped out of sight behind the trees which screened the boating pond. During the next days he collected spare bits of bread and threw them in the pond on his way to school. One morning he saw something that kept him on the shore longer than usual. Beside the island two swans faced each other in such an intent way that he thought they were going to fight. Spreading their wings they rose from the water almost to the tail, pressed their breasts together, then their brows, then their beaks. Pointing their faces skyward they twined necks, then untwisted and coiled them backward, each reflecting the other like a mirror. Together they made and unmade with their bodies the shapes of Greek lyres and renaissance silverware. Suddenly one of them broke the pattern, slipped adroitly behind the other, mounted her tail and thrust his body up and down it while she plunged across the water in a thresh of wings and waves. As they passed Thaw he saw the male push the female's head under water with his beak, perhaps to make her more docile. At the end of the loch they separated, straightened necks and sailed indifferently apart. The female, being more dishevelled, was readjusting her feathers when the male, in a remote bay, started probing unenthusiastically for minnows.

Ten minutes later Thaw joined the lines in the playground full of grey depression. In class he looked coldly on the pupils, the teacher, and Kate Caldwell most of all. They were part of a deceptive surface, horrifying this time not because it was weak and could not keep out Hell but because it was transparent and could not hide the underlying filth. That evening he walked with Coulter along the canal bank and told him about the swans. Coulter said, "Have you seen slugs do it?"
"*Slugs?*"
"Aye, slugs. When I was on MacTaggart's farm in Kinlochrua I came out one morning after some rain and here were all these slugs lying in the grass in couples. I took them apart and put them together again tae see how they did it. They seemed so human. Much more human than your swans."
Thaw stood still for a moment and then cried aloud, "I wish to God I would never want another human being in my whole life! I wish to God I was . . ."
He paused. A word from a recent botany lesson entered his head. ". . . self-fertilizing! Oh, Lord God Maker and Sustainer of Heaven and Hell make me self-fertilizing! If you exist."
Coulter looked at him, slightly awestruck, then said, "You scare me sometimes, Duncan. The things you say arenae altogether sane. It all comes of wanting to be superior to ordinary life."

CHAPTER 17. The Key

Mr. Thaw worked as a labourer and then as a wages clerk for a firm building housing estates round the city edge. The Korean war began, the cost of living rose and Mrs. Thaw got a job as a shop assistant in the afternoons. She came to feel very tired and suffered depressions which her doctor thought were caused by the change of life. When the tea things had been cleared away in the evenings she would sew or knit, glancing occasionally at Thaw, who sat frowning at the pages of a textbook and fingering his brow or cheek. His inattention drew comments from her.

"You're not working."

"I know."

"You ought to be working. The exams are coming off soon. You've made up your mind not to pass and you won't."

"I know."

"And you could pass if you tried. Your teachers all say you could. And you sit there doing nothing and you'll make us all ashamed of you."

"I'm afraid so."

"Well, do something! And don't scratch! You sit there clot-clot-clotting at your face till it's like a lump of raw meat. Think of your sister Ruth if you won't think of yourself or me. She's ashamed enough as it is of a brother who creeps about the school like a hunchback."

"I can't help my asthma."

"No, but if you did the exercises the physiotherapist at the Royal told you to do you could walk about like a human being. You were told to do five-minutes exercise each morning and evening. How often did you do them? Once."

"Twice."

"Twice. And why? Why don't you want to improve yourself?"
"Laziness, I suppose."
"Hm!"
Thaw pretended once more to study a page of mathematics but found himself brooding on a talk with the head English teacher about the school curriculum. Thaw said much of it was neither interesting in itself nor useful in a practical way. Mr. Meikle had looked thoughtfully across the bent backs and heads of his class and said, "Remember, Duncan, when most people leave school they have to live by work which can't be liked for its own sake and whose practical application is outside their grasp. Unless they learn to work obediently because they're told to, and for no other reason, they'll be unfit for human society."
Thaw sighed, picked up a textbook and read:

> A man and his wife clean their teeth from the same cylindrical tube of toothpaste on alternate days. The interior diameter of the nozzle through which the paste is squeezed is .08 of the interior diameter of the tube, which is 3.4 cms. If the man squeezes out a cylinder of toothpaste 1.82 cms in length each time he uses it, and his wife a cylinder 3.13 cms in length, find the length of the tube to the nearest mm. if it lasts from the 3rd of January to the 8th of March inclusive and the man is the first to use it.

A hysterical rage gripped him. Dropping the book, he clutched at his head and rubbed and scratched and towzled it until his mother shouted "Stop!"
"But this is absurd! This is ludicrous! This is unb-unb-unb-unb-unb-unb"—he choked—"unbearable! I don't understand it, I can't learn it, what good will it do me?"
"It'll get you through your exams! That's all the good it needs to do! You can forget it when you've got your Higher Leaving Certificate!"
"Why can't they examine me in standing on my head balancing chairs on my feet? Homework for that might improve my health."
"And do you really think you know what's good for you better than the teachers and headmasters who've studied the subject all their lives?"
"Yes. Yes. Where my own needs are concerned I do know better."
Mrs. Thaw put a hand to her side and said in a strange voice, "Oh, bloody hell!" Then she said, "Why did I bring

children into the world?'' and began weeping.

Thaw was alarmed. It was the first time he had heard her curse or seen her weep and he tried to sound reasonable and calm. "Mummy, it doesnae matter if I fail those exams. If I leave school and get a job you won't need to work so hard."

Mrs. Thaw dabbed her eyes and resumed sewing, her lips pressed tight together. After a pause she said, "And what job will you get? An errand boy's?"

"There must be other jobs."

"Such as?"

"I don't know, but there must be!"

"Hm!"

Thaw shut his books and said, "I'm going for a walk."

"That's right, run away. Men can always run away from work. Women never can."

There was daylight in the sky but none in the streets and the lamps were lit. Boys of his own age strolled on the pavements in crowds of three and four, girls walked in couples, groups of both sexes gossiped and giggled by café doors. Thaw felt inferior and conspicuous. Overheard whispers seemed to mock the absent look he wore to disarm criticism, overheard laughter seemed caused by the upright hair he never brushed or combed. He walked quickly into streets with fewer shops where people moved in enigmatic units. His confidence grew with the darkness. His face took on a resolute, slightly wolfish look, his feet hit the pavement firmly, he strode past couples embracing in close mouths feeling isolated by a stern purpose which put him outside merely human satisfactions. This purpose was hardly one he could have explained (after all he was just walking, not walking to anywhere) but sometimes he thought he was searching for the key.

The key was small and precise, yet in its use completely general and completely particular. Once found it would solve every problem: asthma, homework, shyness before Kate Caldwell, fear of atomic war; the key would make everything painful, useless and wrong become pleasant, harmonious and good. Since he thought of it as something that could be contained in one or two sentences, he had looked for it in the public libraries but seldom on the science or philosophy shelves. The key had to be recognized at once and by heart, not led up to and proved by reasoning. Nor could it be an article of religion, since its discovery would make churches and clergy unnecessary.

Nor was it poetry, for poems were too finished and perfect to finish and perfect anything themselves. The key was so simple and obvious that it had been continually overlooked and was less likely to be a specialist's triumphant conclusion than to be mentioned casually by someone innocent and dull; so he had searched among biographies and autobiographies, correspondences, histories and travel books, in footnotes to out-dated medical works and the indexes of Victorian natural histories. Recently he had thought the key more likely to be found on a night walk through the streets, printed on a scrap of paper blown out of the rubble of a bombed factory, or whispered in a dark street by someone leaning suddenly out of a window.

Tonight he came to a piece of waste ground, a hill among tenements that had been suburban twenty years earlier. The black shape of it curved against the lesser blackness of the sky and the yellow spark of a bonfire flickered just under the summit. He left the pallid gaslit street and climbed upward, feeling coarse grass against his shoes and occasional broken bricks. When he reached the fire it had sunk to a few small flames among a heap of charred sticks and rags. He groped on the ground till he found some scraps of cardboard and paper and added them to the fire with a torn-up handful of withered grass. A tall flame shot up and he watched it from outside the brightness it cast. He imagined other people arriving one at a time and standing in a ring round the firelight. When ten or twelve had assembled they would hear a heavy thudding of wings; a black shape would pass overhead and land on the dark hilltop, and the messenger would walk down to them bringing the key. The fire burned out and he turned and looked down on Glasgow. Nothing solid could be seen, only lights—streetlamps like broken necklaces and bracelets of light, neon cinema signs like silver and ruby brooches, the ruby, emerald and amber twinkle of traffic regulators—all glowing like treasure spilled on the blackness.

He went back down to the dingy streets and entered a close in one of the dingiest. The stair was narrow, ill lit and smelling of cat piss. Before a lavatory door on a half landing he stepped over two children who knelt on a rug, playing with a clockwork toy. The top landing had three doors, one with FORBES COULTER on it in Gothic script among gold vine leaves, framed behind glass which the passage of years had blotched with mildew on the inside. The door was opened by a small woman with an angry cloud of curly grey hair. She said plaintively, "Robert's down in the lavatory Duncan, you'll just have to come in and wait."

Thaw stepped across a cupboard-sized lobby into a tidy comfortable crowded room. Wardrobe, sideboard, table and chairs left narrow spaces between them. A tall window had a sink in front and a gas cooker beside it. A shadow was cast over the fireplace by drying clothes on a pulley in the ceiling, and the table held the remains of a meal.

Mrs. Coulter began moving plates to the sink and Thaw sat by the fire and stared into a bed-recess near the door. Coulter's father lay there, his shoulders supported by pillows, his massive sternly lined blind enduring face turned slightly toward the room.

Thaw said, "Are you any better, Mr. Coulter?"

"In a way, yes, Duncan; but then again, in a way, no. How's the school doing?"

"I'm all right at art and English."

"Art is your subject isn't it? I used to paint a bit myself. During the thirties a few of us—we were unemployed, you know— we got together on Thursday evenings in a room near Brigton Cross and we'd get a teacher or a model along from the art school. We called ourselves the Brigton Socialist Art Club. Have you heard of Ewan Kennedy? The sculptor?"

"I'm not sure, Mr. Coulter. Mibby. I mean the name's familiar but I'm no' sure."

"He was one of us. He went to London and did quite well for himself. A year ago. . . . No. Wait."

Thaw looked at Mr. Coulter's big gnarled hand lying quietly on the quilt, a cigarette with a charred tip between two fingers. "It was three years ago. His name was in the *Bulletin*. He was making a bust of Winston Churchill for some town in England. I thought when I read it, I used to know you."

Mr. Coulter hummed a quiet tune then said, "My father was a picture framer to trade. He did everything in those days, carving the wood, gilding it, even hanging the picture sometimes. Some of his work must be in the Art Galleries to the present day. I used to help him with the hanging. Hanging a picture is an art in itself. What I meant to tell you was this: I was hanging these pictures in a house in Menteith Row on the Green. It's a slum now but the wealthiest folk in Glasgow once lived in those houses, and in my time some of them still did, and this house belonged to Jardine of Jardine and Beattie, the shipbuilders. Young Jardine was a lawyer and became Lord Provost, and *his* son proved tae be a bit of a rogue, but never mind. I was hanging these pictures in the entrance hall: marble floor, oak-panelled walls. The frames were carved walnut covered with gold leaf, but the hall was dark because there were no windows opening into it, apart from a wee skylight window that was no use at all because it was stained glass. When I had finished I opened the front door and went down the steps onto the pavement outside and stood looking in through the open door. It was a morning in the early spring, cold, but the sun quite bright. A girl came along and said, 'What are ye staring at?' I pointed through the door and said 'Look at that. It looks like a million dollars.' The sun was shining intae the hall and the gold frames were shining on the walls. It really did look like a million dollars.''

Mr. Coulter smiled a little.

Coulter entered and said, ''Hullo, Duncan. Hullo, Forbes. Forbes, your cigarette's out. Will I light it for you?''

''Ye can light it if you like.''

Coulter got a match and lit the cigarette, then went to the sink, put an arm round his mother's waist, and said, ''My ain wee mammy, how about a fag? You've given my daddy a fag, give me a fag.''

Mrs. Coulter took a cigarette packet from her apron pocket and handed it over, grumbling, ''You're no' old enough tae smoke but.''

''True, but my wee mammy can refuse me nothing. Have these two been discussing art?''

''Aye, they've been talking about their art.''

''Well, Thaw, my intellectual friend, what's it to be? A game of chess or a dauner along the canal bank?''

''I wouldnae mind a dauner.''

They walked on the towpath talking about women. Coulter had dropped the hard cheerful manner he wore at home. Thaw said, ''The only time I reach them is when I speak at the debating society. Even Kate Caldwell notices me then. She was in the front row of desks last night, staring at my face with her mouth and eyes wide open. I felt dead witty and intellectual. I felt like a king or something. She sits behind me at maths now. I've made a poem about it.''

He paused, hoping that Coulter would ask him to recite. Coulter said, ''Everybody writes poems about girls at our age. It's what they call a phase. Even big Sam Lang writes poems about girls. Even I occasionally—"

"Never mind. I like my wee poem. Bob, if I ask you a question will ye promise to answer truthfully?"

"Ask away."

"Is Kate Caldwell keen on me?"

"Her? On you? No."

"I think she's mibby a bit keen on me."

"She's a wee grope," said Coulter.

"What?"

"A grope. A feel. Lyle Craig in the fifth year is supposed to be winching her steady, and last Friday I saw her being lumbered by a hardman up a close near the Denistoun Palais."

"Lumbered?"

"Groped. Felt. She's nothing but a wee—"

"Don't use that word!" cried Thaw.

They walked in silence until at last Coulter said, "I shouldnae have told you that, Duncan."

"But I'm glad. Thank you."

"I'm sorry I told you."

"I'm not. I want to know every obstacle, every obstacle there is. There's the obstacles of not being attractive, not having money to take her out, not knowing how to talk to her, and now it seems she's a flirt. If I ever reach her she'll shift elsewhere and keep on shifting."

"Mibby it's a mistake to start with Kate Caldwell. You should practise on someone else first. Practise on my girl, big June Haig."

"Your girl?"

"Well, I've only been out with her once. There's a big demand for her."

"What's she like?"

"She's got a back like an all-in wrestler. Her arms are as thick as my thighs and her thighs as thick as your waist. Cuddling her is like sinking intae a big sofa."

"You hardly make her sound attractive."

"Big June is the most attractive girl I know. She's exciting and she's comfortable. Ask her to the third-year dance."

Thaw remembered June Haig. She was a sulky-looking girl and not as large as Coulter pretended, but she had failed to get out of the second year and was called Big June to distinguish her from the less developed girls she sat among. Thaw felt a pang of interest. He said, "Big June wouldnae come to a dance with me."

"She might. She doesnae like you but she's intrigued by your reputation."

"Have I a reputation?"

"You've two reputations. Some say you're an absentminded professor with no sex life at all; others say that's just a disguise and you've the dirtiest sex life in the whole school."

Thaw stood still and held his head. He cried, "I see no way out, no way out. I want to be close to Kate, I want to be valued by her, I suppose I want to marry her. What bloody good is this useless wanting, wanting, wanting?"

"Don't think your problems would be solved by marrying her."

"Why not?"

"Fornication isnae just sticking it in and wagging it around. You've tae time things so that when you're pushing hardest she's exactly ready to take it. If ye don't get this exactly right she feels angry and disappointed with you. It needs a lot of practice tae get right."

"Examinations!" cried Thaw. "It's all examinations! Must everything we do satisfy someone *else* before it's worthwhile? Is everything we do because we enjoy it selfish and useless? Primary school, secondary school, university, they've got the first twenty-four years of our lives numbered off for us and to get into the year above we've to pass an exam. Everything is done to please the examiner, never for fun. The one pleasure they allow is anticipation: 'Things will be better after the exam.' It's a lie. Things are never better after the exam. You'd think love was something different. Oh, no. It has to be studied, practised, learnt, and you can get it wrong."

"You're eloquent tonight," said Coulter. "You've got me almost as mixed up as yourself. But not quite. You see there's really no connection between—"

"*What's that?*"

"That? A kid singing."

They were beside a fence of old railway sleepers planted upright at the towpath edge. From the other side a clear tuneless little voice sang:

"Ah've a laddie in Ame-e-e-rica,
Ah've a laddie ower the sea;
Ah've a laddie in Ame-e-e-rica,
And he's goantae marry me."

They looked through a gap in the sleepers onto a road with the canal embankment on one side and the black barred win-

dows of a warehouse on the other. A small girl was skipping
with a rope and singing to herself in a circle of light under a
lamp. Coulter said, "That kid's too young to be up at this
hour. What are ye grinning at?"
"I thought for a moment her words might be the key."
"What key?"
Thaw explained about the key, expecting it would send Coulter
into a fit of annoyance, as most of his less practical concepts
did. Coulter frowned and said, "Has this key to be words?"
"What else could it be?"
"When I was staying with auld MacTaggart in Kinlochrua during the war I remember two or three nights when I got a
good view of the stars. Ye can always see more stars when
you're in the country, especially if there's a nip of frost in
the air, and these nights the sky was just hotching with stars.
I felt this . . . this coming nearer and nearer me till I almost
had it, but when I tried tae think what it was, it had gone.
And this happened more than once."
"I don't know what you mean. What sort of thing was it?
Did it tie up everything you believed? Could ye test things
with it?"
"You could test nothing with it. It was a feeling, I suppose.
It was gentle, and permanent, and more like a friend than
anything else."
Thaw was unable to think of a similar experience and felt envi-
ous. He said, "It sounds a bit sentimental. Did you only feel
it when you were seeing stars?"
"That was the only time."
Thaw looked at the sky. Though at first sight it was merely
dark his eyes gradually resolved it into brownish-purple, turning dull orange on the horizon toward the city centre. Thaw
said, "Why is it that colour?"
"I suppose it's the electric light reflected back from the gas
and soot in the air."
They reached a point halfway between their homes and said
goodbye. After Thaw had gone forward a few yards by himself
he heard a cry from behind. He turned and saw Coulter wave
and shout, "Don't worry! Don't worry! Tae hell with Kate
Caldwell!"

Thaw walked onward with a small perfect image of Kate
Caldwell smiling and beckoning inside him. Such a fog of desperate emotions was wrapped round it that at last he had to
halt and gasp for breath. On the far bank of the canal stood

the vast sheds of the Blochairn ironworks. Dull bangs and clangs
came from these, an orange glare flickered on the sky above
them, the canal water bubbled blackly and wisps of steam
waltzed on the surface and flew in a cloud over the towpath.
A high railing divided the path from the Alexandra park. Taking
a great breath he rushed at this, gripped two spikes on top,
pulled himself up and jumped down onto the golf course. He
ran along the fairways feeling exalted and criminal and came
to a place where trees grew from smooth turf around the pagoda
of an ornamental fountain. The grey lawns with dim galaxies
of daisies on them, the silhouettes of the trees and fountain,
were excitingly unlike themselves as he had seen them on the
way from school a few hours before. Stepping over a "Keep
Off the Grass" sign he went to a tree he had often wished to
climb. It had no branches for the first twelve feet but it was
craggy and crooked and he climbed high into it before the
impetus which had driven him over the railing ran out and
left him astride a high bough with his arms round the trunk.
He recalled Greek stories about female spirits who lived inside
trees. It was possible to imagine that the trunk between his
arms contained the body of a woman. He hugged it, pressed
his face against it and whispered, "I'm here. I'm here. Will
you come out?" He imagined the woman's body pressing the
other side of the bark, her lips wrestling to meet his lips, but
he felt nothing but roughness so he let go and climbed higher
until the branches swung under his feet. Overhead the purple-
brown sky had been pricked by a star or two. He tried to
feel something gentle, permanent and friendly in them until
he felt absurd, then climbed down and went home.

Mrs. Thaw opened the door to him. She said, "Duncan,
how did you get in that mess?"
"What mess?"
"Your face is pot black, pot black all over!"
He went to the bathroom and looked in the mirror. His face
was smeared with sooty grime, especially round the mouth.

CHAPTER 18. Nature

The manageress of the Kinlochrua Hotel was a friend of Mrs. Thaw and invited her children north for the summer holidays. They boarded a bus one morning in a garage on the Broomielaw and it took them through shadows of warehouses and tenements into bright sunlight on the broad, tree-lined Great Western Road. They hurled past Victorian terraces and gardens and hotels, past merchants' villas and municipal housing schemes into a region which (though open to the sky) could not be called country. New factories stood among tracts of weed and thistle, pylons grouped on hillsides and wire fences protected rows of grassy domes joined by metal tubes. The Clyde on their left widened to a firth, the central channel marked by buoys and tiny lighthouses. A long oil tanker moved processionally seaward between tugboats and was passed by a cargo ship going the other way. The hills on the right got steeper and nearer, the road was pinched between the river and a wooded crag, then they saw ahead of them the great rock of Dumbarton upholding the ancient fort above the roofs of the town. The bus turned north up the Vale of Leven, sometimes travelling between fields and sometimes through the crooked streets of industrial villages, then it reached the broad glittering water of Loch Lomond and ran along the western shore. Islands lay with trees, fields and cottages on them like broken-off pieces of the surrounding land, and on the far side arose the great head and shoulders of Ben Lomond. Fields gave way to heather and the islands grew small and rocky. The Loch became a corridor of water between high-sided bens, with the road twisting through trees and boulders at the feet of them.

The bus was full of folk going north for the holidays. Climbers sat at the back singing bawdy mountaineering songs

and Thaw pressed his brow to the cool window and felt desperate. On leaving home he had taken a grain of effedrine and boarded the bus feeling fairly well, but beyond Dumbarton his breathing worsened and now he tried to forget it by concentrating on the ache the vibrating glass made in the bones of his skull. In the passing land outside the colours were raw green or dead grey: grey road, crags and tree trunks, green leaves, grass, bracken and heather. His eyes were sick of dead grey and raw green. The yellow or purple spots of occasional roadside flowers shrieked like tiny discords in an orchestra where every instrument played over and over again the same two notes. Ruth said, "Feeling cheesed off, brother mine?"
"A bit. It's getting worse."
"Cheer up! You'll be fine when we arrive."
"It's not easy."
"Ach, you're too pessimistic. I'm sure you wouldnae get so bad if you were less pessimistic."

The bus stopped on a hillside in Glencoe to let climbers off and the passengers were told they could stretch their legs for five minutes. Thaw got laboriously out and sat on a sun-warmed bank of turf at the roadside. Ruth stood with climbers taking their rucksacks from the boot and talked to someone she had met when climbing with her father. The other passengers gossiped and glanced at the surrounding peaks with expressions of satisfaction or puzzled resentment. An elderly man said to his neighbour, "Aye, a remarkable vista, a remarkable vista."
"You're right. If these stones could talk they would tell us some stories, eh? I bet they could tell us some stories."
"Aye, from scenes like these Auld Scotia's grandeur springs."
Thaw looked upward and saw huge chunks of raw material hacked about by time and weather. From cracks in the highest a rocky rubble spilled over heathery slopes like stuff poured down slag-bings. A boy and girl in shorts and climbing boots strode past him down the road, the boy with a small rucksack bumping between his shoulders. The climbers by the bus cheered and whistled after them: they joined hands and grinned without embarrassment. The assurance of the boy, the ordinary beauty of the girl, the happy ease of both struck a pang of rage and envy into Thaw which almost made him choke. He glared at a granite slab on the turf beside him. It carried patches of lichen the shape, colour and thickness of scabs he had scratched from his thigh the night before. He imagined the

lichen's microscopic roots poking into imperceptible pores in
what seemed a solid surface, making them wider and deeper.
'A disease of the rock,' he thought, 'A disease of matter like
the rest of us.'

Back in the bus Ruth said, "That was Harry Logan and
Sheila. They're going to do the Buchail and spend the night
in Cameron's bothy. I wouldnae mind being Sheila for today.
Not for tonight, but for today." She laughed and said, "Are
you very bad, Duncan? Why not take another pill?"
"I've done that."
Ten minutes later he knew the asthma had grown too strong
for pills and he began fighting it with his only other weapon.
Withdrawing to the centre of his mind he recalled images from
bookshop windows and American comics: a nearly naked
blonde smiling as if her body was a joke she wanted to share,
a cowering dishevelled girl with eyes and mouth apprehensively
open, a big-breasted woman with legs astride and hands on
hips and a sullen selfish stare which seemed to invite the most
selfish kind of assault. His penis stiffened and he breathed easily.
He fixed on the last of these women and her face became
the face of big June Haig. He imagined meeting her in the
precipitous waste landscapes through which the bus was rushing.
She wore white shorts and shirt but high-heeled shoes instead
of climbing boots, and he raped her at great length with complicated mental and physical humiliations. To stop these thoughts
from coming to a climax of masturbation he sometimes
wrenched his mind from them and sat amazed that thought
could make such strong bodily changes. As his penis shrank
the asthma got hard and heavy in chest and throat; then his
mind gripped the image of the woman once more and a tingling
chemical excitement spread again through his blood, widening
all its channels and swelling the penis below and the air passages
above. And behind it all suffocation waited like an unfulfilled
threat.

The bus stopped in a street of uninteresting houses on
the shore of a loch. Thaw and Ruth got out and found their
mother's friend awaiting them in a car. Ruth sat in front beside
her. She was a small lady with a tight mouth and an abrupt
way with the gear lever. Thaw, dumb with sexual broodings,
sat in the back seat hardly listening to the conversation.
"Is Mary still working in that drapery?"
"Yes, Miss Maclaglan."

"A pity. A pity your father can't get a better job. Won't these
open-air organizations he does so much for *pay* him anything?"
"I don't think so. He only works for them in his spare time."
"Hm. Well, I hope you're very helpful to your mother around
the house. She isn't at all well, you know."
Ruth and Thaw gazed out of the window in embarrassment.
The road undulated in slanting sunlight over a great boggy
moor with small irregular lochans in the folds of it. The summit
of a conical peak arose beyond the curve of the moor's horizon,
and Thaw saw, with distaste, it was Ben Rua. To keep sexually
excited he had been forced to imagine increasingly perverse
things and now whatever in the outer world recalled other
experiences upset him by its irrelevance. They came to the
height of the moor and descended toward an arm of the sea
with Kinlochrua on the other side, a strip of cottage-flecked
lands beneath a grey and grey-green mountain. The tide was
out and the clear shallow brine, reflecting blue sky over yellow
sands, made a colour like emeralds. A sudden muffled clattering
hurt their eardrums. Miss Maclaglan said, "They're testing
something at the munition factory. Let's hope it isn't atomic."
"Wasn't the munition factory shut down when the war stopped?"
said Ruth.
"Yes, it was shut for almost a year; then the Admiralty took
it over. They've taken over the hostel too but they haven't
opened it yet, more's the pity. The hostel was the best thing
that ever happened here, it shook up their ideas a bit. Kinlochrua was dead before and it's been dead since. Do you know
that Mary Thaw is the only real friend I've made in the place?
How can you be friendly with women who're afraid to knit
on Sundays because of what the minister will say? What has
nosey old McPhedron to do with their knitting? Your brother
isn't too well, is he?"
Ruth turned and gave Thaw a glance which meant, Pull yourself
together. She said, "He's having one of his wheezy spells, but
he's got pills for it."
"Well, I think he should go straight to bed the moment we
get to the hotel."

    At the hotel Miss Maclaglan showed him upstairs to a small
clean flower-patterned bedroom. He undressed slowly, removing a shoe and staring for ten minutes through the window,
postponing from moment to moment the effort of removing
the next. Outside lay a mossy ill-kept garden hidden by a wing
of the building from the well-kept gardens in front. It was

hemmed in by dark green cypresses and pines. Small paths and hedges were arranged round a square half-stagnant pond with a broken sundial in the middle. The whole place fascinated him with a sense of sluggish malignant life. The hedges were half withered by the grasses pushing up among them; the grasses grew lank and unhealthy in the shadows of the hedges. With more fibrous limbs than the millipede has legs various plants struggled in the poor soil, fighting with blind deliberation to suffocate or strangle each other. Between the roots moved insects, maggots and tiny crustaceans: jointed things with stings and pincers, soft pursy things with hard voracious mouths, hard-backed leggy things with multiple eyes and feelers, all gnawing holes and laying eggs and squirting poisons in the plants and each other. In the corruption of the garden he sensed something friendly to his own malign fantasies. Convulsively, he wrenched off the other shoe, undressed and got into bed. Miss Maclaglan brought in a hot-water bottle and asked if he would like anything to read. He said no, he had his own books. Ruth brought up a meal on a tray. He ate, then lay and masturbated. Ten minutes later he masturbated again. After that he had no weapons to use against the asthma at all.

The garden behind the hotel was overlooked by a dusty porch containing a massive table and some chairs too worn for use inside. Next day he sat there with books and painting tools. Breathing heavily, he made pencil drawings, emphasized the best ones with India ink and tinted the result with watercolours. While he worked the asthma came to bother him less, and as he had hardly slept the night before he shut his eyes, leaned over the table and rested his brow upon clenched fists. He could hear the air lightly stirring the branches of the trees, the infrequent call of a bird and a wasp buzzing in the corner of the porch, but he listened most intently to a murmuring in his own head, a vague remote sound like the conversation of two people in an adjacent room. One speaker was excited and raised his voice so much above the steady drone of the other that Thaw almost heard the words: ". . . ferns and grass what's wonderful about grass . . ."

An external sound made him look up. The minister stood on the sunlit path beyond the shadow of the porch watching him in an interested way. His buttoned-up black figure was as Thaw remembered, but smaller, and the face more kindly. He said, "They tell me you are not well."

"I'm a lot better this morning, thanks."

The minister stepped into the porch and looked at a drawing. "And who is this fellow?"

"Moses on Sinai."

"What a wild wee man he looks among all that rock and thunder. So you are illustrating the bible."

Thaw spoke tonelessly to keep the note of pride out of his voice. "No. I'm illustrating a lecture I'm to give to the school debating society. It's called 'A Personal View of History.' The pictures will be enlarged onto a screen by epedaiescope."

"And what place has Moses in your view of history?"

"He's the first lawyer."

The minister laughed and said, "In a sense, yes, no doubt, Duncan; but then again, in a sense, no. What's this you are reading?" He picked up a thin book with a glossy cover.

"Professor Hoyle's lectures on continuous creation."

The minister sat down on a chair with his hands on the umbrella handle and his chin resting on his hands. "And what does Professor Hoyle tell us about the creation?"

"Well, most astronomers think all the material in the universe was once compressed in a single gigantic atom, which exploded, and all the stars and galaxies in the universe are bits of that old atom. You know that all the galaxies in the universe are rushing away from each other, don't you?"

"I have heard rumours to that effect."

"It's more than rumour, Dr. McPhedron, it's proved fact. Well, Professor Hoyle thinks all the material of the universe is made out of hydrogen, because the hydrogen atom is the simplest form of atom, and he thinks hydrogen atoms are continually coming into existence in the increasing spaces between the stars and forming new stars and galaxies and things."

"Dear me, is that not miraculous! And you believe it?"

"Well, it isn't definitely proved yet, but I like it better than the other theory. It's more optimistic."

"Why?"

"Well, if the first theory is true then one day the stars will burn out and the universe will be nothing but empty space and cold black lumps of rock. But if Professor Hoyle is right there will always be new stars to replace the dead ones."

The minister said politely, "I am fortunate to be rescued from a dying universe at the moment of finding myself menaced by it."

When Thaw had worked out what the minister meant he felt oppressed and angry. He said "Dr. McPhedron, you talk and—

and smile as if everything I say is stupid. What do you believe
in that makes you superior? Is it God?"
The minister said gravely, "I believe in God."
"And that he's good? And made everything? And loves what
he made?"
"I believe those things too."
"Well, why did he make baby cuckoos so that they can only
live by killing baby thrushes? Where's the love in that? Why
did he make beasts that can only live by killing other beasts?
Why did he give us appetites that we can only satisfy by hurting
each other?"
The minister grinned and said, "Dear me. God himself might
be afraid to sit an examination like this. However, I'll do my
best. You talk, Duncan, as if I believed that the world as it is
is the work of God. That is not true. The world was made
by God, and made beautiful. God gave it to man to look after
and keep beautiful, and man gave it to the Devil. Since then
the world has been the Devil's province, and an annexe of
Hell, and everyone born into it is damned. We have either
to earn our bread by the sweat of our brow or steal it from
our neighbours. In either case we live in a state of anxiety,
and the more intelligent we are the more we feel our damnation
and the more anxious we become. You, Duncan, are intelligent.
Mibby you've been searching the world for a sign of God's
existence. If so, you have found nothing but evidence of his
absence, or less, for the spirit ruling the material world is callous
and malignant. The only proof that our Creator is good lies
in our dissatisfaction with the world (for if the God of nature
had made us the life of nature would suit us) and in the works
and words of Jesus Christ, someone you may have read of.
Has Christ a place in your view of history?"
"Yes," said Thaw boldly. "I regard him as the first man to
make a religion of the equal worth of each individual."
"I'm glad you present him as something so respectable, but
he's more than that. He is the way, the truth and the life. To
find God you must believe Christ *was* God and discard every
other knowledge as useless and vain. Then you must pray for
grace."
Thaw shifted several times uncomfortably during this speech,
for it embarrassed him; also, he was finding it hard to keep
his eyes open. After a half minute of silence he realized a question was expected and said, "What's grace?"
"The Kingdom of Heaven in your own heart. The sure knowledge that you are no longer damned. Freedom from anxiety.

God does not send it to all believers, and to few believers for very long."

"Do you mean that even if I become a Christian I can never be sure of . . . of . . ."

"Salvation. Dear me, no. God is not a reasonable man like your grocer or bank manager, giving an ounce of salvation for an ounce of belief. You can't bargain with him. He offers no guarantee. I see I am boring you, Duncan, and I'm sorry for it, though I've said nothing that almost every Scotsman did not take for granted from the time of John Knox till two or three generations back, when folk started believing the world could be improved."

Thaw held his head between his hands feeling depressed and dull. The minister's answer was more thorough than he had expected and he felt trapped by it. Though certain there were many sound counter arguments, the only one he could think of was "What about the cuckoos?"

The minister looked puzzled.

"Why did God make cuckoos so that they have to live by killing thrushes? Did they give the world to the Devil too? Or did the thrushes?"

The minister got up and said, "The life of brute beasts, Duncan, is so different from ours that strong feelings for them are bound to be vanity and self-deception. Even your father the atheist would agree with me in that. I understand you will be here a week or two. Mibby we can discuss these matters another time. Meanwhile, I hope you have better health."

"Thank you," said Thaw. He pretended to scribble on a piece of paper till the minister had gone then folded his arms on the edge of the table and laid his head on them. He was very tired but if he lost consciousness for a moment the beast of suffocation might pounce on his chest, so he tried to rest without actually sleeping. This was difficult. He got up, collected his things and went slowly to bed.

That afternoon his memory of what is was like to be well faded and hope of improvement faded with it. The only imaginable future was a repetition of a present which had shrunk to a tiny painful act, a painful breath drawn again and again from an ocean of breath. No longer companioning erotic fancies (which, like the pills, had got useless through overuse) the sluggish resolute life of the garden grated on him as it grated on the soil feeding it. He felt the natural world stretching out from each wall of the hotel in great tracts of lumpy earth and rock coated thickly with *life,* a stuff whose parts renewed themselves by eating each other. Two or three hundred miles to the south was a groove in the earth with a gathering of stone and metal in it—Glasgow. In Glasgow he had been aided a little by a feeling that among many people someone might hear and help if he screamed loudly enough. But among these mountains screaming was useless; his pain was as irrelevant as the pain of the thrush starved out by the cuckoo, the snail crushed by the thrush. He started screaming but stopped at once. He tried to think but his thoughts were trapped by the minister's speech. How could the world be justified except as punishment? Punishment for what?

That evening Miss Maclaglan phoned for a doctor. He entered Thaw's room and sat by the bed, a not quite middle-aged man in plus fours with a black moustache and squarish head sunk so far into his shoulders that he seemed unable to move it independently of his body. He took Thaw's pulse and temperature, asked how long he had been like this and grunted sombrely. Miss Maclaglan brought a pan of boiling water with a small metal cage clipped inside it. He took glass and metal parts from the cage, fitted them together into a hypodermic syringe, filled this from a rubber-capped bottle then asked Thaw to pull up his pyjama sleeve. Thaw stared at a corner of the ceiling, trying to think of nothing but a crack in it. He felt the muscle of his upper arm wiped with something cold and then the needle running in. The steel point breaking through layers of tissue set his teeth on edge. There was a faint ache as the muscle swelled with pumped-in fluid, then the needle was withdrawn and an amazing thing started to happen. There spread through his body from the arm, but this time unsustained by thought, the tingling liberating flood he had only been able to make erotically. Each nerve, muscle, joint and limb relaxed, his lungs expanded with sufficient air, he sneezed twice and lay back feeling altogether comfortable and well. There was no sense of asthma waiting to return. He could not believe he would ever be unwell again. He looked out into the sun-warm garden. An overgrown rosebush beside the pond had put out white blossoms, and the black dot of a bee moved over one. Surely the bee was enjoying itself? Surely the bush grew because it liked to grow? Everything in the garden seemed to have grown to its appropriate height and now rested a moment, preserved in the amber light of the evening sun. The garden looked *healthy.* Thaw turned with servile gratitude to the ordinary depressed-looking man who had made this change in things. The doctor was examining books and drawings on the bedside table and frowning slightly. He said, "Any better?"

"Yes, thanks. Thanks a lot. I'm a lot better. I can sleep now."

"Mm. I suppose you know that your kind of asthma is partly a psychological illness."

"Yes."

"You do a lot of reading, don't you?"

"Yes."

"Do you abuse yourself?"

"Certainly, if I've been stupid in public."

"No no. I mean, do you masturbate?"

Thaw's face went red. He stared down at the quilt.

"Yes."

"How often?"

"Four or five times a week."

"Mm. That's quite often. It's not widely agreed upon yet, but there is evidence that nervous diseases are aggravated by masturbation. The inmates of lunatic asylums, for instance, masturbate very often indeed. I would try to cut it out if I were you."

"Yes. Yes, I will."

"Here's a bottle of isoprenaline tablets. If you get bad again, break one in two and let half dissolve under your tongue. I think you'll find it'll help."

Thaw was left feeling faintly worried, but fell asleep almost at once.

He woke late at night and worse than ever. The isoprenaline tablets had no effect and the image of June Haig occurred to him, potent and burning like a hot poker in the blood of his stomach. He thought, 'If only I think things about her it will be all right. I don't need to masturbate.' He thought things about her and masturbated ten minutes later. The beast of suffocation pounced at once. He clenched his fists against his chest and dragged breath into it with a gargling sound. Fear became panic and broke his mind into a string of gibbering half-thoughts that would not form: I can't you are I won't it does it will drowning no no no no drowning in no no no no air I can't you are it does. . . .

A thundering hum filled his brain. He was about to faint when a sudden thought formed complete—*If I deserve this it is good*—and around the thought his mind began exultingly to reassemble. He grinned into the bulb of the bedside lamp. He was

in pain, but not afraid. Breathing hoarsely, he took a notebook
and pen from the bedside table and wrote in big shapeless
words:

> *Lord God you exist you exist my punishment proves it. My*
> *punishment is not more than I can bear what I suffer is*
> *just already the pain is less because I know it is just I*
> *won't ever do that thing again, it will be a hard fight but*
> *with your help I am able for it I won't ever do that thing*
> *again.*

Next day he did it three times. Miss Maclaglan sent a
telegram to his mother, who came north by bus the day after.
She stood by the bed and smiled sadly down at him. "So you're
not too well, son."
He smiled back.
"Ach," she said, "You're a poor auld man. Get a bit better
and I'll stay on with you awhile. It'll be an excuse for me to
have a holiday too."
He was moved to a big low-ceilinged room with two beds in
it. One was his, and Ruth and his mother shared the other.
That night when the lights were out Ruth said, "Sing to us,
Mummy. It's a long time since you sang to us."
Mrs. Thaw sang some lullabies and sentimental lowland songs:
Ca' the Yowes, Hush-a-baw Birdie, This is No' My Plaid. She
had once won certificates at musical festivals with her singing,
but now she only managed the high notes by singing
them very softly, almost in a whisper. She tried to sing *Bonnie*
George Campbell, which starts with a loud wild lamenting note,
but her voice cracked and went tuneless and she stopped and
laughed: "Ach, it's beyond me now. I'm getting an auld
woman."
"No! you're not!" Thaw and Ruth shouted together. Her words
alarmed them. She said, "I think we should try to sleep."
He lay against his pillows breathing heavily. When he coughed
Mrs. Thaw said hopefully, "That's right son, bring it up," and
afterward, "There now, that's better, isn't it?"
But he had brought up hardly anything, and nothing was better,
and the sense of her lying awake attending to the pains in
his chest made them harder to bear. He tried to be as still as
possible, keeping the small lumps in his gullet until the silence
from the other bed made him think she was asleep, but as
soon as he coughed, however stealthily, the creak of a mattress
told him she was awake and listening.

Suddenly he was sitting up and laughing in the darkness. He had been thinking about the key, or perhaps dreaming of it, and now he saw the universe and the meaning of things. It was hard to put his vision into words but he wanted to share it. "Everything is hate," he gabbled dreamily. "We are all hate, big balloons of hate. Tied together by Ruth's hair ribbons."

The two women screamed. Mrs. Thaw said in a high-pitched voice, "That settles it. We're going back. We're going back tomorrow. There must be *somebody* who knows how to cure him."

Ruth yelled, "You're selfish, utterly selfish! You just don't care about anyone but yourself!" and started crying. Thaw felt puzzled, knowing the words had not conveyed what he meant to convey. He tried again.

"Men are pies that bake and eat themselves, and the recipe is hate. I seem to be buried in this rockery . . ." for though he could dimly see the bedroom, and knew where his mother and sister lay, he also felt buried up to the armpits in a heap of earth and rocks. Mrs. Thaw shouted, "Shut up! Shut up!"

Next morning Thaw and his mother returned to Glasgow. Ruth was allowed to stay behind. That day a boat called at Kinlochrua and Miss Maclaglan drove them to the pier and waved from it as they put to sea. The sun shone as bright as when he had arrived five days before, and for the first time since arriving he saw the great green side of Ben Rua. A clean hard wind was blowing. A member of the crew, a thin boy of Thaw's age, leaned against the funnel playing a concertina. Gulls with spread wings hung above in the rushing air. Thaw sat on a ventilator which stuck out of the deck like an aluminium toadstool, and nearby his mother waved to the figure on the receding pier. On the mountaintop he could make out the white dot of the triangulation point. He thought of the previous night and tried to recover from the muddle of darkness and crying his vision of the key. He seemed to have thought that, just as hydrogen was the basic stuff of the universe, so hatred was the basic material of the mind. In the fresh sunlight it was not a convincing idea. He felt amazingly weak, yet liberated, and while sitting still was not conscious of asthma at all.

Two days later Thaw walked jauntily into town with Coulter to visit the Art Galleries. He talked about the visit to Kinlochrua and what the doctor said. Coulter became angry. "That's daft!" he said. "Everybody masturbates at our age. It's natural. We produce the stuff; how else can we get rid of it? Five times a week sounds about normal to me."

"But that doctor said that in lunatic asylums they do it all the time."

"I believe him. Lunatics are like us. They arenae allowed to have sex in other ways. And what else can they do with their time?"

"But whenever I do it nowadays I have another attack."

"I can believe it. That doctor made you think you would have asthma when you masturbate so you have asthma. Anybody can make you believe anything if they try hard enough. I remember once making you think I was a German spy."

Thaw started grinning. "The funny thing is," he said, "that doctor had me believing in God as well."

"How? No, don't tell me, I see how," said Coulter with disgust, "I bet you felt very special and superior, being punished by God for something he doesnae give a damn for in other folk. Well, I hate to disappoint you, but ye may as well leave God and masturbation out of it and go back to having asthma in the normal way."

CHAPTER 19.
Mrs. Thaw Disappears

Thaw opened his diary and wrote:

"Love seeketh not itself to please Nor for itself hath any care But for another gives its ease and builds a Heaven in Hell's despair." So sung a little Clod of Clay trodden by the cattle's feet, but a Pebble of the brook warbled out these metres meet. "Love seeketh only Self to please, to bind another to Its delight, Joys in another's loss of ease, and builds a Hell in Heaven's despite."

Blake doesn't choose, he shows both sorts of love, and life would be easy if women were clods and men were pebbles. Maybe most of them are but I'm a gravelly mixture. My pebble feelings are all for June Haig, no, not real June Haig, an imaginary June Haig in a world without sympathy or conscience. My feelings for Kate Caldwell are cloddish, I want to please and delight her, I want her to think me clever and fascinating. I love her in such a servile way that I'm afraid to go near her. This afternoon Mum was operated on for something to do with her liver. It seems that for the past year or two old Doctor Poole has been treating her for the wrong illness. I'm ashamed to notice that yesterday I forgot to record that she'd been taken into hospital. I must be a very cold selfish kind of person. If Mum died I honestly don't think I'd feel much about it. I can't think of anyone, Dad, Ruth, Robert Coulter, whose death would much upset or change me. Yet when reading a poem by Poe last week, Thou wast that all to me, love, for which my soul did pine, etc., I felt a very poignant strong sense of loss and wept six tears, four with the left eye, two with the right. Mum isn't going to die of course but this coldness of mine is a bit alarming.

They entered a vast ward in the Royal Infirmary flooded, through tall windows, with grey light from the sky outside. Mrs. Thaw leaned on her pillows looking sick and gaunt yet oddly young. Many lines of strain had been washed from her face by the anaesthetic. She looked more mournful than usual but less worried. Thaw got behind the bed and carefully combed the hair which lay matted around her head and neck. He took a strand at a time in his left hand and combed with the right, noticing how its darkness had been given a dusty look by the grey threads in it. He could think of nothing to say and the combing gave a feeling of closeness without the strain of words. Mr. Thaw said, holding his wife's hand and looking through a nearby window, "You've quite a view from here."

Below them stood the old soot-eaten Gothic cathedral in a field of flat black gravestones. Beyond rose the hill of the Necropolis, its sides cut into by the porches of elaborate mausoleums, the summit prickly with monuments and obelisks. The topmost monument was a pillar carrying a large stone figure of John Knox, hatted, bearded, gowned and upholding in his right hand an open granite book. The trees between the tombs were leafless, for it was late autumn. Mrs. Thaw smiled and whispered wanly, "I saw a funeral go in there this morning." "No, it's not a very cheery outlook."

Mr. Thaw explained to his children that it would be weeks before their mother was well enough to come home and some months after that before she was able to leave her bed. The household would need to be reorganized, its duties distributed between the three of them. This reorganization was never effectively managed. Thaw and Ruth quarrelled too much about who should do what; moreover, Thaw was sometimes prevented by illness from working at all and Ruth thought this a trick to make her work harder and called him a lazy hypocrite. Eventually nearly all the housework was done by Mr. Thaw, who washed and ironed the clothes at the weekend, made breakfast in the morning and kept things vaguely tidy. Meanwhile, the surfaces of linoleum, furniture and windows became dirtier and dirtier.

At Whitehill School the pressure of work seemed to slacken for Thaw. The Higher Leaving Examination, the culmination of five years of schooling, was a few months away, and all around him his schoolmates crouched over desks and burrowed like moles into their studies. He watched them with the passionless regret with which he saw them play football or go to dances: the activity itself did not interest, but the power to share it would have made him less apart. The teachers had stopped attending to pupils who would certainly pass or certainly fail and were concentrating on the borderline cases, so he was allowed to study the subjects he liked (art, english, history) according to his pleasure, and in Latin or mathematics classes sat writing or sketching in a notebook as far from the teacher as possible. After Christmas he was told he would not be put forward for his leaving certificate in Latin, and this gave an extra six hours a week to use as he pleased. He used them for art. The art department was in whitewashed low-ceilinged rooms at the top of the building, and nowadays he spent most of his time there making an illuminated version of the Book of Jonah. Sometimes the art teacher, a friendly old man, looked over his shoulder to ask a question.

"Er . . . is this meant to be humorous, Duncan?"

"No sir."

"Why have you given him a bowler hat and umbrella?"

"What's humorous about bowler hats and umbrellas?"

"Nothing! I use an umbrella myself, in wet weather. . . . Do you mean to do anything special with this when you have completed it?"

Thaw meant to give it to Kate Caldwell. He mumbled, "I don't know."

"Well, I think you should make it less elaborate and finish it as soon as possible. No doubt it will impress the examiner, but he's more likely to be impressed by another still life or a drawing of a plaster cast."

Occasionally at playtime he went onto the balcony outside the art room and looked into the hall below where the captain of the football team, the school swimming champion and several prefects usually stood laughing and chatting with Kate Caldwell, who sat with a girlfriend on the edge of a table under the war memorial. Her laughter and hushed breathless voice floated up to him; he thought of going down and joining them, but his arrival would produce an expectant silence and revive the rumour that he loved her.

One day he came from the art room and saw her walk along the balcony on the other side of the hall. She smiled and waved and on an impulse he glared back timidly, opened the door behind him and beckoned. She came round, smiling

with her mouth open. He said, "Would you like to see what
I'm doing? In art, I mean?"

"Oh, that would be lovely, Duncan."

The only other student in the art room was a prefect called
MacGregor Ross who was copying a sheet of Roman lettering.
Thaw brought a folder of work from a locker and laid the
pictures one after another on a desk in front of her.

"Christ arguing with the doctors in the temple," he said. "The
mouth of Hell. This is a fantastic landscape. Mad flowers. These
are illustrations I did for a debating society lecture. . . ."

She greeted each picture with small gasps of admiration and
surprise. He showed her the unfinished Book of Jonah. She
said, "That's wonderful, Duncan, but why have you given him
a bowler hat and an umbrella?"

"Because he was that kind of man. Jonah is the only prophet
who didn't want to be a prophet. God forced it on him. I
see him as a fat middle-aged man with a job in an insurance
office, someone naturally quiet and mediocre whom God has
to goad into courage and greatness."

Kate nodded dubiously.

"I see. And what will you do with it when it's finished?"

Duncan's heart started thumping against his ribs. He said, "I'll
mibby give it to you. If you'd like it."

She smiled flashingly and said, "Oh, thank you, Duncan, I'd
love to have it. That's wonderful of you. It really is. . . . And
what are *you* so busy with?" she asked, going over to MacGregor
Ross. She pulled a stool up to MacGregor Ross's desk and
spent twenty minutes with her head close beside his while he
showed her how to use a lettering pen.

Mrs. Thaw left the Infirmary early in the new year. Mrs.
Gilchrist downstairs and one or two other neighbours came
into the house to prepare it for her, and dusted, washed and
polished into the obscurest corner of every room.

"You'll have to be specially nice to your mother and help
her all you can now," they said severely. "Remember, she
won't be able to leave bed for a long time."

"Interfering old bitches," said Ruth.

"They mean well," said Thaw tolerantly. "They just have an
unfortunate way of putting things."

Mrs. Thaw came home by ambulance and was tucked into the
big bed in the front bedroom. She was allowed to sit by the
fire in the evenings and soon gained enough strength for her
children to quarrel with her without feeling very guilty. Thaw

brought home the completed "Book of Jonah." She took it on her knee, looked thoughtfully through, asked him to explain certain details then said seriously, "You know, Duncan, you would make a good minister."

"A minister? Why a minister?"

"You have a minister's way of talking about things. What are you going to do with this?"

"I'm giving it to Kate Caldwell."

"Kate Caldwell! Why? *Why?*"

"Because I love her."

"Don't be stupid, Duncan. What do you know about love? And she certainly won't appreciate it. Ruth tells me she's nothing but a wee flirt."

"I'm not giving it to her because she'll appreciate it. I'm giving it because I love her."

"That's stupid. Totally stupid. You'll have the whole school laughing at you."

"The school's laughter is no concern of mine."

"Then you're a bigger fool than I thought. You've no sense or pride or backbone at all and you'll marry and be made miserable by the first silly girl who takes a fancy to ye."

"You're probably right."

"But I shouldn't be right! You ought not to let me be right! Why can't you . . . oh, I give up. I give up. I give up."

The skin disease returned and his throat looked as if he had made an incompetent effort to cut it. Each morning he went to his mother's bedside and she wound a silk scarf tightly round up to his chin and fixed it with small safety pins, giving his head and shoulders a rigid look. One morning he entered a classroom and found Kate Caldwell's eyes upon him. Perhaps she had expected someone else to come in, or perhaps she had looked to the door in a moment of unfocused reverie, but her face took on a soft look of involuntary pity, and seeing it he was filled by pure hatred. It stamped his face with an implacable glare which stayed for a second after the emotion faded. Kate looked puzzled, then turned with a toss of the head to some gossiping friends. That night, without any sense of elation, Thaw gave the "Book of Jonah" to Ruth and afterward sat glumly by his mother's bed.

"Do you know something, Duncan?" said Mrs. Thaw. "Ruth will appreciate that a thousand times more than Kate Caldwell."

"I know. I know," he said. There was an ache between his heart and stomach as if something had been removed.

"Ach, son, son," said Mrs. Thaw, holding out her arms to him, "never mind about Kate Caldwell. Ye've always your auld mither."
He laughed and embraced her saying, "Yes, mither, I know, but it's not the same thing, it's not the same thing at all."

The Higher Leaving Examination arrived and he sat it with no sense of special occasion. In the invigilated silence of the examination room he glanced through the mathematics paper and grinned, knowing he would fail. It would be too conspicuous to get up and walk out at once so he amused himself by trying to solve two or three problems using words instead of numbers and writing out the equations like dialectical arguments, but he was soon bored with this, and confronting the supervising teacher's raised and condemning eyebrows with an absentminded stare he handed in his papers and went upstairs to the art room. The other examinations were as easy as he had expected.

Mrs. Thaw had grown gradually stronger but at the time of the exams she caught a slight cold and this caused a setback. She only got up now to go to the lavatory. Mr. Thaw said, "Don't you think you should use the bedpan?"
She laughed and said, "When I can't go to the lavatory myself I'll know I'm done for."
One evening when Thaw was alone with her in the house she said, "Duncan, what's the living room like?"
"It's quite warm. There's a good fire on. It's not too untidy."
"I think I'll get up and sit by the fire for a bit."
She pulled the bedclothes back and put her legs down over the edge of the bed. Thaw was disturbed to see how thin they were. The thick woollen stockings he pulled on for her would not stay up but hung in folds round her ankles.
"Just like two sticks," she said, smiling. "I've turned into a Belsen horror."
"Don't be *daft!*" said Thaw. "There's nothing wrong that another month won't cure."
"I know, son, I know. It's a long, slow process."
At this time Thaw slept with his father in the bed settee. He did not sleep well, for the mattress had a hollow in the middle which Mr. Thaw, being heavier, naturally filled, and Thaw found it hard not to roll down on top of him. One night after the lights were out he remarked how pleasant it would be to get back to the usual sleeping arrangements when his

mother was better. After a pause, Mr. Thaw said strangely,
"Duncan, I hope you're not . . . hoping too much that your
mother will get better."
Thaw said lightly, "Oh, where there's life there's hope."
"Duncan, there's no hope. You see, the operation was too
late. She's been recovering from the effects of the operation,
but it's a recovery that can't last. Her liver is too badly dam-
aged."
Thaw said, "When will she die then?"
"In a month. Mibby in two months. It depends on the strength
of her heart. You see, the liver isn't cleaning the blood, so
her body is getting less and less nourishment."
"Does she know?"
"No. Not yet."
Thaw turned his face away and wept a little in the darkness.
His tears were not particularly passionate, just a weak bleeding
of water at the eyes.

He was wakened by a crash and a great cry. They found
his mother struggling on the lobby floor. She had been trying
to go to the lavatory. "Ach, Daddy, I'm done. I'm done. Finished," she said as Mr. Thaw helped her back to bed. Thaw
stood transfixed at the living-room door, his brain ringing with
echoes of the cry. At the moment of waking to it he had felt
it was not an unexpected thing, but something heard ages ago
which he had waited all his life to hear again.

Two days later Thaw and Ruth came home from school
together and had the door opened to them by Mr. Thaw. He
said, "Your mother has something to tell you."
They entered the bedroom. Mr. Thaw stood by the door watching. The bed had been moved to the window to give her a
view of the street, and she lay with her face toward them and
said timidly, "Ruth, Duncan, I think that one day soon I'll
just . . . just sleep away and not wake up."
Ruth gasped and ran from the room and Mr. Thaw followed
her. Thaw went to the bed and lay on it between his mother
and the window. He felt below the covers for her hand and
held it. After a while she said, "Duncan, do you think there's
anything afterwards?"
He said, "No, I don't think so. It's just sleep."
Something wistful in the tone of the question made him add,
"Mind you, many wiser folk than me have believed there's a
new life afterwards. If there is, it won't be worse than this
one."

For several days on returning from school he took his shoes off and lay beside his mother holding her hand. It would have been untrue to say he felt unhappy. At these times he hardly thought or felt at all, and did not talk, for Mrs. Thaw was becoming unable to talk. Usually he looked out at the street. Although joining a main road it was a quiet street and usually lit by cold spring sunshine. The houses opposite were semi-detached villas with lilacs and a yellow laburnum tree in the gardens. If he felt anything it was a quietness and closeness amounting to contentment. During this time Ruth, who had never taken much interest in household things, became very busy at cleaning and cooking and made her mother many light sorts of foods and pastries, but soon Mrs. Thaw had to be nourished on nothing but fluids and was too weak to speak clearly or open her eyes. Nobody in the household talked much, but once Thaw made a remark to his sister beginning. "When Mummy's dead . . ."

"She's not going to die."

"But Ruth . . ."

"She's not *going* to die. She's going to get better," said Ruth, staring at him brightly.

At school oral examinations were held to corroborate the results of the written exams. The English teacher told his students to learn by heart some passages of prose, preferably from the bible, since they might be asked to recite aloud. Thaw decided to shock the examiner by learning the erotic verses from the Song of Solomon which begin, "Behold thou art fair, my love, behold thou art very fair." On the morning of the English oral he went after breakfast to say cheerio to his mother. Mr. Thaw was sitting by the bed holding one of her hands between both of his. She lay back on the pillows, a line of white showing below her almost closed eyelids. She was mumbling desperately, "I aw ie, I aw ie."

"All right, all right, Mary," said Mr. Thaw. "You won't die. You won't die."

"Uh I *aw* ie, I *aw* ie."

"Don't worry, you're not going to die, you're not going to die."

For the first time in two weeks Mrs. Thaw shuddered and sat up. Her eyes opened to the full, she pulled her lips back from her teeth and shrieked, "I want to die! I want to die!" and fell back. Thaw collapsed on a chair, holding his head between his hands and sobbing loudly. Ten minutes later he ran to

school across the sunlit slope of the park, loudly chanting verses from the Song of Solomon. When he got home that afternoon Mrs. Thaw lay more quiet and still than ever and breathed with a faint wheezy sound. He put his lips to her ear and whispered urgently, "Mum! Mum! I've passed in English. I've got Higher English."
A faint smile moved her mouth, then sank into her blind face like water into sand. Next morning when Mrs. Gilchrist downstairs came in to wash her and pulled the curtain behind the bed she heard a very faint whisper: "Another day," but in the afternoon word that Thaw had passed in Art and History did not reach the living part of her brain, or else she had grown indifferent.

She died three days later, very early on a Saturday morning. The previous night Mrs. Gilchrist downstairs and Mrs. Wishaw from across the landing sat waiting in the living room and did not move out when Thaw went to bed there. Mr. Thaw sat in the bedroom holding his wife's hand. When Thaw awoke the light was filtering through the curtains and the neighbours had left and he knew his mother was dead. He got up, dressed, ate a bowl of cornflakes and switched the wireless on to a comedy programme. Mr. Thaw came in and said, slightly embarrassed, "Would you mind turning it down a bit, Duncan? The neighbours might be offended if they heard."
Thaw switched off the wireless and went for a walk to the canal. He stood at the edge of a deep stone channel and watched without thought or feeling the foam-flecked water swirl between rotting timbers.

In the afternoon he called on Coulter as he had arranged to do some while before. Mrs. Coulter had taken her husband for a walk, and Thaw sat by the fire while Coulter, in vest and trousers, washed at the sink. Thaw said awkwardly, "By the way, Bob, my mother died last night."
Coulter turned slowly round. He said "You're joking, Duncan."
"No."
"But I saw her two weeks ago. She was talking to me. She seemed all right."
"Aye."
Coulter towelled his hands, looking at Thaw closely. He said, "You shouldn't hold it in, Duncan. It'll be worse for you later."
"I don't think I'm holding anything in."

Coulter pulled a shirt and pullover on and said in a worried way, "The bother is, I arranged tae meet Sam Lang at Tollcross playing fields at three. We were going to do some running practice. I thought you wouldnae mind coming along."

"I don't mind coming along."

When he got home the undertaker had called. A coffin lay on a pair of trestles on the rug before the bedroom fireplace. The lid was placed to leave a square hole at the top and Mrs. Thaw's face stuck up through the hole. Thaw looked at it with puzzled distaste. The features had been his mother's but though he saw no difference in the shape all resemblance had vanished. The thing was without even the superficial life of a work of art and its material lacked the integrity of bronze or clay. He touched the brow with a fingertip and felt cold bone under the cold skin. This dense pack of dead tissues was not his mother's face. It was nobody's face.

In the days before the funeral the bedroom was pervaded by a sweet fusty odour which spread to other parts of the house. Air fresheners of the kind used in lavatories were placed under the coffin but made little difference. On Tuesday the minister of Mrs. Thaw's church conducted a short service in the living room while the coffin was screwed tight and taken deftly downstairs to the hearse. The living room was crowded with neighbours and old friends and relatives whom Thaw had heard his parents speak of but hardly ever met. Twice or thrice during the service the door was furtively opened and those beside it shifted to admit a stealthily breathing old man or woman. Thaw stood by the sideboard wearing his newest suit. It struck him that the minister had not visited his mother during the last weeks, and this not through failure of duty (he was a young earnest nervous man) but because his presence would have been an intrusion. To Mrs. Thaw and her friends the church had been a gathering place. They went to a service on Sunday, and on Thursday to a social club in the church hall, but none could have been accused of piety. Mrs. Thaw had been shocked when, some years before, Thaw called himself an atheist, but no more shocked than when, shortly afterward, he called himself a Christian and started turning the other cheek in his fights with Ruth. A phrase came into his head: "The consolations of religion." As far as he could see, his mother had lived and died without consolations of any kind at all.

The service ended and he went down to the cars with his father, the minister and a few others. The cars were shining black Rolls-Royces with silent engines and as they sped through the streets of the northern suburbs he looked out of the window feeling comfortable and privileged. It was a grey day, a lid of grey sky had shut down on Glasgow and thin smirr fell from it. They came to a municipal cemetery so precisely on the edge of the city that on three sides it was surrounded by open fields. There was a delay at the gate. The cars halted in a line behind the cars of a funeral party ahead. After a while the cars in front disappeared and they went up a curving drive between dripping rhododendrons and stopped outside a miniature Victorian-gothic church with a smokestack behind. More neighbours and relatives were waiting at the porch and followed Thaw and his father inside. They stood in the front row of pews and everyone else crowded into the pews behind. Just before them was a tall pulpit, and to the right of it a low platform with the coffin on top. Coffin and platform were covered by a heavy red cloth. After a moment of silence Thaw began to wonder why nobody sat down. The same thought must have struck his father, for he sat down and everyone followed his example. The minister, in the black gown and white bands of a doctor of divinity, climbed into the pulpit, said a prayer and announced a hymn. Everyone stood and sang and sat down again. The minister produced a sheet of paper and said, "Before we proceed with the service I have been asked—er, to read this to you:

"During the last few months of her illness Mary Thaw was completely confined to her bed. I would like to thank those many good friends and neighbours who made these months as pleasant for her as they could. They brought gifts of fruit and of cake, and the even more precious gift of their company. I would like to tell them on her behalf how very much she appreciated their attentions, and to extend to them the thanks that she herself is unable to extend today."

In the pews behind somebody sniffed and blew their nose. Thaw looked sideways at his father and whispered, "That was very good." The service continued. At the words "Dust to dust and ashes to ashes," there began a lumbering rumbling sound and the red cloth began to sag as the coffin was drawn down under it. For a second it bulged up again with a rush of air from below, then flopped so that a rectangular depression appeared where the coffin had been. Thaw was struck by a poignant sense of loss neutralized at once by a memory of a conjuror who had made a scone disappear from under a hand-kerchief.

Outside the church people squared their shoulders and began talking in loud cheerful voices.

"Well, that didn't go too badly, did it?"

"A beautiful service, beautiful."

"Hullo, hullo! There's a voice I've not heard in many a long day. How are ye, Jim?"

"No' too bad. A beautiful service, wasn't it?"

"Aye, beautiful. I liked that bit the minister read out in the middle."

"Ye cannae beat good neighbours."

"Aye, but she deserved good neighbours. She was one hersel'."

"Who's that waiting by the gate? Don't tell me it's auld Neil Bannerman?"

"Aye, it's Neil Bannerman."

"My God, he looks done. Really done. Fancy auld Neil Bannerman surviving Mary Thaw. Last time I saw him was at her father's funeral ten years back."

"Is it true, er, there's a quantity of refreshment, er, available somewhere?"

"Aye, man, there's a tea laid on at the Grand Hotel at Charing Cross. Come in my car."

The male relations gathered in a private room of a hotel in Sauchiehall Street and ate a high tea of cold ham and warm vegetables. They chattered about old acquaintances and football and the days when the local churches had their own football teams. Thaw sat silent among them. At one point Bernard Shaw was mentioned and he was asked to tell an anecdote about him. It was well received. Afterward he returned with his father in someone's car. The rain was falling heavily now. He thought how pleasant it would be to get home and sit by the bedroom fire drinking tea with his mother, then remembered this was impossible.

Mr. Thaw wanted his wife's ashes scattered on a hillside overlooking Loch Lomond where they had walked together in their courting days. One windy and sunny spring morning he journeyed with his children to Loch Lomond by train. Thaw held the oblong deal box with the ashes in it upon his knee.

The lid lacked hinge or fastening, and he raised it once or twice and looked curiously at the soft grey stuff inside. It was exactly like cigarette ash. Mr. Thaw said, "Be careful, Duncan." Duncan said, "Yes, we don't want to spill her before we get there."

He was surprised to see his father look shocked. They climbed the hillside by a stony lane sunk among bracken and budding hedges. Higher up this became a cart track over a green field, then they went through a gap in a dry-stone dyke and it became a sandy path among heather with curlews crying around it. Near the path lay a flat rock with a hole in the middle where the Colquhoun clan once stuck their banner pole when gathering to fight.

"I suppose this place is as good as any," said Mr. Thaw.

They sat and rested, looking down on the loch and the green islands in it. Northward the jagged wall of the highland bens looked distinct and solid enough to bang the knuckles against. They waited till a young couple who had paused to see the view passed out of sight, then opened the box and flung handfuls of ash into the air. The wind whisked it away like smoke into the heather.

A fortnight after Mr. Thaw sat at his desk in the living room and said, "Duncan, come here. I want ye to look at this. It's the bill for your mother's funeral. A fantastic figure, isn't it? You'd think cremation would be a lot cheaper than burial, but no. The costs are practically the same."

Thaw looked at the bill and said, "Aye, it does look a bit extravagant."

"Well, I'm not going to have that sum of money wasted on me, so I'm arranging to give my body to science. Would ye sign this paper? It's to prove that as next of kin you have no objection."

Thaw signed.

"Good. The arrangement is that when I die you inform the medical faculty of the university and they call and collect me with an iron coffin. If you do that within twenty-four hours, you and Ruth will be given ten pounds to divide between you, so you see it's not only cheaper, it's profitable."

"I'll spend the money drinking to the health of your memory," said Thaw.

"If you've sense you'll spend it otherwise."

Almost a year later Thaw was looking through a drawer when he found a letter in his mother's handwriting. It was written very faintly in pencil and was a rough draft of a letter she probably never got round to sending. It was superscribed to the correspondence page of a cheap woman's magazine.

I have enjoyed very much the letters from your readers telling about the funny mistakes some children make. I wonder if you would like to print an experience of mine. When my wee son was six or seven, we left the house one night quite late and were looking up at the stars. Suddenly Duncan said, "Where's the tractor?" His father had been teaching him the names of the stars, and he had got mixed up with the plough. I have not been very well recently and have had to spend most of the time in bed. I find my main pleasure nowadays in memories like these.

Thaw stood awhile with the letter in his hand. He remembered the night she spoke of. It had been at the hostel in Kinlochrua at Christmas. The family had been going to a concert in the main building, and the question had been asked by Ruth. Mrs. Thaw had always preferred him to Ruth and had unconsciously transferred the incident. He put back the letter and shut the drawer. Grief pulled at an almost unconscious corner of his mind like a puppy trying to attract its master's attention by tugging the hem of his coat.

CHAPTER 20. Employers

The Higher Leaving Examination results were not yet published, but almost everyone knew how well or badly they had done and the school was full of excited discussions about maximum salaries and minimum qualifications. Employment officers came and lectured on careers in accountancy, banking and the civil service. A lawyer talked about law, an engineer about engineering, a doctor about medicine and a major about the army. A Scottish Canadian lectured on the advantages of emigration. Students argued in groups about whether it was best to stay a sixth year at school and win more certificates or leave at once for university or commercial or technical colleges. Mr. Thaw said, "So what are you going to do?"

"I don't know."

"What do you want to do?"

"That's irrelevant, isn't it?"

"Face facts, Duncan. If you can't live by doing what you want, you must take the nearest thing to it you can get."

"I want to write a modern Divine Comedy with illustrations in the style of William Blake."

"Well, surely the sensible thing to try for is work as a commercial artist?"

"For that I need four years at art school and you cannae afford to send me."

Mr. Thaw looked thoughtful. He said, "When I worked for Laird's, the box-makers, I was fairly friendly with Archie Tulloch, who was head of the art department. They used to take in boys of sixteen or seventeen then. They designed labels for packages and cartons, you know, and patterns for wrapping paper. That might not gratify your bohemian soul, but it would be a start. If I wrote to Archie Tulloch he would likely look your work over."

Thaw got an afternoon off school and walked down into Bridgeton wearing a newly cleaned overcoat and with a folder of work under his arm. The factory was near the river and he descended to it by narrow streets where many small factories stood between tenements and scrapyards. The sky was grey and beyond the rooftops the Cathkin Braes looked flat and dark like a wall shutting the city in, though he could make out the silhouettes of trees on the skyline. He remembered his mother talking about these trees when he was very small. They had reminded her of a line of camels in the desert. The ceiling of cloud pressed lower and released a thin smirr like a falling mist. It glazed the streets until they reflected the pale sky, a seagull skimming above the street appeared as far below it. The city seemed hung among distances of grey air, and windows were raised from the bottom and hands placed potted ferns on the sills to be watered. The rain soothed Thaw's misery. He started to feel confident, and to imagine coming often this way to Laird's. Even when very rich he would walk through these streets with such regularity that folk who lived there would set their clocks by him. He would be part of their lives. He came to a factory which was a huge brick cube at the junction of two streets. He straightened his tie, ran a hand through his hair, gripped the folder tightly and pushed through a revolving door of brass, glass and carved mahogany.

The entrance hall was a bare place with a small door marked INQUIRIES. He turned the knob and entered a wedge-shaped room with a switchboard and an elderly lady shut in a corner by a counter of polished yellow wood. The lady said, "Yes?"
"I've an appointment; that's to say I'm expected. Mr. Tulloch expects me."
"What is your name, please?"
He said shyly, "I am Duncan Thaw."
The lady moved her fingers among clicking plugs and said, "Mr. Tulloch? A Mr. Thaw to see you. He says he has an appointment. . . . Very well."
She deftly fingered more switches.
"Would you send down a junior? To take a Mr. Thaw to the waiting room? . . . Very well. . . . Would you wait here a little while, sir?"
"Yes, please," said Thaw, humbled at being called sir. He went to a low table with magazines arranged neatly on top in overlapping rows. Lacking the courage to disturb their order, he was content to look at the covers:

The Executive—A MAGAZINE FOR THE MODERN BUSINESSMAN.

Modern Business—A MAGAZINE FOR THE EXECUTIVE.

Ingot—THE THUNDERHAUGH STEEL GROUP MONTHLY BULLETIN.

Automobile—THE CAR DEALERS' MONTHLY BULLETIN.

They had the thin glossy covers of obscene novelettes and were mostly pictures of people in expensive clothes sitting behind desks.

A small neat pretty girl came in and said, "Mr. Thaw? Will you come this way, please?"
He walked behind her across the bare hall and climbed some wide metallic stairs. She hurried ahead of him through corridors of glass and cream-coloured metal, smiling downward as if sharing a tender secret with her bosom, and left him at a door labelled WAITING ROOM. Inside four men sat round a table, one of them saying in an English Midland dialect, "Yes, but what I don't understand is—"
"Will you excuse us?" said another man swiftly to Thaw. Thaw sat down in a comfortable chair and said, "Certainly. Please go on. I'm only here to wait."
"Then would you wait outside?" said the swift man, rising and opening the door. Thaw sat feeling insulted on a sofa against the corridor wall. It occurred to him that the men inside were capitalists plotting something. This floor of the factory was cut up into offices by glass screens supported by metal walls. The glass was rippled so that only shadows could be seen through it, and the bleakness, coldness, metallicness of the place gave a resounding quality to footsteps, clattering typewriters, ringing telephones, and the mutter of administrative voices. Two long spectacled men paused at a corner.
"I think I'd better check that teller."
"No no. No need for that at all."
"Still, if the figures aren't exact—"
"No no. Even if his figures are a hundred percent out, that's enough for my purpose."

Thaw realized Mr. Tulloch was beside him. He was a weary, paunchy man who said, "Duncan Thaw? . . . Yes . . ." and sat down.

"I haven't much time. Show me your stuff."

Thaw suddenly felt competent and businesslike. He opened his folder and said "Here is a series of watercolours, a series dealing with acts of God. The Deluge. The Tower of Babel. The Walls of Jericho Falling Flat."

"Um. Mmm. Next?"

"Penelope unweaving. Circe. Scylla and Charybdis. The last is least successful because at the time I was equally influenced by Blake and Beardsley and the two sorts of outline—"

"Yes. And this?"

"The Cave Artist. Moses on Sinai. Greek Civilization. Roman Imperialism. The Sermon on the Mount. Vandals. The Cathedral City. John Knox preaching to Mary Queen of Scots. The Factory City. The—"

Mr. Tulloch suddenly sat back and Thaw grinned at the air before him and shuffled the pictures back into the half-emptied folder. Mr. Tulloch was saying, ". . . take them at intervals of five years, so you see we really have no room for you. Your work, however, is very promising. Yes. Perhaps something in the illustrative line. Have you tried McLellan the publisher?"

"Yes, but—"

"Oh, yes, ha, ha, well of course the business is overcrowded just now. . . . Have you tried Blockcrafts, Bath Street? Well, try them. Ask for Mr. Grant and say I sent you. . . ." They stood up together. "Apart from that, you see, there's nothing I can do."

"Yes," said Thaw. "Thankyou very much."

He smiled and wondered if the smile looked bitter. It felt bitter. Mr. Tulloch conducted him to the head of the staircase and gave him a tired smile and an unexpectedly firm handshake. "Goodbye. I'm sorry," he said.

Thaw hurried into the drab street, feeling cheapened and defeated. He remembered with an odd pang that Mr. Tulloch had not once asked about his father.

A week later Thaw and his father saw the headmaster of Whitehill School, a white-moustached man who regarded them kindly from behind his desk. He said "Duncan, Mr. Thaw, has very strong imaginative powers. And undoubted talent. And his own way of seeing things, unfortunately." He smiled. "I say unfortunately because this makes it hard for plodding mediocrities like you and me to help him. You agree?"

Mr. Thaw laughed and said, "Oh, I agree all right. However, we must do our best."

"However, we must do our best. Now I think Duncan would be happiest in some job without too much responsibility, a job that would leave him plenty of spare time to develop his talents as he pleases. I see him as a librarian. He's good with books. I see him as a librarian in some small highland town like Oban or Fort William. What do you think, Mr. Thaw?"

"I think, Mr. McEwan, it is a very satisfactory *idea*. But is it a *possibility?*"

"I think so. To enter the library service two higher and two lower certificates are required. Duncan's higher art and english and lower history are guaranteed.The maths results aren't out yet. How do you think he did?"

Mr. Thaw said, "Well, Duncan?"

As the firm responsible voices passed his future gravely backward and forward between them Thaw sank into a fatalistic doze. It took him a moment to notice he was expected to speak. He said, "I've failed in maths."

"Why are you sure?"

"To pass I need full marks for everything I wrote, and what I wrote was mostly nonsense."

"Why does someone of your intelligence write nonsense after four years of study?"

"Laziness, I suppose."

The headmaster raised his eyebrows. "Indeed? The problem is, would you continue to be so lazy if your father was prepared to allow you another year at school?"

Mr. Thaw said, "In other words, Duncan, will you study for a certificate in lower maths if Mr. McEwan allows you another year at school?"

As Thaw considered this a grin began upon his face. He tried to suppress it and failed. The headmaster smiled and said to Mr. Thaw, "He's thinking of all the reading and painting he'll be able to do with practically no supervision at all. Is that not so, Duncan?"

Thaw said, "And mibby I'll be able to go to evening classes at the art school."

The headmaster struck the desk with his hand and leaned over it. "Yes!" he said seriously. "A year of freedom! But it has to be bought. The price is not high, but are you prepared to pay it? Do you faithfully promise your father to study and

master your trigonometry and algebra and geometry? Do you
promise to attend your mathematic lessons, not only in body
but in spirit?"

Thaw hung his head and muttered, "Yes, sir."

"Good, good. Mr. Thaw, I think you have an assurance you
can depend upon."

Next day Thaw met the mathematics teacher as he crossed
the hall. She looked at him brightly and said, "What happened
to you, Thaw?"

He was puzzled. She smiled and said, "Haven't you been going
around telling people you'd failed in maths?"

"Yes, Miss."

"Well, the official results have just been published. You've
passed. Congratulations."

Thaw stared at her in horror.

Later that week he walked into the white marble entrance
of the Mitchell Library. He had often come to this place to
see facsimiles of Blake's prophetic books, and as a plump man
in a brass-buttoned coat led him upstairs the air of scholastic
calm and polite attention produced a lightening of the spirit.
It might not be a bad thing to work in this place. He was
conducted to a door at the end of a corridor with chequered
marble floor and low white vaulted ceiling. The room within
was thickly carpeted, with a vase of flowers on the marble
mantelpiece and another on a desk at the window. A small
old man behind the desk was reading a document. He said
in a clogged voice, "Mr. Thaw? Pleaze take a zeat. I'll be
able to attend to you in a minute."

Thaw sat uneasily. The man had a hole in the right side of
his face where the cheek should have been and most of the
face was twisted toward it. His right eye had been pulled out
of line with the left and the eyeball was so exposed that when
he blinked, which was often, the eyelid could not cover it.
He laid the document down and said, "Zo you want to become
a librarian."

The muscles working his tongue moved awkwardly and beads
of saliva kept bouncing from it onto the desk. Thaw watched
them in fascination, nodding and making quiescent sounds when
these seemed appropriate.

". . . . . hourz nezezzarily ztaggered. You will work two
eveningz per week till half pazt eight, but theze will be compen-

zated for by morningz off. You will be eczpected to attend
night glazzez on two other eveningz."

"To learn what?" said Thaw, with effort.

"Bookkeeping and cataloguing. There are zeveral zyztems of
cataloguing, each a world in itzelf. Each year you will zit an
eczamination and be promoted accordingly, and within five
yearz you zhould qualify for a zertificate qualifying you to aczept
the pozt of zenior librarian anywhere in the United Kingdom."

"Oh. Oh, good," said Thaw feebly.

"Yez, it *iz* good. *Very* good. But I'm afraid you can't ztart
for another zicz weeks. Only the head librarian can employ
you and he's viziting the You Ezz Ay juzt now. But he'll be
back in zicz weekz, and you'll zertainly be able to ztart then."

As Thaw left the building a change came upon him. It
was as if several pounds had been added to his weight, and
his heart had begun beating more sluggishly, and the air had
thickened in his lungs. His thoughts also became heavy and
thick. At home over tea he told his father about the interview.
Mr. Thaw sighed with relief.

"Thank God for that!" he said.

"Yes. Yes, thank *God*. Thank *God*. Yes, indeed, let us give
thanks to *God*."

"Duncan, what's wrong? What's the matter?"

"Nothing. Nothing. Things are as finely arranged as they can
be in a world of this sort. Praise be to the Maker and Upholder
of all things. Yes! Yes! Yes! Yes! Yes! Yes! Ye—"

"Stop! You're talking like a madman! If you won't state the
matter honestly then keep your mouth shut!"

Duncan shut his mouth. After a few minutes Mr. Thaw said
on a note of pleading, "Tell me the matter, Duncan."

"I had a wish to be an artist. Was that not mad of me? I had
this work of art I wanted to make, don't ask me what it was,
I don't know; something epic, mibby, with the variety of facts
and the clarity of fancies and all of it seen in pictures with a
queer morbid intense colour of their own, mibby a gigantic
mural or illustrated book or even a film. I didn't know *what*
it would have been, but I knew how to get ready to make it.
I had to read poetry and hear music and study philosophy and
write and draw and paint. I had to learn how things and people
felt and were made and behaved and how the human body
worked and its appearance and proportions in different situa-
tions. In fact, I had to eat the bloody moon!"

"Duncan, remember what your headmaster said! In four years

you can be head librarian in some small country town and *then* you can make yourself an artist. Surely a *real* artist could wait four years?"

"I don't know if he could. I know that none ever did. People in Scotland have a queer idea of the arts. They think you can be an artist in your *spare* time, though nobody expects you to be a spare-time dustman, engineer, lawyer or brain surgeon. As for this library in a quiet country place, it sounds hellishly like Heaven, or a thousand pounds in the bank, or a cottage with roses round the door, or the other imaginary carrots that human donkeys are shown to entice them into all kinds of nasty muck."

Mr. Thaw rested his elbows on the table and held his head in his hands. After a while he said, "Duncan, what do you want me to do? I want to help you. I'm your father, even though you've been haranguing me as if I was a social system. If I was a millionaire I'd gladly support ye in idleness while you developed your talents, but I'm a costing and bonus clerk, and fifty-seven years old, and my duty is to make you self-supporting. Show me an alternative to the library service and I'll help you toward it."

Tears slid down Thaw's immobile face. He said harshly, "I can't. There's no alternative. I have no choice but to cooperate with my damnation."

"Stop being melodramatic."

"Am I melodramatic? I'm saying what I believe as succinctly as I can."

They finished the meal in silence. Then Mr. Thaw said, "Duncan, go to the art school tonight. Join the evening classes."

"Why?"

"You've six weeks before you start work for the libraries. Use them for what you like doing most."

"I see. Get a taste of that life before I give it up for good. No thanks."

"Duncan, join the evening classes."

"No thanks."

That evening he waited in a corridor of the art school outside the registrar's office in a queue of other applicants. When his turn came he entered a spacious room and started walking toward a desk at the far end, conscious of pictorial and statuesque objects on either side. The man at the desk looked up as he approached. He had a large, spectacled face and a wide mouth with amused corners. He spoke drawlingly, with an expensive English dialect. "Good evening. What can I do for you?"

Thaw sat down and pushed onto the desk a filled in application form. The registrar looked at it and said, "I see you want to go to life classes, ah, Thaw. How old are you?"

"Seventeen."

"Still at school?"

"I've just left it."

"I'm afraid you're rather young for life drawing. You'll have to convince us that your studies are sufficiently advanced to fit you for it."

"I've some work here."

Thaw pushed his folder onto the desk. The registrar looked through it examining each picture carefully. He said, "Are the mounted ones part of a series?"

"They illustrate a lecture I once gave."

The registrar put a few pictures aside and looked at them again. He said, "Don't you think you should join us as a day student?"

"My father can't afford it."

"We could arrange a grant from the Corporation, you know. What are you intending to do?"

"Join the library service."

"Do you like the idea?"

"It seems the only thing possible."

"Honestly, I think you would be wasted in the library service. This is remarkable work. Quite remarkable. I take it you would *prefer* to come to the art school as a full-time day student?"

"Yes."

"Your address is on this form, of course. . . . What school did you go to?"

"Whitehill Senior Secondary."

"Have you a telephone?"

"No."

"Has your father's place of work a telephone?"

"Yes. Garngash nine-three-one-three."

"Well, Thaw, I'll be seeing you again. I'll keep this work if I may. I want to show it to the director."

Thaw shut the door behind him. He had entered the building in an exhausted mood and had maintained through the interview a colourless, almost listless manner. Now he eyed the corridor outside with an excited speculation. It was lined with salt-white casts of renaissance nobility and nude and broken gods and goddesses. A door among these opened and a hectic

little group of girls marched out and surrounded him for a
moment with swinging skirts and hair, scent, chatter, thighs
in coloured slacks and the sweet alien abundances of breasts.
". . . . charcoal charcoal charcoal always charcoal. . . . ."
". . . Did you see the way he posed the model? . . ."
". . . . . Wee Davie gives me the horrors. . . ."
He ran down a staircase, through the entrance hall and into
the street. Too elated to wait for the tram he walked home
by a route which took in Sauchiehall Street, Cathedral Square
and the canal bank. He saw himself at the school of art, a
respected artist among artists: prominent, admired, desired. He
entered corridors of glamorous girls who fell silent, gazing at
him and whispering together behind their hands. He pretended
not to notice but if his look fell upon one she blushed or turned
pale. He soared into dreams of elaborate adventure all dimly
associated with art but culminating in a fancy that culminated
all his daydreams. There was a great hall lit by chandeliers
and floored with marble and with a vast staircase at the end
rising into the dark of a starless sky. On each side of the hall
stood all the women he had loved or who had loved him, all
the men they had loved and married, everyone superbly evil,
virtuous, wise, famous and beautiful and all magnificently
dressed. Then he himself, alone and in ordinary clothes, walked
down the centre of the hall and started unhurriedly climbing
the staircase toward some huge and ultimate menace at the
top. This menace overhung all humanity but only he was fit
to encounter it, although it was an encounter from which he
would not return. He climbed to a tragic crescendo in which
organs, solo voices and orchestras blended in a lament which
combined the most impressive effects of Beethoven, Berlioz,
Wagner and Puccini.

He got home after dark. Mr. Thaw said, "What kept you?"
"I walked back."
"Did they let you join the life class?"
"I'm not sure. The registrar asked me a lot of questions. He
thought I should join the day school. I told him it was impossi-
ble. He asked for your office telephone number."
Thaw spoke expressionlessly. Mr. Thaw said, "Well, well."
They ate supper in silence.

Mr. Thaw came home next day slightly earlier than usual
and slightly breathless. He sat facing Thaw across the living-
room hearth rug and said, "He phoned me this morning—

Peel, the registrar, I mean. He asked me if I could call and
see him. I'd been talking over this business with Joe McVean,
and Joe said, 'Duncan, you take the afternoon off. I'll manage
fine here myself.' So I went and saw Peel there and then.''
Mr. Thaw brought out his pipe and pouch and began filling
one from the other.
"You seem to have made an impression on that man. He said
your work was unusually good. He said it was rare for the
art school authorities to *persuade* someone to join. It had only
happened once in the last ten years. He said the director agreed
with him that you would be wasted as a librarian, and that
you could get a grant from the Corporation of a hundred and
fifty pounds a year. I said to him, 'Mr. Peel, I know nothing
about art. I do not appreciate my son's work. However, I can
vouch for his sincerity, and I accept your opinion as an expert
when you vouch for his ability. But tell me one thing: what
prospects has he when he finishes this four-year course of yours?'
"Well, he hummed and hawed a bit at that, then told me that
for someone of your talent there might well be a chance of
teaching in the art school when you had qualified. 'However,'
he said, 'the boy will be unhappy anywhere else, Mr. Thaw.
Let him decide himself what to do when the four years are
up. Don't rush him into a job he'll hate at this stage.' I said
I would think it over and tell him tomorrow. I went straight
from the art school to Whitehill and saw your headmaster.
Do you know what I found? Peel had phoned him and had a
talk with him. McEwan said to me, 'Mr. Thaw, that man is
better equipped to decide Duncan's future than you or I.' So
I phoned the art school and said you could join.''
"Thanks," said Thaw, and left the room. A minute later Mr.
Thaw came to him in the front bedroom, kneeling by the bed
with his face pushed into the coverlet. Indrawn moans came
from his muffled face and his back shuddered spasmodically.
Mr. Thaw said in a puzzled voice, "What's wrong, Duncan?
Don't you want to go to the art school? Aren't you glad?"
"Yes. Very glad."
"Then why are ye greeting?"
Thaw stood up and dried his face with a handkerchief.
"I don't know. Relief, mibby."
Mr. Thaw patted his son affectionately under the chin with
his clenched fist. "Cheer up!" he said. "And if you don't make
another Picasso of yourself, I'll—I'll—I'll knock your block
off so I will.''

One hot afternoon Thaw and Coulter came down a woodland path veined by tree roots and freckled with sunlight. Birds called in the green shadows above them. Coulter was talking about work. "At first the novelty made it not too bad. It was different from school, and you were getting paid, and you felt a *man;* you know, getting up and intae your clothes at seven, pulling at the day's first fag while your mother fried your breakfast, then down the road to the tram with your wee packet of sandwiches and sitting in your overalls with the other workers, crowding in at the gate and clocking on and then intae the machine shop—'Hullo,' 'Hullo, here it goes again,' 'You're fuckin' right it does'—and then the thumping and banging and feeling of danger—"

"Danger?" said Thaw.

"There's a bit of danger. You'll be battering away at something when the folk nearby start shouting. You wonder who they're yelling at this time, and they yell louder and it strikes you, 'Christ, what if it's me?' and you turn and there's a ten-ton girder swinging toward you on the overhead crane."

"That's hellish! Are there no rules against that sort of thing?"

"There's meant tae be a lane kept clear up the middle of the shed, but in a work like McHargs it's not easy."

Coulter chuckled.

"A weird thing happened the other day. This bloke was directing the lowering of a girder from the crane; you know, he was standing underneath directing the lowering with his hands (you cannae hear a word in that din); you know—lower, lower, a bit to the left; all right, let it go now. The funny thing was, he was looking up at the bloke at the controls most of the time and he didnae notice that at the last moment he directed the girder to be lowered ontae his foot. He gave a scream like a soprano hitting a top note. We all looked to see what the matter was, but it took a while tae find out. He was standing up like the rest of us, only his foot was crushed under this girder. He couldnae even fall down!"

Thaw gave an appalled laugh and said, "You know that's very funny but—"

"Aye. Well, anyway, this business of being a *man* keeps you happy for mibby a week, then on your second Monday it hits you. To be honest the thought's been growing on you all through Sunday, but it really hits you on Monday: I've tae go on doing this, getting up at this hour, sitting in this tram in these overalls dragging on this fag, clocking on in this queue at the gate. 'Hullo, here we go again!' 'You're fuckin' right we go!' and back intae the machine shop. You realize you'll be spending more of your life in this place than anywhere, excepting mibby bed. It's worse than school. School was compulsory—you were just a boy, you neednae take it seriously, you could miss a day if your mammy was agreeable and wrote a note. But engineering isnae compulsory. I chose it. And I'm a man now. I have tae take it seriously, I *have* tae keep shoving my face against this grindstone."

Coulter was silent for a while.

"Mind you, this feeling doesnae last. You stop thinking. Life becomes a habit. You get up, dress, eat, go tae work, clock in etcetera etcetera automatically, and think about nothing but the pay packet on Friday and the booze-up last Saturday. Life's easy when you're a robot. Then accidents happen that start you *thinking* again. You know the Royal visit last week?"

"Aye."

"Well, there's a railway line at the back of the works, and the Royal train was to go along it at three in the afternoon, so the whole work got time off tae see it. So when the train comes along there are four or five hundred of us at the edge of the line in our greasy overalls. The Queen's in the first carriage looking dead cool and gracious and waving; and in the middle are a lot of old men like Lord Provosts with chains round their necks, all waving like mad; and in a sort of observation car at the end sits the Duke in his wee yachting cap. He's sitting at a table with a glass of something on it, and he gives us a wave, but more offhand. And we all just stand there, glowering."

Thaw laughed. "Did nobody wave? I think I'd have waved. Just out of politeness."

"With the whole Union there? They'd have hanged ye. You can laugh, Duncan, but the sight of the Duke set me back a good three weeks. I havenae recovered from it yet. Why should he be enjoying a dram in a comfortable train while I . . . ach!" said Coulter disgustedly. "It's enough to make you rob a bank. I've thought a lot about bank robbery recently. If I'd even a remote chance of succeeding I'd try it too. I've no faith in football pools."

Thaw said, "You're an apprentice. You won't be in the machine shop for good."

"No. Six months in the machine shop, six months in the drawing office, two nights a week at the technical college, and if I pass the exams I'll be a qualified engineering draughtsman in three years."

"And then things won't be too bad."

"Won't they? How did you feel about becoming a librarian?"

They crossed a stream by a plank bridge and came to an acre or two of level turf with a white flagpole in the middle. Lovers and picnic parties sat in the shade at the edge of the wood and children charged about playing anarchic ball games. A few benches on the other side of this green space overlooked the sky and had one or two elderly couples on them. Thaw and Coulter crossed to the benches and sat on one. They were on the edge of a plateau near the top of the Cathkin Braes, and a small rocky cliff went down from their feet to another level space noisy with child play and fringed by trees. From there the land sank in steep wooded terraces to a valley floor carpeted with rooftops and prickly with factory chimneys. To the east the Clyde could be seen meandering among farms, fields, pitheads and slag-bings, then Glasgow hid it till the course was marked by a skeletal procession of cranes marching into the west. Behind the city stood the long northern ridge of the Campsie Fells, bare and heather-green and creased by watercourses, and at this height they could see the Highland bens beyond them like a line of broken teeth. Everything looked unusually distinct, for it was Fair fortnight when big foundries stopped production and the smoke was allowed to clear.

"D'ye see Riddrie?" asked Thaw. "That reddish patch? Look, there's my old primary school on one side and Alexandra Park on the other. Where's your house?"

"Garngad's too low to be seen from here. I'm trying to see McHargs. It should be near those cranes behind Ibrox. Aye, there! There! The top of the machine shop is showing above those tenements."

"I should be able to see the art school, it's on top of a hill behind Sauchiehall Street—Glasgow seems all built on hills. Why don't we notice them when we're in it?"

"Because none of the main roads touch them. The main roads run east and west and the hills are all between."

On the grass at the foot of the cliff a big strong-bodied girl of about fourteen stood with legs apart and hands on hips between two piles of jackets. She wore a blue dress and grumbled impatiently as her younger brothers placed a football some distance in front of her and prepared to kick it at the goal mouth. Thaw stared at her in admiration. He said, "She's great. I'd like to draw her."

"Nude?"

"Anyhow."

"She's not exactly an oil painting. She's no Kate Caldwell."

"Damn Kate Caldwell."

They got up and walked on.

"Yes," said Coulter glumly. "You know what you want and you're in a place where they'll help you get it."

"It was an accident," said Thaw defensively. "If the head librarian hadnae been in America, and my Dad hadnae insisted I go to night classes, and the registrar hadnae been English and liked my work—"

"Aye, but it was an accident that *could* happen to you. Not to me. No accident but an atom bomb can get me out of engineering. I've no ambitions, Duncan. I'm like the man in Hemingway's story, I don't want to be special, I just want to feel good. And I'm in work that's only bearable if I feel as little as I can."

"In four months you'll be in the drawing office and learning something creative."

"Creative? What's creative about designing casings for machine units? I'll be better off, but because it's better wearing a clean suit than dirty overalls. And I'll get more money. But I won't *feel* good."

"It'll be years before I earn money."

"Mibby. But ye'll be doing what you want."

"True," said Thaw. "I'll be doing what I want. I suppose"— he turned and waved toward the city—"I'm nearly the luckiest man living here."

They re-entered the wood and came to a clearing with the iron structure of a child's swing in it. Thaw ran and jumped onto the wooden seat, grabbed the chains on each side and swung violently backward and forward in greater and greater arcs.

"Yah—yip—yeaaaaaaaaaaah!" he shouted. "I'll be doing what I want, won't I?"

Coulter leaned against the trunk of a tree and watched with a slight ironical grin.

INTERLUDE

The swing with Thaw on it flew high and stopped, leaving
him in an absurd position with his knees higher than his back-
flung head. The tree no longer rustled. Each branch and leaf
was locked photographically in a single moment and as in old
photographs the colour faded out, leaving the scene mono-
chrome and brownish. Lanark stared at it through the ward
window and said thoughtfully, "Thaw was not good at being
happy."

The oracle said He was bad at it.

"Yet that is almost a happy ending."

A story can always end happily by stopping at a cheerful moment. Of course in nature the only end is death, but death
hardly ever happens when people are at their best. That is
why we like tragedies. They show men ending energetically
with their wits about them and deserving to do it.

"Did Thaw die tragically?"

No. He botched his end. It set no example, not even a bad
one. He was unacceptable to the infinite bright blankness, the
clarity without edge which only selfishness fears. It flung him
back into a second-class railway carriage, creating you.

Lanark spread cheese on a slice of rye bread and said, "I don't
understand that."

Rima's head stirred among the waves of blond hair on the
pillow. Without opening her eyes she murmured, "Go on with
the story."

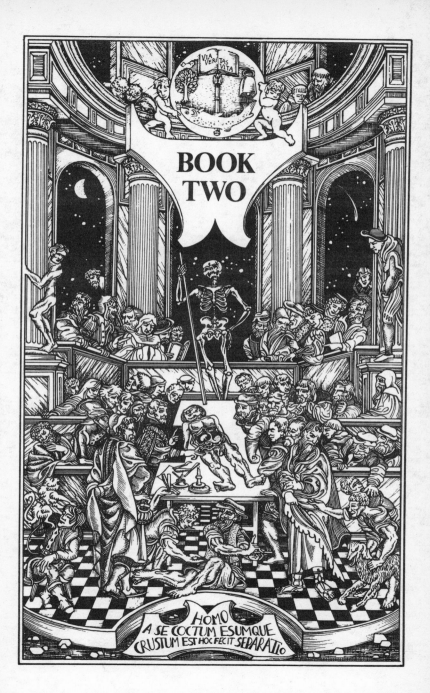

VIA VERITAS VITA

BOOK TWO

HOMO A SE COCTUM ESUMQUE CRUSTUM EST HOC FECIT SEPARATIO

CHAPTER 21. The Tree

The front bedroom was dusty, the curtains unclean, books and papers overlapped the tortoise-shell combs and pin trays on the dressing table. On the wall near the bed a black-bordered photograph of the late king was stuck beside the only picture by Thaw his mother much liked: a childish one of a tree shedding leaves in an autumn gale. These remained because their presence brought Mrs. Thaw less to mind than their removal would have done.

On the first day of art school he woke to the sweet rotten odour which had come when the corpse lay coffined on the hearth-rug. It had taken two or three weeks to vanish and he still sometimes found it on entering the room unexpectedly, though he knew by now it must be altogether ghostly and subjective. Through a gap in the curtains he saw a slice of colourless sky with dark rags of cloud moving across like the shadows of smoke. The ten-to-eight factory horns mourned over the city roofs and he curled more tightly into the nest of warmth his body made in the mattress, for like all bad sleepers he enjoyed bed most in the minutes before leaving it. Faint sounds came from the kitchen where his father prepared breakfast. Hundreds of thousands of men in dirty coats and heavy boots were tramping along grey streets to the gates of forges and machine shops. He thought with awe of the energy needed to keep up a civilization, of the implacable routines which started drawing it from the factory worker daily at eight, from the clerk and shopkeeper at nine. Why didn't everyone decide to stay in bed one morning? It would mean the end of civilization, but in spite of two world wars the end of civilization was still an idea, while bed was a warm immediate fact. He heard his father approach the door and shut his eyes. Mr. Thaw entered quietly, pulled back the curtains, came to the bed and laid a hand on Thaw's brow. Thaw smiled and opened his eyes. His father smiled and said, "Were you really asleep?" "Not really."

Over breakfast they talked about money.
"How much will you need for materials?"
"I don't know. I don't yet know what materials I'll need. But I can get them on account at the school shop."
"That's a very bad idea. It's too easy. I can see you buying something, losing it and buying another."
Thaw said stiffly, "Have you reasons for doubting my honesty?"
"I don't doubt your honesty but I distrust your memory. If you get goods on account be sure to keep the invoices as a reminder. How much will you need for the midday meal?"
"Two shillings."
"Ten bob a week for food. Your tram fares won't come to more than five shillings, so here's a pound."
"That's too much."
"Regard the extra as pocket money. No doubt you'll want a coffee with a friend sometime."
Thaw had hoped for more pocket money. He said in no particular tone of voice, "Thanks very much."
"And Duncan, five shillings a week isn't much pocket money for a boy who'll soon be eighteen. If you ever want to take a lassie out, let me know and I'll give you more."

Garnethill was one of several whale-shaped hills lying parallel to the Clyde and the school was on a quiet street along the spine of it. The main part was an elegant building designed by Mackintosh in the eighteen-eighties but Thaw entered the annexe across the road: a terrace of old houses with new additions among them. He walked down a twisting corridor with so many unexpected descents that it seemed underground. The studio at the end was filled with clear grey morning light from windows in the girder-supported roof. Among tall easels, plaster statues and draught screens some girls crowded loosely in a space like a forest clearing, and boys sat on stools talking nonchalantly in couples. Some smoked and Thaw envied them, for a cigarette would have employed his hands. He could have opened a book and sat behind something reading it, but he was tired of being thought a bookish hermit and meant to forge a new, confident, sardonic, mysterious character for himself; so frowning and leaning against the wall he pretended to see nobody, though glancing furtively at one of the girls. She sat cross-kneed on the pedestal of the discus thrower, sometimes talking to the girls nearby, sometimes tilting her head back to exhale smoke from her nostrils. She wore a suède jacket and tight skirt, and a blond curl curved down to half hide her left eye. Thaw covered his own eyes with his hands as if shielding them from light and stared between the fingers at the other girls. Altogether they gave an impression of bright mirthful sexuality, but separately their attraction was lessened by something schoolgirlish in the dress or markedly individual in the face. From the babble of their conversation only the voice of the blond girl reached him distinctly. Her low notes impressed his ear as velvet impresses fingertips. "I'm glad they couldn't send me to university, actually, 'cause actually art school is more relaxing. . . ."

A brisk white-haired little lady entered and softly called their names from a register. She told them their curriculum, dictated a list of materials and gave the numbers of lockers to store them in.

"Each month you will paint a picture in your own time to be exhibited in the assembly hall. We on the staff look forward to these exhibitions with great interest and even excitement, for they show how well you have grasped what we teach you in class. The theme of your first painting is"—she took a slip of paper from her register and examined it—"the subject is *Washing Day* and must contain a minimum of three figures." Then she ordered them to get paper and a drawing board from the school shop, made them sit in twos before high-legged narrow tables, and went round with a basket of burned-out light bulbs, placing one on each table to be drawn in careful outline. Later she moved among them, giving quiet words of correction and encouragement and making feathery little sketches on the sides of papers to show how the bulbs should be represented. Thaw worked stolidly, his face sometimes expressionless, sometimes bewildered as he fought a gathering rage and disgust. Once he muttered to his neighbour, a square-faced, fair-moustached, well-dressed student, "This is incredible."

"What is?"

"Art from a dead light bulb."

"Not exciting, I admit, but perhaps we should learn to walk before we run."

He had a bland fee-paying school dialect and Thaw detested him.

Halfway through the morning the bell rang and they straggled through the corridor to the refectory, a large low-ceilinged place packed with students who seemed at home there. Thaw stood for ten minutes at the end of an untidy queue. People kept leaving the head of it with coffee and biscuits while others kept joining friends in the middle, so he returned to the studio. Two boys sat in a corner drinking tea from thermos flasks and discussing landladies in a severe border dialect whose words seemed cut in coarse granite. They fell silent as Thaw approached. He nodded at the flasks and said, "That's a good idea. The refectory's too crowded for comfort."
"Aye, and too dear. On a grant like ours we've to economize." The other said accusingly, "Judging by your face you don't think much of the lesson."
"No. It's rotten, isn't it?"
"Is it? Have we not to master the techniques before practising them?"
"But technique and practice are the same thing! We can draw nothing well unless it interests us, and we only learn to draw it well by first drawing it badly, not by drawing what bores us stiff. Learning to draw from dead bulbs and boxes is like learning to make love with corpses."
One student grinned and muttered that that depended on the corpses. The other said sternly, "Are you a Communist?"
"No."
"Are you a Bevanite?"
"I agree with Bevan that Britain should not make atomic bombs."
"I thought so."
The teacher entered and Thaw returned to his seat feeling that he had somehow betrayed himself.

At noon he put the new materials in his locker, left the building and went down to Sauchiehall Street where the pavement was busy with a crowd he could feel anonymous among. He bought a pie from a dairy and wandered, eating thoughtfully, into Sauchiehall Lane, which was quiet except for pigeons cooing and pecking casually between the cobbles. The morning had been like the first morning at any school. It had left a feeling of anxiety, overcrowding and dry curriculums, of minds herded into grooves. Nothing had enriched or warmed except the sight of a certain girl, and that had less warmed than scorched him into a different kind of unease. But now he began to relax, feeling (in that obscure channel between tenement backs) a comfort he sometimes found in graveyards, the canal and other neglected parts of the city. The stone walls, stapled over with iron pipes, seemed to hold something grander and stranger than the builders knew. He looked through a doorway and saw a huge unhealthy tree. It grew in a patch of bare earth among pale-green rhubarb-shaped weeds; it divided at the roots into two scaly limbs, one twisting along the ground, the other shooting up to the height of the third-storey windows; each limb, almost naked of branches, supported at the end a bush of withered leaves. Thaw stared and munched for several minutes then moved away feeling triumphant. It was not a feeling he understood. It might have come from identifying with the tree, with the confining walls or with both.

The afternoon was spent in the modelling department making a clay copy of a plaster lip. At four-thirty he went to his locker and found it empty. He stared dispassionately at the vacant space, knowing the shock of it would break on him in three or four minutes. To prepare for this he said aloud, "I have done a stupid thing."

A student at a nearby locker said smoothly, "We all do, from time to time."

"I have let myself be robbed of three pounds' worth of goods."

The student came over and looked at the empty locker. He said, "You should have got a padlock before leaving anything valuable there. You can get a fairly good one for two or three shillings in Woolworth's."

Thaw recognized his fair-moustached neighbour of the morning who had wanted to walk before running. A flash of intuition separate from logic or evidence made him sure this man was the thief. He said harshly, "You are right," and left the building.

At home over the teatable Mr. Thaw said cheerfully, "Well? How did it go?"

"All right."

"You don't sound very sure."

"I'm tired."

"Did you get much in the way of materials?"

"A drawing board, a folder, cartridge paper, a metal-edged ruler. I . . . I had them stolen."

"My God! How? How?"

Thaw told him how.

"And how much did they cost?"

Thaw put a hand in his pocket and grasped the crumpled invoice tight. "Nearly a pound."

"*Nearly* a pound? *Nearly* a pound? How much did they cost?"

"Fifteen shillings."

Mr. Shaw stared at him disgustedly then said, "Never mind. Just get another lot on account tomorrow."

In bed that night Thaw realized his father would expect the stolen goods to be replaced for fifteen shillings, so to keep his lie a secret he would need to save three pounds minus fifteen shillings multiplied by two. It struck him that if he had a key in the side of his head and could die by turning it, he would gladly turn it now.

Next morning he rose at seven, walked to school to save tram fares and dined on a cheap pie. This left him hungry but came to seem sufficient in two or three days, then he lost appetite for it and drank a cup of milk instead. Daily his stomach grew content with less. His mind was clenched, his surface reinforced against surrounding life. Normal hesitancies of voice and manner vanished. Often a line of words sounded in his head: *clean bleak exact austere rigorous implacable.* Sometimes he whispered these words as though they were a tune his body moved to. Walking down streets and corridors his feet hit the ground with unusual force and regularity. All sounds, even words spoken nearby, seemed dulled by intervening glass. People behind the glass looked distinct and peculiar. He wondered what they saw in gargoyles, masks and antique door knockers that they couldn't see in each other. Everyone carried on their necks a grotesque art object, originally inherited, which they never tired of altering and adding to. Yet while he looked on people with the cold interest usually felt for things, the world of things began to cause surprising emotions. A haulage vehicle carrying a huge piece of bright yellow machinery swelled his heart with tenderness and stiffened his penis with lust. A section of tenement, the surface a dirty yellow plaster with oval holes through which brickwork showed, gave the eerie conviction he was beholding a kind of flesh. Walls and pavements, especially if they were slightly decayed, made him feel he was walking beside or over a body. His feet did not hit the ground less firmly, but something in him winced as they did so.

He could only rest when working properly. After sketching bulbs and boxes the class was given plants, fossils and small stuffed tropical birds. Thaw let his eyes explore like an insect the spiral architecture of a tiny seashell while his pencil point marked some paper with the eye's discoveries. The teacher tried to correct him by rational argument. She said, "Are you trying to make a pattern out of this, Duncan? I wish you wouldn't. Just draw what you see."

"I'm doing that, Miss Mackenzie."

"Then stop drawing everything with the same black harsh line. Hold the pencil lightly; don't grip it like a spanner. That shell is a simple, delicate, rather lovely thing. Your drawing is like the diagram of a machine."

"But surely, Miss Mackenzie, the shell only seems delicate and simple because it's smaller than we are. To the fish inside it was a suit of armour, a house, a moving fortress."

"Duncan, if I were a marine biologist I might care how the shell was used. As an artist my sole interest is in the appearance. I insist that it appears beautiful and delicate and should be drawn beautifully and delicately. There's no need to show these little cracks. They're accidental. Ignore them."

"But Miss Mackenzie, the cracks show the shell's nature—only this shell could crack in this way. It's like the wart on Cromwell's lip. Leave it out and it's no longer a picture of Cromwell."

"All right, but please don't make the wart as important as the lip. You've drawn these cracks as clearly as the edges of the shell itself."

Behind the teacher's back several classmates made gestures like spectators at a boxing match, and later Thaw was approached by Macbeth who said, "Where do you go after school these days?"

"Home, usually."

"Why not come to Brown's? A few of us meet there. It's a change from the concentration camp."

Thaw felt excited. Macbeth was the only first-year student who looked like an artist. He walked with a defiant slouch, wore a beret, rolled his own cigarettes and smelled of whisky in the afternoon. He was often seen on the edge of older groups of students: elegant tight-trousered girls and tall bearded men who laughed freely in public places. In class he did what the teachers wanted with an ease which looked contemptuous, but he impressed Thaw most by keeping company with Molly Tierney, the velvet-voiced girl with blond curls. He sat beside her in class, gave her cigarettes and carried her drawing board from place to place. His face usually had an anxious, babyish look.

Brown's cakeshop in Sauchiehall Street had a narrow staircase going down to a wide low-ceilinged room. The tobacco
smoke and faded luxury were so dense here that Thaw, like
a diver in the saloon of a sunk liner, felt them press against
his eardrums. In an alcove to his right Molly Tierney reclined
on a sofa, smiling and lightly fingering the curl overhanging
her brow. Others from Thaw's class sat at a table beside her
sipping coffee and looking bored. Thaw slid into a chair next
to Macbeth without being specially noticed. Sounds of people
moving and conversing at other tables blurred and receded,
but tiny noises nearby (Macbeth's breathing, a spoon striking
a saucer) were magnified and distinct. Molly Tierney came
into sharp focus. The colours of her hair, skin, mouth and
dress grew clearer like a stained-glass figure with light increasing
behind it. Second by second her body was infused with the
significance of mermaids on rocks and Cleopatra in her barge.
He heard someone say, "Has anyone started their monthly
painting yet? I haven't even thought of it."
Molly said, "I began mine last night. At least I meant to, only
my mother wanted me to watch television and we had a fight.
It ended with me being pushed out of doors into the co-o-ld
bla-a-a-ck night." She giggled. "Me! In my high-heeled shoes."
A voice said venomously, "Parents just won't allow you a life
of your own."
Other voices supported this.
"My father won't let me . . ."
"My mother keeps saying . . ."
"Last week my mother . . ."
"Last year my father . . ."
He thought of entering the conversation by recalling fights
with his mother but the details had grown dim; all he remem-
bered was their inevitability. Molly Tierney sighed and said,
"I think I'll become a nun."
Thaw said, "I think I'll become a lighthouse keeper."
There was silence, and then someone asked why.
"So I'll be able to walk in spirals."
Molly giggled and Thaw leaned toward her. He criticized the
theme of the monthly painting, quoting Blake and Shaw and
describing shapes in the air with his hands. People raised objec-
tions and he quoted folk tales from many lands to show how
fact and fancy, geography and legend were linked. Molly was
clearly listening. She put her feet on the floor and leaned toward
him saying, "You know a lot of fairy stories."

"Yes. They used to be my favourite reading."

"Mine too." She chuckled huskily. "In fact they still are. I like Russian tales best. Have you noticed how many of them are about children?"

They talked of ugly and beautiful witches, enchanted mountains, magic gifts, monsters, princesses and lucky younger sons. With feelings of wonder and freedom he found she loved and remembered much that he loved himself. Suddenly she curled her legs back on the sofa and said to Macbeth, "Give me a cigarette, Jimmy."

Macbeth rolled a cigarette and held a match to the tip while she inhaled it.

"And Jimmy, would you do me a favour? Please, Jimmy, a very special favour?"

"What is it?"

Her voice became a mixture of babyish and whorish. "Jimmy, it's my architecture homework. This model cathedral we've to make. I've tried to make it but I can't, I don't know how to begin, it's too complicated for my tiny mind and I've to hand it on Friday. Will you make it for me? I'll pay for the materials, of course."

No one else at the table looked at each other. A voice in Thaw's head raved at Macbeth, "Spit in her face! Go on, spit in her face!"

Macbeth looked down at his cigarette with a faint smile and said, "All right."

"Oh Jimmy, you're a pet."

Thaw got up and walked home. The sun had set. He felt cold and light-bodied and the streets semed to flow through him on a current of dark air. Clock dials glowed like fake moons on invisible towers. On Alexandra Parade by the Necropolis a drunk man lurched past muttering, "Useless."

"Right," said Thaw. "Useless."

He woke often that night to find his legs grinding against each other and his fingernails tearing healthy parts of his skin. In the morning the sheets were bloodstained and his body felt so heavy he had trouble bringing it out of bed. At school he went through the routines like a sleepwalker. At noon he went to the refectory and drank a cup of black coffee at a crowded table. A girl nearby shouted, "Hullo Thaw!"

He smiled feebly.

"Enjoying yourself, Thaw?"

"Well enough."

"You like the life here, do you, Thaw?"

"Well enough."

A boy leaned against her laughing, and whispered in her ear. She said, "Thaw, this man is saying rude things about you." The boy said quickly, "No, I'm not."

Thaw said flatly, "I'm sure you're not."

He looked at them and saw their faces did not fit. The skin on the skulls crawled and twitched like half-solid paste. All the heads in his angle of vision seemed irregular lumps, like potatoes but without a potato's repose: potatoes with crawling surfaces punctured by holes which opened and shut, holes blocked with coloured jelly or fringed with bone stumps, elastic holes through which air was sucked or squirted, holes secreting salt, wax, spittle and snot. He grasped a pencil in his trouser pocket, wishing it were a knife he could thrust through his cheek and use to carve his face down to the clean bone. But that was foolish. Nothing clean lay under the face. He thought of sectioned brains, palettes, eyeballs and ears seen in medical diagrams and butcher's shops. He thought of elastic muscle, pulsing tubes, gland sacks full of lukewarm fluid, the layers of cellular and fibrous and granular tissues inside a head. What was felt as tastes, caresses, dreams and thoughts could be seen as a cleverly articulated mass of garbage. He got quickly out of the tearoom trying to see nothing but the floor he walked on.

At home he stood in the kitchen after the evening meal, sometimes putting dishes away but mostly standing stock-still, his face open-mouthed and aghast. Mr. Thaw entered and said impatiently, "Haven't you finished yet? You've been here over an hour. Is my company so disagreeable that you can't share a room with me?"

"No, but I'm thinking things I don't like to think about and I can't stop."

"What sort of things?"

"Diseases, mostly. Skin diseases and cancers and insects that live in people's bodies. Some of them are real but I've been inventing new ones. I can't stop."

"For God's sake do your homework or go for a walk. Do *something,* at any rate."

"How can I, with my mind full of these things?"

"Then go to bed."

"But when I shut my eyes I see them. They're so active. They gnaw and gnaw. Surely this is how people go mad."

Mr. Thaw stared at his son with mingled impatience and worry.
"Will I call the doctor then?"
"How would that help? 'Doctor Tannahill, I'm having thoughts I don't like to think!' How would that help?"
"He might send you to a psychiatrist."
"When? I'm thinking these things now."
"But what makes you think them?"
"That's easy. I don't need a psychiatrist to tell me that. Frustration. If a man hath these two, honesty and intelligence, and hath not sex appeal, then he is as sounding brass and tinkling cymbal."
"You're talking hysterically."
"Yes. That's unlucky, isn't it?"
"Get to bed, Duncan, and I'll bring you a toddy."

He sat in bed propped up with pillows to make sleep difficult. He invented a maggot called the Flealouse. It was white and featureless except on the underside, which was all mouths. It bred in connective tissues and moved by eating a trench in the surfaces it travelled among. It spread through bodies without upsetting them at first, for it sweated a juice which worked on the nerves like a drug, making diseased people plumper and rosier, more cheerful and active. Then it started feeding on the brain. The victims felt no less happy but their actions became mechanical and frenzied, their words repetitive and trite. Then the lice, whose movement so far had been sluggish and gradual, suddenly attacked the main bodily organs, growing hugely as they did so. Infected people turned white, collapsed in the street, swelled and burst like rotten sacks of rice, each grain of which was a squirming louse. Then the lice themselves split open releasing from their guts swarms of winged insects so tiny that they could enter anybody through pores in the skin. In less than a century the Flealouse infected and ate every other sort of life on the globe. The earth became nothing but rock under a heaving coat of lice of every size, from a few inches up to five hundred feet. Then they began to eat each other. In the end only one was left, a titan curled round the equator like a grub round a pebble. The body of the last Flealouse contained the flesh of everything that had ever lived. It was content.

While elaborating this fantasy he fell asleep several times and continued it in dreams, sometimes being a victim of the Flealouse, sometimes a Flealouse himself. The dreams were so detailed that horror made him recoil into wakefulness and fix wide-open eyes on the electric light, hoping the pain of the dazzle would keep him conscious. Meanwhile part of his mind tried to get free with the desperation of a rat roasting in a revolving cage.

"Stop! Stop! Stop!"

"You can't."

"Why? Why? Why?"

"Your mind is rotting. Minds without love always breed these worms."

"How can I get love?"

"You can't. You can't."

Something happened shortly after five in the morning. He was struggling against thoughts of the lice and against the sleep which made them seem solid when the image of Molly Tierney came like coolness to a heated brow. He lay down filling slowly with relief. He would go to her the next day and explain calmly, without pathos, that only she could stop him going mad. If she refused to love him what happened after that would be her responsibility, not his. And she might help. This was not a world of certainties but of likelihoods, so the glorious lovely accident must happen *sometimes.* The Flealouse vanished from his mind. He fell into a smooth, wholly dreamless sleep.

He woke as his father was drawing the curtains.

"How's your mind this morning?"

"It's all right now. It's fine."

"But will it last?"

"I think so."

"And you don't want a doctor?"

"Certainly not."

"Good. Three weeks ago, Duncan, you told me you had been robbed of goods worth fifteen shillings. That was a lie. Now I want the truth."

"The goods cost three pounds."

"I know. I was looking in your pocket for handkerchiefs to wash when I found the invoice. I was shifting it to its proper place on the spike in the scullery when I noticed the true amount."

Mr. Thaw went to the window and stood, hands in pockets, looking down the street. There was a small distinct frenzied sound in the room like a mouse gnawing wood or a steel nib scribbling on paper.

"For God's sake stop scratching!" said Mr. Thaw. "Aren't there enough bloodstains on the sheets?"

"Sorry."

"I don't understand why you had to lie about it, unless from a love of lying for its own sake. You could have hidden the truth just by keeping your mouth shut."

"I came as near truth as I dared."

"Dared? What were you afraid of? Did you think I'd thrash you?"

"I deserve to be thrashed."

"But Duncan, I've not thrashed you since you were a wee boy!"

Thaw considered this and said, "True."

"Furthermore, how could you keep hiding the right amount from me? Sooner or later I'd have had to pay the bill."

"I'm paying that myself. I've already saved thirty-five shillings."

"Thirty-five shillings in three weeks! You've saved it out of food money. No wonder you're sick. How can you expect to be well if you starve yourself? *How? How?*"

"Please don't attack me."

"What else can I do?" said Mr. Thaw piteously. "When you were wee you could be beaten, but you're a man now. How else can I bring home your wrongdoing but by driving at you and driving at you with words?"

After a moment he added quietly, "I would be glad in future if you would trust me with the facts of your condition, however disastrous they may be."

"I'll try to."

"Then get up for your breakfast, son."

"I want to stay in bed. I feel feeble."

His father stared at him then left the room saying, "I'll bring your breakfast in."

Thaw lay and remembered the night before. Asking for Molly Tierney's love seemed foolish and unnecessary now, but the decision to do it had cured his fear of decay and disease. When such thoughts came in future he would entertain them calmly, and move on to other thoughts.

For two days his father, before going to work, brought him breakfast in bed. At noon Mrs. Colquhoun downstairs brought up a tray of dinner. Between meals his body basked in unhurried time: time to scribble in notebooks or read or lie thoughtfully dreaming. It was good to be free from the tensions of art school, yet the place haunted him. He had been part of the life of the students there, a voice among voices heard by attractive girls, a face among the faces surrounding them. He wrote:

From under loose sweaters and tight blouses their breasts threaten my independence like the nosecaps of atomic missiles. Cannibal queens carnivorous nightingales why should I feel my value depends on being valued by women, what makes them *the bestowers of value? Oh I want to grip them somehow and show them the universe is bigger, stranger, more sombre, colourful and distinct than they know. And how can I do this in a picture called "Washing Day" with a minimum of three figures? Yah what grandeur can be shown in that? I want to make a series of paintings called* Acts of God *showing the deluge, the confusion of Babel, the walls of Jericho falling flat, the destruction of Sodom. Yes, yes, yes, a hymn to the Old Testament Catastropher who makes things well but hurts and smashes them just as well. Or I would make a set of city scapes with the canal through them. Or*

His pen paused above the page then descended and sketched the tree on Sauchiehall Lane, making it larger, and leafless, and among the tenements and back greens of Riddrie. Around it three dwarfish housewives were stretching ropes between iron clothes-poles, and he drew them from a memory of a home help who had looked after the house while his mother was dying. They wore headscarves, men's boots, and big aprons covered their chests and skirts giving them a sexless, surgical look. At the top of the picture the tree's highest branch stuck into a strip of sky among the tenement chimneys. He remembered a Blake engraving of a grey ocean with an arm sticking out of a wave, the hand clutching at the empty sky. Another Blake engraving showed a tiny pair of lovers watching a small frenzied figure set foot on a ladder so thin and high that the top rested in the sickle of a moon. A caption said, "I want! I want!" Thaw drew a moon in the sky above the treetop.

Next day he rose after breakfast and sat in a thick dressing gown before the living-room fire turning the sketch into a picture. In the evening Ruth called from the kitchen, where she was making the tea, "It seems to me if you're well enough to paint you're well enough to help with the housework."
"True," said Thaw.
"Then will you kindly set the table?"
"I'm too busy."
"For Pete's sake! It won't take ten minutes."

•

"If I stop now I won't work so well when I start again."

"I suppose you think your old picture is more important than anything else?"

Ruth stood in the kitchen doorway with a milk jug in her hand. Thaw looked at her and said coldly, "Yes. What I'm doing just now is more important than anything else happening in this whole city."

"You're mad!"

"Mibby."

He turned back to the picture. Ruth came over and held the full milk jug above it.

"How would you like a dirty big puddle in the middle of your important picture?"

"Your actions aren't on my conscience," said Thaw, working. Ruth tipped the jug slowly forward until a trickle of milk spattered onto the centre of the paper, leaving a small puddle. Thaw rose and went into the kitchen saying, "That was a wrong and childish thing to do."

He brought back a clean cloth, wiped up the milk and continued working. Ruth watched him ominously, jug in hand, then said, in a low vibrating voice, "God, how I hate you! How I hate you!"

"At present, yes, but you'll soon stop. It's a tiring emotion."

"Oh, I'll keep it going! Don't you *worry*."

She flung the jug to smash in the hearth and ran from the room, slamming the door after her. Four minutes later she returned with homework notebooks and sat studying them by the fire, her lips pressed tightly together.

Suddenly Thaw jumped up, crying out on a rising note, "Oh! Oh! *Oh!*"

He had been drawing with waterproof ink on stiff paper. He had thought the milk had fallen on a dry part of the picture, but it was not completely dry, and now that the damp had evaporated a grey smear stained the centre. He had not expected this. He turned to Ruth, his head craning toward her and swaying a little at the end of the neck. With fists clenched he advanced on her whispering, "By God I'll hurt you for this, my dear."

She retreated into the bay window. In former fights she was usually the aggressor and he coldly or hysterically defensive. Now she sank to the floor, protecting her head with her hands, and he stooped and twice drove his fist hard into her stomach, then went back and glowered at the picture. A new wave of rage rose in him and he turned vengefully to her again. She lay curled on herself with her eyes shut, drawing choking breaths and looking very white. He went to the front bedroom and lay on the bed, feeling nothing now but listlessness and defeat, and the fading daylight in the room, and the occasional shout of children playing in the street. After a while he heard Ruth go to the lavatory and taps rushing and the cistern flushing. She looked into the bedroom for a moment and said sobbingly, "Duncan, you've hurt me. You don't know how you've hurt me."

He said coldly, "I'm sorry."

He could only think of the grey smear on the picture. Coldness and indifference spread through him like a stain. Later he heard his father come in and murmurs of conversation from the living room. Mr. Thaw opened the bedroom door abruptly saying, "Duncan! Did you punch Ruth in the stomach?"

"Yes. We were fighting."

"Look, Duncan, I'm glad you're prepared to defend yourself but you should *never* punch a *woman* in the *stomach*."

"I'm sorry. I don't know how to hurt women properly yet." His father left and he lay inert, thinking of the picture. 'I can't do it all again' he thought, then sat up, shaken by a new idea. For an hour before Ruth spoiled the picture his pleasure in it had vanished and now he knew why. The moon was wrong. It did not belong to such a picture; it was a piece of sentimental overemphasis, like a serenader with a guitar. The picture should be made bigger with no sky showing at all.

Mr. Thaw made tea that evening and the family ate in silence. Inside himself Thaw was very cheerful indeed but hid the feeling because the others could not share it. Afterward he began the picture again and finished it three days later.

He brought it to art school and it hung in the assembly hall, where he moved about among the other thoughtful or chattering students. He was sick of it now, it seemed overworked and dull, but he had still expected it to eclipse the work of everyone else and was depressed to see two other pictures equally good. They showed ordinary kitchen interiors. Their paint was carefully used to represent solid figures and the space between, and their common depth of light and air was finer and saner than the unique sombreness of his own rigid composition. Other pictures interested by their oddity.

Molly Tierney showed a tropical landscape where twenty or thirty blondes like herself washed their hair in a waterfall. Macbeth's picture looked like a forgery of a painting by Van Gogh. A plump white-haired white-moustached teacher entered and walked up and down before the pictures talking in a lordly way about the aims of art and indicating with a plump white hand those paintings whose qualities or flaws illustrated his ideas. Once or twice he paused and regarded the tree picture thoughtfully, then moved on leaving Thaw's nerves jangling with colliding messages of anticipation and resentment. The criticism ended without his picture being mentioned and for several hours disappointment worked in him like a speck of acid.

CHAPTER 22.
Kenneth McAlpin

Once a week they queued outside the lecture theatre for a talk on the history of art. Everyone seemed friendly; lightly chattering currents of emotion flowed easily between them and Thaw stood in the flow feeling as dense and conspicuous as a lump of rock. One day he arrived when the queue had gone in but before the lecturer came. Pausing outside the door he made his face expressionless, softened it with a thoughtful frown and entered. There was an explosion of laughter and someone shouted, "This was the noblest Roman of them all!" The theatre confronted him with a collection of grinning, glaring and roaring heads. The mirth crashed like a wave into his shell of loneliness and gravity. He grinned and said, "Is my nose green or something?" sitting down beside the fair-moustached student he had once instinctively hated.

"No, but you looked like Caesar pondering over the head of Pompey."

After the lecture they walked to the refectory together. The moustached student was called Kenneth McAlpin. Thaw said, "It's queer to be enjoying a coffee here."

"I've noticed you hardly ever use the place."

"I never know where to sit. The world sometimes seems a chessboard where the pieces move themselves. I'm never sure what square to go to. Yet it can't be a difficult game, most folk play it instinctively."

"The rules are fairly simple," said McAlpin. "You stick near pieces like yourself and move along with them. The people at that table are in the school choir. The clan over there are highlanders. These four in the corner are serious Catholics. After the second year your group is usually decided by the subject you specialize in."

"Have you a group?"

McAlpin pursed his lips then said, "Yes. I suppose I'm a snob. My family used to be rather well off so I've grown up feeling a bit grander than the majority, and I'm slightly uncomfortable when I'm in a group who don't feel the same. I suppose the people I sit with are snobs too. They'll be here soon, so you can judge for yourself."

Thaw smiled and said, "I'll leave when they come. I don't want to embarrass you."

"Actually I'd be glad if you stayed. I enjoy your conversation more than theirs. With the exception of Judy, of course."

"Judy?"

"My girlfriend. Don't mistake me, they're nice people, you know some of them already. But it's snobbery which keeps us together, I sometimes think."

Judy and Rushford arrived. Judy was a handsome, sturdy girl with a vaguely displeased expression. Rushford wore an embroidered waistcoat copied from one worn by Benjamin Disraeli. "The Victorians were far from being the stuffy monsters we used to assume," he said in a fluting, meticulous voice. Molly Tierney arrived followed by Macbeth and some others, and the group was complete. Macbeth looked lost and unhappy because Molly ignored him but Thaw felt perfectly comfortable. The conversation was about people he never met and parties he never visited but his occasional remarks were heard politely.

After this Thaw and McAlpin worked side by side in the studio, drank coffee together, brought to school books they enjoyed and read the best parts aloud to each other. Thaw preferred poetry and drama, McAlpin music and philosophy. They discussed these but avoided politics in case their opinions divided them. Once or twice they had tea in each other's homes. McAlpin lived in the small posh suburban town of Bearsden. The house had a garden round it and warm well-carpeted rooms. The furniture was large and beautifully kept with Indian cabinets and Chinese ornaments. Mrs. McAlpin was small, brisk and cheerful. "This is the tiniest of the houses we owned when Kenneth's father died," she said with a faint sigh, pouring tea into thin cups. "Not that I wanted the others, even if I could have afforded to keep them. We really were rather prosper-ous once. Kenneth, for instance, had a nanny when he was small . . ."

"We keep it, stuffed, in a cupboard under the stairs," murmured McAlpin.

". . . we had a chauffeur too, Stroud, a delightful character, a real Cockney. I do miss the car. Still, if I had it I would probably use it all the time because I'm naturally terribly lazy. I suppose running up and down to the shops helps keep me young. Another thing we don't do much nowadays is entertain. Still, I want Kenneth's twenty-first birthday party to be one he'll really enjoy. You'll come to it, Duncan, I hope? Kenneth often talks of you."

"I'd like to," said Thaw. He sat on a sofa so deep that it supported the whole length of his legs, and he sipped tea and wondered why he felt so much at home. Perhaps when he was small his own house had seemed as spacious and secure.

At the refectory table he often heard parties and excursions planned. McAlpin took little share in the plans for in that group practical details were left to the girls, but Judy brought him in by asking, "What do you think, Kenneth?" or "Have you any ideas about that?" while Thaw sat hoping to be invited and wondering why Aitken Drummond was always invited. Aitken Drummond was not a member of the group. He was over six feet tall and usually wore green tram conductor's trousers, a red muffler and an army greatcoat. His dark skin, great arched nose, small glittering eyes, curling black hair and pointed beard were so like the popular notion of the Devil that on first sight everyone felt they had known him intimately for years. Drummond was always asked to parties and next day stories were told of him amid mocking, slightly horrified laughter. Thaw envied him, but the question "Can I come to the party, Kenneth?" though often in his mind, was never asked. He was sure McAlpin would answer "Yes, why not?" with hurtful coolness. Yet coolness was the quality in McAlpin he most admired. It showed in his polished solidity, his relaxed confidence which nothing, nobody, seemed to perturb. It showed in his calm robust body, his good manners and good clothes, in the finely rolled umbrella he carried with careless ease when the weather was cloudy. It showed most of all on the few occasions he spoke of his private life, as if that life were entertainment he watched, with ironical sympathy, from a distance. One day he said to Thaw, "I behaved badly last night."

"How?"

"I took Judy to a party. I got rather drunk and started kissing the host's daughter on the floor behind the sofa. She was drunk too. Then Judy found us and was furious. The trouble is I was enjoying myself so much I couldn't even pretend to be sorry."

He frowned and said, "That was bad, wasn't it?"

"If Judy loves you, yes, of course it was bad."

McAlpin looked gravely at Thaw for a moment, then flung his head back and roared with laughter.

One morning Thaw and McAlpin went into the Cowcaddens, a poor district behind the ridge where the art school stood. They sketched in an asphalt playpark till small persistent boys ("Whit are ye writing, mister? Are ye writing a photo of that building, mister? Will ye write *my* photo, mister?") drove them up a cobbled street to the canal. They crossed the shallow arch of a wooden bridge and climbed past some warehouses to the top of a threadbare green hill. They stood under an electric pylon and looked across the city centre. The wind which stirred the skirts of their coats was shifting mounds of grey cloud eastward along the valley. Travelling patches of sunlight went from ridge to ridge, making a hump of tenements gleam against the dark towers of the city chambers, silhouetting the cupolas of the Royal infirmary against the tomb-glittering spine of the Necropolis. "Glasgow is a magnificent city," said McAlpin. "Why do we hardly ever notice that?" "Because nobody imagines living here," said Thaw. McAlpin lit a cigarette and said, "If you want to explain that I'll certainly listen."

"Then think of Florence, Paris, London, New York. Nobody visiting them for the first time is a stranger because he's already visited them in paintings, novels, history books and films. But if a city hasn't been used by an artist not even the inhabitants live there imaginatively. What is Glasgow to most of us? A house, the place we work, a football park or golf course, some pubs and connecting streets. That's all. No, I'm wrong, there's also the cinema and library. And when our imagination needs exercise we use these to visit London, Paris, Rome under the Caesars, the American West at the turn of the century, anywhere but here and now. Imaginatively Glasgow exists as a music-hall song and a few bad novels. That's all we've given to the world outside. It's all we've given to ourselves."

"I thought we had exported other things—ships and machinery, for instance."

"Oh, yes, we were once the world's foremost makers of several useful things. When this century began we had the best organized labour force in the United States of Britain. And we had John McLean, the only Scottish schoolteacher to tell his students what was being done to them. He organized the housewives' rent strike, here, on Clydeside, which made the government stop the landlords getting extra money for the duration of World War One. That's more than most prime ministers have managed to do. Lenin thought the British revolution would start in Glasgow. It didn't. During the general strike a red flag flew on the city chambers over there, a crowd derailed a tramcar, the army sent tanks into George Square; but nobody was hurt much. Nobody was killed, except by bad pay, bad housing, bad feeding. McLean was killed by bad housing and feeding, in Barlinnie Jail. So in the thirties, with a quarter of the male workforce unemployed here, the only violent men were Protestant and Catholic gangs who slashed each other with razors. Well, it is easier to fight your neighbours than fight a bad government. And it gave excitement to hopeless lives, before World War Two started. So Glasgow never got into the history books, except as a statistic, and if it vanished tomorrow our output of ships and carpets and lavatory pans would be replaced in months by grateful men working overtime in England, Germany and Japan. Of course our industries still keep nearly half of Scotland living round here. They let us exist. But who, nowadays, is glad just to exist?''

"I am. At the moment," said McAlpin, watching the sunlight move among rooftops.

"So am I," said Thaw, wondering what had happened to his argument. After a moment McAlpin said, "So you paint to give Glasgow a more imaginative life."

"No. That's my excuse. I paint because I feel cheap and purposeless when I don't."

"I envy your purpose."

"I envy your self-confidence."

"Why?"

"It makes you welcome at parties. It lets you kiss the host's daughter behind the sofa when you're drunk."

"That means nothing, Duncan."

"Only if you can do it."

"Ten weeks is a long, long holiday," said Mr. Thaw that summer. "What's your friend Kenneth doing?"

"Working on the trams. Almost everyone I know is taking some kind of job."

"And what are you going to do?"

"Paint, if you let me. There's an exhibition when we go back with a competition for a picture of the Last Supper. The prize is thirty pounds. I think I can win it."

He walked the streets looking at people. He used the underground railway where passengers faced each other in rows and could be examined without seeming to stare. Folk near the river were usually gaunter, half a head shorter and had cheaper clothes than folk in the suburbs. He had not seen the connection between physical work, poverty and bad feeding before because he came from Riddrie, an in-between district where tradesmen and petty clerks like his father lived. He noticed too that the sleek office faces and roughened workshop ones had the same tight mouths. Nearly everyone looked anxious, smug or grimly determined. Such faces would suit the disciples, who had been chosen from labourers and clerks, but they wouldn't suit Jesus. He began looking for harmonious faces whose mouths closed serenely. Most children had these when they sat still, but the people who kept them after adolescence were usually women with a mild, mysterious, knowing look. For a while he thought this might be the incarnate God's expression, for Leonardo and the carvers of oriental Buddhas had thought so. One morning he found it on the face of a three-inch embryo in the university medical museum. The huge little head nodding over the bent-up knees, the great closed eyes and subtly smiling mouth seemed dreaming of a satisfying secret as big as the universe. And he saw such an expression could not belong to Christ, who had looked steadily at the people around him. He needed the face of a mature, sane, outward-looking man whose love abolished all advantage over whom he beheld, a face without triumph or blame in it because triumph is smug and condemnation is Devil's work. He raked for a Christian expression among old drawings. A sketch of Coulter showed a calm unafraid friendly face but was far too wistful, and one of McAlpin was calm and strong but had disdainful eyelids. He decided to steal a face from a masterpiece, but in Glasgow Art Gallery the only good Christs were infants, apart from Giorgione's "Christ and the Adulteress," where the painter's modesty or restorer's cowardice had kept the holy face in shadow. He took a day trip to the National Gallery in Edinburgh and at last found the face in a trinity by Hugo Van der Goes. It came from the fifteenth century when the Flemish masters discovered oil paint and made brown the subtlest colour of all while keeping the crisp brightness of tempera. God sat on a clumsy gold and crystal throne floating among gaudy turbulent clouds. He wore a plain red robe with green lining and was preventing, by a hand under each armpit, a pained, thin, dead, nearly nude Christ from sliding off the seat beside him. A white pigeon hovered between their heads. God had the same ordinary thin brown face as his son and a look of pure sorrow without bitterness or blame. In spite of the golden seat neither he nor his son looked like well-paid men. They had the thin faces of providers, not owners or directors. And the suffering father, not the dead son, had Thaw's sympathy. This was the face of his Christ, and he knew he could never paint it. Nobody can paint an expression that is not potentially their own, and this face was beyond him.

In the end he decided to imagine the supper as Jesus would see it from the head of the table. On each side of the board the disciples, anxious, hopeful, doubting, delighted, hungry, replete, were craning and leaning for a glimpse of the viewer's face. The only visible part of Jesus was his hands on the table-cloth. They entered the picture from the bottom margin, and Thaw copied them from his father. He took so long preparing this picture that there was no time to paint it so he submitted the black and white cartoon.

The picture won no prize but was easy to photograph, and *The Bulletin* showed Molly Tierney and Aitken Drummond in front of it. A caption said, "Art students discuss Douglas Shaw's interpretation of the Last Supper at the opening of Glasgow Art School's summer exhibition." Thaw took a copy of the paper into a lavatory cubicle to gloat over it. Though sick of the picture the published photograph gave him a moment's pleasure of almost sexual potency. He went over to the refectory in a mood of unusual confidence and sat by Judy, who asked in a friendly way, "Duncan, did you enjoy drawing those unpleasant people? Or does your picture shock you as much as us?"
Her interest delighted him. He said, "No, I didn't try to paint unpleasant people. After all, Christ picked his disciples at random, like a jury, so they must have been an ordinary representative lot. I may have drawn them grotesque. Not many of us are as we should be, even in our own estimations, so how can we help being grotesque? But we aren't often unpleasant."
Judy said, "Draw a portrait of me Duncan, here, on the table-top." She kept her head still while Thaw scribbled on the formica surface. He said, "I've finished, but it's not a success."

Judy said, "You see, you've made me look evil. You've shown my bad qualities."
Thaw looked at the drawing. He thought he had only shown the shape of her face, and not well. She said, "I know I have more bad qualities than good. . . ." He started to protest but she said, "Look at Kenneth!"
Thaw looked across at McAlpin who had put his head back to laugh at a joke. He had grown a beard over the holidays and the gold spire of it wagged at the ceiling. Judy said, "Kenneth has no bad qualities. If he hurt anyone it would be from stupidity, not deliberately."
"He's a gentleman," said Thaw. "It's civilizing to know him."

In the tramcar that evening he felt unusually conscious of his appearance: the paint-stained trousers like a labourer's below the waist, the collar and tie like an office worker above. Passing the park someone plucked at his sleeve. He turned and saw a plump pretty girl who said, "Hullo there. How are you doing?"
"Fine thanks. And yourself?"
"Not too bad. D'ye live out here?"
"Aye. Opposite the chapel."
"I'm visiting my auntie. I'll be seeing you."
She went downstairs and Thaw wondered who she could be. Suddenly he realized she was Big June Haig who had been to Whitehill School. He went downstairs and stood beside her on the platform. She said, "Oh, there you are."
"I usually get off farther up the hill," said Thaw, as if explaining something.
"Your house faces the Chapel?"
The tram halted and they got off.
"No, it's in the street which runs into the road just opposite the Chapel."
He stood still, describing this geography with his hands. She gripped his lapel and drew him onto the pavement out of the path of a lorry, saying, "I don't want to be held as a witness to a road accident."
"Where are you working just now?"
"Brown's. I'm a waitress in the dining room."
"Oh I go there sometimes, but downstairs to the smokeroom."
Thaw described his eating habits in detail and she seemed to listen intently. He showed her the photograph in the paper and she was less impressed than he expected. There were gaps in the conversation in which he expected her to say cheerio,

but she stayed quiet until he thought of something new to
say. He said, "I'll walk you to your auntie's house," and they
set off side by side. June moved with chin held up and vivid
mouth set haughtily as if disdaining herds of admirers, and
Thaw's heart thumped hard against his ribs. They turned some
corners and stopped at a close. June explained that she visited
her aunt twice a week; the aunt was an old lady who had recently
had an operation. Thaw made an unsubtle reference to her
unselfishness. There was another silence. He said desperately,
"Look, could I meet you sometime?"
"Oh sure."
"Where do you live nowadays?"
"Langside, near the monument."
"Hm . . . Where will we meet?"
After a pause she suggested Paisley's corner near Jamaica Street
Bridge.
"Good!" said Thaw firmly, then added, "But we haven't fixed
the night or the hour have we?"
June said, "No. We haven't."
After some silence she suggested Thursday night at seven
o'clock.
"Good!" said Thaw firmly again. "I'll see you then."
"Yes."
"Well . . . cheerio."
"Cheerio, Duncan."
That night Thaw kept stopping work to walk up and down
the living room, chuckling and singing. Mr. Thaw said, "What's
got into ye? Did a lassie look at ye sideways?"
"My painting aroused a certain interest."

Next morning Thaw told McAlpin about June as they sat
in the school library. McAlpin studied the page of a glossy
magazine, then said, "Does she smell of the bakery, the brew-
ery, or the brothel?"
Thaw felt shocked and cheapened and cursed himself for speaking. McAlpin glanced at him and said, "All women have an
odour, you know. The deodorant adverts pretend it's a bad
thing, which is all balls. If the girl is clean it's a very attractive
thing. Judy has an odour."
"Good."
"What you need, Duncan, is a friendly, experienced older
woman, not a silly wee girl."
"But I don't like being condescended to."
"I admit she'd have to handle you cleverly. I'm sure there

are many women in continental brothels who could do it. Of
course there are no brothels deserving the name in Scotland.
This is such a bloody *poor* country."
Thaw said, "Your mind is full of brothels this morning."
"Yes. . . . What do you think will happen to you when you
leave art school?"
"I don't know. But I can't teach children and I won't go to
London."
McAlpin said, "I don't want to teach but I probably will. I
would like to travel and have freedom before I settled down,
visit Paris, Vienna, Florence. There are a lot of quiet little
cities in Italy with frescoes by minor masters in the churches
and their own wine served under awnings in the squares outside.
I'd like to wander around exploring these with a girl, not necessarily a girl I'd marry. Think! After sunset the air is as warm
as a fine summer afternoon here . . . but I can't leave my
mother for long. At least when I do leave her it will be to
marry Judy, which—as far as freedom is concerned—will
be leaving the frying pan for the fire. Meanwhile I'm getting
older."
"Blethers."
"Does time never worry you?"
"No. Only feelings worry me, and time isn't a feeling."
"I feel it."
After a moment McAlpin said on a baffled note, "I suspect
that if I started living in a slum, and consorting with a prostitute,
and wore nothing but a leopard skin, Judy and my mother
would visit me four days a week with baskets of food."
"I envy you."
"Don't."

That afternoon in the lecture theatre Thaw's body came
to an uneasy compromise with the wooden bench and he dozed.
Later he heard the lecturer say ". . . something of a thug. In
fact he broke Michelangelo's nose once, in a brawl, when they
were young. It is consoling to remember that he died, most
unhappily, a raving lunatic in a Spanish prison, ha-ha. However,
that will do for today."
The lights went on and people crowded to the exits. Thaw
noticed McAlpin and Judy ahead of him; they ran hand in
hand across the street to the annexe and he followed slowly.
They were not in the refectory. He sat down at a table near
Drummond and Macbeth. Drummond was saying, "I can't understand why I've been asked. I hardly know Kenneth."

"When is it?" said Macbeth.

"Tomorrow night. We go to his house for a meal and a booze-up, then to a fancy-dress party at a hotel."

"How old is he?" said Macbeth.

"Twenty-one."

A sad kind of shock flowed through Thaw like water. He sat still, not saying much, then went to the counter and brought food back to the table. Drummond left and Macbeth sat in a way which told Thaw he was depressed at not being asked to the party. Macbeth said, "You're quiet tonight, Duncan."

"I'm sorry. I was thinking."

"I suppose you've been asked to Kenneth's party tomorrow?"

"No."

Macbeth became cheerful. "No? That's queer. You and Kenneth are always about together. I thought you were friends."

"I thought that."

He walked a lot around the streets that evening and let himself into the house after midnight.

"Is that you, Duncan?" said his father from the bed settee in the living room.

"I think so."

"Is anything wrong?"

Thaw explained what had happened. He said, "I can't get used to this. An acquaintance becomes a friend in a gradual, genial way. The reverse is . . . shocking."

"What's that noise?"

"I'm fiddling with ornaments on the lobby table. In God's name how can I face him tomorrow? What can I say?"

"Don't say much, Duncan. Quietly and politely wish him many happy returns of the day."

"That's a good idea, Dad. Goodnight."

"And go straight to sleep. No writing."

He went to bed, grew breathless, took two grains of ephedrine, slept for an hour and woke feeling excited. He opened his notebook and wrote, *The future demands our participation. To participate willingly is freedom, unwillingly is slavery.*

He scored this out and wrote:

The universe compels cooperation. To cooperate consciously is freedom, unconsciously is. . . .

Nature always has our assistance. To assist eagerly is freedom, resistingly is. . . .

God needs our help. Giving it joyfully is freedom, resentfully is. . . .

We have God's help. To know this is freedom, not to notice is . . . .

He snarled and threw the notebook at the ceiling where it

rebounded onto the top of the wardrobe, dislodging an avalanche of books and papers. He lay feeling happy about the changes in life, then masturbated and fell asleep. His happiness had gone when he awoke.

McAlpin was not at school that day. At tea break Judy, Molly Tierney and Rushford discussed the costumes they would wear at the fancy-dress dance. Thaw was unsure how to behave. He drew on the tabletop and grinned with the left side of his mouth.
"You should see my costume!" said Molly gleefully. "It's terrible. All pink and nineteen-twentyish, with a cigarette holder three feet long. Here, give me a pencil."
She seized the pencil from Thaw's fingers and drew the costume on the tabletop. That evening he went into town to meet June and stood in an entry to a clothes shop looking at suave dummies in evening dress and sportswear. Grey dusk became black night. The entrance was a common place for appointments, and he often had the company of people waiting for boy or girlfriends. None waited longer than fifteen minutes. When it was not possible to pretend June would come he walked home feeling horribly insulted.

McAlpin entered the classroom briskly next day with a new book in one hand. He hooked his neatly rolled umbrella on a radiator, laid his coat and bag on a pedestal and came briskly to Thaw. He said, "Listen to this!" and read out the first paragraph of *Oblomov*.
Thaw heard him with embarrassment then said, "Very good" and went into a corner to sharpen a pencil. That morning he and McAlpin worked apart from each other. At lunchtime Thaw went to the main building and obtained an interview with the registrar. In a careful voice he said he thought the school's anatomy course inadequate, that he was going to ask permission to sketch in the dissection room of the university, that he would be grateful for a letter from the registrar saying that such permission would be useful to his art. The registrar swung reflectively from side to side in his swivel chair. He said, "Well, I'm not sure, Thaw. Morbid anatomy certainly was in our curriculum till shortly after the fourteen-eighteen war. I was trained in it myself. I don't think I benefitted from it, but of course I was not so dedicated an artist as you. But would such training do you good psychologically? I honestly think it would do harm."
"I am not—" Thaw said, then cleared his throat and knelt before the electric fire near Mr. Peel's desk. He stared into

the red-hot coil and plucked fibres out of the coconut matting.
"I am not a complete person. A good painter one day, mibby,
but always an inadequate man. So my work is important to
me. If that work is to develop I must see how people are made."
"Your 'Last Supper' showed a detailed grasp of anatomy,
gained, I assume, by the usual methods?"
"Yah. That detail was bluff. I padded out the definite things
I knew with imagination and pictures in books. But now my
imagination needs more detailed knowledge to work on."
"I am not convinced that morbid anatomy will be good for
you, Thaw, but I suppose you must convince yourself of that.
I'm remotely acquainted with the head of the university medical
faculty. I'll get in touch with him."
"Thank you, sir," said Thaw, standing up. "Some sketching
in the vivisection room is really necessary at this stage."
"Dissection room."
"Pardon?"
"You said vivisection room."
"Did I? I'm sorry," said Thaw, confused.

He ran back to the classroom to work off his exhilaration.
McAlpin stood at an easel near the door. Thaw stopped and
muttered to him, "Peel's getting me permission to sketch in
the university dissection room."
"Good! Good!"
"I've not felt so happy since I invented the bactro-chlorine
bomb."
McAlpin bent over and emitted muffled bellowing laughter.
Thaw went to his seat thinking what a waste of time unfriendli-
ness was. Later on their way to the refectory he said to McAlpin,
"Why didn't you ask me to your party?"
"We had only a few tickets for the fancy-dress ball and had
to give them to people who had asked Judy and me to their
parties. I wanted to invite you but—er, it just wasn't possible.
I thought you wouldn't mind because you were taking out
that girl you picked up. How did you get on with her?"

CHAPTER 23. Meetings

One evening Thaw came down to Sauchiehall Street when the air was mild and the lamps not yet lit. So fine a lake of yellow sky lay behind the western rooftops that he walked toward them in a direction opposite home and was overtaken by Aitken Drummond at Charing Cross.
"This isn't your usual territory, Duncan."
"I'm just walking."
"I suppose you're waiting for the ball to start?"
"Is there a ball tonight? No, I cannae afford a ticket."
"I admit money is useful but don't bother about a ticket. Come with me."
They walked past the Grand Hotel then turned down a stunted unlit lane into a cluttered little yard. Thaw made out heaps of coke and coal, bins overflowing with garbage, stacks of milk, beer and fish crates. Drummond opened a door.

They entered so hot an air that Thaw felt stifled for a minute or two. Below a weak electric bulb an old man in a boiler suit sat smoking a pipe beside the furnace door. Drummond said, "This is Duncan Thaw, Dad. We're going to the art school ball."
Mr. Drummond took the pipe from his mouth and directed Thaw to an empty chair with the stem. His amused sunken mouth indicated a lack of teeth; his nose was almost as big as his son's but more craggy; spectacles were pushed up on his brow, the legs mended with insulating tape. He said, "So you're going dancing? It's a waste of time, Douglas, a damned waste of time."
"He's called Duncan!" shouted Drummond.
"That doesn't matter, it's still a waste of time."

"Who's in the kitchen tonight?"

"Eh? Luigi."

"Why not get Duncan and me something to eat? He's hungry."

"No, I'm not," said Thaw.

Mr. Drummond left the room. Drummond pulled his father's chair to the furnace door and opened it, showing a red-hot gullet of flame-roaring coal. He sat and spread his palms to the blaze saying, "It's only a coincidence that I look like the Devil but I do enjoy heat. Pull your chair nearer, Duncan."

Mr. Drummond returned with a big plate of sandwiches and placed it on the floor between Thaw and Drummond. He said, "There's cheese, there's egg, there's salmon, there's meat paste. Help yourselves."

He brought another chair from a corner, sat down and lifted a library book from the floor. "Do you read this man, Duncan?" he asked, showing the title of a novel by Aldous Huxley.

"Yes, but he annoys me. He shows a world with too little in it to believe or enjoy."

"Too little?" said Mr. Drummond with a cackle of anarchic glee. "He leaves you with *nothing*, Duncan. Nothing whatsoever. Nothing at all. And he's right."

He turned a page and read while Thaw and Drummond ate.

"Tonight's pay night!" said Drummond suddenly in a loud voice. Mr. Drummond looked up.

"I said you got paid tonight. Can I have some money?"

"The Glasgow Corporation, Duncan, gives this man one hundred and twenty pounds a year. He spends it on nothing but clothes and pocket money. He lives—"

"And materials," said Drummond.

"And painting materials. He lives at home—he's twenty-four—he pays nothing toward his rent or rates or fuel or light or food—"

"Food!" cried Drummond triumphantly. "I'm glad you mentioned food! Do you know what my father gave me for dinner today, Duncan? Fried kippers. Kippers, mind you, and fried with their heads and tails on."

"Well, if you don't like it you know what to do," said Mr. Drummond mildly, returning the pipe to his mouth.

"Give me ten shillings," said Drummond. His father fished four half crowns from his overalls pocket, handed them over, saw the plate was empty and stood up.

"Have some more sandwiches," he told Duncan.

"No thanks, Mr. Drummond. That was good, but more would
be too much."

"Well, the cook's a friend of mine. I'm not buying them and
I'm not stealing them. You wouldn't like some more?"

"No thanks, Mr. Drummond."

"Duncan has to go now, Dad. We've an appointment. Would
you like more coal?"

"If you can spare the time from your *urgent appointment.*"

A wooden hatch opened upon the coal heap outside. Thaw
and Drummond pulled lumps onto the boiler-room floor with
clumsy wooden rakes. Drummond shovelled them into the furnace and they left after washing their hands below a tap in
the darkened yard.

They walked into the Cowcaddens and entered a close
where the narrow stairs were worn to such a slant that the
foot trod them uneasily. Thaw grew breathless and leaned a
moment on a windowsill. He could see the flat back of a dingy
church across a window box in which the soot-freckled crests
of three stunted cauliflowers rose above a clump of weeds.
On the top landing, Drummond pushed open a bright yellow
door (the lock was broken), stuck his head inside and shouted,
"Ma!" After a moment he said, "Come in, Duncan. I have
to be careful in case my mother's at home. If she dislikes someone she's liable to retire to her bedroom and burn a pheasant's
tail feather."

"What does that do?"

"I shudder to think."

Thaw entered the queerest house he had ever seen. Parts
of it were very like a home but these lay like valleys between
piled furniture and objects salvaged from scrap heaps, middens
and junk shops. As he edged into the kitchen he felt threatened
by empty picture frames, stringless instruments and old wireless
sets. The ceilings were loftier than in his own home but there
was no open space and no planning.

"Excuse the mess," said Drummond. "I haven't had time to
tidy up. I'm hoping to get a studio nearer the art school soon.
What can we use?"

He began shifting things from in front of a cupboard. Thaw
bent to help but Drummond said, "Leave it to me, Duncan.
If you shift these I won't know precisely where to find them."
When the cupboard door could be opened about twelve inches

Drummond thrust his arm into the crevice and brought out, one at a time, a top hat, a Roman helmet, a pith helmet, a deerstalker, a mortarboard and an Indian feathered headdress, all with labels saying they belonged to the Acme Costume Hiring Agency.

"I used to work there," said Drummond. "They stored their best things with an almost criminal carelessness."

Drummond put on the top hat, a tail coat and spats. He cut himself a gleaming shirtfront, collar and cuffs from a sheet of glossy cardboard and fixed these in place with pins and drops of glue, then took a long pair of green rubber fangs from a drawer and inserted them carefully between his teeth and upper lip. He rubbed green greasepaint into his cheeks and, glaring balefully, asked with difficulty, "Dracula?"

"Oh yes," said Thaw, nodding.

Drummond slipped the rubber teeth into his pocket and said, "Who do you want to be?"

"A sorcerer. But I'll settle for an academic."

He put on the mortarboard.

"Not enough," said Drummond. "Go in there."

He moved a tailor's dummy and opened another door. Thaw entered a neat little room which clearly belonged to a woman. There were flowered curtains, striped wallpaper and a pink satin quilt on the bed. There was a scrolled and gilded bird cage, an ashtray shaped like a skull, and sweet peas blooming in a window box.

"Open the wardrobe," commanded Drummond from outside.

"I don't think I should be here."

"You should do exactly what I tell you."

The wardrobe door was ajar and as Thaw opened it a ginger cat strolled out.

"Is there a black silk dressing gown among the coats to the right?" called Drummond.

"Yes."

"Bring it here. Touch nothing else."

Thaw returned to the chaotic kitchen. Drummond said, "Sorry, I would have fetched it myself but my mother made me promise not to go into her bedroom. Put it on. It'll work rather well as an academic robe."

"Won't she find out?"

"No no. She's managing a tearoom in Largs and her visits home are erratic, to say the least."

Drummond took a knobbed cane in one hand and they set off for the ball.

Outside the lamps were lit and tramcars clanged and sparkled. A cryptic drama seemed unfolding throughout the city.
An old woman and man argued quietly at a street corner
watched by two little girls keeking round the corner of a lighted
fruit shop. In a firelit room, seen through a ground-floor window, a man stood with a towel round his neck, shaving perhaps.
Near the school they stepped into a room full of smoke, noise
and people. Drummond forced a way to the bar and Thaw
slid after him between backs and shoulders. Drummond handed
him a large whisky and told him to knock it back in one. A
blonde and a brunette leaned smiling toward Thaw and the
blonde said, "Does your mother know you're here?"
He said, "Mibby. She's dead," and turned away, pleased by
his harshness. Drummond bought two cigars. They lit them,
went out and marched up Sauchiehall Street issuing smoke like
chimneys. Thaw was surprised to find the stares of the bypassers
amusing. He began laughing violently but coughed violently
instead.
"For God's sake don't inhale, Duncan!" said Drummond, slapping his back.
"There's prestige in looking ridiculous with you, Aitken."
The door of the annexe was thronged with people trying to
buy tickets or bribe an entrance from the doorkeepers. Drummond and Thaw mounted the steps side by side, Drummond
cleaving a path with his great axe-blade-edged nose, Thaw opening one with the pallid inclined carapace of his brow. Officials
in exotic costumes shouted "It's the Drummond!" "It's the
Thaw!" and cheerily ushered them in. The janitor gripped
Thaw's sleeve, drew him aside and indicated Drummond, saying, "Beware of that lad. When drunk he's fit company for
neither man nor brute."

The triumph of arrival faded. He sat at the edge of the
dance hall grinning unhappily at the revolving carnival of couples brushing past his knees, his eyes sucking visions of thighs
and hips, fluttering breasts, throats and glances. Molly Tierney,
dressed like an oriental dancing girl, spun gleefully in the arms
of a white-robed Arab who was McAlpin and saluted Thaw
with a raised forefinger. Suddenly two girls said "Hullo!" and
sat on each side of him. "Don't you recognize us?" asked the
smaller girl on the left.
"I'm sorry, I've a poor memory for people."
"You met us in the pub, don't you remember?"

"Are you the girls who asked that question? No, I don't remember your faces."

"Why?" asked the girl on his right. "Did we look awfully hard and experienced?"

"Not at all," said Thaw hurriedly. "Are you at the university?"

"No, the art school."

"Are you in the first year?"

They laughed.

"No, the fourth."

The pale girl said to the dark, "It makes you feel terribly ageing," and then, to Thaw, "Why aren't you dancing?"

"I've no sense of bodily rhythm."

"Oh, we'll soon teach you *that*," said the dark girl, rising to her feet. She led him to a corner and showed him how to move his feet; then she took him onto the floor where he partnered her, feeling clumsy and apologetic and desperately wishing she was the pale girl; then she took him back and gave him to her friend. He felt the difference at once. Her body was firmer, supple without fragility, her hair was pale gold, drawn smoothly back from pale brows to the back of her head. She wore earrings made from small stones hung on thin chains, her dress was black with a square-cut neckline. Sometimes she spoke words directing his steps, sometimes words of congratulation. He looked straight into her eyes, imagined being married to her, thought of Molly Tierney and felt no regret at all. He thought, I'm being ridiculous, and kept looking in her eyes; the dark pupils grew very clear and her face and head became a dim white and gold shape around them. He thought, She's like marble and honey, and shaped the words with his lips. The music stopped and he had to dance with the smaller girl again. He looked straight across her shoulder and talked about painting and the art school. She said, "Is your father a minister?"

"No, my father's a pious atheist. Do I look like a minister's son?"

"You look like a kid of twelve. But you sound like an old highland minister."

He danced again with the pale girl in a silence which grew desperate, for he knew it must end. So he said, "You're like marble and honey."

"What?"

"You're like marble and honey."

"Oh. Am I? Thank you."

She looked at him without smiling and said, "You should dance more often."

"No, really, I can't."
"If you come to more balls I'll dance with you."
He grew more worried, feeling she could not dance with him all evening, wondering when and how she would break from him. When the music stopped he excused himself and hurried from the hall.

He went upstairs thinking, 'I love her,' and, 'You're daft.' He wondered if she had a boyfriend and why he wasn't around. Anyway, she had danced with him from kindness; their connection had no equality in it. He imagined her friends mocking the lost look on his face when he danced with her. She would laugh and say, "He's just a kid!" He looked for a place to hide. Intimate whispers came from all the dark corridors so he opened a door onto the dance hall balcony, a small place used as a store for chairs. A man was slumped there with arms on the balustrade and head on arms. It was Drummond. Thaw had never seen him alone or depressed before. Drummond smiled faintly and pointed to a chair.
"How are you, Duncan? Why aren't you dancing?"
"I can't."
From up here the dancers seemed blind caps of hair with projecting hands and feet like the limbs of starfish. The linked couples twitched and turned as if the music was a fluid vibrating them. When it stopped they hurried to the side of the hall like corpuscles into a clot. Drummond sighed and said, "They're villainous, Duncan, downright villainous, absolutely villainous."
"Who are?"
"Women."
Drummond gazed down on the dancers and said, "One kept following me around tonight and looking at me . . . she went off with someone else ten minutes ago. I think I could have had her if I'd wanted. But I saw Molly dancing, and I'd no heart for anything of that kind. I don't know why. She's past her best and engaged to an Irish vet and flirting away. . . ."
"Molly Tierney?"
"I used to go about with her. You must admit she's good-looking. She avoids me now."
"Why?"
"I suppose because her parents are nice and mine aren't. My mother told her she wasn't fit to sleep with a pig. Which forced me into the unenviable position of declaring she *was* fit to sleep with a pig."
They were silent again, gazing on the dancers. Then Drum-

mond said, "I tried to cure myself by imagining her pissing and excreting and menstruating, but the connection made these acts beautiful to me."

"How do women menstruate? At regular times on regular days?"

"When they reach Molly's age they can do it running for a tram, or standing before an easel, or at dinner or talking quietly to a friend, as we are. She let me watch her sometimes."

"*What?*"

"We shared many little secrets of that kind," said Drummond gloomily. This aspect of love had never entered Thaw's fantasies. He rubbed his face in frustration. Drummond said, "You'll be happier with women when you're better known—prestige makes a lot of them randy. Janet Weir used to go around with the president of the students' representative council, but when Jimmy Macbeth grew famous for drinking himself to death she kept company with him for a day or two. Then the film *Cyrano de Bergerac* popularized long noses and she turned to me. A lot of girls like me because I'm supposed to be a symbol of something. It's humiliating in some ways but lucky in others. What do you think of Janet?"

"I don't know her."

"She looks like the Mona Lisa but has nicer legs. She invited me into her room last night and told me she loved me."

"Oh, *God,*" said Thaw, beating his brow. It felt like a gate which had been locked and soldered shut. Drummond stretched his arms and yawned. "Yes, I was embarrassed too. Girls who say they love you expect all sorts of irrational things, like sincerity, in exchange. Still, we passed a pleasant night. She's a virgin, you know. I'd seen her with so many men that I hadn't expected that. I was careful not to destroy it. I like virginity; it seems a pity to destroy it for fun. But I suppose she'll get me doing it eventually. Virgins are terribly single-minded."

"I'm going to the lavatory."

Two hours later Thaw leaned despondently on the railings by the entrance watching the last dancers leave in ones and twos. He had stowed the mortarboard and gown in a locker. Drummond, still dressed like Dracula, capered on the pavement among laughing friends.

"I must get a woman to take home," he was saying. "I must take *some* woman home. Lorna, Lorna, Lorna!"

He tried to embrace a girl who slipped under his arm, laughing and saying, "Not tonight, Aitken, not tonight!"

A girl in a blue coat came out and paused, looking vaguely
from side to side. Drummond took her hand politely and said,
"Let us walk you home, Marjory."
The girl's face crinkled in a shy amused smile. She said, "I'm
sorry, Aitken. My father is coming for me in the car."
"Phone him up, he may not even have left yet. Tell him we're
walking you home. I'll hold one hand and Duncan the other.
Two is a perfectly safe escort."
The girl hesitated.
"It's only half past eleven. And a warm night," said Drummond
with soft urgency.
"All right," said the girl. She smiled quickly at Thaw and went
indoors to phone.
"Marjory is a nice girl, a really nice girl," said Drummond
musically. "I don't know why people think I'm incapable of
liking nice girls."
Thaw yawned at the sky. One or two stars were visible. He
said, "Goodnight, Aitken."
"Don't go," said Drummond quickly. "Don't you *like*
Marjory?"
"That's not the point," said Thaw; yet when Marjory came
out Drummond took her right hand and Thaw her left, holding
it lightly and carefully. It was small, faintly warm, neither dry
nor quite moist, and he was very conscious of it.

They walked, talking about ordinary things, across the arch
of the hill and followed the lamp-reflecting steel of the tramlines
over the River Kelvin into a district of trees and terraces. Somewhere beyond the university they heard some sharp barks and
a black dog ran toward them round a curving pavement.
"It's Gibbie!" said Marjory, and squatting down on her
haunches received the dog's head in her lap. "How are you,
Gibbie? Eh, Gibbie? Good dog, Gibbie," she whispered, rubbing its cheeks with her hands. The dog panted and lolled its
tongue out, grinning up at her with shut ecstatic eyes. She
stood up and it shot back the way it had come. They followed
until they reached a tall, slightly gawky woman standing by a
gate in a hedge. She smiled amiably and gave her hand to
the students in turn.
"Oh, I've met you before, Aitken, of course. So this is Duncan.
How are you, Duncan? Thank you both for seeing our little
daughter so safely home. My husband is just bringing the car
round to drive you back to the city centre. Neither of you
live near here, do you?"

A car drove slowly toward them along the edge of the kerb. It stopped and the back door was pushed open. They said goodbye to Marjory and her mother and climbed in.

Though Marjory had given him no more than some friendly glances and a squeeze of the hand he spent the weekend cleaning paint stains from his clothes and started brushing his teeth before going to bed. On Monday he stood with friends on the staircase of the main building when she went swiftly by. He followed her down to the entrance hall, across the street and into the annexe, where, singing, she turned unexpected corners. Her voice echoed along an unseen corridor until silenced by the remote slam of a door. He stood for a while as if still listening. The song had been tuneful but without definite tune, a line of melodious notes as casual as bird notes. On the staircase he had glimpsed her throat in silhouette, the outline pulsing like a plucked string. He felt baffled and wondered whether to feel insulted. She must have known he was following; why hadn't she stopped? But then he could have reached her side by walking faster; why hadn't he walked faster?

At noontime she was several places ahead of him in the refectory queue and smiled and raised her hand in greeting. He nodded, looked casually elsewhere, and three minutes later arrived beside her in a way that seemed accidental. He waited until she noticed him before smiling. She said, "Hullo, Duncan. How are you?"

"Well. How are you?"

"Oh! Well."

A pleasant little giggle suggested, not that he amused her, but that it was amusing for them to be talking there. He said, "I enjoyed our walk on Friday."

"I enjoyed it a lot too."

"Aitken is good company."

"You were not bad company yourself, Duncan."

A dangerous silence widened between them. He drew breath and plunged over it.

"Can I . . . eat at your table?"

"Of course, Duncan."

She smiled so kindly that he felt he had said nothing difficult or strange. They took their plates to a table and ate beside Janet Weir and a couple of other girls who were attractive and welcoming. He enjoyed the meal for it was easier talking to several girls than one, but when Janet left to get cigarettes he leaned towards Marjory and his face went red.

"Would you . . . let me take you to the pictures some night?"

"Of course, Duncan."

"Will tomorrow night do?"

"Yes. . . . yes, I think so."

"I'll call about seven, will I?"

She frowned vaguely. "I . . . think so, Duncan. Yes."

After tea next evening he took from his wardrobe a blue pin-striped double-breasted suit, a gift of a neighbour whose son had outgrown it. Thaw had enraged his mother by saying he would never wear it because it was the kind of suit businessmen and American gangsters wore. Tonight he put it on, slid a clean white folded handkerchief into the breast pocket and set off for Marjory's home, buying a box of chocolates on the way. Aboard the bus his heart beat loudly and his knees trembled, but entering the district where she lived he was unable to find the house. It had been at the end of a curving terrace but there were many of these. He searched for a phone box to look up her address in the directory and found one near the docks, but with the book in hand he discovered he didn't know her second name. He punched his brow violently for a while, then phoned McAlpin who said, "Her father's Professor Laidlaw, who does biochemistry at Gilmorehill. I'll look up the address for you. You sound rather . . . distraught."

Half an hour later Thaw rang a doorbell and Mrs. Laidlaw opened to him, saying, "Come in, Duncan."

Having despaired of getting there he felt his arrival was insubstantial. He said, "I'm sorry I'm late. I lost my way."

"Are you late? Marjory's still upstairs getting ready."

The lobby had shining dark furniture and dark landscapes in guilt frames. A golf club and umbrella lay in a huge blue earthenware vase, and on the polished floor nearby a golf ball was tethered by a cord to a rubber mat. Mrs. Laidlaw led him into a room with a bright fire in the hearth and switched on the light. A massive man hoisted himself out of an armchair and said in a gentle voice, "How do you do?"

Thaw said, "How do you do?"

"This is Marjory's father—oh, but you met last Friday. Now sit down, both of you, and I'll see if I can hurry up my daughter a little."

Thaw sat down and tried to seem at ease. The professor had sounded small and clerkly in the car but here the quiet voice emphasized his suave bulk. He was leaning forward and tickling with one finger the ear of the dog, Gibbie, who sprawled on the hearth rug.

"Do you play golf?" he asked gently.

"No. But my father does—did, I mean, during the war. He's mainly a climber, though."

"Ah."

Thaw cleared his throat and said, "I received some golfing lessons at my secondary school, but the game required more care, concentration and precision than I was prepared to bring to it." The professor said, "Yes. It is an exacting game and requires . . . . . patience."

They were silent until a small yellow budgerigar landed with a thump on Thaw's shoulder and said "Hurry up, Marjory! Good old Mr. Churchill! Hurry up, Marjory!"

Thaw said, "Ah. A budgerigar."

"Yes indeed. We call him Joey. I'm sure I've seen you around the university."

"I sometimes sketch in the medical building."

"Why?"

"To see the insides of people. And death too, of course."

"Why?"

"Because it's stupid to share the world with something you're afraid to look at. You see I want to like the world, life, God, nature, et cetera, but I can't because of pain."

"Pain poses no problem. It warns individuals that they're defective."

"Oh, I know pain is usually good for us," said Thaw, "but what good is it to a woman who bears a limbless baby with a face on top of its head? What good is it to the baby?"

"I deal with life at a cellular level," said the professor.

A little later he and Thaw said simultaneously, "How is Marjory—" "Tell me about golf—"

"I beg your pardon," said Thaw. "How is Marjory?"

"Getting on at school."

"I . . . I don't know. What year is she in?"

"The second, I think."

"Then she's probably doing quite well," said Thaw. "Hardly anyone fails their second year," he added.

"I thought you were in her class," said the professor, faintly hostile.

"Indeed no," said Thaw coldly.

Marjory came in with her mother. She wore a flower-patterned dress and long earrings and her breasts seemed more prominent than usual. The budgerigar fluttered to her shoulder twittering, "Hurry, hurry up, Marjory! Good old Mr. Churchill!"

She blushed and smiled.

"Naughty Joey's giving away secrets," said Mrs. Laidlaw.

"I'm sorry I kept you waiting, Duncan."

"I was very late myself," said Thaw.

"Off the pair of you go now," said Mrs. Laidlaw kindly. She stood in the doorway watching them go down the path. Thaw felt like a child going to school with his sister. On the pavement Marjory hesitated and said nervously, "Duncan—I hope you won't be annoyed about this—when I said I could go out with you tonight I'd forgotten I'd arranged to see a friend. . . . She's very nice. . . . Would it be all right if she came with us? She lives quite near."

"Of course!" said Thaw, and talked heartily to cover the stoical adjustments happening inside him. They reached a gate in a thick hedge and Marjory whispered that she wouldn't be long and left him outside. The night was chilly and glints of frost shone in the pavement under the street lamp. He heard a door open and the light murmur of Marjory's voice, then the darker tones of someone else. Eventually the door shut and Marjory joined him with a slight vertical crease between her eyebrows. "I'm sorry, Duncan—she wasn't able to come. I think maybe she has a cold."

"Don't worry about it."

She gave a quick polite smile. He was disturbed by the strained lines it made near the corners of her mouth. If she often smiled like that a wrinkle would come there in ten or twelve years.

They were late for the film. It had love scenes which made him very conscious of Marjory beside him. He leaned toward her but she sat so upright and stared so straight ahead that he dispiritedly brought out the chocolates and resignedly popped one at intervals into her mouth. After the film the nearby cafés had queues outside so they boarded the bus home. He sat on the upper deck watching the pure line of her face and throat against the black window. They filled him with delight and terror for he would need to cross over to them and he hadn't much time. He stared desperately, trying to learn what to do by intensity of vision. Her eyes were downcast under a brown feathery brow, her mouth had a lost remote look but the chin was strong, her brown hair was drawn into a flat coil at the back of her skull and the tip of an ear peeped through like a delicate section of seashell. The head turned and faced him enquiringly. Sweat trickled down his brow.

"Can I . . . hold your hand?"

"Of course, Duncan."

"It's queer. When I ask for something I'm usually sure you'll give it, but I sweat as if I'd no chance at all."

Her throat was shaken by a note of bitten-back laughter.

"Do you, Duncan?"

The handhold was mainly pleasing for symbolic reasons, but where their shoulders touched so soft a silence and relaxation flowed into him that his mind bathed in vacancy for a while, untroubled by thoughts of what to do when they reached her house.

They paused at the garden gate. She shut her eyes suddenly and tilted her blind face upward. He put his mouth on hers. After a moment she slipped away, saying "Goodnight, Duncan."

"Goodnight—I'll see you tomorrow, won't I?"

"Yes, tomorrow. Goodnight."

He walked thoughtfully home, for the last tram had gone. Frost stiffened the substance of the pavement so that his feet hit the glittering surface with a tweeting note. Crossing the hill by the university he was struck by the clarity of the stars. They were not like lights stippling the inner surface of a dome but like galactic chandeliers hung at different levels in black air. He felt vaguely happy, yet vaguely puzzled and flat, and very cold. The kiss had meant nothing, nothing books, films and gossip had made him expect. Was it his fault? Or Marjory's? Did it matter? He reached home, went to bed and slept.

He was standing on the golf course of Alexandra Park shortly after dawn, listening to a lark in the grey air overhead. The song stopped and the bird's corpse thumped onto the turf at his feet. He walked downhill through a litter of sparrows and blackbirds on the paths to the gate. On Alexandra Parade a worker's tram, apparently empty, groaned past the traffic lights. He watched the lights change from red and amber to green, then to green and amber, and then go out. The tramcar came to a halt.

Not everything died at once for the lowlier plants put on final spurts of abnormal growth. Ivy sprouted up the Scott monument in George Square and reached the lightning conductor on the poet's head; then the leaves fell off and the column was encased in a net of bone-white bone-hard fibre. Moss carpeted the pavements, then crumbled to powder under his feet as he walked alone through the city. He was happy. He looked in the windows of pornography shops without wondering if anyone saw him, and rode a bicycle through the halls of the art galleries and bumped down the front steps, singing. He set up easels in public places and painted huge canvases of buildings and dead trees. When a painting was completed he left it confronting the reality it depicted. The weather had also died. There was no rain or wind. The sky was always grey and warm and the time mid-afternoon.

He sat in the courtyard of Holyrood Palace in Edinburgh painting a view of Arthur's Seat. A harsh beak whispered gratingly in his left ear, "This is all much as Queen Mary remembered it."
A white speck appeared high on the crags and moved down the path toward the courtyard's southern gate. A load of depression settled in his heart. He leaned toward the canvas and worked with his face against it, determined to see nobody. A chilling shock went through him and he knew she had laid her hand on the back of his neck. He tried to ignore her but work was intolerable under her suffering eyes, so he motioned her to stand before the easel. She did so, thinking he meant to put her in the picture. He took a rifle and shot her. She stared at him reproachfully, then broke, crumpled, crumbled into a turd.

Great beetles emerged. The city was full of them. They were five feet long and shaped like rowing boats with antennae and had mouths in their stomachs. They were in every building throwing furniture and the bodies of the dead out of the windows. They feared open spaces and crossed these at a quick scuttling run. In the angle between a wall and pavement Thaw crouched between two who flickered their antennae incuriously over him. Since they had no eyes they thought him one of themselves as he squatted down and moved as they did.

He awoke with a chill that kept him in bed for a week.

CHAPTER 24. Marjory Laidlaw

Convalescence was sweetened by the thought of Marjory and he returned to school full of anxious hope. Once again he was standing on the staircase talking to McAlpin and Drummond when she passed without noticing him wave and call. He gaped after her, wondering if he should chase and strike her. Surely she must have seen him! Why did she pretend not to? Or was the fault his? Perhaps on their night out together he had bored or disappointed her beyond any hope of forgiveness. An hour later in the school shop she said "Hello, Duncan!" and stood looking at him with a shy gay open amused smile.

"Hullo!" he said, gazing joyfully back.

"Have you been ill, Duncan?"

"Just a bit."

"What a shame."

She still smiled, but her voice sympathized.

In the following weeks she brought him increasing splendour and discontent. He told her of a studio he was sharing near Kelvingrove Park.

"It's a great big attic and by clubbing together it only costs a few shillings a week each. On Friday nights we go there from school and take turns at making a big meal. Most of the others get help from their girlfriends but Kenneth is a great chef. Last week he made Spanish onion soup with toast on top. Next week it's my turn and I'm going to boil a haggis. A shop in Argyle Street has good big cheap ones and they're nice with tatties and turnip. Afterwards we put off the lights and play records by the fire, jazz and classical. You should come."

"It sounds marvellous." She sighed. "I wish I could come."

"Why can't you?"

"Well . . . there's a friend I always have to see on Fridays."
At tea breaks and lunch time they sat in the refectory or went
to a café and returned holding hands and talking. He joined
the school choir because she sang there, and after late practices
they walked to her home. At the garden gate conversation
suddenly failed, their mouths met in a ritual pressure and she
slipped away with a soft "Goodnight," leaving him as baffled
as the first time they kissed. When they left the school together
she always murmured "Excuse me a minute," slipped into the
ladies' lavatory and left him outside for a quarter of an hour.
She never recognized him if he was with friends. These insults filled reservoirs of rage which evaporated whenever she
smiled at him. And when their bodies accidentally touched
a current of stillness and silence flowed in from her and he
felt that before touching Marjory he had never known rest.
His calmest moods had been full of fear, hope, lust and memory, all clashing to make a discord of ideas and words. Her
touch silenced these, letting him know nothing for a while but
the pressure of hand or knee, and Marjory beside him,
and sunlight on rooftops or a cloud seen through a window.
That didn't happen often. His frequentest pleasure was waking
in the morning, hearing pigeons among the chimneypots and
being warmed by the thought of soon seeing her. When words
came at these times the memory of Marjory orchestrated them
into phrases. He wrote poems and slid copies into her hands
as they passed in the school corridors. He started combing
his hair, brushing his teeth, polishing his shoes, changing underwear twice a week and (to the annoyance of Mr. Thaw, who
laundered them) shirts four times a week. He wore the pin-
striped suit to school and cleaned off the stains with turpentine,
though this made temporary rashes on the skin. His manner
with other girls grew more playful. He thought they were interested in him.

After school one evening he saw her on the edge of a
group outside the annexe. She smiled and raised her hand and
he said, "Remember tonight, Marjory?"
She grew agitated and distressed. "No, Duncan. . . . Duncan
I think I . . . I'm sure I've something to do tonight. . . . This
isn't an excuse; I really have too much work to do."
"Never mind," said Thaw amiably. He entered the refectory
and found McAlpin alone at a table. Thaw sat down, folded
arms on the tabletop and hid his face in them. "Damn her,"

he said muffledly. *"Damn* her. *Damn* her. *Damn* her."

"What happened this time?"

Thaw explained. McAlpin said, "She's afraid of you."

"That's impossible. I'm not aggressive. Even in masturbation fantasies I never dream of being cruel to *real* girls."

After a pause, McAlpin said, "Imagine you are quiet, timid, rather conventional, and not long out of a middle-class fee-paying school which prides itself on producing genteel young ladies. You are chased by a clever peculiar boy. He's polite but his clothes and hair have paint on them, he breathes heavily and his skin is often . . . mmmm . . . medically interesting. How would you react? Remember, you've been brought up not to hurt people."

Thaw said, "I've thought of that. And next time we meet I'll nod to her distantly and she'll be specially inquiring and charming. She'll suggest we have coffee together. Oh, she wants me. Slightly. Sometimes."

"Maybe she's frigid."

"Of course she's frigid. So am I. But nobody stays the same forever and even lumps of ice, surely, will melt if they rub together long enough. Perhaps she's not frigid. Perhaps she loves someone else."

"She's honest, Duncan—I doubt if there's anyone else."

"Do you? I would doubt but . . . she's so much more bonny each time I see her that I feel she must love somebody."

McAlpin said, "Hm!" and glanced sideways at Thaw beneath lethargic eyelids.

He sat on the top deck of the homeward tramcar and his rage at her increased with the distance between them. A voice said, "Hullo, Duncan."

It took a moment to recognize June Haig, who was going downstairs. He rose and followed, saying, "Hullo, June. You are a bad girl."

"Oh? Why that?"

"Last year you kept me waiting for nothing for a whole hour at Paisley's corner."

She gave him a quick startled smile. "Did I? Oh, yes. Something happened."

He saw that she didn't remember. He grinned and said "Don't worry. The point is . . ." —the tramcar stopped and they crossed to the pavement—"the point is, will you forget again if we arrange to meet again?"

"Oh no."

"Yes you will, if we don't meet soon. What about Paisley's corner tomorrow night? About seven?"

"Yes, all right, then."

"Good. I'll be there."

He turned and walked quickly home. June had aroused him like an erotic fantasy, yet he hadn't once blushed or stammered. He wondered why this arousal made him her equal when his feeling for Marjory made him subordinate. In the living room he walked up and down for a while, then said, "Dad, tomorrow night I'm taking out a girl. I want you to give me five pounds."

Mr. Thaw turned slowly and stared at him.

"What kind of girl is this?"

"Her kind is no business of yours. I want to be free and openhanded. A few shillings will keep me mean and cautious and I'll get no pleasure at all. I need pleasure."

"And how often do you intend to have it?"

"I don't care. I don't know. I'm only thinking of tomorrow night."

Mr. Thaw scratched his head. "Your grant is a hundred and twenty a year. With that I'm to clothe, house, feed you and pay for materials and pocket money. You won't work in the holidays because it interferes with your artistic self-expression—"

"Don't talk to me about self-expression!" cried Thaw fiercely. "Do you think I'd paint if I'd nothing better to express than this rotten *self*? If my self was made of decent material I could relax with it, but self-*disgust* keeps forcing me out after the truth, the truth, the truth!"

"I can make neither head nor tail of that," said Mr. Thaw, "but I know the result. The result is that I toil so that you can paint. And now you want over a quarter of my weekly salary to spend on pleasure. What kind of fool do you think I am?"

After a moment Thaw said, "In future I'll handle my grant money myself. I know you don't mind me sleeping here, but I'll try not to ask for other favours."

"You'll try and you'll fail because you're so damned impractical. But all right, all right. Try anyway."

"Thank you. It'll be two months before the next grant comes through. Please give me five pounds, Dad."

His father looked hard at him, then brought out a wallet and handed over the money.

In Paisley's shop door next night he knew after ten minutes that June would not come, yet numbness in his limbs and heart kept him waiting an hour longer. A lame old man in a dirty coat approached and asked for money. Thaw stared resentfully into bloodshot eyes, a twisted helpless mouth and a tangled beard slimy with spittle. He could not think why he should own a five-pound note and this man not, so he handed it over and walked quickly away. He felt his soul was being deliberately crushed, yet there was nobody to blame. He could not bear to face his father. He walked to the Cowcaddens, climbed the stair to Drummond's house, pushed the door open and went into the kitchen.

Drummond and Janet Weir sat on each side of the kitchen range looking at a crate on the hearth rug. The ginger cat sprawled on a sheet of glass covering this and stared down at two white mice among cheese rinds at the bottom. Drummond said, "Hullo, Duncan. Ginger's at his television set."
"How did this happen?" said Thaw.
"My mother visited us yesterday. She brought the mice as a present for the cat, since it was his ninth birthday. My father and I took them away from her."
"And now Ginger sits there, foiled of his rightful prey," said Mr. Drummond. He lay in the recess bed with spectacles on his craggy nose, a flat cap on his head, an open library book propped on the quilt over his knees. Janet shivered and said, "Surely it's cruel, having him on top of them like that."
Drummond said, "What? Make the tea, Duncan looks tired. These mice are nearly blind, Duncan. If anyone is suffering it's Ginger."

Drummond left the room and came back with a picture of himself chalking a cue beside a snooker table. He propped the painting on the sideboard, took paint and brushes and began altering the position and number of the balls. The air was permeated by the pleasant smell of linseed oil and turpentine. At intervals Drummond stood back and said, "How's that, Duncan?"
Janet handed Thaw a cup of tea and a bacon sandwich, and when he had drunk and eaten he began to draw her. She crouched near the fire with the cat on her lap, copious hair overhanging and surrounding her subtle face. She looked rather like Marjory, but Marjory moved with childish carelessness and Janet seemed to feel eyes watching the secretest parts of her.

"What o'clock is it?" said Thaw.

"I don't know," said Drummond. "None of the clocks in this house can be relied on, least of all the ones that go. It's a pity Ma isn't here. She could estimate the time by things like passing aeroplanes. Couldn't she, Dad?"

"What?"

"I said Ma could always tell the time."

"Oh, aye. She would shake my shoulders in bed in the morning. 'Hector! Hector! It's ten past four. There's Mrs. Stewart going to her work in the bakery—I'd know her step anywhere.' Or it would be 'It's a quarter to eight—I can hear the horse of Eliot's milk cart two streets away.'"

"Do you know the time, Mr. Drummond?" said Thaw.

Mr. Drummond lifted an alarm clock which lay face down on a pile of books by the bed. He held it to his ear, shook it and put it carefully down saying, "The hands have ceased to go round and round, and no trust whatever can be placed in it." He closed his eyes, opened his mouth, lay back on the pillow and at last said definitely, "We are in the region of midnight."

"Then the trams have stopped, you'll have to stay here tonight," said Drummond.

"The trams haven't stopped. I can hear them," said Janet.

"Can't you keep your mouth shut?" cried Drummond savagely. "I don't know why I tolerate you! You're the epitome of all . . . of all . . . Duncan! You aren't going to let this woman drive you out of my house?"

"No. I'm going home to bed. Goodnight."

Drummond followed Thaw into the lobby. "Let's be sensible about this, Duncan. Why should you go to bed?"

"To sleep."

Drummond stood erect, folded his arms, drew his black eyebrows together at the bridge of his nose and said in a firm quiet voice, "I'm telling you not to go out of that door, Duncan."

"Heech! You're in a bad way when you have to resort to commanding," said Thaw, but lingered. "Why should I *not* go out that door?" he asked plaintively.

"Because you'd rather not," said Drummond, ushering him back into the kitchen.

"I'm being weak," said Thaw, settling into a chair by the fire. *"No, damn me!"* he cried, jumping up. "Why should I be commanded by you or by any man? Goodnight!"

"Janet, ask him to stay!" said Drummond. "Tell him it's stupid going back to Riddrie at this hour of night."

"I think you should stay, Duncan," said Janet.

"Well, if you're convinced of that . . ." said Thaw, sitting down. For the first time since waiting for June he felt relaxed and cheerful.

Thaw drew, Drummond painted, they gossiped and improvised jokes and sometimes chuckled continuously for many minutes. They had spells of listlessness when Janet made the tea. Each time he drew her his hand moved more easily and depicted more of the surrounding room. It was as if Janet's body gave out light which clarified nearby things and turned the cluttered furniture, Drummond working at the sideboard, Mr. Drummond reading or dozing, even stale breadcrusts on the table, into parts of a cunning harmony. She sat still easily under his concentrated stare. Sometimes her eyes returned it for a second, then glanced slyly sideways at Drummond. Thaw said, "You're a flower beneath the foot, Janet."

"What do you mean, Duncan?"

"You're beautiful and neglected and dishevelled."

"Don't encourage her," said Drummond grimly. "Don't you know it's deliberate? She probably wants the girls at school to think I beat her."

"Why have you always to be offensive?" said Janet.

"Why have I . . .? Why have you always to be offensive? Stupid!" said Drummond, almost kindly, for he was staring at his painting. He had taken out all but one white ball and said, "How's that, Duncan?"

"Good. But I preferred it with more balls."

Drummond frowned at the picture, took a saw from a drawer and cut off the part with the snooker table on it. He placed the self-portrait on the mantelpiece and said "How about that, Duncan?"

"More perfect but less worthwhile."

Drummond said, "Make the tea, Janet."

He took a small gilt frame from under the sideboard, measured it, sawed the head off the portrait and fitted it into the frame. He hung it on the wall and stood back regarding it with arms folded and head on one side. He said, "More perfect? You're right, Duncan, it is more perfect. Yes, I'm pleased with my night's work."

"All sheer bloody nonsense!" snorted Mr. Drummond from his bed.

"Yes, I'm pleased with my night's work," said Drummond, accepting a cup of tea from Janet.

The darkness outside the window paled and soft pink came into the sky behind the pinnacles of the dingy little church. Drummond shot up the window to let in a cool draught. From grey rooftops on the left rose the mock Gothic spire of the university, then the Kilpatrick hills, patched with woodlands and with the clear distant top of Ben Lomond behind the east-ward slope. Thaw thought it queer that a man on that summit, surrounded by the highlands and overlooking deep lochs, might see with a telescope this kitchen window, a speck of light in a low haze to the south. The dim sky broke into cloudbergs with dazzling silver between. Mr. Drummond lay back on his pillow snoring wheezily through open mouth.

"The dairy will be open now," said Drummond. "Janet, here's half a crown. Go and buy something nice for breakfast. Duncan and I will get ready for bed."

Thaw and Drummond went into a room with an open bed settee in the middle. They undressed to their underwear, removed their socks and got between rough blankets. They heard Janet return and do something in the kitchen, then she entered with three plates of stewed pears and cream. She ate on the edge of the bed and when Thaw and Drummond lay down she wrapped herself in a khaki greatcoat and lay across their ankles with the cat curled against her stomach. Thaw said sleepily, "I would now be getting out of my bed at home if—"

Suddenly he was struck by an image, not of June Haig but of Marjory. He imagined her breasts trembling under skilful hands and sat up, saying, "Janet! You're Marjory's friend. Is she carrying on with somebody else?"

"I don't think so, Duncan."

"Then what is wrong with her? What is wrong with her?"

"I think she's too contented at home, Duncan. She's very happy with her father and mother."

"I see. She's in love with her parents. Instead of learning to be adult by teaching me to be adult she basks idly at home. Oh, God, if you exist, *hurt* her, *hurt* her, God, let her find no comfort but in me, make life afflict her as it afflicts me. Oh, Aitken! Aitken! How *dare* she be happy without me?"

Thaw lay back glaring at the ceiling. After a pause Drummond said bitterly, "I understand your feelings."

Janet sneered and said, "In case you don't know, Duncan, he's thinking about Molly—*oh!*"

Drummond's foot below the blankets had struck her chin. She put her hands to her face and wept quietly. They stewed in their separate miseries and gradually fell asleep.

Thaw dreamed he was fornicating awkwardly with Marjory, who stood naked and erect like a caryatid. He rode astride her hips, holding himself off the ground by gripping her sides with knees and arms. The cold rigid body stayed inert at first, then gradually began to vibrate. He had a thin, lonely sensation of triumph.

He awoke late in the afternoon. Slowly drawing his feet from below Janet without disturbing her he carried his clothes into the kitchen, washed at the sink, dressed, gave water and cheese to the mice in the crate and rolled up the drawings he had made the night before. On the way to the front door he glanced into the bedroom. Janet no longer lay on the bed foot and there was movement under the blankets. In the close he met Mr. Drummond returning from the hotel, tall, spectacled, flat-capped, raincoat open over boiler suit.

"Hullo, Duncan. You're not leaving? I'm just going to make dinner. I've some cod roe here."

He indicated a paper parcel under his armpit.

"No thanks, Mr. Drummond."

"Well, it's a present from the chef. I neither pinched it nor paid for it. You're sure you won't have some?"

"No thanks. If I go back to your house I'm afraid I'll never get away."

Mr. Drummond laughed and started filling a short-stemmed pipe. "You're a reader, aren't you?"

"I read books, yes."

"I'm inclined that way myself. I tried to make Aitken a reader, but I failed. Do you know how he passed his English exams?"

"No."

"I read his schoolbooks, Scott, Jane Austen, and so on, and told him the stories. He can remember anything he hears, you see, but he's never read a book from start to finish in his life, unless it was about art. Consequently his mind is cramped, narrow and lacking in sympathy for his fellow man. He'll never prosper. But you'll prosper, Duncan."

"I hope so, Mr. Drummond."
"Oh, yes, you'll prosper, Duncan."

Cheered by this prophecy Thaw walked quickly uphill to
the school and passed Marjory in the entrance hall. He nodded
coldly but she stopped him, smiled and said, "Where have
you been, Duncan?"
"I've been sleeping."
"Are you coming for a coffee?"
He was filled with relief and delight. She gave him her hand
to hold on the way to the refectory. He thought, 'This is an
interesting world.'

CHAPTER 25. Breaking

He took the 1875 *Imperial Gazetteer of Scotland* from his father's bookcase and read:

MONKLAND CANAL, an artificial navigable communication between the city of Glasgow and the district of Monkland in Lanarkshire. The project of the canal was suggested in 1769 as a measure for securing to the inhabitants of Glasgow, at all times, a plentiful supply of coals. The Corporation of the city immediately employed the celebrated James Watt to survey the ground, obtained an act of parliament for carrying out the measure, and subscribed a number of shares to the stock. The work was begun in 1771. Previous to its formation the lands in the neighbourhood were comparatively shut up, the mineral fields unproductive, and only a thatched cottage was seen here and there to dot the surface. But once the canal was in operation a change, as if effected by magic, came over the face and feelings of the district, a change accelerated by the establishment of ironworks in the district of Monkland. Public works were erected, population gathered in masses by thousands, splendid edifices were called into existence, a property once considered valueless, except for the scanty returns of its tillage or hortage, became a mine of wealth which may enrich many succeeding generations.

When the project of opening the district by railways was first mooted it created much alarm in the canal company, lest traffic be wholly diverted from their navigation. The alarm was not unfounded, but it only induced the company to reduce their dues by two thirds and expend large sums on improvements to facilitate traffic. New locks were made at Blackhill, of a character excelling all works of their class in Great Britain. They comprised two entire sets of four double locks each, either set being worked independently of the other; and were formed at the expense of upward of £30,000. In 1846, when the Monkland Canal became one concern with the Forth and Clyde Canal, the purchase price was £3,400 per share.

The canal had closed to traffic before he was born. From a channel carrying trade into the depth of the country it had become a ribbon of wilderness allowing reeds and willows, swans and waterhens into the heart of the city. He was puzzled by the phrase "splendid edifices were called into existence." The only splendid building he knew east of the city was the canal itself, a ten-mile-long artwork shaped in stone, timber, earth and water. He went to sketch the Blackhill locks.

This was difficult. He knew how the two great water stair-cases curved round and down the hill, but from any one level the rest were invisible. Moreover, the weight of the architecture was seen best from the base, the spaciousness from on top; yet he wanted to show both equally so that eyes would climb his landscape as freely as a good athlete exploring the place. He invented a perspective showing the locks from below when looked at from left to right and from above when seen from right to left; he painted them as they would appear to a giant lying on his side, with eyes more than a hundred feet apart and tilted at an angle of 45 degrees. Working from maps, photographs, sketches and memory his favourite views had nearly all been combined into one when a new problem arose.

He had meant to people the canvas with Sunday afternoon activity: children fishing for minnows with jam-jars, a woman clipping a hedge round an old lockkeeper's cottage, a pensioner exercising a dog on the towpath. But the locks now looked so solid that he wanted them to frame something vaster. He opened the last book of the bible and read of ultimatums and proclamations, of war, starvation, profiteering and death, of flaming bodies hurled through the sky to poison whole nations. The politics of the book seemed as modern as in the days of St. John and Albrecht Dürer. The final splitting of people into good and bad and the survival of the good into a luxurious new world was unconvincing, but politicians usually talk like that in a crisis. He changed the time of day from afternoon to gloaming and made a black descending dart high up between the moon and the roof of his old primary school. Being painted on the sky it could not fall, nor could the crowds under it escape. They fled along towpaths, over bridges, and collected on heights, yet there was no brutality in their fearful rush: mothers still clung to children, fathers shielded both, on open spaces single figures pointed to doors in the hillside. To show the crowds properly he made great changes in the landscape and these were nearly complete when a new need arose. In that huge multitude only *types* were visible, and he suddenly wanted a life-size figure in the foreground, someone whose bewildered face looked straight at the viewers, making them feel part of the multitude too.

Thaw stopped to think, for the whole composition would have to be rearranged again if the new figure was to fit it and not be just stuck on top. His painting teacher, a conscientious man, approached and said, "How much longer will you be on this? It's all you've done this term. The others have finished three or four paintings by now."

"Mine is bigger than theirs, sir."

"Bigger, yes. Ridiculously big. When will you finish it?"

"Mibby next week, Mr. Watt. It looks nearly finished."

"Quite. It looked nearly finished three weeks ago. It looked finished a fortnight before that. Each time you suddenly painted most of it out and began what seemed a different picture."

"I got ideas for improvement."

"Quite so. If you get any more ideas, ignore them. I want that picture finished next week."

Thaw stared uneasily at his feet and said in a low voice, "I'll try to finish it next week, sir, but if I get a good idea I can't promise to reject it."—He was filled with sudden gaiety and tried hard not to grin.—"If I did that, God might not give me others."

After a pause Mr. Watt said, "Show me your folder of work."

Thaw brought over a folder of drawings and the teacher looked slowly through them.

"Why all the ugly distortions?"

"I may have over-emphasized some shapes to make them clearer, but surely you don't think all my work distorted, sir?"

Mr. Watt looked through the folder again, frowning slightly, and set aside a sheet of hands drawn in pencil. He said, "I like these. They're well observed and carefully described."

Thaw hunted through the folder and brought out a foreshortened drawing of a woman seen from the feet. He said, "Don't you think she is beautiful?"

"No. I honestly think you've made her ugly and tortured-looking."

Thaw shuffled the drawings back into the folder and said embarrassedly, "I'm sorry. I can't agree."

"We're going to discuss this later," said the teacher in a muffled voice, and left the room. McAlpin, who was working nearby, looked up and said, "I enjoyed that. I kept wondering which of you would burst into tears first."

"It was nearly me."

"It's a good thing the registrar likes your work."

"Why?"

"It would take too long to explain."

They worked in silence, then Thaw asked in a pleading voice, "Kenneth, am I impudent?"

"Oh, no. You obviously dislike having to hurt their feelings."

On the way to the classroom next morning Thaw met Mr. Watt who said, "One moment, Thaw! I'd like a word with you."

They stepped into a window recess and sat on a bench. Mr. Watt sucked grimly at his lower lip, then said, "I've just been talking about you to Mr. Peel. I told him that you rejected my advice, were a disturbing influence on other students, and that I didn't want you in my class."

Thaw's heart began beating hard and heavily. He said, "I like you to advise me, sir, I like advice from anyone, but advice which can't be rejected doesn't deserve the name. Moreover—"

"Let's not discuss it. McAlpin tells me you share a studio near the park."

"Yes."

"I have asked Mr. Peel to let you paint there. You'll come to school as usual for lectures, but the rest of the time you'll work by yourself. At the end of the term we'll see what you have to show."

Thaw took a moment to digest this, then gave his teacher a look of such delight, affection, and pity that Mr. Watt stirred impatiently and said, "I'd be grateful for an answer to a strictly unofficial question, Thaw. Do you have the faintest notion what you're trying to do?"

"No sir, but this new arrangement will help me find out. Can I start shifting my things today?"

"Start when you like."

At home that evening Thaw packed books and papers he had not yet taken to the studio. To Mr. Thaw, who was helping, he said, "Could I take the spare mattress from the single bed?"

"So I'm to see even less of you than usual?"

"It helps to be in the same room as my work when I wake in the morning."

"All right. Take the mattress. And sheets. And blankets. And why not the bed when you're about it?"

"No. A mattress and sleeping bag are easily rolled out of the way. A real bed would be a waste of space."

"All right, all right. But I'll consider it a favour if you come home to see me sometimes, and not only when you need money."

These words held such humility and bitterness that Thaw felt an unfamiliar pang. He said sadly, "I respect and admire you, Dad. I even like you. But I'm afraid of you, I don't know why."

"Perhaps we chastised you too much when you were wee."

"Chastised . . . ?"

"Thrashed."

"Did you do it often?"

"Quite often. You took it badly. We had to give you cold baths to stop your hysterics."

This struck Thaw as an odd way to treat a small child. He hid his embarrassment by saying heartily, "I'm sure I deserved it."

On Saturday morning he waited for Marjory in Central Station, for she had agreed to lunch with him, then help clean the studio. He felt lively and excited though he knew she was coming because he had asked for help, not pleasure. This would be their first time alone in a private place, and if they ever considered marriage her work in the studio would give him a notion of her domestic stamina. She was an hour and five minutes late and he could not look at her grimly, for the nearly hopeless wait gave her the appearance of a splendid surprise. She explained that she had worked hard the night before, her mother thought it best not to wake her, and the alarm clock had failed to ring. The waitress serving them in the restaurant they visited was June Haig.

"It's a while since I saw you, June," he said while Marjory considered the menu.

"Hello, Duncan. And er you still et the ert school?" she said, tapping her ruby underlip with a pencil end. She spoke drawlingly, for her accent had turned Anglo-Scottish.

"I've been twice jilted by that girl," said Thaw when June left with the order.

"When was that, Duncan?" said Marjory, looking interested.

"I'll tell you one day. It's a sordid wee story," said Thaw jovially. He enjoyed a vision of himself as a worldly man who could joke about being jilted by a waitress. While they ate Marjory looked up once or twice and saw his face intent on hers and smiled a small strained smile. He remembered when that smile had seemed ugly. Now it seemed lovely, and he was sure that after twelve years the wrinkle it caused would seem lovely too.

"Duncan," said Marjory, "you won't mind if I . . . well, I may have to leave you early this afternoon."

After a pause Thaw said dryly, "If that's so it can't be helped."

"Well anyway, we'll see," said Marjory vaguely.

The studio was a long whitewashed attic. Two windows allowed a view of trees, paths and lawns sloping up to the mansions of Park Terrace. A gas cooker, table, sofa and some chairs stood round a fireplace at one end. The other end was filled by a canvas stretched on the wall which bore the first strokes of a bigger version of the Blackhill locks landscape. The middle of the floor held the grime and rubbish which comes when a few young men use a room carelessly. Among it were easels, Thaw's bedding and a heavy old sideboard loaded with paint material. There was a figurine of a dancing faun on the mantelpiece and several sentences drawn on the sloping ceiling.

IF MORE THAN 5% OF THE PEOPLE LIKE A PAINTING THEN BURN IT FOR IT MUST BE BAD
James McNeil Whistler

I DO NOT PRETEND TO UNDERSTAND ART BUT I BELIEVE MOST SO-CALLED MODERN ART IS THE WORK OF LAZY, HALF-BAKED PEOPLE
President Truman

GOING DOWN TO HELL IS EASY: THE GLOOMY DOOR IS OPEN NIGHT AND DAY. TURNING AROUND AND GETTING BACK TO SUNLIGHT IS THE TASK, THE HARD THING
Vergil

HUMANITY SETS ITSELF NO PROBLEM WHICH CANNOT EVENTUALLY BE SOLVED
Marx

Thaw lit the fire, folded back the carpet, swept the floor, carried boxes of rubbish down to the midden, shook mats out of the window and washed the panes. Marjory cleaned the rusty stove, then washed pans and utensils and scrubbed the floor. It was six o'clock when they finished. The room looked wonderfully neat and clean.

"Wash yourself and we'll have tea," said Thaw. He brought parcels out of a cupboard. "Chops," he said. "Onions. Cakes. Bread. Real butter. Jam."

"Oh, Duncan! How lovely! But . . . Mummy expects me for tea. . . ."

"Run down to the phone box at the corner and tell her you're having it here. Here's three pennies for the call."

When Marjory returned the meal was almost ready. They ate hungrily and washed up, then Marjory sat on the sofa by the fire. Thaw occasionally went to the other end of the room and returned with folders. He opened them and spread the contents on the rug at her feet: paintings, drawings and sketches, reproductions and photographs clipped from newspapers and magazines.

"Goodness, Duncan. What a lot of good work. You make me feel very lazy."

He put the work away and returned to the hearth. It was nearly dark outside and most of the light came flickering from a sheaf of vivid flames in the grate. Marjory looked up at him and smiled. Her hands were folded in her lap. Thaw stood by the table and felt a silence like the silence in the mathematics room when the teacher had asked a question he couldn't answer.

"You know I'm afraid of you, Marjory," he blurted.

"Why, Duncan?"

"I suppose because I . . . I like you very much."

"I like you too, Duncan."

There was more silence. He thought to break it with a joke. He said derisively, "Do you know that a while ago I actually believed you were going out with another man—"

She interrupted at once. "Oh, Duncan, I meant to tell you about that. I know a boy at the university, he . . . takes me sometimes to dances and things, but I—I don't know how to say this without seeming vain—I think he . . . likes me more than I like him."

"That's all right," said Thaw abstractedly. He sat on the hearth rug by her feet and laid his head against her knee.

"I . . . oh, I . . ." he murmured.

His intellect had dissolved. He shaped words with his lips but only one or two became sound: "mother" he said once, and shortly after that "world," but he was unconscious of thoughts and later could not remember thinking.

"And yet you . . ." he murmured, reaching up and touching

her cheek curiously. She stirred a little. "I think I'll have to be going home now," she said.

"Of course," he said, standing up. "I was dreaming. I'll see you home."

He helped her on with her coat and they went downstairs.

He stopped outside the close mouth and pointed across at the sighing silhouette of the park trees. "Let's go through the park."

"But Duncan, the gates are locked."

"There's a railing missing here. Come on. It'll be a shortcut." He helped her through the narrow gap and down an embankment on the other side. Their feet rustled dead leaves. They crossed dark smooth lawns and walked round a splashing fountain among the dumpy bodies of holly trees. Two glimmering swans paddled drowsily in the black water of the ornamental pond and they heard the somnolent squawk of a goose from the island in the middle. There was a wide bridge over the Kelvin with lightless iron candelabra on plinths at each end. Thaw rested his elbows on the parapet and said, "Listen."

Nearby an almost full moon was freckled by the top leaves of an elm. The river gurgled faintly against its clay bank, the distant fountain tinkled. Marjory said, "Lovely."

He said, "I've once or twice felt moments when calmness, unity and . . . and glory seemed the core of things. Have you ever felt that?"

"I think so, Duncan. I once went with friends onto the Campsies and I got separated from them. It was a lovely warm day. I think I felt it a little then."

"But must these moments always be lonely? Won't love let us enjoy them with somebody else?"

"I don't know, Duncan."

Thaw looked at her. "Yah. Come on," he said genially. "And please put your arm through mine."

Beyond the bridge the road divided and a monument to Carlyle stood in the fork. It was a rough granite pillar with the top cut in the shape of the prophet's upper body. Moonlight lay like white frost on brow, beard and shoulders and left the hollow cheeks and concave eye sockets in gloom. Thaw shook his free fist and shouted, "Go home, ye spy! Go home, ye traitor to democracy! . . . He follows me everywhere," he explained to Marjory, and helped her over a locked gate into the lighted street.

As they passed the university Marjory said, "Duncan, have you had much experience of girls?"

"Not much, and all of one sort."

He told her about Kate Caldwell, Molly Tierney and June Haig, speaking lightly and jokingly. She punctuated the story with murmurs of "Oh, Duncan."

"And there you have my experience of girls," he ended.

"Oh, Duncan."

The phrase was so loaded with affectionate pity that he began to think he had done a stupid thing. She said, "You see, Duncan, I think you're too afraid. Do you remember in the bus back from the pictures when you asked if you could hold my hand?"

"Yes."

"You needn't have asked. I knew you wanted to. Any girl would have known and let you do it."

"I see."

"And to a certain extent it's the same with kissing. When a girl feels you're worried and frightened she gets upset too."

"Like life models who only feel embarrassed when an embarrassed student draws them."

"Yes, it's like that."

He stopped and gripped her arm. "Marjory, can I draw you? Naked, I mean?"

She stared. He said eagerly, "I won't be embarrassed—my picture needs you. The professional models are good to practise on but they come out like film actresses. I need someone who's beautiful but not fashionable."

"But Duncan . . . I'm not beautiful."

"Oh, you are. If I paint you I'll show you you are."

"But Duncan, I . . . I . . . I have an ugly birthmark down my side."

He shook his head impatiently. "Surface discolourations aren't important." He gave a slight, helpless laugh and added, "You ought to do it, to make us equal again. I stripped naked in front of you just now, in words."

"Oh, Duncan!"

She gave him an affectionate pitying smile and sighed.

"All right, Duncan."

They walked on.

"Good. When? Next week?"

"No, the week after. I'm very busy just now."

"Monday?"

"No. Well . . . Friday."

"Good. About seven?"

"Yes."

"And should I keep reminding you till then?"

"No, I . . . I really will remember, Duncan."

"Good."

At the garden gate she tilted up her mouth. He brushed his cheek on hers and murmured, "We're not mature enough for mouths. Mine hardens when I touch you with it. Please hold me."

They clasped, and her ear against his cheek made a point of tingling excitement. He began breathing deeply. She whispered, "Are you happy, Duncan?"

"Aye."

A car stopped at the kerb. Glancing sideways they saw the profile of the professor sitting immobile behind the wheel. They broke apart, laughing.

The enlarged landscape would show Blackhill, Riddrie, the Campsie Fells, the Cathkin Braes and crowds from both sides mixing around the locks in the middle. Over 105 square feet of canvas he wove, unwove and rewove a net of blue, grey and brown guidelines. He was contemplating them glumly one night when McAlpin entered and said, "What's wrong?"

"I wish the shapes weren't so restless."

"A landscape seen simultaneously from above and below and containing north, east and south can hardly be peaceful. Especially if there's a war in it."

"True, but I'm making a point of rest in the middle foreground: Marjory, looking at us."

"What expression will she have?"

"Her usual expression. I hope you remember she's posing tomorrow. I don't want interruptions."

"Don't worry, you'll be left to yourselves. What exactly do you expect from tomorrow evening? You seem to be building a lot on it."

"I expect an evening of good sound work. I'll be glad to get more but I'm not hoping for it so I can't be disappointed. I love the slight gawkiness in her. She doesn't seem to feel she has breasts and that emphasizes them. She's pretty, isn't she?"

"Yes. Mind you, she could dress to show it more."

"What do you mean?"

"Her clothes are a bit schoolgirlish, don't you think?"

"No, I don't think that."

"You don't? I see."

"My grapes are not sour, you foxy plutocrat."
"Sour gra—? Why, you shabby socialist!"
They laughed at each other.

Next morning he prepared his drawing board, brought
in a bottle of wine and carefully set the fire so that it would
flare at the touch of a match; but he was restless and went to
school for the coffee break. In the refectory he met Janet Weir
and asked if she had seen Marjory.
"No, Duncan. She's not at school today."
"Did she—yesterday, I mean—look a bit tired and ill?"
"I don't think so, Duncan."
He returned to the studio and at half-past six lit the fire and
sat by it trying to read. The doorbell rang at ten to eight.
Making an effort not to run he strolled down and casually
turned the knob. It took him two or three seconds to see that
the girl on the mat was Janet. She said, "Duncan, Marjory
sent me to say she's terribly sorry. She was working very hard
last night and isn't feeling very well."
After a moment Thaw said heavily, "Tell her I'm not surprised,"
and closed the door. He went upstairs and uncorked the wine,
intending to drink himself silly, but after one glass he felt so
dull that he spread his mattress and slept.

There was a sound of wind and of seagulls squabbling
above the park. He woke in a square of sunlight and saw blue
air and white clouds through the window. Turning his back
to it he curled tightly into the mattress and deliberately remembered his friendship with Marjory from the time she first passed
him on the stairs to the evening before. It seemed such a history
of insult that he bit his fingers with rage and at the end his
eyes were warm with tears. He grew calmer by moving onto
the dais of the lecture theatre and talking in a quiet, distinct
voice.
". . . an art school without classes or examinations where life
drawing, morbid anatomy, tools, material and information are
free to whoever wants them. I am ready to lay these plans
before the director and the board of governors, but without
your loyalty I can do nothing."
Her face was in the cheering crowd which parted to let him
through. He noticed her with a slight nod, having more important things to think about. A Labour administration made him
Secretary of State for Scotland, and arising in the House of
Commons he announced his plan for a separate Scottish parlia-

ment: "It is plain that the vaster the social unit, the less possible is true democracy."

A stunned silence was broken by the Prime Minister denouncing him as a renegade. Thaw strode from the chamber and an amazing thing happened. All seventy-one Scottish MPs—Labour, Liberal and Tory—rose and followed him. On the terrace above the Thames he was turning to address them when McAlpin came in and said, "Hullo. Having a long lie?"

"She didn't come."

"The bitch! Listen, it's a glorious day, come out sketching with me."

"I don't feel like moving."

"Make yourself. You'll be better for it."

"I can't."

McAlpin stretched paper on a drawing board. Thaw said abruptly, "I've finished with her."

"Very wise."

"But I haven't worked out how to say 'Goodbye.' "

"Don't bother. Just don't say 'Hello' again."

"No. I must be definite."

"It's useless brooding, Duncan. The light will have gone in three or four hours. Come out sketching."

"No."

McAlpin left, and after the civil war Thaw became head of the reconstruction committee. Fountains splashed and trees grew where the demolished banks had stood. Backcourts were given benches and open-air draughtboards for the old, paddling ponds and sand pits for infants, communal non-profitmaking launderettes for housewives. Pleasure boats with small orchestras sailed down the canal from Riddrie to the Clyde islands. Marjory read his name in newspapers, heard his voice on the wireless, saw his face in cinemas; he surrounded her, he was shaping her world, yet she could not touch him. Then he dozed and dreamed of a fearful twilit country dripping with rain. He was trying to escape from it with a little girl who insulted and betrayed him. She grew tall and sat wearing jewellery on a throne in a dark ancient house. She had sent her club-footed butler to catch him. Tiny Thaw fled from room to room, slamming doors behind him, but the slow limping sound drew nearer all the time. He came at last to a cupboard with no way out and clutched the doorknob, trying to hold it shut. Freezing water swirled up his legs.

He woke in darkness with half the bedding on the floor. Three stars shone through the window and geese sang discordantly from the pond. Pulling the blankets round him, he eased his breathing with an ephedrine pill and imagined her a slave in a luxurious brothel where he tortured her into making shameless love to him. The second time he masturbated she changed into June Haig, the third time became a boy. Disgusted with himself he stared at the ceiling till dawn, then fell asleep again. It was Sunday, and that afternoon other students came and made coffee, painted and gossiped. Thaw lay pretending to read but actually composing farewell speeches for Marjory, speeches amused, pathetic, stoical, coldly insulting and madly violent. In the evening Macbeth arrived. The art school had expelled him for drunkenness and he sagged into a chair saying, "Wha's wrong wi' Duncan? Why's he curled up like that?"

"Shh. He's breaking with Marjory," murmured McAlpin.

"Why're you breaking, Duncan? Can you not get your hole, is 'at it! Will she not give you your hole?"

"No. Partly, mibby. I don't know."

"Listen to me, Duncan. Listen. Listen. Holes don't matter. I've had my hole regular since I was seventeen, just because Molly wouldnae look at me don't think I've gone without my hole. I go to Bath Street. I get it twice, three times, four times a week and it doesnae matter *that* much."

He snapped his fingers. "Marjory is a nice girl. You stick to her, hole or no hole."

"She isn't kind to me," said Thaw from under the blankets.

"I admit that is depressing. I admit that no hole, with no kindness on top of it, can be depressing."

On Monday he went to art school and met Marjory on the steps. His mind had split with her so completely that the pretty smiling girl before him was as confusing as a resurrection. "Hello, Duncan! I'm sorry about Friday. Janet told you why, didn't she?"

"She told me, yes."

"There's a choir practice after lunch today. Are you going to the refectory?"

"I suppose so."

Her smile was so direct and bright that his face had to reflect it, but in the refectory he sat beside her and Janet Weir without talking and drew on the tabletop. Marjory said, "Janet and I are going to the opera tonight, Duncan."

"Good."

"We haven't booked seats, we're going to queue for the balcony."

"Good."

Janet went to get cigarettes. Marjory said, "Aitken isn't coming—he hates opera. But you like it, Duncan, don't you?"

"Yes."

She moved nearer.

"Duncan, you know I'll pose for you whenever you like."

"Marjory, we must stop this."

He drew a dark shadow under an eye, pressing hard on the pencil and saying, "We'll be better rid of each other."

He glanced sideways. Her quiet profile seemed to examine the drawing. Janet returned saying, "No Gauloise! I wish they'd sell us Gauloise."

Thaw said, "There's no satisfaction in the present way of things."

"Shall we go over to the choir, Duncan?" Marjory asked.

As they crossed the street she said, "I'm sorry, Duncan."

"It doesn't matter. I spent the weekend getting used to leaving you and now I'm used to it."

They paused at the door of the theatre where the choir rehearsed. He said, "So there's nothing to be done."

"I see. Oh, Duncan, I'm sorry you've liked me so much. And Duncan, I'm sorry I haven't—"

"Oh, don't be sorry," he said, taking her hands and leaning his brow on hers. "Don't be sorry! You gave me friendship, and for a long time I was grateful."

"But Duncan, can't we still be friends? Not now, perhaps, but later?"

They put their cheeks together and he murmured, "Later, mibby, when I have a real girlfriend I can . . . perhaps. . . ."

"Yes. Then."

She clasped his waist and he caressed her easily, moving his mouth into the soft nook between her neck and shoulder. Janet and two friends went past saying, "Oho!" "Aha!" "Hurry up, you're late."

He wondered why his mouth and hands had never done these things before. More footsteps sounded along the corridor and they separated.

"I'm leaving the choir," he said. "So go through that door, and goodbye."

She smiled and went quickly through the door. He set out briskly for the studio, meaning to start work at once. Their parting had been so kind that for three minutes he was almost

happy, but as time and space widened between them resentment
developed. Along Sauchiehall Street the glances of passers-by
made him notice he was chanting aloud, "If you *exist* let me
kill her, if you *exist* let me kill her."

At the studio he saw nothing in his picture but a tangle of
ugly lines. He sat and stared at them till it was dark.

CHAPTER 26. Chaos

He waited a long time next morning for an impulse to get out of bed, and at last crawled to the larder, and to the lavatory, and back to bed again. He lay like a corpse, his brain rotten with resentful dreams. He tortured her in sexual fantasies, and revised and enlarged the farewell speeches he had failed to make when parting, and minutely remembered and resented every moment they had passed together. He wondered why his thoughts were so full of a girl who had given him so little. The aching emotions gradually became muscular tightness, his limited movement a way of saving breath. He kept wanting her to enter the dark, dusty, muddled room, switch on the light and glance round it, smiling. His own face would stay hard and immobile but she would remove her coat, give a small pat to the back of her hair and start to clean up. She would make a warm drink, sit by the mattress and hold the cup for him to sip like a child. With a sardonic smile he would submit to this but at last he would take her hands and press them to where she could feel the heart knocking on his ribs. They would lean against each other. The sweat would go from his brow, the tension from his body and he would sleep. He was afraid of sleep now and sat as rigid as possible to keep it away.

One day during the summer holidays McAlpin, who was painting in a corner, said, "I know advice is always useless but wouldn't you feel better if you got up and tackled your picture?"

"It's ludicrous to think anyone in Glasgow will ever paint a good picture."

"You should go home, Duncan."

"Afraid to move."

Later McAlpin went out and returned with Ruth. Thaw stared at her fearfully for she often called his illness a disgusting way of grabbing attention. She asked kindly, "How are you, old Duncan?" and gently helped him to dress and led him downstairs to a taxi. As they sped homeward she spoke of her training college in Aberdeen. She had been a year there, her intelligent bright bounciness had no aggression in it and he sensed he need never fear her again. Mr. Thaw had laid the table for tea. As they sat round it Ruth said "I like Aberdeen, I've got so many boyfriends! I go swimming with Harry Docherty, who was the Scottish Junior Breaststroke Champion, and I go dancing with Joe Stewart, and I go to parties with anybody—anybody I like, I mean. The girls at college think I'm a scarlet woman but I think they're daft. Most of them have only one boyfriend and talk about nothing but marriage. I'm not going to marry for four or five years, and there's safety in numbers, I say."

"Quite right," said Mr. Thaw. "Don't commit yourself to another human being until you're able to be independent. You're young, enjoy yourself."

"On Sunday I go for walks with Tony Gow, who's a medical student. You'd like him, Duncan. He knows all about animals and flowers and folk songs. He's not much use in the back row of a cinema but he's really interesting. Our walks haven't been much fun lately because of this new rabbit disease the farmers are spreading. All along the country roads you find these poor dying rabbits, gasping for breath with their eyes bulging out. Tony takes them by the hind legs and brains them on the ground. I can't do it. I know it's the kind thing to do but I can't even look. Tony—"

Thaw screamed, "Stop!"

After a moment Mr. Thaw said, "Go to bed son. I'll get the doctor."

The doctor ordered rest and new kinds of pill. Thaw sat in bed, unable to concentrate on reading but willing to argue. "I wish I was a duck."

"What?"

"I wish I was a duck on Alexandra Park pond. I could swim, and fly, and walk, and have three wives, and everything I wanted. But I'm a man. I have a mind, and three library tickets, and everything I want is impossible."

"My God, what are you saying? What's this I've fathered? Look at penicillin and the national health service, look at all these books and pictures you're so keen on! And you want to be a bird!"

"Look at Belsen!" cried Thaw. "And Nagasaki, and the Russians in Hungary and Yanks in South America and French in Algeria and the British bombing Egypt without declaring war on her! Half the folk on this planet die of malnutrition before they're thirty, we'll be twice as many before the century ends, and the only governments with the skill and power to make a decent home of the world are plundering their neighbours and planning to atom bomb each other. We cooperate in millions when it comes to killing, but when it comes to generous, beautiful actions we work in tens and hundreds."

Mr. Thaw rubbed the side of his face and said, "You've read more books than me. How long have there been men in the world?"

"About three hundred thousand years."

"How long have we had cities?"

"About six thousand years."

"And how long have there been governments with worldwide powers? I know the answer to that one. Hardly more than a century."

"Well?"

"Duncan, modern history is just beginning. Give us another couple of centuries and we'll build a *real* civilization! Don't worry, son, others want it beside yourself. There's not a country in the world where folk aren't striving and searching. Don't be fooled by the politicians. It isn't the loud men on platforms but the obscure toilers who change things. And if a few damned power cliques start an atomic war in the next ten or twenty years, humanity will survive. We may take centuries to breed out the effects of radiation, but ordinary folk will do it and start the steep upward climb once more."

"Yah, I'm *sick* of ordinary people's ability to eat muck and survive. Animals are nobler. A fierce animal will die fighting against insults to its nature, and a meek one will starve to death under them. Only human beings have the hideous versatility to adapt to lovelessness and live and live and live while being exploited and abused by their own kind. I read an essay by a little girl in a book about children in wartime. Her house had been bombed. She wrote, 'I am nothing and nobody. My cat was stuck to the wall. I tried to pull her off but they threw my cat away.' Worse things have happened to children every day for the last quarter million years. No kindly future will ever repair a past as vile as ours, and even if we do achieve a worldwide democratic socialist state it won't last. Nothing decent lasts. All that lasts is this mess of fighting and pain and I object to it! I object! I object!"

"Stop pitying yourself."

Thaw opened his mouth to protest, noticed he was pitying himself and shut it again. Mr. Thaw sighed and said, "Let's agree the world is one helluva mess. What do you think will improve it?"

"A memory and a conscience. I hate the heedless way it puts on life without noticing or caring, like a rotten fruit putting on mould."

"But Duncan, memory and conscience are human things!"

"Unluckily."

"Is it a God you want?"

"Yes. Yes, it's a big continual loving man I want who shares the pain of his people. It's an impossibility I want."

Mr. Thaw pushed flat some wisps of hair on his head and said, "My father was elder in a Congregationalist church in Bridgeton: a poor place now but a worse one then. One time the well-off members subscribed to give the building a new communion table, an organ and coloured windows. But he was an industrial blacksmith with a big family. He couldnae afford to give money, so he gave ten years of unpaid work as church officer, sweeping and dusting, polishing the brasses and ringing the bell for services. At the foundry he was paid less the more he aged, but my mother helped the family by embroidering tablecloths and napkins. Her ambition was to save a hundred pounds. She was a good needlewoman, but she never saved her hundred pounds. A neighbour would fall sick and need a holiday or a friend's son would need a new suit to apply for a job, and she handed over the money with no fuss or remark, as if it were an ordinary thing to do. She got a lot of comfort from praying. Every night we all kneeled to pray in the living room before going to bed. There was nothing dramatic in these prayers. My father and mother clearly felt they were talking to a friend in the room with them. I never felt that, so I believed there was something wrong with me. Then the 1914 war started and I joined the army and heard a different kind of prayer. The clergy on all sides were praying for victory. They told us God wanted our government to win and was right there behind us, with the generals, shoving us forward. A lot of us in the trenches let God go at that time. But Duncan, all these airy-fairy pie-in-the-sky notions are nothing but aids to doing what we want anyway. My parents used Christianity to help them behave decently in a difficult life. Other folk used it to justify war and property. But Duncan, what men believe isn't important—it's our actions which make us right or wrong. So if a God can comfort you, adopt one. He won't hurt you."

"Will he not?" said Thaw sullenly. "The only God I can imagine is too like Stalin to be comforting."

"I don't condone Stalin's methods, of course, but I firmly believe anyone else ruling Russia in the thirties would have had to behave like him."

The new pills stopped working and the doctor prescribed others which didn't work either. On the worst nights Mr. Thaw sat by the bed wiping trickles of sweat from Thaw's face with a towel and holding out a basin to take the thick yellow phlegm. Thaw was wholly occupied by the disease now. He felt it in him like civil war sabotaging his breathing and allowing only enough oxygen to feel pain, helplessness and self-disgust. Once after midnight he said, "Doctor thinks . . . this illness . . . mental."

"Aye, son. He's hinted at it."

"Fill bath."

"What?"

"Fill bath. Cold water."

With difficulty he explained that maybe (like a land forgetting inner differences when attacked by another) the clenched air tubes might relax if his whole skin was insulted by cold water. Mr. Thaw reluctantly filled the bath and helped Thaw to the edge. Thaw dropped his pyjamas, placed one foot in the water and stood, breathing heavily. After a while he brought in the other foot and with a spasmodic effort knelt on one knee.

"Hurry up, Duncan. Put yourself under!" said Mr. Thaw and moved to thrust him down.

"No!" screamed Thaw, and five minutes later managed to lie on his back with nose and lips above the surface. Breathing was as hard as ever. Mr. Thaw dried him and helped him back to bed. "You should have lain down at once, Duncan. If shock treatment *can* work, it has to come as a shock."

Thaw sat for a while, then said, "You're right. Hit me."

"What?"

"Hit me. On face."

"Duncan! . . . I *cannae.*"

After more minutes of sore breathing, Thaw cried, "Please!"

"But Duncan—"

"Can't stand . . . more this. Can't stand."

Mr. Thaw struck his face with his open palm.

"No good. Could hit . . . *myself* . . . harder. Again!"

Mr. Thaw struck harder. Thaw reeled, recovered, compared the painful cheek to the pain in his chest and muttered, "No bloody good."

Mr. Thaw bowed his head and wept. He was sitting on the edge of the bed and Thaw embraced him, saying, "Sorry, Dad. Sorry."

He felt his father's body shake with the sobs erupting inside. It did not feel a large body, and looking down at the thin white hair strands on the freckled scalp he sensed it was an ageing body, and was puzzled to find his own, for a moment, the stronger.

"Go to bed, Dad," he said. "I'm better now."

The tension in his chest had eased.

"My God, Duncan, if I could take your damned illness myself I would! I would!"

"What good would that do? Who would support us then? No, this is the best arrangement."

Mr. Thaw went to bed and the breathing worsened again. When he tried to ignore it by staring at things in the surrounding room they became unstable, as if walls, furniture and ornaments were pieces of a destructive force gripped into shape by a hostile force which could only just hold them. A glazed jug before the window seemed about to explode. Its shiny green hardness threatened him across the room. Everything he saw seemed made of panic. He stared at the ceiling and gathered his thoughts into an intense, silent cry: 'You exist. I surrender. I believe. Help me please.'

The asthma worsened. He gave a fearful moan, then controlled himself enough to make an amused sound and say, "Nobody. There. At all."

He said it again, louder, but it sounded like a lie. Without comfort he found himself condemned to a faith which would never again let him end a prayer by saying, 'If you exist.'

Again he fired his thoughts through the ceiling.

'This belief comes from my cowardice, not from your glory. You won it by a torturer's trick. But you are far from winning my approval. And I will never, never, never, never pray to you again.'

Next day the doctor said, "This has gone on far too long. He should be in hospital. Have you a neighbour with a telephone?"

Ruth and his father helped him dress. The neighbours stood at their doors as the ambulance men carried him downstairs. Mrs. Gilchrist called out glumly, "A fine way to go your holidays, Duncan."

It was a fresh July morning. He sat clutching the edge of the ambulance bench while Mr. Thaw on the bench opposite grunted and prized at the lock of a suitcase with a propelling pencil. Thaw said, "What's wrong?"

"The bloody lock's stuck."

"I won't need a case in hospital."

"Of course you won't. This is to take away your clothes."

The frosted glass window was slightly open at the top and he watched the streets of Blackhill through the slit. The sun shone and children shouted. He said, "That was quick."

"Yes," said his father, putting the case down. "I can't help feeling relieved. When Ruth and I are climbing in Zermatt we'll know you're being better cared for than you could be at home."

"I don't suppose I'll be in long."

"If I were you, Duncan, I wouldn't be too anxious to get out. It might be wise to tell the doctor in charge that there's nobody to look after you outside. Give them time to discover the fundamental root cause of the trouble."

"It doesn't have a fundamental root cause."

"Don't make up your mind about that. Modern hospitals have all kinds of resources, and Stobhill is the biggest in Britain. I was in it myself in 1918: a shrapnel wound in the abdomen. Don't worry, I'll make sure you've plenty of books. I read a lot in Stobhill, authors I couldnae face now, Carlyle, Darwin, Marx. . . . Of course I was on my back for five months."

Mr. Thaw looked out of the window a while, then said, "There's a railway cutting in the grounds which goes to a kind of underground station below the clock tower. The army sent us there in trains. Would you like me to bring you Lenin's *Introduction to Dialectical Materialism?*"

"No."

"That's shortsighted of you, Duncan. Half the world is governed by that philosophy."

The ward was so long that the professor and his company took over an hour to inspect the beds on one side and come down the other to where Thaw lay, near the door. The professor was robust and bald. He stood with folded arms and tilted head as if studying a corner of the ceiling. His quiet speech reached patient, staff doctor, sister, staff nurse and medical students equally, though a bright glance at one of them sometimes underlined a remark or question.

"Here we have a pronounced bronchial infection based on a chronic weakness which may be hereditary, since the father's sister died of it. . . . *You* won't die of it. Nobody dies of asthma unless they've a weak heart, and your ticker should keep you running another half century, with ordinary care. There may be a psychological factor—the illness first appeared at the age of six, when the family was split by war."

"My mother was with us," said Thaw defensively.

"But the father wasn't. Note the eczema on scrotum and behind knee and elbow joints. Typical."

"Has he had skin tests?" asked a student.

"Yes. He reacts violently to all pollens, all hair, fur, feather, meat, fish, milk and every kind of dust. So these can only be irritations. If they were causes he'd have spent his whole life in bed and he frequently gets by without asthma. . . . Don't you?"

"Yes," said Thaw.

"As to treatment: penicillin to reduce the infection, a course of aminophylline suppositories for long-term relief and isoprenaline for temporary relief. Physiotherapy to encourage breath control, that's quite important if they're young, and later a course of de-allergizing injections to cope with the irritation. Coal tar for the skin. It's messy, it's old-fashioned, but the best we can do till we get our hands on this new American cortisone cream. And a sedative to help him relax. . . . Are you a nervous type?"

"I don't know," said Thaw.

"Do you lose yourself in daydreams, then jump violently at ordinary noises?"

"Sometimes."

The professor lifted a drawing of a winged woman from Thaw's locker. "Artistic, too. Would you mind chatting to a psychiatrist?"

"No."

"Good. I know you're not bonkers, but a few talks about family, sex, money and so on can cut down feelings which might interfere with the more straightforward treatments. Your teeth need attention too. You don't brush them often enough, do you?"

"No," said Thaw.

The ward was murmurous with conversations which coalesced, once or twice a week, into political arguments in which lumps of language were hurled backward and forward across great distances. Sometimes in the morning a distant clanking drew near and a huge man toiled past, bowing low over a tiny complicated crutch. His face was shrunk to a bright animal eye, a lump of nose and a mouth twisted over toothless gums. He kept muttering, "God knows how I got this way." "I've been a hard worker all my life." "I've earned every penny I owned" and "I do *nut* like hospitals."

The men in the beds on each side were more self-absorbed. On the left Mr. Clark frowned thoughtfully, moving his hands in slow descriptive gestures or lifting and letting fall the bed-clothes in different folds. In the afternoon he made croaking sounds which the nurses interpreted as requests for a urine bottle, bedpan or cigarette; he was allowed to smoke if someone was there to see he didn't burn himself. His face and neck were leathery and corded like a turtle's, his nose high-bridged and imperious. Propped up by pillows he sometimes dozed, his head dithering in space a fraction away from them, then lurched awake with a faint cry of "Agnes!" Nobody visited him. Mr. McDade on Thaw's left was a small man whose chest bulged like a fat stomach against his chin. He had wiry red hair and a severe face made clerkly by steel spectacles without lenses. These held up each nostril a rubber tube from an oxygen cylinder behind the bed. He removed them to sleep, and some-times at night rose up in bed on all fours like a dog, making an orchestral noise as if forcing breath through hundreds of tiny flutes and whistles. The nurses would turn him over and restore the spectacles for a while. A small brisk wife and some very tall sons came to see him regularly and before visiting hour he was given an injection which let him talk knowledge-ably about grandchildren and prizefighting in a low, clogged voice. He and Thaw often exchanged a slight, negative heads-hake, and one day when his relatives were late he said, "Some business this, eh?"

"Aye."

"A bad bugger, thon."

"Who?"

"Clark."

Thaw glanced the other way and saw Mr. Clark holding up the top edge of his sheet and studying it like a newspaper. Mr. McDade muttered, "Have you noticed? When the nurses have tucked him in he untucks himself and croaks for a bottle. Outside he'd get six months for it. Outside they call that inde-cent exposure."

"He's old."
"Aye, he's old. When old men reach that state there's a place for them."

Twice a week Thaw put on slippers and dressing gown and was pushed in a wheelchair to the psychiatric block, or walked there if he was well enough. The psychiatrist was a well-dressed man of about forty with no special characteristics. He said, "During our conversations you may experience several unexpected emotions toward me. Please don't be ashamed to mention them, however bizarre they seem. I won't be at all offended. They'll be part of the treatment."
Thaw talked about parents, childhood, work, sexual fantasies and Marjory. The words poured from him, and once or twice he burst into tears. The psychiatrist said, "In spite of your blinding resentment of women I suspect you are basically heterosexual," and, later, "The truth, you know, isn't black *or* white, it's black *and* white. I keep a ceramic zebra on my mantelpiece to remind me of that," but usually he said "Why?" or "Tell me more about that," and Thaw felt no emotions toward him at all. He enjoyed the visits but returned to the ward feeling slightly anxious and flat, like an actor whose performance has been neither applauded nor booed. When able to walk he prolonged his return through the hospital grounds. The long low red-brick wards lay on the slopes of an airy hill. Seagulls were always circling overhead or perched on gables, perhaps because of stale bread flung out by the kitchens. There was a high red clock tower with a tinny chime, and all was gardened around with shrubberies, gravel paths and beds of bee-humming, dazzling, blue and scarlet flowers. It was a summer of extraordinary heat. Patients in dressing gowns walked carefully on the lawns or brooded on benches. Most of them were aging and solitary, and when white-clad nurses passed briskly in chattering couples and threes, Thaw was startled by the mercy of these bright young women caring for so many made lonely, feeble and repulsive by disease.

Each week his breathing improved for a few days, then worsened. Mr. Clark stopped smoking and calling for Agnes and lay perfectly still. The deep lines cut by experience were fading from his face; each day he was more like a young man though his eyes looked different ways and one side of his mouth opened in a grin while the other was firmly shut. Mr. McDade in the right-hand bed was aging. The hollows between the cords of his cheeks and neck grew deeper. He stared at passing doctors and nurses with unusually wide red-rimmed eyes. He spoke less to his wife and sons but often glanced toward Thaw, muttering, "Some . . . business . . . this . . . eh?"

He plainly wanted companionship in pain, but Thaw muttered "Aye" without looking up from scribbling. The notebook had become a neutral surface between the pain of the ward and the pain of breathing. He hated leaving it to feed or to sleep. At night, when a lamp shone on the nurses' table far down the ward, enough gloaming filtered in from the summer sky to make a pale tablet of his page, and his hand continued shading enigmatic female heads, and grotesque male ones, and monsters that were part bird, part machinery, and huge cities mingling every style and century of architecture. After midnight he put the books aside and sat erect, clinging so tightly to consciousness that for many nights he thought himself sleepless. Then he noticed that though he heard the remote melancholy *ding-dong* of the clock tower sounding the quarters, they never seemed to sound the hour, and once he saw the two night nurses whispering near a corner bed, and then, without crossing the floor, one was reading a book at the central table and the other sat crocheting nearby. All night he was dipping in and out of sleep, but at such a shallow angle he never noticed. Sometimes he slept soundly and then waking was difficult, for it was hard at first to recognize the shapes and sounds of the ward and breathing was a vile science to be relearned by a lot of choking.

Late one night the nurse in charge led round a sister he had never seen before. They stopped at Mr. McDade's bed. He was sleeping in the oxygen spectacles, his mouth continually gulping air and a sound like distant bagpipes coming from his chest. Below her stiff, white, sphinx-like cap the sister's face looked keen and fiftyish. She said, "Poor McDade! God help him!" on a low note of such stern pity that warmth gushed in Thaw's chest and he gazed at her lovingly. She moved to his bed-foot, smiled and said, "And how are you tonight, Duncan?"

He whispered, "Fine, thanks."

"Would you like a cup of cocoa?"

"Very much, thanks."

"You'll see to it, nurse?"

They moved on and later the nurse brought sweet warm cocoa and two pink pills on a teaspoon.

He awoke in sunlight breathing easily amid the bright clangour of washbasins being passed round. For the first time since entering hospital he felt well enough to shave, but after fondling the shrub of hair on his chin he merely freshened his face and hands and lay basking in the kind light and air. Mr. Clark looked much better. His face was old and thoughtful again and he appeared to be conducting a tiny orchestra with his right forefinger. Mr. McDade's bed was empty and stripped down to the wire mattress. Thaw imagined the small pigeon-chested body being carried away by the quiet, black-suited young man who replaced the oxygen cylinders but he was too happy to feel anything but relief. He wanted to talk to people and make them laugh. When the nurse brought breakfast he tasted and said, "Nurse! I refuse to eat this porridge without proper anesthetic!"

He said it again, louder. Nobody noticed, so he wrote it down to tell Drummond or McAlpin and went on eating.

CHAPTER 27. Genesis

Slanting sunshine lit a cut-glass vase of cowslips and canterbury bells on Mr. Clark's table. Thaw sat in an armchair admiring the butter-yellow cowslips with pale green drooping stems, the dark spear-leaved stalks with transparent blue-purple bells. He whispered, "Purple, purple," and the word felt as purple to his lips as the colour to his eyes. A nurse making Mr. McDade's old bed said, "You'll have to be on your best behaviour today, Duncan. You're getting a new neighbour. A minister."

"I hope he isn't talkative."

"Oh, he'll be talkative. Ministers are paid to be talkative."

She placed screens round the bed and someone with a suitcase went behind them. The screens were removed and a small grey-haired man in pyjamas sat against his pillow receiving elderly lady visitors. These talked in quick, low, consoling voices while the minister smiled and nodded absentmindedly. When they left he put on spectacles with lenses like half-moons and read a library book.

After dinner that day Thaw sat in bed sketching when a voice said, "Excuse me, but are you an artist?"

"No. An art student."

"I'm sorry. I was misled by your beard. Would you mind showing me that drawing? I'm fond of flowers."

Thaw handed over the notebook, saying, "It's not very good. I'd need more time and materials to make it good."

The minister held up the book before his face and after nodding once or twice began turning the earlier pages. Thaw felt worried but not annoyed. The minister had the quality of a mildly shining, useful, grey, neglected metal; his accent was the one Thaw liked best, the accent of shopkeepers, schoolteachers, and working men with an interest in politics and religion. He said, "Your flowers are beautiful, really beautiful, but—I hope you're not offended—the earlier drawings confuse me a little. Of course I can see they're very clever and modern."

"They're doodles, not drawings. I haven't been fit enough to draw properly."

"How long have you been here?"

"Six weeks."

"Six weeks?" said the minister respectfully. "That's a long time. I expect to be only a few days myself. They want to make certain tests and see how I react. The heart, you know, but nothing serious. Now tell me, because I've often wondered, what makes people artists? Is it an inborn talent?"

"Certainly. It's born into everyone. All infants like playing with pencils and paints."

"But not many of us take it further than that. I, for instance, would like nothing better than to sketch a nice view, or the face of a friend, but I couldnae draw a straight line to save my life."

"There are very few good jobs for handworkers nowadays," said Thaw, "so most parents and teachers discourage that kind of talent."

"Did your parents encourage you?"

"No. They allowed me paper and pencil when I was an infant, but apart from that they wanted me to do well in life. My father only let me go to art school because he heard I might get a job there."

"So your talent *must* be inborn!"

After pondering awhile, Thaw said, "Someone might work and work at a thing, not because they were encouraged, but because they never learned to enjoy anything else."

"Dear me, that sounds very bleak! Tell me, just to change the subject, why are modern paintings so hard to understand?"

"As nobody employs us nowadays we've to invent our own reasons for painting. I admit art is in a bad way. Never mind, we've some good films. So much money has been put into the film industry that a few worthwhile talents have got work there."

The minister said slyly, "I thought artists didn't work for money."

Thaw said nothing. The minister said, "I thought they toiled in garrets till they starved or went mad, then their work was discovered and sold for thousands of pounds."

"There was once a building boom," said Thaw, growing excited, "In north Italy. The local governments and bankers of three or four towns, towns the size of Paisley, put so much wealth and thought into decorating public buildings that half Europe's greatest painters were bred there in a single century. These bosses weren't unselfish men, no, no. They knew they could only win votes and stay popular by giving spare wealth to their neighbours in the form of fine streets, halls, towers and cathedrals. So the towns became beautiful and famous and have been a joy to visit ever since. But today our bosses don't live among the folk they employ. They invest surplus profits in scientific research. Public buildings have became straight engineering jobs, our cities get uglier and uglier and our best paintings look like screams of pain. No wonder! The few who buy them, buy them like diamonds or rare postage stamps, as a form of non-taxable banking."

His voice had grown shrill and he gulped rapidly from a glass of water. The minister said, "That sounds rather communistic, but in Russia I believe—"

"Russia," cried Thaw, "has a more rigid ruling class than ours, so while western art is allowed to be hysterical, eastern art is allowed to be merely dull. No wonder! Strong, lovely, harmonious art has only appeared in small republics, republics where the people and their bosses shared common assemblies and a common—"

He coughed violently.

"Well, well," said the minister soothingly. "You've given me a lot to think about."

He began reading again. Thaw stared back at the flowers, but delight and freshness had leaked out of them.

Next morning Thaw sat in the armchair while the minister, hands clasped on chest, lay gazing at the ceiling. He said suddenly, "I've been thinking that maybe you should talk to Arthur Smail."

"Who?"

"He's our session clerk, a young man, very enterprising and full of modernistic ideas. Would you open the drawer of my locker, please? I'm not supposed to move. Do you see a wallet? Take it out and look inside and you'll find some snapshots. No, put that one back, that's my sister. It's my church I want you to see."

Thaw looked at two photographs showing the inside and outside of an ordinary Scottish church.

"Cowlairs Parish Church. Not grand maybe, but I've been there thirty-two years so I like it. I like it. Since the engine works closed the district has gone sadly downhill, I'm afraid. And the Presbytery have decided that next year our congregation and the congregation of St. Rollox must combine, for there aren't enough members to justify the upkeep of two establishments. St. Rollox is a church round the corner from us. Do you follow me?"

"Yes."

"Now the two congregations are nearly equal size, so Arthur Smail thought that if we cleaned and rewired our fabric, the Presbytery would send the congregation of St. Rollox to us instead of we to them. Am I boring you?"

"No."

"Mr. Smail belongs to a firm of shopfitters and we have Mr. Rennie, a painter and decorator, and two electricians, so we had the necessary skill and any number of willing helpers. The church is cleaner and brighter than I've known it for years. Unluckily, however (though quite understandably), St. Rollox have done the same thing and done it better. A member of theirs who did well in Canada sent a donation which let them clean the outside stonework, a thing we can't afford. So Mr. Smail came up with a new idea. . . . Have you ever attended a church of Scotland?"

"When I was at school."

"Then you may have observed that in the last century a lot of features were brought back which our ancestors had cast out. Nothing harmful, of course, like prayer books and bishops, just small embellishments: side pulpits, organs, stained-glass windows and even, in a few cases, crucifxes on the communion table. But a modern mural painting would be a complete novelty; newspapers, wireless and even television might take note, which would put an extra card up our sleeve in dealing with the Presbytery. So Mr. Smail wrote to the director of the art school asking if he could recommend a student who would like to take on the job. Because, you see, we couldn't pay him. The director wrote back saying it would be a shame to spoil an old building with the work of inexperienced hands. Mr. Smail was much annoyed. Excuse me telling you this, I have very little to do with it."

Thaw stared into the photographs. From in front the church looked like a blackened stone dog kennel with a squat little tower, a tower no taller than the tenements on each side. The interior was surprisingly spacious, the exact pattern of the church used by Thaw's old school. A balcony surrounded three sides and the fourth was pierced by a high arched chancel with three lancet windows in the back wall and an organ in the left. Intuitively he stood under the arch appraising the flat plaster surfaces. A sudden dread filled him that he wouldn't be allowed to decorate this building. He returned the snapshots, muttered "Excuse me," and hurried off down the ward.

He crossed bright lawns between vivid flowerbeds and sank, wrestling for breath, upon a bench. He shut his eyes and saw the inside of the church. Images were flowing up the walls like trees and mingling their colours like branches on the ceiling. He opened his eyes and stared across fields and woodland at the dip in the heat-dimmed Campsies. Self-pitying tears sprung on his cheeks and he whispered at the blue sky, *"Bastard,* giving me ideas without the strength to use them." He punched the side of his head, muttering, "Take that for having ideas. And that."
He broke into a fit of giggling, got up and returned to the ward.

"I must explain something," he said, sitting down by the minister. "I am not a Christian. I have a sort of faith in God but I can't believe he came down and made wheelbarrows in a shop. I like most of what Christ taught and I prefer him to Buddha, but only because Buddha started life with exceptional social privileges. I also want very, very much to paint this mural."
Thaw wondered if the minister was smiling, for he had hidden his face by a hand adjusting the spectacles, but when he lowered it he said gravely, "If you are willing to help and your design satisfies the kirk session we'll be perfectly content. There are no inquisitors among us."
"Good. The chancel ceiling is divided by plaster ribs into six panels. The most suitable theme for them is surely the six days of creation: Genesis, chapter one."
"The ceiling? . . . Mr. Smail thought the wall facing the organ would be the best place."
"The wall facing the organ will show the world on the seventh day, when God looks at it and likes it."
"That sounds acceptable."
"Good. I'll make sketches."

The ideas he scribbled in the notebook grew so fast that they burned up energy needed for breathing and he had to stop twice for injections. God was the easiest part of the design. He came out strong and omniscient, like Mr. Thaw, but with

an unexpected expression of reckless gaiety got from Aitken
Drummond. Next evening he showed sketches to the minister.
"I've decided to begin with the universe before creation starts,
when the spirit of God moves on the face of the deep. I'll
paint it on the back wall round the three windows."
"Dear me, that's a very large area."
"Yes, but I'll make it a simple deep, dark blue with silver
ripples. Modern science thinks the primordial chaos was hydrogen. I can't paint hydrogen so I'll stick to the old Jewish notion
of a universe filled with water. The Greeks believed everything
was made of water too."
"I thought they believed the original chaos was a mixture of
atoms and strife, with love outside it. Then love worked its
way in, driving strife out and linking the atoms."
"You refer to Empedocles. I refer to Thales, who was earlier."
"You're very erudite."
"We have to be. Nowadays we cannae depend on the education
of our patrons. Traditionally, in the chaos stage, the spirit of
God is shown as a bird. I'm making him a man above the
point of the middle window. He's small, and shaped like a
falling diver, and in black silhouette so we can't see if he's
swooping toward us or away. He is the seed fertilizing chaos,
the word that will order it into worlds."
"Perfectly orthodox."
"Here is the ceiling. The first panel shows Monday's work,
the making of light. A golden egg with God inside floats on
the dark water. He's naked and fully visible and represented
conventionally as a middle-aged vigorous man."
"His expression is rather alarming."
"I can soften it. On Tuesday we have the making of space. A
firmament is set up dividing the waters above it from the waters
below. God wades waist deep in the lower waters, raising a
tent-shaped sky above his head. The light fills the tent. On
Wednesday the lower waters are drawn back and the dry land
fixed in the middle and clothed with grass, flowers, herbs and
trees. The early Jews seemed obsessed with water, they have
God grappling with it for one and a half working days."
"They lived in the Euphrates delta," said the minister. "Where
water not only fell from the sky but in seasons of flood actually
bubbled out of the soil. It nourished their crops and flocks
and often drowned them too."
"I see. Thursday: night and day, sun, moon, stars. Friday: fishes
and birds. With each addition to his universe God is more
hidden behind it, till on Saturday all we see are his nostrils

in a cloud, breathing life into Adam who is wakening among
the creatures below. Adam is shaped like God but more pensive.
Lastly, here is the wall facing the organ. Adam and Eve kneel
cuddling beside the river which springs from under the tree
of life. The bird in the tree is a phoenix. I've several other
details to work out yet."

After a long pause the minister said, "I admire, of course,
the skill and thought you have put into this and so, I'm sure,
will the kirk session. But I'm afraid they won't allow your
depiction of God. No. You see, he'll frighten the children.
Everything else is just fine however: light, space, oceans, mountains, all these birds and animals—but not God. Oh, no."

"But without God we have a purely evolutionary picture of
creation!" cried Thaw.

"There is a lot to be said for the Mosaic notion that the Almighty
is most present when least imagined. And it would be a pity
to frighten the children," said the minister, closing his eyes.

"Very well," said Thaw, after a pause. "I'll take him off the
ceiling. But I *must* show him diving through chaos. That is
essential."

"Hardly anyone will notice him there. I'm sure that Arthur
Smail will raise no objection."

At medical inspection next morning the professor paused
by Thaw's bed and said, "Mr. Clark and Mr. Thaw here are
our oldest inhabitants. Everyone else in the ward when they
were admitted has cleared out or kicked the bucket but these
two have got into a repetitive cycle of improvement and deterioration. Mr. Clark is seventy-four, there's some excuse for him.
There's none for you, Duncan. Why do you do it?"

"I don't know," said Duncan.

"Then I'll tell you," said the professor cheerfully. "And don't
get angry. You're intelligent and tough enough to understand
me, which is why I'm not whispering behind your back. This
patient, gentlemen, is suffering from adaption. Let me give
you an example of adaption. A hardworking man of thirty loses
his job through no fault of his own. For two or three months
he hunts for work but can't find any. His national insurance
money runs out and he goes on the dole. In these circumstances
his energy and initiative are a burden to him. They make him
want to break things and punch people. So instinctively his
metabolism lowers itself. He grows slovenly and depressed.
A year or two passes, he's offered a job at last and refuses it.
Unemployment has become his way of life. He's adapted to

it. In the same way some people come here with commonplace
illnesses which, after an initial improvement, stop responding
to treatment. Why? In the absence of other factors we must
assume that the patient has adapted to the *hospital itself*. He
has reverted to an infantile state in which suffering and being
regularly fed feel actually safer than health. And mind you,
he's not a malingerer. The adaption has occurred in a region
where mind and body are indistinguishable. So what do we
do? In your case, Duncan, we're going to do this. No more
ephedrine, isoprenaline, aminophylline suppositories, sedatives
or sleeping pills. From now on we give you nothing: nothing
but an injection if the attacks are really bad. And if you aren't
well by next Friday we'll give you a hypodermic needle, a
bottle of adrenalin and sling you out. Of course if this were
America, and your father were rich, we could make a packet
by hanging on to you till you croaked. So think yourself lucky.
And now we will look at the heart of the minister of Cowlairs
Parish Church. Screens, please."

Thaw lay trembling with indignation. When the professor
left the ward he scrambled up, put on his dressing gown and
hurried outside. He found himself running through the grounds
muttering, "All right, I'll leave. I'll leave now. I'll demand a
taxi and leave now."
He leaned on the parapet of a bridge across a cutting near
the clock tower. Rails at the bottom were hidden by lank grass
and a litter of broken wicker baskets. The banks were overhung
by elders and brambles, but he glimpsed through them a station
platform, cracked, mossy and strewn with rubbish. He returned
thoughtfully to the ward.

A spruce fresh-faced man of about thirty sat by the minister,
who said, "Duncan, this is Mr. Smail, our session clerk. I've
been showing him your new designs and he's quite pleased
with them."
"Very impressive," said Mr. Smail, "though, of course, I'm
no judge of painting. My concern is with the practical side,
and I'm heartily glad we've got it moving at last. With your
permission I'll show these sketches to the kirk session next
Sunday."
He patted a glossy briefcase on his lap.
"I can make more elaborate designs if you like," said Thaw.
"Oh, no need at all. If the minister's pleased nobody else will

complain—not openly, at any rate. You know, of course, that we're a poorly endowed church and can't pay you. However, I think I've enough contacts to ensure a fair bit of publicity when the work's complete. No, we won't hide your light under a bushel. Now, how long will you take?"

Thaw pondered. He had no idea at all. He said cautiously, "Perhaps three months."

"And when can you start?"

"As soon as I'm well again," said Thaw, suddenly feeling well, "In fact I'm getting out on Friday."

"So you'll be finished by Christmas. Good. That will give us time to clear the scaffolding out for the Watch Night service. Perhaps the dedication ceremony and the Christmas service might be combined?"

"I don't think so," said the minister. "No. But it could be combined with the service at Hogmanay."

"Good. A newly decorated church by the new year. That will give the Presbytery something to think about."

Thaw felt a hidden alarm within him. He said, "It's a huge area. I'll need a lot of help. Not skilled help—just folk who can lay a colour inside the shapes I chalk for them."

"Oh, I'll help you myself. I've been practising on the kitchen ceiling. And Mr. Rennie, who's going to lend the scaffolding, I'm sure will lend a hand as well. We'll have no shortage of helpers."

Thaw took nail scissors from the minister's locker and snipped a corner from his dressing gown. He said, "First of all the plaster surfaces in the chancel must be painted this colour, a dark blue inclining to violet, in good-quality oil paint, eggshell finish, at least two coats."

Mr. Smail made a note in a pocket diary and shut the half-inch of cloth between the pages saying, "Leave it to me. And mibby sometime next week you'll give me a list of your materials. With my contacts I'm sure I can get them at a discount." Thaw lay down on his bed with a sensation of Napoleonic power.

On Friday he was ill again. The night before, the ward sister had given him a hypodermic needle, cotton wool, surgical spirit and a rubber-capped adrenalin bottle. She had shown him how to use them and later his father arrived with clothes and money. Now he laboriously dressed, glanced unhappily at Mr. Clark (who was smoking again) and said goodbye to the minister. In the reception hall he phoned for a taxi, then huddled on the back seat, soothed by the sizzling of the tyres on the wet roads, for at last the weather had broken.

He got out at the art school and slowly climbed to the hall called "the museum" where several students were writing at tables. He filled the registration form for his final year and carried it down a corridor, noticing that the dark panelled walls, white plaster gods and tight-trousered girls no longer seemed excitingly solid but shallow, like a photograph of a once-familiar street. There was a queue outside the registrar's door so he stepped into an empty studio and squirted six minims of adrenalin into his calf muscle. He entered the registrar's office shortly after, feeling businesslike on the outside but relaxed and dreamy within. He handed over the form and was asked to sit down.

"Well, Thaw, how are you getting on?"

"Not badly, sir. I've been offered a really big job." He explained about the mural and said, "Do you think I could work on it till Christmas?"

"I see no reason why not. When your diploma exam comes along next June the school could take the assessors to the church to see what you've done. Talk it over with Mr. Watt."

"Can I tell him you approve of the idea?"

"No. I neither approve or disapprove; it has nothing to do with me. Mr. Watt is your head of department."

"He may not want to give me permission."

"Oh? Why not?"

"He has already allowed me a great deal of freedom—freedom to paint in my own studio, I mean."

"Well?"

"I have nothing to show for it; no finished work, I mean."

"Why?"

"Ill health. But I've recovered now. If you like I can prove it with doctors' certificates."

The registrar sighed, rubbed his brow and said, "Go away, Thaw, go away. I'll speak to Mr. Watt."

"Thank you, Mr. Peel," said Thaw, briskly standing. "That is abnormally decent of you."

In the tram home he sat beside a lady with a shopping bag who eyed him for a while out of a sharp profile and at last said, "You're Duncan Thaw, of course."

"Yes."

"You don't remember me."

"Were you a friend of my mother?"

"A friend of your mother? I was the best friend Mary Needham had. I worked beside her in Copland and Lyes long, long, long before your father appeared on the scene. Mind you," she added musingly, "a lot of folk thought they were Mary's best friend. She knew so many and they all trusted her. Neighbours would confide in her who hated each other like poison. But there, she's gone. And so has your grampa, that good old man."

Her tone irritated Thaw. He could hardly remember his mother's father, a tall man with a white moustache who lived in a semi-detached villa a block away. The woman sighed and said, "Of course, your granny was the first to go. You were very fond of your granny."

"Was I?" said Thaw, startled, because he couldn't remember having a granny.

"Oh, yes. Whenever you quarrelled with your mother (you were always a difficult lad) you ran to your granny's house and she petted and spoiled you and gave you everything you liked. You were very upset when she died. You would go to her back door and lie there crying for her."

"Aren't you mixing me with someone else?"

"Who else? Surely not your sister. She was barely two at the time. A wild girl, your sister."

A moment later the woman chuckled and said, "Mind you, Mary was a wild one too in her day. Oh, she shocked me all right. I was one of the mousey kind. I remember two lads from haberdashery arranged to meet us at the Scott monument one Saturday. It was my first date and I was there punctual to the minute, dolled up to the nines. So were the lads. We waited half an hour and then by strolls Mary, arm in arm with a six-foot Australian soldier. Glasgow was full of them that summer. She strolled past without a word, just a sort of sideways wink at me. Wee Archie Campbell was heartbroken. Next day I asked her, 'How can you be so cruel?' She said, 'Ach, how else can you treat men who wear spats?' Another time she was out three nights running with three different boys. 'How can you?' I asked. She said, 'It's the opera this week. I cannae afford to go three nights running by myself.' One of these boys was your father. Nobody was more surprised than me when Mary Needham married Duncan Thaw. Well, she learned."

"Learned what?"

"Nothing, but it was surprising. He was the last man I'd have thought she'd marry. Four years passed before you appeared on the scene."

Thaw got home three hours before his father returned from work. The fire was set. He lit it then took a pile of sheet music from the piano stool and spread it on the hearth rug: cheap adaptations from Rossini and Verdi, the songs of Burns and sentimental translations from the Gaelic: *Ca' the Yowes* and *By the Light of the Peat-Fire-Flame.* His mother's unfamiliar maiden name was written in neat copperplate in faded brown ink on the inside cover, and his grandparents' address on the Cumbernauld Road, and the dates of purchase: none earlier than 1917 or later than 1929, when she married.
With sudden curiosity he looked at a wedding photograph on the mantelpiece. His father (shy, pleased, silly and young-looking) stood arm in arm with a slender laughing woman in one of the knee-length bridal dresses fashionable in the twenties. Her high-heeled shoes made her look the taller of the two. Thaw could think of no connection between this lively shop girl full of songs and sexual daring and the stern gaunt woman he remembered. How could one become the other? Or were they like different sides of a globe with time turning the gaunt face into the light while the merry one slid round into shadow? But only a few old people remembered her youth nowadays and soon both her youth and her age would be wholly forgotten. He thought, 'Oh no! No!' and felt for the only time in his life a pang of pure sorrow without rage or self-pity in it. He could not weep, but a berg of frozen tears floated near his surface, and he knew that berg floated in everyone, and wondered if they felt it as seldom as he did.

He fell asleep with his head on the heap of music and woke an hour later feeling so fit that he flung the syringe and adrenalin into the rubbish bin and drank a mouthful of the surgical spirit. It affected him like a glass of whisky taken in good company but the taste was so abominable that he poured the rest onto the packet of cotton wool and flung it on the fire. It boomed up the chimney in a satisfying flame.

CHAPTER 28. Work

Two and a half weeks later he stood with chalk and measuring rod on a plank platform forty feet above the chancel floor. As he scribbled on the blue vault he sang aloud:

> "Immortal, invisible, God only wise,
> In light inaccessible hid from our eyes,
> Most blessed, most glorious, the Ancient of Days,
> Almighty, victorious, you knew what you were about
> when you created me."

There was laughter from the helpers on the lower levels of scaffolding and on the ladders against the walls. They came two evenings a week: Mr. Smail, Mr. Rennie the decorator, a young electrician and a girl of sixteen who wanted to go to art school. Mr. Rennie was the most useful, a robust man of sixty who had attended evening classes in sign writing. With a skilled hand and loving patience he covered the tall arched deep-blue window wall with a fluid pattern of silver scrolling ripples. The others worked less finely but just as hard, excepting the girl, who had no head for heights. Most of the time she sat in the front row of the pews sketching the others at work. They liked her because she was good-looking and made tea and sandwiches.

At the start of November the ceiling was so full of different shapes that the delicately patterned window wall looked insipid, so Thaw chalked boulders, flames and clouds on it and prepared new cans of colour to paint them. When his helpers came that evening Mr. Smail climbed to the platform and said, "I'm afraid you've hurt Mr. Rennie's feelings."
"Why?"

"He put a lot of hard work into that wall. He was proud of it."

"No wonder. It was beautiful. I was only able to think of this better idea because he carried out my first one so well. And a quarter of his water will still be visible when the fire, clouds and rock are painted in. I'll go down and explain."

But when Thaw got down Mr. Rennie had left, and he didn't return. After that the other helpers stopped coming. Thaw missed them, for he liked working with people and enjoyed chatting over tea and sandwiches. But the main areas had been filled so he could now starting changing and refining by himself.

Each morning his palette, cleaned and laid out with new paint, looked prettier than any picture. While climbing to the platform he almost regretted that these tear-shaped pats of intense colour (Naples and marigold yellow, Indian red and crimson lake, emerald green and the two blues) could not be spread on the walls in their tropical vividness. To show distance and weight they had to be mixed with each other and white, black or umber. Yet it was magical that pig bristles fastened to a stick, spreading oily brown mud on a pale grey surface, could make a line of hills appear against a dawn sky. As he applied the paint his mind became a mere link between hand, colour, eye and ceiling. On descending to see the work from the church floor he had sometimes moments of selfish excitement, but his mind was sick of domineering over something as ramshackle as himself and glad to climb up again to where sight, thought, limbs, paint, feelings and brushes were a kit of tools the picture needed to complete itself. When busiest in this pure kind of work he was often visited by bizarre sexual fantasies. He got rid of them by quickly masturbating a few times, which left him free for a couple of days afterward.

When he paused to listen the usual sounds were from traffic outside and the *clicklick* . . . *clicklick* of the clock in the tower. Sometimes steps resounded from a warren of meeting rooms, kitchens and corridors at the back of the building and around noon on weekdays came a muffled clangour from a hall used as a dining centre by a local school. The only regular visitor was the old minister, who came in the evening after seeing people in his vestry. He sat so still in the front pew, staring so quiet and open-mouthed at the ceiling, that he was usually forgotten until Thaw, finding some flaw in a cloud, wave, or animal, yelled, "That's not how you should be!" then looked down and added, "I'm sorry," but the minister only

smiled and nodded. One evening when Thaw descended to
wash brushes he said, "You won't have it finished for the Watch
Night service, will you?"

"I'm sorry. Probably not."

"Oh, that's a pity. You see, people are starting to complain.
When do you think it *will* be finished?"

Thaw winced and said, "When will the Presbytery need to
see it?"

"June, I suppose, at the latest. But surely you can finish before
then? How about Easter Sunday? That gives you at least four
extra months."

Thaw said cautiously, "Oh, I'll probably have it done by then."

"Now is that a promise? Can I tell the kirk session that?"

"Yes. A promise," said Thaw gloomily.

Shortly before Christmas he was eating lunch at the communion table when a middle-aged lady came in. Her hair was
a cloud of angry grey curls. She wore a white smock, and
stared at him, glanced once at the mural and stared back. He
hurried over saying "Mrs. Coulter!"

"Well, Duncan?"

"What are you doing here? Are you working on the school
dinners?"

"It brings in the pennies."

"How are you? How's Robert?"

"Not bad, I suppose. Of course, he's not very pleased with
you. You could at least have come to the wedding."

"Robert married? I never knew."

"You were sent an invitation three weeks ago."

"But I've not been home. I'm sleeping here just now."

"Here?"

"I've a mattress behind that pew over there. How's the engineering?"

"Oh, he gave that up a year ago. He's in Dundee writing
the sports page for the *North East Courier*."

"Robert a journalist?"

"Aye. He was always keen on the writing."

"He never told me that!"

"He didn't want to. When you get onto your high horse, Duncan, nobody else gets a word in edgeways. Well, the Thomson
press was advertising for journalists, and he sent them a story
he'd written. I don't know why, he was doing all right at engineering. Anyway, they took him on, and now he's married a
girl in one of their offices."

"I must write to him."

"Oh, you'll never write to him. You're too full of yourself. But I suppose that's how people get on in the world . . . not that you seem to have got very far."

She stared at the paint-stained dressing gown he wore on top of his overalls. His mother had made it from a thick grey army blanket and it was warm and draught-proof. He said awkwardly, "Tell Robert I'm sorry I missed the wedding."

The pulpit was draught-proof with an electric foot warmer. In frosty weather he found it cosier sleeping curled on its octagonal floor than extended on the mattress, and grew so used to this that he continued there when spring came. Small corns embossed the palms of his hands from climbing the tubular steel. The ceiling was finished and the scaffolding removed before Easter, and now he worked from ladders upon the great wall facing the organ. One day Mr. Smail came and asked crisply, "When will you finish this, Duncan?"

"I don't know."

"But good heavens, you asked for three months and have taken seven! And the Presbytery are coming to inspect this in June and we should be arranging favourable publicity as soon as possible!"

After a pause Thaw said, "You can show it to journalists in a fortnight. It won't be finished then, but it will look as if it is."

"I have your solemn word on that?"

"Oh, yes, my solemn word, if you want it."

When Mr. Smail left he climbed down and glumly considered the tall arched panel. At the top a phoenix sank into flames among the leaves and yellow fruit of the tree of life, whose branches sheltered crows, pigeons, wrens and squirrels. The straight dark trunk divided the wall in half and grew from a lawn in the foreground. Rabbits nibbled cowslips, a mole delved and a roe deer nursed her fawn. There was enough killing to keep predators alive and the herbivores jumpy: a fox brought a pheasant to its cubs, a tawny owl in the tree of knowledge held a vole in a claw while other voles played among dead leaves between the roots. The naked man and woman embracing under the great tree of knowledge were clearly reflected in a pool of rushes and irises. This pool, the source of a river, contained a salmon rising to a gnat and mosaic turrets of caddis larvae on weedy pebbles. So far he was satisfied. His trouble began in the background where history was acted in the loops and delta of the river on its way to the ocean. The more he worked the more the furious figure of God kept popping in and having to be removed: God driving out Adam and Eve for learning to tell right from wrong, God preferring meat to vegetables and making the first planter hate the first herdsman, God wiping the slate of the world clean with water and leaving only enough numbers to start multiplying again, God fouling up language to prevent the united nations reaching him at Babel, God telling a people to invade, exterminate and enslave for him, then letting other people do the same back. Disaster followed disaster to the horizon until Thaw wanted to block it with the hill and gibbet where God, sick to death of his own violent nature, tried to let divine mercy into the world by getting hung as the criminal he was. It was comical to think he achieved that by telling folk to love and not hurt each other. Thaw groaned aloud and said, "I don't enjoy hounding you like this, but I refuse to gloss the facts. I admire most of your work. I don't even resent the ice ages, even if they did make my ancestors carnivorous. I'm astonished by your way of leading fertility into disaster, then repairing the disaster with more fertility. If you were a busy dung beetle pushing the sun above the skyline, if you had the head of a hawk or the horns and legs of a goat I would understand and sympathize. If you headed a squabbling committee of Greek departmental chiefs I would sympathize. But your book claims you are a man, the one perfect man of whom we are imperfect copies. And then you have the bad taste to put yourself in it as a character and show that you're socially repulsive. You've never been house-trained. Very few men are as nasty to their children as you are to yours. Why didn't you give me a railway station to decorate? It would have been easy painting to the glory of Stevenson, Telford, Brunel and a quarter million Irish navvies. But here I am, illustrating your discredited first chapter through an obsolete art form on a threatened building in a poor province of a collapsing empire. Only the miracle of my genius stops me feeling depressed about this, and even so my brushes are clogged by theology, that bastard of the sciences. Let me remember that a painting, before it is anything else, is a surface on which colours are arranged in a certain order. There is too much blue in this picture and I'd better not cover it with more birds. There could be no harm in another cloud, a thundercloud over Sinai, shaped like a chariot with you standing in it, very black-coated and Presbyterian. If I make you small enough Mr. Smail might not notice you and the composition doesn't need a big man there."

Two days later a telegram was handed to him which said, RETURN TO ART SCHOOL AT ONCE. DIPLOMA EXAM STARTED YESTERDAY. PETER WATT. The art school looked flimsier than ever and as he entered the old studio the other students gave an ironical cheer. Mr. Watt muttered, "Better late than never, Thaw," and handed him a paper which required him to design a decorative panel for the dining room of a luxury liner. He took a sheet of hardboard and spent the morning filling it with a merman and a mermaid chasing each other's tails with a knife and fork, then he said, "That's the best I can do, Mr. Watt. I'll go back to the church now."

"Wait a minute! You're allowed six weeks for this examination. Half the diploma assessment is based on it."

"I know, sir. I'm sorry, but I must return to Cowlairs. You see—"

"You will not return to Cowlairs. You will come with me, now, to the registrar."

Thaw was left outside the office door for ten or fifteen minutes and ushered in by the registrar's secretary, an unusual formality. Mr. Peel and Mr. Watt were seated on the same side of a long table, a single chair facing them at a distance. Thaw sat on it and some seconds of tribunal silence ensued. The two men looked so solidly forbidding that he instinctively blurred them by unfocusing his eyes. At last the registrar said, "Have you any complaint about your treatment in this school, Thaw?"

"None. I have been treated very well."

"Correct. Yet you have ignored our advice, flouted our authority and not only obliged us to bend our rules but actually to improvise new ones to avoid expelling you. Of course we have been influenced by consideration of your health: and I don't mean merely your physical health."

There was more silence, so Thaw said, "Thank you, sir."

"When you started here you signed an application form. That form was a contract, a contract you have renewed at the start of each school year. Society is upheld by contracts, Thaw. All government, all business, all industry is the result of people making promises and working to keep them. In return for a steady grant of money you promised to qualify for the Scottish Education Department Diploma of Painting. This school exists to award that diploma. Mr. Watt tells me you refuse to sit the examination."

"But I've finished it."

Mr. Watt said, "What will the other students think of the exam
if you are allowed to pass on half a day's work?"
Thaw said, "Mr. Watt, I realize that schools need examinations,
and admit that many students wouldn't work at all if they
weren't rewarded with paper rolls printed by the government.
And, Mr. Peel, I've been thrilled to hear you defending contracts and promises, because if these weren't defended we'd
have mere anarchy. I cannot deny your truths, I can only oppose
them with mine. This exam is endangering an important painting. It would be blasphemy to waste my talent making frivolous
decorations for a non-existent liner. But I see your difficulty.
You must uphold the art school, while I am upholding art.
The solution is simple. Don't award me this diploma. I promise
not to feel offended. The diploma is useless, except to folk
who want to be teachers."
Thaw leaned forward to see the pleased light of agreement
on the registrar's face but it was so compressed and wrinkled
that he sank back feeling lonely. The registrar said, "I have
never in my life heard such a display of intellectual arrogance.
You've made me more miserable than I've felt for many years.
You have sat smugly declaiming that black is white and evi-
dently expecting me to agree. I have no advice to give, but I
tell you this: If you do not return at once to the examination
your connection with the art school ends today, and for good."
Thaw nodded and left the office feeling dazed. He went upstairs
to the studio trying to think of entertaining nonsense to add
to the background of the examination panel. He climbed slower
and slower, then stopped and turned. On the way down he
passed Mr. Watt coming up. They pretended not to see each
other.

      The following evening his father entered the church and
cried, "Come down and read this, Duncan!"
Thaw wiped his brush and descended the ladder.
"Read this!" commanded Mr. Thaw, stiffly holding out a letter.
"No need."
"Damn you, read it!"
"No. It's from Mr. Peel explaining why I've been expelled."
"My God, you've made a mess of your life."
"It's too early to judge."
"How do you intend to eat in future?"
"I've still some of my grant money. And the minister says
the congregation may hold a collection for me when the mural's
done."

"What will that bring you? Twenty pounds? Fourteen? Eight?"
"There's going to be a lot of good publicity, Dad. I may get
other mural jobs, paying ones, in cafés and pubs. The ceiling's
finished. What do you think of it?"
"I don't appreciate painting, Duncan! I take my opinion from
the experts. And you've quarrelled with your experts."
"The experts who matter are you and me, the only people
here. Please look at my ceiling! Don't you enjoy it? Look at
the hedgehog! I copied her from a cigarette card you stuck
in an album for me when I was five. Don't you remember?
Will's *Wild Animals of Britain?* She fits that corner perfectly.
Don't you like her?"
Mr. Thaw sat on a corner of the communion table and said,
"Son, when will I be footloose?"
Thaw was puzzled by the word. He said, "Footloose?"
"Yes. When can I live as I want? I don't enjoy working as a
costing clerk in a city. This summer I meant to get a job with
the Scottish Youth Hostels or the Camping Club. The money's
poor but I'd be among hills and able to walk and climb and
mix with the sort of folk I like. I'm nearly sixty, but thank
God I have my health. I expected you to get a job at the art
school. Peel told me it was a probability four years ago. Instead
you've chosen to become a social cripple. Not like Ruth! She's
independent."
"I'm independent too. If I've recently eaten your food or slept
under your roof it's because I was sick," said Thaw sullenly.
He was disconcerted, for he had never expected his father to
become a man who lived by doing what he liked. Mr. Thaw
said mildly, "Son, I don't hate helping you. Listen, I'm prepared
to pay the rent of the house for at least another year, even if
I'm not living there. We can both use it as a base, a point of
departure. Of course, I'd prefer you to pay for the electricity
you burn."
"That's fair enough."
"Another thing. Since you were wee I've put a few bob a
month into a couple of insurance policies for you. It's time
you did that yourself. Keep up the payments, and you'll get
five pounds a week from the time you're sixty. Of course, if
you realize it right away you'll get less than fifty pounds. That's
up to you."
"Thank you, Dad," said Thaw and nearly smiled. He had not
lied in saying he still had some grant money left, but it was
only a few shillings.

A week later a group containing Mr. Smail and the minister entered. Mr. Smail said jovially, "Here's a young lady who wants to speak to you, Duncan."

Thaw came down from the ladder. The lady was dwarfed by a tall man with an expensive camera. The details of her person and dress were slightly sloppy, but she moved with such smiling confidence that this wasn't seen at first. She held out her hand, saying, "Peggy Byres of the *Evening News*."

Thaw laughed and said, "Are you going to make me famous?" He talked for six or seven minutes about the ceiling. She glanced at it, scribbled in a note pad and said, "Is your family very religious, Duncan?"

"Oh, no. I've never been christened."

"Then why are you so religious?"

"I'm not. I never go to church services. Sunday is my day of rest."

"Then what makes you paint a religious work without payment?"

"Ambition. The Old Testament has everything that can be painted in it: universal landscapes and characters and dreams and adventures and histories. The New Testament is more single-minded. I don't enjoy it so much."

"Look at these rabbits beside the pool, Miss Byres," said Mr. Smail. "You can almost hear them nibbling."

The reporter looked at the Eden wall and said, "Who's that behind the bramble bush with a lizard at his feet?"

"God," said Thaw, glancing uneasily at the minister and Mr. Smail. "The lizard is the serpent before his legs were removed. God has his back to us—you can hardly see his face."

"But what we can see looks very . . . looks rather . . ."

"Enigmatic," said Thaw. "He's not just watching Adam and Eve make love, he can see the expulsion afterward and the river of bloody history down to the wars of the apocalypse. We've had a lot of these wars recently. He can even see past them to the just city predicted by St. John, Dante and Marx. I haven't read Marx but—"

"These birds in the tree of life are miracles of delicacy, aren't they, Miss Byres?" said Mr. Smail from a distance.

"But why is Adam a Negro?"

"He's actually more red than black," the minister murmured, "and the name 'Adam' derives from a Hebrew word meaning 'red earth.'"

"But Eve is white!"

"Pearly pink," said Thaw. "I'm told that for a few moments

love makes different people feel like one. My outline shows
the oneness, my colours emphasize the difference. It's an old
trick. Rubens used it."

"Did you draw Eve from a model?"

"Yes."

"A girlfriend?" asked the reporter, with an arch smile.

"No, a friend of a friend," said Thaw, who had drawn Janet
Weir. He added glumly, "Most girls will pose naked for an
artist if he only wants to draw them."

The reporter tapped her lip with the pencil, then said, "Do
you find life a tragedy or really more of a joke?"

Thaw laughed and said, "That depends on the part of it I'm
looking at."

"And what will you do when you've finished here?"

"I hope to paint some commercial murals. I'll need the money."

"Do you like the mural, Miss Byres?" said Mr. Smail.

"I'm afraid I'm not an art critic. The *Evening News* doesn't
have a regular art critic. Duncan, would you go up your ladder
and pretend to paint Adam and Eve for a minute? We'll take
a photograph, anyway."

He bought the paper on Saturday and carried it eagerly
into the pulpit. The article began:

ATHEIST PAINTS
FACE OF GOD

Most people think artists are mad.
The wild-bearded figure in the
paint-stained dressing gown who
haunts Cowlairs Parish Church will
hardly reassure them on that point.
And Duncan Thaw, a self-proclaimed atheist and Marxist, freely
admits he is painting a large mural
there with nothing in mind but the
lust for fame.

His eyes clenched shut in horror. Eventually he opened them
and skimmed quickly through the rest.

He has a terrifying laugh, like the
bark of an asthmatic sea lion, and
produces it unexpectedly for no reason at all. I sometimes wondered
if it was caused by something I had
said, but on reflection I saw this was
impossible. . . .

Was Adam a Negro? Duncan Thaw
thinks so. . . .

"I have no trouble finding nude
models," he remarks, with something suspiciously like a wink. . . .

He hopes this will be the first of
many murals. He hopes to make a
lot of money this way. He says he
needs it.

He felt as if there was poison in his chest, as if half his blood
had been removed. He sat still until the old minister wandered
in and asked, "Have you read . . . ?"
"Yes."
"It's unfortunate. Unfortunate."
"Surely she was trying to be cruel!"
"No, I don't think so. I met many reporters when I was chaplain
at Barlinnie Jail and on average they're no more wicked than
other people. But their job depends on being entertaining,
so they make everything look as clownish or as monstrous as
they can. If any more reporters come, Duncan, my advice is
to tell them nothing you really feel or believe."

A reporter came that evening, took Thaw for a drink in
a pub and explained that he too would have been an artist if
his uncle hadn't opposed the idea. Thaw said, "Please tell your
readers I am not an atheist. I may have my own conception
of God, but it doesn't clash with the opinions of the church,
my employer."
This appeared two days later under the heading:

NOT AN
ATHEIST

The Cowlairs "mad muralist," Duncan Thaw, has denied he is an atheist. He says he has his own conception of good but it doesn't clash.

After this Thaw noticed that journalists weren't interested in
his thoughts, though they asked him what it felt like to sleep
alone in a big building and kept photographing Adam and
Eve. An exception was a tall man in a beautifully cut grey
suit from the *Glasgow Herald*. He sat for half an hour in the

front pew staring at the ceiling, then sat on the organ stool and gazed at the Eden wall. At last he said, "I like this."

"I'm glad."

"Of course it will be almost impossible for me to criticize it. It isn't cubist or expressionist or surrealist, it isn't academic or kitchen sink or even naive. It's a bit like Puvis de Chavannes, but who nowadays knows Puvis de Chavannes? I'm afraid you're going to pay the penalty of being outside the main streams of development."

"The best British painters are that."

"Eh?"

"Hogarth. Blake. Turner. Spencer. Burra."

"Oh, you like these? Turner *is* good, of course. His handling of colour anticipates Odilon Redon and Jackson Pollock. Well, I'll do my best for you, though this is one of my busy weeks. The Glasgow and Edinburgh schools are having their diploma shows, so I haven't much space."

At the end of an article about other people the *Herald* said this:

> It isn't easy to discover Cowlairs Parish Church in the depths of northeast Glasgow, but hardy souls who make the effort will find Duncan Thaw's (unfinished) Genesis mural worth a great deal more than a passing glance.

The newspapers sickened him of the mural. He had taken months to make every shape as clear and harmonious as possible, putting in nothing he didn't feel lovely or exciting. He knew that reports must always simplify and twist, but he also felt that the most twisted report gives some idea of its cause, and his work had caused nothing but useless gossip. He lay curled on the pulpit floor, dozing and waking till afternoon, then rose and stared, biting his thumb knuckle, at the unfinished wall. All he could see in it now were complicated shapes. With a slam and clattering McAlpin and Drummond came in followed by Macbeth. Thaw gazed at them astonished and relieved.

"We are here," said Drummond, "because we read in the papers that you are holding weekday services in which Negroes are raped by white women."

"You will gather that we are slightly puggled," said McAlpin.

"Stotious," said Drummond.

"Miraculous," said McAlpin.

"Full," said Drummond.

They starting running round the church along the backs of pews, zigzagging through the nave and up into the gallery, pausing for new views of the mural and shouting to each other: "I can see the whole window wall from here."

"Good God, there's a diver in it."

"The tree looks best from above."

"But I see a dung beetle you can't see."

Macbeth sat heavily beside Thaw saying, "They've got their diplomas. They can laugh."

They came down at last and Drummond said soberly "It's all right, Duncan, you've nothing to worry about."

"You like it?"

"We're envious," said McAlpin. "At least I am. Come for a drink."

"Gladly! Where to?"

"Remember I've only half a crown," said Drummond.

"I've twenty-six pounds," said Thaw. "But it has to last till my next mural."

Drummond said, "This is clearly a Wine 64 night."

"What is Wine 64?"

"Not a drop of it is drunk before it's sixty-four days old, yet a tumblerful costs only fourpence. It's so strong I only drink it once a year. Twice would damage the health. The only pub selling it is in Grove Street, but we'll be safe because there's three of us."

"Four," said Macbeth, standing up firmly.

Sliding patches of evening sunshine mingled with flurries of so warm a rain that nobody thought of sheltering from it. Drummond led them round Sighthill cemetery, across some football pitches and up a wilderness of slag bings called Jack's Mountain. From the top they saw the yellow-scummed lake called the Stinky Ocean, then came down near a slaughterhouse behind Pinkston power station, along the canal towpath, between bonded warehouses, across Garscube Road and into a public house. The customers sat on benches against the wall, staring at each other across the narrow floor like passengers in a train. They were all older than forty with very creased faces and clothes. An old lady sitting beside Thaw said quietly, "All God's people, sonny."

He nodded.

"And he loves every one of us."

Thaw frowned. She said, "You neednae be afraid to speak to a granny, son."

"I'm not afraid. I was wondering about what you said."

She took his hand. "Listen, son, God was the humblest man who ever walked the earth. He didn't care who you were or what you did, he still sat with you and drank with you and loved you."

Thaw was astonished. He imagined the creator as an erratically generous host, not as a friendly fellow guest, but the old woman's faith had been tested by more life than his so he said gently, "He drank with you?"

She nodded and smiled at a sherry on the table before her and squeezed his hand, saying, "Yes, he did, because it lifts the heart. I was reading the *Sunday Post,* and a doctor writing in it said a lot of people died of drink but more died of worry. Now I can come in here on a Saturday night and have a half or two, and I hear folk talking and I feel I love everyone in the room."

Macbeth leaned toward her. "If God loves us why are we in such a mess?"

He smiled at her as if she was a joke, but she was not offended and not only reached out to squeeze his hand but stroked his hair.

"Because we don't love God, we mock and despise him. But he still loves us, no matter what we do."

"Even if we kill someone?"

"Even if we kill someone."

"Even if you're a Communist?"

"It doesn't matter who you are. When God meets you at the gates of pearl and asks who you are and you say to him, 'God forgive me,' then it's 'Come in. You're welcome.' "

Thaw had never before met a religious person who thought God's love an easy thing. He said abruptly, "What if we can't forgive ourselves?"

She didn't understand the question and he repeated it. She said, "Of course you can't forgive yourself! Only God can forgive you."

"Tell me this," said Macbeth. "Are you a Catholic?"

"I come from Ireland—I'm Irish through and through."

"But are you a Catholic?"

"It doesn't matter who you are. . . ."

Thaw sipped Wine 64 which tasted like watered strawberry jam. In leaning forward to speak Macbeth left a gap through which McAlpin was visible. Thaw told him quietly, "I left the church tonight for a complete change of air and the first stranger I meet is a friend of God."

"Ah!" said McAlpin cheerfully, setting down his glass. "Shall I tell you about God? I'm unusually lucid tonight."

Beyond him a haggard man was discussing with Drummond the chances of selling one's body for medical research while still alive. Thaw said, "Will you take long?"

"Certainly not. God, you see, is a word. It is the word for everything not speaking when someone says 'I think.' And by Propper's Law of Inverse Exclusion (which enables a flea in a matchbox to declare itself jailor of the universe) every single 'I think' has intimate knowledge of the surface of what it is not. But as every thinker reflects a different surface of what he isn't, and as God is our word for the whole, it follows that all agreement about God is based on misunderstanding."

"You're a liar," cried Macbeth, who had caught some of this, "The old woman is right. God is not a word, God is a man! I crucified him with these hands!"

McAlpin said soothingly, "Since competitive capitalism split us off from the collective unconscious we've all been more or less crucified."

"Don't talk to me about crucifixion," snarled Macbeth. "How can a man with a diploma understand crucifixion? A year ago a friend said to me, 'Jimmy, if you go on like this you'll end in the gutter, the madhouse or the Clyde.' Since then I have been in all three."

McAlpin raised a forefinger and said, "To a sensitively poised intelligence like me a wrong note in a Beethoven quartet is as excruciating as a boot up the backside or a fall from Clyde Street suspension bridge is to you."

"You think you're fucking clever, don't you?" said Macbeth. Meanwhile the old lady had jumped up and was shaking everyone by the hand. When she came to Drummond he grinned at her and sang with surprising sweetness:

> "The Lord's my shepherd: I'll not want.
>   He makes me down to lie
>   In pastures green. He leadeth me
>   The quiet waters by."

Several people joined in, others laughed and a few frowned and muttered. The old lady caressed Drummond's hair and said he looked like Christ, then said her name was Molly O'Malley and danced a jig on the narrow floor, calling out to Thaw from the middle of it, "God love you, my boy! God love you, my bonny boy!"

"You're after the auld woman, eh?" asked an old man nearby.

"Me?" said Thaw. "No!"

"Blethers. I'd have ridden a cat at your age."

A stout bartender arrived and said firmly, "Right, lads, you've had your fun."

"Fun?" cried Macbeth querulously. "What fun have I had?" But they were forced to leave.

There was a chill wind outside and a sky bright with the green and gold of a slow summer sunset. Drummond said he knew of a party and led them up Lynedoch Street, a normally shallow hill which tonight seemed perpendicular. They avoided falling off by clinging to each other, except Macbeth who drifted away down a sidestreet. The party was in a large, well-furnished house and Thaw found the other guests daunting. They were his own age but had the clothes and conversation of adults with monthly salaries. He found a corner in a dim room where couples clung and turned to the sound of a gramophone. Suddenly a woman in a black dress said loudly, "Good heavens, is that you, Duncan? Won't you dance with me?"

They danced and he gazed fascinated at her blond hair and naked shoulders. She giggled and said, "You don't remember me, but you should. I was the first girl you ever danced with. Ever, ever, ever."

He grinned thankfully and said, "I'm very glad."

"Do you remember what you thought I was like?"

"Marble and honey."

"Am I still like that?"

"Yes."

"What a relief. You see, I'm marrying a solicitor next month. He's very rich and sexy and what more can a woman want?" Her manner was strained and cheerful and he didn't understand it. She said, "I'm a terrible woman, Duncan. I've still four or five boyfriends and I play them against each other, and at the moment I rather fancy that woman talking to Aitken. Have you ever fancied a man?"

"Not in the cuddling way," said Thaw.

His head lay on her shoulder and his hands clasped the halves of her bottom. She said, "Stop touching me, Duncan."

He said, "I'm sorry," and went over to a table of drinks, filled a tumbler of whisky and forced it quickly down him like medicine. It tasted horrible. The words "Stop touching me,

Duncan'' were sounding in the centre of him. He couldn't
bear them, but they were in his centre. He filled and drank a
tumbler of sherry, which tasted better; then one of gin, which
tasted much worse; then he went upstairs to the lavatory.

When he got inside the room was visibly whirling. He
closed his eyes and felt it drop like a crashing aeroplane. He
fell to the wall, then to the floor. He embraced the narrow
part of the lavatory pan and lay shivering and wishing he was
unconscious. Whenever he opened his eyes he saw the room
whirl: when he closed them he felt it fall. There were hammer-
ings and voices shouting, "Open the door," but he said, "Go
away, I'm cold,'' and after a while they went away. Later he
heard such an odd scratching and tapping that he sat up. The
tapping was mingled with faint cries of "Let me in!" and the
bluster of strong wind. There was a white mouthing face behind
the black glass of the window and he felt a pang of superstitious
terror, for he remembered the lavatory was on the second or
third floor. At last he crawled over, reached up a hand and
raised a catch. The window swung in and Drummond jumped
through with a gust of rain. He said, "Don't worry, Duncan,''
and wiped Thaw's face and shirt with a sponge. Thaw said,
"I'm cold, leave me alone.''
Two people helped him downstairs through an empty house.
A door was opened and he was taken into a dark shed with
a concrete floor. He screamed, "This is a cold place, I don't
want to be here.''
He was laid on the skin of a cold sofa, some doors slammed
and a voice said, "Where do you live?''
"Cowlairs Parish Church.''
"For Christ's sake where does he live?''
A voice gave an address on the Cumbernauld Road and the
sofa throbbed and swung forward. It was clearly part of a car,
and when it stopped outside the close in Riddrie he was able
to get out and walk upstairs alone. Luckily his father no longer
lived there.

A week later he recovered enough self-esteem to return
to the church. The mural broke upon him in an altogether
fresh way. He chuckled and skipped about, looking at it from
different angles, his mind brightening with new ideas. He was
laying paint on his palette when the minister came in. He said,
"You took a holiday, Duncan. Good. You needed a rest. . . .
I'm afraid I have bad news. The Glasgow Presbytery have been

here and . . . they've seen it and they're not very happy. Of course, our publicity was bad and the colour of Adam was rather a shock. I told them you could change that, but it was the *principle* of the thing they disliked. I'm afraid we're going to lose our church."

Anger flooded Thaw's veins with adrenalin. He laid his ladder against the wall and said, "When?"

"In another six or seven months. Sometime early in the coming year."

"At least it gives me time to finish the mural," said Thaw, mounting the ladder.

"I'm sorry, but you'll have to stop."

"Why?" said Thaw, staring.

"We've had complaints from the congregation. They'd like to worship without this mess of ladders and pots and drips on the chancel floor. The session say you must stop. Even Mr. Smail says so, and he was a great supporter of yours."

"When?"

"Next Sunday."

On Sunday the minister came an hour before the service and said, "Well, Duncan."

Thaw climbed wearily down the ladder for he'd been working all night. He said, "That's the best I can do in the time."

"It looks just fine."

"If anyone wonders about these marks tell them they would have become a herd of cattle."

"Oh, no one will ask. It looks fine."

"And if they say the sky is cluttered, tell them I meant to simplify it."

"It's beautiful, Duncan, but you could be an eternity on it. An eternity."

"And if they say the events on the horizon distract from the big simple foreground shapes, tell them I'd begun to notice that, but this was my first mural, I'd seen nobody else paint one, and I'd to teach myself as I went along. Tell them I couldn't afford assistants."

The minister hesitated, then said firmly, "Finish the mural when you like, Duncan. Pay no attention to them. Work on it as much as you like."

"Oh!" said Thaw, and wept with relief. The minister patted his shoulder and said kindly, "Just you go ahead and pay no attention to them."

CHAPTER 29. The Way Out

He could no longer ask the church to pay for materials. When only ten pounds remained he knew he would be a desperate man when it was spent; on the other hand if he survived without touching it he could probably last forever. A smell of boiled cabbage from the depths of the building suggested an idea. In the early afternoon he went to a lane behind the church where rubbish bins stood and found scraps from the school dinners tipped there. He started bringing a plate round and picking out slices of bread and mutton, lumps of macaroni and dumpling. One day he heard someone cry "Duncan Thaw!" and looked into the accusing eyes of Mrs. Coulter. He said defensively, "I'm not stealing this. Nobody wants it."
"You should be ashamed, a well-brought-up boy like you!" He walked past her with the heaped plate, but around noon the next day she brought a large covered bowl into the church and set it on the end of a pew saying, "Your dinner."
He said irritably, "You don't need to do that Mrs. Coulter." She snorted and went out and did the same every following weekday except Friday, when she left two bowls. And the decorator, Mr. Rennie, arrived one evening and said abruptly, "Do you still want help?"
"More than ever."
"Right. I'll give you a couple of nights a week."
He began changing into overalls and Thaw, who wept easily nowadays, hurried to a quiet corner of the church. Then he returned and said, "You see my tree of life, Mr. Rennie? It's big and beautiful and in the wrong place. Far too central. It must be shifted two and a quarter inches to the left, fruit, birds, squirrels and all. Do you see why?"

"Don't ask me why, just show me how to do it."

"I will, Mr. Rennie. Excuse me if I chatter nervously, I'm afraid of you vanishing. And could you lend me scaffolding again for a few days? I want to get back to the ceiling."

"That won't please the minister."

"Just for a few days."

The help of Mr. Rennie, though only six hours a week, was so welcome that Thaw found comfort in addressing him when he wasn't there.

"We aren't working on the rim of the universe, are we, Mr. Rennie? No, no, Cowlairs is a historic region. A cinema down the road has a granite slab set in the wall above a bunged-up drinking fountain. It must have lain flat once, for the inscription says James Nisbet lies under it who suffered martyrdom there in 1684. I suppose the district was wild moorland then. He was shot by government troops for worshipping God without a prayerbook, just making up the words as he went along. . . . A bad business? No, a question of law and order. Men who refused to pray out of a properly licensed book might undermine the government by asking God to change it. So *bang-bang,* cheerio, Jimmy Nisbet. But four years later came a different lot of politicians who found it easy to govern Scotland without prayerbooks. So the troops stopped chasing Presbyterians, who wouldnae pray out of books, and returned to chasing Catholics, who prayed out of Latin ones. And a slab was laid over Nisbet's bones on the site of the Carlton picture house (they're turning it into a bingo hall next year) and a slipshod verse was carved on it which ends with the rousing words:

> As Britain lyes in guilt, you see,
> 'Tis asked o reader, art thou free?

Are we free, Mr. Rennie? Of course we are. We're making our own model of the universe and nobody gives a damn for us. . . ."

"Yes, a great ground for martyrs, Mr. Rennie. Overby in the cemetery is a monument to Baird, Hardie and Wilson, some weavers who nearly overturned the British government around 1820. The government was very insecure in those days. It had just won a large war and there was widespread unemployment. Mechanization was making the owning classes richer and the working classes poorer—especially the weavers. A secret organization grew up in the weaving towns which planned to call a general strike, assassinate the cabinet, attack the barracks and give everybody the vote. Cunning, eh? The details of the revolt were mostly worked out by government agents, and when the great day dawned they had trouble getting anyone to move. However, in the villages of Strathaven and Bellshill some enthusiasts set out with red flags. Four of them actually hoisted one on Cathkin Braes and then went home to their teas, for clearly nothing was happening. So Baird, Hardie and Wilson were arrested, tried and hung, and the bloody tide of revolution receded. Then one day the government noticed it could give the vote to almost everyone without losing power. The unemployed got assisted passages to Canada, Australia, Asia and Africa, where they prospered by grabbing land from the natives. Britain became an empire, everyone lived happily ever after, and a monument was erected to Baird and Hardie and Wilson who had died to make us free. But don't think this red-hot radicalism made us less religious, Mr. Rennie. Glasgow is still full of churches built in the last century. Half of them have been turned into warehouses. Perhaps you and I are painting what will become the best decorated motorcycle and television accessories depot in the United Kingdom."

Later he said, "I apologize, Mr. Rennie, I don't believe that. I believe this church will be knocked down, but first the mural must be made perfect. When a thing is perfect it is eternal. It can be destroyed afterward, or slowly decay, but its perfection is safe in the past, which is the only inevitable part of the universe. No government, no force, no God can make what has been not have been. The past is eternal and every day our abortions fall into it: love affairs we bungled, homes we damaged, children we couldn't be kind to. Let you and I, Mr. Rennie, make eternity a present of a complete, perfect, harmonious, utterly harmless thing; something whose every part is the result of intelligent, loving care; something which isn't a destructive weapon and can't be sold at a profit by public-spirited businessmen. And remember, Mr. Rennie, we're doing nothing novel. For five or six thousand years Egyptian and Etruscan and Chinese artists put their best work into graves which were never opened. The old Greeks and Romans had as many Leonardos, Rembrandts and Cézannes as we have, all painting on plaster that's turned to powder now, apart from a few square yards in Pompeii. I'm not sorry. There are too many colour photographs of the Great Art of the Past. If it didn't have colour reproduction, the mid-twentieth century would have no reason to think itself artistic at all . . . and if it didn't have you and me, Mr. Rennie."

"Stop condescending to me," said a voice.

Thaw started and dropped his brush, for it was three o'clock in the morning. He laughed shakily and climbed down the ladder, saying, "I will never condescend to you again, Mr. Rennie, if you promise not to speak to me when you aren't here. Excuse me, I'm a little tired."

Sleeping had become as easy as work, for he dreamed he was in the mural. "Here it is: land, sky and sunlight," he said to God his father as they strolled round the bramble bush, the serpent wagging its tail behind them. It was a clear day and anemones were singing in the tidal pools. "You'll get it back when I've put it in decent order. I don't like being in debt. As you see I've had no trouble with rational pain and death." They looked up at a hawk with a young rabbit hanging from its claws, then paused on the summit of a cliff. On the river below two swans twined their necks and the first lovers knelt to each other on the far shore. On the western horizon arose the great stump of the Babylonian tower, tiny figures waved flags on the summit; to the east, on Ben Sinai, in a patch of bad weather, the minister was carving the triangulation tables of the law. "Sex and history are problems I can't solve, so I'm returning them in the form you gave them, though stated a little more clearly. I'll finish by the new year and then I'll owe you nothing. Though I'll be grateful if you give me some paying customers after that, I'll need the money. Excuse me a moment." He went up and moved the lightning over Sinai two and a quarter inches to the right, making it echo the rift in the tree of knowledge. He had no sensation of waking. As he lay with closed eyes his mind circled the chancel walls with lazy power, pausing in the vault to choose the area he would work upon that day. He even had a plan view of his body, curled in the pulpit like a grub in a nut, and knew it would soon bring his working weight up the ladder to join his thoughts. Body and mind so completely served the mural that sexual fancies never came to him now and he only knew he needed food when the brush felt too heavy to hold. His strangest, most dreamlike times happened away from the mural. He sat at the communion table eating lumps of custard from Mrs. Coulter's bowl while the old minister stared at him murmuring, "Oh yes, you're a real artist. A real artist."

Later he was in a crowded art shop in the city centre stealing

tubes of paint without haste or panic. Later still he stood on
a pavement arranging to meet June Haig.
"You won't come!" he said, laughing in her face. "I know
you won't come."
"Oh, don't worry, I'll be there. Paisley's corner by the bridge.
I'll be there."
"So will I, but you won't come."
He laughed again because he felt he was not talking to her
in the present but two or three years earlier.

      The afternoon darkened early and he was working peer-
ingly in the semi-dusk when someone coughed behind him.
A man and a woman stood in the aisle, and when his eyes
were used to the better light on the church floor he noticed
the woman was Marjory. The man said heartily, "Hullo, Duncan," and Marjory raised her hand and smiled. Thaw said
"Hullo" and looked down on them, smiling slightly. The man
said, "We were visiting friends in Lenzie and we thought, old
times and so forth, why not run in and see Duncan? So here
we are."
The man peered up through the ladders.
"You must have çat's eyes to work in this light."
"The switches are behind the door."
"No no. No no. I quite like it in this dimness, more mysterious,
if you know what I mean. . . . Very impressive. Very impres-
sive."
Marjory said something he couldn't hear. He said, "What?"
"This isn't your usual style of work, Duncan."
After a short silence Thaw said, "I'm trying to show more
air and light."
The man said, "So you are. So you are." He moved back
into the body of the church, looking at the mural and quietly
humming. He said, "You're nearly finished."
"Far from it."
"It looks finished to my untutored eye."
Thaw indicated bits to be repainted.
"How much longer will you be on it?"
"A few weeks."
"Then what will you do. Teach?"
"I don't know."
He turned round and pretended to work. After a moment
he heard the man cough and say, "Well, Marjory," and, "I
think we'll be getting along now, Duncan."
Thaw looked round and said goodbye. The two people had

moved back into the middle of the church. The man said, "By the way, did you know Marjory and I are thinking of getting married?"

"No."

"Yes, we're thinking about it."

"Good."

There was silence then the man said, "Well, goodbye, Duncan. When we're married you must look in on us. We still think of you now and again."

Thaw shouted, "Good."

The syllable clattered upon the ceiling and walls. At the door he saw Marjory look back and raise her hand, but couldn't see if she was smiling or not.

It was too dark to work now. He lay on the planks, his thoughts returning to Marjory in a puzzled way, like a tongue tip returning to a hole from which a tooth has been pulled. He was sure he had just seen a girl without special beauty or intelligence. He wondered why she had been all he wanted in a woman. She was as unlike Marjory as Mrs. Thaw's corpse had been unlike his mother. He wished he had said something ironic and memorable but she had given him no chance.

"This isn't your usual style of work, Duncan."

He shivered and climbed slowly down. His body felt unusually heavy. He switched on the lights and stared at the mural. It looked horrible. He went up into the gallery where he kept a large mirror for such emergencies. Reflected in it, the left and right sides transposed, the mural sometimes looked new and exciting when he had been working too close to it for too long. Now it appeared even worse than his naked eyes had seen. He flung the mirror onto the pews beneath shouting, "Not beauty! Not beauty! Nothing but hunger!"

He tried to cram all his knuckles into his mouth, then went downstairs and picked the biggest mirror fragment from among the pews and hurried about trying to catch a fresh new glimpse of the work. He had wanted to make a harmony of soft blue, brown and gold livened here and there by sparks of pure colour, but he could see only clumsy black and grey, glaring reds and greens. He had tried to show bodies in a depth of tender light, sharing space with clouds, hills, plants and creatures, but his space was hardly a foot deep and his people were crushed in it as if into a narrow cupboard. His mural showed the warped rat-trap world of a neurotic virgin. He hurled the mirror fragment into the chancel.

"That is not art," he shouted, bending his head and wildly scratching. "Not art, just hungry howling. Oh, why did she hunt me out? Why didn't she stay? How can I make her a beautiful world if she refuses to please me? Oh, God, God, God, let me kill her, kill her! I must get out of here."

He went into the lavatory beside the vestry, stripped off dressing gown and overalls and started washing. From upstairs the voices of Cowlairs Women's Social Club were bawling a chorus of "Who's Sorry Now?" As he rubbed a paint stain from his knee with newspaper soaked in turpentine he noticed an advertisement for a film called *Test Pilot*. A strong, slightly pained male head looked skyward out of a padded husk hung with microphones, cables and dials. A woman stood nearby in profile, her back to the pilot but glancing at him with a sidelong inviting provocative smile. She had short dark hair and lips like June Haig. She was barefoot and wore bangles and black gauze trousers with a slit from ankle to waist. A sleeveless black gauze shirt covered her breasts but left bare the valley between them and her throat and midriff. Stealthily arising, his sexual imagination began slowly to rip and toy with her, but he crumpled the paper and flung it aside, thinking, "Women are never like that. Or they seem to be and then, 'Stop touching me, Duncan.' But that's my fault. I've seen them with other men at bus stops, leaning toward them, looking into their faces, nakedly wanting to be liked or happy because they see they're wanted. But I'm unattractive. Never mind. Prostitutes make a living from men like me. I must go to Bath Street."

He put on his suit, noticing the two five-pound notes still in the jacket pocket. Returning to the church to switch the lights off he noticed the place was stinking, stinking so powerfully he thought for a moment it was on fire. Then he recognized the corrupt sweet odour that had come after his mother's death. He laughed mournfully and said, "Still there, auld woman? And bigger than ever, if my nose is any judge. I must see if I can get rid of you in Bath Street."

It was ten o'clock and the tram into town was nearly empty. He sat chewing a knuckle and staring out of the window. Visions of viciously exciting intercourse were blurred by thoughts of peaceful sleep in the arms of someone pretending to like him. He left the tram and walked up West Regent Street. Two women stood at opposite corners of Blythswood Square. He

quickened as he passed them, then slowed up, cursing his cowardice. It occurred to him that he hadn't eaten for two or three
days. He bought a poke of chips in a shop near Charing Cross
and walked, eating them, up Bath Street. A woman stood at
a corner wearing a red coat and carrying a big black handbag.
She looked too old and dignified to be a prostitute but though
on the far side of the road she seemed to be noticing him
sideways. He stood against some railings, finishing the chips
while the heart hammered in his chest. He crumpled and dropped the cardboard container and was about to cross the road
when he saw someone coming. A small man walked lurchingly
toward the woman along the opposite pavement. She turned
to look at him. He slowed down, fumbled in several pockets
and brought out a cigarette case. For a moment they stood
talking then she took a cigarette, the man lit it and they set
off toward Sauchiehall Street. Thaw walked on full of anger
and relief and entered a café near Green's Playhouse. He ordered a coffee and sat till the Italian behind the counter started
to stand chairs on tables and sweep the floor. The idea of prosti-
tution was wholly depressing now but there was nowhere to
retreat. Church and home were places he never wanted to visit
again. He went out into Renfield Street.

It was midnight but there were people about: one or two
smart-suited men walking briskly, a lounger in a dirty coat
reading a newspaper at a street corner. Two women halted
across the road from him. They were young, tall and wore
fur-trimmed black coats open over their dresses. One of them
put a leg forward, pulled the hem of her dress halfway up
her thigh and did something for a while to the top of her
stocking. The woman at her side glanced around disdainfully.
Thaw stopped, his stomach transbarbed by a shaft of nervous
excitement. He raised his hand and crossed over, trying to
smile. He said to the woman, who was now pulling down the
hem of her dress, "Hullo. I think we know each other."
The other woman said, "You're wrong. It's me ye know,"
and stared at him. He said, "All right."
The bending woman stood up and said, "I'll be seeing ye,
Greta."
"Aye, all right. Wait, come here a minute."
They moved aside and whispered together. Both had bright
bronze hair permed exactly alike. Greta wore a tight dress
which showed the urn-like curves of her thighs and hips. It
was fastened down the front with buttons from which creases

ran round her body like lines of latitude. Thaw was excited
and puzzled that things were going so easily. The smaller girl
said, "Goodnight, Greta. Goodnight, big boy," and walked
away. The other took his arm. His nostrils were buffeted by
cheap sweet perfume. He said, "Have you a place of your
own?"

"Sure I've a place."

"Will we take a taxi?"

"Aye. Let's be stylish."

He waved to an approaching taxi and with a feeling of compe-
tence saw it come to the kerb. They entered and the woman
gave an address. He leaned back, feeling cared for. The woman
said, "Is it a short time you're after?"

"All night, please. I'm a bit tired."

"It'll cost ye."

"How much?"

"Oh, ten pounds, easy."

Thaw was slightly shocked. "As much as that? . . . I've only
nine pounds sixteen and tenpence. Less, when I've paid for
the taxi."

"I suppose that'll have to do."

He hesitated, then said, "You'll have trouble warming me up.
I'm as cold as a fish."

She patted his knee. "Oh, I'll warm you up. I'm good."

The taxi stopped at the white portico of a church. He paid
the driver and joined the woman on the pavement saying, "Are
we getting married?"

"I live just round the corner."

They entered a close in the block of buildings which held
his old studio. He had difficulty climbing the stairs. She said,
"You aren't well, are you?"

"Just a bit tired."

A frosted glass window beside the door had a black triangular
hole in it. She put her hand through the hole and took out a
key. She opened the door, carefully closed it behind them,
and whispered to Thaw to be quiet. She led him in darkness
up narrow creaking stairs, opened another door, closed it behind them, touched a switch and he saw the rosy light of a
table lamp in a pink satin shade. They were in a cosy attic
bedroom with a sloping ceiling. The woman switched on an
electric fire, took off her coat and sat down on the bed looking
at him. He started to undress.

Sometime later she said in a sudden suspicious voice, "What's that?"
Thaw was breathing hard and didn't answer. She said, "Stop! What's that?"
"Nothing."
"You call that nothing?"
"It's eczema, it isn't infectious, look—"
"No you don't! Stop! Stop it!"
She got up and started to dress, saying, "I cannae afford to take chances."
Thaw watched her, his mouth hanging stupidly open. He couldn't quite believe what was happening. She buttoned up her dress.
"Get up!" she said roughly.
He sat up slowly and started dressing. His mouth still hung open. Once or twice he stopped and stared hard at the floor and she told him to hurry up. He felt dizzy and said, "Let me sit for a bit."
He heard her say in a kindlier voice, "I cannae afford to take chances."
"It wasn't what you thought. Not contagious or infectious."
He took three pound notes from his hip pocket and laid them on the table.
"What's that for?"
"Your time."
"Take it back."
He stared at the money without moving. She seized it and shoved it into the pocket of his jacket. He stood up and put the jacket on. She led him downstairs.

He went slowly by back streets to Drummond's house, opened the broken-locked door and moved stealthily into a room off the lobby. Light, reflected from a street lamp, showed a leatherette armchair with china ornaments on the seat. He moved these and sat, elbows on knees, chin on knuckles, until cold sunlight dawned on the roofs outside the window and his teeth were chattering. In occasional waking dreams he seemed another object in the room, like the clock on the mantelpiece, the ornaments at his feet. The sound of conversation from the kitchen struck him as it struck the objects. Once Mr. Drummond passed the door muttering loudly, "Sheer bloody nonsense . . . " then came noises of the lavatory being used. Thaw wrapped a small carpet round himself as protection from the cold. He began to dream he was a carpet himself, a mat of flesh with a hole in it. Something dreadful was going to emerge from that hole, he could smell its cold breath. He heard quick footsteps and a voice shouted, "Sponger and scrounger!"

He opened his eyes and saw a brisk, erect, fairly old woman staring at him accusingly. One hand was on her hip; the other held a bird cage with a stuffed canary on the perch. She glanced down at it and tears came to her eyes.

"Poor wee Joey," she whispered softly. "Poor wee Joey. That bloody cat. Sponger and scoundrel!" she yelled again. "I won't stand it!"

Drummond strode in saying, "Pull yourself together Ma. Oh, hullo Duncan. Ma, for God's sake make yourself a cup of strong black coffee."

"I won't stand any more! You fill the house with Mollys and Janets till I'm driven out by the stink of bloody women, then your lazy friends come crawling in and shift all my good sister's china, I won't stand it!"

"Sorry about this, Duncan," said Drummond grimly. He picked up his mother and wrestled her out of the room. Thaw went away.

It was a bright morning and the city stank of cheap perfume. He wandered eerily round to Brown's tearoom and sat an hour or two in the teaspoon-tinkling warmth. His head ached. A small girl sat by him and said, "Hullo, Duncan, you look very well dressed today. Crumpled, perhaps, but quite smart really."

He stared at her. She said, "Do you remember you once said illness was useful sometimes?"

He stared at her.

"Well, my doctor's told me the same thing. You see, my mother committed suicide when I was three which probably . . . and then I lived with an aunt and the doctor thinks I made myself ill to . . . to be attended to. He said first I gave myself pleurisy and then anæmia and then colds, so now I'm going to a psychiatrist. Are you all right?"

Thaw stared at her. He heard the words but they seemed meaningless.

"Did you know that somebody, I forget his name, said you were a genius? Do you know who said that?"

Thaw stared at her.

"I forget his name but he's a painter. . . . I think his first name begins with B. He's quite well known. Anyway, that should make you feel . . . rather . . . I'm expecting Peter here soon. Did you know I was married?"

Thaw stood up awkwardly and climbed to the street. A Riddrie tram stopped at nearby traffic lights and he boarded with an effort. His seat in the downstairs cabin seemed to be a dog. When he looked at it or stroked it with his hand it was clearly a seat, but when he closed his eyes against the glare it seemed a huge dog. Getting up to the house was difficult. Inside he squatted on the hearth rug and pressed his fists to his aching brow. After a while he felt the rug get up, walk to the bedroom and tip him onto the bed. He got his clothes and shoes off and pulled the blankets over him. Oblivion seemed to fall on him from the ceiling like a ton of bricks.

He wakened in the air above his body which lay with open mouth and eyes, the head lolling sideways off the pillow. He wondered whether to leave it but it moved, groaned, and at once he became part of it and sat up. He was full of dull peace. No noise came from the main road outside, not the faintest sound from upstairs or down. Air flowed in and out of his lungs so easily that he would have imagined himself dead if he hadn't felt hungry. He pulled the heavy bedclothes aside, lowered his feet to the floor, tried carefully to stand and fell down. He lay awhile with his head under a chair, shuddering with laughter, and later drew his clothes on without standing and crawled into the kitchen, shaking his head from side to side and muttering, "All for a bit of skin, all for a bit of dried skin." Pulling himself upright with difficulty he ate two oatcakes, washed and ate a shrivelled carrot, and that was all his stomach could hold. He sat on a chair and tried to arrange the thoughts in his head like pieces on a chessboard, but the thoughts were few and small and kept slipping between his fingers, so he stared at a spider which sat on the electric stove twitching far too many legs. He loathed it and brought the weight of his clenched fist down on it, yet when he withdrew the hand the insect sat there, twitching and unhurt. He struck many times in a fit of rage but the blows did not flatten it, and he stopped when the metal-topped stove had bruised his fist.

Suddenly words came to him out of the air, whispered by an invisible beak. He became tense, said "Yes," walked upright out of the house, shut the door behind him and started fingering his pockets to learn if he had the key.
"Too many pockets," he mumbled. "Must sew some up. Oh."
Mrs. Colquhoun's cat sat in the opposite doorway looking at him. Part of her head and throat was missing. The right side was cut away and he saw the brain in section, white and pink

and pleated like the underneath of a mushroom. The cat yawned, opening her half-mouth wide and unrolling her tongue across the white needle teeth. Thaw could see the tongue down to its root in the thin corridor of her throat. His lips moved, speaking indistinct words about his terror. His fingers shut upon the key's cold steel. Clutching it for comfort he went down to the street. The air was warm and the sky as black as tar. A red planet in the middle put out rings of dark air like ripples from a stone dropped in a pond. Thaw obeyed the whisper and turned left. The whisperer was a black crow which flew behind his head. In the great silence its orders were very distinct. He was himself that black bird looking down on Duncan Thaw and the streets he walked through. Sometimes he soared to the end of a street, leaving the small walking figure behind, or he would drop back and follow at a distance. At corners he came up, bringing his beak close to an ear to whisper: *turn this way, turn that.* At the end of one street a rusty gate was chained shut and twined with convolvulus, but he squeezed between some bent railings. He saw the crimson planet between pagoda-shaped growths whose brittle fleshy stalks sweated white syrup. The crow flapped up the cinder path in front of his feet, chattering wildly:

> *"Eenty teenty haligalum*
> *the head is hatched, the sky is crackit*
> *and John Knox boozed up a kee-kark lum*
> *and all the Gods are humpy-kee-kark, kee-kark, kee-kark."*

Thaw staggered, slipped and was flying. The crow soared a hundred feet below him. His position and speed depended on it. They passed above the dull ribbon of the weedy canal and he saw into rooms where women ironed beneath pulleys hung with washing, men in shirtsleeves read newspapers, children and lovers lay under quilts in dim bedrooms. He swung as if on trapezes across the city's cut honeycomb. The intricate compact life fascinated, then appalled him. He covered his eyes. His feet touched ground at once.

He leaned his stomach on a baluster of the bridge and folded his arms on the parapet. He felt sick. The river had shrunk to a narrow trickle among cracked mudflats. A thin cloud of gulls screamed above something dead under the suspension bridge to the east. A subterranean murmuring began as a vibration in the soles of the feet, increased until it thrummed on his eardrums and welled over the horizon like the thunder of a gong. He raised his head and saw the warehouses on the left bank. The city beyond them was growing into the sky. First the towers of the municipal building ascended, and beyond them the hump of Rotten Row with all the tenement windows lit, and then the squat cathedral spire with tower and nave and a nearby cluster of Royal infirmary domes and beyond those, like the last section of a telescope, the tomb-rotten pile of the Necropolis slid up with the John Knox column overtopping the rest. The book in the hand of the stone man struck across the throbbing planet and a blue shadow sped from the book to Thaw's heart, chilling it. The city was forcing itself into the sky on every side. Factory, university, gasometer, slagbing, ridges of tenements, parks loaded with trees ascended until he looked up at a horizon like the rim of a bowl with himself at the bottom. The rim was crowded with watchers. He felt a rage of self-pity that so many were focussing on as few as he and saluted them with two fingers. One of the watchers left the rim and passed down out of sight behind rooftops. Thaw shut his eyes and imagined her descending the streets like a water drop sliding down the side of a basin, then he walked over the bridge and met her at Paisley's corner.

She smiled and took his arm and he was competent. He grinned to see himself shift his arm to her waist as they walked and how his remarks made her giggle. He flapped and tumbled in the air above their heads, helpless and screeching with laughter, then brought his beak close to an ear and made suggestions. They climbed a narrow road between staring crowds. Sometimes he recognized a face to the left or right, but he had to keep his whole attention on Marjory, feeding her with the talk which made her smile and being careful not to laugh. She did not notice that the hand holding hers was as senseless as granite and prevented by an effort from crushing her fingerbones. They crossed the rocking planks of the canal bridge, passed some warehouses and climbed a grassy slope. Thaw went first, pulling her behind. She was laughing when he forced her down and rubbed her body and neck with his stone hands. She struggled.

"Quick quick quick!" screamed the crow. "Cut her off quick." He moved his stone mouth across her throat into the angle of the jaw near the ear and cut her off quick.

He woke in drizzling rain with a crust on his lips and something beside him he did not want to see. He attempted to fly home but was too breathless to do it for more than short distances, otherwise he crawled on the slimy towpath. Coming upstairs he kept falling from side to side and inside the house he lay on the lobby floor and started grunting, mainly for breath but partly for attention. He grunted louder and louder until a policeman broke the lock of the door. He expected to go to prison, but a doctor was there and they lifted and laid him in bed. The doctor gave a morphine injection and he fell into a sweet sleep. He woke in the Southern General Hospital and was nearly a fortnight there.

CHAPTER 30. Surrender

Lanark stared through the ward window at a bed which seemed a reflection of his own except that the figure in it was under the sheets. He said, "Did Thaw really kill someone or was that another hallucination?"
I'm only able to tell the story as he saw it.
"But did the police arrest him?"
No. In hospital he kept vaguely expecting them to, but they didn't come, which worried him. He wanted to get away from everything he knew, and arrest would have made that easy.
"Then it was a hallucination."
Not necessarily. In 1956 there were a hundred and fifty officially recognized murders in Britain, a third of them unsolved. Thaw certainly felt he had done something foul but denouncing himself to the police needed effort, so he thought as little and slept as much as possible. He didn't dream nowadays. His mind was under a cold bandage of dullness.

He had a bruised hand, malnutrition and bronchial asthma, and received cortisone steroids, a new drug which healed the asthma in two days. The other things took longer. The hospital almoner wanted to contact his father but Thaw withheld the address. He said he would visit Mr. Thaw when he got out, not really meaning to.

He was released, went home, and packed a small canvas knapsack with some clothes and a shaving kit.
"You said he had given up shaving."
He resumed it after the *Evening News* article in order not to look like his newspaper photograph. The knapsack contained one of Mr. Thaw's old compasses. With over nine pounds in

his pocket he went to the bus station at the end of Parliamentary Road. He thought of going to London, of sliding down the globe into the cluttered and peopled south, but at the station the needle of his mental compass swung completely and pointed to the northern firths and mountains. He decided to visit his father after all.

Consider him passing along the route described at the start of Book One, Chapter 18 only he dozes most of the way and gets out at Glencoe village. He walks up a narrow road to the youth hostel, a road through a tunnel of branches. It is autumn, when the highlands are rich with purples, oranges and greeny-golds which would look gaudy if the grey light didn't soften them.
"Leave out the local colour."
All right.

It isn't yet five o'clock and some climbers are waiting on the hostel steps. Thaw walks round the side of the building to the warden's quarters at the back, but before knocking at the door he looks through a window. The room is a neat one with small watercolours of Loch Lomond on the walls which used to hang in the living room at Riddrie. He recognizes also a bookcase, writing desk and wooden tobacco jar carved in the shape of an owl. His father sits reading in an easy chair by a warm stove. There is a teapot under a cosy on a low table at his elbow, some cups, a cut-glass sugar bowl, milk jug and plate of biscuits. Two women sit on a sofa opposite. One is grey-haired and sixtyish; the other might be her daughter and is dark-haired and fortyish. The older woman knits, the younger reads. The quiet interior has a completeness, a calm contented polish, which Thaw feels should not be touched. He can break it, not add to it, so he finds a gap in the hedge leading to the road and returns to the village.

He has tea in a restaurant for tourists and wonders what to do. Going back to Glasgow feels impossible so he goes toward Fort William.

The lochside road is a dull one and at the dreary slate-bings by Ballachulish his breathing worsens and later makes him sit on a low wall beside a line of cars queuing for the ferry. An American lady stands by her car staring up the hill at a whitish stone thing like an old-fashioned petrol pump in

the woods above. She asks, "Do you know what that is?"
He tells her he thinks it marks the spot where Colin Campbell,
nicknamed the Red Fox, was murdered. She smiles slowly and
says, "Did I read about that in Robert Stevenson's *Kidnapped?*"
Thaw says it is possible. She says, "You don't look too well.
Can I do anything to help?"
He mentions the illness and says it will pass. She says, "My
husband is also a sufferer," and gets back into the car. Then
she comes out and hands him a paper tissue with some blue
and pink torpedo-shaped pellets in it. She says, "Try one of
these, they're new."
He swallows one and a moment later a happy warmth spreads
through him. He looks at her lovingly. She says, "Don't take
more than four a day, they can make you high. We're going
to Mallaig, can we give you a lift?"

He steps into a detached part of America. The seats seem
upholstered in soft buffalo hide, the climate is five degrees
above skin heat, somewhere a tiny orchestra is playing. The
engine is inaudible and, once over the ferry, the lochs and
mountains, like films projected onto the windows, pass backward at great speed. The driver, a taciturn man with a thick
neck, asks Thaw where he's heading. After a while Thaw says
he's going to Stirr. The lady says, "You may find Henry a
little taciturn. There's a blood clot in President Eisenhower's
brain and the market's responding badly."

Thaw shuts his eyes and dimly sees his father and sister
in a grey field. Mr. Thaw holds out a skein of wool which
his sister winds into a ball. When he opens his eyes it is dark
and the car climbs a long winding drive to a building like
Balmoral Castle but with a neon hotel sign on the front. He
is breathless again. The lady says, "We've looked up Stirr on
the map and you'll never make it tonight. We're going to stay
here and we suggest you do the same. It's a little expensive
but—"
She is clearly going to make a generous suggestion so Thaw
interrupts by saying that a good night's rest is worth any expense. They all get out of the car and enter the hotel. At the
reception desk he says he isn't hungry and will go straight to
bed. They bid him goodnight.

The hotel is vast and he is surprised by the smallness of
his room. He is very breathless but gets into bed, takes two
torpedo pills and sinks into sleep at once.

Twice or thrice next morning he dimly hears someone knocking and calling the time and he rises at last about eleven. He breathes easily but his mind is stupid, his body heavy. He has missed breakfast and takes coffee and toast uneasily in the corner of a huge lounge. He pays his bill at the reception desk and goes outside. The day is windy and overcast. A dislike of returning makes him unwilling to face the long drive-way; besides, the wind is pushing him the other way. He walks round the hotel and over some lawns, fingering the last half-crowns and coppers in his pocket. Passing a rectangular pool of waterlilies he flings them in. A path leads through a rhododendron shrubbery to a gate onto a moor. He goes through.

The moor rises to a ridge between two rocky hills. There is no path, and sometimes the heather gives way to mossy patches where his feet sink and squelch. He takes two or three hours to reach the ridge and rests on the leeward side of an untidy heap of stones. The heather before him slopes down to the ocean, but a hump of it hides the shore. He sees arms of land dividing the grey water, some patched with fields, others rocky and sloping up into mountains. He thinks one might be Ben Rua. He notices that a nearby stone in the heap has a surface carved with words:

Upon
THIS SPOT
King Edward
had lunch after stalking
28th August, 1902

For some reason this seems funny and he laughs a lot but isn't really happy. He takes another pill which makes him slightly happy, but not much, so he throws the rest away. The wind feels colder. He stands and idly consults the compass. The needle directs him downhill.

After walking for a while he sees the ground sloping away on each side as well as in front. He seems to be on a promontory, but the wind and the slope and his instinct make it easier to go on. The promontory ends in many little cliffs with slopes of heather and tumbled rocks between. Descent is easy at first, then he comes to steeper rocks and must scramble down gullies of loose stones that collapse and slide. He falls the last few yards and lies under boulders among withered bracken, thinking, I'm sore and don't like it. There is a bleeding scratch along one leg and a shoulder aches. He feels sticky and sweating, his heart hammers and he thinks, I need a bath. He pulls off knapsack, coat, jacket, jersey, and then feels the cold and walks down a steep beach of big pebbles like stone eggs and potatoes. They slide awkwardly. He stumbles across them.

The first wave is no shock but the beach shelves steeply and the next, which is large and sudden, slaps his chest, floats him off his legs and knocks him backward onto the sliding pebbles in two or three feet of water. He rises spluttering, the shirt sticking and rasping on his skin. Laughing with rage he pulls it off and wades out against the sea shouting, *"You can't get rid of me!"* He bows his head into the slapping waves, struggles through them with his arms and finds he is rising higher and higher out of the water. His feet are on a submerged ridge, he is waist deep when he reaches the end and steps forward onto fluid. He wallows under, gasping and tumbling over and over in salt sting, knowing nothing but the need not to breathe. A humming drumming fills his brain, in panic he opens eyes and glimpses green glimmers through salt sting. And when at last, like fingernails losing clutch on too narrow a ledge, he, tumbling, yells out last dregs of breath and has to breathe, there flows in upon him, not pain, but annihilating sweetness.

Foremost of the Beasts of the Earth for Pride

Job xli. 24

FORCE

BOOK FOUR

Or THE MATTER,
FORM and POWER of
a COMMONWEALTH

CHAPTER 31. Nan

Lanark opened his eyes and looked thoughtfully round the ward. The window was covered again by the Venetian blind and a bed in one corner was hidden by screens. Rima sat beside him eating figs from a brown paper bag. He said, "That was very unsatisfying. I can respect a man who commits suicide after killing someone (it's clearly the right thing to do) but not a man who drowns himself for a fantasy. Why did the oracle not make clear which of these happened?"

Rima said, "What are you talking about?"

"The oracle's account of my life before Unthank. He's just finished it."

Rima said firmly, "In the first place that oracle was a woman, not a man. In the second place her story was about me. You were so bored that you fell asleep and obviously dreamed something else."

He opened his mouth to argue but she popped a fig in, saying, "It's a pity you didn't stay awake because she told me a lot about you. You were a funny, embarrassing, not very sexy boy who kept chasing me when I was nineteen. I had the sense to marry someone else."

"And you!" cried Lanark, angrily swallowing, "were a frigid cock-teasing virgin who kept shoving me off with one hand and dragging me back with the other. I killed someone because I couldn't get you."

"We must have been listening to different oracles. I'm sure you imagined all that. Is there anything else to eat?"

"No. We used it all up."

With a clattering of purposeful feet a stretcher was pushed into the ward among a crowd of doctors and nurses. Munro marched in front; technicians followed dragging cylinders and apparatus. They went behind the screens in the corner and nothing could be heard but low hissing and some phrases which seemed to have drifted from the corridors.

". . . the conceived conceiving in mid conception . . ."

". . . . inglorious Milton, guiltless Cromwell . . . . ."

"Why inglorious? Why not guilty?"

"She came naked. That helped."

Munro came over and stood at the bed's foot regarding them gravely. He said, "I've arranged a meeting with Lord Monboddo three hours from now to authorize your departure from the institute. I had meant you to wait here till then but we've had an unexpected delivery of human beings. They're in good condition, but feeble, and will die if someone puts them off their food. A nurse is bringing your clothes. You can dress and wait in the staff club."

"No need," said Lanark. "We wouldn't spread our opinions in a case like this."

Munro asked Rima, "Do you agree?"

"Of course, but I'd like to see the staff club."

"If I can trust you I'd like you to stay here. This is a lonely ward and company would help the woman feel at home."

Rima said brightly, "I'll be delighted to help you, Dr. Munro, but will you do something for us? Get Monsignor Noakes to send more of his lovely food. It will be easy to not mention food when we have some."

Munro walked away saying grimly, "I promise nothing, but I'll do what I can."

Lanark stared at her and said, "You are unscrupulous!"

She asked in a hurt voice, "Aren't you glad I'm not like you?"

"Very glad."

"Then show it, please."

They heard the technicians and their apparatus leave the ward. Only a few doctors were busy behind the screens when a nurse came to Rima and Lanark with an armful of clothes and a couple of fat rucksacks and said, "Dr. Munro wants you to dress now. He says the rucksacks are full of food for your journey and you can start eating it when you like."

Rima seized the female garments and stroked them with her fingertips. They were blond and velvety. A small excited smile curved her lips. She sprang naked from bed, saying, "I'll dress in the bathroom." She ran to the door at the end of the ward and Lanark examined the rucksacks. Each contained a rolled-up leather overcoat and hard little blocks of compressed fruit and meat wrapped in rice paper. One held a red thermos flask of coffee and a flat steel flask of brandy, the other a first-aid kit and an electric torch. Departure from this far too warm, too insulated place seemed disturbingly near. Lanark got up and carried his clothes to the bathroom.

Rima stood before a mirror, brushing her hair downward over a shoulder with slow, even strokes. She wore a short, amber-coloured, long-sleeved dress, and sandals of yellow leather, and Lanark stood half-hypnotized by her cool golden elegant figure. She murmured, "Well?"

He said, "Not bad," and started washing at a basin.

"Why don't you say I'm beautiful?"

"When I do you disparage me."

"Yes, but I feel lonely when you don't."

"All right. You're beautiful."

He dried himself and began putting on a grey tweed suit and pullover. She tied her hair carefully with a dark yellow ribbon, looking sad and thoughtful. He kissed her and said, "Cheer up! You're the light and I'm the shadow. Aren't you glad we're different?"

She pulled a face and went out, saying, "It's hard to shine without encouragement."

When he re-entered the ward, the doctors, nurses and screens had gone and Rima was talking to a woman in the corner bed. He joined them, noticing a small bald wrinkled head sticking from under a coverlet. The mother lay half sunk in a bank of pillows. Her body was slight, there were grey glints in her brown hair and youth and age were equally mingled in her gaunt little face. She smiled wanly and said, "It's strange seeing you again, mystery man."

He stared blankly. Rima said, "It's Nancy. Don't you remember Nan?"

He sat by the bed almost laughing with surprise. He said, "I'm glad you escaped from the Elite."

He could not stop grinning. Since entering the institute he had forgotten Sludden and his harem, and now these tangled love-lives seemed wonderfully funny. He pointed at the cot. "You've a nice-looking baby."

"Yes! Isn't she like her father?"

"Don't be silly," said Rima gently. "Babies aren't like people.

Who is the father anyway? Toal?"
"Of course not."
"Then who is he?"
"Sludden."
Rima peered at what was visible of the baby's face.
"Are you sure?"
Nan smiled sadly. "Oh, yes. I wasn't his fiancée, like Gay, or
his vulgar mistress, like Frankie, or his clever mistress, like
you. I was the poor little girl he had been kind to, but he
loved me most, though I had to keep that a secret. Whenever
I was tired of being neglected and tried to escape he would
come to my lodgings and climb drainpipes and break in through
windows. Sludden was tremendously athletic. He would hold
me tight and tell me that though we'd slept together so often
our lovemaking was still fresh and adventurous and it would
be stupid to give it up because of the other girls. He said he
needed all of you so that he could be lively with me. He was
the first man I ever loved and I never really wanted anyone
else, though I was always planning to leave him, before my
illness got bad."
"What illness?"
"I began to grow mouths, not just in my face but in other
places, and when I was alone they argued and shouted and
screamed at me. Sludden was very good with them. He could
always get them singing in tune, and when we slept together
he even made me glad of them. He said he'd never known a
girl who could be pierced in so many places."
Nan smiled in an almost motherly way and Lanark, with a
pang of jealousy, saw the same soft, remembering look on Rima's face. Nan sighed and said, "But they drove even Sludden
away in the end (the mouths did), because as I grew worse I
needed him more and he didn't like that. He was going into
politics and he had a lot to do."
Lanark and Rima cried out together, "Politics?" and Rima said,
"He always made fun of people who went into politics."
"I know, but when you disappeared he replaced you with a
protest girl, a big brassy blonde who played the guitar and
kept telling us her father was a brigadier. I didn't like her at
all. She said we should prepare to seize the reins of the economy,
and it was very important to care for people, but she always
talked too much to listen to anyone. While she was speaking
Sludden would wink at us behind her back. A lot of the Elite
crowd went protestant then. Hundreds of new cliques appeared
with names and badges I can't even remember. Even criminals

wore badges. Suddenly Sludden came in wearing a badge
and laughing his head off. He'd gone with the blonde to a
protest meeting and been elected to a committee. He said we
should all become protestants because nobody had confidence
nowadays in Provost Dodd and we had a real chance of seizing
the city. None of that made sense to me. You see I was pregnant
and Sludden wouldn't allow me near enough to tell him. When
I managed it at last he grew very serious. He said it was a
crime to bring children into the world before it had been redeemed by revolution. He wanted the baby killed before it
was born but I wouldn't allow that. Pass her to me, please."
Rima lifted the baby into Nan's arms. It opened its eyes, gave
a small mew of complaint and returned to sleep against her
breast. She said, "He called me selfish, and he was right, I
suppose. I had never known anyone who wanted me before
I met Sludden, and now he didn't want me at all, and I needed
someone else, though the thought of the coming baby often
made me quite mad and sick. I felt I was being crushed under
a whole pile of women with Sludden jumping up and down
on top, wearing a crown and laughing. Then the baby would
move inside me and I would suddenly feel calm and complete.
I was sorry for Sludden then. He seemed a frantic greedy child
running everywhere looking for breasts to grab and mothers
to feed him and who would never, never have enough. Did
you feel that, Rima?"
Rima said shortly, "No."
"Why did you like him so much?"
"He was clever and amusing and kind. He was the only man
among us who hadn't a disease."
Lanark said, "He had no disease because he *was* a disease.
He was a cancer afflicting everyone who knew him."
Rima snorted. "Huh, you don't know who you're talking about.
Sludden liked you. He tried to help you, but you wouldn't
let him."
Nan smiled. "You're making Lanark jealous."
"Oh yes, she's making me jealous. But I can be jealous and
correct."
Rima said, "How did you get here, Nancy?"
"Well, I was in my lodgings when the pains began and I knew
my baby was coming. I asked the landlord to help but he was
frightened and ordered me out of the house, so I shut myself
in my room and managed (I can't remember how) to drag a
heavy wardrobe in front of the door. That nearly killed me.
The pains were so bad I fell down and couldn't move. I was

sure the baby had died after all. I felt I was nothing then, nothing and nobody, a nobody feeling nothing but horror, a piece of dirt as evil as the world. I suppose I screamed to get out because an opening appeared in the floor beside me."

Lanark shuddered and said, "Going through *that* nearly killed me. I knew a soldier who jumped in with his revolver and was gored to death by it. I don't see how a pregnant woman could survive at all."

"But it was easy. It was like sinking through warm dark water that could be breathed. Every bit of me was supported. I still felt the labour pains but they weren't sore, they were like bursts of music. I felt my little girl break free and float up to my breast and cling there. No, she must have drifted down for I was coming head first. I felt all kinds of muck flow out of me and vanish in the darkness. That darkness loved me. It was only when the light returned that the music became pain again and I fainted. That was a long time ago, and here I am, talking to you, in a lovely clean room."

Lanark said abruptly, "You'll be well cared for here."

He rose and walked through the nearest archway. Nan's story had recalled his own crushing descent in a way which made him long for sunlit landscapes of hill and water. Hopefully he raised the great Venetian blind, but the screen he had once thought a window was no longer there. In the centre of the wall, from floor to ceiling, was a double door of dark wood with panels of ornamental bronze. He pressed it but it was immovable, without handles or keyhole. He returned to the ward.

Nan breast-fed the baby and gossiped quietly to Rima. Lanark sat on his bed and tried to finish *The Holy War* but found it irritating. The writer was unable to imagine an honest enemy, and his only notion of virtue was total obedience to his strongest character. A nurse brought Nancy's lunch. She only ate part and a moment later Lanark was startled to see Rima eat the rest, glancing at him defiantly between forkfuls. He pretended not to notice and nibbled a block of dense black chocolate from the rucksack. The sour taste was so unwelcome that he lay down and tried to sleep, but his imagination projected cityscapes on the insides of his eyelids: sliding views of stadiums, factories, prisons, palaces, squares, boulevards and bridges. Nancy and Rima's conversation seemed like the murmur of distant crowds with fanfares sounding through it. He opened his eyes. The noise was not imaginary. An increasing

din of trumpets shook the air. Lanark stood up and so did
Rima. The trumpets grew deafening, then silent as a black
and silver figure entered and stood under the central arch. It
was a man in a black silver-buttoned coat, black knee breeches
and white stockings. He wore white lace at the throat and
wrists, silver-buckled shoes and a snowy periwig with a three-
cornered black hat on top. He held a portfolio in his left hand
and in his right an ebony staff tipped with a silver knob. His
face was the most surprising thing about him for it was Munro's.
Lanark said, "Dr. Munro!"
"At the moment I am not a doctor, I am a chamberlain. Bring
your rucksacks."
Lanark slung a rucksack on his shoulder and carried the other
in his hand. Rima said goodbye to Nan, who was comforting
her crying baby. Munro turned and rapped his staff against
the great doors, which clanged and swung inward. Munro led
them through, Rima pressing against Lanark's side. The doors
closed.

CHAPTER 32.
Council Corridors

They were in a wood-panelled, low-ceilinged, circular room, thickly carpeted and smelling like an old railway carriage. An upholstered bench went round the wall and a mahogany pillar in the centre supported a bald bronze head wearing a laurel wreath. Munro said loudly, "The northern lobby."

The head nodded and a faint rumbling began. Lanark realized they were in a carriage travelling sideways. Munro said, "The machinery joining the institute to the council chambers is rather antiquated. Take a seat, we'll be some minutes here."

They sat and Rima murmured, "Isn't this exciting?"

Lanark nodded. He felt strong and sure of himself and thought that a lord president director could have frightened him once, but not now. He was too old. Munro was pacing round the pedestal and Lanark called out, "Where do we go when we've seen Lord Monboddo?"

"We'll see what he says first."

"But these rucksacks have been packed for a particular kind of journey!"

"You're leaving at your own request, so you'll have to travel on foot. It's too late to discuss it now."

The doors opened and someone dressed like Munro led in two plump men in evening dress. Soon after the lift stopped again and another chamberlain brought in a group of worried men in crumpled suits. The three chamberlains talked quietly by the pedestal while the rest babbled in clusters on the bench.

". . . . not honouring us, it's the creature he's honouring . . . ."

"His secretary is an algolagnics man."

". . . . . but he'll maintain the differential. . . . ."

"If he doesn't he's opening the floodgates to a free-for-all."
Munro approached Lanark and said grimly, "Bad luck! I expected to have the director to ourselves but he's receiving a deputation and conferring a couple of titles. He's available for ten minutes, I'll have to settle our business in three, so when we leave the lift stay close to me and say as little as possible."

"But this meeting will shape our whole future!"

"Don't worry, I won't let you down."

The doors opened and the chamberlains led them out onto such a bright floor that Lanark's heart lurched, thinking he was in open daylight.

It was a floor of coloured marble inlaid in geometrical patterns. It was nearly a quarter of a mile across, but as the eye took in the height of the ceiling the width seemed insignificant. It was an octagonal hall where eight great corridors met below a dome, and looking down them was like looking down streets of renaissance palaces. The place seemed empty at first, but when his eyes got used to the scale Lanark noticed a great many people moving like insects about the corridor floors. The air was cool and, except for the remote sonorous echoes of distant footfalls, refreshingly quiet. Lanark looked around with open mouth. Rima sighed, slid her fingers out of his and stepped elegantly away across the marble floor. She seemed to grow taller and more graceful as she receded. Her figure and colouring blended perfectly with her surroundings. Lanark followed, saying, "This place suits you."

"I know."

She turned and walked past him, smoothing the amber velvet over her hips, her chin raised and face dreamy. Feeling excluded he stared around once more. Some benches upholstered in red leather lay about the floor and Munro sat on the nearest looking intently along a corridor, the staff and portfolio across his knees. Some distance behind stood a wooden medieval throne on top of three marble steps. The other chamberlains had brought their parties to it, and now the plump men in evening dress knelt side by side on the lowest step in an attitude of prayer. Close by, with folded arms, the deputation stood in a tight cluster. Their chamberlain was photographing them. Rima continued walking past Lanark in an aimless dreamy way till he said sharply, "It's impressive, of course, but not beautiful. Look, at those chandeliers! Hundreds of tons of brass and glass pretending to be gold and diamonds and they don't even light the place. The real light comes from behind the columns round the walls. I bet it's neon."

"You're jealous because you don't belong here."

He was hurt by the truth of this and said in a low voice, "Quite right."

She laid a hand on his chest and stared excitedly into his eyes. "But Lanark, we could live here if you wanted to! I'm sure they'd give you a job, you can be very clever when you try! Tell Munro you want to stay. I'm sure it's not too late!"

"You've forgotten there's no sunlight here and we don't like the food."

Rima said wistfully, "Yes, I had forgotten that."

She walked away from him again.

He sat beside Munro and tried to keep calm by looking up into the deep blue dome. It was painted with angels blowing trumpets and scattering blossoms around figures on clouds. He specially noted four ponderous horsemen on some puffs of cumulus. They wore Roman armour, curly wigs and laurel wreaths and managed the horses with their knees, for each held a sword in the left hand and a mason's trowel in the right. On similar clouds facing them stood four venerable men in togas holding scrolls and queerly shaped walking sticks. Both groups were gazing at the height of the dome where a massive man sat upon a throne. His strong face looked benevolent, but something peering in it suggested he was shortsighted or deaf. The painter had tried to distract from this by loading him with impressive instruments. A globe lay in his lap and a sword across his knees. He held scales in one hand and a trowel in the other. An eagle with a thunderbolt in its beak hovered over his head and an owl looked out from under the hem of his robe. A turbaned Indian, a Red Indian, a Negro and a Chinaman knelt before him with gifts of spice, tobacco, ivory and silk. Lanark heard Munro ask, "Do you like it?"

"Not much. Who are these horsemen?"

"Nimrod, Imhotep, Tsin-Shi Hwang and Augustus, early presidents of the council. Of course the titles were different then."

"Why the wigs and armour?"

"An eighteenth-century convention—the mural was painted then. The men facing them are former directors of the institute: Prometheus, Pythagoras, Aquinas and Descartes. The figure on the throne is the first Lord Monboddo. He was an insignificant legislator and an unimportant philosopher, but when council and institute combined he was a member of both, which made him symbolically useful. He knew Adam Smith."

"But what is the institute? What is the council?

"The council is a political structure to lift men nearer Heaven. The institute is a conspiracy of thinkers to bring the light of Heaven down to mankind. They've sometimes been distinct organizations and have even quarrelled, though never for long. The last great reconciliation happened during the Age of Reason, and two world wars have only united us more firmly."

"But what is this heavenly light? If you mean the sun, why doesn't it shine here?"

"Oh, in recent years the heavenly light has never been confused with an actual *sun*. It is a metaphor, a symbol we no longer need. Since the collapse of feudalism we've left long-term goals to our enemies. They're misleading. Society develops faster without them. If you look closely into the dome, you'll see that though the artist painted a sun in the centre it's almost hidden by the first Monboddo's crown. Stand up, here comes the twenty-ninth."

A tall man in a pale grey suit was crossing the smooth marble floor accompanied by three men in dark suits. A herald in medieval tabard marched in front with a sword on a velvet cushion; another came behind carrying a coloured silk robe. The whole party was advancing briskly to the throne when Munro stepped into the path and bowed saying, "Hector Munro, my lord."

Monboddo had a long narrow face with a thin, high-bridged nose. His hair was pale yellow and his eyes grey behind gold-rimmed spectacles, yet his voice was richly, resonantly masculine. He said, "Yes, I know. I never forget a face. Well?"

"This man and woman have applied for relocation."

Munro handed his portfolio to someone at Monboddo's side, who pulled out a document and read it. Monboddo glanced from Lanark to Rima.

"Relocation? Extraordinary. Who's going to take them?"

"Unthank is keen."

"Well, if they understand the dangers, let them go. Let them go. Is that paper in order, Wilkins?"

"In perfect order, sir."

Wilkins held out the document at an angle supported by the portfolio. Monboddo glanced at it and made snatching movements with his right hand until Munro placed a pen between the fingers. He was going to sign when Lanark shouted, "Stop!"

Monboddo looked at him with raised eyebrows. Lanark turned
on Munro and cried, "You know we don't want to return to
Unthank! There's no sunlight in Unthank! I asked for a town
with sunlight!"
"A man with your reputation can't be allowed to pick and
choose."
Monboddo said, "Has his chief given him a poor report?"
"A very poor report."
There was a silence in which Lanark felt something vital being
filched from him. He said fiercely, "If that report was written
by Ozenfant it ought not to count. We dislike each other."
Munro murmured, "It is written by Ozenfant."
Monboddo touched his brow with a fingertip. Wilkins mur-
mured, "The dragonmaster. A strong energy man."
"I know, I know. I never forget a name. An abominable musi-
cian but an excellent administrator. Here's your pen, Munro.
Uxbridge, give me that cape, will you?"
A herald placed a heavy green cloak lined with crimson silk
round Monboddo's shoulders and helped him adjust the folds.
Monboddo said, "No, we won't go against Ozenfant. Look,
Wilkins, sort this out while I attend to these other chaps. We
haven't much time, you know."
Monboddo strode onward to the throne, the cape billowing
behind him. Most of his retinue followed.

Wilkins was a dark, short, compact man. He said, "What
seems to be the problem?"
Munro said crisply, "Mr. Lanark does not know what relocation
involves. He has asked to leave. I have found a city whose
government will take him in spite of his poor record. He refuses
to go because of the climate."
Lanark said obstinately, "I want sunlight."
"Would Provan suit you?" asked Wilkins.
"I know nothing of Provan."
"It is an industrial centre surrounded by farming country but
in easy distance of highlands and sea. The climate is mild and
damp with a yearly average of twelve hours' sunlight per day.
The inhabitants speak a kind of English."
"Yes, we'll go there gladly."
Munro said, "Provan won't take him. Provan was the first place
I asked."
Wilkins said, "Provan will have to take him if he goes to Un-
thank first."
Munro rubbed his chin and began to smile. "Of course. I had
forgotten."

Wilkins turned to Lanark and said smoothly, "Industrially speaking, you see, Unthank is no longer profitable, so it is going to be scrapped and swallowed. In a piecemeal way we've been doing that for years, but now we can take it *en bloc* and I don't mind telling you we're rather excited. We're used to eating towns and villages but this will be the first big city since Carthage and the energy gain will be enormous. Of course people like you who've joined us already won't need to go through that messy business again. You'll be moved to Provan, which has a lively expanding economy. So visit Unthank with a clear mind. Think of it as a stepping stone to the sun."

"But how long will we have to live there?"

Wilkins glanced at his wristwatch.

"In eight days a full meeting of council delegates will give the go-ahead. We start work two days after."

"Then Rima and I will be in Unthank for twelve days?"

"No longer. Only a revolution can change our programme now."

"But I've heard Unthank is a more political place nowadays. Are you sure a revolution can't happen?"

Wilkins smiled.

"I meant that only a revolution *here* can change our programme."

"But have I no other choices?"

"Stay with us if you like. We can find work for you. Or leave and just wander about. Space is infinite to men without destinations."

Lanark groaned and said, "Rima, what should we do?"

She shrugged impatiently.

"Oh, don't ask me! You know I like it here and that hasn't influenced you so far. But I refuse to wander about in space. If you want to do that you can do it alone."

Lanark said in a subdued voice, "Right. We'll return to Unthank."

Wilkins and Munro straightened their backs and spoke in louder voices. Wilkins slid the paper into the portfolio and said, "Leave this with me, Hector. Monboddo will sign it."

Munro said, "They'd better not go without visas."

"Give me the ink, I'll stamp them."

Munro unscrewed the silver knob from his staff (it was shaped like a pair of spread wings) and held it upside down. Wilkins stuck his thumb in the socket and drew it out with a glistening blue tip. Rima was leaning forward to watch and Wilkins dabbed his thumb at her forehead, making a mark between the brows

like a small blue bruise. She gave a little shriek of surprise.
Wilkins said, "That didn't hurt, did it? Now you, Lanark."
Lanark, too depressed to ask for explanations, received a similar
mark; then Wilkins put his thumb in the knob a second time
and brought it out clean. He said, "It's not a conspicuous sign
but it tells educated people that you've worked for the institute
and are protected by the council. They won't all like you for
that but they'll treat you with respect, and when Unthank falls
you'll have no trouble getting transport to Provan."
Rima said, "Will it wash off?"
"No, only strong sunlight can erase it, and you won't find
that till you reach Provan. Goodbye."
He walked away across the floor, diminishing toward the tiny
distant throne where Monboddo, like a green and scarlet doll,
was graciously receiving a paper from the leader of the pygmy
deputation. Munro screwed the knob onto his staff and beckoned Rima and Lanark in the opposite direction.

Beyond the northern lobby the corridor was crossed by
a wrought-iron screen ten feet high. A gate in the middle was
guarded by a policeman who saluted as Munro led them
through. The corridor grew busier. Black and silver chamberlains led past small groups of people, some of them negro and
oriental. From windows overhead came the applause of distant
assemblies, faint orchestras and fanfares, the rumble and hum
of machinery. Brisk, well-dressed men and women came and
went through doorways on either side, and Lanark's rucksacks
made him feel unnatural among so many people carrying brief-
cases and portfolios. If Rima had offered to carry hers he would
have felt he had an ally, but she moved along the corridor
like a swan down a stream. Even Munro seemed a servant
clearing the way for her, and Lanark felt he would be unkind
not to trudge alongside like a porter. After twenty minutes
they came to another high octagonal hall where corridors met.
The blue dome here was patterned with stars and a lamp in
the height cast a white beam down on a granite monument
in the centre of the floor, a rough block carved with giant
figures and with water trickling from it into ornamental pools.
Girls and boys lounged smoking and chatting on steps surrounding this, and on the smooth tiled floor older people ate and
drank at tables among orange-trees in tubs. Soft laughter and
music sounded from windows overhead and blended with the
conversation, clinking cutlery, splashing fountains and whistling
of canaries from cages in the little trees.

Munro halted and said, "What do you think of it?"

Lanark no longer trusted Munro. He said, "It's better than the staff club," but the leisurely air of the place made his heart swell and eyes water. He thought, 'Everyone should be allowed to enjoy this. In sunlight it would be perfect.'

Munro said, "Since we're beside the exit we may as well rest while I give you advice on your journey."

He stuck his staff into the soil of a tub, sat at a table and beckoned a waiter. Rima and Lanark sat down too. Munro said, "I suppose you won't refuse a light refreshment?"

Rima said, "I'd love it."

Lanark looked round for the exit. Munro said, "Lanark appears to be angry with me."

Rima laughed. "No wonder! I liked hearing him argue with you and Monboddo and that secretary. I thought 'Good! I'm being defended by a strong man!' But you were too clever for him, weren't you?"

"He won't lose by it."

As Munro ordered from the waiter Lanark had the feeling of being watched. At nearby tables sat a mother, her twelve-year-old son and an old couple playing chess. None of these seemed specially attentive, so he gazed up at the rows of windows above the doors where waiters ran in and out. They were curtained with white gauze and seemed empty, but overhead, not far below the dome, a balcony projected and a group of men and women in evening dress were leaning over the parapet. The distance was too great to distinguish faces but a stout man in the centre dominated the party with wide gestures of the hands and arms, and appeared to point in Lanark's direction. Something like a pair of binoculars was produced and clapped to the face of a woman at the stout man's side. Feeling exasperated Lanark seized a newspaper on a nearby chair, opened it and started reading, presenting the back of his head to the watchers above. The paper was called *The Western Lobby* and was soberly printed in neat columns without spreading headlines or large photographs. Lanark read:

ALABAMA JOINS
THE COUNCIL

By accepting the creature's help in constructing the continent's largest neuron energy bank, New Alabama becomes the fifth black state to be

fully represented on the council. Inevitably this will strengthen the hand of Multan of Zimbabwe, leader of the council's black bloc. Asked last night if this would not lead to increased friction in the council's already unwieldy conferences, the president, Lord Monboddo, said, "All movement creates friction if it doesn't happen in a vacuum."

Farther down the page his eye was caught by a name he knew.

OZENFANT RAMPANT

When presenting the energy department's quinquennial audit yesterday, Professor Ozenfant roundly condemned the council's adoption of decimal time. The old duodecimal time scale (declared the fiery Professor) had been more than an arbitrary subdivision of the erratic and unstable solar day. The duodecimal second had allowed more accurate readings of the human heartbeat than decimal seconds. Predictions of deterioration on the decimal scale had a 1.063 greater liability to error, which accounted for the recent reduction in the energy surplus. Sabotage by a rogue element in the intake had also been responsible, but the main culprit was the new time scale. Professor Ozenfant insisted that his words must not be taken as a criticism of Lord Monboddo. In committing us to decimal time the lord president director had simply ratified the findings of the expansion project committee. It was unfortunate that nobody in that committee had first-hand experience of the lonely, difficult and dangerous work of sublimating dragons. The whole business was one more example of a council rule undermining an institute process.

Lanark folded the paper into his pocket and peered upward again. The party still leaned upon the balcony wall, and the gestures of the man in the centre had a familiar, mocking, flamboyant quality. Rima had accepted a cigarette from Munro who was holding a lighter to the tip. Lanark said sharply, "Is that Ozenfant watching us? There, on the balcony?"
Munro looked upward.
"Ozenfant? I don't know. It's hardly likely; he isn't popular on the eighth floor. It might be one of his imitators."
"Why do people imitate him if he isn't popular?"
"He's successful."
The waiter placed a full glass of wine before each of them and a plate of something like an omelette. Rima took her fork and began eating. After a gloomy pause Lanark was about to follow her example when there came a sound of booing, laughter and ironical cheers. Along the space between the tables and the monument marched a procession of shaggy young men and women holding placards with slogans:

EAT RICE, NOT PEOPLE

EATING PEOPLE IS WRONG

FUCK MONBODDO

MONBODDO CAN'T FUCK

A policeman marched on either side and behind them slid a platform loaded with men and filming equipment.
"Protestants," said Munro without looking up. "They march every day to the barrier about this time."
"Who are they?"
"Council employees or children of council employees."
"What do *they* eat?"
"The same as everyone else, though that doesn't stop their denouncing us. Their arguments are ludicrous, of course. We don't eat people. We eat the processed parts of certain life forms which can no longer claim to be people."
Lanark saw Rima push her plate away. There was a tearful look on her face, and when he reached out and grasped her hand she grasped his in turn. He said sternly, "You were going to give us advice about our journey."
Munro looked at them, sighed and laid down his fork. "Very well. You will walk to Unthank across the intercalendrical zone. This means the time you take is unpredictable. The road is fairly distinct, so keep to it and trust nothing you can't test

with your own feet or hands. The light in this zone travels at different speeds, so all sizes and distances are deceptive. Even the gravity varies."

"Then the journey could take months?"

"I repeat, you will cross an intercalendrical zone. A month is as meaningless there as a minute or a century. The journey will simply be easy or strenuous or a combination of both."

"What if our supplies give out?"

"Some reports suggest that people who find the journey difficult reach the other side in the moment of final despair."

Rima said faintly, "Thank you. That's very encouraging."

"Better put your coats on. It's cold down there."

The coats were ankle-length with hoods and a thick fleecy lining. They pulled on their rucksacks, smiled anxiously at each other, kissed quickly, then followed Munro across the floor and up the steps to the monument. The giant rock overhung the steps like a boulder balanced on a pyramid. Shadows cast by the light defined figures brooding in crevices, declaiming from ledges and emerging from a cave in the centre. A figure on top seemed to represent the sculptor. His face looked up at the light but his fists drove a chisel with a mallet into the stone between his knees. Lanark touched Munro's shoulder and asked what this represented.

"The Hebrew pantheon: Moses, Isaiah, Christ, Marx, Freud and Einstein."

They passed through a group of young people who stared and murmured, "Where are they going?" "The emergency exit?" "Look at those crazy coats!" "Surely not the emergency exit!" Someone shouted, "What's the emergency, Granddad?"

Munro said, "No emergency, just relocation. A simple case of relocation."

There was silence then a voice said, "They're insane."

They reached the summit where water trickled down into gold-fish ponds. The great boulder was supported by a surprisingly small pedestal with an iron door in it. Munro struck the door with his staff. It opened. They stooped and passed through.

CHAPTER 33. A Zone

In watery green light, between narrow cement walls, they descended a metal staircase for many minutes. The air grew chilly and at length they came into a cavernous low-ceilinged place which gave a sense of width without spaciousness, for the floor was covered by pipes and tubes of every size from the height of a man to the thickness of a finger, while the ceiling was hidden by cables and ventilation ducts. They emerged from a door in a brick pillar onto a metal walkway leading across the pipes. Munro moved down this and Lanark and Rima followed, sometimes clambering over an unusually large pipe by an arched metal ladder. For a long time the only sound was a distant pulsing hum mingled with gurgles and clanking and their echoing footsteps. Rima said, "This bending hurts my back."

"I see a wall in the distance. We'll soon be out of here."

"Oh, Lanark, how dreary this is! I was excited when we went up to Monboddo. I expected a glamorous new life. Now I don't know what to expect, except horror and dullness."

Lanark felt that too. He said, "It's just a zone we've got to cross. Tomorrow, or the next day, we'll be in Unthank."

"I hope so. At least we've friends there."

"What friends?"

"Our friends at the Elite."

"I hope we can make better friends than those."

"You're a snob, Lanark. I knew you were insensitive, but I never thought you were a snob."

They forgot their misery in the heat of a small quarrel until the walkway reached a platform before an iron door in a wall of damp-streaked cement. It was the first door they had seen for many days with hinges and a key in the lock. It was stencilled with large red letters:

EMERGENCY EXIT 3124
DANGER! DANGER! DANGER! DANGER!
YOU ARE ABOUT TO ENTER
AN INTERCALENDRICAL
ZONE

Munro turned the key and opened the door. Lanark expected darkness but his eyes were dazzled by an amazingly bright white mist. A road began at the threshold with a yellow stripe down the middle, but it was only visible for five or six feet ahead. He stepped outside and a wave of coldness hit his face and hands making him draw deep breaths of freezing air. They exalted him. He cried, "It's good to be in the open at last! Surely the sun is up there!"
"Several suns are up there."
"There's only one sun, Munro."
"It's been shining a long time. The light of many days keeps returning to zones like this."
"Then it ought to be even brighter."
"No. When light rays meet at certain speeds and angles they negate each other."
"I'm not a scientist, that means nothing to me. Come on, Rima."
"Goodbye Lanark. Maybe you'll trust me when you're a little older."
Lanark didn't answer. The door slammed behind him.

They walked into the mist guided by the yellow line on the road between them. Lanark said, "I feel like singing. Do you know any marching songs?"
"No. This rucksack hurts my back and my hands are freezing."
Lanark peered into the thick whiteness and sniffed the breeze. The landscape was invisible but he could smell sea air and hear waves in the distance. The road seemed to rise steeply for it became difficult to walk fast, so he was surprised to see Rima vanishing into the mist a few paces ahead. With an effort he came beside her. She didn't seem to be running, but her strides covered great distances. He caught her elbow and gasped, "How can . . . you go . . . so quickly?"
She stopped and stared.
"It's easy, downhill."
"We're going uphill."
"You're mad."

Each stared at the other's face for a sign that they were joking until Rima backed away saying fearfully, "Keep off! You're mad!"

He stepped after her and felt acutely dizzy. At the same time something shoved him sideways. He staggered but kept his feet and stood swaying a little. He said weakly, "Rima. The road slopes downhill on this side of the line and uphill on the other."

"That's impossible!"

"I know. But it does. Try it."

She came near, put a foot hesitantly across, then withdrew it saying, "All right, I believe you."

"But why not test it? Hold my hand."

"Since we're both on the downhill side we may as well keep to it. We'll travel faster."

She began walking and he followed.

He now had sensations of descending steeply. Each stride covered more and more ground until he shouted, "Rima! Stop! Stop!"

"I'll fall if I try to stop!"

"We'll fall if we don't. It's getting too steep. Give me your hand."

They grabbed hands, dug heels in, slithered to a standstill and stood precariously swaying. He said, "We'll have to take this slowly and carefully. I'll go first."

He released her hand, stepped slowly and carefully forward, his feet slid from under him, he grabbed her for support and pulled her heavily down. They rolled over each other then he was tumbling sideways with a rhythmical bumping each time the rucksack passed under his body. When he came to rest and managed to stand up the ground seemed level and he was alone in the mist. Not even the yellow line was visible. He yelled "Rima! Rima! Rima!" and listened, and heard the distant sea. For a moment he felt utterly lost. He took the torch from his rucksack, switched it on and found the yellow line a yard away from him; then he remembered that if Rima had fallen over the line she would have rolled the opposite way. This was a cheering thought for it made events seem logical. He turned and climbed the hill, torch in hand, and after a lot of effort reached a summit where he heard a sound of weeping. Ten steps farther he found her squatting on the far side of the line, her hands covering her face. He sat down and put an arm round her shoulders.

After a while she looked up and said, "I'm glad it's you."
"Who else could it have been?"
"I don't know."
Her knuckles were bleeding. He brought out the first-aid kit,
cleaned the grazes and put on sticking plaster. Then they sat
side by side, tired out and waiting for the other to suggest a
move. At last Rima said, "What if we walked on different sides
of the line but held hands across it? Then when one of us
went downhill we'd be steadied by the one going up."
Lanark stared at her and cried, "What a clever idea!"
She smiled and stood up. "Let's try it. Which way do we go?"
"To the left."
"Are you sure?"
"Yes. You slid over the line without noticing."
The new way of walking was a strain on the linking arm but
worked very well. Eventually the road grew level on both sides
and part of a huge rocky wall could be seen through the mists
ahead. The yellow line ran up to an iron door painted with
these words:

EMERGENCY EXIT 3124
NO ADMITTANCE

Lanark kicked the door moodily. It was like kicking rock. He
said "It was me who slid over the yellow line, not you."
They turned round and set off again.

They had not gone far when they heard a strange wavering
sound, a sound Lanark seemed to recognize. Rima said, "Someone's crying."
He took the torch from his pocket and shone it ahead and
Rima drew a sudden breath. A tall blond girl, wearing a black
coat and a knapsack, squatted on the road with her hands over
her face. Rima whispered, "Is it me?"
Lanark nodded, went to the girl and knelt beside her. Rima
gave a little hysterical giggle. "Aren't you forgetting? You've
done that already."
But the grief of the girl before him made him ignore the one
behind. He held her shoulders and said urgently, "I'm here,
Rima! It's all right. I'm here!"
She paid no attention. The upright Rima walked past him, saying coldly, "Stop living in the past."
"But I can't leave a bit of you sitting on the road like this."
"All right, drag her along. I suppose helpless women make

you feel strong and superior, but you'll find her a bore eventually."

Her voice throbbed with such scorn, helplessness and humour that it drew him to his feet. Since the crouching Rima seemed unable to notice him he followed the moving one.

They joined hands and silently travelled a great distance. Nothing was visible but the pallor of the mist, nothing audible but the sighing sea. The cold air stung their faces; shoulder, elbow and fingers grew sorely cramped and burning, especially in mid-gradient when one was straining downhill to drag the other steeply up. They passed into a stupor in which they knew nothing but the pain in their arms and the ache of their feet on the road. Sometimes they entered a real sleep from which they were wakened by a pang of vertigo as one or the other wandered onto the line. These pangs, as strong as electric shocks, at last conditioned them into sleepwalking straight forward because Lanark had been unconscious for a long time when something cut him hard on the knee. He blinked and saw a huge tilted shape in the whiteness ahead. He brought out the torch and shone it down. His knee had struck the rim of a rusty iron wheel, flat on its side and blocking the roadway. He helped Rima onto it, led the way along one of the spokes, climbed over the hub and shone the torch at the shape overhanging them. He expected to see something heavily industrial, like the tower above a derelict mine shaft, so the object confused him. It was made of timber bound with iron into a shape like a tub cut away on one side. Rima said, "It's a chariot."

"But there's room inside for twenty or thirty men! What beasts could ever pull it? The head of that bolt is bigger than *my* head."

"Maybe you've shrunk."

"And it's ancient—look at the rust! Yet it's lying on top of a modern road. We'll have to walk round."

He jumped down between the chariot and the severed wheel and sank to his knees in dry sand. Rima landed near him, dropped her rucksack and flopped beside it, saying, "Goodnight."

"You can't sleep here."

"Tell me when you find somewhere better."

He hesitated but the narrow space shielded them from the cold air and the sand was very soft. He dropped his own rucksack and lay beside Rima, saying, "Rest your head on my arm."

"Thanks. I will."

They wriggled to make the sand fit their bodies and lay still for a while. Lanark said, "Last night I lay on a goosefeather bed with the sheets turned down so bravely. Tonight I'll sleep in a cold open field along with the raggle-taggle gypsy."

"What's that?"

"A song I remember. Are you sorry we left the institute?"

"I'm too exhausted to feel sorry about anything."

A little later her voice seemed to reach him from a distance. "I'm glad I'm exhausted. I couldn't sleep here if I wasn't exhausted."

He was wakened by musical whirring which came from far away, passed overhead and faded into silence. Rima stirred and sat up, spilling sand from her shoulders, then stretched her arms and yawned. "Ooyah, how fat and sticky and stale I feel."

"Fat?"

"Yes, my stomach's swollen."

"It must be wind. You'd better eat."

"I'm not hungry."

"Could you drink hot coffee? There's a flask of it in your rucksack."

"Oh, I could drink that, yes."

She unbuckled the rucksack, put her hand in and drew out, with a disgusted look, the red thermos flask which tinkled and shed a stream of brown droplets. She tossed it away and began brushing sand from her hair with her hands. Lanark said, "You must have smashed it when you fell. You'd better take your food out, the damp will spoil it."

Nothing he said would persuade her to touch the food so he removed it himself, peeled off the sodden wrappings and repacked it in his own rucksack along with the brandy flask. Then they rose, walked around the chariot and saw the shadowy prow of another chariot. The road was hidden by a wilderness of broken chariots which loomed in the mist like a fleet of sunk battleships, the shafts, axles, broken rims and naked spokes sticking up between sand-logged hulls like masts, anchors and titanic paddlewheels. It was impossible to climb through so they trudged round, often stopping at first to pour sand from their shoes but soon tiring of this and plodding uncomfortably on. Many hours seemed to pass before they stepped onto asphalt again. They sat and had a nip of brandy before emptying their shoes for the last time, then they joined hands over the yellow line and resumed walking.

New freshness filled them. There was little or no strain on their arms, the mist grew warm as if the sun was about to come through and they were soothed by pleasant sounds: first larksong overhead, then the crooning of pigeons and a swishing as if heavy rain were falling in a forest. Once they heard such a loud gurgling and creaking of oars that Lanark groped with his torch to the roadside, expecting to see the bank of a wide river, but though the water noise grew louder he saw nothing but sand. Farther on they were passed by footsteps and voices going the opposite way. The voices travelled in clusters of two and three and spoke quietly and indistinctly except for a couple who seemed to be arguing.

". . . a form of life like you or me."

". . . here's ferns and grass. . . ."

"What's wonderful about grass?"

As they passed through an invisible crowd of chattering children some real raindrops dashed in their faces and the mist turned golden and lifted. The straight road, embanked in places, ran without undulation across undulating sand to a mountain on the horizon. Tiny farms, fields and woodlands covered foothills which glittered in the rain as though dusted with silver: the summit was split into many snowy peaks with clouds drifting down between them, and all this was seen under a rainbow, a three-quarter violet blue green yellow orange red arc shining sweetly in a shining sky. Rima smiled at the distance and gripped both his hands. She said, "It was good of you to bring me out of that place. You're very wise sometimes."

They kissed and walked onward. The mist descended and the strange gravities of the road strained their arms once more. Again they avoided the strain by walking in a half-conscious daze. At last Rima said, "We're nearly there."

Lanark jerked awake and saw a rocky wall above them in the mist. He switched on the torch and an iron door appeared with these words on it:

EMERGENCY EXIT 3124
NO ADMITTANCE

Rima sat down with her back to the door and folded her arms. Lanark stood staring at the words, trying not to believe what he saw. Rima said, "Give me something to eat."

"But—but—but this is impossible! Impossible!"

"You led us right round these chariots and back along the road."

"I'm sure it's a different door. It's rustier."

"The same number's on it. Give me that rucksack."

"But Munro said the road was clearly marked!"

"Are you deaf? I'm starving! Pass the bloody rucksack!"

He sat down and laid the rucksack between them. She opened it and began eating with tears flowing down her cheeks. He laid a hand on her shoulder. She shook it off so he started eating too. Hunger and thirst hadn't troubled him much since entering the zone and now he found the food so tasteless that he returned it to the rucksack, but Rima chewed as fast and savagely as if eating were a sort of revenge. She devoured dates, figs, beef, oatmeal and chocolate and all the time the tears poured down her cheeks. Lanark stared in awe and at last said timidly, "You've eaten more than half the food."

"Well?"

"We've still a long way to travel."

She made a noise between a howl and a laugh and went on eating till nothing was left, then she uncorked the brandy flask, drank two mouthfuls and got up and staggered into the mist. He dimly saw her kneel at the roadside and heard vomiting sounds. She returned looking pale, lay down with her head in his lap and fell asleep at once.

The weight on his lap was comforting at first. Her face, childish in sleep, filled him with the tender, sad superiority we usually feel for the sleeping; but the road was hard, his position uncomfortable and he began to feel trapped. His thoughts kept exploring the road ahead, wondering how to escape from it. His muscles ached with the effort of keeping still. At last he kissed her eyelids until she raised them and asked "What's wrong?"

"Rima, we must get away from here."

She sat up and pressed her hair back with her hands.

"If you don't mind I'll just stay and wait for you to come wandering back."

"You may wait a long time. I refuse to die at the door of a place where I've acted wickedly."

"Wickedly? Wickedly? You use more meaningless words than anyone I've ever met."

He wondered how to be soothing and said experimentally, "I love you."

"Shut up."

His anger rose to the surface. "I love the reckless way you abandon courage and intelligence whenever things get really difficult."

"Shut up! Shut up!"

"Since we're determined to behave badly, please pass the brandy."

"No, I need it."

He got to his feet and said, "Are you coming, then?"

She folded her arms. He said sharply, "If you need the first-aid box, you'll find it in the rucksack."

She didn't move. He said humbly, "Please come with me."

She didn't move.

"If you knock the door hard enough, somebody might open it."

She didn't move. He laid the torch beside her, said quickly, "Goodbye," and walked away. He was descending the first hill in great strides when something punched his back. He turned and saw her, tearstained and breathless. She cried, "You'd have left me! You'd have left me alone in the fog!"

"I thought you wanted that."

"You're a cruel nasty idiot."

He said awkwardly, "Anyway, give me your hand."

They joined hands and all at once his body felt aching-feeble. He even lacked strength to hold her fingers. It was Rima who kept them together and moving along the road. He loathed her. He wanted to lie down and sleep so he disguised his staggers as a carefree way of walking and thought malignantly, 'She'll soon tire of dragging me along,' but Rima continued for a great distance without complaining. At last, feeling lightheaded, he pretended to hum a tune to himself. She stopped and cried, "Oh, Lanark, let's be friends! Please, please, why can't we be friends?"

"I'm too tired to be friendly. I want to sleep."

She stared at him, then her face relaxed into a smile. "I thought you hated me and wanted to get away."

"At the moment that is perfectly true."

She said cheerfully, "Let's sit down. I'm tired too," and sat on the road. He would have preferred the sand at the roadside but was too tired to say so. He lay beside her. She stroked his hair and he was almost sleeping when he felt something strange and sat up.

"Rima! This asphalt is cracked! It's covered with moss!"

"I thought it was more comfortable than usual."

He looked uneasily around and saw through the mist a thing which shocked him out of tiredness. A dark humped headless creature, about four feet high with many legs, stood perfectly

still in front of them. The feet were gathered together and
the legs bent as if to jump. Lanark felt Rima grip his shoulder
and whisper, "A spider."
His scalp tightened. There was a thudding in his ears. He stood
up and whispered, "Give me the torch."
"I haven't a torch. Come away."
"I'm going nowhere with that behind me."
He took a breath and stepped forward. The dark body became
a cluster of bodies, each with its own leg. He called happily,
"Rima, it's toadstools!"
A clump of big toadstools grew on the yellow line so that
half the domed heads tilted left and the other half to the right.
Lanark bent down and stared between the stems. They were
rooted in a heap of rotten cloth with rusty buckles and a blis-
tered blue cylinder in it. He pointed: "Look, the thermos flask!
That pile of old clothing must be your rucksack!"
"Don't touch! It's horrible!"
"How did they come here? We left them beside the chariots.
They can't have crawled along the road to meet us."
"Can any dreadful thing not happen here?"
"Be sensible, Rima. Strange things have happened here but
nothing dreadful. This fungus is a form of life, like you and
me."
"Like you, perhaps. Not like me."
Lanark was fascinated. Peering closely he moved round the
cluster and felt his ankles brushed by something light.
"And, Rima, here's ferns and grass."
"What's wonderful about grass?"
"It's better than a desert full of rusty wheels. Come on, there's
a slope. Let's climb it."
"Why? My back's sore, and you're supposed to be tired."
Beyond the toadstools the road vanished under an overgrown
embankment. Lanark scrambled upward and Rima, grumbling,
came after.

They climbed through gorse, brambles and bracken, feeling glad of the protective coats. The white mist faded until
they emerged into luminous darkness under an immense sky
of stars. They stood beside a ten-lane motorway which lay across
the mist like a causeway across an ocean of foam. Vehicles
were whizzing along too quickly to be recognized: tiny stars
in the distance would suddenly expand, pass in a blast of wind,

shrink to stars on the opposite horizon, and vanish. There was a thirty-feet-high road sign on the grassy verge:

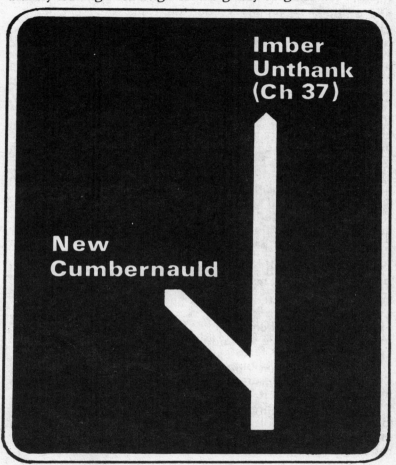

Imber
Unthank
(Ch 37)

New
Cumbernauld

"Good," said Lanark happily. "We're on the right road at last. Come on."

"It seems a general rule that when I'm able to walk you feel exhausted and when I need a rest you keep dragging me along."

"Are you really tired, Rima?"

"Oh, no. Not at all. Me tired? What a strange idea."

"Good. Come along, then."

As they started walking a glow appeared on the misty horizon to their left and a globe of yellow light slid up into the sky from behind a jagged black mountain. Rima said, "The moon!"

"It can't be the moon. It's going too fast."

The globe was certainly marked like the moon. It swung upward across Orion, passed near the Pole Star and sunk down below the horizon on the far side of the road. A little later, with a piece of rim missing from one side, it rose again behind the mountain on the left. Rima stood still and said desperately "I can't go on. My back hurts, my stomach's swollen, and this coat is far too tight."

She unbuttoned it frantically and Lanark stared in surprise. The dress had hung loose from her shoulders, but now her stomach was swollen almost to her breasts and the amber velvet was as tight as the skin of a balloon. She gazed down as if struck by something and said faintly, "Give me your hand."

She pressed his hand against the lower side of her belly, staring wildly at his face. He had begun to say, "I feel nothing," when his palm received, through the tense stomach wall, a queer little pat. He said, "Somebody is in there."

She said hysterically, "I'm going to have a baby!"

He gaped at her and she glared accusingly back. He struggled to keep serious and failed. His face was stretched by a huge happy grin. She bared her teeth and shrieked, "You're *glad!* You're *glad!*"

"I'm sorry, I can't help it."

In a low intense voice she said, "How you must hate me. . . ."

"I love you!"

". . . grinning when I'm going to have horrible pains and will split open and maybe die . . ."

"You won't die!"

". . . beside a fucking motorway without a fucking doctor in fucking sight."

"We'll get to Unthank before then."

"How do you know?"

"And if we don't I'll take care of you. Births are natural things, usually."

She knelt on the grass, covered her face and wept hysterically while Lanark started helplessly laughing, for he felt a burden lifted from him, a burden he had carried all his life without noticing. Then he grew ashamed and knelt and embraced her, and she allowed him. They squatted a long time like that.

CHAPTER 34. Intersections

When he next looked at the sky a half-moon was sailing over it. He said, "Rima, I think we should try to keep moving." She got to her feet and they started walking arm in arm. She said miserably, "It was wrong of you to be glad."

"There's nothing to worry about, Rima. Listen, when Nan was pregnant she had nobody to help her, but she still wanted a baby and had one without any bother."

"Stop comparing me with other women. Nan's a fool. Anyway, she loved Sludden. That makes a difference."

Lanark stood still, stunned, and said, "Don't you love me?"

She said impatiently, "I like you, Lanark, and of course I depend on you, but you aren't very inspiring, are you?"

He stared at the air, pressing a clenched fist to his chest and feeling utterly weak and hollow. An excited expression came on her face. She pointed past him and whispered, "Look!"

Fifty yards ahead a tanker stood on the verge with a man beside it, apparently pissing on the grass between the wheels. Rima said, "Ask him for a lift."

Lanark felt too feeble to move. He said, "I don't like begging favours from strangers."

"Don't you? Then I will."

She hurried past him, shouting, "Excuse me a minute!"

The driver turned and faced them, buttoning his fly. He wore jeans and a leather jacket. He was a young man with spiky red hair who regarded them blankly. Rima said, "Excuse me, could you give me a lift? I'm terribly tired."

Lanark said, "We're trying to get to Unthank."

The driver said, "I'm going to Imber."

He was staring at Rima. Her hood had fallen back and the

pale golden hair hung to her shoulders, partly curtaining her
ardently smiling face. The coat hung open and the bulging
stomach raised the short dress far above her knees. The driver
said, "Imber isn't all that far from Unthank, though."
Rima said, "Then you'll let us come?"
"Sure, if you like."
He walked to the cab, opened the door, climbed in and reached
down his hand. Lanark muttered, "I'll help you up," but she
took the driver's hand, set her foot on the hub of the front
wheel and was pulled inside before Lanark could touch her.
So he scrambled in after and shut the door behind him. The
cabin was hot, oil-smelling, dimly lit and divided in two by a
throbbing engine as thick as the body of a horse. A tartan
rug lay over this and the driver sat on the far side. Lanark
said, "I'll sit in the middle, Rima."
She settled astride the rug saying, "No, I'm supposed to sit
here."
"But won't the vibration . . . do something?"
She laughed.
"I'm sure it will do nothing nasty. It's a nice vibration."
The driver said, "I always sit the birds on the engine. It warms
them up."
He put two cigarettes in his mouth, lit them and gave one to
Rima. Lanark settled gloomily into the other seat. The driver
said, "Are you happy then?"
Rima said "Oh, yes. It's very kind of you."
The driver turned out the light and drove on.

The noise of the engine made it hard to talk without shout-
ing. Lanark heard the driver yell, "In the pudding club, eh?"
"You're very observant."
"Queer how some birds can carry a stomach like that without
getting less sexy. Why you going to Unthank?"
"My boyfriend wants to work there."
"What does he do?"
"He's a painter—an artist."
Lanark yelled, "I'm not a painter!"
"An artist, eh? Does he paint nudes?"
"I'm *not* an artist!"
Rima laughed and said, "Oh, yes. He's very keen on nudes."
"I bet I know who his favourite model is."
Lanark stared glumly out of the window. Rima's hysterical de-
spair had changed to a gaiety he found even more disturbing
because he couldn't understand it. On the other hand, it was

good to feel that each moment saw them nearer Unthank. The speed of the lorry had changed his view of the moon; its thin crescent stood just above the horizon, apparently motionless, and gave a comforting sense that time was passing more slowly. He heard the driver say, "Go on, give it to him," and Rima pushed something plump into his hands. The driver shouted, "Count what's in it—go on count what's in it!"

The object was a wallet. Lanark thrust it violently back across Rima's thighs. The driver took it with one hand and yelled, "Two hundred quid. Four days' work. The overtime's chronic but the creature pays well for it. Half of it yours for a drawing of your girl here in the buff, right?"

"I'm not an artist and we're going to Unthank."

"No. Nothing much in Unthank. Imber's the place. Bright lights, strip clubs, Swedish massage, plenty of overtime for artists in Imber. Something for everybody. I'll show you round."

"I'm not an artist!"

"Have another fag, ducks, and light one for me."

Rima took the cigarette packet, crying, "Can you really afford it?"

"You saw the wallet. I can afford anything, right?"

"I wish my boyfriend were more like you!"

"Thing about me, if I want a thing, I don't care how much I pay. To heck with consequences. You only live once, right? You come to Imber."

Rima laughed and shouted, "I'm a bit like that too."

Lanark shouted, *"We're going to Unthank!"* but the others didn't seem to hear. He bit his knuckles and looked out again. They were deep among lanes of vast speeding vehicles and container trucks stencilled with cryptic names: QUANTUM, VOLSTAT, CORTEXIN, ALGOLAGNICS. The driver seemed keen to show his skill in overtaking them. Lanark wondered how soon they would reach the road leading off to Unthank, and how he could make the lorry stop there. Moreover, if the lorry did stop, he (being near the door) must get out before Rima. What if the driver drove off with her? Perhaps she would like that. She seemed perfectly happy. Lanark wondered if pregnancy and exhaustion had driven her mad. He felt exhausted himself. His last clear thought before falling asleep was that whatever happened he must not fall asleep.

He woke to a perplexing stillness and took a while understanding where he was. They were parked at the roadside and an argument was happening in the cabin to his right. The driver

was saying angrily, "In that case you can clear out."
Rima said, "But why?"
"You changed your mind pretty sudden, didn't you?"
"Changed my mind about what?"
"Get out! I know a bitch when I see one."
Lanark quickly opened the door saying, "Yes, we'll leave now.
Thanks for the lift."
"Take care of yourself, mate. You'll land in trouble if you
stick with her."
Lanark climbed on the verge and helped Rima down after him.
The door slammed and the tanker rumbled forward, becom-
ing a light among other lights whizzing into the distance.
Rima giggled and said, "What a funny man. He seemed really
upset."
"No wonder."
"What do you mean?"
"You were flirting with him and he took it seriously."
"I wasn't flirting. I was being polite. He was a terrible driver."
"How does the baby feel?"
Rima flushed and said, "You'll never let me forget that, will
you?"
She started rapidly walking.

The road ran between broad shallow embankments. Rima
said suddenly, "Lanark, have you noticed something different
about the traffic? There's none going the opposite way."
"Was there before?"
"Of course. It only stopped a minute ago. And what's that
noise?"
They listened. Lanark said, "Thunder, I think. Or an aero-
plane."
"No, it's a crowd cheering."
"If we walk on we may find out."

It became plain that something strange was happening
ahead, for lights had begun clustering on the horizon. The
embankment grew steeper until the road passed into a cutting.
The verge was now a grassy strip below a dark black cliff with
thick ivy on it. Wailing sirens sounded behind them and police
cars sped past toward the light and thunder. The cutting ahead
seemed blocked by glare, and vehicles slowed down as they
neared it. Soon Rima and Lanark reached a great queue of
trucks and tankers. The drivers stood on the verge talking in

shouts and gestures, for the din increased with every step. They passed another road sign:

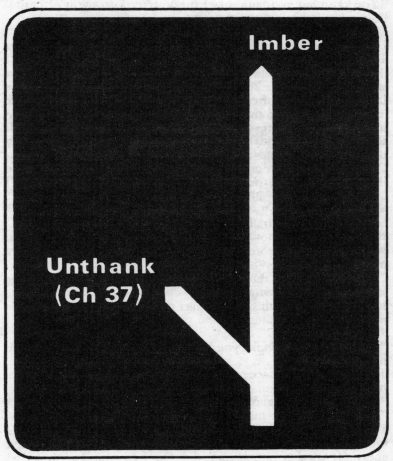

:and eventually Rima halted, pressed her hands over her ears, and by mouthings and headshakings made it clear she would go no farther. Lanark frowned angrily but the noise made thought impossible. There was something animal and even human in it, but only machinery could have sustained such a huge screeching, shrieking, yowling, growling, grinding, whining, yammering, stammering, trilling, chirping and yacacawing. It passed into the earth and jarred painfully on the soles of the feet. Still holding her ears Rima turned and hurried back and Lanark, after a moment of hesitation, was glad to follow.

Many more vehicles had joined the queue and drivers were standing on the road between them, for the backs of the trucks gave shelter from the sound. A young policeman with a torch was speaking to a group and Lanark gripped Rima's sleeve and drew her over to listen. He was saying, "A tanker hit an Algolagnics transporter at the Unthank intersection. I've never seen anything like it—nerve circuits spread across all the lanes like bloody burst footballs and screaming enough to crumble the road surface. The council's been alerted but God knows how long they'll take to deal with a mess like that. Days—weeks, perhaps. If you're going to Imber you'll need to go round by New Cumbernauld. If you're for Unthank, well, forget it."

Someone asked him about the drivers.

"How should I know? If they're lucky they were killed on impact. Without protective clothes you can't get within sixty metres of the place."

The policeman left the group and Lanark touched his shoulder saying, "Can I speak to you?"

He flashed his torch on their faces and said sharply, "What's that on your brows?"

"A thumb print."

"Well, how can I help you, sir? Be quick, we're busy at the moment."

"This lady and I are travelling to Unthank—"

"Out of the question sir. The road's impassable."

"But we're walking. We needn't keep to the road."

"Walking!"

The policeman rubbed his chin. At length he said, "There's the old pedestrian subway. It hasn't been used for years, but as far as I know it isn't *officially* derelict. I mean, it isn't boarded up."

He led them across the grass to a dark shape on the cutting wall. It was a square entrance, eight feet high and half hidden by a heavy swag of ivy. The policeman flashed his torch into it. A floor, under a drift of withered leaves, sloped down into blackness. Rima said firmly, "I'm not going in there."

Lanark said, "Do you know how long it is?"

"Can't say, sir. Wait a minute. . . ."

The policeman probed the wall near the entrance with his torch beam and revealed a faded inscription:

**EDESTRIAN UNDER ASS
UNTHAN 00 ETRES**

The policeman said, "A subway with an entrance like this can't be very long. A pity the lights are broken."

"Could you possibly lend me your torch? We mislaid ours and Rima—this lady—is pregnant, as you see."

"I'm sorry sir. No."

Rima said, "It's no use discussing it. I refuse to go in there."

The policeman said, "Then you'll have to hitch a lift back to New Cumbernauld."

He turned and walked away. Lanark said patiently, "Now listen, we must be sensible. If we use this tunnel we'll reach Unthank in fifteen minutes, perhaps less. It's unlit but there's a handrail on the wall so we can't lose our way. New Cumbernauld may be hours from here, and I want to get you into hospital as quickly as possible."

"I hate the dark, I hate hospitals and I'm not going!"

"There's nothing wrong with darkness. I've met several dreadful things in my life, and every one was in sunshine or a well-lit room."

"Yet you pretend to *want* sunshine!"

"I do, but not because I'm afraid of the opposite."

"How wise you are. How strong. How noble. How useless."

Bickering fiercely they had moved into the tunnel mouth to escape the blast of the din outside. Lanark abruptly paused, pointed into the dark and whispered, "Look, the end!"

Their eyes had grown used to the black and now they could see, in the greatest depth of it, a tiny, pale, glimmering square. Rima suddenly gripped the handrail and walked down the slope. He hurried after her and silently took her arm, afraid a wrong word would overturn her courage.

The roaring behind them sank into silence and the withered leaves stopped whispering under their feet. The ground levelled out. The air grew cold, then freezing. Lanark had kept his eyes fixed on the glimmering little square. He said, "Rima, have you let go the handrail?"

"Of course not."

"That's funny. When we entered the tunnel the light was straight ahead. Now it's on our left."

They halted. He said, "I think we're moving along the side of an open space, a hall of some kind."

She whispered, "What should we do?"

"Walk straight toward the light. Can't you button your coat?"

"No."

"We must get out of this cold as fast as we can. Come on. We'll go straight across the middle."

"What if . . . what if there's a pit?"

"People don't build pedestrian subways with pits in the middle. Let go of the rail."

They faced the light and stepped cautiously out, then Lanark felt himself slipping downward and released Rima's arm with a yell. Head and shoulder met a dense, metal-like surface with such stunning force that he lay on it for several seconds. The hurts of the fall were far less than the intense freezing cold. The chill on his hands and face actually had him weeping.

"Rima," he moaned, "Rima, I'm sorry . . . I'm sorry. Where are you, please?"

"Here."

He crawled in a circle, patting at the ground until his hand touched a foot. "Rima . . . ?"

"Yes."

"You're wearing thin sandals and you're standing on ice. I'm sorry, Rima, I've led you onto a frozen lake."

"I don't care."

He stood up, his teeth chattering, and peered about, saying, "Where's the light?"

"I don't know."

"I can't see it . . . I can't see it anywhere. We must find our way back to the handrail."

"You won't manage it. We're lost." Her body was beside him but her voice, low and dull, seemed to come from a distance. She said, "I'm a witch. I deserve this for killing him."

Lanark thought she had gone mad and felt terribly weary. He said patiently, "What are you talking about, Rima?"

After a moment she said, "Pregnant, silent, freezing, all dark, lost with you, feet that might fall off, an aching back, I deserve all this. He was driving badly to impress me. He wanted me, you see, and at first I found that fun; then I got tired of him, he was so smug and sure of himself. When he made us get out I wanted him to die, so he went on driving badly and crashed. No wonder you mean to lock me in a hospital. I'm a witch."

He realized she was weeping desperately and tried to embrace her, saying, "In the first place, the tanker that crashed may not be the one that gave us the lift. In the second place, a man's bad driving is nobody's fault but his own. And I'm not going to lock you up anywhere."

"Don't touch me."

"But I love you."

"Then promise not to leave when the baby comes. Promise you won't give me to other people and then run away."

"I promise. Don't worry."

"You're only saying that because we're freezing to death. If we get away from here you'll hand me over to a gang of bloody nurses."

"I won't! I won't!"

"You say that now, but you'll run away when the real pains begin. You won't be able to stand them."

"Why shouldn't I stand them? They'll be your pains, not mine."

She gasped and shrieked, "You're glad! You're glad! You evil beast, you're glad!"

He shouted, "Everything I say makes you think I'm evil!"

"You are evil! You can't make me happy. You *must* be evil!"

Lanark stood gasping dumbly. Every comforting phrase which struck him was accompanied by a knowledge of how she would twist it into a hurt. He raised a hand to hit her but she was with child; he turned to run away, but she needed him; he dropped down on his hands and knees and bellowed out a snarling yell which became a howl and then a roar. He heard her say in a cold little voice, "You won't frighten me that way."

He yelled out again and heard a distant voice shout, "Coming! Coming!"

He stood up, drawing breath with effort and feeling the chill of the ice on his hands and knees. A light was moving toward them over the ice and a voice could be hear saying, "Sorry I'm late."

As the light neared they saw it was carried by a dark figure with a strip of whiteness dividing head from shoulders. At last a clergyman stood before them. He may have been middle-aged but had an eager, smooth, young-looking face. He held up the lamp and seemed to peer less at Lanark's face than at the mark on his brow. There was a similar mark on his own. He said, "Lanark, is it? Excellent. I'm Ritchie-Smollet."

They shook hands. The clergyman looked down on Rima, who had sunk down on her heels with her arms resting wearily on her stomach. He said, "So this is your good lady."

"*Lady,*" snarled Rima contemptuously.

Lanark said, "She's tired and a bit unwell. In fact she'll be having a baby quite soon."

The clergyman smiled enthusiastically.

"Splendid. That's really glorious. We must get her into hospital."

Rima said violently, "No!"

"She doesn't want to go into hospital," explained Lanark.

"You must persuade her."

"But I think she ought to do what she likes."

The clergyman moved his feet and said, "It's rather chilly here. Isn't it time we put our noses above ground?"

Lanark helped Rima to her feet and they followed Ritchie-Smollet across the black ice.

It was hard to see anything of the cavern except that the ceiling was a foot or two above their heads. Ritchie-Smollet said, "What tremendous energy these Victorian chaps had. They hollowed this place out as a burial vault when the ground upstairs was filled up. A later age put it to a more pedestrian use, and it still is a remarkably handy short cut. . . . Please ask any questions you like."

"Who are you?"

"A Christian. Or I try to be. I suppose you'd like to know my precise church, but I don't think the sect is all that important, do you? Christ, Buddha, Amon-Ra and Confucius had a great deal in common. Actually I'm a Presbyterian but I work with believers of every continent and colour."

Lanark felt too tired to speak. They had left the ice and were climbing a flagged passage under an arching roof. Ritchie-Smollet said, "Mind you, I'm opposed to human sacrifice: unless it's voluntary, as in the case of Christ. Did you have a nice journey?"

"No."

"Never mind. You're still sound in wind and limb and you can be sure of a hearty welcome. You'll be offered a seat on the committee, of course. Sludden was definite about that and so was I. My experience of institute and council affairs is rather out of date—things were less tense in my time. We were delighted when we heard you had chosen to join us."

"I've chosen to join nobody. I know nothing about committee work and Sludden is no friend of mine."

"Now, now, don't get impatient. A wash and a clean bed will work wonders. I suspect you're more exhausted than you think."

The pale square of light appeared ahead and enlarged to a doorway. It opened into the foot of a metal staircase. Lanark and Rima climbed slowly and painfully in watery green light. Ritchie-Smollet came patiently behind, humming to himself. After many minutes they emerged into a narrow, dark, stone-built chamber with marble plaques on three walls and large wrought-iron gates in the fourth. These swung easily outward, and they stepped onto a gravel path beneath a huge black sky. Lanark saw he was on a hilltop among the obelisks of a familiar cemetery.

CHAPTER 35. Cathedral

After they had gone a little way Lanark stopped and declared, "This isn't Unthank!"

"You are mistaken. It is."

They looked down a slope of pinnacled monuments onto a squat black cathedral. The floodlit spire held a gilt weathercock above the level of their eyes, but Lanark was more perplexed by the view beyond. He remembered a stone-built city of dark tenements and ornate public buildings, a city with a square street plan and electric tramcars. Rumours from the council corridors had made him expect much the same place, only darker and more derelict, but below a starless sky this city was coldly blazing. Slim poles as tall as the spire cast white light upon the lanes and looping bridges of another vast motorway. On each side shone glass and concrete towers over twenty floors high with lights on top to warn off aeroplanes. Yet this was Unthank, though the old streets between towers and motorlanes had a half-erased look, and blank gables stood behind spaces cleared for carparks. After a pause Lanark said, "And Unthank is dying?"

"Dying? Oh I doubt it. The population has shrunk since they scrapped the Q39 project, but there's been a tremendous building boom."

"But if a place is losing people and industry how can it afford new buildings?"

"Ah, I know too little about chronology to say. I feel that what happens between *hearts* matters more than these big public ways of swapping energy. You tell me, no doubt, that this is a conservative attitude. On the other hand, radicals are the only people who'll work with me. Odd, isn't it?"

Lanark said irritably, "You seem to understand my questions, but your answers make no sense to me."

"That's typical of life, isn't it? But as long as you've a good heart and keep trying there's no need to despair. *Wer immer streband sich bemüht, den können wir erlösen.* Oh, you'll be a great deal of use to us."

Rima suddenly leaned on a stone and said quietly, without bitterness, "I can't go on."

Lanark, alarmed, clasped her waist though it worried him to be clasping two people instead of one. Ritchie-Smollet said softly, "A giddy spell?"

"No, my back hurts and I . . . I can hardly think."

"In my missionary phase I took a medical degree. Give me your pulse."

He held her wrist in one hand, beat time with the other, then said, "Eighty-two. Considering your condition that's quite good. Could you manage down to that building? A sleep is what you need most, but I'd better examine you first to make sure everything's in order."

He pointed to the cathedral. Rima stared at it. Lanark murmured, "Could we join hands and carry her?"

Rima pushed herself upright and said, "No, give me your arm. I'll walk."

The clergyman led them down dim weedy paths past the porticoes of mausoleums cut into the hillside. Gleams of light from below lit corners of inscriptions to the splendid dead:

"... His victorious campaign ..."
"..... whose unselfish devotion ....."
"... revered by his students ..."
"..... esteemed by his colleagues ....."
"... beloved by all ..."

They crossed a flat space and walked along a cobbled lane. Ritchie-Smollet said, "A tributary of the river once flowed under here."

Lanark saw that a low wall beside him was the parapet of a bridge and looked over onto a steeply embanked road. Cars sped up this to the motorway but there seemed to be a barrier: after slowing and stopping they turned and came back again. A tiny distinct throbbing in the air worked on the eardrum like the point of a drill on a tooth.

"What's that noise?"

"There appears to be a pile-up at the intersection: a burst transporter, one of these huge dangerous God-the-Father jobs. The
council ought to ban them. The city looks like being sealed
off for quite a while. However, we've adequate food stocks.
Come through here, it's a short cut."

The parapet had given way to a wall screened by bushes.
Ritchie-Smollet parted two of these uncovering a hole into
brighter air. Lanark helped Rima through. They were in the
grounds of the cathedral where gravestones lay flat like a pavement. Vans and private cars stood on them against the surrounding wall, and Rima sank down on the step of a mobile crane.
Ritchie-Smollet thrust hands into trouser pockets and stared
ahead with a small satisfied smile.

"There she stands!" he said. "Our centre of government once
again."

Lanark looked at the cathedral. At first the floodlit spire seemed
too solid for the flat black shape upholding it, a shape cut
through by rows of dim yellow windows; then his eye made
out the tower, roofs and buttresses of a sturdy Gothic ark,
the sculpted waterspouts broken and rubbed by weather and
the hammers of old iconoclasts.

"What do you mean, centre of government? Unthank has a
city chambers."

"Ah, yes, we use it nowadays for property deals. Quite a lot
of work is done there, but the *real* legislators come here. I
know you're keen to meet them but first you'll have to sleep.
I speak as a doctor now, not as a minister of the gospel, so
you mustn't argue with me."

They walked over inscriptions more laconic than in the higher
cemetery.

"William Skinner: 5½ feet North × 2¼ West."

"Harry Fleming, his wife Minnie, their son George, their
daughter Amy: 6 feet West × 2½ North."

They reached a side entrance and crossed a shallow porch into
the cathedral.

A long-haired young man wearing blue overalls sat reading
a book on a lidded stone font near the door. He glanced up
and said, "Where have you been, Arthur? Polyphemus is going
berserk. He thinks he's discovered something."

"I'm in a hurry, Jack," said Ritchie-Smollet crisply. "These

people need rest and attention. Will anywhere be clear for a
while? I mean really clear?"
"Nothing scheduled for the arts lab."
"Then get blankets and pillows into it and clean sheets, really
clean sheets, and make up a bed."
"Yes but" —the youth laid down his book and slid to the
floor—"what will I tell Polyphemus?"
"Tell him politics is not man's chief end."
The youth hurried off between rows of rush-bottomed chairs
covering the great flagged floor. The cathedral seemed vaster
inside than out. The central pillars upholding the tower hid
what lay beyond, but organ tones and blurred hymnal voices
indicated a service there. At the same time the hard beat of
wilder music sounded from somewhere below. Ritchie-Smollet
said, "Not a bad God kennel, is it? The October Terminus
are having a gig in the crypt. Some people don't approve of
that, but I tell them that at the Reformation the building was
used by three congregations simultaneously and in my father's
house are many mansions. Do you need the lavatory?"
"No," muttered Rima, who had sunk into a chair. "No, no,
no, no."
"Come on, then. Not far now."

They moved slowly down a side aisle and Lanark had
time to notice that the cathedral had clearly been used in several
ways since its foundation. Torn flags hung overhead; against
the walls stood ornate memorials to soldiers killed while invad-
ing remote continents. Before the arches under the tower they
turned left and went down some steps, then right and descended
others into a small chapel. An orange light hung in the stone-
ribbed ceiling but the stone was whitewashed and the effect
was restful. The air was warmed and scented by paraffin heaters
in the corners; a stack of plastic mattresses against a wall nearly
touched the ceiling. Three of these were laid edge to edge
and Jack was making a bed on the middle one. Rima lay down
on it when he finished and Lanark helped remove her coat.
"Don't go to sleep yet—I'll be back in a jiff," said Ritchie-
Smollet and went out. Jack adjusted the wicks of the heaters
and followed him. Lanark shed his own coat and sat with Rima's
head on his lap. He was weary but couldn't relax because his
clothes felt sticky and foul. He fingered the matted beard on
his cheeks and chin and touched the thinning hair on his scalp.
Clearly he had grown older. He looked down at Rima, whose

eyes were closed. Her hair was black once more, and apart
from the big belly her whole figure seemed slighter than in
the council corridors. A small insulted frown between the brows
suggested an angry little girl, but her lips had the beautiful
repose of a mature, contented woman of thirty or forty. He
gazed and gazed but couldn't decide her age at all. She sighed
and murmured, "Where's Sludden?"
He overcame a pang of anger and said gently, "I don't know,
Rima."
"You're nice to me, Lanark. I'll always trust you."

Ritchie-Smollet and Jack brought basins of hot water, towels, clean nightshirts, and went out again. Rima lay on the
towels while Lanark sponged and dried her, taking special care
of the great belly, which looked more normal naked than
clothed. She slid between the sheets and Ritchie-Smollet returned with a black leather case. He knelt by the bed and
took out thermometer, stethoscope and sterilized gloves in a
transparent envelope. He slipped the thermometer below
Rima's armpit and was tearing the envelope when she opened
her eyes and said sharply, "Turn round Lanark."
"Why?"
"If you don't turn round I won't let him touch me."
Lanark turned round and walked to the far side of a pillar,
his feet cold on the bare stone. He stopped and stared at the
ceiling. The arching ribs came together in carved knops, and
one showed a pair of tiny snakes twining across the brow of
a very cheerful skull in the middle of a wreath of roses. Nearby
on the vault someone had scribbled in pencil:
GOD = LOVE = MONEY = SHIT.
"Well, that seems all right," said Ritchie-Smollet loudly. Lanark
turned and saw him repacking the case. "The little fellow seems
the correct way up and round and so forth. If she insists on
having it here I suppose we can manage."
"*Here?*" said Lanark, startled.
"Not in hospital, I mean. Anyway, I'll leave you to some well-
earned rest."
He went out, pulling a red curtain across the door. Rima murmured, "Get in behind me."
He obeyed and she pressed her freezing soles greedily to his
shins, but her back was familiar and cosy and soon they grew
warm and slept.

He wakened among whispering and rustling. Chains of bright spots flowed zigzag over the dark vault and pillars and crowded floor. They were cast by a silver-faceted globe revolving where the orange lamp had hung, and now the only steady light shone on the steps to the entrance. These were the breadth of the wall. Young men in overalls were arranging electrical machines on them which sometimes filled the chapel with huge hoarse sighs. Three older men sat on the lower steps holding instruments joined by wires to the machinery, and a fourth was setting up a percussion kit with BROWN'S LUGWORM CASANOVAS printed on the big drum. Lanark saw he was part of an audience: the whole floor was paved with mattresses and covered with people squatting shoulder to shoulder. Beside him a delicate girl in a silver sari was leaning on a hairy, barechested man in a sheepskin waistcoat. Just in front a girl in the tartan trews and scarlet mess jacket of a highland regiment was whispering to a man with the braided hair, headband and fringed buckskin of an Indian squaw. People from every culture and century seemed gathered here in silk, canvas, fur, feathers, wool, gauze, nylon and leather. Hair was frizzed out like the African, crewcut like the Roman, piled high like Pompadour, straightened like the Sphinx or rippled over the shoulders like periwigs. There was every kind of ornament and an amount of nakedness. Lanark looked unsuccessfully for his clothes. He felt he had rested a long time but Rima was still sleeping, so he decided not to move. Other couples were reclining at length and even caressing in the shelter of sleeping bags.

There was applause and a small gloomy man with a heavy moustache stood with a microphone on the steps. He said, "Glad to be back, folks, in legendary Unthank where I've had so many legendary experiences. I'm going to lead off with a new thing, it bombed them in Troy and Trebizond, it sank like stone-cold turkey in Atlantis, let's see what happens here. 'Domestic Man.' "
He threw his head back and shouted:

"The cake she baked me bit me till I cried!"

The instruments and machines said BAWAM so loudly that hearing and thought were destroyed for a second.

"The bed she made me was so hard I nearly died!"
(BAWAM)

"The shirt she washed me folded its arms and tied me up inside!"

(BAWAM)

"She's going domestic, she's got a great big domestic plan, But *please* baby believe me lady I am
                not a domestic man
                not a domestic man
                not a domestic man."
(BAWAM BAWAM BAWAM BAWAM BAWAM BAWAM BAWAM BAWAM BAWAM)

Rima was sitting up, hands pressed over ears and tears pouring down her cheeks. She spoke but the words were inaudible. Lanark saw Ritchie-Smollet beckoning violently from the doorway behind the singer. He pulled Rima up and they stumbled through the audience. The singer shouted:

"She cleans windows till they shine so I can't see!"
                (BAWAM)
"She polishes floors till they suck my foot in up to the knee!"
                (BAWAM)
"She papers rooms till the walls start squeezing in on me!"
                (BAWAM)

As they passed the singer Rima waved so threateningly at a bank of loudspeakers that someone grabbed her arm. Lanark pulled him off and clumsy punches were exchanged on the way to the door. Ritchie-Smollet separated them, his voice coming through the BAWAMing like a far-off whisper: ". . . entirely my fault . . . delicate condition . . . failure of liaison. . . ."

    It was quieter outside the door where Jack waited with dressing-gown and slippers. Rima kept muttering "Bastards" as she was helped into these.
"They dislike space, you see, and noise fills that up," said Ritchie-Smollet, leading them across the nave. "The fault is really mine. I went out with a man who thought I could save his marriage because I'd performed the ceremony. Illogical, really. Didn't know him from Adam. I hadn't expected you to sleep so long—if we had a clock it would be safe to say you snoozed right round the bally thing. Contractions started yet?"
"No," said Rima.
"Good. In a brace of shakes you'll have a bed and a bite in

the triforium. I'd have put you there when you came but I
feared you were too feeble to face the stairs."

He opened a little door and they saw a stair hardly two feet
wide spiralling upward in the thickness of the wall. Lanark
said, "Excuse me, but can't we get a decent room in a decent
house?"

"Rooms are hard to find just now. The house of God is the
best I can offer."

"When I was last here a quarter of the city stood empty."

"Ah, that was before the new building programme started.
Someone on the committee may offer you a spare room eventually. Anyway, we can wait for them in the triforium—your
clothes are there."

Ritchie-Smollet ducked through the doorway and climbed.
Rima followed and Lanark came after. The stairs were laboriously steep. After several turns they passed through another
door onto the inner sill of a huge window. Rima gasped and
clutched a handrail. Far below a man moved like a beetle over
the flagged floor and the echoing throbs of "Domestic Man"
added to the insecurity. Ritchie-Smollet said, "That's Polyphemus on his way to the chapterhouse. My word, but the Lugworms are going it some."

A few steps took them onto a walkway between rows of organ
pipes, and a few more into the end of a very long low attic.
The ceiling slanted from the floor to a wall of arches overlooking the nave. As they walked down it Lanark saw partitions
dividing the loft on his left into cubicles, each containing a
little furniture. In one a man in a dirty coat sat trying to mend
an old boot. In another a haggard woman lay drinking from
a flat-sided bottle. Ritchie-Smollet said, "Here we are," stepped
into one and squatted on the carpet.

The cubicle had a homely look mitigated by a smell of
disinfectant. It was lit by a pink silk-shaded lamp above a low
bed that covered a third of the floor. The seats were stools
and cushions but there was a low table, a chest of drawers
and a tiny sink. The boards between the ceiling joists were
covered by forget-me-not patterned paper, and on one of the
two walls a hanger on a hook held Lanark's clothes, newly
cleaned and pressed.

"Small but snug," said Ritchie-Smollet. "A regrettable lack of
headroom but nobody will disturb us. I suggest Rima slip into
bed (she'll find a hot-water bottle there) and you get dressed.
Then Jack will bring us a meal, a companion will arrive for

your good lady, and we two can attend the meeting in the
chapterhouse. The provost should be there by now."
Lanark sank on a stool with elbows on knees and chin on hands.
He said, "You keep moving me about and I don't know why."
"Yes, it's difficult. In the present state of chronological confusion it's impossible to state things clearly. As secretary I can
only arrange meetings by keeping members here till the rest
arrive. But Gow's come, and poor Scougal and Mrs. Schtzngrm
and the ubiquitous Polyphemus. And chairman Sludden, praise
God."
Lanark looked at Rima. The sight soothed him. She lay smiling
against the pillows, a hand touching her full breast. There was
a soft calmness about her; the dimples at the corners of her
mouth were unusually deep. She said fondly, "It's all right,
Lanark. Don't worry."
He sighed and started dressing.

Jack entered with a loaded tray and Ritchie-Smollet poured
coffee into cups and passed plates around, chatting as he did
so.
"All out of tins, of course, but good of its kind. Easy to serve,
too, which is handy because there's only room for a very tiny
kitchen. There was amazing opposition when we set up this
little refuge—even more than to the arts lab in the lady chapel.
Yet these lofts have lain empty since the old monks marched
round them telling their beads. And what could better con-
form to the wishes of the founder? You know the poem, of
course:

"If at the church they would give us some ale,
and a pleasant fire our souls to regale,
we'd sing and we'd pray all the livelong day,
nor ever once wish from the church to stray,

"And God, like a father, rejoicing to see,
His children as pleasant and happy as He,
would have no more quarrel with Devil or barrel,
But kiss him and give him both drink and—"

"What the hell am I eating?" shouted Lanark. ·
"Enigma de Filets Congalés. Is it underdone? Try this pink
moist crumbly stuff. I can heartily recommend it."
Lanark groaned. A stink of burning rubber was fading from
his nostrils and his limbs were invaded by a familiar invigorating
warmth. He said, "This is institute food."

"Yes. The Quantum group delivers nothing else to us nowadays."

"We left the institute because we hate this food."

"I admire you for it!" cried Ritchie-Smollet enthusiastically. "And you've moved in the right direction! We have two or three millennialists on the committee and who's to blame them? Has not the prayer of humanity in all ages been for innocent and abundant food? Impossible, of course, but *wer immer strebend sich bemüht* et cetera. And one has to eat, unless one feels with Miss Weil that anorexia nervosa is a sacred duty."

"Yes I will eat!" cried Lanark savagely. "But please stop bombarding me with funny names and meaningless quotations!" He finished all the plates that Rima and Ritchie-Smollet left untouched and in the end felt bloated, drugged and horribly tricked. A voice cried, "Rima!" A plump woman of about forty wearing tarty clothes came in. Rima laughed and said, "Frankie!"

Frankie dropped a huge embroidered handbag on the floor, sat on the bed and said, "Sludden told me you were here— he's coming later. So the mystery man has put a bun in your oven, has he? Actually you don't look too bad—quite surprisingly winsome, really. Hullo, mystery man, I'm glad you've grown a beard. You look less vulnerable."

"Hullo," said Lanark ungraciously. He was not pleased to see Frankie.

CHAPTER 36. Chapterhouse

Ritchie-Smollet led them to the far end of the attic, through a small kitchen where Jack was washing dishes, and down another spiral stair in the thickness of the wall. They came into a square room with vaulted ceiling upheld by a great central pillar. A row of stone chairs with wooden backs were built into the length of each wall. Lanark thought this an awkward arrangement: if all the seats were occupied everyone would find the central pillar hiding three or four people opposite. A small, fit-looking man stood with feet apart and hands in pockets warming his back at an electric fire. Ritchie-Smollet spoke with less than usual enthusiasm.

"Ah, Grant. This is Lanark, who has news for us."

"Council news, no doubt," said Grant with a sarcastic emphasis, "I've been waiting over an hour."

"Remember the rest of us haven't got your knack of timing things. The provost may be in the crypt; I'll go and look."

Ritchie-Smollet left by a door in a corner. Grant and Lanark stared at each other. Grant seemed about thirty though there were some deep vertical wrinkles on his cheeks and brow. His short crisp hair was carefully combed and he wore a neat blue suit and red necktie. He said, "I know you. When I was a lad you used to hang around the old Elite with Sludden's mob."

"Not for long," said Lanark. "How do you time things? Have you a watch?"

"I've a pulse."

"You count your heartbeats?"

"I estimate them. We all developed that talent in the shops when the old timekeeping collapsed."

"You keep a shop?"

"I'm talking abut workshops. Machine shops. I'm a maker, not a salesman."

Lanark sat on a seat near the fire. Grant's voice offended him. It was loud, penetrating and clearly used to addressing crowds without help from the equipment which lets a man talk softly to millions. Lanark said, "Where's Polyphemus?"

"Eh?"

"I heard that someone called Polyphemus was here."

Grant grinned and said, "I'm here all right. Smollet calls me that."

"Why?"

"Polyphemus was a one-eyed ogre in an old story. I keep reminding the committee of a fact they want to forget, so they say I have only one way of seeing things."

"What fact is that?"

"None of them are makers."

"Do you mean workers?"

"No, I mean makers. Many hard workers make nothing but wealth. They don't produce food, fuel, shelter or helpful ideas; their work is just a way of tightening their grip on folk who do."

"What do you make?"

"Homes. I'm a shop steward with the Volstat Mohome group."

Lanark said thoughtfully, "These groups—Volstat, Algolagnics and so on—are they what people call the creature?"

"Some of us call it that. The council is financed by it. So is the institute. So it likes to call itself the foundation."

"I'm sick of these big vague names that power keeps hiding behind," said Lanark impatiently.

"So you prefer not to think of them," said Grant, nodding amiably. "That's typical of intellectuals. The institute has bought and sold you so often that you're ashamed to name your masters."

"I have no masters. I hate the institute. I don't even like the council."

"But it helped you come here, so it still has a use for you."

"Blethers!" cried Lanark. "People usually help each other if they can do it without troubling themselves much."

"Try a cigarette," said Grant, offering a packet. He had grown friendlier as Lanark grew angrier.

"Thank you, I don't smoke," said Lanark, cooling a little.

A while later Lanark said, "Would you tell me exactly what the creature is?"

"A conspiracy which owns and manipulates everything for profit."

"Are you talking about the wealthy?"

"Yes, but not the wealthy in coins and banknotes—that sort of wealth is only coloured beads to keep the makers servile. The owners and manipulators have smarter ways of banking energy. They pay themselves with time: time to think and plan, time to examine necessity from a distance."

An old man leaning on a stick and a dark young man with a turban entered and stood talking quietly by the pillar. Grant's loud voice had been even and passionless, but suddenly he said, "What I hate most is their conceit. Their institute breaks whole populations into winners and losers and calls itself *culture*. Their council destroys every way of life which doesn't bring them a profit and calls itself government. They pretend culture and government are supremely independent powers when they are nothing but gloves on the hands of Volstat and Quantum, Cortexin and Algolagnics. And they really think they are the foundation. They believe their greed holds up the continents. They don't call it greed, of course, they call it profit, or (among themselves, where they don't need to fool anyone) *killings*. They're sure that only their profit allows people to make and eat things."

"Maybe that's true."

"Yes, because they make it true. But it isn't necessary. Old men remember when the makers unexpectedly produced enough for everyone. No crop failed, no mine was exhausted, no machinery broke down, but the creature dumped mountains of food in the ocean because the hungry couldn't pay a *profitable* price for it, and the shoemaker's children went shoeless because their father had made too many shoes. And the makers accepted this as though it was an earthquake! They refused to see they could make what they needed for each other and to hell with profit. They would have seen in the end, they would have had to see, if the council had not gone to war."

"How did that help?"

"As the creature couldn't stay rich by selling necessary things to the folk who made them it sold destructive things to the council. Then the war started and the destructive things were used to wreck the necessary things. The creature profited by replacing both."

"Who did the council fight?"

"It split in two and fought itself."

"That's suicide!"

"No, ordinary behaviour. The efficient half eats the less efficient half and grows stronger. War is just a violent way of doing what half the people do calmly in peacetime: using the other half for food, heat, machinery and sexual pleasure. Man is the pie that bakes and eats himself, and the recipe is separation."

"I refuse to believe men kill each other just to make their enemies rich."

"How can men recognize their real enemies when their family, schools and work teach them to struggle with each other and to believe law and decency come from the teachers?"

"My son won't be taught that," said Lanark firmly.

"You have a son?"

"Not yet."

The chapterhouse had filled with chattering groups and Ritchie-Smollet moved among them collecting signatures in a book. There were many young people in bright clothing, old eccentric men in tweeds and a large confusion of in-between people. Lanark decided that if this was the new government of Unthank he was not impressed. Their manners were shrill and vehement or languid and bored. Some had the mark of the council on their brow but nobody displayed the calm, well-contained strength of men like Monboddo, Ozenfant and Munro. Lanark said, "Could you tell me about this committee?"

"I'm getting round to it. The war ended with the creature and its organs more dominant than ever. Naturally there was a lot of damage to repair, but that only took half our time and energy. If industry and government had been commanding us for the common good (as they pretend to do), the continents would have become gardens, gardens of space and light where everyone had time to care for their lovers, children and neighbours without crowding and tormenting them. But these vast bodies only cooperate to kill or crush. Once again the council began feeding the creature by splitting the world in two and preparing a war. But it ran into unexpected trouble—"

"Stop! You're simplifying," said Lanark. "You talk as if all government was one thing, but there are many kinds of government, and some are crueller than others."

"Oh, yes," said Grant, nodding. "An organization which encloses a globe must split into departments. But you're a very ordinary victim of council advertising if you think the world is neatly split between good governments and bad."

"What was the council's unexpected trouble?"

"The creature supplied it with such vast new weapons that a few of them could poison the world. Most folk are dour and uncomplaining about their own deaths, but the death of their children depresses them. The council tried to pretend the new weapons weren't weapons at all but homes where everyone could live safely, but for all that an air of protest spread even to the council corridors. Many who had never dreamed of governing themselves began complaining loudly. This committee is made of complainers."

"Has complaint done any good?"

"Some, perhaps. The creature still puts time and energy into vast weapons and sells them to the council, but recent wars have been fought with smaller weapons and kept to the less industrial continents. Meanwhile the creature has invented peaceful ways of taking our time and energy. It employs us to make essential things badly, so they decay fast and have to be replaced. It bribes the council to destroy cheap things which don't bring it a profit and replaces them with new expensive things which do. It pays us to make useless things and employs scientists, doctors and artists to persuade us that these are essential."

"Can you give me examples?"

"Yes, but our provost wants to speak to you."

Lanark stood up. A lean, well-dressed man with bushy grey hair came through the crowd and shook his hand, saying briskly, "Sorry I missed you upstairs, Lanark—you were too quick for me. Don't worry—she's all right."

The voice was familiar. Lanark stared into the strange, haggard, bright-eyed face. The provost said reassuringly, "It's all right—she's in excellent spirits. I'm glad there was someone dependable like you with her. Frankie will tell us when the contractions start."

Lanark said, "Sludden."

"You didn't recognize me?" asked the provost, chuckling. "Well, none of us are the men we were."

Lanark said harshly, "How's your fiancée?"

"Gay?" said Sludden ruefully. "I hoped *you* could tell me about Gay. The marriage didn't work. My fault, I'm afraid; politics puts strain on a marriage. She joined the institute. The last I heard of her was that she had gone to work for the council. If you didn't see her in the corridors she's probably with a

foundation group, Cortexin perhaps. She had a talent for com-
munications."
Lanark felt baffled and feeble. He wanted to hate Sludden but
couldn't think of a reason for doing it. He said accusingly,
"I saw Nan and her baby."
"Rima told me. I'm glad they're well," said Sludden, smiling
and nodding.
"The committee is convened," said Ritchie-Smollet. "Please
be seated."

People moved to the walls and sat down. Sludden took
a chair with a high carved back and armrests; Ritchie-Smollet
led Lanark to a seat on Sludden's right and himself sat on his
left. Grant sat beside Lanark. Ritchie-Smollet said, "Silence,
please. The internal secretary has failed to make an appearance,
so once again we must take the minutes of the last meeting
as read. Never mind. The reason for the present meeting is
. . . but I call on our chairman, provost Sludden, to explain
that."
"We are privileged to have among us," said Sludden, "a former
citizen of Unthank who till recently worked for the institute
under the famous—perhaps I should say infamous—Ozenfant.
Lanark—here he is beside me—has elected to return here of
his own free will, which is no doubt a testimonial to the charm
and friendliness of Unthank but proves also the strength of
his own patriotic spirit."
Sludden paused. Ritchie-Smollet cried, "Oh, jolly good!" and
clapped his hands. Sludden said, "I understand he has had personal consultations with Monboddo."
A voice behind the pillar shouted, "Shame!"
"Monboddo certainly has no friends here, but information
about where Unthank stands in the council is hard to obtain,
so we welcome any source of light on the subject. Also with
me is Grant, sufficiently known to us all."
A voice behind the pillar shouted, "Up the makers, Poly!"
"Grant feels he has important news for us. I don't know what
it is, but I suppose it will keep till we have heard our guest
speaker?"
Sludden looked at Grant, who shrugged.
"So I will call on Lanark to take the floor."

Lanark rose confusedly to his feet. He said, "I'm not sure
what to say. I'm not patriotic. I don't like Unthank, I like
sunshine. I came here because I was told Unthank would be

scrapped and swallowed in a few days, and anybody here
with a council passport would be transferred to a sunnier city."
He sat down. There was silence, then Ritchie-Smollet said,
"Monboddo told you this?"
"No, one of his secretaries did. A man called Wilkins."
"I strongly object to the tone of the last speaker's remarks,"
cried a bulky, thick-necked man in a voice twice as penetrating
as Grant's.
"Though he openly boasts of being no friend to Unthank, our
provost has introduced him as if he was some sort of ambassador, and what news does the ambassador bring? Gossip. Nothing but gossip. The mountain has laboured and given birth
to a small obnoxious rodent. But what is the *tendency* of the
speech by this self-proclaimed enemy of the city which nurtured
him? He tells us that after some vague but imminent doomsday
those who carry a council passport will be transferred to a
happier land while the majority are *swallowed,* whatever that
means. I will, however, say this. *I* have a council passport,
like several others on the committee, and like the speaker himself. His statements are clearly devised to spread distrust among
our brothers and dismay and dissension in our rank and file.
Let me assure this messianic double agent that he will not suc-
ceed. Nobody is better able to fight the council than men like
Scougal and me. We love our people. We will sink or swim
with Unthank. Meanwhile I propose that the committee combat
the demoralizing tendency of the guest speaker's tirade by pretending we never heard it."
"Oh, not a tirade, Gow!" said Ritchie-Smollet mildly. "Lanark
spoke four short sentences. I counted them. We ought to hear
a little more before dismissing him totally. Wilkins said Unthank
would be scrapped and swallowed. Did he indicate why?"
"Yes," said Lanark. "He said you were no longer profitable,
and scrapping you would bring some kind of energy gain. He
said his people were used to eating towns and villages, but
Unthank would be their first city since Carthage."
A howl of laughter went up from different parts of the room.
A voice behind the pillar cried, "Carthage? What about Coven-
try?" and others shouted "Leningrad!" "Berlin!" "Warsaw!"
"Dresden!" "Hiroshima!"
"I would like also to menshun," said a slow-voiced, white-haired
lady, "Münster in 1535, Gonstantinoble in 1453 and 1204,
ant Hierusalem more vrequently than vun cares to rememper."
"Please, please! A little more moderation!" cried Ritchie-Smol-
let. "These unhappy rationalizations took place when the coun-

cil was split in two or menaced by sectarian extremists. I am sure Lanark is not lying when he tells us what he heard. I do suggest his informant misled him."

"The peaceful destruction of a modern city would be something new," said Sludden thoughtfully. "It would have to be a city with no effective government. And the creature would have to provide a lot of powerful new machinery. And the destruction would have to be approved by a full meeting of the council, a meeting where Unthank was represented."

"Wilkins said a meeting of council delegates would approve the action in eight days," said Lanark. "That was a while ago. The creature has delivered large suction delvers to something called the expansion project. I saw one. As for your government, you know it better than I do."

"Utter nonsense!" cried Gow. "The council has no heartier opponent in Unthank than myself. As the oldest and most active member of the committee I have wrestled with it since the last world war, and never till recently have we obtained from it such enormous concessions. A short while ago our roads and buildings were a century out of date. Now look at them! Modern motorways. High-rise housing. A city centre full of towering office blocks. We could have done none of this without council aid. Yet you suggest the council plans to smash us!"

"These new developments do not greatly veigh with me," said the slow-voiced lady. "The profits of this building vork haf gone to the creature. A city lives by its industry ant ours still declines. But ve cannot, on the vort of von man, assume the vorst. Ve neet documentary corroboration."

Gow said, "I have no wish to stoop to personal invective but—"

"Excuse me, Gow, Jack would like a chance to speak," said Sludden, indicating Ritchie-Smollet's helper who was waving from a corner.

"I was cleaning the guest speaker's suit," said Jack, "and I noticed a council paper in the pocket. Maybe that could tell us something."

Lanark pulled out the newspaper he had lifted in the council café. Sludden took it and started reading. Gow said, "I don't like using insulting language, but the welfare of the community drives me to it. This guest speaker of ours, this would-be plenipotentiary, is no stranger to *me*. On a recent delegation to the council *I* saw this so-called Lanark sniffing around Monboddo's throne with his long-haired girlfriend and his shabby little rucksack. He made no very creditable impression on the powers that be, I don't mind telling you. Is it likely, if there

was a plot to dismantle this city, that they would trust the details to someone like *this*?"
"Give him laldy, Gow!" yelled a voice behind the pillar. Lanark gaped and stood up. He heard Grant at his side murmuring, "Careful now!" but a growing unease in his stomach had nothing to do with the debate. He said sharply, "Nobody trusted me with details. Wilkins would have told anybody these plans; he said only a revolution could change them. I don't care if you believe me or not."
He walked toward the door he had entered by.

Before he reached it Sludden cried, "Wait, everyone should hear this!" so he paused by the pillar. Sludden said, "This is from the chronology section of the *Western Lobby*.

Nobody but a fanatic would suggest that the material of time is moral, but on occasions like the present, when the boundaries of the most stable continents seem melting into intercalendrical mist, it seems probable that a working timescale needs a higher proportion of common decency than the science of chronology has hitherto assumed. Decency is a vague term, and at present we suggest no more by it than a little more brotherhood between colleagues of equal or nearly equal standing.

The authority of the council has always depended on the support of the creature, and until recently it was widely felt that Monboddo's connections with the Algolagnics–Cortexin group merely ratified his standing as a strong president. Recent disclosures, however, by the fiery energy chief Ozenfant show that recent loans of creature energy have been absorbed by the lord president's office to the almost total exclusion of the normal power corridor network.

Although respect for the president director and respect for the decimal hour are not connected in logic, they seem to feed irrationally on each other in a state of collapsing

confidence. There is deep alarm in
council corridors that speculation
against the new timescale has now
exceeded the boundaries of reason
and may no longer be susceptible
to rational remedy. Only one thing
is certain. The swift dismantling of
a certain darkened district, which
once seemed a daring and debatable
act of rationalization, has become
a matter of urgent necessity."

"What's that supposed to mean?" asked Gow. "There are hundreds of darkened districts. What conceivable reason have you
for thinking they've chosen Unthank?"

"I came here to tell you that," said Grant. "Nearly two days
ago a Cortexin tanker and an Algolagnics transporter collided
at the intersection. All incoming traffic is diverted to Imber.
We have food supplies for three more days. By 'day' I mean
the old fashioned solar day of twenty-four hours, with roughly
seventeen hundred heartbeats an hour."

"Pull yourself together, Grant!" said Ritchie-Smollet. "Do you
suggest these vehicles were smashed in a criminal plot between
Algolagnics and the council? That is pure paranoia. The council
is sending experts to deal with the damage."

"You don't need a plot to cause crashes on a motorway," said
Grant. "They happen all the time. When they happen on the
council's doorstep they're cleared at once. Why the delay with
us?"

"Because we are not on the council's doorstep. From the council's viewpoint we are a remote and unimportant province, but
that does not mean they are out for our blood. The council
traffic commissioner has talked to me on the phone. His clear-
ance teams are fighting an imbalance at the Cortexin cloning
plant. Half West Atlantis will sink if that isn't stabilized first.
But he's moving heaven and earth to get the right men quickly
here too. He said so. I know him. He is an honest man."

"Haven't you seen how the council works in peacetime?" asked
Grant. "It never behaves badly. It never destroys a country
of peasant villages, for example, but it lets the creature turn
whole forests into paper so there are no roots to hold the
water back. And when an accidental storm arises (as they always
will), half a million people drown or die in the following famine,
and the council helps the survivors, and the helpers organize
the country's industry in ways the creature finds profitable. I'm
sure your traffic commissioner honestly wants to clear the inter-

section. I'm sure his honest experts have more urgent work
to do. And I'm sure that three days from now, when our administration crumbles and the city is a horde of starving rioters,
the council will introduce an honest emergency-aid programme
and honestly evacuate Unthank down whatever gullet the creature offers."

There was a long silence.

"It is true," said the slow-voiced lady softly, "that with efery
passing moment a broken nerf circuit of the new Algolagnics
model becomes a more dangerous object. Virst ve haf only
the fibrations, but after two days, on the old timescale, sublima-
tion produces radioactive fumes of an unusually lethal ant vide-
spreading type."

"Why not clear up the mess yourselves?" said Lanark impatiently.

"We lack protective clothing. Vithout it nothing is able to lif
vithin sixty metres of these objects."

"Are they heavy?" asked Lanark. "Could you flood the road
and float them off it?"

"Powerhoses," said Grant to Sludden. "Open a storm drain
and order the fire brigade to flush the mess down it with powerhoses."

"Impossible!" bellowed Gow. "Even if Unthank *is* menaced
in the way you suggest, which I do *not* for one moment admit,
the forcing of unqualified firemen to do the dangerous work
of trained nerve-circuit experts is in flagrant defiance of all
normal and democratic procedure. I am sure our provost is
not going to be led astray by the jeremiads of the guest speaker
and the rantings of brother Grant. Once again we see extremists
of the right and left combining in an unholy alliance against
all that is most stable in—"

"Blood will have to flow," said a loud dull voice behind the
pillar. "I'm sorry, I see no other way."

"Whose blood will have to flow, Scougal?" asked Ritchie-Smollet gently, "and when, and where, and why will it flow, Scougal?"

"I'm sorry if my remarks upset people" said the dull voice,
"I apologize. But blood will have to flow, I see no other way."

Lanark walked over to the little door, opened it, ducked under
the lintel and closed it behind him.

CHAPTER 37.
Alexander Comes

Finding no light-switch he climbed the narrow steep spiral in blackness, patting the wall as he neared the level of the attic. At last his hand touched a clumsy wooden bolt. He slid it back, shoved hard and stepped out into fresh air with a few stars overhead. Either he had left the chapterhouse by the wrong stairs or the stairs by the wrong door for he now stood in a gutter between two dim slopes of roof. He could hear muffled kitchen noises of water and clinking dishes, so the attic was nearby. The gutter was clearly a walkway too, so he moved along it toward the noise and came to a stone parapet overlooking a city square. It was a quiet square with a couple of tiny figures walking across. The houses on the far side were the old tenement kind with shops on the ground floor and some upper windows curtained and lit from inside. These seemed so pleasantly familiar that he stared, perplexed. Unthank was the only city he remembered, but he had always wanted a brighter place: why should he like the look of it now? The yattering noise from the intersection was very audible. So were the kitchen sounds which came from a door in a gable behind him. He knocked on this, and a moment later Frankie opened it. He was so delighted that he seized her waist and kissed her surprised mouth. She pushed him away after a while, laughing and saying, "Passionate, eh?"

"How is she?"

"She was sleeping when I left, but I sent for the nurse to be on the safe side."

"Thanks, Frankie, you're a good girl."

He walked beside the arches along the attic and softly entered the bright little cubicle. Rima smiled at him softly from her pillow. He said "Hullo" and squatted on a cushion by the bed. She whispered, "The contractions have begun."

"Good. A nurse is coming."

He held her hand under the bedclothes. A stout lady came busily in and frowned at him, then bent over Rima with a very wide smile.

"So you're going to have a wee baby!" she said in the loud slow voice some people use when speaking to idiots. "A wee baby just like your *mummy* had when *you* were born! Isn't that nice?"

"I'm not going to speak to her," said Rima to Lanark, then drew a sharp breath and seemed to concentrate on something.

"That's right!" said the nurse consolingly. "It doesn't *really* hurt now, does it?"

"Tell her my back's sore!" said Rima sharply.

"Her back's sore," said Lanark.

"And do you really want your husband to stay here? Some men find it very, very difficult to take."

"Tell her to shut up!" said Rima and a moment later added bitterly, "Tell her I've wet the bed."

"It isn't what you think," said the nurse. "It's perfectly natural." She turned the mattress and changed the sheets while Rima sat on a cushion wrapped in a blanket. Rima said, "I'm having a girl."

"Oh," said Lanark.

"I don't want a boy."

"Then I do."

"Why?"

"So that one of us will welcome it, whoever comes."

"You must always put me in the wrong, mustn't you?"

"Sorry."

She returned to bed, scowled, ground her teeth and worked hard for a while, holding his hand tight; then she relaxed and cried desperately, "Tell her to stop this pain in my back!"

"Things must get worse before they get better," said the nurse soothingly. She was drinking tea from a thermos flask.

"Ha!" snarled Rima. She thrust Lanark's hand away, clenched her fists outside the covers and started working again, sweating hard. For a long time spells of fretful repose were followed by spells of silent, urgent, determined labour.

At last she raised her knees high, spread them wide and said sharply, "What's happening?"

The nurse folded back the covers. Lanark leaned against the wall by the bed foot and stared into the red widening gash between Rima's thighs. She gasped and cried, "My back! My back! What's happening?"

"He's coming. I can see the face," said Lanark, for in the depth of the gash he seemed to see a squeezed-thin face emerging, six inches high and less than half an inch wide, the nose thin as a string and ending in an absurd little flap, the eyes on each side sunk in vertical creases. The mouth was a tight-pursed hole and the nurse kept sticking her finger in it, presumably to help it breathe. Then the mouth opened into an oval with something flat inside, and the oval grew and filled the whole gash, and the flatness was a dome coming out, and the dome was a head gripped by the nurse's hand. Then the universe seemed to go slow and silent. In slow silence a small, pale-lavender, enraged little person was lifted up, dragging after him a meaty cable. He had a penis, and his elbows and knees were bent, and his fists and eyes clenched tight, and his aghast mouth was yelling a soundless scream of fury. Rima, whose face seemed to have been scrubbed by a storm, turned on him a slow smile of loving recognition. The small person flushed red, opened an eye, then another, and after some hiccups his scream wavered out into angry sound. The universe returned to the usual speed. The nurse gave the baby to Rima and told Lanark sternly, "Go and get two soup plates from the kitchen."

"Why?"

"Do what you're told."

He ran along by the arches hearing sounds of a service from the cathedral floor. A remote ministerial voice was chanting, "My buird thou hast hanselled in face o' my faes; thou drookest my heid wi' ile, my bicker is fou an' skailin. . . ." Jack sat in the kitchen listening to Ritchie-Smollet, who was leaning on a table. "I would have advised more caution, but we've burned our boats and must abide the issue. Ah, Lanark! How are things with you?"

"Fine. Can I have two soup plates, please?"

"Congratulations! Boy or girl? How's the mother?" asked Ritchie-Smollet, handing over plates from a pile.

"Thank you. A boy. She seems all right."

"One has become two: the first and best miracle of all, eh? I hope you'll allow me the privilege of christening the little chap."

"I'll mention it to his mother but she isn't religious," said Lanark going to the door.

"Are you sure of that? Never mind. Come back when you can and we'll drink their health. I believe we've some cooking sherry in the larder."

The cubicle seemed full of women. Rima suckled the baby, Frankie poured water from a kettle into a basin, the nurse seized the plates and said, "That's fine, you can go now."
"But—"
"We can hardly move as it is, there's no room for you."
He watched his son enviously for a moment then went slowly away, but not toward the kitchen, for he didn't want company. He suddenly wanted to use himself vigorously, to run fast or climb high. He found a spiral stair near the organ loft and climbed quickly to another open walkway under the stars. It led through a chilling wind to another little door. He opened this and entered a large, dim, square, dusty room lit by hurricane lamps on the floor. A steep iron ladder slanted upward near the centre, and six Lugworm Casanovas lay smoking in sleeping bags along a wall. One of them said, "Shut it, man, nobody's too hot in here."
Lanark said, "Sorry," closed the door and crossed to the ladder. Its rungs were cold and gritty with rust, it shuddered at each step. When the upper shadows hid him from the eyes below he climbed more slowly, not lifting a foot until both hands gripped a rung, not raising a hand till both feet were firmly placed. He came to a floor of narrow planks set an inch apart. Light shining up between them showed the foot of a steeper ladder. He climbed this more slowly than ever. In the wall before, to each side, and behind him, were huge windows barred by horizontal stone slats. He looked down through them onto the black cathedral roof edged with city lights. He stood on thin rungs high up in an old stone cage and listened to the faintly whistling breeze. With each extra step he tried to remember that the ladder was solid, and braced by an occasional rod against a wall that had stood for many centuries, and would probably not collapse suddenly without warning. At last he reached, not a floor, but a narrow metal bridge. Black machinery overhung it. He made out timber beams, a big wheel and a bell whose rim, when he stepped underneath, came down to his shoulders. He raised a hand to the massive clapper and carefully pushed it forward, meaning gently to touch the side, but the weight increased with the angle, he had to use unexpected force and the shock of contact bathed him in a sudden sonorous *Dong*. Half deafened, half intoxicated by the sound,

he laughed aloud, let the clapper fall back and shoved it at the rim with both hands, ducked as it swung back again and then reached up again to hurl it forward. The detonation of the strokes grew inaudible. He felt only a great droning reverberating the bell, the bridge, his bones, the tower, the air. His arms were tired. He ducked out from under the bell and gripped a handrail for support, though at first the sound in it hurt his palms like an electric current.

The droning faded. He seemed to hear protesting cries from below and, ashamed of the noise he had made, climbed a ladder away from them. He came to a higher floor of wooden slats where the blackness was total, except for a chink of light below a door. He groped toward it, slid the bolt and went out onto a windy platform at the foot of the floodlit steeple. The racket from the intersection was audible again, sometimes louder, sometimes fainter. He wondered if this was caused by the blustering wind and stepped to the parapet facing the Necropolis, for the din seemed to come from behind it. The highest monuments were silhouetted against a pulsing glow in the sky. Wedges of shadow moved over this like the arms of a windmill. The yattering noise sank to a dull stutter, hesitated, coughed and stopped. The majestic beams of shadow swept the sky in silence for a while, then suddenly widened as the glow faded. The main light now was cast by the great lamp standards on the motorway. A remote mechanical braying began and came swiftly nearer. A line of red fire engines with braying sirens appeared round a curving bridge from the intersection and sped down the gorge between Necropolis and cathedral. The air began filling with traffic sounds. Lanark walked round the platform to the far side of the tower and looked down onto the square. A couple of trucks rumbled across it pulling trailers with metal wreckage on them; then a trickle of cars began flowing in the opposite direction. A mobile crane drove through a gateway to the cathedral grounds, crossed the stones of the old graveyard and parked against a wall. Lanark suddenly felt his chilled ears, hands and body and returned to the door in the spire.

Coming down on the ladders he found the light from below much stronger than before. The room where the Lugworms had lain was lit by bulbs hung from improvised brackets. Two electricians were working near the door and one of them said, "A bloke was looking for you, Jimmy."

"Who was he?"

"A young bloke. Long hair."

"What did he want?"

"He didnae say."

Near the cubicle he heard a strange, steady little song. Sludden lay on the bed singing "Dadadada" and dandling a robust little boy in a blue woollen suit. Rima, in a blouse and skirt, sat knitting beside them. The sight filled Lanark with a large cold rage. Rima gave him an unfriendly glance and Sludden said brightly, "The wanderer returns!"

Lanark went to the tiny sink, washed his hands, then turned to Sludden and said, "Give him to me."

He took the child, who started wailing. "Oh, put him down!" said Rima impatiently. "He needs a rest and so do I."

Lanark sat on the bed foot and sang quietly, "Dadadada." The boy stopped complaining and settled in his arms. The small compact body was warm and comforting and gave such a pleasant feeling of peace that Lanark wondered uneasily if this was a right thing for a father to feel. He laid the boy in a pram by the bed and tucked a soft blanket round him.

Sludden stood up and stretched his arms, saying, "Great! That's really great. I came here for several reasons, of course, but one is to congratulate you on your performance. Don't sneer at him, Rima, he's a good committee man when he accepts discipline. He jostled Gow, and that allowed us to act. The committee is in permanent session now. I don't mean we're all in the chapterhouse all the time, but some of us are in the chapterhouse all the time."

Lanark said, "Listen, Sludden, I want the company of my wife and child. Do you understand me?"

"Of course!" said Sludden cheerily. "I'm just leaving. I'll come back for you all later."

"What do you mean?"

"Sludden has offered us room in his house," said Rima.

"We're not taking it."

"I don't want to force anything on you," said Sludden. "But this seems a strange place to bring up a child."

"Unthank is dead and done for, don't you realize that?" cried Lanark. "The boy and Rima and I are leaving for a much brighter city. Wilkins promised us."

"Don't trust your council friends too far," said Sludden gravely. "We've cleared the motorway, the food trucks are rolling in again. And even if Wilkins did tell the truth, you're forgetting

differences in timescale. The decimal calendar hasn't been introduced here and what the council calls days can be months—
years, where we're concerned. And remember, Alexander was
born here. You have a council passport. He hasn't."
"Who is Alexander?"
Sludden pointed to the pram. Rima said, "Ritchie-Smollet chris-
tened him that."
Lanark jumped up shouting, *"Christened?"*
Alexander started crying. "Shushush," whispered Rima, reach-
ing for the pram handle and gently rocking it. "Shushushush."
"Why Alexander?" whispered Lanark furiously. "Why couldn't
you wait for me? Why the bloody hurry?"
"We waited as long as we could—why didn't you come when
we called?"
"You never called me!"
"We did. Jack went to the tower when you started your row
and shouted up the ladder, but you wouldn't come down."
"I didn't know that was Jack shouting," said Lanark, confused.
"Were you drunk?" asked Rima.
"Of course not. You've never seen me drunk."
"Perhaps, but you often act that way. And Ritchie-Smollet says
a bottle of cooking sherry has vanished from the kitchen."
"I'm leaving," said Sludden with a chuckle. "Outsiders should
never mix in a lovers' quarrel. I'll see you later."
"Thank you," said Lanark. "We'll manage by ourselves."
Sludden shrugged and left. Alexander gradually fell asleep.

Rima sat with tight-shut lips, knitting hard. Lanark lay on
the bed with hands behind his head and said gloomily, "I didn't
want to leave you. And I didn't think I was long."
"You were away for hours—ages, it seemed to me. You've
no sense of time. None at all."
"Alexander is quite a good name. We can shorten it to Alex.
Or Sandy."
"He's called *Alexander.*"
"What are you knitting?"
"Clothes. Children need clothes, hadn't you noticed? We can't
always live on Ritchie-Smollet's charity."
"If Sludden is right about calendars," Lanark mused, "we'll
be a long time in this place. I'll have to look for work."
"So you're going to leave me alone again. I see. Why did
you ring that bell? Are you sure you weren't drunk?"
"I rang it because I was happy then. Why are you attacking
me?"

"To defend myself."

"I'm sorry I shouted at you, Rima. I was surprised and angry. I'm very glad to be back with you."

"Yes, it's easy for you to live in a box, you can run off to your towers and committee meetings whenever you like. When will I get some freedom?"

"Whenever you need it."

"And you'll stay here and look after Alex?"

"Of course. That's only fair."

Rima sighed and then smiled and rolled up her knitting. She came to the bed, kissed him quickly on the brow, then went to the chest of drawers and peered at her face in a mirror.

Lanark said, "Are you leaving already?"

"Yes, Lanark. I really do need a change."

She made up her mouth with lipstick. Lanark said, "Who gave you that?"

"Frankie. We're going dancing. We're going to get ourselves picked up by a couple of young young young boys. You don't mind, do you?"

"Not if you only dance with them."

"Oh, but we'll flirt with them too. We'll madden them with desire. Middle-aged women need to madden somebody some times."

"You aren't middle-aged."

"I'm no chicken, anyway. When Alex wakens you can change his nappy—there's a clean one in the top drawer. Put the dirty one in the plastic bag under the bed. If he cries you must heat some milk in the kitchen—not too hot, mind. Test it with your finger."

"Aren't you breastfeeding him?"

"Yes, but he has to learn to drink like an ordinary human being. But I'll probably be back before he wakens. How do I look?"

She posed before him, hands on hips. He said, "Very young. Very beautiful."

She kissed him warmly and left. He lay back on the bed, missing her, and fell asleep.

He was wakened by Alexander crying so he changed his nappy and carried him to the kitchen. Jack and Frankie were eating a meal at a table there. Frankie said, "Hullo, passionate man. How's Rima?"

He stared at her, confused, and blushed hotly. He muttered, "Gone for a walk. The boy needs milk."

"I'll make him a bottle."

Lanark strayed round the kitchen murmuring nonsense to Alexander, for there was a strange appalling pain in his chest and he didn't want to talk to adults. Frankie handed him a warm bottle with teat folded in a white napkin. He muttered some thanks and went back to the cubicle. He sat on the bed and held the teat to Alexander's mouth but Alexander twisted aside, screaming, "NonononoMumumumum!"

"She'll be back soon, Sandy."

"NononononononononoMumumumumumumumumum!"
Alexander kept screaming and Lanark walked the floor with him. He felt he was carrying a dwarf who kept hitting him on the head with a stick, a dwarf he could neither disarm nor put down. People in neighbouring cubicles began banging their walls, then a man came in and said, "There are folk trying to sleep in this building, Jimmy."

"I can't help that, and I'm not called Jimmy."

The man was tall and bald with white stubble on his cheeks, a single black tooth in his upper jaw, and wore a dirty grey raincoat. He stared at Lanark for a while then pulled a brown bottle from his pocket and said, "Milk's no use. Give him a slug of this—it's a great quietener."

"No."

"Then take a slug yourself."

"No."

The man sighed, squatted on a stool and said, "Tell me your woes."

"I have no woes!" yelled Lanark who was too plagued to think. Alexander was screaming "Mumumumumumumumumum!"

"If it's woman trouble," said the man, "I can advise you because I was married once. I had a wife who did terrible things, things I cannae mention in the presence of a wean. You see, women are different from us. They're seventy-five percent water. You can read that in Pavlov."

Alexander fastened his gums on the teat and started sucking. Lanark sighed with relief. After a moment he said, "Men are mostly water too."

"Yes, but only seventy percent. The extra five percent makes the difference. Women have notions and feelings like us but they've got tides too, tides that keep floating the bits of a human being together inside them and washing it apart again. They're governed by lunar gravity; you can read that in Newton. How can they follow ordinary notions of decency when they're driven by the moon?"

Lanark laid Alexander in the pram with the bottle beside him and gently rocked the handle.

The man said, "I was ignorant when I was married. I hadnae read Newton, I hadnae read Pavlov, so I kicked the bitch out—pardon the language, I am referring to my wife. I wish now that I'd cut my throat instead. Do me a favour, pal. Give yourself a holiday. Have a drink."

Lanark glanced at the brown bottle held toward him, then took it and swigged. The taste was horrible. He passed it back, trying to say thank you, but there were tears in his eyes and he could only gulp and pull faces. A warm stupidity began to spread softly through him. He heard the man say, "You have to like women but not care for them: not care what they do, I mean. Nobody can help what they do. We do as things do with us."

"What is for us," said Lanark, with a feeling of profound understanding, "will not go past us."

"A hundred years from now," said the man, "it'll all be the same."

Lanark heard Alexander asking sadly, "When will she come?"

"Soon, son. Very soon."

"When is soon?"

"Near to now but not now."

"I need her now."

"Then you need her badly. You must try to need her properly."

"What is proply?"

"Silently. Silence is always proper. When I understand this better I'll stop talking. You won't be able to hear me for miles. I will radiate silence like a dark star shining in the gaps between syllables and conversation."

"You're ignoring politics," said the man aggressively. "Politics depend on noise. All parties subscribe to *that* opinion, if to no other."

Alexander screamed, "They're biting me!"

"Who's biting you?" said Lanark leaning unsteadily over the pram.

"My teeth."

Lanark put a finger in the small mouth and felt a tiny bone edge coming through the gum. He said uneasily, "We age quickly in this world."

"You must remember one important thing," said the man, "You've emptied the bottle. I'm not complaining. I know where to get another, but it costs a coupla dollars. A dollar a skull. Right?"

"I'm sorry. I've no money."

"What's happening here?" asked Rima, coming angrily in.
"Sandy is teething," said Lanark.
"I'm just leaving, missus," said the man, and left.

Rima changed Alexander's nappy, saying grimly, "I can't trust you to do a thing."
"But I've fed him. I've cared for him."
"Huh!"
Lanark lay on the bed watching her. He was sober now and some of the ache had returned to his chest, but he was also thankful and relieved. After a while he said, "Did you enjoy the dancing?"
"Dancing?"
"You said you were going dancing with Frankie."
"Did I? Maybe I did. Anyway I missed Frankie and went house-hunting with what's-his-name. The fat soldier. McPake."
"McPake?"
"He used to hang around the old Elite with us. The Elite has vanished under a motorway now. Nothing there but a great concrete trench. They really are making a mess of this place."
"Did you find any houses?"
"Hundreds of them, all furnished and all beautiful. But we've no money so I was wasting my time. Is that what you're going to say?"
"Of course not!"
She had settled Alexander in the pram and was sitting despondently with drooping head and arms folded under breasts. He was pricked by tenderness and desire and went to her with arms outstretched, whispering, "Oh, Rima dear, let's love each other a little. . . ."
She smiled, jumped up and danced toward him with hands outstretched and nipping. "Oh, Rima dear!" she moaned through pursed-out lips. "Oh, lovey-dovey earie-dearie Rima, let's lovey-dovey an itsy-bitsy little. . . ."
Her nips were painful and he fended them off, laughing until they both fell side by side and breathless on the bed. A moment later he asked sadly, "Do I really seem like that?"
"I'm afraid you do. You're too nervous and pathetic."
She sighed, then unfastened her blouse, saying, "However, since you want it, let's love each other a little."
He stared, astonished, and said, "I can't make love when you've made me feel small and absurd."
"I've made you fell absurd, have I? I'm glad. I'm delighted. You make me feel small all the time. You've never paid

attention to my feelings, never once. You dragged us here from a perfectly comfortable place because you disliked the food, and what good did it do? We still eat the same food. You laughed when I gave you a son and you can't even give him a home. You use use use me all the time, and you're so smugly sure you're right all the time. You're heavy and dismal and humourless, yet you want me to pet you and make you feel big and important. I'm sorry, I can't do it. I'm too tired." She went to the seat by the pram and resumed knitting.

Lanark sat on the bed with his face in his hands. He said, "This is Hell."
"Yes. I know."
"I wish you could love me."
"You take me for granted, so I can't. You don't know how to make me love you. Some men can do it."
He looked up and said, "Which men?"
She continued to knit. He stood up and cried, *"Which men?"*
"I might tell you if you wouldn't get hysterical."
Alexander sat up and asked in an interested voice, "Is Dad going to get hysterical?"
Lanark shook his head dumbly then whispered, "I must get out of here."
"Yes, I think you should," said Rima. "Look for a job. You need one."
He went to the entrance and turned, hoping for a look of friendship or recognition, but her face was so full of stony pain that he could only shake his head.
"Goodbye Dad," said Alexander casually. Lanark waved to him, hesitated, then left.

CHAPTER 38.
Greater Unthank

The shadowy nave seemed vast and empty till he neared the door and saw Jack sitting on the font. Lanark meant to pass him with a slight nod but Jack was watching with such a frank stare that he stopped and said tensely, "Could you please direct me to a labour exchange?"

"They're not called labour exchanges now, they're called job centres," said Jack, springing down. "I'll take you to one."

"Can Ritchie-Smollet spare you?"

"Maybe not, but I can spare him. I change bosses when I like."

Jack led him through the cathedral grounds to a bus stop on the edge of the square. Lanark said, "I can't afford a bus fare."

"Don't worry, I've got cash. What do you want at a job centre?"

"An unskilled job doing something useful exactly the way I'm told."

"Not many jobs like that in Unthank nowadays. Except in cleansing, perhaps. And cleansing workers have to be young and healthy."

"How old do you think I am?"

"Past the halfway mark, at least."

Lanark looked down at the prominent veins on the back of his hands and muttered after a while, "No dragonhide, anyway."

"What did you say?"

"I may not be young but I don't have dragonhide."

"Of course you don't. We aren't living in the dark ages."

Lanark felt like the victim of a sudden horrible accident. He thought, 'Over halfway through life and what have I achieved? What have I made? Only a son, and he was mostly his mother's work. Who have I ever helped? Nobody but Rima, and I've only helped her out of messes she'd have missed if she had been with someone else. All I have is a wife and child. I must make them a home, a secure comfortable home.'

As if answering the thought a bus crossed a corner of the square with a painting on the side of a mother and child. Printed over it were the words **A HOME IS MONEY. MONEY IS TIME. BUY TIME FOR YOUR FAMILY FROM THE QUANTUM CHRONOLOGICAL. (THEY'LL LOVE YOU FOR IT.)**

"I need a lot of money," said Lanark. "If I can't get work I'll have to beg from the security people."

"The name's changed," said Jack. "They're called social stability now. And they don't give money, they give three-in-one."

"What's that?"

"A special kind of bread. It nourishes and tranquillizes and stops your feeling cold, which is useful if you're homeless. But I don't think you should eat any."

"Why?"

"A little does no harm, but after a while it damages the intelligence. Of course the unemployment problem would be a catastrophe without it. Here comes our bus."

"This *is* Hell," said Lanark.

"There are worse hells," said Jack.

The bus was painted to look like a block of Enigma de Filets Congelés. On the side it said **NOW EVERYONE CAN TASTE THE RICH HUMAN GOODNESS IN FROZEN SECRETS, THE FOOD OF PRESIDENTS.**

Jack led Lanark to a seat on the top deck and brought out a cigarette packet labelled POISON. He said, "Like one?"

"No thanks," said Lanark and stared as Jack lit a white cylinder with DON'T SMOKE THIS printed along it.

"Yes, they're dangerous," said Jack, inhaling. "That's why the council insisted on the warning."

"Why doesn't it stop them being made?"

"Half the population is hooked on them," said Jack. "And the council gets half the money spent on them. They're an Algolagnics product. There are less dangerous drugs, of course, but they wouldn't be so profitable if they were legalized."

A bus going the other way carried a sentence past the window: **QUICK MONEY IS TIME IN YOUR POCKET—BUY**

MONEY FASTER FROM THE QUANTUM EXPONENTIAL.

Jack said, "You were being sarcastic—weren't you?—when you asked if Ritchie-Smollet could spare me?"

"I'm sorry."

"I don't mind. Yes, he depends on me, does old Smollet. So does Sludden. I choose my bosses carefully. *That* bloke was my boss once."

Jack pointed through the window at a tattered poster covering the end of a derelict tenement. It showed a friendly-looking man behind a desk with telephones on it. The words below said **ARE YOU LOOKING FOR A FACTORY SITE, A FACTORY OR A LABOUR FORCE? PHONE 777-7777 AND SPEAK TO TOM TALLENTYRE, CHAIRMAN OF THE WORK FOR UNTHANK BOARD.**

"Tallentyre was a very big man after they scrapped the Q39 project," said Jack. "In fact he was provost for a while. But Sludden did for him in the end. Sludden pointed out that the posters were put up in parts of Unthank where the unemployed lived, and folk with power to start new factories didn't live in Unthank anyway. So the action shifted to Sludden and Smollet, and so did I. I enjoy being where the action is. That's why I'm with you, just now."

"Why are you with me?"

"You aren't what you pretend, are you? I agree with Gow. You're some sort of agent or investigator. Why ask about cleansing and social stability when you work for Ozenfant and carry a council passport?"

"I don't work for Ozenfant. And what use is a council passport to me?"

"It could get you a very well-paid job."

"I want that!" said Lanark excitedly. "How do I get one? I want that!"

"Ask the employment centre to put you on the professional register," said Jack sulkily. He seemed disappointed.

Lanark looked out of the window, feeling more hopeful. The bus was passing busy new shops whose fronts spread along whole blocks and showed brightly packaged food and drugs and records and clothes. He noticed many restaurants with oriental names and many kinds of gambling shops. In some he glimpsed people sitting with bags and baskets at counters, apparently gambling for food. The gaps left by demolished buildings were crammed with parked cars and surrounded by

fences with wild threats scrawled on them in bright paint.
CRAZY MAC KILLS, they said and **MAD TOAD RULES,**
and **THE WEE MALCIES ARE COMING,** but they didn't
distract from the larger message of the posters. These showed
pictures of family life, sex, food and money, and their words
were more puzzling.
**BOOST YOUR THERMS WITH NULLITY GREEN—BAG
HER IN YOUR BLOCKAL BLOOPER-MARKET.
GRIND YOUR SPECTACLES WITH METAL TEA, THE
SEX CHAMP ON THE CHILIASM.
THE SWEETEST DREAMERS INHALE BLUE FUME,
THE POISON WITH THE WARNING.
WISE BUYERS ARE THE BEST SEXERS—BUY HER A
LONG LIFE, AN EASY DEATH FROM QUANTUM
PROVIDENTIAL. (SHE'LL LOVE YOU FOR IT.)**
Lanark said, "What a lot of instructions."
"Don't you like advertisements?"
"No."
"The city would look pretty dead without them—they add to
the action. Read that."
Jack pointed to a small poster on the bus window which said:

**ADVERTISING OVERSTIMULATES,
MISINFORMS,
CORRUPTS.**
If *you* feel this, send your name and address
to the Council Advertising Commission and
receive your free booklet explaining why we
can't do without it.

They got off the bus in a large square Lanark knew well,
though it was brighter and busier than he remembered. He
gazed at the statues on their massive Victorian pedestals and
reflected that he had seen them before he saw Rima. The square
was still enclosed by ornate stone buildings except where he
and Jack stood before a glass wall of shining doors. Above
this great horizontal strips of concrete and glass alternated to
a height of twenty or thirty floors. Jack said, "The job centre."
"It's big."
"All the central job centres are housed here, and it's the central
centre of stability and surroundings too. I'll leave you now,
right?"
Lanark felt he was reliving something which had happened
once before, perhaps with Gloopy. He said awkwardly, "I'm

sorry I'm not what you thought—not a man of action, I mean.''
Jack shrugged and said, "Not your fault. I'll give you a bit
of advice—"
He was interrupted by sudden siren blasts and a rattling like
thin thunder. The traffic halted round the square. Pedestrians
stood staring as an open truck sped past full of khaki-clad men
wearing black berets and holding guns. It had caterpillar treads
of a sort Lanark had seen rolling slowly over rough ground
in films, but on the smooth road it raced so swiftly that it
was past as soon as recognized.
"The army!" cried Jack with a smile of pure appetite. "Now
we'll see some action. Hoi! Hoi! Hoi!"
He ran along the pavement shouting and waving to a taxi in
the resuming traffic. It came to the kerb and he leaped in.
Lanark watched it turn a corner, then stood awhile feeling sickened and uneasy. He was thinking about Alex, Rima and the
soldiers. He had never seen armed soldiers in a street before.
At last he turned and entered the building.

To a uniformed man in the entrance hall he said, "I'm
looking for work."
"Where do you live?"
"The cathedral."
"The cathedral's in the fifth district. Take lift eleven to floor
twenty."
The lift was like a metal wardrobe and packed with poorly
dressed people. When Lanark got out he had another feeling
of entering the past. He saw a dingy expanse tiled with grey
rubber and covered by men of all ages crowded together on
benches. A counter divided into cubicles by partitions ran along
one wall, and the cubicle facing the lift contained a chair and
a sign saying INQUIRIES. As Lanark walked toward this he felt
the air of the place resisting him like transparent jelly. The
men on the benches had a statuesque, entranced look as though
congealed there. All movement was exhausting—it would have
been equally tiring to go back. He reached the chair, slumped
onto it and sat, upright but dozing, until someone seemed to
be shouting at him. He opened his eyes and said thickly, "I
. . . am not . . . an animal."
An old clerk with bristling eyebrows behind the counter said,
"Then you ought to be on the professional register."
"Eh? . . . How?"
"Go down to the second floor."

Lanark got back to the lift and only wakened properly inside it. He wondered if all offices in that building had the same deadening influence.

But the second floor was different. It was covered by a soft green carpet. Low easy chairs clustered round glass tables with magazines on them, but nobody was waiting. There were no counters. Men and women too elegant to be thought of as clerks chatted to clients across widely spaced desks divided from each other by stands of potted plants. A girl receptionist showed him to the desk of a slightly older woman. She pushed a packet labelled BLUE FUME toward him, saying, "Please sit down. Do you inhale this particular poison?"
"No thank you."
"How very wise. Tell me about yourself."
He talked for a while. She opened her eyes wide and said, "You've actually worked with Ozenfant? How exciting! Tell me, what kind of man is he? In private life, I mean."
"He overeats and he's a bad musician."
The woman chuckled as if he had said something clever and shocking, then said, "I'm going to leave you for a moment. I've just had rather a good idea."
She came back saying, "We're in luck—Mr. Gilchrist can see you right away."
As they walked between the other desks she murmured, "Strictly between ourselves, I think Mr. Gilchrist is very keen to meet you. So is Mr. Pettigrew, though he doesn't show it, of course. You'll enjoy Mr. Pettigrew, he's a *tremendous* cynic."
She led him to a door but didn't follow him through.

Lanark entered an office with two desks and a secretary typing at a table in the corner. A tall bald man sat telephoning on the edge of the nearest desk. He smiled at Lanark and pointed to an easy chair, saying, "He must be suffering from *folie de grandeur.* Provosts are buffers between us and the voters; they aren't supposed to *do* things. But nobody wants a riot, of course."
At the desk behind him a stout man leaned back smoking a pipe. Lanark sat looking through the window at the floodlit roof of a building across the square. A dome at one end had a glittering wind-vane shaped like a galleon. The tall man put the receiver down, saying, "That's that. My name is Gilchrist— I'm very pleased to meet you."

They shook hands and Lanark saw the council mark on Gilchrist's brow. They sat down in chairs beside a coffee table and Gilchrist said, "We want coffee, I think. Black or white, Lanark? See to that, Miss Maheen. I hear you are looking for professional employment, Lanark."
"Yes."
"But you've no definite idea of the kind of work you want."
"Correct. I'm more concerned about the salary."
"Would you like to work here?"
Lanark looked round the room. The secretary was attending to an electric percolator on top of a filing cabinet. The man behind the other desk had a large, dolorous, clownish face and winked at Lanark with no change of expression. Lanark said, "I'm very willing to consider it."
"Good. You mentioned salary. Unluckily salaries are a vexed question with us. It's impossible to pay a monthly or yearly sum when we can't even measure the minutes and hours. Until the council sends us the decimal clocks it's been promising for so long Unthank is virtually part of the intercalendrical zone. At present the city is kept going by force of habit. Not by rules, not by plans, but by habit. Nobody can rule with an elastic tape measure, can they?"
Lanark shook his head impatiently and said, "I've a family to feed. What can you offer me?"
"Credit. Members of our staff receive a Quantum credit card. That's much more useful than money."
"Will it let me rent a comfortable home for three people?"
"Easily. You could even buy a home. The energy to pay for it would be deducted from your future."
"Then I'll be glad to work here."
"I should explain the range of our activities."
"No need. I'll do whatever I'm told."
Gilchrist smiled and shook his head, saying "Social ignorance is only a virtue in the manufacturing classes. We professionals must understand the organism as a whole. That is our burden and our pride. It justifies our bigger incomes."
"Blethers!" said the stout man at the other desk. "Who in this building understands the organism as a whole? You and me and an old woman upstairs, perhaps, but the rest have forgotten. They were told, but they've forgotten."
"Pettigrew is a cynic," said Gilchrist, laughing.
"A *lovable* cynic," muttered Pettigrew. "Remember that. Pettigrew is everybody's lovable cynic."

The secretary laid a tray of coffee things on the table. Gilchrist carried his cup to the window, sat on the ledge and said oracularly, "Employment. Stability. Surroundings. Three offices, yet properly understood they are the same. Employment ensures stability. Stability lets us reshape our surroundings. The improved surroundings become a new condition of employment. The snake eats its tail. Nothing has precedence. This great building—this centre of all centres, this tower of welfare—exists to maintain full employment, reasonable stability and decent surroundings."

"Animals," said Pettigrew. "We deal with animals here. The scruff. The scum. The lowest of the low."

"Pettigrew is referring to the fact that there are not enough jobs and houses for everyone. Naturally—as in all freely competing societies—the unemployed and homeless tend to be less clever, or less healthy, or less energetic than the rest of us."

"They're a horde of stupid, dirty layabouts," said Pettigrew. "I know them, I grew up among them. You middle-class liberals like to pet them, but I wouldn't even let them breed. What we need is an X-ray device under the turnstiles at the football stadiums. Each man going through gets a blast of 900 roentgens right on the testicles. It would be perfectly painless. They wouldn't know what had happened till they got a wee printed card along with their entrance ticket. 'Dear Sir,' it would say. 'You may now ride your wife in perfect safety.'"

Gilchrist laughed until his coffee spilled into the saucer. "Pettigrew, you're incorrigible!" he said. "You talk as if a man's misery was all his own fault. You must admit that poverty, insanity and crime have multiplied since our major industry shut down. That isn't coincidence."

"Blame the unions!" said Pettigrew. "Prosperity is made by the bosses struggling with each other for more wealth. If they have to struggle with their workers too, then everybody loses. No wonder the big groups are shifting their factories to the coolie continents. I'm only thankful that the folk who lose most in the end are the envious sods who own the least. Greed isn't a pretty thing but envy is far, far worse."

"You're talking politics. It's time you shut up for a while," said Gilchrist amicably. He put down his cup on the window ledge, sat beside Lanark and said quietly, "Don't let his rough tongue upset you. Pettigrew is something of a saint. He's helped more widows and orphans than we've had good breakfasts."

"There's no need for excuses," said Lanark. "I realize now that nobody does well in this world if they don't belong to a big strong group. Your group handles the people who don't have one. I want to be with you, not under you, so tell me what to do."

"You're very abrupt," said Gilchrist. "Please remember we are here to help the unfortunate, and we *do* help them, as far as we can. Our problem is lack of funds. The recent Greater Unthank reorganization has given us a much larger staff to deal with the increasing number of unfortunates, so we have thousands of experts—planners, architects, engineers, artists, renovators, conservers, blood doctors, bowel doctors, brain doctors—all sitting on their bottoms praying for funds to start working with."

"So what can *I* do?"

"You can start as a grade D inquiry clerk. You will sit behind a desk hearing people complain. You must note their names and addresses and tell them they'll hear from us through the post."

"That's easy."

"It's the hardest job we have. You must give an appearance of listening closely. You must prod them with questions to keep the words flowing if they look like drying up. You must keep each one talking till they're exhausted—longer, if possible."

"And I write a report on what they tell me?"

"No. Just note their name and address and tell them they'll hear from us through the post."

"Why?"

"I was afraid you would ask that," said Gilchrist, sighing slightly. "As I already indicated, there are many whom we cannot help through lack of funds. A lot of these are still strong and vigorous, and it is a dangerous thing to suddenly deprive a man of hope—he can turn violent. It is important to kill hope *slowly,* so that the loser has time to adjust unconsciously to the loss. We try to keep hope alive till it has burned out the vitality feeding it. Only then is the man allowed to face the truth."

"So a grade D inquiry clerk does nothing but postpone."

"Yes."

Lanark said loudly, "I don't want—" then hesitated. He thought of the credit card, and a home with three or four rooms, perhaps in walking distance of this great building. Perhaps he would be able to go home for lunch and eat it with Sandy and Rima.

He said feebly, "I don't *want* this job."

"Nobody wants it. As I said, it's the hardest job we have. But will you take it?"

After a moment Lanark said, "Yes."

"Excellent. Miss Maheen, come over here. I want you to smile at our new colleague. He's called Lanark."

The secretary sat down facing Lanark and looked into his eyes. She had a smooth, vacant, fashionably pretty face and her hair was so golden and perfectly brushed that it looked like a nylon wig. For a split second her mouth widened in a smile, and Lanark was disconcerted by a click inside her head. Gilchrist said, "Show her your profile." Lanark stared at him and heard another click. Miss Maheen slid two fingers inside a pocket of her crisp white blouse above her left breast and drew out a plastic strip. She handed it to Lanark. There were two clear little pictures of him at one end, a disconcerted full face and a perplexed profile. The rest was covered by fine blue parallel lines with LANARK printed on top and a long number with about twelve digits.

"She's a reliable piece," said Gilchrist, patting Miss Maheen's bottom as she returned to her table. "She issues credit cards, makes coffee, types, looks pretty and her hobby is oriental martial arts. She's a Quantum-Cortexin product."

Lanark said bitterly, "Can't Quantum-Cortexin make something to work as a grade D inquiry clerk?"

"Oh, yes, they can. They did. We tried it out at a stability sub-centre and it provoked a riot. The clients found its responses too mechanical. Most people have a quite irrational faith in human beings."

"Roll on, Provan," said Pettigrew.

"Amen, Pettigrew. Roll on, Provan," said Gilchrist.

"What do you mean?" said Lanark.

"*Roll on* is a colloquialism whereby an anticipated event is conjured to occur more quickly. We're looking forward to our transfer to Provan. You know about that, of course?"

"I was told I could go there because I'd a council passport."

"Yes indeed. We'll manage things much better from Provan. I'm afraid this big expensive building has been a great big expensive mistake. Even the air conditioning doesn't work very well. But let's go to the twentieth floor."

They went through the desks of the outer office to a large and quiet lift. It brought them to a long narrow office containing about thirty desks. Half were occupied by people typing or

phoning; many were empty, and the rest surrounded by talkative groups. Gilchrist led Lanark to one of these and said,
"Here is our new inquiry clerk."
"Thank God!" said a man who was carefully folding a paper
form into a dart. "I've just faced six of the animals, six in a
row. I'm not going out there again for a long, long time."
He launched the dart which drifted sweetly down the length
of the office. There was scattered applause.
"Good luck!" said Gilchrist, shaking Lanark's hand. "I promise
you'll be promoted out of here as soon as we find a replacement
for you. Pettigrew and I drink in the Vascular Cavity. It's a
vulgar pub but handy for the office and one always gets a good
eyeful." (He winked.) "So if you call there later we'll have a
jar together."
He went out quickly. The dart thrower led Lanark to the last
of a long row of doors in one wall. He softly opened it a
little way, peeked through the crack and whispered, "He seems
quiet. I don't think there's anything to worry about. You know
what to do?"
"Yes."
Lanark stepped through the door into a cubicle behind a counter
with an inquiries sign on it.

    A thin, youngish man sat facing him. He had short ruffled
hair, a clean suit of cheap cloth, his eyes were closed and he
seemed barely able to avoid falling sideways. Lanark took the
knob of the door he had just come through, slammed it hard
and sat down. The man opened his eyes and said, "No no
no no . . . no no, you've got me wrong."
As his eyes focused on Lanark's face his own face began to
change. Vitality flooded into it. He smiled and whispered, "Lanark!"
"Yes," said Lanark, wondering.
The man almost laughed with relief. "Thank Christ it's you!"
He leaned over the counter and shook Lanark's hand, saying,
"Don't you know me? Of course not, I was a kid at the time.
I'm Jimmy Macfee. Granny Fleck's wee Macfee. You remember
the old Ashfield Street days when me and my sisters played
at sailing ships on your bed? My, but you've put on the beef.
You were thin then. You had pockets full of seashells and
pebbles, remember?"
"Were you that boy?" said Lanark, shaking his head. "How's
Mrs. Fleck? Have you seen her lately?"
"Not lately, no. She hardly goes out these days. Arthritis. It's

her age. But thank Christ it's you. I've seen six of these clerks, and every one of them has tried to put me off by sending me to another. The problem is, see, that I'm married, see, and me and the wife have a mohome. *And* we've two weans, six years and seven years, boy and girl. Now I'm not criticizing mohomes—I *make* the bloody things—but there's not much room in them, right? And when we took this one the housing department definitely said that if I paid my rent prompt and kept my nose clean we'd get a proper house when we needed it. Well we've had an accident. The wife's pregnant again. So what can we do? Four of us and a screaming wean in a mohome? And having to use a public lavatory when we need a wash or a you-know-what? So what can we do?"

Lanark stared down at a pen and a heap of forms on the counter. He picked up the pen and said hesitantly, "What's your address?" Then he dropped the pen and said firmly, "Don't tell me. It's no use. This place isn't going to help you at all."

"What?"

"You'll get no help here. If you need a new house you'll have to find a way of getting it yourself."

"But that needs money. Are you advising me . . . to steal?"

"Perhaps. I don't know. But whatever you do please be careful. I haven't met the police yet, but I imagine they're fairly efficient when dealing with lonely criminals. If you decide to do something, do it with a lot of other people who feel the same way. Perhaps you should organize a strike, but don't go on strike for more money. Your enemies understand money better than you do. Go on strike for things. Strike for bigger houses."

Macfee screwed his face up incredulously and shouted, "Me? Organize a . . . ? Thanks for bloody nothing!"

He sprang up, turned and went toward the lift.

"Wait!" cried Lanark, climbing over the counter. "Wait! I've another idea!"

He forced his way through the dead air of the floor and managed to press into the lift before the doors shut. He was pushed against Macfee's shoulder in a mass of older men and younger women.

"Listen, Macfee," he whispered. "My family and I are shifting into a new place soon—you could get the old one."

"Where is it?"

"In the cathedral."

"I'm not a bloody squatter!"

"But this is legal—it's run by a very helpful minister of religion."

"How big is it?"

"About six feet by nine. The ceiling slopes a bit."

"Christ, my mohome's nearly that size. *And* it has a flat roof and two rooms."

"But it would suit us fine, mister!" said a haggard woman holding a baby. "Six feet by nine? My man and his brother and me *need* a place like that."

"Tell me one thing," said Macfee belligerently. "What do they pay you for working here?"

"Enough to buy my own house."

"Why do they pay you anything?"

"I think they employ a lot of well-educated people to keep us comfortable," said Lanark. "And because they're afraid we'd be dangerous if we had no work at all."

"Fucking wonderful!" said Macfee.

"Honest, mister, that room you're leaving sounds very, very nice. Where did you say it was?"

The door opened and they hurried across the entrance hall, Lanark keeping close to Macfee's shoulder. As they came onto the pavement three armoured trucks full of soldiers thundered past. "What's happening?" cried Lanark. "Why all these soldiers?"

"How do I know?" shouted Macfee. "I'm pig-ignorant, all I hear is the news on television and funny noises in the street. They were ringing the cathedral bell like madmen a short while back. How do I know what's going on?"

They walked in silence till they reached a corner where a sign projected above a door. It was a fat red heart with pink neon tubes running into it and *The Vascular Cavity* underneath. Lanark said, "At least let me buy you a drink."

"Can you afford it?" said Macfee sarcastically. Lanark fingered the credit card in his pocket, nodded and pushed the door open.

The room was lit by a dim red glow with some zones of gaudy brightness. Most of the tables and chairs were partitioned off by luminous grilles shaped and coloured like pink veins and purple arteries. A revolving ball cast a flow of red and white corpuscular spots across the ceiling, and the music was a low, steady, protracted throbbing like a lame giant limping up a thickly carpeted stair.

"What kind of boozer is this?" said Macfee.

Lanark stood and stared. He would have turned and walked out if it hadn't been for women. They filled the place with laughing, alert, indifferent young faces and throats, breasts, midriffs and legs in all kinds of clothing. He felt he had never seen so many girls in his life. Looking closely he saw there were as many men but they made a less distinct impression. For all he cared they were duplicates of the same confident long-haired youth and Lanark hated him. He stood transfixed between fascination and envy until someone shouted his name from a corner. He looked across and saw Gilchrist, Pettigrew and Miss Maheen standing at a bar quilted with red plastic.

"Listen," he told Macfee. "That tall man is my boss. If anyone can help you it's him. Let's try anyway."

He led the way to the bar, and said "Mr. Gilchrist, this is an old friend of mine—Jimmy Macfee—I knew him as a boy. He's a client of mine, a really deserving case, and—"

"Now, now, now!" said Gilchrist cheerfully. "We're here on pleasure, not business. What would you both like?"

"A whisky as big as yours," said Macfee.

"The same, please," said Lanark.

Gilchrist gave the order. Macfee was clearly attracted by Miss Maheen who turned her head at regular intervals, smiling at each of them in turn.

"Why are you not drinking?" he asked when her split-second smile reached him.

"She doesn't drink," said Pettigrew dourly.

"Can't she speak for herself?" said Macfee.

"She doesn't need to."

"Are you her husband or something?" said Macfee.

Pettigrew coolly emptied his whisky glass and said, "What do you do?"

"I'm a maker. I make mohomes," said Macfee boldly. *"And I live in one."*

"Mohome makers aren't real makers," said Pettigrew. "My father was a real maker. I respect real makers. You're in the luxury trade."

"So you think a mohome is a luxury?"

"Yes. I bet yours has colour television."

"Why shouldn't it have?"

"I suppose you came to us because you wanted a house you could stand up in, with an inside lavatory, and separate bedrooms, and wooden window frames, and maybe a fireplace?"

"Why shouldn't I have a house like that?"

"I'll tell you. When mohome users get a house like that they crowd into one room and sublet the others, and rip out the plumbing to sell as scrap metal, and rip out the window frames and chop up the doors and burn them. A mohome user isn't fit for a decent house.''

''I'm not that sort! You know nothing about me!'' cried Macfee.
''I knew all about you as soon as I clapped eyes on you,''
said Pettigrew softly. *''You,* are an obnoxious, little, bastard.''
Macfee stared at him, clenching his fists and inhaling loudly.
His shoulders swelled and he seemed to grow taller.

''Miss Maheen!'' said Pettigrew loudly. ''If he threatens me,
chop him.''

Miss Maheen stepped between Macfee and Pettigrew and raised
her right hand to throat level, holding it flat and horizontal
with the small finger outward. Her smile widened and remained. Gilchrist said hastily, ''Oh, there's no need for violence,
Miss Maheen. Just *look* at him.''

Lanark heard a snapping sound inside Miss Maheen's head.
He couldn't see her face but he saw Macfee's. His mouth fell
open, the lower lip trembled, he clapped his hands over his
eyes. Gilchrist said quietly, ''Lead him out, Lanark. This isn't
his kind of pub.''

Lanark gripped Macfee's arm and led him through the
crowd.

Outside the door Macfee leaned against the wall, dropped
his hands and shuddered. ''Wee black holes,'' he whispered.
''Her eyes turned into wee black holes.''

''She's not a real woman, you see,'' said Lanark. ''She's a tool,
an instrument *shaped* like a woman.''

Macfee bent forward and was sick on the pavement; then he
said, ''I'm going home.''

''I'll take you there.''

''Better not. I'm going to hit someone tonight. I *need* to hit
someone tonight. If you don't keep away it'll probably be you.''

He sounded so feeble that Lanark took his arm and walked
with him along several busy streets, then several quiet ones.
They passed a parked truck beside three workmen cementing a
concrete block over a sewer grating. A soldier with a gun stood
smoking nearby. Lanark asked the foreman, ''What are you
doing?''

''Cementing a block over this stank.''

''Why?''

''Just don't interfere,'' said the soldier.

''I'm not interfering, but couldn't you tell us what's happening?''

''There's going to be an announcement. Just go to your homes
and wait for the announcement.''

Lanark noticed that every drain they passed was blocked up. A hollow shouting began in the distance and drew nearer. It came from a loudspeaker on top of a slow-moving van. It said, "SPECIAL EMERGENCY ANNOUNCEMENT. IN FIFTEEN MINUTES NORMAL HEARTBEAT TIME, PROVOST SLUDDEN WILL MAKE A SPECIAL EMERGENCY ANNOUNCEMENT. IF YOU HAVE NEIGHBOURS WITHOUT TELEVISION OR WIRELESS, CALL THEM IN TO HEAR PROVOST SLUDDEN'S SPECIAL EMERGENCY ANNOUNCEMENT IN FIFTEEN MINUTES NORMAL HEARTBEAT TIME. ALL SHOPS, OFFICES, FACT-ORIES, DANCEHALLS, CINEMAS, RESTAURANTS, CAFÉS, SPORT CENTRES, SCHOOLS AND PUBLIC HOUSES ARE ASKED TO RELAY PROVOST SLUDDEN'S EMERGENCY ANNOUNCE-MENT OVER THEIR LOUDSPEAKER SYSTEMS IN FOURTEEN AND A HALF MINUTES NORMAL HEARTBEAT TIME. THIS IS URGENT. . . ."

"What's *happening* to this city?" asked Macfee, shaking his arm free. They passed a long queue of people outside a public lavatory, then a wall of gigantic posters. Macfee said "Here" and they stepped through a gap between two posters onto a great area of gravel covered by rows of parked cars. He stopped beside one and opened the door. Lanark opened the door on the other side.

The front seat of the car extended the whole width and a plump young woman with a thin face sat in the middle. She said, "Come in. Sit down. Shut the door and shut up, both of you. Excuse my manners. I'll make tea in a minute but I don't want to miss my garden."

Lanark shut the door and leaned back with a feeling of relief. Sunlight streamed in through the windows and the car seemed to be thrusting slowly forward through a shrubbery of rose-bushes. Green leaves and heavy white blossoms brushed across the windscreen and past the windows of the doors. He saw golden-brown bees working in the hearts of the roses and heard their drowsy humming, the rustle of leaves, some distant bird calls. Mrs. Macfee took a small can from a shelf and pressed the top. A fine mist smelling like roses came out. She sighed and leaned back with closed eyes saying, "I don't need to see it. The sound and scent are good enough for me."

The car had no clutch or steering column, and the seat was the sort that could slide forward while the back flattened to form a bed. A glass panel and a blind shut out the back seat where the children were probably sleeping. Under the windscreen was a set of drawers, shelves and compartments. One compartment held an electric plate, another a plastic basin with a small tap above it. Macfee opened a tiny refrigerator door, took out two cans of beer and passed one to Lanark.

The roses parted before the windscreen and the car, with a sound of gurgling water, floated like a yacht onto a circular lake surrounded by hills sloping up from the water's edge and clothed from base to summit in a drapery of the most gorgeous flower blossoms, scarcely a green leaf visible among the sea of odorous and fluctuating colour. The lake was of great depth but so transparent that the bottom, which seemed to be a mass of small round pearly pebbles, was distinctly visible whenever the eye allowed itself *not* to see, far down in the inverted heaven, the duplicate blooming of the hills. The whole impression was of richness, warmth, colour, quietness, softness and delicacy, and as the eye traced upward the myriad-tinted slope, from its sharp junction with the water to its vague termination in the cloudless blue, it was difficult not to fancy a wide cataract of rubies, sapphires, opals and golden onyxes rolling silently out of the sky. Mrs. Macfee took another little can and sprayed the interior with a scent of pansies. Macfee shouted "Sentimental rot!" and violently twisted a switch.

The interior became part of a sharp red convertible speeding down a multi-lane freeway under a dazzling sun. A swarm of dots grew visible in the heat haze ahead. The dots became a pack of motorcyclists. The car accelerated, moving in sideways toward the bikes.

"Jimmy!" said Mrs. Macfee. "You know I don't like this."

"You're unlucky, aren't you?" said Macfee. She pressed her lips together, pulled open a drawer in the dashboard, took out a sock and needle and started darning. Looking past her profile Lanark saw the car drawing level with the leader of the pack. He wore leather clothes with skull and swastika badges. A girl like Miss Maheen dressed in leather clung behind him. Then *froom!*—a glittering barbed dart shot out from Macfee's side of the car and entered the cyclist's body under the armpit. With a great screech the car swung round sideways and ploughed into the pack. The scene outside went suddenly slow. Slowly crashing and screaming cyclists were tossed into the air or fell and clung in agony to the car bonnet until they slid slowly off. Lanark shoved open the door beside him and stared with relief at the dingy gravel park and a row of quiet mohomes.

"Shut the door, we're freezing," yelled Macfee. Lanark reluctantly closed it. Bodies still spun ballet-like through swirling clouds of dust. Two bikes crashed with a tremendous explosion; then the scene was replaced by the head and shoulders of a man with a vividly patterned necktie. He said, "We are sorry to interrupt this programme but here is an emergency announcement by Provost Sludden, the chief executive officer of Greater Unthank. As this announcement contains a warning of serious health hazards for inhabitants of the Greater Unthank region, it is vital that everyone—especially those with children—gives it very special attention. Provost Sludden."
Sludden appeared, sitting on a leather sofa under a huge map of the city. His hands were clasped between his knees, and he looked gravely at the camera a while before speaking.

"Hullo. Not many of you have seen me face to face like this, and I promise you I regret having to appear. A provost is a public servant, and a good servant should never march into the living room when the family is enjoying an evening of television and complain about the difficulties of his job. Good servants work quietly behind the scenes, providing their employers with what the employers need. But sometimes an unforeseen accident occurs. Perhaps a bath falls through the kitchen ceiling, and then no matter how competent a servant is, he must tell the boss and the boss's wife what has happened, because the household routine is going to be upset and everyone has a right to know why. Something unexpected has happened to the plumbing of the Unthank region, and as chief executive officer I am going to take you into my confidence and explain why.

"But first I must tell you how your elected servants recently defeated a much greater problem: starvation. Yes. Starvation. The council was allowing a heap of poisonous muck from a burst transporter to isolate the city. Our foodstocks were nearly exhausted. We might have introduced severe rationing in the hope that the council would intervene to save us at the last minute, but we decided not to risk that. We decided to act ourselves. We told our heroic fire brigade to sweep the poison into the sewers—there was nowhere else for it to go. They did. Unthank was saved. We didn't publicize this triumph. It was enough reward for us that nobody would go hungry.

"Now for the bad news. The poison from the motorway is creeping backward through the sewage system in the form of a very lethal and corrosive gas. It is undermining our streets, our public buildings and our houses."

Sludden stood up and pointed to an area of the map outlined in red.

"Here is the danger area: central Unthank inside the ring road and the district east of the cathedral."

"That's us, all right," said Macfee.

"To prevent loss of life we must stop the gas from spreading. Every drain and sewer-opening in the danger area must be blocked. This work is proceeding in the streets and will soon start in houses and other buildings. Sanitary workers will call in to seal up every sink, urinal and lavatory pan. Naturally this takes time, so we invite your cooperation. Tubes of plastic cement will soon be obtainable, on demand, from your local police station and post office. The homes of householders who block their own drains will receive nothing more than a routine inspection. Meanwhile everyone should immediately plug their sinks and fill them with water. Lavatory pans will also stay safe for a while if they are not actually employed. I will now pause for three minutes to let everyone attend to their sink."

Three sentences appeared on the screen:

PLUG YOUR SINK.
FILL IT WITH WATER.
DON'T FLUSH YOUR LAVATORY PAN.

"Have another beer," said Macfee, passing a can across. "You too, Helen,"
She said, "I'm frightened, Jimmy."
"Frightened? Why? We're in luck at last. Mohomes don't have lavatories. Our sink isn't connected to the sewage system."
"But what will we do if we cannae use the public toilet?"
"I think the provost will announce plans for that," said Lanark. The speech had greatly impressed him. He thought, 'I'm glad Rima and Sandy are in the cathedral. Ritchie-Smollet will have taken the necessary precautions by now.' He sipped from the can. The inscription vanished and Sludden appeared once more.

"There is one question I am sure you are all asking yourselves: How are we to get rid of our bodily waste? Well, you know, that question is as old as humanity itself. We tend to forget that interior flush lavatories are comparatively recent inventions, and three quarters of the world doesn't have them. For a while we must be content to use one of these, as our great-grandparents did."

He held up a chamberpot.

"Those of you with small children probably have one already. New stocks are being rushed to the shops from the Cortexin Adhoc Sanitation plant at New Cumbernauld. Large orders have been placed with a small factory in Unthank which still makes the old-fashioned earthernware article, thus giving a much-needed boost to a neglected part of the city's economy. And though many will have to manage without one for a short period, I am sure they will be able to improvise with some other domestic utensil. As to the removal of the waste, you will receive through the post, if you have not received it already, a packet of these."

He held up a black plastic bag.

"This is large enough to comfortably hold
the contents of one full chamberpot. When
tied at the neck it is both damp proof and
odour proof. These should be stacked *beside,* not *inside,* your usual midden or dust-
bin. To speed collection, the cleansing
workers will be helped by the army. That
is why you have seen so many soldiers
on the street lately."

"Soldiers don't need guns to shift shit," said Macfee.

"Washing, if kept to a minimum, will present no problem. Once your sink is blocked
it can be used in the usual way, except
that the dirty water (which should be employed more than once) should be ladled
into a pail and emptied into a gutter or
convenient piece of ground. The same
goes for urine. Fortunately a spell of mild
weather is forecast, and our liquid waste
will either evaporate or flow into districts
where the drains still work."

"What if it rains?" said Macfee.

"But we must also tackle the *causes* of this
dangerous annoyance. We have already
demanded action from the council, whose
slowness caused this disaster in the first
place. We have appealed to the Cortexin
Group, who manufactured the poison.
Both reply that experts are being con-
sulted, the matter will be considered, that
in due course we will hear from them.
This is not good enough. So Professor Eva
Schtżngrm has been made leader of a team
who are working to gain the technology
to clear the gas themselves, and we are
choosing a delegate to speak up boldly
for Unthank at the general assembly of
council states soon to be held in Provan.
The fact is that the council has treated Unthank badly. It is a long time since they

introduced their decimal calendar based on the twenty-five-hour day. They promised us new clocks, so we rashly scrapped the old ones, and the new clocks failed to arrive. I was a young man then and I confess that, like most people, I didn't care. Everyone likes to feel they have plenty of time; nobody likes seeing how fast it passes. But we can't cope with a public emergency without clocks, so we have created a new department, our own department of chronometry. This department has commandeered a television channel—this television channel—and I will show you what it is going to transmit."

Sludden walked over to a clock hanging on a wall, a pendulum clock with a case shaped like a small log cabin.

"Fucking miraculous," said Macfee, opening another beer can. Helen said, "Don't you think you've had enough?"

"This is one of many clocks recently unearthed from museums, lumber-rooms and antique shops. It may not look very impressive, but it is the first to be restored to perfect working order. When the others have been repaired they will be installed in the head offices of our essential services, and each one of them will be synchronized with this."

Sludden pointed to a weight shaped like a fir cone.

"Notice that the weight has been wound up and placed on a small shelf immediately under the case. At the end of this announcement, I will suspend it, and the clock will strike the hours of midnight: the time when an old day dies and a new day begins. The sound will be reinforced by a long blast upon police and factory sirens, who will repeat the noise at noon tomorrow. Employees of the chronometry department have also taken over ninety-two church towers with bells in them, and from now on they too will broadcast the message of this little clock.

"I know that quiet-minded people will find this a rude intrusion on their privacy; that intellectuals will say that a return to a solar timescale, when we don't have sunlight, is putting clocks backward, not forward; and that manual workers, who time themselves by their pulses, will find the whole business irrelevant. Never mind. This clock allows me to make definite promises. By eight o'clock tomorrow every house, mohome, office and factory will have received an envelope of plastic wastebags. By ten o'clock the first free tubes of plastic cement will be available at your local post office. And at every hour I or some other corporation representative will appear on this channel to tell you how things are going. And now—"

Said Sludden taking the weight in his hand—

"I wish you all a very good night. Eternity, for Greater Unthank, is drawing to an end. *Time* is about to begin."

He suspended the weight. The pendulum swung left with a tick, then right with a tock. The clock face grew till it nearly filled the windscreen. Both hands pointed straight upright to a small door above the dial, which flapped open. A fat wooden bird popped out and in shouting "Cuckoo! Cuckoo! Cuck—" Macfee turned a switch and the windscreen went transparent. The three of them sat in a row and stared through it at the darkened carpark. Sirens, hooters and distant clanging could be heard outside. Helen switched on a light.

"A maniac!" said Macfee. "The man's a maniac."

"Oh no," said Lanark. "I've known him a long time, and he's not a maniac. As a private person I don't trust him, but he seems to have thoroughly grasped the political situation. And that speech sounded honest to me."

"He's a friend of yours?"

"No, a friend of my wife."

Macfee leaned over and grabbed Lanark's lapels and said, "What's the score?"

"Jimmy!" cried Helen.

Lanark cried, "What's wrong?"

"That's what I'm asking you! You've a council passport, right?

And you work for social stability, right? You know Sludden, right? So just tell me what you folk are trying to do!''

Lanark had been half dragged across Helen's lap, his ear was pressed against her thigh and comforting warmth began flowing through it. He said dreamily, "We're trying to kill Unthank. Some of us."

"Christ, that isn't news. We've known that for ages in the shops! 'All right,' I said. 'Let the place die as long as my weans are spared.' But you bastards are really putting the boot in now, aren't you? *Aren't you?*''

Macfee shifted a hand to grip Lanark's nostrils and cover his mouth. Lanark found he was watching a bulging reflection of his face and Macfee's hand on the side of a shiny kettle on a shelf a few inches away. The reflection flickered and grew dim and he supposed that when it went black he would be unconscious. He felt no pain so he was not much worried. Then he heard slapping sounds and Helen panting, "Let *go*, let him *go*." he was released and heard much louder slapping sounds. Helen moaned, then yelled, "Clear out, mister! Leave us! Leave us alone!"

He found and pulled a handle and scrambled sideways out the door and slammed it shut. He hesitated beside the mohome, which was rocking slightly. Muffled noises came from the front seat and a frail childish wailing from the back. His eye was distracted by a lit poster on a gable showing an athletic couple in bathing costume playing beach ball with two laughing children. The message above said MONEY IS TIME. TIME IS LIFE. BUY MORE LIFE FOR YOUR FAMILY FROM THE QUANTUM INTERMINABLE. (THEY'LL LOVE YOU FOR IT.)

CHAPTER 39. Divorce

"Let the place die as long as my weans are spared." Jimmy's words had brought Sandy alarmingly to mind. Lanark ran from the park and along some empty streets, trying to retrace his steps. A warm heavy rain began falling and the gutters filled rapidly. The surrounding houses were unfamiliar. He turned a corner, came to a railing and looked down over several levels of motorway at the dark tower and bright spire of the cathedral. He sighed with relief, climbed the rail and scrambled down a slope of slippery wet grass. The water was nearly two feet deep at the edge of the road and flowing swiftly sideways like a stream. He waded through to the drier lanes. The only vehicle he saw was a military jeep which whizzed round a curve sending out sizzling arcs of spray, then slowed down and stopped beside him.

"Come here!" cried a gruff voice. "I've a gun, so no funny business."

Lanark went closer. A fat man in a colonel's uniform sat beside the driver. The fat man said, "How many of you are there?"

"One."

"Do you expect me to believe that? Where are you going?"

"The cathedral."

"Don't you know you're trespassing?"

"I'm just crossing a road."

"Oh, no! You are crossing a freeway. Freeways are for the exclusive use of wheeled carriages propelled by engines burning refined forms of fossilized fuel, and don't forget it. . . . Good heavens, it's Lanark, isn't it?"

"Yes. Are you McPake?"

"Of course. Get inside. Where did you say you were going?"

Lanark explained. McPake said, "Take us there, Cameron," then he leaned back, chuckling. "I thought we had a riot on our hands when we saw you. We're on the watch for them, you know, at times like these."

The jeep turned down toward the cathedral square. Lanark said, "I suppose Rima told you about Alexander?"

McPake shook his head. "Sorry, I only know one Rima. She used to hang about with Sludden in the old Elite days. Had her myself once. What a woman! I thought she took off for the institute when you did."

"Sorry, I'm getting confused," said Lanark.

He sat in a state of miserable excitement until the jeep put him down at the cathedral gates. In the doorway he heard organ strains, and the floor inside held a scattering of elderly and middle-aged people (But *I'm* middle-aged, he thought), standing between the rows of chairs and singing that time, like an ever-rolling stream, bears all her sons away, they fly, forgotten, as the dream dies at the opening day. He hurried past them with his mouth shaping denunciations, opened the small door, and rushed up the spiral stair, and along the window ledge, through the organ loft and past the cubicles of the attic. Rima and Alex were in none of them. He rushed to the kitchen and stared at Frankie and Jack, who looked up, startled, from a card game. He said, "Where are they?" There was an embarrassed silence; then Frankie said in a small voice, "She said she left a note for you."

He hurried back and found the empty cubicle. A note lay on the carefully made bed.

Dear Lanark,
I expect you won't be surprised to find us gone. Things haven't been very good lately, have they. Alexander and I will be living with Sludden, as we arranged, and on the whole it's better that you aren't coming too. Please don't try to find us—Alex is naturally a bit upset by all this and I don't want you to make him worse.

You probably think I've gone with Sludden because he has a big house, and is famous, and is a better lover than you in most ways, but that isn't the real reason. It may surprise you to hear that Sludden needs me more than you do. I don't think you need anybody. No matter how bad things get, you will always plod on without caring what other people think or feel. You're the most selfish man I know.

Dear Lanark, I don't hate you but whenever I try to write something friendly it turns out nasty, perhaps because if you give the devil

*your little finger he bites off the whole arm. But you've often been
nice to me, you aren't really a devil.*

Love

Rima

P.S. *I'm coming back to collect some clothes and things. I may see
you then.*

He undressed slowly, got into bed, switched off the light and
fell asleep at once. He woke several times feeling that something
horrible had happened which he must tell Rima about, then
he remembered what it was. Lying drearily awake he sometimes
heard the cathedral bell tolling the hours. Once it struck five
o'clock and when he awoke later it was striking three, which
suggested that the regular marking of time had not slowed it
down much.

     At last he opened his eyes to the electric light. She stood
by the bed quietly taking clothes from the chest of drawers.
He said, "Hullo."

"I didn't mean to wake you."

"How's Sandy?"

"Very quiet but quite happy, I think. He has plenty of room
to run about and Sludden lives outside the danger zone so
there's no stink, of course."

"There's no stink here."

"In another twenty-four hours I'm sure even you will begin
to notice it."

She snapped the suitcase shut and said, "I wanted to pack this
before I left but I was afraid you would suddenly come in
and get hysterical."

"When have you seen me hysterical?" he asked peevishly.

"I don't remember. Of course that's partly your trouble, isn't
it? Sludden and I often discuss you, and he thinks you would
be a very valuable man if you knew how to release your emotions."

He lay rigid, clenching his fists and teeth in order not to scream.
She placed the suitcase by the bed foot and sat on it, twisting
a handkerchief. She said, "Oh, Lanark, I don't like hurting
you but I must explain why I'm leaving. You think I'm greedy
and ungrateful and prefer Sludden because he's a far better
lover, but that's not why. Women can live quite comfortably
with a clumsy lover if he makes them happy in other ways.
But you're too serious all the time. You make my ordinary
little feelings seem as fluffy and useless as bits of dust. You
make life a duty, something to be examined and corrected.

Do you remember when I was pregnant, and said I wanted a girl, and you said you wanted a boy so that someone would like the baby? You've always tried to *balance* me as if I were a badly floating boat. You've brought no joy to my happiness or sorrow to my misery, you've made me the loneliest woman in the world. I don't love Sludden *more* than you, but life with him seems open and free. I'm sure Alex will benefit too. Sludden plays with him. You would only explain things to him."
Lanark said nothing. She said, "But we enjoyed ourselves sometimes, didn't we? You've been a friend to me—I'm not sorry I met you."
"When can I visit Sandy?"
"I thought you were going away to Provan soon."
"Not if Sandy isn't going."
"If you phone us first you can come anytime. Frankie has the number and the address. We'll be needing a babysitter."
"Tell Sandy I'll see him soon and I'll visit him often. Goodbye."
She stood, lifted the case, hesitated and said, "I'm sure you would be happier if you complained more about things."
"Would complaining make you like me and want to stay? No, it would make it easier for you to leave. So don't think—"
He stopped with open mouth, for heavy grief came swelling up his throat till it broke out in loud, dry choking sobs like big hiccups or the slow ticking of a wooden clock. Wetness flooded his eyes and cheeks. He stretched a hand toward her and she said softly, "Poor Lanark! You really are suffering," and went softly out and softly closed the door behind her. Eventually the sobbing stopped. He lay flat with a leaden weight in his chest. He thought wistfully of getting drunk or smashing furniture, but all activity seemed too tiring. The leaden weight kept him flat on his back till he fell asleep.

     Later someone laid a hand on his shoulder and he opened his eyes sharply saying, "Rima?"
Frankie stood by the bed with food on a tray. He sighed and thanked her and she watched him eat. She said, "I've taken your clothes away—they were terribly dirty. But there's a new suit and underthings laid out for you downstairs in the vestry."
"Oh."
"I think you need a shave and a haircut. Jack was a barber, once. Will I ask him to see to it?"
"No."
"Can Sludden speak to you?"
He stared at her.

She flushed and said, "I mean, if he comes to see you, you won't lose your temper or attack him, will you?"
"I certainly won't lose my dignity because I'm faced by someone with none of his own."
She giggled and said, "Good. I'll tell him that."

She removed the tray and later Sludden entered and sat by the bed, saying, "How do you feel?"
"I don't like you, Sludden, but the only people I do like depend on you. Tell me what you want."
"Yes, in a minute. I'm glad you agreed to see me, but of course I knew you would. What Rima and I admire in you is your instinctive self-control. That makes you a very, very valuable man."
"Tell me what you want, Sludden."
"We're sensible modern men, after all, not knights who've been jousting for the love of a fair lady. I dare say the fair lady picked you up somewhere, but you were too weighty for her so she dropped you and picked me up instead. I'm a lightweight. Women enjoy lifting me. But you're made of sterner stuff, which is why I'm here."
"Please tell me what you want."
"I want you to stop pitying yourself and get out of bed. I want you to do a difficult, important job. The committee sent me here. They ask you to go to Provan and speak for Unthank in the general assembly of council states."
"You're joking!" said Lanark, sitting up. Sludden said nothing. "Why should they ask me?"
"We want someone who's been through the institute and knows the council corridors. You've worked for Ozenfant. You've spoken to Monboddo."
"I've quarrelled with the first and I don't like the second."
"Good. Stand up in Provan and denounce them for us. We don't want to be represented by a diplomat now, we want someone tactless, someone who will tell delegates from other states exactly what is happening here. Use your nose and take back some of our stink to its source."
Lanark sniffed. The air had an unpleasant familiar smell. He said, "Send Grant. He understands politics."
"Nobody trusts Grant. He understands politics, yes, but he wants to change them."
"Ritchie-Smollet."
"He doesn't understand politics at all. He believes everyone he meets is honestly doing their best."

"Gow."

"Gow owns shares in Cortexin, the company that fouled us up. He makes belligerent noises but he would only pretend to fight the council."

"And you?"

"If I left the city for more than a week our administration would collapse. There would be nobody in control but a lot of civil servants who want to clear out as soon as they can. We're under very strong attack, inside and out."

"So I've been chosen because nobody else trusts one another," said Lanark. An intoxicating excitement began to fill him and he frowned to hide it. He saw himself on a platform, or maybe a pedestal, casting awe over a vast assembly with a few simple, forceful words about truth, justice and brotherhood. He said suddenly, "How would I get to Provan?"

"By air."

"But do I cross a zone, I mean an incaldrical zone, I mean—"

"An intercalendrical zone? Yes, you do."

"Won't that age me a lot?"

"Probably."

"I'm not going. I want to stay near Sandy. I want to help him grow up."

"I understand that," said Sludden gravely. "But if you love your son—if you love Rima—you'll work for them in Provan."

"My family isn't in the danger area now. It's living with you."

Sludden smiled painfully, stood up and walked the floor of the cubicle. He said, "I will tell you something only one other person knows. You'll have to be quiet about it till you reach Provan, but then you must tell the world. The whole of the Greater Unthank region is in danger, and not just from a typhoid epidemic, though that is probable too. Mrs. Schtzngrm has analyzed a sample of the poison—two firemen died getting it for her—and she says it has begun filtering down through the Permian layer. As you probably know, the continents, though not continuous with it, are floating on a superdense mass of molten—"

"Don't blind me with science, Sludden."

"If the pollution isn't cleared up we're going to have tremors and subsidences in the earth's crust."

"Something must be done!" cried Lanark, aghast.

"Yes. The knowledge of what to do belongs to the institute. The machinery to do it belongs to the creature. Only the council can force them to act together."

"I'll go," said Lanark quietly, and mainly to himself. "But first I must see the boy."

"Get dressed in the vestry and I'll take you to him," said Sludden briskly. "And by the way, if you've no objection we'll have you declared provost: Lord Provost of Greater Unthank. It doesn't mean anything—I'll still be senior executive officer—but you'll be going among people with titles, and a title of your own helps to impress that kind."

Lanark pulled on the old greatcoat like a dressing gown, thrust his bare feet into the mud-caked shoes and followed Sludden downstairs to the vestry. His feelings were pulled between a piercing sad love for Sandy and an excited love of his own importance as a provost and delegate. Nothing interrupted the colloquy between these two loves. A warm bath was ready for him, and afterward he sat in a bathrobe while Jack shaved and trimmed him and Frankie manicured his fingernails. He put on clean new underwear, socks, shirt, a dark blue necktie, and a three-piece suit of light grey tweed, and beautifully polished black shoes; then he withdrew to the lavatory, excreted into a plastic chamberpot fitted inside the lavatory pan and had the comfortable feeling that someone else was expected to empty it. There was a mirror above the blocked lavatory sink; a medicine cabinet with a mirror for a door hung on the wall facing it. By moving the door to an angle he managed to see himself in profile. Jack had removed the beard and trimmed the moustache. His greying hair, receding from the brow, swept into a bush behind the ears: the effect was impressive and statesmanlike. He placed his hands on his hips and said quietly, "When Lord Monboddo says that the council has done its best for Unthank he is lying to us—or has been lied to by others."

He returned to the vestry and Sludden escorted him out to a long black car by the cathedral door. They climbed into the back seat and Sludden said, "Home, Angus," to the chauffeur.

They sped swiftly through the city and Lanark was too occupied with himself to notice much, except when the pervading stink grew unusually strong as the car crossed the riverbed by a splendid new concrete bridge. Heaps of bloated black plastic bags were scattered across the cracked mud. Sludden said glumly, "Nowhere else to dump them."

"On television you said these bags were odour-proof."

"They are, but they burst easily."

They came to a private housing scheme of neat little identical bungalows, each with a small garden in front and a garage alongside. The car stopped at one with a couple of old-fashioned ornamental iron lampposts outside the gate. Sludden led the way to the front door and fumbled awhile for his key. Lanark's heart beat hard thinking he would meet Rima again. Through an uncurtained plate-glass window on one side he saw into a firelit sitting room where four people sat sipping coffee at a low table before the hearth. Lanark recognized one of them. He said, "Gilchrist is in there!"

"Good. I invited him."

"But Gilchrist is on the side of the council!"

"Not on the sanitary question. He's on our side on that, and it's important to present a broad front when dealing with journalists. Don't worry, he's a great fan of yours."

They entered a small lobby. Sludden took a note from a telephone stand, read it and frowned. He said, "Rima's gone out. Alex will be upstairs in the television room. I suppose you'd prefer to see him first."

"Yes."

"Go through the first door on your right at the top."

He climbed a narrow, thick-carpeted stair and quietly opened a door. The room he entered was small and had three armchairs facing a television set in the corner. Two dolls wearing different kinds of soldier uniform lay on the floor among a litter of plastic toy weapons. A table had a monopoly game spread on it and some drawings on sheets of paper. Alexander sat on the arm of the middle chair, stroking a cat curled on the seat and watching the television screen. Without turning he said, "Hullo, Rima," and then, glancing round, "Hullo." "Hullo, Sandy."

Lanark went to the table and looked at the drawings. He said, "What are these?"

"A walking flower, a crane lifting a spider over a wall, and a space invasion by a lot of different aliens. Would you like to sit down and watch television with me?"

"Yes."

Alexander shoved the cat off the seat and Lanark sat down. Alexander leaned against him and they watched a film like the film Lanark had seen in Macfee's mohome, but the people killing each other in it were soldiers, not road users. Alexander said, "Don't you like films about killing?"

"No, I don't."

"Films about killing are my favourites. They're very real, aren't they?"

"Sandy. I'm going to leave this city for a long time."

"Oh."

"I wish I could stay."

"Mum said you would come and see me often. She doesn't mind us being friends."

"I know. When I told her I would visit you often I didn't know I would have to go away."

"Oh."

Lanark felt tears behind his eyes and realized his mouth was straining to girn aloud. He felt it would be horrible for a boy to remember a pitiable father and turned his face away and hardened the muscles of it to keep the grief inside. Alexander had turned his face to the television set. Lanark got up and moved clumsily to the door. He said, "Goodbye."

"Goodbye."

"I've always liked you. I always will like you."

"Good," said Alexander, staring at the screen. Lanark went outside, sat on the stairs and rubbed his face hard with both hands. Sludden appeared at the foot and said, "I'm sorry but the press are in a hurry."

"Sludden, will you look after him properly?"

Sludden climbed some steps toward him and said, "Don't worry! I know I played around a lot when I was younger but I've always liked Rima and I'm past wanting a change. Alex will be safe with me. I *need* a home life nowadays."

Lanark looked hard into Sludden's face. The shape seemed the same but the substance had changed. This was the eager, slightly desperate face of a burdened and caring man. With a pang of pity Lanark knew Sludden would have very little domestic peace with Rima. Lanark said, "I don't want to talk to journalists."

"Don't worry. Just appearing to them is the main thing."

A shaded lamp on the mantelpiece cast an oval of soft light on the small group before the hearth. Sludden, Gilchrist, a quiet-looking man and a reckless-looking man sat on a long leather sofa facing the fire. A grey-haired lady Lanark had seen in the chapterhouse sat on an armchair with a briefcase on her lap. Lanark pushed his own chair as far back into the shadow

as possible. Sludden said, "These two gentlemen fully understand the situation. They're on our side, so there's no need
to worry."

The quiet man said quietly, "We aren't interested in the detailed
character stuff. We just want to convey that the right man has
been found for the right job."

"A new figure strides into the political arena," said the reckless
man. "Where does he come from?"

"From Unthank," said Sludden. "He and I were close friends
in our early days. We hung about sowing our wild oats with
the same bohemian crowd, measuring out our life with coffee
spoons and trying to find a meaning. I did nothing at all in
those days but Lanark, to his credit, produced one of the finest
fragments of autobiographical prose *and* social commentary it
has been my privilege to criticize."

"No use to our readers," said the reckless man. The quiet
man said, "We can use it. What happened then?"

"He entered the institute and worked with Ozenfant. Although
a mainstay of the energy division, his qualities were *not*
appreciated and eventually, sickened by bureaucratic ineptitude,
he returned to Unthank: but not before registering a strong
personal protest to the lord president director."

"Room for a bit of dramatic detail here," said the reckless
man. "Exactly why did you quarrel with Ozenfant?"

Lanark tried to remember. At last he said, "I didn't quarrel
with him. He quarrelled with me, about a woman."

"Better leave that out," said Sludden.

"All right," said the quiet man. "He returned to Unthank.
And then?"

"I can tell you what happened then," said Gilchrist amiably.
"He devoted himself to public service by working in the Central
Centre for Employment, Stability and Surroundings. I was his
boss and I soon realized he was something of a saint. When
confronted by human suffering he had absolutely no patience
with red tape. To be frank, he often went too fast for me,
and that is why he is exactly the lord provost the region needs.
I can imagine no better politician to represent Greater Unthank
at the forthcoming general assembly."

"Good!" said the reckless man. "I wonder if Provost Lanark
would care to say something quotable about what he is going
to *do* at the Provan assembly?"

After thinking for a while Lanark said boldly, "I will try to
tell the truth."

"Couldn't you make it more emphatic?" said the reckless man.

"Couldn't you say, 'Come hell or high water, I will tell the world the **TRUTH**'?"

"Certainly not!" said Lanark crossly. "Water has nothing to do with my visit to Provan."

"Come what may, the world will hear the truth," murmured the quiet man. "We'll quote you as saying that."

"Very good, gentlemen!" said Sludden, standing up. "Our provost is leaving now. It's a very ordinary departure so you needn't watch. If you want a photograph Mr. Gilchrist's secretary can provide one. I'm sorry my wife was not here to offer you stronger refreshment, but you will find a bottle of sherry and a half bottle of whisky on the telephone-stand outside. Consume them at your leisure. Mr. Gilchrist will drive you back into town."

Everybody stood up.

Sludden showed Gilchrist and the journalists out. The grey-haired lady sighed and said, "Communicating with the press is a science I will nefer understand. This briefcase, Mr. Lanark, holts passcart, identification paper and three reports relating to the Unthank region. Before you speak in Provan I advise you to master them. There is a seismological report on the effect of pollution upon the Merovicnic discontinuity. There is a sanitary report on the probability of typhoid and related epidemics. There is a social report cuffering all the olt ground— no region our size has so much unemployment, uses so much corporal punishment in schools, has so many children cared for by the state, so much alcoholism, so many adults in prison or such a shortage of housing. It is all very olt stuff but people should be reminded. The seismological report is the only von whose language is at all technical because it contains an analysis of certain deep Permian samples vich *may* haf a commercial value. I haf put in a dictionary of scientific terms to help you out."

"Thank you," said Lanark, taking the case. "Are you Mrs. Schtzngrm?"

"Eva Schtzngrm, yes. There is von other matter personal to your*self,*" she said, lowering her voice. "In crossing the intercal-endrical zone by air I think you vill pass very rapidly through the menopause barrier."

"What?" said Lanark, alarmed.

"No neet to worry. You are not a voman and so vill not be greatly changed. But you may haf very odd experiences of contraction and expansion which neet not be referred to after-vards. Don't vorry about them. Don't vorry."

Sludden looked round the door and said, "Angus has set up the lights. Let's go to the airfield."

They went through a kitchen to a back door and followed an electric cable which snaked up a path between seedy cabbage stumps.

"Remember," said Sludden, "your best tactic is open denunciation. It's pointless complaining to the council chiefs when the other delegates aren't present, and vice versa. The leaders must be shamed into making concrete promises in the hearing of the rest."

"I wish you were going instead," said Lanark. They reached an overgrown privet hedge whose top leaves were black against a low glowing light. Sludden, then Lanark, then Mrs. Schtzngrm pushed through a gap onto the airfield. This was almost too narrow to be called a field, being a grassy triangular space on the summit of a hill completely surrounded by back gardens. A square tarpaulin was spread on the grass with three electric lights placed round it, and in the centre of the tarpaulin, upon very broad feet and short bowed legs, stood something like a bird. Though too large for an eagle it had the same shape and brownish gold feathers. The figures U-1 were stencilled on the breast. In the back between the folded wings was an opening about eighteen inches wide, though overlapping feathers made it seem narrower. As far as Lanark could see the interior was quilted with blue satin. He said, "Is this a bird or a machine?"

"A bit of both," said Sludden, taking the briefcase from Lanark's hand and tossing it into the cavity.

"But how can it fly when it's hollow inside?"

"It draws vital energy from the passenger," said Mrs. Schtzngrm.

"I haven't enough energy to fly that to another city."

"A credit cart vill allow the vehicle to draw energy from your future. You haf a cart?"

"Here," said Sludden. "I took it from his other suit. Angus, the chair, please."

The chauffeur brought a kitchen chair from the darkness and placed it beside the bird; Lanark, feebly protesting, was helped onto it by Sludden.

"I don't like doing this."

"Just step inside, Mr. Delegate."

Lanark put one foot in the cavity, then the other. The bird rocked and settled as he slid down inside; then the head came up and turned completely round so that he was faced by the down-curving dagger point of the great beak. "Give it this," said Sludden, handing him the credit card. Lanark held it by an extreme corner and thrust it shyly toward the beak, which snapped it up. A yellow light went on in the glassy eyes. The head turned away and lowered out of sight. Mrs. Schtzngrm said, "He cannot fly till you haf put yourself mostly inside. Remember, the less you think the faster he vill go. Do not fear for your goot clothing, the interior is sanitizing and vill launder and trim you while you sleep."

The smooth strong satin inside the bird supported Lanark as though he sat in a chair, but when he pulled his arms in it stretched him out and the rear end sank until his feet inside the neck felt higher than his face. This looked out of the cleft between two brown wings, which started rising higher and higher on each side. Squinting forward he could see a bungalow roof with a yellow square of window. The black shape of some-one's head and shoulders looked out of this, and if the window belonged to Sludden's house the watcher was surely Sandy and at once the grotesque flimsy aircraft and being a delegate and a provost seemed stupid evasions of the realest thing in the world and he shouted "No!" and began struggling to get out but at that moment the arching wings on each side thrashed down and with a thunderous *wump-wump-wump* he was flung upward feet first like a javelin and a sore blast of cold air on the brow knocked him out of his senses.

CHAPTER 40. Provan

He wakened cradled in stillness and looking at a bright full
moon. The surrounding sky held a few big stars. His eyes
were so dazzled that he rested them on the deep spaces between,
but other stars started glittering there, and then whole constella-
tions; he could not watch a space, however tiny, without the
silver dust of a galaxy coming to glimmer in it. With outspread
wings his aircraft seemed hanging, slightly tilted, between the
ceiling of stars and a floor of smooth clouds which spread,
like them, from horizon to horizon, and was that most mysteriously splendid of all colours, whiteness seen by a dim light.
This thinned and opened under him and for a moment the
craft seemed to overturn, for the bright moon shone through
the opening. He was looking down into the sky reflected in
a circular lake, reflected and magnified, for a black speck in
the centre of the lower moon was clearly a reflection of his
bird-machine. The lake, though sombre, had colour of its own.
A jet black halo surrounded the reflected moon, and a ring
of deep blue water flecked with stars surrounded that. To left
and right was a beach of pure sand as pearly-pale as the clouds,
and the round lake and its beaches were enclosed by two curving
shores which made the shape of an eye. And Lanark saw that
it was an eye, and the feeling which came to him then was
too new to have a name. His mouth and mind opened wide
and the only thought left was a wonder if he—a speck of a
speck floating before that large pupil—was seen by it. In an
effort to think something else he looked up at the stars but
looked down again almost at once, and the eye was nearer
now, he could only see the stars reflected in the depth. There
was a sound like remote thunder or the breathings of wind
in the ear. *"Is . . . is . . . is . . ."* it said. *"Is . . . if . . .
is. . . ."* He knew that half the stars were seeing the other

half and smiled slightly, not knowing up from down or caring which was which. Then, dazed by infinity, he did not fall asleep but seemed to float out into it.

He wakened next in pale cold azure. He was above a plain of snowy clouds with a blue bird-like shadow skimming over them on one side and on the other, not far above the horizon, a small piercing sun which seemed to shoot golden wires at his eyes when he glimpsed it. Sometimes he passed through fountains of birdsong squirting up through rifts in the clouds and looked down for a moment on grass or rocks a mile or so beneath, but the only steady sound was the quietly thudding wings of the eagle-machine muted by the thin air. His body lay relaxed and warm on the firm satin. His face lay in a pool of cold air as refreshing as a rinse of cold water. On the horizon ahead he saw a mountain of white cloud as single as a milk jug on the edge of a bare table. A bird-shaped black dot, casting a fleck of shadow, seemed to cross the side of it. Later, when the peak and precipices of the mountain floated above him, creamy and dazzling toward the sun and toning into blue shadow away from it, he saw that the cloudy plain ended here and a real mountain stood under the cloud one. It had a sharp summit and granite precipices and was highest of a jagged range rising from heathery purple moors. It combined the massiveness of great sculptures with the most delicately imagined detail. A drifting movement on the shadowy side of a glen resolved into a herd of deer. A small loch on the moor had a waterfall spilling out of it and an angler, knee deep, near the edge. He saw differently coloured fields with white farmhouses along a shore, and a bay where the sand under shallow water was lemon-yellow with reddish gardens of weed. Farther out the water was ribbed by sea swells and ruffled all over by little waves that sparkled where the sunlight caught them. He passed over a pale green, slow-foaming triangle of wake with a long tanker moving onward at the tip. Then conversational sounds came from inside his eagle-machine, and he pulled his head in out of the sunlight.

A small voice near his toes was saying ". . . identify self. This is Provan Air Authority addressing the U-1 flight from Unthank. Repeat: will passenger please identify self. Over." "I am the Lord Provost of the Greater Unthank region," said Lanark firmly, yet with elation, "and delegate to the general assembly of council states."
"Please rep—please rep—please repeat. Over."

Lanark said it again.

"The U-1 flight from Unthank may proceed to Hampden as
planned on beam co—beam co—beam coordinate zero flux
zero parahelion 43 minutes 19 point nought 7 seconds epihelion
ditto neg—ditto neg—ditto negating impetus reversal flow 22
point nought 2—nought 2—nought 2—nought 2—nought 2
beyond the equinoctial of Quebus on the international nerve—
national nerve—national nerve-circuit-decimal-calendar-cor-
texin-quantum-clock. Message understood? Over."

"It sounds like gibberish to me," said Lanark.

"Proceed as planned. Repeat: as planned. Repeat: as planned.
Out."

There was a click and silence. He lay thinking of how he kept
being pushed into certain actions, and how people kept talking
to him as though he had planned them. But perhaps the message
had not been for him but for his aircraft. It had sounded very
like a machine talking to a machine. He pushed his head out
into sunlight again.

He was flying up a wide and winding firth with very different coasts. To the right lay green farmland with clumps of
trees and reservoirs in hollows linked by quick streams. On
the left were mountain ridges and high bens silvered with snow,
the sun striking gold sparkles off bits of sea loch between them.
On both shores he saw summer resorts with shops, church spires
and crowded esplanades, and clanging ports with harbours full
of shipping. Tankers moved on the water, and freighters and
white-sailed yachts. A long curving feather of smoke pointed
up at him from a paddle steamer churning with audible chunk-
ing sounds toward an island big enough to hold a grouse moor,
two woods, three farms, a golf course and a town fringing a
bay. This island looked like a bright toy he could lift up off
the smoothly ribbed, rippling sea, and he seemed to recognize
it. He thought, 'Did I have a sister once? And did we play
together on the grassy top of that cliff among the yellow gorse-
bushes? Yes, on that cliff behind the marine observatory, on
a day like this in the summer holidays. Did we bury a tin
box under a gorse root in a rabbit hole? There was a half-
crown piece in it and a silver sixpence dated from that year,
and a piece of our mother's jewellery, and a cheap little notebook with a message to ourselves when we grew up. Did we
promise to dig it up in twenty-five years? And dug it up two
days later to make sure it hadn't been stolen? And were we
not children then? And was I not happy?'

The shores grew steeper, more wooded and close together; the firth was pinched between them to a water-lane marked by buoys and light-towers. In places docks embanked it and vessels were being built or unloaded beneath the arms of cranes. Then the high land sloped away left and right and he came to a valley, a broad basin of land filled by a city with the river gleaming toward a centre of spires, towers and high white blocks. The eagle-machine left the river and soared in a long curve over sloping hills to the south, then to the east, then to the north. It crossed tenements of clean stone enclosing gardens where children played and lines of washing flapped in a slow breeze. There was a holiday in this city for the air was transparent and the bowling greens and tennis courts busy with players. The width and beauty of the view, its clearness under the sun seemed not only splendid but familiar. He thought, 'All my life, yes, all my life I've wanted this, yet I seem to know it well. Not the names, no, the names have gone, but I recognize the places. And if I really lived here once, and was happy, how did I lose it? Why am I only returning now?'

Sometimes he heard a sound like a slow explosion, a huge soft roaring from the city centre, and looking over there he saw tiny bird shapes moving to and fro. A shadow touched him and looking upward he saw, overhead toward the east, a great eagle crossing his course with the sign Z-1 on the underside of the breast. He realized his own craft was following a spiral path aimed at the city centre and getting lower all the time. It soared down the tree-filled gorge of another river, a small one linking parks full of strollers and sunbathers. Children on a grassy slope waved handkerchiefs at him and he thought, 'Soon I'll see the university.' A moment later he looked down on twin quadrangles framed by pinnacled rooftops. He thought, 'Soon we'll reach the river with the big dock basin and cranes and warehouses', but this time he was wrong. The small river entered a mainstream which spread out into arms of quiet water, but these lay among paths and trees surrounding a gigantic sports stadium. Figures were racing and vaulting round the tracks, on the rich green grass of the centre rested athletes in variously coloured suits, from the crowded terraces a dull hubbub of applause welled into a roar. Lanark's aircraft joined five or six others circling overhead. At intervals one would drop toward a white canvas square spread before the main grandstand with red, blue and black target rings painted on

it. A voice over a loudspeaker was saying ". . . and now Posky, Podgorny, Paleologue and Norn are entering the last lap; and just descending, bang on target, is Premier Kostoglotov of the Scythian People's Republic; and Norn and Paleologue are passing, yes, passing Podgorny into second place, almost neck and neck, and the gap between them and Posky is closing fast"— here a great roar went up—
"and the Toltec of Tiahuanaco dips toward the target just as Posky falls into third place and now Norn leads, then Paleologue, then Posky with Podgorny a very poor fourth; and here comes the Provost of Unthank—I'm sorry the *Lord* Provost of *Greater* Unthank—dropping toward the target just as Norn, yes, Norn, yes, Norn of Thule breaks the tape, closely followed by Paleologue of Trebizond and Posky of Crim Tartary."

Lanark's eagle-machine thumped down on the canvas and stood rocking slightly. Six men in dust coats seized it and carried it a few yards to a row of similar machines standing against a long narrow platform. Lanark gripped his briefcase and was helped onto the platform by a girl in a scarlet skirt and blouse who said hurriedly, "The Unthank delegate, yes?"
"Yes."
"This way, please, you're half a minute behind schedule."
She led him down some steps, through groups of relaxing athletes, across a momentarily bare cinder track and into a doorway under the terracing of the main grandstand. After the wide spaces of the sky it was perplexing to trot up a narrow passage in artificial light. He decided that whatever happened he would remain dour, sceptical and unimpressed. They came to a hall with open lifts along the walls. The girl ushered him into one, saying, "Go up to the executive gallery, they're expecting you. Leave your luggage with me; I'll make sure it reaches your room in the delegates' repose village."
"No, I'm sorry, these documents are vital," said Lanark. He saw a row of buttons in a polished metal panel and touched one beside the words EXECUTIVE GALLERY. The lift ascended and he watched his reflection in the polished panel with satisfaction. Though older he was even more dignified than in the vestry lavatory. He had grown a pointed, compact, captainish little white beard, his cheeks were smooth and rosy, the effect was of well-groomed efficiency. The lift door opened and Wilkins, looking exactly as Lanark remembered him, shook his hand, saying, "Provost Sludden! Am I right?"
"No, Wilkins. My name is Lanark. We've met before."

Wilkins peered closely and said, "Lanark! My God, so you are. What's happened to Sludden?"

"He is coping at present with a very dangerous sanitary problem. The Greater Unthank regional committee have judged it wiser for me to represent the city."

Wilkins smiled crookedly and said, "That man is a fox: a ninth-generation ecological fox. Never mind. Join the queue, join the queue."

"Wilkins, our sanitary problem is assuming catastrophic dimensions. I have more than one report in this briefcase which shows that people will start dying soon and—"

"This is a social reception, Lanark, public health will be debated on Monday. Just join the queue and say hello to your hosts."

"Hosts?"

"The Provan executive officer and Lord and Lady Monboddo. Join the queue, join the queue."

They were in a broad curving corridor with glass double-doors on one side and a queue moving steadily through. Lanark noticed a woman in a silver sari and a brown man in a white toga but most people wore sober uniforms or business suits and had the wary look of important people who, without showing friendship, are prepared to respond judiciously to it in others. They were an easy crowd to join. At the glass door a loud voice announced the arrivals to a company beyond: "Senator Sennacherib of New Alabama. Brian de Bois Guilbert, Grand Templar of Languedoc and Apulia. Governor Vonnegut of West Atlantis. . . ."

He reached the door and heard the satisfying cry, "Lord Provost Lanark of Greater Unthank," and shook hands with a hollow-cheeked man who said, "Trevor Weems of Provan. Glad you could come."

A stately woman in a blue tweed gown shook his hand and said, "Had you a nice trip?"

Lanark stared at her and said, "Catalyst."

"Call her Lady Monboddo," said Ozenfant, who was standing beside her. He shook Lanark's hand briskly. "Time changes all the labels, as you yourself are proving also."

A girl in a scarlet skirt and blouse took Lanark's arm and led him down some steps saying, "Hello, I'm called Libby. I expect you need some refreshment. Shall I get you a snack from the buffet? Pâté de something? Breast of something? Locusts and honey?"

"Was Ozenfant . . . ? Is Ozenfant . . . ?"

"The new lord president director, yes hadn't you heard?
Doesn't he look tremendously fit? I wonder why his wife is
wearing that hairy frock? Perhaps you aren't hungry. Neither
am I. Let's tuck into the booze instead, there's heaps of it.
Just sit there a minute."
He sat down at the end of a long leather sofa and looked
perplexedly around.

He was on the highest and largest of four floors which
descended like steps to a wall of window overlooking the stadium. Half the people standing around seemed to be delegates
and stood talking in quiet little groups. Girls in scarlet lent
some liveliness to the company by carrying trays between the
groups with flirtatious quickness, but they were balanced by
silent, robust men who stood watchfully by the walls wearing
black suits and holding glasses of whisky which they did not
sip. On a glass-topped table near the sofa lay a sheaf of pamphlets
entitled **ASSEMBLY PROGRAMME.** Lanark lifted and
opened one. He read a printed letter from Trevor Weems
welcoming the delegates on behalf of the people of Provan
and trusting their stay would be a happy one. There was no
possibility of danger to life or limb, as the newest sort of security
staff had been rented from the Quantum-Cortexin group; the
Red Girls, however, were human and anxious to help with
any difficulty the delegates could bring to them. Then came
six pages of region names listed alphabetically from Armorica
to Zimbabwe. Lanark saw that the Greater Unthank delegate
was given as Provost Sludden. Then came a page headed:

FIRST DAY

**HOUR 11. Arrival and reception of delegates by Lord
    and Lady Monboddo**

After this a press conference was listed, a lunch, an "opportunity
for social and informal lobbying," a sheepdog trial, a pipe band
contest, a dinner with speeches, a performance by the Erse
Opera Company of Purser's *Misfortunes of Elphin,* a firework
display and a party. Lanark turned a page impatiently and found
something less frivolous.

SECOND DAY

HOUR 8.50.   Breakfast. Lobbying.

HOUR 10.   **World Education Debate.**
                                Chairman, Lord Monboddo.
Opening speech: "Logos into Chaos." The Erse
delegate and sociosophist Odin MacTok analyzes
the disastrous impact of literacy on the undereducated.
Speeches.   Motions.   Voting.

HOUR 15.   **Lunch. Lobbying.**

HOUR 17.   **World Food Debate.**
                                Chairman, Lord Monboddo.
Opening speech: "Excrement into Aliment." The
Bohemian delegate and Volstat research scholar
Dick Otoman explains how organic pollutions can
be pre-processed to revitalize each other within
the human body.
Speeches.   Motions.   Voting.

HOUR 22.   **Dinner. Lobbying.**

THIRD DAY

HOUR 8.50.   **Breakfast. Lobbying.**

HOUR 10.   **Public Order Debate.**
                                Chairman, Lord Monboddo.
Opening speech: "Revolutionary Stasis." Kado
Motnic, sociometrist and delegate of the People's
Republic of Paphlogonia describes the application
of short-nerve-circuitry to libido-canalization in the
infra-supra-25-40 spectrum.
Speeches.   Motions.   Voting.

HOUR 15.   **Lunch. Lobbying.**

HOUR 17.   **World Energy Debate.**
                                Chairman, Lord Monboddo.
Opening speech: "Biowarp." South Atlantis delegate and Algolagnics director Timon Kodac presents gene-warping as the solution to the fossil-fuel failure.
Speeches.   Motions.   Voting.

HOUR 22.   **Dinner. Lobbying.**

FOURTH DAY

HOUR 8.50.   **Breakfast. Lobbying.**

HOUR 10.   **World Health Debate.**
                         Chairman, Lord Monboddo.
         Opening speech: "Kindness, Kin and Capacity."
         Hanseatic delegate and sociopathist Moo Dackin
         explains why healthy norms must be preserved
         by destroying other healthy norms.
         Speeches.   Motions.   Voting.
HOUR 15.   **Lunch, social and informal.**
HOUR 17.   **The Subcommittees report. Voting.**
HOUR 21.   **Press conference.**
HOUR 22.   **Dinner. Speeches.**
                         Master of Ceremonies, Trevor Weems.
         Opening speech: "Then, Now and Tomorrow." Six
         millennia of achievement will be outlined by the
         Chairman of the Assembly, Moderator of the Ex-
         pansion Project, Director of the Institute and Presi-
         dent of the Council, the Lord Monboddo. Trevor
         Weems, Chief Executive Officer of the Provan Ba-
         sin, will propose a vote of thanks. Toadi Monk,
         Satrap of Troy and Trebizond, will move the vote
         of thanks to the hosts.
HOUR 25.   **The delegates depart.**

Before reading all this Lanark had been gripped by a large
undirected excitement. Since wakening to sunlight in his aircraft
that morning he had felt himself nearing the centre of a great
event, approaching a place where he would utter, publicly, a
word that would change the world. The sight of Wilkins, the
catalyst and Ozenfant-Monboddo had not damaged this feeling.
He had been startled, but so had they, which was satisfying.
But the assembly programme disconcerted him. It was like seeing the plans of a vast engine he meant to drive and finding
he knew nothing about engineering. What did "Speeches. Motions. Voting" mean? What was "Lobbying" and why did it
happen at mealtimes? Did the other delegates understand these
things?

     The gallery was very crowded now and two men sat at
the other end of the sofa sipping pint glasses of black beer
and gazing at the active little figures on the sunlit sports field
below. One of them said cheerfully, "It's great to see all this
happening in Provan."

"Is it?"

"Oh, come now, Odin, you've worked as hard as anyone to bring the assembly here."

The other said morosely, "Bread and circuses. Bread and circuses. A short spell of reasonable wages and long holidays while they plunder us and then *wham!* The chopper. Provan will be turned into another Greater Unmentionable Region."

Lanark said eagerly, "Excuse me, are you complaining about the condition of this city?"

The morose man had thick white hair, a body like a wrestler's and a pinkish battered face like a boxer's. He looked at Lanark balefully for a moment, then said, "I think I've a right to do that. I live here."

"Then you don't know how lucky you are! I'm from a region with an unusually dangerous sanitary problem, and Provan strikes me as the most splendidly situated—"

"Are you a delegate?"

"Yes."

"So you've just arrived by air."

"Yes."

"Then don't talk to me about Provan. You're in the early stages of a Gulliver complex."

Lanark said coldly, "I don't understand you."

"The first recorded aerial survey happened when Lemuel Gulliver, a plain, reasonable man, was allowed to stand on his feet beside the capital of Lilliput. He saw well-cultivated farms surrounding the homes, streets, and public buildings of a very busy little people. He was struck by the obvious ingenuity and enterprise of the rulers, the officials and the workmen. It took him two or three months to discover their stupidity, greed, corruption, envy, cruelty."

"You pessimists always fall into the disillusion trap," said the cheerful man cheerfully. "From one distance a thing looks bright. From another it looks dark. You think you've found the truth when you've replaced the cheerful view by the opposite, but true profundity blends all possible views, bright as well as dark."

The morose man grinned and said, "Since nearly everyone clings to the cloud-cuckoo view it's lucky one or two of us aren't afraid to look at the state of the sewers."

"Sorry I took so long," said the Red Girl, placing a tray on the table. "I thought it might be fun to try a gaelic coffee."

"I'm glad you mentioned sewers," said Lanark eagerly, "I come from Unthank, which is having trouble with its sewers. In fact the future of the whole region is being menaced—I mean, decided—by this assembly, and I've been sent here as advocate for the defence. But the programme"—he waved it—"tells me nothing about where and when to speak. Can you advise me?"

"There's no need to be so serious on the first day," said the Red Girl.

"The future of a crippled region," said the morose man slowly, "is usually hammered out by one of the subcommittees."

"Which subcommittee? When and where does it meet?"

"This is a friendly social reception!" said the Red Girl, looking distressed. "Can't we keep all this heavy stuff till later? There's going to be *such* a lot of it."

"Shut up, dear," said the morose man. "Wilkins knows all the ropes. You'd better ask him."

"Listen," said the Red Girl. "I'll take you to Nastler. He knows everything about everything, and he's expecting to see you soon in the Epilogue room. He told me so."

"Who is Nastler?"

"Our king. In a way. But he's not at all grand," said the Red Girl evasively. "It's hard to explain."

The morose man guffawed and said, "He's a joker. You'll get nothing out of him."

Lanark opened his briefcase, locked the assembly programme inside and stood up.

"I understand that you are employed to help me with my difficulties," he told the Red Girl. "I will speak to both Wilkins and this Nastler person. Which can I see first?"

"Oh Nastler, definitely," said the red girl, looking relieved. "He's an invalid, anyone can see him anytime. But won't you drink your coffee first?"

"No," said Lanark, and thanked the morose man, and followed the Red Girl into the crowd.

Weems and the Monboddos were still shaking hands with the queue by the door, which was a short one now. As Lanark passed them the announcer was saying, "Chairman Fu of Xanadu. Proto-Presbyter Griffith-Powys of Ynyswitrin. Premier Multan of Zimbabwe."

The Red Girl led him along the outer corridor till they came to a white panel without hinges or handle. She said, "It's a door. Go through it."

"Aren't you coming?"

"If you're going to talk politics, I'm going to wait outside."

As Lanark pressed the surface he noticed a big word on it:

EPILOGUE

He entered a room with no architectural similarity to the building he had left. The door on this side had deeply moulded panels and a knob, the ceiling was bordered by an elaborate cornice of acanthus sprays, there was a tall bay window with the upper foliage of a chestnut tree outside and an old stone tenement beyond. The rest of the room was hidden by easels holding large paintings of the room. The pictures seemed brighter and cleaner than the reality and a tall beautiful girl with long blond hair reclined in them, sometimes nude and sometimes clothed. The girl herself, more worried and untidy than her portraits, stood near the door wearing a paint-stained butcher's apron. With a very small brush she was adding leaves to a view of the tree outside the window, but she paused, pointed round the edge of the picture and told Lanark, "He's there."

A voice said, "Yes, come round, come round."

Lanark went behind the picture and found a stout man leaning against a pile of pillows on a low bed. His face, framed by wings and horns of uncombed hair, looked statuesque and noble apart from an apprehensive, rather cowardly expression. He wore a woollen jersey over a pyjama jacket, neither of them clean, the coverlet over his knees was littered with books and papers, and there was a pen in his hand. Glancing at Lanark in a sly sideways fashion he indicated a chair with the pen and said, "Please sit down."

"Are you the king of this place?"

"The king of Provan, yes. And Unthank too. And that suite of rooms you call the institute and the council."

"Then perhaps you could help me. I am here—"

"Yes, I know roughly what you want and I would like to help. I would even offer you a drink, but there's too much intoxication in this book."

"Book?"

"This world, I meant to say. You see I'm the king, not the government. I have laid out landscapes, and stocked them with people, and I still work an occasional miracle, but governing is left to folk like Monboddo and Sludden."

"Why?"

The king closed his eyes, smiled and said, "I brought you here to ask that question."

"Will you answer it?"

"Not yet."

Lanark felt very angry. He stood up and said, "Then talking to you is a waste of time."

"Waste of time!" said the king, opening his eyes. "You clearly
don't realize who I am. I have called myself a king—that's a
purely symbolic name, I'm far more important. Read this and
you'll understand. The critics will accuse me of self-indulgence
but I don't care."[1]

With a reckless gesture he handed Lanark a paper from the
bed. It was covered with childish handwriting and many words
were scored out or inserted with little arrows. Much of it seemed
to be dialogue but Lanark's eye was caught by a sentence in
italics which said: *Much of it seemed to be dialogue but Lanark's
eye was caught by a sentence in italics which said:*

Lanark gave the paper back asking, "What's that supposed to
prove?"

"I am your author."

Lanark stared at him. The author said, "Please don't feel embarrassed. This isn't an unprecedented situation. Vonnegut has it
in *Breakfast of Champions* and Jehovah in the books of Job and
Jonah."

"Are you pretending to be God?"

"Not nowadays. I used to be part of him, though. Yes, I am
part of a part which was once the whole. But I went bad and
was excreted. If I can get well I may be allowed home before
I die, so I continually plunge my beak into my rotten liver
and swallow and excrete it. But it grows again. Creation festers
in me. I am excreting you and your world at the present moment. This arse-wipe"—he stirred the papers on the bed—"is
part of the process."

"I am not religious," said Lanark, "but I don't like you mixing
religion with excrement. Last night I saw part of the person
you are referring to and it was not at all nasty."

"You saw part of God?" cried the author. "How did that happen?"

Lanark explained. The author was greatly excited. He said,
"Say those words again."

"*Is . . . is . . . is . . .* , then a pause, then *Is . . . if . . .
is. . . .*"

"If?" shouted the author sitting upright. "He actually said if?
He wasn't simply snarling 'Is, is, is, is, is,' all the time?"

Lanark said, "I don't like you saying 'he' like that. What I saw
may not have been masculine. It may not have been human.
But it certainly wasn't snarling. What's wrong with you?"

The author had covered his mouth with his hands, apparently

1. To have an objection anticipated is no reason for failing to raise it.

to stifle laughter, but his eyes were wet. He gulped and said, "One *if* to five *is*es! That's an incredible amount of freedom. But can I believe you? I've created you honest, but can I trust your senses? At a great altitude *is* and *if* must sound very much alike."

"You seem to take words very seriously," said Lanark with a touch of contempt.

"Yes. You don't like me, but that can't be helped. I'm pri*ma*rily a literary man," said the author with a faintly nasal accent, and started chuckling to himself.

The tall blond girl came round the edge of the painting wiping her brush on her apron. She said defiantly, "I've finished the tree. Can I leave now?"

The author leaned back on his pillows and said sweetly, "Of course, Marion. Leave when you like."

"I need money. I'm hungry."

"Why don't you go to the kitchen? I believe there's some cold chicken in the fridge, and I'm sure Pat won't mind you making yourself a snack."

"I don't want a snack, I want a meal with a friend in a restaurant. And I want to go to a film afterward, or to a pub, or to a hairdresser if I feel like it. I'm sorry, but I want money."

"Of course you do, and you've earned it. How much do I owe?"

"Five hours today at fifty pence an hour is two pounds fifty. With yesterday and the day before and the day before is ten pounds, isn't it?"

"I've a poor head for arithmetic but you're probably right," said the author, taking coins from under a pillow and giving them to her. "This is all I have just now, nearly two pounds. Come back tomorrow and I'll see if I can manage a little extra." The girl scowled at the coins in her hand and then at the author. He was puffing medicinal spray into his mouth from a tiny hand-pump. She went abruptly behind the painting again and they heard the door slam.

"A strange girl," murmured the author, sighing. "I do my best to help her but it isn't easy."

Lanark had been sitting with his head propped on his hands. He said, "You say you are creating me."

"I am."

"Then how can I have experiences you don't know about?

You were surprised when I told you what I saw from the aircraft."

"The answer to that is unusually interesting; please attend closely. When *Lanark* is finished (I am calling the work after you) it will be roughly two hundred thousand words and forty chapters long, and divided into books three, one, two and four."

"Why not one, two, three and four?"

"I want *Lanark* to be read in one order but eventually thought of in another. It's an old device. Homer, Vergil, Milton and Scott Fitzgerald used it.[2] There will also be a prologue before book one, an interlude in the centre, and an epilogue two or three chapters before the end."

"I thought epilogues came after the end."

"Usually, but mine is too important to go there. Though not essential to the plot it provides some comic distraction at a moment when the narrative sorely needs it. And it lets me utter some fine sentiments which I could hardly trust to a mere character. And it contains critical notes which will save research scholars years of toil. In fact my epilogue is so essential that I am working on it with nearly a quarter of the book still unwritten. I am working on it here, just now, in this conversation. But you have had to reach this room by passing through several chapters I haven't clearly imagined yet, so you know details of the story which I don't. Of course I know the broad general outline. That was planned years ago and mustn't be changed. You have come here from my city of destruction, which is rather like Glasgow, to plead before some sort of world parliament in an ideal city based on Edinburgh, or London, or perhaps Paris if I can wangle a grant from the Scottish Arts Council[3] to go there. Tell me, when you were landing this morning, did you see the Eiffel Tower? Or Big Ben? Or a rock with a castle on it?"

"No. Provan is very like—"

"Stop! Don't tell me. My fictions often anticipate the experiences they're based upon, but no author should rely on that sort of thing."

Lanark was so agitated that he stood and walked to the window

2. Each of the four authors mentioned above began a large work *in medias res*, but none of them numbered their divisions out of logical sequence.
3. In 1973, as a result of sponsorship by the poet Edwin Morgan, the author received a grant of £300 from the Scottish Arts Council for the purpose of helping him write his book, but it was never assumed that he would use the money to seek out exotic local colour.

to sort out his thoughts. The author struck him as a slippery
person but too vain and garrulous to be impressive. He went
back to the bed and said, "How will my story end?"
"Catastrophically. The Thaw narrative shows a man dying because he is bad at loving. It is enclosed by your narrative which
shows civilization collapsing for the same reason."
"Listen," said Lanark. "I never tried to be a delegate. I never
wanted anything but some sunlight, some love, some very ordinary happiness. And every moment I have been thwarted by
organizations and things pushing in a different direction, and
now I'm nearly an old man and my reasons for living have
shrunk to standing up in public and saying a good word for
the only people I know. And you tell me that word will be
useless! That you have *planned* it to be useless."
"Yes," said the author, nodding eagerly. "Yes, that's right."
Lanark gaped down at the foolishly nodding face and suddenly
felt it belonged to a horrible ventriloquist's doll. He raised a
clenched fist but could not bring himself to strike. He swung
round and punched a painting on an easel and both clattered
to the floor. He pushed down the other painting beside the
door, went to a tall bookcase in a corner and heaved it over.
Books cascaded from the upper shelves and it hit the floor
with a crash which shook the room. There were long low shelves
around the walls holding books, folders, bottles and tubes of
paint. With sweeps of his arm he shoved these to the floor,
then turned, breathing deeply, and stared at the bed. The author
sat there looking distressed, but the paintings and easels were
back in their old places, and glancing around Lanark saw the
bookcases had returned quietly to the corner and books, folders,
bottles and paint were on the shelves again.
"A conjuror!" said Lanark with loathing. "A damned conjuror!"
"Yes," said the conjuror humbly, "I'm sorry. Please sit down
and let me explain why the story has to go like this. You can
eat while I talk (I'm sure you're hungry) and afterward you
can tell me how you think I could be better. Please sit down."
The bedside chair was small but comfortably upholstered. A
table had appeared beside it with covered dishes on a tray.
Lanark felt more exhausted than hungry, but after sitting for
a while he removed a cover out of curiosity. There was a bowl
beneath of dark red oxtail soup, so taking a spoon he began
to eat.

"I will start," said the conjuror, "by explaining the physics
of the world you live in. Everything you have experienced

and are experiencing, from your first glimpse of the Elite café to the metal of that spoon in your fingers, the taste of the soup in your mouth, is made of one thing."

"Atoms," said Lanark.

"No. Print. Some worlds are made of atoms but yours is made of tiny marks[4] marching in neat lines, like armies of insects, across pages and pages and pages of white paper. I say these lines are marching, but that is a metaphor. They are perfectly still. They are lifeless. How can *they* reproduce the movement and noises of the battle of Borodino, the white whale ramming the ship, the fallen angels on the flaming lake?"

"By being read," said Lanark impatiently.

"Exactly. Your survival as a character and mine as an author depend on us seducing a living soul into our printed world and trapping it here long enough for us to steal the imaginative energy which gives us life. To cast a spell over this stranger I am doing abominable things. I am prostituting my most sacred memories into the commonest possible words and sentences. When I need more striking sentences or ideas I steal them from other writers, usually twisting them to blend with my own. Worst of all I am using the great world given at birth— the world of atoms—as a ragbag of shapes and colours to make this second-hand entertainment look more amusing."

"You seem to be complaining," said Lanark. "I don't know why. Nobody is forcing you to work with print, and all work involves some degradation. I want to know why your readers in their world should be entertained by the sight of me failing to do any good in mine."

"Because failures are popular. Frankly, Lanark, you are too stolid and commonplace to be entertaining as a successful man. But don't be offended; most heroes end up like you. Consider the Greek book about Troy. To repair a marriage broken by adultery, a civilization spends ten years smashing another one. The heroes on both sides know the quarrel is futile, but they continue

---

4. This is a false antithesis. Printed paper has an atomic structure like anything else. "Words" would have been a better term than "print," being less definably concrete.

INDEX OF PLAGIARISMS

There are three kinds of literary theft in this book:
BLOCK PLAGIARISM, where someone else's work is printed as a distinct typographical unit, IMBEDDED PLAGIARISM, where stolen words are concealed within the body of the narrative, and DIFFUSE PLAGIARISM, where scenery, characters, actions or novel ideas have been stolen without the original words describing them. To save space these will be referred to hereafter as Blockplag, Implag, and Difplag.

ANON.
Books 3 and 4. These owe much to *Monkey*, the Chinese comic classic eclectic novel, first Englished by Arthur Waley, which shows the interplay between an earthly pilgrimage and heavenly and hellish supernatural worlds which parody it. (*See also* KAFKA.)
ANON.
Chap. 29, para. 2. The couplet

ends a verse on a monument
now standing beside a pedestrian lane under a flyover of an
intersection of the Monkland
Motorway and Cathedral
Street, Glasgow.
ANON.
Chap. 30, para. 12. Blockplag
of inscription on cairn on moor
beside the String Road near
Black-waterfoot on Isle of
Arran, Firth of Clyde.
ANON.
Chap. 43. Ozenfant's speech.
Blockplag of first stanza of Mid-
dle English epic poem *Gawain
and the Green Knight*, omitting
3rd and 4th lines, "The tyke
that the trammels of treason
there wrought/Was tried for
his treachery, the truest on
earth" (the translation is also
anonymous).
BLACK ANGUS
See Macneacail, Aonghas.
BLAKE, WILLIAM
Chap. 19, para. 1. Implag of
poem "The Clod and the Peb-
ble" from *Songs of Experience*.
Chap. 35, last paragraph. Im-
plag. Ritchie-Smollet quotes
"The Little Vagabond" from
Songs of Experience.
BORGES, JORGE LUIS
Chap. 43. Ozenfant's speech.
Blockplag from short essay
"The Barbarian and the City."
BOYCE, CHRISTOPHER
Chap. 38, para. 16. The en-
counter between the "sharp red
convertible" and the motorcy-
clists is an Implag from the short
story "Shooting Script."
**BROWN,
GEORGE DOUGLAS**
Books 1 and 2 owe much to
the novel *The House with the
Green Shutters* in which heavy
paternalism forces a weak-
minded youth into dread of
existence, hallucination, and
crime.
BUNYAN, JOHN
Chap. 9, para. 10. Blockplag of
first paragraph of the *Relation of
the Holy War Made by Shaddai
Upon Diabolus for the Regaining
of the Metropolis of the World; or
the losing and taking again of the
town of Mansoul*.
BURNS, ROBERT
Robert Burns' humane and lyri-
cal rationalism has had no impact upon the formation of this

it because they think willingness to die
in a fight is proof of human greatness.
There is no suggestion that the war does
anything but damage the people who
survive it.

"Then there is the Roman book
about Aeneas. He leads a group of refu-
gees in search of a peaceful home and
spreads agony and warfare along both
coasts of the Mediterranean. He also visits Hell but gets out again. The writer
of this story is tender toward peaceful
homes, he wants Roman success in warfare and government to make the world
a peaceful home for everyone, but his
last words describe Aeneas, in the heat
of battle, killing a helpless enemy for
revenge.

"There is the Jewish book about
Moses. It's very like the Roman one
about Aeneas, so I'll go on to the Jewish
book about Jesus. He is a poor man
without home or wife. He says he is
God's son and calls all men his brothers.
He teaches that love is the one great
good, and is spoiled by fighting for
things. He is crucified, goes to Hell,
then to Heaven which (like Aeneas's
peaceful world) is outside the scope of
the book. Jesus taught that love is the
greatest good, and that love is damaged
by fighting for things; but if (as the song
says) "he died to make us good" he
too was a failure. The nations who wor-
shipped him became the greediest conquerors in the world.

"Only the Italian book shows a living man in Heaven. He gets there by
following Aeneas and Jesus through
Hell, but first loses the woman and the

home he loves and sees the ruin of all his political hopes.

"There is the French book about the giant babies. Pleasing themselves is their only law so they drink and excrete in a jolly male family which laughs at everything adults call civilization. Women exist for them, but only as rubbers and ticklers.

"There is the Spanish book about the Knight of the Dolorous Countenance. A poor old bachelor is driven mad by reading the sort of books *you* want to be in, with heroes who triumph here and now. He leaves home and fights peasants and innkeepers for the beauty which is *never* here and now, and is mocked and wounded. On his deathbed he grows sane and warns his friends against intoxicating literature.

"There is the English book about Adam and Eve. This describes a heroic empire-building Satan, an amoral, ironical, boundlessly creative God, a lot of warfare (but no killing) and all centered on a married couple and the state of their house and garden. They disobey the landlord and are evicted, but he promises them accommodation in his own house if they live and die penitently. Once again success is left outside the scope of the book. We are last shown them setting out into a world to raise children they know will murder each other.

"There is the German book about Faust, an old doctor who grows young by witchcraft. He loves, then neglects, a girl who goes mad and kills his baby

book, a fact more sinister than any exposed by mere attribution of sources. See also Emerson.

CARLYLE, THOMAS
Chap. 27, para. 5. "I can't believe," etc., is an Implag of the youthful sage of Ecclefechan's query of his mother, "Did God Almighty come down and make wheelbarrows in a shop?" The device of giving a ponderous index to a work of ponderous fiction is taken from *Sartor Resartus*.

CARROLL, LEWIS
Chap. 41, para. 3. The taste of the white rainbow is a Difplag of the taste in the bottle marked "drink me" in *Alice in Wonderland*.

CARY, JOYCE
Chaps. 28 and 29. Difplags of the novel *The Horse's Mouth*. Here and elsewhere Duncan Thaw is a hybrid formed by uniting Gulley Jimson (the Blake-quoting penniless painter of a mural illustrating the biblical Genesis in a derelict church) with his untalented working-class disciple, Nosey Barbon.

CHASE, JAMES HADLEY
Chap. 9, para. 1. Blockplag of first two paragraphs of *No Orchids for Miss Blandish*.

COLERIDGE, SAMUEL TAYLOR
Chap. 26, para. 12. The warmth that gushes in Thaw's chest is the same spring of love which releases *The Ancient Mariner* from the nightmare life-in-death.
Chap. 41, para 12. This reference to God, orphans and Hell is a debased Implag of "An orphan's curse would drag to hell/A spirit from on high," from *The Rime of the Ancient Mariner*.

CONRAD, JOSEPH
Chap. 32, para. 4. This difplags the meeting of the Assistant Commissioner and Sir Ethelred in *The Secret Agent*.
Chap. 41, para 6. Kodac's speech contains a dispersed Implag of names and nouns from the novel *Nostromo*.

DISNEY, WALT
In Book 3, the transforming of Lanark's arm and the turning of people into dragons is a Difplag

of the transformed hero's nose and turning of bad boys into donkeys from the film *Pinocchio*. So is the process of purification by swallowing in the last paragraphs of Chap. 6. (*See also* GOD and JUNG.)

ELIOT, T. S.
Chap. 10, para. 4. "I'm something commonplace that keeps getting hurt" is a drab Difplag of the "notion of some infinitely gentle,/Infinitely suffering thing" in *Preludes*.

EMERSON, RALPH WALDO
Ralph Waldo Emerson has not been plagiarized.

EVARISTI, MARCELLA
Chap. 45, para. 3. "Dont knife the leaf" is from the song *Lettuce Bleeds*.

FITZGERALD, F. SCOTT
Epilogue, para. 1. The sentence "You don't like me" etc. is from McKisco's bedroom dialogue with Rosemary Hoyte in Book 1 of *Tender Is the Night*. Chap. 10, para. 6. "We think a lot of new friends" etc. echoes Dick Diver's remark to Rosemary on the beach.

FREUD, SIGMUND
Difplags in every chapter. Only a writer unhealthily obsessed by all of Dr. Freud's psycho-sexual treatises would stuff a novel with more oral, anal and respiratory symbols, more Oedipal encounters with pleasure-reality/Eros-thanatos substitutes, more recapitulations of the birth-trauma than I have space to summarize. (*See also* DISNEY, GOD and JUNG.)

GLASHAN, JOHN
Chap. 38, para. 13. The snapping noise in Miss Maheen's head is an Implag from the "Snapping Song" from "Earwigs Over the Mountains" sung by the Social Security choir in *The Great Meths Festival*.

GOD
Chap. 6, paras. 11, 12, 13, 14. The purification by swallowing is a Difplag from the verse drama *Jonah*. (*See also* DISNEY and JUNG.)

GOETHE, JOHANN WOLFGANG VON
Chap. 35, para. 1. "*Wer immer strebend*" etc. is from the verse drama *Faust*, angel chorus Act V, Scene VII. Bayard Taylor translates this as "Whoe'er as-

son. He becomes banker to the emperor, abducts Helen of Troy and has another, symbolic son who explodes. He steals land from peasants to create an empire of his own and finances it by piracy. He abandons everything he tires of, grabs everything he wants and dies believing himself a public benefactor. He is received into a Heaven like the Italian one because 'man must strive and striving he must err' and because 'he who continually strives can be saved.' Yah! The only person in the book who strives is the poor devil, who does all the work and is tricked out of his wages by the angelic choir showing him their bums.[5] The writer of this book was depraved by too much luck. He shows the sort of successful man who captains the modern world, but doesn't show how vilely incompetent these people are. *You* don't need that sort of success.

"It is a relief to turn to the honest American book about the whale. A captain wants to kill it because the last time he tried to do that it bit off his leg while escaping. He embarks with a cosmopolitan crew who don't like home life and prefer this way of earning money. They are brave, skilful and obedient, they chase the whale round the world and get themselves all drowned together: all but the storyteller. He describes the world flowing on as if they had never

5. "*Von hinten anzusehen—Die Racker sind doch gar zu appetitlich*" is little more than a line. Louis MacNeice omits it from his translation as inessential because it reduces the devil's dignity. The author's amazing virulence against Goethe is perhaps a smokescreen to distract attention from what he owes him. *See* GOETHE and WELLS in the Index of Plagiarisms.

existed. There are no women or children in this book, apart from a little black boy whom they accidentally drive mad.

"Then there is the Russian book about war and peace. That has fighting in it, but fighting which fills us with astonishment that men can so recklessly, so resolutely, pester themselves to death. The writer, you see, has fought in real battles and believed some things Jesus taught. This book also contains"— the conjuror's face took on an amazed expression—"several believable happy marriages with children who are well cared for. But I have said enough to show that, while men and women would die out if they didn't usually love each other and keep their homes, most of the world's great stories[6] show them failing spectacularly to do either."

6. The index proves that *Lanark* is erected upon an infantile foundation of Victorian nursery tales, though the final shape derives from English language fiction printed between the 40's and 60's of the present century. The hero's biography after death occurs in Wyndham-Lewis's trilogy *The Human Age,* Flann O'Brien's *The Third Policeman* and Golding's *Pincher Martin.* Modern afterworlds are always infernos, never paradisos, presumably because the modern secular imagination is more capable of debasement than exaltation. In almost every chapter of the book there is a dialogue between the hero (Thaw or Lanark) and a social superior (parent, more experienced friend or prospective employer) about morality, society or art. This is mainly a device to let a self-educated Scot (to whom "the dominie" is the highest form of social life) tell the world what he thinks of it: but the glum flavour of these episodes recalls three books by disappointed socialists which appeared after the second world war and centred upon what I will call dialogue under threat: *Darkness at Noon* by Arthur Koestler, *1984* by George Orwell, and *Barbary Shore* by Norman Mailer. Having said this, one is compelled to

pires unweariedly is not beyond redeeming"; John Anster as "Him who, unwearied, still strives on/We have the power to save" and Hopton Upcraft as "It's a great life/If you don't weaken."
Epilogue, para. 1. "I am part of that part which was once the whole" is an Implag from Mephistopheles' speech in *Faust* Act I, Scene III: *"Ich bin ein Theu des Theus, der Angango alles war."*
GOLDING, WILLIAM
See footnote 6.
GOODMAN, LORD
Chap. 38, para. 9. "Greed isn't a pretty thing but envy is far, far worse" is a slightly diffuse Implag from the speech in which the great company lawyer compared those who fight for dividends with those who fight for wages and declared his moral preference for the former.
GUARDIAN
Chap. 36, para. 8. The newspaper extract is a distorted Blockplag of the financial report from Washington, July 9, 1973.
HEINE, HEINRICH
Chap. 34, para. 5. "screeching, shrieking, yowling, growling, grinding, whining, yammering, skammering, trilling, chirping" etc. contains Implag from the Hellnoise described in Chap. 1 of *Reisebilder* in Leland's translation.
HIND, ARCHIE
Epilogue, para. 14. The disciplines of cattle slaughter and accountancy are dramatized in the novel *The Dear Green Place.*
HOBBES, THOMAS
Books 3 and 4 are Difplags of Hobbes's daemonic metaphor *Leviathan,* which starts with the words "By art is created that great Leviathan called a Commonwealth or State (in Latin, *Civitas*), which is but an artificial man." Describing a state or tribe as a single man is as old as society—Plutarch does it in his life of Coriolanus—but Hobbes deliberately makes the metaphor a monstrous one. His state is the sort of creature Frankenstein made: mechanical yet lively; lacking ideas, yet directed by cunning brains; morally and physically clumsy, but full of strength got from

people forced to supply its belly, the market. In a famous title page this state is shown threatening a whole earth with the symbols of warfare and religion. Hobbes named it from the verse drama *Job*, in which God describes it as a huge water beast he is specially proud to have made because it is "king of all the children of pride." The author of *The Whale* thought it a relation of his hero. (*See* MELVILLE.)

HOBSBAUM, DR. PHILIP
Chap. 45, paras. 6, 7, 8. The battle between the cloth and wire monkeys is a Difplag of *Monkey Puzzle*:

Wire monkeys are all
          elbows, knees and teeth.
Cloth monkeys can be leant
          upon.

Wire monkeys endure,
          repel invaders.
Cloth monkeys welcome all
          comers.

They set up wire monkeys to
  test the youngsters' hunger,
Cloth monkeys their loneliness.

Wire monkeys suckle, give food.
Cloth monkeys are barren.

You will see the youngster
          turn to the wire monkey
For sustenance merely
Then go back and embrace
          the cloth monkey
Who affords nothing.

When frightened the youngster
  will bury its head in
          the soft
Warm protruding bosom of the
          cloth.
The wire monkey stands
          against the blast.
Everyone prefers cloth monkeys.

HUME, DAVID
Chap. 16, para. 9. Blockplag from treatise: *An Enquiry Concerning Human Understanding.*

IBSEN, HENRIK
Books 3 and 4. These owe much to the verse drama *Peer Gynt*, which presents an interplay between a petit-bourgeois universe and supernatural regions which parody and criticise it. (*See also* KAFKA.)

IMPERIAL GAZETTEER OF SCOTLAND, 1871
Chap. 25, para. 1. This is not

"Which proves," said Lanark, who was eating a salad, "that the world's great stories are mostly a pack of lies." The conjuror sighed and rubbed the side of his face. He said, "Shall I tell you the ending you want? Imagine that when you leave this room and return to the grand salon, you find that the sun has set and outside the great windows a firework display is in progress above the Tuileries garden."
"It's a sports stadium," said Lanark.
"Don't interrupt. A party is in progress, and a lot oi informal lobbying is going on among the delegates."
"What is lobbying?"
"Please don't interrupt. You move about discussing the woes of Unthank with whoever will listen. Your untutored eloquence has an effect beyond your expectations, first on women, then on men. Many delegates see that their own lands are threatened by the multinational companies and realize that if something isn't quickly done the council won't be able to help them either. So

ask why the "conjuror" introduces an apology for his work with a tedious and brief history of world literature, as though summarizing a great tradition which culminates in himself! Of the eleven great epics mentioned, only one has influenced *Lanark*. Monboddo's speech in the last part of *Lanark* is a dreary parody of the Archangel Michael's history lecture in the last book of *Paradise Lost* and fails for the same reason. A property is not always valuable because it is stolen from a rich man. And for this single device thieved (without acknowledgement) from Milton we find a confrontation of fictional character by fictional author from Flann O'Brien; a hero, ignorant of his past, in a subfuse modern Hell, also from Flann O'Brien; and, from T. S. Eliot, Nabokov and Flann O'Brien, a parade of irrelevant erudition through grotesquely inflated footnotes.

How to Make us All Happy

491

tomorrow when you stand up in the great assembly hall to speak for your land or city (I haven't worked out which yet), you are speaking for a majority of lands and cities everywhere. The great corporations, you say, are wasting the earth. They have turned the wealth of nations into weapons and poison, while ignoring mankind's most essential needs. The time has come etcetera etcetera. You sit down amid a silence more significant than the wildest applause and the lord president director himself arises to answer you. He expresses the most full-hearted agreement. He explains that the heads of the council have already prepared plans to curb and harness the power of the creature but dared not announce them before they were sure they had the support of a majority. He announces them now. All work which merely transfers wealth will be abolished, all work which damages or kills people will be stopped. All profits will belong to the state, no state will be bigger than a Swiss canton, no politician will draw a larger wage than an agricultural labourer. In fact, all wages will be lowered or raised to the national average, and later to the international average, thus letting people transfer to the jobs they do best without artificial feelings of prestige or humiliation. Stockbrokers, bankers, accountants, property developers, advertisers, company lawyers and detectives will become schoolteachers if they can find no other useful work, and no teacher will have more than six pupils per class. The navy and air forces will be set to providing children everywhere with free meals. The armies will dig irrigation ditches and plant trees. All human excrement will be returned to the land.

the simple Blockplag it seems. It unites extracts from the *Monkland Canal* entry and the *Monkland and Kirkintilloch Railway* entry which preceeds that.
JOYCE, JAMES
Chap. 22, para. 5. This monologue by a would-be artist to a tolerant student friend is a crude Difplag of similar monologues in *A Portrait of the Artist as a Young Man.*
JUNG, CARL
Nearly every chapter of the book is a Difplag of the mythic "Night Journey of the Hero" described in that charming but practically useless treatise *Psychology and Alchemy.* This is most obvious in the purification by swallowing at the end of chapter 6. (*See also* DISNEY, GOD and FREUD.) But the hero, Lanark, gains an unJungian political dimension by being swallowed by Hobbes's Leviathan. (*See* HOBBES.)
KAFKA, FRANZ
Chap. 39, last paragraph. The silhouette in the window is from the last paragraph of *The Trial.*
KELMAN, JIM
Chap 47. God's conduct and apology for it is an extended Difplag of the short story *Acid:*

In this factory in the north of England acid was essential. It was contained in large vats.

Gangways were laid above them. Before these gangways were made completely safe a young man fell into a vat feet first. His screams of agony were heard all over the department. Except for one old fellow the large body of men was so horrified that for a time not one of them could move. In an instant this old fellow who was also the young man's father had clambered up and along the gangway carrying a big pole. Sorry Hughie, he said. And then ducked the young man below the surface. Obviously the old fellow had had to do this because only the head and shoulders . . . in fact, that which had been seen above the acid was all that remained of the young man.
KINGSLEY, REVEREND CHARLES
Most of *Lanark* is an extended Difplag of *The Water Babies,*

a Victorian children's novel thought unreadable nowadays except in abridged versions. *The Water Babies* is a dual book. The first half is a semi-realistic, highly sentimental account of an encounter between a young chimney sweep from an industrial slum and an upper-class girl who makes him aware of his inadequacies. Emotionally shattered, in a semi-delirious condition, he climbs a moorland, descends a cliff and drowns himself, in a chapter which recalls the conclusion of Book 2. He is then reborn with no memory of the past in a vaguely Darwinian purgatory with Buddhist undertones. At one point the hero, having stolen sweets, grows suspicious, sulky and prickly all over like a seaurchin! The connection with dragonhide is obvious. He is morally redeemed by another encounter with the upper-class girl, who has died of a bad cold, and then sets out on a pilgrimage through a grotesque region filled with the social villainies of Victorian Britain. (*See also* MacDONALD.)

KOESTLER, ARTHUR
See footnote 6.

LAWRENCE, D. H.
See footnote 12.

LEONARD, TOM
Chap. 50, para. 3. "In a wee while, dearie" is an Implag of the poem "The Voyeur."
Chap. 49. General Alexander's requiem for Rima is a Blockplag of the poem *Placenta*.

LOCHHEAD, LIZ
Chap. 48, para. 25. The android's discovery by the Goddess is a Difplag of *The Hickie*:

I mouth
sorry in the mirror when I see
the mark I must have
                    made just now
loving you.
Easy to say it's alright
adultery
like blasphemy is for
                    believers but
even in our
situation simple etiquette
                    says
love should leave us
                    both unmarked.
You are on loan to me
                    like a library book
and we both know it.

I don't know how Monboddo would propose to start this new system, but I could drown the practical details in storms of cheering. At any rate, bliss it is in this dawn to be alive, and massive sums of wealth and technical aid are voted to restore Unthank to healthy working order. You board your aircraft to return home, for you now think of Unthank as home. The sun also rises. It precedes you across the sky; you appear with it at noon above the city centre. You descend and are reunited with Rima, who has tired of Sludden. Happy ending. Well?"

Lanark had laid down his knife and fork. He said in a low voice, "If you give me an ending like that I will think you a very great man."
"If I give you an ending like that I will be like ten thousand other cheap illusionists! I would be as bad as the late H. G. Wells! I would be worse than Goethe.[7] Nobody who knows a thing about life or politics will believe me for a minute."
Lanark said nothing. The conjuror scratched his hair furiously with both hands and said querulously, "I understand your resentment. When I was sixteen or seventeen *I* wanted an ending like that. You see, I found Tillyard's study of the epic in Dennistoun public library, and he said an epic was only written when a new society was giving men a greater chance of liberty. I decided that what the *Aeneid* had been to the Roman Empire my epic would be to the Scottish Cooperative Wholesale Republic, one of the many hundreds of

7. This remark is too ludicrous to require comment here.

small peaceful socialist republics which would emerge (I thought) when all the big empires and corporations crumbled. That was about 1950. Well, I soon abandoned the idea. A conjuror's best trick is to show his audience a moving model of the world as it is with themselves inside it, and the world is not moving toward greater liberty, equality and fraternity. So I faced the fact that my world model would be a hopeless one. I also knew it would be an industrial-west-of-Scotland-petitbourgeois one, but I didn't think that a disadvantage. If the maker's mind is prepared, the immediate materials are always suitable.

"During my first art school summer holiday I wrote chapter 12 and the mad-vision-and-murder part of chapter 29. My first hero was based on myself. I'd have preferred someone less specialized but mine were the only entrails I could lay hands upon. I worked poor Thaw to death, quite cold-bloodedly, because though based on me he was tougher and more honest, so I hated him. Also, his death gave me a chance to shift him into a wider social context. You are Thaw with the neurotic imagination trimmed off and built into the furniture of the world you occupy.[8] This makes you much more capable of action and slightly more capable of love.

"The time is now"—the conjuror glanced at his wristwatch, yawned and lay back on the pillows—"the time is

8. But the fact remains that the plots of the Thaw and Lanark sections are independent of each other and cemented by typographical contrivances rather than formal necessity. A possible explanation is that the author thinks a heavy book will make a bigger splash than two light ones.

Fine if you love both of us
but neither of us
        must too much show it.

In my misted mirror
you trace two toothprints
on the skin of your
        shoulder and sure
you're almost quick enough
to smile out bright and
        clear for me
as if it was O.K.

Friends again, together in
        this bathroom
we finish washing love away.

McCABE, BRIAN
Chap. 48, para. 2. The Martian headmaster is from the short story *Feathered Choristers*.
MacCAIG, NORMAN
Chap. 48, para. 22. The cursive adder is from the poem *Movements*.
MacDIARMID, HUGH
Chap. 47, para. 22. Major Alexander's remark that "Inadequate maps are better than no maps; at least they show that the land exists" is stolen from *The Kind of Poetry I Want*.
MacDONALD, REVEREND GEORGE
Chap. 17, *The Key*, is a Difplag of the Victorian children's story *The Golden Key*. The journey of Lanark and Rima across the misty plain of Chap. 33 also comes from this story, as does the death and rebirth of the hero halfway through (*see also* KINGSLEY) and the device of casually ageing people with spectacular rapidity in a short space of print.
MacDOUGALL, CARL
Chap. 41, para. 1. *Poxy nungs* is the favourite expletive of the oakumteaser in the colloquial verse drama *A View from the Rooftops*.
McGRATH, TOM
Chap. 48, para. 22. The android's circuitous seduction of God is from the play, *The Android Circuit*.
MacNEACAIL, AONGHAS
See Nicolson, Angus.
MANN, THOMAS
Chap. 34, para. 5. "Screeching, shrieking, yowling, growling, grinding, whining, yammering, stammering, trilling, chirping" etc. contains Implag of the devil's account of Hellnoise in the novel. *Doktor Faustus*, translated by H. T. Lowe-Porter.

MAILER, NORMAN
See footnote 6.
MARX, KARL
Chap. 36, paras. 3 and 4.
Grant's long harangue is a Dif-
plag of the pernicious theory of
history as class warfare embod-
ied in *Das Kapital.*
MELVILLE, HERMAN
See footnote 12.
MILTON, JOHN
See footnote 6.
MONBODDO, LORD
Chap. 32, para. 3. The reference to James Burnett, Lord
Monboddo, demonstrates the
weakness of the fabulous and al-
legorical part of *Lanark.* The
"institute" seems to represent
that official body of learning
which began with the ancient
priesthoods and Athenian acad-
emies, was monopolized by the
Catholic Church and later dispersed among universities and
research foundations. But if the
"council" represents government, then the most striking
union of "council" and "institute" occurred in 1662 when
Charles II chartered the Royal
Society for the Advancement of
the Arts and Sciences. James
Burnett of Monboddo be-
longed to an Edinburgh Cor-
responding Society which advanced the cause of science
quite unofficially until granted
a royal charter in 1782. He was
a court of session judge, a friend
of King George and an erudite
metaphysician with a faith in sa-
tyrs and mermaids, but has only
been saved from oblivion by the
animadversions against his theory of human descent from the
ape in Boswell's *Life of Johnson.*
By plagiarizing and annexing
his name to a dynasty of scientific Caesars the author can only
be motivated by Scottish chau-
vinism or a penchant for resounding nomenclature. A
more fitting embodiment of
government, science, trade and
religion would have been Robert Boyle, son of the Earl of
Cork and father of modern
chemistry. He was founder of
the Royal Society, and his
strong religious principles also
led him to procure a charter for
the East India Company, which
he expected to propagate Christianity in the Orient.

1970, and although the work is far from
finished I see it will be disappointing
in several ways. It has too many conversations and clergymen, too much
asthma, frustration, shadow; not enough
countryside, kind women, honest toil.
Of course not many writers describe
honest toil, apart from Tolstoy and Lawrence on haymaking, Tressel on house-
building and Archie Hind on clerking
and slaughtering. I fear that the men
of a healthier age will think my story
a gafuffle of grotesquely frivolous para-
sites, like the creatures of Mrs. Radcliffe,
Tolkien and Mervyn Peake. Perhaps my
model world is too compressed and
lacks the quiet moments of unconsid-
ered ease which are the sustaining part
of the most troubled world. Perhaps I
began the work when I was too young.
In those days I thought light existed to
show things, that space was simply a gap
between me and the bodies I feared or
desired; now it seems that bodies are
the stations from which we travel into
space and light itself. Perhaps an illu-
sionist's main job is to exhaust his restless audience by a show of marvellously
convincing squabbles until they see the
simple things we really depend upon:
the movement of shadow round a globe
turning in space, the corruption of life
on its way to death and the spurt of
love by which it throws a new life clear.
Perhaps the best thing I could do is
write a story in which adjectives like
commonplace and *ordinary* have the significance which *glorious* and *divine* carried in earlier comedies. What do you
think?"
"I think you're trying to make the readers admire your fine way of talking."
"I'm sorry. But yes. Of course," said
the conjuror huffily. "You should know

by now that I have to butter them up[9] a bit. I'm like God the Father, you see, and you are my sacrificial Son, and a reader is a Holy Ghost who keeps everything joined together and moving along. It doesn't matter how much you detest this book I am writing, you can't escape it before I let you go. But if the readers detest it they can shut it and forget it; you'll simply vanish and I'll turn into an ordinary man. We mustn't let that happen. So I'm taking this opportunity to get all of us agreeing about the end so that we stay together right up to it."

"You know the end I want and you're not allowing it," said Lanark grimly. "Since you and the readers are the absolute powers in this world you need only persuade them. My wishes don't count."

"That *ought* to be the case," said the conjuror, "but unluckily the readers identify with your feelings, not with mine, and if you resent my end too much I am likely to be blamed instead of revered, as I should be. Hence this interview.

"And first I want us all to admit that a long life story cannot end happily. Yes, I know that William Blake sang on his deathbed, and that a president of the French Republic died of heart-failure while fornicating on the office sofa,[10] and that in 1909 a dental patient in Wumbijee, New South Wales, was struck by lightning after receiving a

9. In this context to butter up means to flatter. The expression is based upon the pathetic fallacy that because bread tastes sweeter when it is buttered, bread enjoys being buttered.
10. The president in question was Felix Fauré, who died in 1909 upon the conservatory sofa, not office sofa, of the Elysée Palace.

NicGUMARAID, CATRIONA
Like all lowland Scottish literateurs, the "conjuror" lacks all understanding of his native Gaelic culture. The character and surroundings of the Rev. McPhedron in Chap. 13, the least convincing chapter in the book, seem to be an effort to supply that lack. As a touchstone of his failure I print these verses by a real Gael. See also MacNeacail, Aonghas.

Nan robh agam sgian
ghearrainn ás an ubhal
an grodadh donn a th'ann
a leòn's a shàraich mise.

Ach mo chreach-s' mar thà
chan eil mo sgian-sa biorach
's cha dheoghail mi ás nas mò
an loibht' a sgapas annad.

NICOLSON, ANGUS
See Black Angus.
O'BRIEN, FLANN
See footnote 6.
ORWELL, GEORGE
Chap. 38. The poster slogans and the social stability centre are Difplags of the Ingsoc posters and Ministry of Love in *1984.*
PLATH, SYLVIA
Chap. 10, para. 10. "I will rise with my flaming hair and eat men like air" is an Implag of the last couplet of "Lady Lazarus," with "flaming" substituted for "red."
POE, EDGAR ALLAN
Chap. 8, para. 7. The "large and lofty apartment" is an Implag from the story *The Fall of the House of Usher.* Chap. 38, para. 16. The three long first sentences are Implag from *The Domain of Arnheim.* The substitution of "pearly" pebbles for "alabaster" pebbles comes from Poe's other description of water with *s.* pebbly bottom in *Eleonora.*
POPE, ALEXANDER
Chap. 41, para. 6. Timon Kodac's statement "Order is heaven's first law" is from the poetic *Essay on Man.*
PRINCE, REV. HENRY JAMES
Chap. 43, Monboddo's speech. "Stand with me on the sun" is from *Letters addressed by H. J. Prince to his Christian Brethren at St. David's College, Lampeter.*
PROPPER, DAN

Chap. 28, para. 7. McAlpin's statement of Propper's law is a distorted Implag from *The Fable of the Final Hour:* "In the 34th minute of the final hour the Law of Inverse Enclosure was rediscovered and a matchbox was declared the prison of the universe, with two fleas placed inside as warders."

QUINTILIANUS MARCUS FABRICIUS

Chap. 45, para. 5. Grant's "form of self-expression second only to the sneeze" is an Implag from Book 11 of the *Institutio Oratoria* translated by John Bulwer in his Chironomia.

REICH, WILHELM

Book 3. The dragonhide which infects the first six chapters is a Difplag of the muscular constriction Reich calls "armouring."

REID, TINA

Chap. 48, para. 15. The android's method of cleaning the bed is a Difplag of *Jill the Gripper* from *Licking the Bed Clean.*

SARTRE, JEAN-PAUL

Chap. 18, para. 6. Chap. 21, para. 12. These are Difplags of the negative epiphanies experienced by the hero of *Nausea.*

SAUNDERS, DONALD GOODBRAND

Chap. 46. The peace-force led by Sergeant Alexander is blocked by God in a land whose shapes and colours come from *Ascent:*

The white shape is Loch Fionn,
Intimate with corners.
From here, the foothills
　　　　　　of Suilven,
The white shape is Loch Fionn.

The green shape is Glencanisp,
Detailed with rocks,
From here, the shoulder
　　　　　　of Suilven,
The green shape is Glencanisp.

The blue shape is the seas.
The blue shape is the skies.
From here, the summit
　　　　　　of Suilven,
My net returns glittering.

SHAKESPEARE, WILLIAM

Books 1 and 2 owe much to the play *Hamlet* in which heavy paternalism forces a weak-minded youth into dread of existence, hallucinations and crime.

SITWELL, EDITH

Chap. 41, para. 12. "Speaking

dose of laughing gas.[11] The God of the real world can be believed when such things happen, but no serious entertainer dare conjure them up in print. We can fool people in all kinds of elaborate ways, but our most important things must seem likely and the likeliest death is still to depart this earth in a 'fiery-pain-chariot' (as Carlyle put it), or to drift out in a stupefied daze if there's a good doctor handy. But since the dismaying thing about death is loneliness, let us thrill the readers with a description of you ending *in company.* Let the ending be worldwide, for such a calamity is likely nowadays. Indeed, my main fear is that humanity will perish before it has a chance to enjoy my forecast of the event. It will be a metaphorical account, like Saint John's, but nobody will doubt what's happening. Attend!

"When you leave this room you will utterly fail to contact any helpful officials or committees. Tomorrow, when you speak to the assembly, you will be applauded but ignored. You will learn that most other regions are as bad or even worse than your own, but that does not make the leaders want to cooperate: moreover, the council itself is maintaining its existence with great difficulty. Monboddo can offer you nothing but a personal invitation to stay in

11. The township of Wumbijee is in southern Queensland, not new South Wales, and even at the present moment in time (1976) is too small to support a local dentist. In 1909 it did not exist. The laughing gas incident is therefore probably apocryphal but, even if true, gives a facetious slant to a serious statement of principle. It will leave the readers (whom the author pretends to cherish) uncertain of what to think about his work as a whole.

Provan. You refuse and return to Un-thank, where the landscape is tilted at a peculiar angle, rioters are attacking the clock towers and much of the city is in flame. Members of the committee are being lynched, Sludden has fled, you stand with Rima on the height of the Necropolis watching flocks of mouths sweep the streets like the shadows of huge birds, devouring the population as they go. Suddenly there is an earth-quake. Suddenly the sea floods the city, pouring down through the mouths into the corridors of council and institute and short-circuiting everything. (That sounds confusing; I haven't worked out the details yet.) Anyway, your eyes finally close upon the sight of John Knox's statue—symbol of the tyranny of the mind, symbol of that protracted male erection which can yield to death but not to tenderness—toppling with its column into the waves, which then roll on as they have rolled for . . . a very great period. How's that for an end-ing?"

"Bloody rotten," said Lanark. "I ha-ven't read as much as you have, I never had the time, but when I visited public libraries in my twenties *half* the science-fiction stories had scenes like that in them,[12] usually at the end. These banal world destructions prove nothing but the impoverished minds of those who can think of nothing better."

The conjuror's mouth and eyes opened wide and his face grew red. He began speaking in a shrill whisper which swelled to a bellow: *"I am not writing*

12. Had Lanark's cultural equipment been wider, he would have seen that this conclusion owed more to *Moby Dick* than to science fiction, and more to Lawrence's essay on *Moby Dick* than to either.

purely as a private person," and much of the religious senti-ment, are Im- and Difplag from the section of *Facade* which starts "Don't go bathing in the Jordan, Gordon."

SMITH, W. C.
Chap. 28. Blockplag from hymn "Immortal, Invisible, God Only Wise" with distorted final line.

SPENCE, ALAN
Chap. 45, para. 9. The fine col-ours are taken from the anthol-ogy *Its Colours They Are Fine.*

THACKERAY, WILLIAM MAKEPEACE
Chap. 11, para. 5. The bag and listed contents are a Plag, Block- and Dif-, from the Fairy Blackstick's bag in *The Rose and the Ring.*

THOMAS, DYLAN
Chap. 29, para. 5. Contains small Implag and Difplag from the prose poem "The Map of Love." Chap. 42, para. 5. La-nark's words when urinating are a distorted Implag of the poem "Said the Old Ramrod."

TOTUOLA, AMOS
Books 3 and 4. These owe much to *The Palm Wine Drink-ard,* another story whose hero's quest brings him among dead or supernatural beings living in the same plane as the earthly. (*See also* KAFKA.)

TURNER, BILL PRICE
Chap. 46, para. 1. "The sliding architecture of the waves" is from *Rudiment of an Eye.*

URE, JOAN
Chap. 48, para. 8. The batman's wife is singing her own version of the song in the review *Some-thing may come of it:* "Nothing to sing about/getting along/very pedestrianly./People in aeroplanes/singing their song/continue to fly over me./Some-thing they've got that I've not?/Something I've got that they've not?/Nothing to sing about./Nothing to sing about."

VONNEGUT, KURT
Chap. 43, Monboddo's speech. The description of the earth as a "moist blue-green ball" is from the novel *Breakfast of Champions.*

WADDEL, REVEREND P. HATELY
Chap. 37, para. 4. The over-heard prayer is from Rev. Wad-del's lowland Scottish transla-tion of Psalm 23.

**WELLS,
HERBERT GEORGE**
The institute described in Books 3 and 4 is a combination of any large hospital and any large university with the London Underground and the BBC Television Centre, but the overall scheme is stolen from 21st-century London in *The Sleeper Awakes* and from the Selenite sublunar kingdom in *The First Men on the Moon.* In the light of this fact, the "conjuror's" remark about H. G. Wells in the Epilogue seems a squid-like discharge of vile ink for the purpose of obscuring the critical vision. See footnote 5.

WOLFE, TOM
Chap. 41, para. 6. The hysterical games-slang in this section is an Implag from the introduction to an anthology, *The New Journalism.*

XENOPHON
Chaps. 45, 46, 47, 48, 49. The mock-military excursion throughout these is an extended Difplag of the *Anabasis.*

**YOUNGHUSBAND,
COL. STUKELY**
Chap. 49, para. 49. "Down the crater of Vesuvius in a tramcar" is a remark attributed to General Douglas Haig in *Quips from the Trenches.*

ZOROASTER
Chap. 50, paras 1, 3, 5, 7, 9, 11, 13, 15, 17, 19, 21, 23, 25, 27, 29, 31 are all spicy bits culled from Sybilene Greek apocrypha edited by Hermippus and translated by Friedrich Nietzsche, but the flowery glade of Sibma thick with vines and Eleale to the asphaltic pool; the sun, wind and flashing foam; the triumph of Galatea and her wedding with Grant; the collapse of the Cocqigrues; the laughing surrender of God; the bloom of the bright grey thistle; the building of Nephelococugia; the larks, lutes, cellos, violets and vials of genial wrath; the free waterbuses on the Clyde; the happiness and good work of Andrew; the return of Coulter, coming of McAlpin and resurrection of Aiken Drummond; the Apotheosis and Coronation of the Virgin AmyAnnieMoraTracy

science fiction! Science-fiction stories have no real people in them, and all my characters are real, real, real people! I may astound my public by a dazzling deployment of dramatic metaphors designed to compress and accelerate the action, but that is not science, it is magic! Magic! As for my ending's being banal, wait till you're inside it. I warn you, my whole imagination has a carefully reined-back catastrophist tendency; you have no conception of the damage my descriptive powers will wreak when I loose them on a theme like THE END."

"What happens to Sandy?" said Lanark coldly.

"Who's Sandy?"

"My son."

The conjuror stared and said, "You have no son."

"I have a son called Alexander who was born in the cathedral."

The conjuror, looking confused, grubbed among the papers on his bed and at last held one up, saying, "Impossible, look here. This is a summary of the nine or ten chapters I haven't written yet. If you read it you'll see there's no time for Rima to have a baby in the cathedral. She goes away too quickly with Sludden."

"When you reach the cathedral," said Lanark coldly, "you'll describe her having a son more quickly still."

The conjuror looked unhappy. He said, "I'm sorry. Yes, I see the ending becomes unusually bitter for you. A child. How old is he?"

"I don't know. Your time goes too fast for me to estimate."

After a silence the conjuror said querulously, "I can't change my overall plan now. Why should I be kinder than my century? The millions of children who've been vilely murdered this century is—*don't hit me!"*

Lanark had only tensed his muscles but the conjuror slid down the bed and pulled the covers over his head; they subsided until they lay perfectly flat on the mattress. Lanark sighed and dropped his face into his hand. A little voice in the air said, "Promise not to be violent."

KatrinaVeronicaMargaretInge IngeIngeIngeIngeIngeIngeInge IngeIngeIngeIngeIngeIngeInge IngeIngeIngeIngeIngeMarian BethLizBettyDanieleAngel TinaJanetKate; the final descent to healthy commonplace and finding a silk smooth you inside that husk are Blockplags, Implags, Difplags of *The Marriage of Heaven and Hell* translated into clear images and sublime distances by William Blake and William Turner for the benefit of all makers of useful good and lovely things.

Lanark snorted contemptuously. The bedclothes swelled up in a man-shaped lump but the conjuror did not emerge. A muffled voice under the clothes said, "I didn't need to play that trick. In a single sentence I could have made you my most obsequious admirer, but the reader would have turned against both of us. . . . I wish I could make you like death a little more. It's a great preserver. Without it the loveliest things change slowly into farce, as you will discover if you insist on having much more life. But I refuse to discuss family matters with you. Take them to Monboddo. Please go away."

"Soon after I came here," said Lanark, lifting the briefcase and standing up, "I said talking to you was a waste of time. Was I wrong?"

He walked to the door and heard mumbling under the bedclothes. He said, "What?"

". . . know a black man called Multan . . ."

"I've heard his name. Why?"

". . . might be useful. Sudden idea. Probably not."

Lanark walked round the painting of the chestnut tree, opened the door and went out.[13]

13. As this "Epilogue" has performed the office of an introduction to the work as a whole (the so-called "Prologue" being no prologue at all, but a separate short story), it is saddening to find the "conjuror" omitting the courtesies appropriate to such an addendum. Mrs. Florence Allan typed and retyped his manuscripts, and often waited many months without payment and without complaining. Professor Andrew Sykes gave him free access to copying equipment and secretarial help. He received from James Kelman critical advice which enabled him to make smoother prose of the crucial first chapter. Charles Wild, Peter Chiene, Jim Hutcheson, Stephanie Wolf Murray engaged in extensive lexical activity to ensure that the resulting volume had a surface consistency. And what of the compositors employed by Kingsport Press of Kingsport, Tennessee, to typeset this bloody book? Yet these are only a few out of thousands whose help has not been acknowledged and whose names have not been mentioned.

CHAPTER 41. Climax

He looked down, startled, at Libby, who lay curled with her legs under her in the angle between wall and carpet looking unconscious. She was a gracefully plump, dark-haired girl. Her skirt was shorter and blouse silkier than he remembered, and her sulky slumbering face looked far more childish than the clothes. She opened her eyes saying "What?" and sat up and glanced at her wristwatch. Without blame she said, "You've been hours in there. Hours and hours. We've missed the opera."

She held out a hand and he helped her up. She said, "Did he feed you?"

"He did. Now I would like to speak to Wilkins."

"Wilkins?"

"Or Monboddo. On second thought, I would prefer to see Monboddo. Is that possible?"

She stared at him and said, "Do you never relax? Don't you ever enjoy yourself?"

"I did not come here to relax."

"Sorry I asked."

She walked down the corridor. He followed, saying, "Listen, if I'm being rude I apologize, but I'm very worried just now. And anyway, I've always been bad at enjoying myself."

"Poor old you."

"I'm not complaining," said Lanark defensively. "Some very nice things have happened to me, even so."

"When, for instance?"

Lanark remembered when Sandy was born. He knew he must have been happy then or he wouldn't have rung the cathedral bell, but he couldn't remember what happiness felt like. His past suddenly seemed a very large, very dreary place. He said tiredly, "Not long ago."

In the hall beside the lift doors she halted, faced him and said firmly, "I don't know where Monboddo and Wilkins are just now. I expect they'll drop in later when the party starts, so I'll give you some advice. Play it gelid. I see you've got it bad, Dad, but the hard sell is no go on day one when everybody's casing each other. The real hot lobbyists start cashing their therms halfway through countdown on day two. And there's something else I'd like to tell you. The Provan executive pays my salary whether I stay with you or not. If you want me to vanish say 'vanish' and I'll vanish. Or else come for a quiet drink with me and talk about *anything* but this general bloody awful assembly. Even their language gives me the poxy nungs."

Lanark stared at her, seeing how attractive she was. The sight was a great pain. He knew that if she let him kiss her petulant mouth he would feel no warmth or excitement. He looked inside himself and found only a hungry ungenerous cold, a pained emptiness which could neither give nor take. He thought, 'I am mostly a dead man. How did this happen?' He muttered, "Please don't vanish."

She took his arm and led him toward the gallery saying slyly, "I bet I know one thing you enjoy."

"What?"

"Bet you enjoy being famous."

"I'm not."

"Modest, eh?"

"No, but I'm not famous either."

"Think I'd have waited all these hours outside Nastler's door if you'd been an ordinary delegate?"

Lanark was too confused to answer. He pointed to a silent crowd of black-suited security men on each side of the glass door and said, "What are they doing here?"

"They're staying outside to make the party less spooky."

Though nearly empty the gallery throbbed with light rhythmical music. In the night sky outside the window the pinktipped petals of several great chrysanthemums were spreading out from golden centres among the stars and dipping down toward the floodlit stadium where tiny figures thronged the terraces and crowded upon dance floors, one at each end of the central field. The chrysanthemums faded and a scarlet spark shot through them, drawing a long tail of white and green

dazzling feathers. The floor along the window was furnished with piles of huge coloured cushions. The floor above that had a twelve-man orchestra at one end, though at present the only player was a clarinettist blowing a humorous little tune and a drummer softly stroking the cymbals with wire brushes. The floor above that had four well-laden buffets along it, and the top floor had many empty little chairs and tables, and a bar at each end, and four girls sitting on stools by one of the bars. Libby led Lanark over to them and said, "Martha, Solveig, Joy and the other Joy, this is you-know-who from Unthank." Martha said, "It can't be."
Solveig said, "You look far too respectable."
Joy said, "Shall I put your briefcase behind the bar? It'll be safe there."
The other Joy said, "My mother is a friend of yours, or says she used to be."
"Is she called Nancy?" said Lanark glumly, handing over the briefcase and sitting down. "Because if she is I met you when you were a baby."
"No, she's called Gay."
"Don't remind him of his age," said Libby. "Be a mother yourself and mix us two white rainbows. (She's good at white rainbows.)"

Solveig was the largest of the girls and the other Joy was the smallest. They were all about the same age and had the same casually friendly manners. Lanark was not very conscious of them as distinct people but he was soothed by being the only man among them. Libby said, "We've got to persuade Lanark that he's famous."
They all laughed and the other Joy, who was measuring drops of liquor into a silver canister, said, "But he knows. He must know."
"What am I famous for?" said Lanark.
"You're the man who does these weird, weird things for no reason at all," said Martha. "You smashed Monboddo's telescreen when he was conducting a string quartet."
"You fought with him over a dragon-bitch and blocked the whole current of the institute," said Solveig.
"You told him exactly what you thought of him and walked straight out of the council corridors into an intercalendrical zone. On foot!" said Joy.
"We're mad keen to see what you do tonight," said the other Joy. "Monboddo's terrified of you."

Lanark started explaining how things had really happened, but
the corners of his mouth had risen and were squeezing out
his cheeks and narrowing his eyes; he could not help his face
being contorted, his tongue gagged by a huge silly grin, and
at last he shook his head and laughed. Libby laughed too. She
was leaning on the bar, her hip brushing his thigh. Martha
told him, "Libby's using you to make her boyfriend jealous."
"No I'm not. Well, just a bit, I am."
"Who's your boyfriend?" asked Lanark, smiling.
"The man with the glasses down there. The drummer. He's
horrible. When his music isn't going right for him nothing
goes right for him."
"Make him as jealous of me as you like," said Lanark, patting
her hand. The other Joy gave him a tall glass of clear drink
and they all watched him closely as he sipped. The first sip
tasted soft and furry, then cool and milky, then thin and piercing
like peppermint, then bitter like gin, then thick and warm like
chocolate, then sharp like lemon but sweetening like lemonade.
He sipped again and the flow of tastes over his tongue was
wholly different, for the tip tasted black currant, blending into
a pleasant kind of children's cough mixture in the centre and
becoming like clear beef gravy as it entered the throat, with
a faint aftertaste of smoked oysters. He said, "The taste of
this makes no sense."
"Don't you like it?"
"Yes, it's delicious."
They laughed as if he'd said something clever. Solveig said,
"Will you dance with me when the music starts?"
"Of course."
"What about me?" said Martha.
"I intend to dance once with everybody—except the other Joy.
I'm going to dance twice with the other Joy."
"Why?"
"Because being unusually kind to someone will give me a feel-
ing of power."
Everyone laughed again and he sipped the drink feeling worldly
and witty. A small man with a large nose arrived and said,
"You all seem to be having a good time, do you mind if I
join in? I'm Griffith-Powys, Arthur Griffith-Powys of Ynyswitrin. Lanark of Unthank, aren't you? I only just missed you
this morning, but I heard you'd been hard at it. It was good
to know somebody was knocking the gelid lark. We've had
too much of that. You'll be sounding off loud and clear tomorrow, I hope?"

The gallery was filling with older people who were clearly delegates or delegates' wives, and others in their thirties who seemed to be secretaries and journalists. There were more red girls too, though few of them now wore the whole red uniform. Groups were forming but the group round Lanark was the largest. Odin, the pink-faced morose man, came over and asked, "Any luck with His Royal Highness?"

"None. In fact he said he wasn't a king at all but a conjuror."

"Young people must find the modern world very confusing," said Powys, patting Martha's arm paternally. "So many single people have different names and so many different people have the same name. Look at Monboddo. We've all known at least two Monboddos and the next one will likely be a woman. Look at me! Last year I was Arch Druid of Camelot and Cadbury. This year, what with ecumenical pressure and regionalization, I'm Proto-Presbyter of Ynyswitrin, yet I'm the same man doing the same job."

Odin said in a low voice, "Here comes the enemy."

Five black men of different heights entered, two in business suits, two in military uniform and the tallest in caftan and fez. Martha shivered and said, "I hate the black bloc—they drink nothing stronger than lemonade."

"Well, I *love* them," said Libby stoutly. "I think they're charming. And Senator Sennacherib drinks whisky by the quart."

"What I can't take is bloody Multan's air of superiority," said Odin. "I know we sold and flogged his ancestors, which proves we're vicious; but it doesn't prove he's much good."

"Is that Multan?" said Lanark. The blacks had descended to the next floor and were standing at one of the buffets. "Excuse me a minute," said Lanark. He passed quickly through the other groups, descended three or four steps and approached the black bloc. "Please," he said to the tall man in the fez, "are you Multan of Zimbabwe?"

"Here is General Multan," said the tall man, indicating a small man in military uniform. Lanark said, "May I speak to you, General Multan? I've been told you . . . we might be able to help each other."

Multan regarded Lanark with an expression of polite amusement. He said, "Who told you that, man?"

"Nastler."

"Don't know this Nastler. How does he say we be useful?"

"He didn't, but my own region—Greater Unthank—is having trouble with—well, many things. Almost everything. Is yours?"

"Oh, sure. Our plains are overgrazed, our bush is underculti-

vated, our minerals are owned by foreigners, the council sends
us airplanes, tanks and bulldozers and our revenues go to Algolagnics and Volstat to buy fuel and spare parts to work them.
Oh, yes, we got problems."
"Oh."
"I don't expect help from your sort, man, but I listen hard
to anything you say."
Multan held a plate of sweet corn and chopped meat in one
hand and ate delicately with the other for a minute or two,
closely watching Lanark, who could now hear the dance orchestra playing very loudly, for the nearest groups had fallen silent
and an attentive and furtive murmuring came from the rest
of the gallery. Lanark felt his face blush hotter and hotter.
Multan said, "Why you go on standing there if you got nothing
to say?"
"Embarrassment," said Lanark in a low voice. "I started this
conversation and I don't know how to end it."
"Let me help you off the hook, man. Come here, Omphale."
A tall elegant black woman approached. Multan said, "Omp-
hale, this delegate needs to talk to a white woman."
"But I'm black. As black as you are," said the woman in a
clear, hooting voice.
"Sure, but you got a white voice," said Multan, moving away.
Lanark and the woman stared at each other then Lanark said,
"Would you care to dance?"
"No," said the woman and followed Multan.

Suddenly, on a note of laughter, all the conversations
started loudly again. Lanark turned, blushing, and saw the two
Joys laughing at him openly. They said "Poor Lanark!" and
"Why did he leave the friends who love him?" Each linked
an arm with him and led him down steps to a side of the
dance floor where Odin, Powys, the other girls and some new
arrivals had gathered. They received him so genially that it
was easy to smile again.
"I could have told you it was useless talking to that bastard,"
said Odin. "Have a cigar."
"But wasn't it exciting?" said Libby. "Everybody expected
something gigantic to happen. I don't know what."
"The opening of a new intercontinental viaduct, perhaps," said
Powys jocularly. "The unrolling across the ocean of a fraternal
carpet on which all the human races could meet and sink into
one human race and get Utopia delivered by parachute with
their morning milk, no?"
"Congratulations! You've done something rather fine," said

Wilkins, shaking his hand. "The rebuff doesn't matter. What counts is that you put the ball fair and square into their arena *and* they know it. One of you girls should get this man a drink."

"Wilkins, I want to talk to you," said Lanark.

"Yes, the sooner the better. There are one or two unexpected developments we must discuss. Shall we breakfast together first thing tomorrow at the delegates' repose village?"

"Certainly."

"You don't mind rising early?"

"Not at all."

"Good. I'll buzz your room before seven, then."

"Please, sir," said Solveig very meekly, "please can I have the dance you promised me earlier, please, please?"

"In a wee while, dearie. Let me finish my drink first," said Lanark kindly.

As he sipped a second white rainbow he looked out at the starry field of the sky where rockets bloomed, tinting thousands of upturned faces in the stadium beneath with purple, white, orange and greenish-gold. He was leaning on a rail guarding the drop to the lowest and narrowest floor and he also saw in the window a dark distinct reflection of himself, the captainish centre of a company standing easily in midair under the flashing fireworks and above the crowd. He nodded down at the people below and thought, 'Tomorrow I will defend you all.' He brought the cigar to his lips, turned round and carefully surveyed the gallery. His group was still the largest, though Wilkins had left it and was moving among the others. Lanark even saw him pause for a word with Multan. He thought tolerantly, 'I must keep my eye on that fellow; he's a fox, an ecological fox of the first water. . . . Fox? Ecological? First water? I don't usually think in words like these but they seem appropriate here. Yes, tomorrow I will talk to Wilkins. There will be some shrewd bargaining but no compromise. No compromise. I'll play it by ear. I'll play it hot, gelid, dirty, depending on how he deals the deck. I'll cash every therm in my suit, and then some, but no compromise! If a region's to be thrown to the crocodiles it won't be Unthank; upon that I am resolved. Monboddo is afraid of me: understandably. The hell with the standings, the top rung is up for grabs! All bets are off, the odds are cancelled, it's anybody's ballgame! The horses are all drugged, the track is glass . . . what is happening to my vocabulary? This cigar is intoxicating. Good thing I noticed: stub it out, stay calm, sip your drink. . . . I know why this is called a white rainbow. It's clear like water, yet on the tongue it spreads out into all the tastes on an artist's peacock palette (badly put). It contains as many tastes as there are colours in the mother of pearly stuff lining an abalone seashell. Poetry. Shall I tell the other Joy? She mixed this drink, she's standing over there, what a clever attractive little . . . I used to prefer big women but . . . oh, if my hand were between her small . . .'

"I am pleased to encounter you, sir," said a quiet, bald man with rimless spectacles, shaking Lanark's hand. "Kodac, Timon Kodac of South Atlantis. God knows why they chose me as a delegate. My true field is research, for Algolagnics. But it's nice to visit other continents. My mother's people hailed from Unthank."

Lanark nodded and thought, 'She is smiling at me just as Libby smiled. I thought Libby meant to seduce me but she had a boyfriend. All young attractive healthy girls have young attractive healthy boyfriends. I've heard that young girls prefer older men, but I've never seen it.'

"That's a very good woman you've got," said Kodac.

Lanark stared at him. Kodac said, "That little old professor. What's her name? Schtzngrm. That was quite a report she sent to the council. You know, the preliminary report with the Permian deep pollution samples. It made us sit up, in Algolagnics, when we got word of it. Oh, yes, we have our sources."

Lanark smiled, nodded and sipped. He thought, 'Surely her face is making me smile at her? It's so merry and intelligent, so quick to be surprised and amused. I will smile back, but not much. A leader should be an audience, not a performer. His crowd should feel he is noticing, assessing, appreciating them, but from a position of strength.'

Kodac said, "Of course what interests us is her *final* report, giving the locations. I believe you are seeing Wilkins tomorrow. He's a very, very shrewd man, best man the council owns. We have a lot of respect for Wilkins at Algolagnics. So far we've always been one or two paces ahead of him, but it's been a hassle. By the way, a lot of us in Algolagnics feel Unthank has had a pretty raw deal from the council. It doesn't surprise us that you and Sludden are taking an independent line. More power to you! And speaking unofficially, I know these are also the sentiments of the Tunc-Quidative and Quantum-Cortexin clusters. But I suppose they've told you that?"

Lanark nodded gravely and thought, 'If she knew what her odd, thoroughly alive young face makes me feel, and how I

envy the seam in her jeans which goes down over her stomach
and over the little mound between the thighs and through
and up between behind . . . if she knew how much less than
a leader I am, I would bore her. I must give her the same
smile I am giving this bald man who is hinting something:
the knowing smile which tells them I know more than they
know I know.'

"Hey!" said Kodac chuckling. "See that little tulip watching
you over there? Bet you she would go like a bomb. Yes, I'm
sure Wilkins is just wild to get his hands on that final report
of yours. If he knows it exists. Does he?"

Lanark stared at him. Kodac laughed, patted Lanark's shoulder
and said, "A straight question at last, eh? I'm sorry, but though
government and industry are interlocking we ain't *fully* interlocking. Not yet. We support each other because order is Heav-
en's first law, but remember Costaguana? Remember when the
Occidental Republic split off from it? That could never have
happened without our support. Of course we weren't called
Algolagnics then; that was in the time of the old Material Interests Corporation. Boy, what a gang of pirates *they* were! And
the mineral was silver, which doesn't thrust as hard as a certain
other mineral, you follow?"

Lanark smiled bitterly and thought, 'The only feeling she gives
me is stony pain, the pain of being slightly alive in a pot-bellied
old body with thinning hair. But leaders need to be mostly
dead. People want solid monuments to cling to, not confused
men like themselves. Sludden was wise to send me. *I* can never
melt.'

"Your glass is empty," said Kodac, taking it. "I'll find a girl
to fill it; I need a drink myself."

"Don't be nasty to me, Lanark," said the other Joy, smiling
in front of him. "You promised me two dances, remember?
Surely you can give me one?"

Without waiting for a reply she drew him out among the dancers.

Bitterness fell from him. The firm bracelet of her fingers
round his wrist gave lightness and freedom. He laughed and
held her waist, saying, "And Gay is your mother? Has the
wound in her hand healed?"

"Was she ever wounded? She never tells me anything."

"What does she do nowadays?"

"She's a journalist. Let's not talk about her; surely I'm enough
for you?"

Holding her was hard, at first, for the music was so quick and
jerky that the other men and women danced without touching
each other. Lanark danced to the slower sound of the whole
room, whose main noise was conversation. Heard all together
the conversations sounded like a waterfall blattering into a pool
and made the orchestra seem the chirping of excited insects.
At first the other dancers collided with him but later they moved
to the side of the floor and stood cheering and clapping. The
orchestra lapsed raggedly into silence and the other Joy broke
away and ran into the crowd. He followed her through laughter to his group and found her talking vigorously to the
other girls. She faced him and asked, "Was that not nearly incest?"
He stared at her. She said, "You are my father, aren't you?"
"Oh, no! Sludden is. Probably."
"Sludden? My mother never tells me anything. Who is Sludden?
Is he successful? Is he good-looking?"
Lanark said gently, "Sludden is a very successful man, and
women find him very attractive. Or used to. But I don't want
to talk about him tonight."
He turned sadly away and looked at the crowded gallery where
the dancing had resumed. On the faces of all these strangers
he saw such familiar expressions of worry, courage, happiness,
resignation, hope and failure that he felt he had known them
all his life, yet they had surprising variety. Each seemed a world
with its own age, climate and landscape. One was fresh and
springlike, another rich, hot and summery. Some were mildly
or stormily autumnal, some tragically bleak and frozen. Someone was standing by his side and her company let him admire
these worlds peacefully, without wanting to conquer or enter
them. He heard her sigh and say, "I wish you were more
careful," and he turned and saw Lady Monboddo. Her face
looked younger, more solemn and lonely than he remembered.
Her breasts were bigger and a floor-length gown of stiff tapestry
patterned with lions and unicorns gave her a pillar-like look.
Lanark said gladly, "Catalyst!"
"That was my job, not my name. I think you should leave
this place and go to bed, Lanark."
"I would, if I could go with you," said Lanark, placing an
arm round her waist. She frowned at him as though his face
was a page she was trying to read. He withdrew his arm awkwardly and said, "I'm sorry if I'm greedy, but I don't think
these little girls like me much. And you and I were nearly
very good friends once."

"Yes. We could have done anything we liked together. But you ran away to a dragon-bitch."

"But good came of it!" said Lanark eagerly. "She didn't stay a dragon long and we have a son now. He's very tall and healthy for his age, and seems intelligent too, and may be quite a kind person when he grows up."

She still stared at his face as if trying to read it. He looked away, saying uncomfortably, "Don't worry about me. I'm not drunk, if that's what you're thinking."

When he looked back she had gone and Martha stood there offering a glass and saying, "I mixed this one. It doesn't taste very nice but it's strong. Please, sir, will it soon be time for me to dance with you?"

"Why do you girls keep replacing each other?" said Lanark moodily, "I've had no time to know any of you yet."

"We think a lot of new friends can have more fun together than a pair of old friends."

"So when will you leave me?"

"Maybe I'll stay with you. Tonight," said Martha, looking at him unsmilingly.

"Maybe!" said Lanark sceptically, and drank.

At first the taste was sickly sweet and then so appallingly bitter that he gulped it hastily. Somewhere he could hear Powys saying ". . . wants the council to ban the manufacture of footwear, because the earth, you see, is like the body of a mother, and direct contact with her keeps us healthy and sane. He says the recent increase in warfare and crime is caused by composition rubber shoe soles which insulate us from the cthonic current and leave us a prey to the lunar current. Once I would have laughed, of course, but modern science is reinstating so much that we regarded as superstition. It seems that hedgehogs really *do* suck the teats of cows. . . ."

Lanark was lying outspread on cushions upon the lowest floor of all. Someone had removed his shoes and his feet gently explored the softer parts of a silk-clad body. His cheek lay on another one, each hand was snug between a pair of canvas-covered thighs and someone caressed his neck. The sounds of the gallery and orchestra were subdued and distant but he could hear two people talking high above his head.

"It's nice to see women combining to make a man feel famous."

"Drivel. They're making him a sot."

"I believe he comes from a region where coitus is often reached through stupefaction."

"And just as often missed."

"I hate these voices," said Lanark. There was whispering and he was gently raised and helped forward. A door closed somewhere and all noises stopped.

He said loudly, "I am walking . . . along a corridor."

Someone whispered, "Open your eyes."

"No. Touch tells me you are near me but eyes talk about the space between."

Another door closed and he lay down among whispers like falling leaves and felt his clothes removed. Someone whispered "Look!" and he opened his eyes long enough to meet a thin-lipped small smiling mouth in a glade of dark hair. Softly, sadly, he revisited the hills and hollows of a familiar landscape, the sides of his limbs brushing sweet abundances with surprisingly hard tips, his endings paddling in the pleats of a wet wound which opened into a boggy cave where little moans bloomed like violets in the blackness. There were dank odours and even a whiff of dung. Losing his way he lay on his back feeling that he too was a landscape, a dull flat one surrounding a tower sticking up into a dark and heavy sky. In the darkness above he felt people climbing off and onto his tower and swinging there with rhythmical gasps or shrieks. He hoped they were enjoying themselves and was glad of the company, and he kissed and caressed to show this; then everything turned over and he was the heavy sky pressing the tower into the land below, yet he felt increasingly lost, knowing the tower could stand for hours and never fire a gun. Someone whispered, "Won't you give yourself?"

"I can't. Half my strength is locked in fear and hatred."

"Why?"

"I don't remember."

"How would you like to show it?"

"I would like to . . . I can't say. You'd be disgusted."

"Tell us."

"I would like . . . I can't tell you. You would laugh."

"Risk it."

"I want you to hate and fear me too, but be unable to escape. I want you captured and bound, and waiting helplessly in perfect dread for the slash of my whip, the touch of my branding iron. And then, at the climax of your terror, what enters you is simply naked me—ah! You would have . . . to . . . be . . . de . . . lighted. Then."

The land and foundation melted and he was thrusting, biting, grunting and clutching among squealing jelly meats like a carnivorous pig with fingers. Later on, feeling expended, he lay again in kindness gently rooting in soft clefts, rocking and drifting on smoothness, afloat and basking in softness. He clasped a waist, his penis nestled between two gentle mounds and he was filled with kind nowhere.

He was knee-deep in a cold quick little burn gurgling over big rounded stones, some black, some grey, some speckled like oatmeal. He was tugging some of the stones out and carefully flinging them onto the bank a yard or two upstream where Alexander, about ten years old, very brown, and wearing red underpants, was building a dam with them. The hot sun on Lanark's neck, the chill water round his legs, the ache in his back and shoulders suggested he had been doing this for a long time. He hauled out an extra large black and dripping boulder, heaved it into the heather, then climbed up and lay flat on his back beside it, breathing hard. He closed his eyes against the profound blue and the dazzle came hot dark red through his lids. He could hear the water and the click of stones. Alexander said, "This water keeps getting through."
"Plug the holes with moss and gravelly stuff."
"I don't believe in God, you know," said Alexander.
Lanark blinked sideways and watched him wrenching clods from the bank. He said, "Oh?"
"He doesn't exist. Grampa told me."
"Which Grampa? Everyone has two."
"The one who fought in France in the first war. Give me a lot of that moss."
Without sitting up Lanark plucked handfuls from a dank mossy cushion nearby and chucked them lazily over. Alexander said, "The first war was the most interesting, I think, even though it had no Hitler or atomic bombs. You see, it mostly happened in one place, and it killed more soldiers than the second war."
"Wars are only interesting because they show how stupid we can be."
"Say that sort of thing as much as you like," said Alexander amiably, "but it won't change me. Anyway, Grampa says there isn't a God. People invented him."
"They invented motorcars too, and there are motorcars."
"That's nothing but words. . . . Shall we go for a walk? I can show you Rima, if you like."
Lanark sighed and said, "All right, Sandy."
He stood up while Alexander climbed out of the burn. Their clothes lay on a flat rock and they had to shake small red ants

off them before dressing. Alexander said, "Of course my real
name is Alexander."
"What does Rima call you?"
"Alex, but my *real* name is Alexander."
"I'll try to remember that."
"Good."

They walked down the burn to a place where it vanished
into a dip in the moor. Lanark saw it fall from his feet down
a reddish rock into a pool at the head of a deep glen full of
bushes and trees, mostly birch, rowan and small oaks. A couple,
partly screened by the roots of a fallen mountain ash, lay on
some grass beside the pool. The woman seemed asleep and
Lanark saw more of the man, who was reading a newspaper.
He said, "That isn't Sludden."
"No, that's Kirkwood. We don't see Sludden nowadays."
"Why not?"
"Sludden became too dependent."
"Kirkwood isn't?"
"Not yet."
"Sandy, do you think Rima would like to see me?"
Alexander looked uncertainly into the glen, then pointed the
other way saying, "Wouldn't you like to walk with me to the
top of that hill?"
"Yes. I would."

They turned and walked uphill toward a distant green
summit. Alexander flung himself down for a rest at the top
of the first slope and did the same thing halfway up the next.
Soon he was resting for two minutes every minute or two.
Lanark said irritably, "You don't need as much rest as this."
"I know how much rest I need."
"The sun won't hang around the sky forever, Sandy. And it
bores me, sitting still so often."
"It bores me walking all the time."
"Well, I'll go on at a slow steady pace and you catch up with
me when you like," said Lanark, standing up.
"Yah!" cried Alexander on a strong whining note. "You must
be right all the time, mustn't you? You won't leave anyone
in peace, will you? You have to spoil everything, haven't you?"
Lanark lost his temper, thrust his face toward Alexander's and
hissed, "You hate visiting the country, don't you?"
"Have I been howling and whining like this all the time? If
I hated the country I would have been, wouldn't I?"

"Stand up."

"No. You'll hit me."

"I certainly will *not*. Stand up!"

Alexander stood up, looking worried. Lanark went behind him, gripped his body under the armpits and with a strong heave managed to sit him on his shoulders. Staggering slightly he set off through a plantation of tiny fir trees. A minute later Alexander said, "You can put me down now."

Lanark plodded on up the slope.

"I said you can put me down. I can walk now."

"Not till . . . we leave . . . these trees."

The weight at first had been so heavy that Lanark told himself he would only walk ten paces, but after that he went another ten, and then another, and now he thought happily, 'I could carry him forever by taking ten steps at a time.' But he put him down at the far side of the plantation and rested on the heather while Alexander hurried ahead. Eventually Lanark followed and overtook him on a ridge where heather and coarse brown grass gave place to a carpet of turf. The land here dipped into a hollow then rose to the steep cone of the summit. Alexander said, "You see that white thing on top?"

"Yes."

"It's a triangle point."

"A triangulation point."

"That's right, a triangule point. Come on."

Alexander started straight toward the summit. Lanark said, "Stop Sandy, that's the difficult way. We'll take this path to the right."

"The straight way in the shortest, I can *see* it is."

"But it's the steepest too. This path keeps to the high ground, it will save a lot of effort."

"You go that way then."

"I will, and I'll reach the top before you do. This path was made by sensible people who knew which way was the quickest."

"You go that way then," said Alexander and rushed straight down into the hollow.

Lanark walked up the path at an easy pace. The air was fresh and the sun warm. He thought how good it was to have a holiday. The only sound was the *Wheep! Wheep!* of a distant moorbird, the only cloud a faint white smudge in the blueness over the hilltop. In the hollow on his left he sometimes saw Alexander scrambling over a ridge and thought tolerantly, 'Silly of him, but he'll learn from experience.' He was wondering sadly about Alexander's life with Rima when the path became a ladder of sandy toeholes kicked in the steepening turf. From here the summit seemed a great green dome, and staring up at it Lanark saw an amazing sight. Up the left-hand curve, silhouetted against the sky, a small human figure was quickly climbing. Lanark sighed with pleasure, halted and looked away into the blue. He said, "Thank you!" and for a moment glimpsed the ghost of a man scribbling in a bed littered with papers. Lanark smiled and said, "No, old Nastler, it isn't you I thank, but the cause of the ground which grew us all. I have never given you much thought, Mr. cause, for you don't repay that kind of effort, and on the whole I have found your world bearable rather than good. But in spite of me and the sensible path, Sandy is reaching the summit all by himself in the sunlight; he is up there enjoying the whole great globe that you gave him, so I love you now. I am so content that I don't care when contentment ends. I don't care what absurdity, failure, death I am moving toward. Even when your world has lapsed into black nothing, it will have made sense because Sandy once enjoyed it in the sunlight. I am not speaking for mankind. If the poorest orphan in creation has reason to curse you, then everything high and decent in you should go to Hell. Yes! Go to Hell, go to Hell, go to Hell as often as there are vicitms in your universe. But I am not a victim. This is my best moment. Speaking purely as a private person, I admit you to the kingdom of Heaven, and this admission is final, and I will not revoke it."

Near the top of the slope he began to grow breathless. The turf of the summit was broken by low gnarls of rock. The concrete triangulation pillar stood on one and Alexander was using it as a backrest. He had the air of man sprawling on a comfortable sofa in his own house and seemed not to see Lanark at first, then patted invitingly the rock beside him, and when Lanark sat down he leaned against him and they looked a long time at the view. In spite of their height the sea was only a soft dark line on the horizon. The land up to it was wide low hills given over to pasture, and there were strips of windbreak wood with half-reaped fields of grain in the valleys between. Lanark and Alexander faced a steep side of the hill which sloped straight down to a red-roofed town with crooked streets and a small ancient palace. This had round towers with conical roofs and a walled garden open to the

public. Many figures were moving between the bright bushes
and flowerbeds, and there was a full car-park outside. Alexander
said, "It would be nice to go down there."
"Yes."
"But Mum might worry."
"Yes, we must go back."
They sat a little longer and when the sun was three-quarters
across the sky they arose and descended to the moor by a
path which led round a small loch. Two men with thick mous-
taches, one carrying a rifle, came up the path and nodded to
Lanark as they passed. The rifle man said, "Will I shoot the
delegate?" and the other laughed and said, "No, no, we mustn't
kill our delegate."
Shortly after, Alexander said, "Some jokes make me tremble
with fear."
"I'm sorry."
"It can't be helped. Are you really a delegate?"
Lanark had been pleased by the recognition but said firmly,
"Not now. I'm on holiday just now."

    The loch was embanked as a reservoir on one side and
on the grass of the embankment a dead seagull lay with outspread wings. Alexander was fascinated and Lanark picked it
up. They looked at the yellow beak with the raspberry spot
under the tip, the pure grey back and snowy breast which seemed
unmarked. Alexander said, "Should we bury it?"
"That would be difficult without tools. We could build a cairn
over it."
They collected stones from the shingle of the lochside and
heaped them over the glossy feathers of the unmarked body.
Alexander said, "What happens to it now?"
"It rots and insects eat it. There are a lot of red ants around
here; they'll pick it to a skeleton quite fast. Skeletons are inter-
esting things."
"Could we come back for it tomorrow?"
"No, it probably needs several weeks to reach the skeleton
stage."
"Then say a prayer."
"You told me you didn't believe in God."
"I don't, but a prayer must be said. Put your hands like this
and shut your eyes."
They stood on each side of the knee-high cairn and Lanark
shut his eyes.
"You begin by saying *Dear God.*"

"Dear God," said Lanark, "we are sorry this gull died, especially as it looks young and healthy (apart from being dead). Let there be many young, living gulls to enjoy the speed and freshness this one missed; and give us all enough happiness and courage to die without feeling cheated; moreover . . ." He hesitated. A voice whispered, "Say amen."
"Amen."

Something cold stung his cheeks. He opened his eyes and saw the sky dark with torn, onrushing clouds. He was alone with nothing at his feet but a scatter of stones with old bones and feathers between them. He said "Sandy?" and looked around. There was nothing human on the moor. The light was fading from two or three sunset streaks in the clouds to the west. The heather was crested with sleet; the wind whipped more of it into his face.
"Sandy!" he screamed, starting to run. "Sandy! Sandy! *Alexander!*"
He plunged across the heather, tripped and fell into darkness. He wrestled awhile with something entangling, then realized it was blankets and sat up.

He was in a square room with cement floor and tiled walls like a public lavatory. It seemed large, perhaps because the only furniture was a lavatory pan in one corner without seat or handle to flush it. He lay in the diagonally opposite corner on part of the floor raised a foot above the rest and covered with red linoleum. The door of the place had a metal surface, and he knew it was locked. He had a headache and felt filthy and was sure something dreadful had happened. He pulled the blankets around him and huddled up, biting the thumb knuckle and trying to think. His main feeling was of filth, disorder and loss. He had lost someone or something, a secret document, a parent, or his self-respect. The past seemed a muddle of memories without sequence, like a confused pile of old photographs. To sort them out he tried recalling his life from the start.

First he had been a child, then a schoolboy, then his mother died. He became a student, tried to work as a painter and became very ill. He hung uselessly round cafés for a time, then took a job in an institute. He got mixed up with a woman there, lost the job, then went to live in a badly governed place where his son was born. The woman and child left him, and for no very clear reason he had been sent on a mission to some sort of assembly. This had been hard at first, then easy, because he was suddenly a famous man with important papers in his briefcase. Women loved him. He had been granted an unexpected holiday with Sandy, then something cold had stung his cheek—

His thoughts recoiled from that point like fingers from a scalding plate, but he forced them back to it and gradually more recent, more depressing memories came to him.

CHAPTER 42. Catastrophe

There had been a sky dark with onrushing clouds. He had been alone with some scattered rocks, old bones and feathers at his feet and had looked round saying "Sandy?" but there was nobody else on the moor and the light was fading from two or three sunset streaks in the clouds to the west. He had run across the heather screaming Alexander's name and tripped and fallen into darkness. He had wrestled a while with something entangling, then realized it was a downy quilt, flung it aside and sat up.

He was in bed in a darkened room with a headache and a feeling of terrible loss. He was sure he had come here with people who had been kind to him, but who were they? Where had they gone? His hand found and flicked the switch of a bedlight. The room was a dormitory with a pair of beds to each wall and dressing tables between them loaded with female cosmetics. The walls had coloured posters of male singers on them and notices saying things like JUST BECAUSE YOU'RE PARANOID DON'T THINK THEY AREN'T PLOTTING AGAINST YOU. His clothes were scattered about the floor. He groaned, rubbed his head, got up and quickly dressed. He felt that something very good had happened recently. It may not have been love, but it had left him ready for love. Delight had opened him, prepared him for someone who wasn't there. He was anguished by the absence of someone to hold and whisper to affectionately, someone to hold him and speak lovingly back. He left the room and hurried along a dark corridor toward a sound of music and voices behind a door. He pushed the door open and stood blinking in the light. The voices stopped then someone shouted, "Look out! Here he comes again!" and a huge explosion of laughter went up.

The gallery was emptier than he remembered. Most people lay on cushions on the lowest floor and he hurried through them looking left and right. He remembered meeting a thin-lipped smiling little mouth in a glade of dark hair and cried to a laughing mouth among dark hair, "Is it you? Were you with me?"

"When?"

"In the bedroom?"

"Oh, no, not me! Wasn't it Helga? The woman dancing up there?"

He rushed onto the dance floor, crying, "Are you Helga? Were you with me in the bedroom?"

"Sir," said Timon Kodac, who was dancing with her, "this lady is my wife."

Laughter came from every side though nobody else was dancing and the only player was a saxophonist. The rest of the orchestra sat with girls on cushions round the floor and he suddenly saw Libby very clearly. She leaned against the drummer, a middle-aged man with horn-rimmed glasses. Her gracefully plump young body yearned toward him, little ripples flowed up it, thrusting her shoulder into his armpit, a breast against his side. Lanark hurried over and said, "Libby, please, was it—was it you, please?"

"Nyuck!" she said with a disgusted grimace. "Certainly not!"

"It's all sliding away from me," wept Lanark, covering his eyes. "Sliding into the past, further and further. It was lovely, and now it has turned to jeering."

A hand seized his arm and a voice said, "Take a grip of yourself."

"Don't let go," said Lanark opening his eyes. He saw a small, lean, young-looking man with crew-cut hair, black sweater, slacks and sandshoes.

The man said, "You're being bloody embarrassing. I know what you need. Come with me."

Lanark let himself be led up to the top floor, which was completely empty. He said, "Who are you?"

"Think a bit."

The voice sounded familiar. Lanark peered closely and saw deep little creases at the corners of the eyes and mouth which showed that this smooth, pale, ironical face belonged to quite an old man.

He said, "You can't be Gloopy."

"Why not?"

"Gloopy, you've changed. You've improved."

"Can't say the same for you."

"Gloopy, I'm lonely. Lost and lonely."

"I'll help you out. Sit there."

Lanark sat at a table. Gloopy went to the nearest bar and returned with a tall glass. He said, "There you are. A rainbow." Lanark gulped it and said, "I thought you were operating as a lift, Gloopy."

"Doesn't do to stay too long at the same thing. What is it you want? Sex, is it?"

"No, no, not just sex, something more gentle and ordinary." Gloopy frowned and drummed his fingers on the tabletop. He said, "You'll have to spell it out more definite than that. Think carefully. Male or female? How old? What posture?"

"I want a woman who knew and liked me a long time ago and still likes me. I want her to take me in her arms easily, casually, as if it was a simple thing to do. She'll find me cold and unresponsive at first, I've lived too long alone, you see, but she mustn't be put off by that. We'll sleep together calmly all night, and then I'll lose my fear of her and toward morning I'll wake with an erection and she'll caress me and we'll make love without worry or fuss. And spend all day in bed, eating, reading and cuddling happily, making love if we feel like it and not *bothered* by each other."

"I see. You want a mother figure."

"No!" yelled Lanark. "I don't want a mother figure, or a sister figure, or a wife figure, I want a woman, an attractive woman who likes me more than any other man in the world yet doesn't pester me!"

"I can probably fix you up with something like that," said Gloopy. "So stop shouting. I'll give you one more drink, and then we visit your rooms in Olympia. All types of attractive bints in Olympia."

"My rooms? Olympia?"

"Olympia is the delegates' repose village. Didn't they tell you?"

"Are you a pimp, Gloopy?" said Lanark, gulping another white rainbow.

"Yeah. One of the best in the business. There's a great need for us in times like these."

"Times like what, Gloopy?"

"Don't you read the glossies? Don't you watch the talk shows?

Ours is an era of crumbling social values. This is the age of alienation and non-communication. The old morals and manners are passing away and the new lot haven't come in yet. Result is, men and women can't talk about what they want from each other. In an old-fashioned flower culture like Tahiti a girl would wear a pink hibiscus blossom behind her left ear, which meant, I got a good boyfriend but I'd like to have two. So the boys understood her, see? The European aristocracy used to have a very sophisticated sex language using fans, snuffboxes and monocles. But nowadays people are so desperate for lack of a language that they've taken to advertising in newspapers. You know the kind of thing! *Forty-three-year-old wealthy but balding accountant whose hobby is astronomy would like to meet one-legged attractive not necessarily intelligent girl who wouldn't mind spanking him with a view to forming a lifelong attachment.* That's just not good enough. Too much room for accident. What society needs is me, a sensitive trustworthy middleman with wide connections and access to a good Tunc-Quidative-Cortexin-Cluster-Computer."

"Smattera fact, Gloop," said Lanark shyly, "sometimes I am a . . . a . . . a . . ."

"Yeah?"

"a . . . a . . . an imaginary sadist."

"Yeah?"

"Not a damaging sadist. Namaginary one. So from standpoint of occasional perverse frolic it would help matters if lady nquestion, along with the other points numerated, which *are* the 'sential points, make no mistake about that, these other points I numerated are the 'sential ones . . . where was?"

"Perverse frolic."

"Good. I'd like her *not* to be namaginary masochist, because I want to give her imaginary pain, not imaginary pleasure."

"Yeah. Defeat whole purpose."

"So I require namaginary *weaker* sadist than myself."

"Yeah, difficult, but I might just manage to swing it. Come on, then."

Gloopy steered him through the dozen Quantum-Cortexin security men who remained outside the gallery and opened a door beside the doors of the lifts. They walked down a paved path between lawns and trees with Chinese lanterns in them. Lanark said, "I thought we were very high up, Gloop."

"Only on the inside. The stadium is built in an old dock basin, you see. The river's down here, Narky boy."

They passed a wharf where small pleasure boats were gently rocking and came to a smooth sheet of water with lamps along the far shore. Lanark stopped and pointed dramatically to the long reflections of the lights in the dark water.

"Gloop!" he cried. "Poem. Listen. 'Magine these lights stars, right? Here goes. Twilit lake, sleek as clean steel—"

"This is a river and it's nearly dawn, Narky boy."

"Doninerrupt. You're not a cricit, Gloop, you're a chamberlain, like Munro. Know Munro, no? Nindividual who delivers folk from one chamber to nother. Listen. Twilit lake, sleek as clean steel, each star a shining spear in your deep. Pottery. I have been twitted, in my time, with solidity, Gloop. Dull solid man of few words, me. But *pottery* is lukring in these dethps, Gloop!" said Lanark, thumping his chest. He thumped too hard and started coughing.

"Lean on me, Nark," said Gloopy.

Lanark leaned on him and they came to a footbridge which crossed the water in one slender white span to a shining arrangement of glass cubes and lantern-hung trees on the other shore.

"Olympia," said Gloopy.

"Nice," said Lanark. In the middle of the bridge he stopped again saying, "No fireworks now, so we have waterworks, yes? It's urgent that I piss."

He did so between two railings and was disappointed to see his urine jet two feet forward and then fall straight down. "When I was a small-bellied boy!" he cried, "tumbling ninepin over the dolly mixture daisies, my piss had an arc of thirteen feet. A greybeard now, belly flabby from abuse of drink, I cannot squirt past my reflection. Piss. A word which sounds like what it means. A rare word."

"Police," muttered Gloopy.

"No, Gloop, you are wrong. Police does not sound like what it means. It is too like polite, please and nice."

Gloopy was running down the slope of the bridge toward the village. When he reached the shore he turned his head for a moment and yelled, "All right, officers! Just a perverse frolic!"

Lanark saw two policemen advancing toward him. He zipped up his trousers and hurried after Gloopy. As he reached the shore two men stepped onto the bridge and stood blocking the way. They wore black suits. One held out a hand and said in a dull voice, "Pass please."

"I can't, you're blocking the way."

"Show your pass, please."

"I don't have one. Or if I do it's in my briefcase—I've left

that somewhere. Do I need a pass? I'm a delegate, I have
rooms here, please let me through."
"Identify self."
"Provost Lanark of Greater Unthank."
"There is no Provost Lanark of Greater Unthank."
Lanark noticed that the man's eyes and mouth were shut and
the voice came from a neatly folded white handkerchief in
his breast pocket. His companion was staring at Lanark with
eyes and mouth wide open. A metal ring with a black centre
poked out between his teeth. With great relief Lanark heard
the voice of an ordinary human policeman behind him: "Just
what's happening here?"
"There is no Provost Lanark of Greater Unthank," said the
security man again.
"There is!" said Lanark querulously, "I know the programme
says the Unthank delegate is Sludden but it's wrong, there
was an unexpected last-minute change. *I* am the delegate!"
"Identify self."
"How *can* I without my briefcase? Where's Gloopy? He'll
vouch for me, he's a very important pimp, you've just let him
through. Or Wilkins, send for Wilkins. Or Monboddo! Yes,
contact the bloody Lord Monboddo, he knows me better than
anyone."
In his own ears the words seemed shrill and unconvincing.
The voice from the security man's pocket sounded like a record
slowing to a stop: "Proof-burden property of putative prover."
"What the hell does that mean?"
"It means, Jimmy, that you'd better come quietly with us,"
said a policeman, and Lanark felt a hand grip each shoulder.
He said feebly, "My name is Lanark."
"Don't let it worry you, Jimmy."

The security men stepped back. The policemen pushed
Lanark forward, then sideways and down to a landing stage.
Lanark said, "Aren't you taking me to the repose village?"
They pushed him onto the deck of a motor launch, then down
into a cabin. He said, "What about Nastler? He's your king,
isn't he? *He* knows me."
They pushed him down on a bench and sat on a bench opposite.
He felt the launch move out into the river and was suddenly
so tired that he had to concentrate to keep from falling down.

Later he saw the planks of another landing stage, and a
pavement which continued for a long time, then a few stone

steps, a doormat and some square rubber tiles fitted edge to edge. He was allowed to lean on a flat surface. A voice said, "Name?"

"Lanark."

"Christian or surname?"

"Both."

"Are you telling me your name is Lanark Lanark?"

"If you like. I mean yes yes yes yes yes."

"Age?"

"Ndtermate. I mean indeterminate. Past halfway."

Someone sighed and said "Address?"

"Nthank cathedral. No, 'Lympia. Olympia."

There was some muttering. He noticed the words "bridge" and "security" and "six fifty." That jerked him awake. He stared across a counter at a police sergeant with a grey moustache who was writing in a ledger. He saw a room full of desks where two policewomen were typing and the number 6.94 very big and black was framed upon the wall. With a click it charged to 6.95. He realized that a decimal clock had a hundred minutes an hour and licked his lips and tried to talk quickly and clearly.

"Sergeant, this is urgent! An important phone call is probably going through just now to my rooms in the delegates' repose village; can it be diverted here? It's from Wilkins, Monboddo's secretary. I've been drunk and foolish, I'm sorry, but there may be a public disaster if I can't speak to Wilkins!"

The sergeant stared at him hard. Lanark had flung out his hands appealingly and now saw they were filthy. His waistcoat was unbuttoned, his suit crumpled. There was a bad smell in the room and he noticed, with a shudder, that it came from a brown crusted stain on his trouser leg. He said, "I know I look detestable but politicians can't always be wise! Please! I'm not asking for myself but for the people I represent. Put me on to Wilkins!"

The sergeant sighed. He took an assembly programme from under the counter and studied a back page printed in small type. He said, "Is Wilkins a surname or a Christian name?"

"Surname, I think. Does it matter?"

The sergeant pushed the programme over the counter saying, "Which?"

A list of names headed COUNCIL STAFF filled ten pages. In the first four Lanark found Wilkins Staple-Stewart, the Acting Secretary for Internal-External Liaison, Peleus Wilkins, Procurator Designate for Surroundings and Places, and Wendel Q.

Wilkins, Senior Adviser on Population Energy Transfer.
"Listen!" said Lanark. "I'll phone every Wilkins in the list till
I get the—no! No, I'll phone Monboddo and get the full name
from him; he knows me even if his damned robots don't. I'm
sorry the hour is so early, but . . ."
He hesitated, for his voice sounded unconvincing again and
the sergeant was slowly shaking his head. "Let me prove who
I am!" said Lanark wildly. "My briefcase is in Nastler's room
in the stadium—no, I gave it to Joy, a Red Girl, a hostess in
the executive gallery; she put it behind the bar for me I must
get it back it contains a vitally important document please this
is vital—"
The sergeant, who was writing in the ledger, said "All right,
lads."
Lanark felt a hand clapped on each shoulder and cried, "But
what am I charged with? I've hurt nobody, molested nobody,
insulted nobody. What am I charged with?"
"With being a pisser," said a policeman holding him.
"All men are pissers!"
"I am charging you," said the sergeant, writing, "under the
General Powers (Consolidation) Order, and what you need
is a nice long rest."
And as he was led away Lanark found himself yawning hugely.
The hands on his shoulder grew strangly comforting. Surely
he had often been pushed forward by strong people who
thought he was wicked? The feeling was less dreamlike than
childlike.

He was led into a small narrow room with what looked
like bunks piled with folded blankets along one wall. He climbed at once to the top bunk and lay down, but they laughed
and said, "No, no, Jimmy!"
He climbed down and they gave him two blankets to carry
and led him to another door. He went through and it was
slammed and locked behind him. He wrapped the blankets
round him, lay on a platform in a corner and slept.

And now he was awake and wildly miserable. He sprang
up and walked in a circle round the floor, crying, "Oh! I have
been wicked, *stupid*, evil, *stupid*, daft daft daft *daft* and stupid,
stupid! And it happened exactly when I thought myself a fine
great special splendid man! How did it happen? I meant to
find Wilkins and talk to him sensibly, but the women made
me feel famous. Did they want to destroy me? No, no, they

treated me like something special because it made *them* feel special but all the time nothing good was being made, nothing useful was done. I was drunk, yes, with white rainbows, yes, but mostly with vanity; nobody is as crazy as a man who thinks he is important. People tried to tell me things and I ignored them. What was Kodac hinting at? Valuable minerals, special reports, government ignorance, it sounded like dirty trickery but I should have listened carefully. And . . . Catalyst . . . why didn't I ask her name? She tried to warn me and I thought she wanted to sleep with me. Yah! Greed and idiocy. *I forgot the reports!* I lost the reports without even reading them, I was seduced by people I can't even remember (but it was lovely). And how did I come to be paddling in that burn with Sandy? What was that but a useless bit of happiness put in to make my fall more dreadful? (But it was wonderful.) Oh, Sandy, what kind of father have you been cursed with? I left you to defend you and have turned into a ludicrous lecherous discredited stinking goat!"

He stopped and stared at some things he had not noticed beside the platform: three plastic mugs of cold tea and three paper plates of rolls with cold fried sausages in them. He grabbed the rolls and with tears trickling down his cheeks gulped and swallowed between sentences, saying, "Three mugs, three plates, three meals: I've been a whole day in here, the first day of the assembly is over. . . . When will I be let out? . . . I was fooled by false love because I never knew the true kind, not even with Rima. Why? I was faithful to her not because I loved her but because I *wanted* love, it is *right* that she left me it is *right* that I'm locked up here, I deserve much worse. . . . But who will speak for Unthank? . . . Who will cry out against that second-hand second-rate creator who thinks a cheap stupid *disaster* is the best ending for mankind? O, heavens, heavens fall and crush me! . . . ."

He noticed that self-denunciation was becoming a pleasure and sprang up and beat his head hard against the door; then stopped because it hurt too much. Then he noticed someone else was shouting and banging too. The door had a slit like a small letterbox at eye level. He looked through and saw another door with a slit immediately opposite. A voice from there said, "Have you a cigarette Jimmy?"

"I don't smoke. Do you know the time?"

"It was two in the morning when they brought me in and that was a while ago. What did they get you for?"

"I pissed off a bridge."

"The police," said the voice bitterly, "are a shower of bastards. Are you sure you don't have a cigarette?"

"No, I don't smoke. What did they get you for?"

"I hammered a man up a close and called the police a shower of bastards. Listen, they can't treat us like this. Let's batter our doors and yell till they give us some fags."

"But I don't smoke," said Lanark, turning away.

His main feeling now was of physical filth. The lavatory pan suddenly flushed and he examined it. The water looked and smelled pure. He undressed, wet a corner of a blanket and scrubbed himself hard all over. He draped a dry blanket round him like a toga, rinsed his underclothes several times in the pan and hung them on the rim to dry. He scraped with his nails the crust of vomit from the trouser leg and rubbed the place with the wettened blanket. The creased cloth offended him. Though thirsty he had only been able to empty one mug of cold tea. He spread the trousers on the platform and rubbed them steadily in small circles with the mug base, pressing down hard. He did this a long time without seeing an improvement, but whenever he stopped there was nothing else to do. The door opened and a policeman entered with a mug and a plate of rolls. He said, "What are you doing?"

"Pressing my trousers."

The man collected the other mugs and plates. Lanark said, "When will I get out, please?"

"That's up to the magistrate."

"When will I see the magistrate?"

The policeman went outside, slamming the door. Lanark ate, drank the hot tea and thought, 'The assembly has begun the work of the second day.' He began pressing again. Whenever he stopped he felt so evil and useless, evil and trivial that he bit his hands till the pain was an excuse for screaming, though he did it quietly and undramatically. Another policeman brought lunch and Lanark said, "When will I see the magistrate?"

"The court sits tomorrow morning."

"Could you take my underclothes please and hang them somewhere to dry?"

The policeman went out, laughing heartily. Lanark ate, drank, then walked in a circle, flapping the underpants in one hand, the vest in the other. He thought, 'I suppose the assembly is discussing world order just now.' A feeling of hatred grew in him, hatred of the assembly, the police and everyone who wasn't in the cell with him. He decided that when he was released he would immediately piss on the police station steps, or smash a window, or set fire to a car. He bit his hands some more, then worked at pressing trousers and drying underclothes till long after the evening tea and rolls. He felt too restless to lie down, and when the underwear was only slightly damp he dressed, polished his shoes with the blanket and sat waiting for breakfast and the magistrates' court. He thought drearily, 'Perhaps I'll be in time for the pollution debate.'

And then he wakened with a headache, feeling filthy again. Three mugs of cold tea, three plates of rolls lay beside the platform. He thought, 'My life is moving in circles. Will I always come back to this point?' He didn't feel wicked any more, only trivial and useless. Another policeman opened the door and said, "Outside. Come on. Outside."
Lanark said feebly, "I would like to stay here a little longer."
"Outside, come on. This isn't a hotel we're running."

He was led to the office. A different sergeant stood behind the counter and an old lady wearing jeans and a fur coat stood in front. Her face was sharp and unpleasant; her thin hair, dyed blond, was pulled into an untidy bun on top of her head and the scalp showed between the strands. She said, "Hullo, Lanark."
The sergeant said, "You have this lady to thank for bailing you out."
She said, "Why didn't he appear in the magistrates court this morning?"
"Pressure of business."
"The court didn't look busy to me. Come on Lanark."
Her voice was harsh and grating. He followed her to the station steps and was slightly blinded by the honey-coloured light of an evening sun sparkling on the river beyond a busy roadway. He stopped and said, "I'm sorry. I don't know who you are."
She pulled off a fur gauntlet and with a queer, vulnerable gesture held out her hand, palm upward. One of the lines across it was deep, like a scar.
He said "Gay!" with immense regret, for though she had been ill when he last saw her she had also been attractive and young. He gazed into her lean old face, shaking his head, and her expression showed she had the same feeling about himself.

She pulled on the glove and slipped her arm round his, saying quietly, "Come on, old man. We can do something better than stand round regretting our age. My car is over there."

As they went toward it she said with sudden violence, "The whole business stinks! Everyone knew you disappeared two days ago; there were plenty of rumours but nothing was done. Twice daily I phoned every police station in the Provan region and they pretended they hadn't heard of you till an hour ago; then the marine police station admitted they had a prisoner who *might* be you. An hour ago! After the subcommittee reports had been read and voted on and all the smiling statements made to the press. Did you know I was a journalist? I write for one of those venomous little newspapers that decent people think should be banned: the sort that print nasty stories about rich, famous, highly respected citizens."

She opened the car door. He sat beside her and she drove off. He said, "Where are we going?"

"To the banquet. We'll be in time for the speeches at the end."

"I don't want to go to a banquet. I don't want the other delegates or anybody to see me or be reminded of me ever again."

"You're demoralized. It'll wear off. My daughter is a stupid, gelid little nung. If she'd looked after you none of this would have happened. Have you guessed who caused all this?"

"I blame nobody but myself."

She laughed almost merrily and said, "That's a splendid excuse for letting bastards walk all over you. . . . Do you really not know who pushed you into that trap?"

"Gloopy?"

"Sludden."

He looked at her. She frowned and said, "Perhaps Monboddo is in it too, but no, I don't think so. The big chief prefers not to know certain details. Wilkins and Weems are more likely, but if so Sludden has been too smart for them. Instead of neatly carving up Greater Unthank for the council my bloody ex-husband has handed it over to Cortexin lock, stock and ballocks."

"Sludden?"

"Sludden, Gow and all the other merry men. Except Grant. Grant objected. Grant may manage to start something."

"I don't understand you," said Lanark drearily. "Sludden sent me here to argue against Unthank's being destroyed. Will it be destroyed?"

"Yes, but not in the way they first planned. The council and creature-clusters meant to use it as a cheap supply of *human* energy, but they won't do that now till they've sucked out these lovely rich juices discovered by your friend Mrs. Schtzngrm."

"What of the pollution?"

"Cortexin will handle that. For the moment, at any rate."

"So Unthank is safe?"

"Of course not. Bits of it have become valuable property again, but only to a few people and for a short time. Sludden has sold your resources to an organization with worldwide power run by a clique for the benefit of a clique. That isn't safety. Why do you think were you sent here as a delegate?"

"Sludden said I was the best man available."

"Ha! Politically speaking you don't know your arse from your elbow. You don't even know what the word 'lobbying' means. You were fucking well *certain* to pox up everything, that's why Sludden made *you* delegate. And while people here got excited about you, and plotted against you, and passed big resolutions about world order and energy and pollution, Sludden and Cortexin were doing with Unthank exactly what they wanted. You aren't very intelligent, Lanark."

"I have begun to notice that recently," said Lanark, after a pause.

"I'm sorry old man, it isn't your fault. Anyway, I'm trying to make you angry."

"Why?"

"I want you to raise hell at this banquet."

"Why? I won't do it, but why?"

"Because this has been the smoothest, politest, most docile assembly in history. The delegates have handled each other as gently as unexploded bombs. All the dirty deals and greedy devices have been worked out in secret committees with nobody watching, nobody complaining, nobody reporting. We need somebody, just once, to embarrass these bastards with a bit of the truth."

"Sludden told me to do that."

"His reasons are not my reasons."

"Yes. He was a politician, you are a journalist, and I like neither of you. I like nobody except my son, and I'm afraid I'll never see him again. So I care for nothing."

The car was passing down a quiet street. Gay parked it suddenly by a vast brick wall and folded her arms on the wheel.

She said quietly, "This is terrible. In the days of the old Elite you were a definite, independent sort of man in your limited way. I was slightly afraid of you. I envied you. I was a silly weakling then, the mouthpiece of someone who despised me. And now that I've lost my looks and gained some sense and self-confidence you've gone as feeble as putty. Did Rima chew your balls off?"

"Please don't talk like that."

Gay sighed and said, "Where will we go?"

"I don't know."

"You're my passenger. Where do you want me to drive you?"

"Nowhere."

"All right," she said, reaching into the back seat. "Here's your briefcase. My daughter found it somewhere. It was empty, apart from a scientific dictionary and this pass with your name on it." She stuck a long strip of plastic into his breast pocket. "Get out."

He got out and stood on the kerb, trying to find comfort in the familiar smoothness of the briefcase handle. He expected the car to drive away but Gay got out too. She took his arm and led him to a double door, the only feature in a wilderness of wall. He said, "What place is this?" but she hummed softly to herself and touched a bell button. Each wing of the door suddenly swung inward and Lanark was appalled by the sight of two tight-mouthed security men. They spoke sharply and simultaneously, the voices springing from their shirtfronts: "Pass, please."

"You can see it in his pocket," said Gay.

"Identify self."

"He's the Unthank delegate, slightly late, and I'm from the press."

"Delegate may enter. No press may enter without the red card. No press may enter without the red card. Delegate may enter."

They moved apart, leaving a narrow space between them. Gay said, "Well, goodbye, Lanark. I'm sorry I won't be able to twist your arm when the right moment comes. But if you manage to improvise some guts, old man, I'll certainly hear about it."

She turned and walked away.

"Delegate may enter. Or Not," said the security men. "Delegate may enter. Or not. Invite expression of intention by progression or retrogression. Request expression of intention. Demand expression of intention. Command expression of intention!"

Lanark stood and pondered.

"Think hard!" said the security men. "In default of expression of intention, delegate demoted to condition of obstruction. Think hard! In def of exp of int del dem to con of ob think, conofobthink, conofobthink."

And although it made him shudder, he stepped through the narrow space between them because he could think of nowhere else to go.

CHAPTER 43. Explanation

A concrete floor, dusty and stained by pigeon droppings, lay under a high roof upheld by iron girders. From the doorway a long blue carpet ran into the shadowy distance. He walked down this till it touched a similar carpet at right angles. He turned the corner round a little gurgling fountain in a glass bowl and heard a hubbub of voices. A dozen security guards stood before the door of a circus tent. He went forward, holding out his pass and saying loudly, "Unthank delegate!"

A displeased-looking girl in red shirt and jeans appeared between the black-clad men and said, "I'm surprised to see *you* here, Lanark. I mean, everything's finished. Even the food." It was Libby. He muttered that he had come for the speeches. "Why? They'll be horribly boring, and you look as if you hadn't washed for a week. Why do you want to hear speeches?"

He stared at her. She sighed and said, "Come inside, but you'll have to hurry."

He followed her through the door. The hubbub grew deafening as she led him along between the inner wall of the tent and a line of waiters carrying out trays laden with used dishes. He glimpsed the backs of people sitting at a table which curved away to the left and right. Libby pointed to an empty chair saying, "That was yours."

He slunk into it as quietly as possible. A neighbor stared at him, said "Good God, a ghost!" and started chuckling. It was Odin. "It's very, very, very good to see you," said Powys, the other neighbour. "What happened? We've been terribly alarmed about you."

The table formed a white-clothed circle filling most of the tent. There was a wineglass to each chair and a sign with

the guest's name and title facing outward. Red girls carried
bottles about inside the circle, filling glasses. Lanark explained
what had happened to him.

"I'm glad it was only that," said Powys. "Some people whispered you'd been shot or abducted by the security guards.
Of course we didn't really believe it. If we had we'd have
complained."

"That rumour did the assembly a power of good," said Odin
cheerfully. "A lot of cowardly loudmouths were afraid to say
a word during the big energy debate. Bloody idiots!"

"Well, you know," said Powys, "I don't mind admitting I was
worried too. These guards are ugly customers, and nobody
seems to know what their precise instructions are. Yes, the
business of the last few days has been settled with unusual
promptness, so you did not piss in vain. But it was reckless
of you to pollute their river. They're very fond of it."

Solveig came along the table filling wineglasses. He stared down
at the tablecloth, hoping not to be noticed. There was a sound
like a colossal soft cough then a perfectly amplified voice said,
"Ladies and gentlemen, you will be glad to hear that after an
absence of three days one of our most popular delegates has
returned. The witty, the venerable, the *not always perfectly sober*
Lord Provost Lanark of Greater Unthank is in his place at last."
Lanark's mouth opened. Though total silence had fallen he
seemed to hear a great roar go up. The multitude of glances
on him—mocking, he was sure, condescending, contemptuous,
amused—seemed to pierce and press him down. Someone
yelled, "Give the man a drink!"

He sobbed and laid his head on the tablecloth. The hubbub
of voices began again, but with more speculation than laughter
in it. He heard Odin murmur, "That wasn't necessary," and
Powys said, "No, they didn't need to rub it in like that."

There was another soft cough and the voice said, "My lords,
ladies and gentlemen, pray silence for Sir Trevor Weems,
Knight of the Golden Snail, Privy Councillor of Dalriada, Chief
Executive Officer of the Greater Provan Basin and Outer Erse
Confederacy."

There was some applause then Lanark heard the voice of
Weems.

"This is a strange occasion for me. The man sitting on
my left is the twenty-ninth Lord Monboddo. He has been many
things in his time: musician, healer, dragon-master, scourge
of the decimal clock, *enfant terrible* of the old expansion project,

stupor mundi of the institute and council debates. I have known
him as all these things and opposed him as every one of them.
A rash, rampant, raving intellectual, that's what I called him
in the old days. Everyone remembers the unhappy circumstances in which his predecessor retired. I won't tell you what
I thought when I heard the name of the new Monboddo. If I
spoke too plainly our excellent Quantum-Cortexin security
guards might be obliged to lead me away under the Special
Powers (Consolidation) Order and lock me in a very small
room for a very long time. The fact is, I was appalled. Our
whole Provan executive was flung into profound gloom when
we realized we would be hosts to a general assembly chaired
by the dreadful *Ozenfant*. But what has been the outcome?"
There was a pause. Weems said fervently, "Ladies and gentlemen, this has been the most smoothly run, clear-sighted, coher-
ent assembly the council has ever convened! There are many
reasons for this, but I believe future historians will mainly as-
cribe it to the tact, tolerance and intelligence of the man sitting
on my left. He need not shake his head! If he is a rebel we
need more of them. Indeed, I might even be persuaded to
vote for a revolution—if the twenty-ninth Lord Monboddo un-
dertook to lead it!"
There was some loud laughter.

By slow degrees Lanark had come to sit upright again.
The centre of the circle was empty. Far to the right Weems
stood beside Lord and Lady Monboddo. Microphones pro-
truded from a low bank of roses on the tablecloth before him.
All the guests on that side of the circle were pink. On the
other side they were sallow or brown, with the five members
of the black bloc directly facing Monboddo. Several dark delegates talked quietly among themselves, not attending to the
speech. Weems was saying, ". . . will be far too deep for me,
I'm afraid, and what I do understand I'll almost certainly disa-
gree with. But he has heard so much from us in the past three
days that it is only fair to allow him his revenge. And so, Lord
Monboddo, I call on you to summarize the work of the council,
Then, Now and Tomorrow."
Weems sat down amid applause. Monboddo had been smiling
down at the table with half-shut eyes. He arose and stood with
one hand resting on the table, the other in his pocket, the
smiling head tilted a little to one side. He waited until applause,
faint conversation, coughs and stirrings sank into silence. As
the silence continued his figure, casual yet unmoving, gained

power and authority until the whole great ring of guests was
like an audience of carved statues. Lanark was amazed that so
many could make so complete a silence. It weighed on him
like a crystal bubble filling the top of the tent and pressing
down on his skull: he could shatter it any time by yelling a
single obscenity, but bit his lips hard to stop that happening.
Monboddo began to speak.

> "Some men are born modest. Some
> achieve modesty. Some have modesty
> thrust upon them. I fear that Sir Trevor
> has firmly placed me in the last of these
> categories."

Laughter went up, especially from Weems.

> "Once I was an ambitious young de-
> partment chief. I launched policies and had
> flashes of creative brilliance which, believe
> me, my friends, verged, I thought, upon
> genius! Well, ambition has met its nemesis.
> I now stand on the top tip of our vast
> pyramid and create nothing. I can only
> receive the brilliant proposals of younger,
> more actively placed colleagues and find
> ways to reconcile and promote them. I ex-
> amine the options and discard, without
> emotions, those which do not fit our sys-
> tem. Such work uses a very *small* part of
> human intelligence."

"Oh, nonsense!" shouted Weems cheerfully.

> "Not nonsense, no, my friend. I
> promise you that in three years all the lim-
> ited skills of a council supremo will be
> embodied in the circuits of a Quantum-
> Cortexin humanoid, just as the skills of
> secretaries and special policemen are em-
> bodied. It may be my privilege to be the
> last of the fully human Lords Monboddo.
> The idea would flatter my very considera-
> ble vanity, were it not for the great im-
> provement people will see in government
> business when the change takes place. Ev-
> erything will suddenly go much faster.

Yes, today human government stands at a very delicate point of balance. But before opening the path ahead I must describe the steps which brought us here.

"So stand with me on the sun some six thousand years ago and consider, with sharper eyes than the eagle, the moist blue-green ball of the third planet. The deserts are smaller than now, the forest jungles much bigger, for where soil is thick, shrubberies clog the rivers and spread them out into swampland. There are no broad tracts of fenced field, no roads or towns. The only sign of men is where the globe's western edge is rolling into the shadow of night. Some far-apart gleams are beginning on that dim curve, the fires of hunters in forest clearings, of fishers at river mouths, of wandering herdsmen and planters on the thin soil between desert and jungle, for we are too few to take good land from the trees. Our tiny tribal democracies have spread all over this world, yet we influence it less than our near relation the squirrel, who is important to the survival of certain hardwoods. We have been living here for half a million years, yet history, with its noisy collisions and divisions of code and property, has not yet started. No wonder the first historians thought men had been created a few centuries before themselves. No wonder later theorists called prehistoric men *childlike, savage, rude,* and thought they had wasted time in fighting and couplings even more ferocious than those of today.

"But big killings, like big buildings, need large populations to support them, and fewer people were born in 500,000 years of the stick-and-stone age than in the first 50 years of the twentieth century. Prehistoric men were too busy cooperating against famine, flood and frost to hate each other very much; yet they tamed fire and

> animals, mastered joinery, cooking, tailoring, painting, pottery and planting. These skills still keep most of us alive. Compared with the sowing and reaping of the first grain crop, our own biggest achievement (sending three men to and from a dead world in a self-firing bullet) is a marvellously extravagant baroque curlicue on the recentest page of human history."

"That's crap, Monboddo! And you know it!" yelled someone across the circle from Lanark. There was laughter from the darker-skinned delegates. Monboddo smirked at them before continuing:

> "I still represent modern government, Mr. Kodac, do not worry. But the tools for harpooning other planets are still in the primitive phase, and it does no harm to admit that clever fellows like ourselves need not be ashamed of our ancestors. All the same, this petit-bourgeois world of gamekeepers and peasant craftmen bores me. Yes, it bores me. I thirst for the overweening exuberance of the Ziggurats and Zimbabwes, the Great Walls and Cathedrals. What is lacking from this prehistoric nature-park where sapient men have lived so long with such little effect? Surplus is lacking: that surplus of food, time and energy, that surplus of *men* we call wealth.
> "So let a handful of centuries pass and look at the globe again. The biggest land mass is split into three continents by a complicated central sea. East of it, a wide river no longer meanders through swamps but flows in a distinct channel across a fertile geometry of fields and ditches. On the glittering surface boats and barges move upstream and down to unload their cargoes beside the cubes, cones and cylinders of the first city. A great house with a tower stands in the city centre. On the summit, high above the hazes of the river, the secretaries of the sky use the turning dome

of heaven as a clock of light where sun, moon and galaxies tell the time to dig, reap and store. Under the tower the wealth of the state, the sacred grain surplus, is banked: sacred because a sack of it can keep a family alive for a month. This grain is stored life. Those who own it can command others. The great house belongs to modern men like ourselves, men, not skilful in growing and making things, but in managing those who do. There is a market beside the great house from which tracks radiate far across plain and forest. These tracks are beaten by tribesmen bringing fleeces, hides and whatever else can be exchanged for the life-giving grain. In time of famine they will sell their children for it. In time of war they can sell enemies captured in battle. The wealth of the city makes warfare profitable because the city managers know how to use cheap labour. More trees are felled, new canals widen the cultivated land. The city is growing.

"It grows because it is a living body, its arteries are the rivers and canals, its limbs are the trade routes grappling goods and men into its stomach, the market. We, whose state is an organization linking the cities of many lands, cannot know what sacred places the first cities seemed. Luckily the librarian of Babylon has described how they looked to a visiting tribesman:

He sees something he has never seen, or has not seen . . . in such plenitude. He sees the day and cypresses and marble. He sees a whole that is complex and yet without disorder; he sees a city, an organism composed of statues, temples, gardens, dwellings, stairways, urns, capitals, of regular and open spaces. None of these artifacts impresses him (I know) as beautiful; they move him as we might be moved today by a complex machine of whose purpose we are ignorant but in whose design we intuit an immortal intelligence.

"Immortal intelligence, yes. That undying intelligence lives in the great house which is the brain of the city, which is the first home of institutional knowledge and modern government. In a few centuries it will divide into law court, university, temple, treasury, stock exchange and arsenal."

"Here here!" shouted Weems unexpectedly, and there was some scattered applause.

"Bugger this," muttered Odin. "He's talked for ten minutes and only just reached the topic."

"I find these large vague statements very soothing," said Powys. "Like being in school again."

"But all tribesmen are not servile adorers of wealth," (said Monboddo). "Many have skill and greed of their own. The lords of the first cities may have fallen before nomads driving the first wheeled chariots. No matter! The new masters of the grain may only keep it with help from the clever ones who rule land and time by rod and calendar, and can count and tax what others make. The great riverine cultures (soon there are five of them) absorb wave after wave of conquerors, who add to the power of the managers by giving them horsemen for companions. So the growth of cities speeds up. Their trade routes interlock and grapple, they compete with each other. Iron swords and ploughshares are forged, metals command the wealth of the grain. The seaside cities arise with their merchant and pirate navies."

"He's getting faster," whispered Powys. "He's covered twelve civilizations in six sentences."

"Men increase. Wealth increases. War increases. Nowadays, when strong governments agree *there must not be* another big war, we can still applaud the old battles and invasions which blended the skills of conquerors and conquered. The are no villains in history. Pessimists point to Attila and Tamerlane, but these active men liquidated unprofitable states which *needed* a destroyer to release their assets. Wherever wealth has been used for mere self-maintenance it has always inspired vigorous people to grasp and fling it into the service of that onrushing history which the modern state commands. Pale pink people like myself have least reason to point the scorning finger. Poets tell us that for two millennia Europe was boisterous with energies released by the liquidation of Asiatic Troy. I quote the famous Lancastrian epic:

"Since the siege and assault was ceaséd
                    at Troy,
The burgh broken and burned to
                    brands and ashes,
It was Aeneas the Able and his high
                    kind
That since despoiled provinces and
                    patrons became
Wellnigh of all the wealth in the West
                    Isles;
For rich Romulus to Rome riches he
                    swipes,
With great bobbaunce that burgh he
                    builds upon first,
And names with his own name as now
                    it hath;
Ticius in Tuscany townships founds,
Langbeard in Lombardy lifts up homes,
And far over the French flood Felix
                    Brutus,
On many banks full broad Britain he
                    builds with his winnings,

> Where war and wreck and wonder
> By turns have waxed therein,
> And oft both bliss and blunder
> Have had their innings.

"Bliss and blunder. The flow of wealth around the globe has involved much of both, but wealth itself has continued to grow because it is always served by the winners."

"Pale pink people," muttered Odin broodingly. "Pale pink people."

"I don't think the blackies and brownies are much amused," said Powys. "Are you all right, Lanark?"

Monboddo's strong quiet voice purred on like a stupefying wind.

". . . so north Africa becomes a desert, with several useful consequences. . . ."

"After the clean camaraderie of the steam bath-house, the new recruits notice that their parents stink. . . ."

". . . but machinists only work efficiently in a climate of hope, so slavery is replaced by debt and money becomes a promise to pay printed by the government. . . ."

". . . by the twentieth century, wealth has engrossed the whole globe, which now revolves in a tightening net of thought and transport woven round it by trade and science. The world is enclosed in a single living city, but its brain centres, the governments, do not notice this. Two world wars are fought in thirty years, wars the more bitter because they are between different parts of the same system. It would wrong the slaughtered millions to say these wars did no good. Old machines, old ideas were replaced at unusual speed. Science, business and government quickly became richer than ever before. We must thank the dead for that."

Monboddo glanced at Weems, who stood up and said solemnly, "This is surely a good time to remember the dead. There are hardly any lands where men have not died this century fighting for what they thought best. I invite all delegates to stand with me for two minutes and remember the friends, relations and countrymen who suffered to make us what we are."

"Bloody farce," muttered Odin, gripping Lanark under the elbow to help him rise.

"Soon be over," whispered Powys, helping at the other side. The whole great circle gradually rose to their feet except the black bloc, who stayed obstinately seated. There was silence for a while; than a distant trumpet sounded outside the tent and everyone sat murmuringly down.

"What's the point of this speech?" said Odin. "It's too Marxian for the Corporate Wealth gang and too approving for the Marxists."

"He's trying to please everyone," said Powys.

"You can only do that with vague platitudes. He's like all these Huns—too clever for his own good."

"I thought he came from Languedoc," said Powys.

"As I reach our present dangerous time," (said Monboddo, sighing), "I fear I have angered almost everyone here by a perhaps too cynical view of history. I have described it as a growing and spreading of wealth. Two styles of government command the modern world. One works to reconcile the different companies which employ their people, the other employs the people themselves. Defenders of the first style think great wealth the reward and necessary tool of those who serve mankind best; to the rest it is a method by which strong people bully weak ones. Can I define wealth in a way which lets both sides agree with me? Easily.

"At the start of my talk I said wealth was a surplus of men. I now say a wealthy state is one which orders its surplus men into great enterprises. In the past extra men were used to invade neighbours, plant colonies and destroy competitors. But the liquidation of unprofitable states

by warfare is not practical now. We all
know it, which is why this assembly has
been a success: *not* because I have been
a specially good chairman but because you,
the delegates of states big and small, have
agreed to order onrushing history, onrushing wealth, onrushing *men* by majority de-
cisions reached through open and honest
debate.''

Weems started clapping again, but Monboddo talked vehe-
mently over him.

"Believe me, this splendid logicalness
has been achieved only just in time! More
men have been born this century than in
all the ages of history and prehistory pre-
ceding. Our man surplus has never been
so vast. If this human wealth is not governed it will collapse—in places it is already collapsing—into poverty, anarchy,
disaster. Let me say at once that I do not
fear wars between any government represented here today, nor do I fear revolution. The presence of that great revolutionary hero, Chairman Fu of the People's
Republic of Xanadu, shows that revolu-
tions are perfectly able to create strong
governments. What we must unite to prevent are half-baked revolts which might
give desperadoes access to those doomsday machines and bottled plagues which
stable governments are creating, not to
use, but to prevent themselves from being
bullied by equals. No land today lacks desperadoes, brave greedy ignorant men who
can no longer be sent to work in less busy
parts of the world and are too ambitious
to join a regular police force. No modern
state lacks irresponsible intellectuals, the
enemies of strong government everywhere. Both types seem anxious to break
the world down into tiny republics of the
prehistoric kind, where the voice of the
dull and cranky would sound as loud as

the wise and skilful. But a reversion to barbarism cannot help us. The world can only be saved by a great enterprise in which stable governments use the skills of institutional knowledge with the full backing of corporate wealth. Council, institute and creature everywhere must work together.

"The fuel supply of the present planet is almost exhausted. The food supply is already insufficient. Our deserts have grown too vast, our seas are overfished. We need a new supply of energy, for energy is food as well as fuel. At present dead matter is turned into nourishment by farming, and by the consumption of uneducated people by clever ones. This arrangement is a failure because it is inefficient; it also puts clever people into a dependent position. Luckily our experts will soon be able to turn dead matter directly into food in our industrial laboratories— *if we give them access to sufficient energy.*

"Where can this energy be found? Ladies and gentlemen, it is all around us, it streams from the sun, gleams from the stars and sings harmoniously in every sphere. Yes, Mr. Kodac! It is time for me to admit that sending ships into space is not just an adventure but a necessity. That greater outer space is not, we now know, a horrid vacuum but a treasure house which can be endlessly, infinitely plundered—if we combine to do it. Once again the secretaries of the sky will be our leaders. We must build them a high new platform, a city floating in space where the clever and adventurous of every land, working in a clean, nearly weightless atmosphere, will reflect heat and sunlight down to the powerhouses of the world.

"It has been suggested we call this enterprise New Frontier or Dynostar. I suggest the Laputa Project. . . ."

Monboddo's speech had hypnotized Lanark. He listened open-mouthed, nodding in the pauses. Whenever he understood a sentence it seemed to say everything was inevitable and therefore right. Yet his body grew less and less easy, his head buzzed, when Monboddo said "a high new platform, a city floating in space," he seemed to hear another voice, harsh and incredulous, say, "The man's a lunatic."

Even so, he was appalled to find himself standing and shouting "EXEXEXEXEXEXEX" at the top of his voice. Powys and Odin gripped his wrists, but he wrenched them free and yelled, "EXCUSE ME! EXCUSE ME but Lord Monboddo lied when he said all the delegates agreed to manage things through open, honest debates! Or else he has been lied to by other people."

There was silence. Lanark watched Monboddo watching him woodenly. Weems stood up and said quietly, "As host of this gathering I apologize to Lord Monboddo and the other delegates for . . . for Provost Lanark's hysterical outburst. He is notorious for his lack of control in civilized company. I also demand that Provost Lanark take back these words."

"I'm sorry I said them," said Lanark, "but Lord Monboddo has deliberately or ignorantly told us a lie. I pissed off a bridge, but I should not have been locked up before I had spoken for Unthank! Unthank is being destroyed with no open agreement at all, jobs and homes are being destroyed, we've begun hating each other, the Merovicnic Discontinuity is threatened—"

He was deafened by a babel of laughter and talk. A row of black-clad men stood behind Weems and Lanark saw two of them walk around the tent toward him. His legs trembled so much that he sat down. Voices were shouting for silence somewhere on his left. Silence fell. He saw Multan of Zimbabwe standing up, smiling at Monboddo, who said shortly, "Speak, by all means."

Multan looked round the table then said, "The Unthank delegate says this assembly has not held free and open debates. That's not news to the black bloc. Is it news to anybody?" He chuckled and shrugged. "Everybody knows three or four big boys run the whole show. The rest of us don't complain, why should we? Words by themselves are no good. When we get organized big, we'll complain and you'll listen. You'll have to listen. So this Lanark is very foolish to speak like he does. But he tells the truth. So on this side of the table we watch what happens. We laugh because it don't matter to us how you claw each other. But we watch closely what happens, all the same."

He sat down. Monboddo sighed and scratched his head. At last he said, "I will answer the Zimbabwe delegate first. He has told us, with admirable modesty, that he and his friends are not yet able to share the work of the council but will do so when they can. That is very good news; may the day come soon. The Unthank delegate's case is less clear. I gather the police arrested him in the circumstances where his exalted rank was not apparent. He has missed our debates, but what can I do? I leave Provan one decimal hour from now. I can grant him a brief personal interview. I can promise that anything he says will be recorded in the assembly minutes for everyone to read. It is all I can offer. Is it sufficient?"

Lanark felt everyone watching him and wanted to hide his face again. He glanced over his shoulder and shivered at the sight of two black-suited men. One nodded and winked. It was Wilkins. Monboddo said loudly, "If you wish this interview, my secretaries will escort you to a convenient place. Otherwise the matter must be dropped. Answer, please, there is not much time."

Lanark nodded. He stood and walked from the tent between the secretaries, feeling old and defeated.

CHAPTER 44. End

As they crossed the wide dim floor Wilkins said cheerily, "That was great fun; you scared the shits out of old M."
The other man said, "These intellectuals have no staying power."
"Lanark has been around for a long, long time," said Wilkins, "I think he deserves a three-syllable name, don't you?"
"Oh, he certainly deserves it," said the other man. "There's nothing wrong with a two-syllable name, I'm called Uxbridge, but Lanark has earned something more melodious. Like Blairdardie."
"Rutherglen, Garscaden," said Wilkins.
"Gargunnock, Carmunnock, Auchenshuggle," said the other man.
"Auchenshuggle has four syllables," said Wilkins.

They went through a narrow door, climbed a dingy stair and crossed a small office into a slightly larger office. It was lit by a neon tube and the walls were hidden by metal filing cabinets, some piled on others. There was a metal desk in the corner. Without much surprise Lanark saw Monboddo sitting behind it with hands clasped patiently on the waistcoat over his stomach. "Bilocation," said Monboddo. "I would be nothing if I did not duplicate. Sit down."
Wilkins placed a straight wooden chair before the desk and Lanark sat.
"Wilkins, Uxbridge, go away. Miss Thing will record us," said Monboddo. Lanark saw a girl exactly like Miss Maheen sitting between two filing cabinets. Wilkins and Uxbridge left. Monboddo tilted his chair back, looked at the ceiling and sighed. He said, "At last the Common Man confronts the Powerful

Lord of this World. Except that you are not very common and I am not very powerful. We can change nothing, you and I. But talk to me. Talk to me."

"I am here to speak for the people of Unthank."

"Yes. You wish to tell me they have too few jobs and homes and social services so stupidity, cruelty, disease and crime are increasing among them. I know that. There are many such places in the world, and soon there will be more. Governments cannot help them much."

"Yet governments can fire great structures into space!"

"Yes. It is profitable."

"For whom? Why can't wealth be used to help folk here and now?"

"It is, but we can only help people by giving less than we take away from them. We enlarge the oasis by increasing the desert. That is the science of time and housekeeping. Some call it economics."

"Are you telling me that men lack the decency and skill to be good to each other?"

"Not at all! Men have always possessed that decency and skill. In small, isolated societies they have even practised it. But it is a sad fact of human nature that in large numbers we can only organize against each other."

"You are a liar!" cried Lanark. "We have no nature. Our nations are not built instinctively by our bodies, like beehives; they are works of art, like ships, carpets and gardens. The possible shapes of them are endless. It is bad habits, not bad nature, which makes us repeat the dull old shapes of poverty and war. Only greedy people who profit by these things believe they are *natural.*"

"Your flood of language is delicious," said Ozenfant, yawning slightly, "and can have no possible effect upon human behaviour. By the way, it was not clever of you to get Multan speaking for you. He is no enemy of the council, he is a weak member plotting to become strong. If he succeeds his aim will be my aim: to manage things as smoothly as possible. His only enemies will be people like you—the babies."

"I am not a baby."

"You are. Your deafness to reasoned argument, your indifference to decent custom and personal dignity, a selfishness so huge and instinctive that it cannot even notice itself, all make you the nearest thing to an adult baby I have ever encountered. And now you may retaliate by calling me as many foul names as you please. Nobody will know. Miss Thing cannot hear what is irrelevant to the business of the council."

Lanark said coldly, "You want me to lose my temper."

"Yes indeed," said Monboddo, nodding. "But only to cut short a useless argument. You suffer from the oldest delusion in politics. You think you can change the world by talking to a leader. Leaders are the effects, not the causes of changes. I *cannot* give prosperity to people whom my rich supporters cannot exploit."

Lanark put his elbows on his knees and propped his face between his hands. After a while he said, "I don't care what happens to most people. All of us over eighteen have been warped into deserving what happens to us. But if your *reason* shows that civilization can only continue by damaging the brains and hearts of most children, then . . . your reason and civilization are false and will destroy themselves."

"Perhaps," said Monboddo, yawning, "but I think we can make them last our time. What have you recorded, Miss Thing? Tell us, please."

The secretary parted her lips and a monotonous voice slid out between them:

> *"Greater Unthank Addendum to General Assembly Minutes: Provost Lanark referred to Unthank's serious employment, housing, health and pollution problems. Chairman Monboddo related them to the supranational crisis in these areas and intimated that the solution of such problems must await the primary solution of the worldwide energy famine. Provost Lanark called for a more urgent approach to local difficulties insofar as they affect the 0–18 spectrum. Chairman Monboddo suggested the outcome of difficulties in this spectrum was less disastrous than Provost Lanark feared."*

Miss Thing's mouth clicked shut. Monboddo slapped his brow and said, "Cryptonite! I forgot the Cryptonite deposits. Put them in, Miss Thing; it will let us end on a cheerful note." Miss Thing opened her mouth again.

> *"Chairman Monboddo suggested the outcome of difficulties in this spectrum would be less disastrous socially than Provost Lanark feared as the development by Cortexin of the Unthank*

> *mineral resources was well on the way to putting*
> *prosperity within the grasp of everyone."*

Lanark stood up and wrung his hands. He cried out, "I am useless. I should never have come here, I did no good to anyone, not to Sandy, Rima or anyone. I need to go home."

"Home?" said Monboddo, raising an eyebrow.

"Unthank. It may be bad but the badness is obvious, not gilded with lies like here."

"You are severe. But I will help you. Open the bolthole, Miss Thing."

There was a grey woollen rug in front of the desk. Miss Thing knelt and pulled it back, uncovering a round steel plate sunk in the linoleum. She put a thumb and forefinger into two small openings at the centre and lifted it easily out, though it was two feet across and four inches thick. "The way home," said Monboddo. "Look inside. You will recognize the interior of a familiar aircraft."

He stood up and rested, hands in pockets, on a corner of the desk. Lanark stooped and stared for a long time into the round hole. There was a cavity under it lined with blue silk. Monboddo said, "You do not trust me. But you will climb inside because you are too reckless to linger. Am I right?"

"You're wrong," said Lanark, sighing. "I will climb inside because I'm too tired to linger."

He stepped into the cavity, sat down and straightened his legs. The space lengthened and narrowed to fit him. He lay staring up at a circle of cream-coloured ceiling surrounded by blackness. He heard Monboddo murmur "Bon voyage," and a round black shape slid sideways across the circle of ceiling and eclipsed it with a low clang. Then the space he lay in dropped.

The drop was a long down-rushing swoop stopped by a jarring jerk. Then came another drop. With an indrawn scream he knew he was going down the great gullet again. The tiny office, the great round table, Provan, Greater Unthank, Alexander, cathedral, Rima, Zone, council corridors, institute had been a brief rest from the horror of endless falling. Monboddo had tricked him back into it. He screamed with hatred. He pissed with panic. He writhed and his face came out into a rush of milky mist. He was plunging downward in the bird-machine. The panic changed. He was the mind of this bird, an old bird

in poor repair. Each wingstroke tore out feathers he needed
for landing and the land was far below. He kept falling as
far as he dared, then levelling in a thrash of pinions which
thinned and flew back like darts. His bald breast and sides
were freezing in the fall. The misty air thinned to black and
the black map of a city lay below, the streets dotted lines of
light. Bits of the map were on fire. A big red flower of flame
drew him down to it. He saw a flaming glass tower, a square
of statues, engines and seething heads; he heard roaring and
sirens, tried to level and crashed sideways on cracking wings
through sparks, heat and choking smoke where a great dim
column swung at him, missed, swung away and swung back
like a mace to strike him down.

He woke, sore and bandaged, in bed with a tube running
into his arm. He lay there dreaming and dozing and hardly
thinking at all. He assumed he was in the institute again but
the ward had windows with darkness outside them, and the
beds were packed together with hardly a foot of space between.
The patients were all very old. All cleaning and some nursing
was done by those fit enough to walk, for there was a very
small staff. The light fittings were peculiar. Electric globes hung
from the ceiling by slim rods which were parallel to each other
but slanted toward a corner of the ward. When a nurse took
the tube from his arm and changed the bandages he said,
"Is the hospital sloping?"
"So you've found your tongue at last."
"Is the hospital sloping?"
"If that was all, we'd be laughing."
The meals were mainly beans and this pleased him, though
he couldn't remember why. The doctor was a hurried, haggard,
unshaven man in a dirty smock. He said, "Have you any friends,
old man?"
"I used to have."
"Where can we contact them?"
"They used to hang around the cathedral."
"Were you one of Smollet's mob?"
"I knew Ritchie-Smollet, yes. I knew Sludden too."
"Best not to mention that, Sludden is far from popular at pres-
ent. But we'll find if Smollet can take you. We have to evacuate
this place, there's going to be another shock. What's your
name?"
"Lanark."

"A common name in these parts. We had a provost called that once. He wasn't much good."

Lanark slept and wakened to screams and shouting. He was sweating and sticky. The air was very hot and the ward was empty except for a bed in a far corner; an old woman sat in it crying, "They shouldn't leave us here, it isn't right." A soldier came in, looking carefully round, avoided the old woman's eye and edged toward Lanark between the empty beds. He was a tall man with a sullen, handsome, slightly babyish face and did not seem to be carrying a weapon. His only insignia was a badge on his beret shaped like a hand with an eye in the palm. He stood looking down at Lanark, then sat on the edge of the bed and said, after a moment, "Hullo, Dad."

Lanark whispered "Sandy?" and smiled and touched his hand. He felt very happy. The soldier said, "We've got to get out of here. The foundation is cracked."

He opened the bedside locker, took out trousers, jacket and shoes and helped Lanark into them, saying, "I wish you'd kept in touch with us."

"I didn't know how."

"You could have written or phoned."

"I never seemed to have time. Yet I did no good, Sandy. I changed nothing."

"Of course you changed nothing. The world is only improved by people who do ordinary jobs and refuse to be bullied. Nobody can persuade owners to share with makers when makers won't shift for themselves."

"I could never understand politics. How do you live, Sandy?"

"I report for movers and menders."

"What kind of work is that?"

"We have to hurry, Dad. Are you able to stand?"

Lanark managed to stand, though his knees trembled. The old woman in the corner bed wailed, "Son, could you help me too, son?"

"Wait here! Help is coming!" shouted Alexander fiercely. He took Lanark's right arm over his shoulder, gripped him round the waist and moved him toward the door, cursing below his breath. They were labouring uphill for the slope of the floor was against them. The screams and yelling grew louder. Alexander halted and said, "Listen, you used to be a sentimental man in some ways, so shut your eyes when you get out of here. Some things are happening which we just can't help."

"Anything you say son," said Lanark, closing his eyes. The arm round his waist gave such a strong feeling of happiness and safety that he started chuckling.

He was helped down many stairs amid loud crying and across a space where his ankles brushed past fingertips and then, though the air was no cooler, an uproar of voices and running feet suggested they were outside. He opened his eyes. The sight threw him off balance and he lost more balance trying to recover it. Alexander held him up, saying, "Steady, Dad." A great loose crowd, much of it children shepherded by women, slid and stumbled down a hillside toward a wide-open gate. But the hillside was a city square. The slanting lamp-standards lighting the scene, the slanting buildings on each side, the slanting spire of the nearby cathedral showed the whole landscape was tilted like a board.
"What happened?" cried Lanark.
"Subsidence," said Alexander, carrying him with the crowd. "There's going to be another soon, a bad one. Hurry."
Whenever Lanark's feet touched the ground he felt a vibration like a continuous electric shock. It seemed to strengthen his legs. He began moving almost briskly, chuckling and saying, "I like this."
"Jesus Christ," muttered Alexander.
"Do I sound senile, Sandy? I'm not. This gate leads to the graveyard, the Necropolis, doesn't it?"
"We'll be safer away from the buildings."
"I know this graveyard well, Sandy. So did your mother. I could tell you a lot about it. This bridge we're coming to, for instance, had a tributary of the river flowing under it once."
"Shut up and keep *moving,* Dad."

In the dim cemetery folk crouched on the grass plots or dispersed up the many little paths. From the height of the hill a loudspeaker was telling people to keep clear of high monuments. Alexander said, "Rima should be up at the top, can you go on?"
"Yes, yes!" said Lanark excitedly. "Yes, we must all get to the top, there's going to be a flood, a huge immense deluge."
"Don't be stupid, Dad."
"I'm not stupid. Someone told me everything would end in a deluge; he was very very definite about it. Yes, we must go as high as possible, if only for the view."
As they climbed the steep little paths Lanark felt more and

more energetic and cheerful. He tried to skip a little.

"Are you married, Sandy?"

"Steady, Dad, I wish you'd call me by my full name. No, I'm not married. I've a daughter, if that's any consolation."

"It is! It is! Will she be at the top of the hill too?"

"No, she's in a safer place than this, thank goodness. Do you hear the guns?"

There was a distant snapping sound.

"How can men fight like that at a time like this?" said Lanark, his voice squeaky with indignation.

"The Corquantal Galaxy are trying to liquidate their Unthank plant but Makers, Movers and Menders backed Defence Command in supporting the One-Wagers against them, so the council rump have sent in the Cocquigrues."

"I understand none of that. What are Cocquigrues?"

"I'll tell you when there's time."

Buildings burned in the city below. The glossy walls of the tower blocks reflected flickering glares upon a small knot of people between the monuments and the summit. Lanark couldn't see them clearly because tears came to his eyes. It struck him that Rima must be an old woman now and the thought was an unexpected pain. He muttered "Must sit" and settled on the edge of a granite slab. The vibration through it irritated his backside. He made out a nearby knot of men wearing armbands and stooping over an old-fashioned radio transmitter. Beside them a stout woman in a black dress waved to Alexander, then came over and laid a hand on Lanark's shoulder. He gazed up, astonished, into her large-eyed, large-nosed face with small straight childishly serious mouth. Though a little weary, and the glossy hair slightly streaked with grey, this seemed exactly the face he had first seen in the Elite Café. He said, "You aren't Rima?"

She laughed and said, "You always found it hard to recognize me. You've grown old, Lanark, but I knew you at once."

Lanark smiled and said, "You've grown fat."

"She's pregnant," said Alexander glumly. "At *her* age."

"You don't know my age," said Rima sharply and added, "I'm sorry I can't introduce you to Horace, Lanark, but he refuses to meet you. He's an idiot sometimes."

"Who is Horace?"

Alexander said dourly, "Someone who doesn't want to meet you. And a rotten wireless operator."

Lanark stood up. The vibration in the ground had become a strong, almost audible throbbing and Rima said tensely, "I'm frightened, Alex, don't be nasty to me."

The throbbing stopped. In a great quietness the hot air seemed to scald the skin. Lanark felt so heavy that he crashed on his knees to the ground, then so light that he rose in the air. When he came down again the ground was not where he expected. He lay listening to rumbling and shouting and looked at the firelit pinnacle of an obelisk; it leaned so far over him that he knew it must crack or topple. He got heavy, then light again, and this time only his head left the ground and fell back with a thump which dazed him slightly. When he next saw the obelisk it pointed perfectly upright and the glow on it was very strong.

"Tell me what's happening, please," said Rima. She lay curled on the ground with her hands over her eyes. Everybody lay on the ground except Alexander, who knelt beside the radio transmitter earnestly turning knobs.

"The ground is level again," said Lanark, getting up, "and the fire is spreading."

"Is it horrible?"

"It's wonderful. It's universal. You should look."

Behind the burning building was a great band of ruddy light with clouds rising into it from collapsed and collapsing roofs. There were no other lights. "First the fire, then the flood!" cried Lanark exultingly, "Well, I have had an interesting life."

"You're as selfish as ever!" shrieked Rima.

"Be quiet, I'm trying to contact Defence Command," said Alexander.

"Nothing can be defended now, I hear the water coming," said Lanark. There was a faraway rushing mingled with faint squeals. He hobbled between two monuments to the edge of a slope and gazed eagerly down, holding himself erect by a branch of a twisty thorn tree.

A blast of cold wind freshened the air. The rushing grew to surges and gurglings and up the low road between Necropolis and cathedral sped a white foam followed by ripples and plunging waves with gulls swooping and crying over them. He laughed aloud, following the flood with his mind's eye back to the river it flowed from, a full river widening to the ocean. His cheek was touched by something moving in the wind, a black twig with pointed little pink and grey-green buds. The colours of things seemed to be brightening although the fiery light over the roofs had paled to silver streaked with delicate rose. A long silver line marked the horizon. Dim rooftops against it grew solid in the increasing light. The broken buildings were fewer than he had thought. Beyond them a long faint bank of cloud became clear hills, not walling the city in but receding, edge behind pearl-grey edge of farmland and woodland gently rising to a faraway ridge of moor. The darkness overheard shifted and broke in the wind becoming clouds with blue air between. He looked sideways and saw the sun coming up golden behind a laurel bush, light blinking, space dancing among the shifting leaves. Drunk with spaciousness he turned every way, gazing with wide-open mouth and eyes as light created colours, clouds, distances and solid, graspable things close at hand. Among all this light the flaming buildings seemed small blazes which would soon burn out. With only mild disappointment he saw the flood ebbing back down the slope of the road.

Rima came beside him and said teasingly, "Wrong again, Lanark."
He nodded, sighed, and said, "Rima, did you ever love me?"
She laughed, held him and kissed his cheek. She said, "Of course I did, even though you kept driving me away so nastily and so often. They've started shooting again."
They stood awhile listening to the snapping and cracklings. She said, "Defence command have called Alex over to maintenance. It's very urgent, but he says he'll come back for you as soon as he can. You're to stay here and not worry if he's late."
"Good."
"I'm sorry you can't come with me, but Horace is an idiot sometimes. Why should a young man like him be jealous of you?"
"I don't know."
She laughed, kissed his cheek and went away.

After a while he hobbled back to the space between the monuments and sat once again on the edge of the granite slab. He was tired and chilly but perfectly content to wait. There was nobody about, but after a while he heard the crunch of a foot on gravel. A figure approached him wearing the black and white clothes and carrying the silver-tipped staff of a chamberlain. Lanark had trouble focusing on the face under the wig: sometimes it seemed to be Munro, sometimes Gloopy. He said, "Munro? Gloopy?"

"Correct sir," said the figure, bowing respectfully. "We have been sent to bestow on you an extraordinary privilege."

"Who sent you?" said Lanark peevishly. "Institute or council? I dislike both."

"Knowledge and government are dissolving. I now represent the ministry of earth."

"Everything keeps getting renamed. I've stopped caring. Don't try to explain."

The figure bowed again and said, "You will die tomorrow at seven minutes after noon."

The words were almost drowned by a squawking gull turning in the sky overhead, but Lanark understood them perfectly. Like a mother's fall in a narrow lobby, like a policeman's hand on his shoulder, he had known or expected this all his life. A roaring like a terrified crowd filled his ears; he whispered, "Death is not a privilege."

"The privilege is knowing when."

"But I . . . I seem to remember passing through several deaths."

"They were rehearsals. After the next death nothing personal will remain of you."

"Will it hurt?"

"Not much. Just now there is no feeling in your left arm; you can't move it. In a moment it will get better again, but at five minutes after noon tomorrow your whole body will become like that. For two minutes you will be able to see and think but not move or speak. That will be the worst time. You will be dead when it stops."

Lanark scowled with self-pity and annoyance. The chamberlain said, respectfully "Have you a complaint?"

"I ought to have more love before I die. I've not had enough."

"That is everyone's complaint. You can appeal against the death sentence if you have something better to do."

"If you're hinting that I should go in for more adventures, no thank you, I don't want them. But how will my son—how will the *world* manage when I'm not here?"

The chamberlain shrugged and spread his hands.

"Well go away, go away," said Lanark more kindly. "You can tell the earth I would have preferred a less common end, like being struck by lightning. But I'm prepared to take death as it comes."

The chamberlain vanishęd. Lanark forgot him, propped his chin on his hands and sat a long time watching the moving clouds. He was a slightly worried, ordinary old man but glad to see the light in the sky.

I STARTED MAKING MAPS WHEN I WAS SMALL
SHOWING PLACE, RESOURCES, WHERE THE ENEMY
AND WHERE LOVE LAY. I DID NOT KNOW
TIME ADDS TO LAND. EVENTS DRIFT CONTINUALLY
                                        DOWN,
EFFACING LANDMARKS, RAISING THE LEVEL, LIKE
                                        SNOW.

I HAVE GROWN UP. MY MAPS ARE OUT OF DATE.
THE LAND LIES OVER ME NOW.
I CANNOT MOVE. IT IS TIME TO GO.

GOODBYE

Fiction in Paladin

The Businessman: A Tale of Terror   £2.95 ☐
Thomas M. Disch
'Each of the sixty short chapters of THE BUSINESSMAN is a *tour de force* of polished, distanced, sly narrative art . . . always the vision of America stays with us: melancholic, subversive and perfectly put . . . In this vision lies the terror of THE BUSINESSMAN'
Times Literary Supplement

'An entertaining nightmare out of Thomas Berger and Stephen King'
Time

Filthy English   £2.95 ☐
Jonathan Meades
'Incest and lily-boys, loose livers and ruched red anal compulsives, rape, murder and literary looting . . . Meades tosses off quips, cracks and crossword clues, stirs up the smut and stuffs in the erudition, pokes you in the ribs and prods you in the kidneys (as in Renal, home of Irene and Albert) . . . a delicious treat (full of fruit and nuts) for the vile and filthy mind to savour'
Time Out

Dancing with Mermaids   £2.95 ☐
Miles Gibson
'An excellent, imaginative comic tale . . . an original and wholly entertaining fiction . . . extremely funny and curiously touching'
Cosmopolitan

'The impact of the early Ian McEwan or Martin Amis, electrifying, a dazzler'
Financial Times

'It is as if Milk Wood had burst forth with those obscene-looking blossoms one finds in sweaty tropical palm houses . . . murder and mayhem decked out in fantastic and erotic prose'
The Times

To order direct from the publisher just tick the titles you want and fill in the order form.

Original Fiction in Paladin

Paper Thin   £2.95 ☐
Philip First
From the author of THE GREAT PERVADER: a wonderfully original
collection of stories about madness, love, passion, violence, sex and
humour.

Don Quixote   £2.95 ☐
Kathy Acker
From the author of BLOOD AND GUTS IN HIGH SCHOOL: a
visionary collage–novel in which Don Quixote is a woman on an
intractable quest; a late twentieth-century LEVIATHAN; a stingingly
powerful and definitely unique novel.

To order direct from the publisher just tick the titles you want
and fill in the order form.

Fiction in Paladin

In the Shadow of the Wind   £2.95 ☐
Anne Hébert
Winner of the Prix Femina
'A bewitching and savage novel . . . there is constant magic in it'
Le Matin

'Beautifully written with great simplicity and originality . . . an
unusual and haunting novel'
London Standard

Love is a Durable Fire   £2.95 ☐
Brian Burland
'Burland has the power to evoke time and place with total authority
. . . compelling . . . the stuff of which real literature is made'
Irish Times

To order direct from the publisher just tick the titles you want
and fill in the order form.

All these books are available at your local bookshop or newsagent, or can be ordered direct from the publisher.

To order direct from the publishers just tick the titles you want and fill in the form below.

Name _____

Address _____

_____

Send to:
Paladin Cash Sales
PO Box 11, Falmouth, Cornwall TR10 9EN.

Please enclose remittance to the value of the cover price plus:

UK 60p for the first book, 25p for the second book plus 15p per copy for each additional book ordered to a maximum charge of £1.90.

BFPO 60p for the first book, 25p for the second book plus 15p per copy for the next 7 books, thereafter 9p per book.

Overseas including Eire £1.25 for the first book, 75p for second book and 28p for each additional book.

Paladin Books reserve the right to show new retail prices on covers, which may differ from those previously advertised in the text or elsewhere.